NEW YORK TIMES **BESTSELLING AUTHOR**

LORI WILDE

TWO GREAT NOVELS FOR ONE LOW PRICE!

D0030603

Happily Ever After

15% OFF COVER PRICE

MEET THE BRIDES OF THE
WEDDING VEIL WISHES SERIES

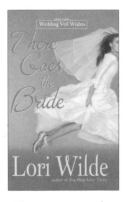

Please turn to the
back of this book
for a preview.

OR ENJOY
BOTH NOVELS
TOGETHER
IN THIS SPECIAL
COLLECTION

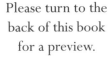

ISBN 978-1-4555-4992-4

$8.00 US / $9.00 CAN.

50800

EAN

DON'T MISS
You Only Love Twice
Mission: Irresistible
Charmed and Dangerous
License to Thrill

**Download the FREE
Forever app—and get
more to love!**

Praise for

LORI WILDE'S NOVELS

THERE GOES THE BRIDE

"A wild ride."   —*Booklist*

"I adored this book! I even kept it in my purse in the hopes that I would have a few minutes in which to squeeze a paragraph or two...I can't wait to read the next in this wonderful new series...Superb!"

—TheRomanceReadersConnection.com

"FOUR HEARTS! Ms. Wilde conquers a whole new part of the romance genre...lots of funny elements and a great cast of characters."

—LovesRomanceandMore.com

"A dynamite novel that readers will treasure for years to come."   —*RT Book Reviews*

ONCE SMITTEN, TWICE SHY

"Lori Wilde at her best...I really loved this story. The writing is wonderful and the plot grabbed my attention from the first page. I fell in love with the characters and couldn't wait to see how they worked everything out."

—ContemporaryRomanceWriters.com

"A definite crowd pleaser...Lori Wilde can write very engaging and quirky romances and *Once Smitten, Twice Shy* is one of them...[A] good read with some suspense to boot."

—FreshFiction.com

"A wild ride on an emotional roller coaster."

—FallenAngelReviews.com

ADDICTED TO LOVE

"Entertaining and humorous...There's a seriousness to it also, as the heroine learns to recognize real love and caring. Wilde again includes secondary romances that are intriguing, entertaining, and hot."

—*RT Book Reviews*

"Wilde brings romance fans a feel-good, laugh-out-loud read...one of the best romantic comedies I've read in a long time."

—NightsandWeekends.com

"Charming...lighthearted fun...strong secondary romances enhance an engaging Valentine tale."

—*Midwest Book Review*

ALL OF ME

"[The characters'] physical attraction heats up the pages, but their personal development forms the heart and soul of the novel, a delicately revealing in-depth character study. Wilde's clever combination of humor, sorrow and love brings a deeply appealing sense of realism."

—*Publishers Weekly*

HAPPILY EVER AFTER

LORI WILDE

FOREVER

NEW YORK   BOSTON

Forever
Hachette Book Group
237 Park Avenue
New York, NY 10017
www.HachetteBookGroup.com

Printed in the United States of America

First Edition: December 2013

10 9 8 7 6 5 4 3 2 1

OPM

Forever is an imprint of Grand Central Publishing.
The Forever name and logo are trademarks of Hachette Book Group, Inc.

The Hachette Speakers Bureau provides a wide range of authors for speaking events. To find out more, go to www.hachettespeakersbureau.com or call (866) 376-6591.

The publisher is not responsible for websites (or their content) that are not owned by the publisher.

Contents

Addicted to Love

In memory of
Frederick Shawn Blalock 1967–2007
Be at peace, my brother.

Acknowledgment

While Valentine, Texas, is a real place, the town of Valentine depicted in the pages of this book is completely fictional. I've taken literary license for story purposes.

Rachael's Story

Chapter 1

The last thing Sheriff Brody Carlton expected to find when he wheeled his state-issued white-and-black Crown Victoria patrol cruiser past the WELCOME TO VALENTINE, TEXAS, ROMANCE CAPITAL OF THE USA billboard was a woman in a sequined wedding dress dangling from the town's mascot—a pair of the most garish, oversized, scarlet puckered-up-for-a-kiss lips ever poured in fiberglass.

She swayed forty feet off the ground in the early Sunday morning summer breeze, one arm wrapped around the sensuous curve of the full bottom lip, her other arm wielding a paintbrush dipped in black paint, her white satin ballet-slippered toes skimming the billboard's weathered wooden platform.

The billboard had been vandalized before, but never, to Brody's knowledge, by a disgruntled bride. He contemplated hitting the siren to warn her off, but feared she'd startle and end up breaking her silly neck. Instead, he whipped over onto the shoulder of the road, rolled down the passenger-side window, slid his Maui Jim sunglasses to the end of his nose, and craned his neck for a better look.

The delinquent bride had her bottom lip tucked up between her teeth. She was concentrating on desecrating the billboard. It had been a staple in Valentine's history for as long as Brody could remember. Her blonde hair, done up in one of those twisty braided hairdos, was partially obscured by the intricate lace of a floor-length wedding veil. When the sunlight hit the veil's lace just right it shimmered a phosphorescent pattern of white butterflies that looked as if they were about to rise up and flutter away.

She was oblivious to anything except splashing angry black brushstrokes across the hot, sexy mouth.

Brody exhaled an irritated snort, threw the Crown Vic into park, stuck the Maui Jims in his front shirt pocket, and climbed out. Warily, he eyed the gravel. Loose rocks. His sworn enemy. Then he remembered his new bionic Power Knee and relaxed. He'd worn the innovative prosthetic for only six weeks, but it had already changed his life. Because of the greater ease of movement and balance the computerized leg afforded, it was almost impossible for the casual observer to guess he was an amputee.

He walked directly underneath the sign, cocked his tan Stetson back on his head, and looked up.

As far as he knew—and he knew most everything that went on in Valentine, population 1,987—there'd been no weddings scheduled in town that weekend. So where had the bride come from?

Brody cleared his throat.

She went right on painting.

He cleared his throat again, louder this time.

Nothing.

"Ma'am," he called up to her.

"Go away. Can't you see I'm busy?"

Dots of black paint spattered the sand around him.

She'd almost obliterated the left-hand corner of the upper lip, transforming the Marilyn Monroe sexpot pout into Marilyn Manson gothic rot.

The cynic inside him grinned. Brody had always hated those tacky red lips. Still, it was a Valentine icon and he was sworn to uphold the law.

He glanced around and spied the lollipop pink VW Bug parked between two old abandoned railway cars rusting alongside the train tracks that ran parallel to the highway. He could see a red-and-pink beaded heart necklace dangling from the rearview mirror, and a sticker on the chrome bumper proclaimed I HEART ROMANCE.

All rightee then.

"If you don't cease and desist, I'll have to arrest you," he explained.

She stopped long enough to balance the brush on the paint can and glower down at him. "On what charges?"

"Destruction of private property. The billboard is on Kelvin Wentworth's land."

"I'm doing this town a much-needed community service," she growled.

"Oh, yeah?"

"This," she said, sweeping a hand at the billboard, "is false advertising. It perpetuates a dangerous myth. I'm getting rid of it before it can suck in more impressionable young girls."

"What myth is that?"

"That there's such things as true love and romance, magic and soul mates. Rubbish. All those fairy tales are complete and utter rubbish and I fell for it, hook, line, and sinker."

"Truth in advertising *is* an oxymoron."

"Exactly. And I'm pulling the plug."

You'll get no argument from me, he thought, but vandalism was vandalism and he was the sheriff, even if he agreed with her in theory. In practice, he was the law. "Wanna talk about it?"

She glared. "To a man? You've gotta be kidding me."

"Judging from your unorthodox attire and your displeasure with the billboard in particular and men in general, I'm gonna go out on a limb here and guess that you were jilted at the altar."

"Perceptive," she said sarcastically.

"Another woman?"

She didn't respond immediately and he was about to repeat the question when she muttered, "The Chicago Bears."

"The Bears?"

"Football."

Brody sank his hands onto his hips. "The guy jilted you over football?"

"Bastard." She was back at it again, slinging paint.

"He sounds like a dumbass."

"He's Trace Hoolihan."

Brody shrugged. "Is that supposed to mean something?"

"You don't know who he is?"

"Nope."

"Hallelujah," the bride-that-wasn't said. "I've found the one man in Texas who's not ate up with football."

It wasn't that he didn't like football, but the last couple of years his life had been preoccupied with adjusting to losing his leg in Iraq, getting over a wife who'd left him for another man, helping his wayward sister raise her young daughter, and settling into his job as sheriff. He hadn't had much time for leisurely pursuits.

"How'd you get up there?" Brody asked.

"With my white sequined magical jet pack."

"You've got a lot of anger built up inside."

"You think?"

"I know you're heartbroken and all," he drawled, "but I'm gonna have to ask you to stop painting the Valentine kisser."

"This isn't the first time, you know," she said without breaking stride. *Swish, swish, swish* went the paintbrush.

"You've vandalized a sign before?"

"I've been stood up at the altar before."

"No kidding?"

"Last year. The ratfink never showed up. Left me standing in the church for over an hour while my wilting orchid bouquet attracted bees."

"And still, you were willing to try again."

"I know. I'm an idiot. Or at least I was. But I'm turning over a new leaf. Joining the skeptics."

"Well, if you don't stop painting the sign, you're going to be joining the ranks of the inmates at the Jeff Davis County Jail."

"You've got prisoners?"

"Figure of speech." How did she know the jail was empty fifty percent of the time? Brody squinted suspiciously. He didn't recognize her, at least not from this distance. "You from Valentine?"

"I live in Houston now."

That was as far as the conversation got because the mayor's fat, honking Cadillac bumped to a stop behind Brody's cruiser.

Kelvin P. Wentworth IV flung the car door open and wrestled his hefty frame from behind the wheel. Merle Haggard belted from the radio, wailing a thirty-year-old country-and-western song about boozing and chasing women.

"What the hell's going on here," Kelvin boomed and lumbered toward Brody.

The mayor tilted his head up, scowling darkly at the billboard bride. Kelvin prided himself on shopping only in Valentine. He refused to even order off the Internet. He was big and bald and on the back side of his forties. His seersucker suit clung to him like leeches on a water buffalo. Kelvin was under the mistaken impression he was still as good-looking as the day he'd scored the winning touchdown that took Valentine to state in 1977, the year Brody was born. It was the first and last time the town had been in the playoffs.

Brody suppressed the urge to roll his eyes. He knew what was coming. Kelvin was a true believer in the Church of Valentine and the jilted bride had just committed the highest form of blasphemy. "I've got it under control, Mayor."

"My ass." Kelvin waved an angry hand. "She's up there defacin' and disgracin' our hometown heritage and you're standing here with your thumb up your butt, Carlton."

"She's distraught. Her fiancé dumped her at the altar."

"Rachael Renee Henderson," Kelvin thundered up at her. "Is that you?"

"Go away, Mayor. This is something that's gotta be done," she called back.

"You get yourself down off that billboard right now, or I'm gonna call your daddy."

Rachael Henderson.

The name brought an instant association into Brody's mind. He saw an image of long blonde pigtails, gap-toothed grin, and freckles across the bridge of an upturned pixie nose. Rachael Henderson, the next-door neighbor who'd followed him around like a puppy dog until he'd moved to Midland with his mother and his sister after their father went to Kuwait when Brody was twelve. From what he recalled, Rachael was sweet as honeysuckle, certainly not the type to graffiti a beloved town landmark.

People change.

He thought of Belinda and shook his head to clear away thoughts of his ex-wife.

"My daddy is partly to blame for this," she said. "Last time I saw him he was in Houston breaking my mother's heart. Go ahead and call him. Would you like his cell phone number?"

"What's she talking about?" Kelvin swung his gaze to Brody.

Brody shrugged. "Apparently she's got some personal issues to work out."

"Well, she can't work them out on my billboard."

"I'm getting the impression the billboard is a symbol of her personal issues."

"I don't give a damn. Get 'er down."

"How do you propose I do that?"

Kelvin squinted at the billboard. "How'd she get up there?"

"Big mystery. But why don't we just let her have at it? She's bound to run out of steam soon enough in this heat."

"Are you nuts? Hell, man, she's already blacked out the top lip." Kelvin anxiously shifted his weight, bunched his hands into fists. "I won't stand for this. Find a way to get her down. Now!"

"What do you want me to do? Shoot her?"

"It's a thought," Kelvin muttered.

"Commanding the sheriff to shoot a jilted bride won't help you get reelected."

"It ain't gonna help my reelection bid if she falls off

that billboard and breaks her fool neck because I didn't stop her."

"Granted."

Kelvin cursed up a blue streak and swiped a meaty hand across his sweaty forehead. "I was supposed to be getting doughnuts so me and Marianne could have a nice, quiet breakfast before church, but hell no, I gotta deal with this stupid crap." Kelvin, a self-proclaimed playboy, had never married. Marianne was his one hundred and twenty pound bullmastiff.

"Go get your doughnuts, Mayor," Brody said. "I've got this under control."

Kelvin shot him a withering look and pulled his cell phone from his pocket. Brody listened to the one-sided conversation, his eyes on Rachael, who showed no signs of slowing her assault on the vampish pout.

"Rex," Kelvin barked to his personal assistant. "Go over to Audie's, have him open the hardware store up for you, get a twenty-five-foot ladder, and bring it out to the Valentine billboard."

There was a pause from Kelvin as Rex responded.

"I don't care if you stayed up 'til three a.m. playing video games with your geeky online buddies. Just do it."

With a savage slash of his thumb on the keypad, Kelvin hung up and muttered under his breath, "I'm surrounded by morons."

Brody tried not to take offense at the comment. Kelvin liked his drama as much as he liked ordering people around.

Fifteen minutes later, Rex showed up with a collapsible yellow ladder roped to his pickup truck. He was barely twenty-five, redheaded as rhubarb, and had a voice deep as Barry White's, with an Adam's apple that protruded like a submarine ready to break the surface. Brody often wondered if the prominent Adam's apple had anything to do with the kid's smooth, dark, ebony voice.

Up on the billboard, Rachael was almost finished with the mouth. She had slashes of angry black paint smeared across the front of her wedding gown. While waiting on Rex to show up with the ladder, Kelvin had spent the time trying to convince her to come down, but she was a zealot on a mission and she wouldn't even talk to him.

"I want her arrested," Kelvin snapped. "I'm pressing charges."

"You might want to reconsider that," Brody advised. "Since the election is just a little more than three months away and Giada Vito is gaining favor in the polls."

The polls being the gossip at Higgy's Diner. He knew the mayor was grandstanding. For the first time in Kelvin's three-term stint, he was running opposed. Giada Vito had moved to Valentine from Italy and she'd gotten her American citizenship as soon as the law allowed. She was a dyed-in-the-wool Democrat, the principal of Valentine High, drove a vintage Fiat, and didn't mince her words. Especially when it came to the topic of Valentine's favored son, Kelvin P. Wentworth IV.

"Hey, you leave the legal and political machinations to me. You just do your job," said Kelvin.

Brody blew out his breath and went to help Rex untie the ladder. What he wanted to do was tell Kelvin to shove it. But the truth was the woman needed to come down before she got hurt. More than likely, the wooden billboard decking was riddled with termites.

He and Rex got the ladder loose and carried it over to prop it against the back of the billboard. It extended just long enough to reach the ladder rungs that were attached to the billboard itself.

Kelvin gave Brody a pointed look. "Up you go."

Brody ignored him. "Rachael, we've got a ladder in place. You need to come down now."

"Don't ask her, tell her," Kelvin hissed to Brody, then said to Rachael, "Missy, get your ass down here this instant."

"Get bent," Rachael sang out.

"That was effective," Brody muttered.

Rex snorted back a laugh. Kelvin shot him a withering glance and then raised his eyebrows at Brody and jerked his head toward the billboard. "You're the sheriff. Do your job."

Brody looked up at the ladder and then tried his best not to glance down at his leg. He didn't want to show the slightest sign of weakness, especially in front of Kelvin. But while his Power Knee was pretty well the most awesome thing that had happened to him since his rehabilitation, he'd never tested it by climbing a ladder, particularly a thin, wobbly, collapsible one.

Shit. If he fell off, it was going to hurt. He might even break something.

Kelvin was staring expectantly, arms crossed over his bearish chest, the sleeves of his seersucker suit straining against his bulky forearms. The door to the Cadillac was still hanging open and from the radio Merle Haggard had given it up to Tammy Wynette, who was beseeching women to stand by their man.

Brody was the sheriff. This was his job. And he never shirked his duty, even when it was the last thing on earth he wanted to do. Gritting his teeth, he gathered his courage, wrapped both hands around the ladder just above his head, and planted his prosthetic leg on the bottom rung.

His gut squeezed.

Come on, you can do this.

He attacked the project the same way he'd attacked physical therapy, going at it with dogged determination to walk again, to come home, if not whole, at least proud to be a man. Of course Belinda had shattered all that.

Don't think about Belinda. Get up the ladder. Get the girl down.

He placed his good leg on the second rung.

The ladder trembled under his weight.

Brody swallowed back the fear and pulled his prosthesis up the next step. Hands clinging tightly to the ladder above him, he raised his head and counted the steps.

Twenty-five of them on the ladder and seventeen on the back of the billboard.

Three down, thirty-nine left to go.

He remembered an old movie called *The Thirty-Nine Steps*. Suddenly, those three words held a weighted significance. It wasn't just thirty-nine more steps. It was also forty-two more back down with Rachael Henderson in tow.

Better get climbing.

Thirty-eight steps.

Thirty-seven.

Thirty-six.

The higher he went, the more the ladder quivered.

Halfway up vertigo took solid hold of him. He'd never had a fear of heights before, but now, staring down at Kelvin and Rex, who were staring up at him, Brody's head swam and his stomach pitched. He bit his bottom lip, closed his eyes, and took another step up.

In the quiet of the higher air, he could hear the soft whispery sound of his computerized leg working as he took another step. Kelvin's country music sounded tinny and far away. With his eyes closed and his hands skimming over the cool aluminum ladder, he could also hear the sound of brushstrokes growing faster and more frantic the closer he came to the bottom of the billboard.

Rachael was still furiously painting, trying to get in as many licks as she could.

When Brody finally reached the top of the first ladder, he opened his eyes.

"You're doing great," Kelvin called up to him. "Keep going. You're almost there."

Yeah, almost there. This was the hardest part of all, covering the gap between the ladder from Audie's Hardware and the thin metal footholds welded to the back of the billboard.

He took a deep breath. He had to stretch to reach the bottom step. He grabbed hold of it with both hands, and took his Power Knee off the aluminum ladder.

For a moment, he hung there, twenty-five feet off the ground, fighting gravity and the bile rising in his throat, wondering why he hadn't told Kelvin to go straight to hell. Wondering why he hadn't just called the volunteer fire department to come and get Rachael down.

It was a matter of pride and he knew it. Stupid, egotistical pride. He'd wanted to prove he could handle anything that came with the job. Wanted to show the town he'd earned their vote. That he hadn't just stumbled into the office because he was an injured war hero.

Pride goes before a fall, his Gramma Carlton used to say. Now, for the first time, he fully understood what she meant.

Arms trembling with the effort, he dragged himself up with his biceps, his real leg tiptoed on the collapsible ladder, his bionic leg searching blindly for the rung.

Just when he thought he wouldn't be able to hold on a second longer, he found the toehold and then brought his good leg up against the billboard ladder to join the bionic one.

He'd made it.

Brody clung there, breathing hard, thanking God for letting him get this far and wondering just how in the hell he was going to get back down without killing them both, when he heard the soft sounds of muffled female sobs.

Rachael was crying.

The hero in him forgot that his limbs were quivering, forgot that he was forty feet in the air, forgot that somehow he was going to have to get back down. The only thing in his mind was the woman.

Was she all right?

As quickly as he could, Brody scaled the remaining rungs and then gingerly settled his legs on the billboard decking. He ducked under the bottom of the sign and peered around it.

She sat, knees drawn to her chest, head down, looking completely incongruous in that wedding dress smeared with black paint and the butterfly wedding veil floating around her head. Miraculously, the veil seemed to have escaped the paint.

"You okay?"

She raised her head. "Of course I'm not okay."

Up close, he saw tear tracks had run a gully through the makeup on her cheeks and mascara had pooled underneath her eyes. She looked like a quarrelsome raccoon caught in a coyote trap, all piss and vinegar, but visibly hurting.

He had the strangest, and most uncharacteristic, urge to pull her into his arms, hold her to his chest, kiss the top of her head the way he did his six-year-old niece, Maisy, and tell her everything was going to be all right.

Mentally, he stomped the impulse. He didn't need any damsel-in-distress hassle.

The expression in her eyes told him anger had propelled her up here, but now, her rage spent, she was afraid to come back down. That fear he understood loud and clear.

Calmly, he held out a hand to her. "Rachael, it's time to go."

"I thought I'd feel better," she said in a despondent little voice as she stared at his outstretched hand. "I don't feel better. I was supposed to feel better. That was the plan. Why don't I feel better?"

"Destruction rarely makes you feel good." His missing leg gave a twinge. "Come on, give me your hand and let's get back on the ground."

"You look familiar. Are you married?" she asked.

He opened his mouth to answer, but she didn't give him a chance before launching into a fast-paced monologue. "I hope you're married, because if you're not married, you need to get someone else to help me down from here."

"Huh?" Had the sun baked her brain or had getting stood up at the altar made her crazy?

"If you're not married, then this is a cute meet. I'm a sucker for meeting cute."

"Huh?" he said again.

"My first fiancé?" she chattered, her glossolalia revealing her emotional distress. "I met Robert in a hot-air balloon. He was the pilot. I wanted a romantic adventure. The balloon hung up in a pecan tree and the fire department had to rescue us. It was terribly cute."

"Sounds like it," he said, simply to appease her. Mentally, he was planning their trip off the billboard.

"And Trace? I met him when he came to the kindergarten

class where I taught. On career day. He was tossing a football around as he gave his speech. He lost control of it and accidentally beaned me in the head. He literally knocked me off my feet. He caught me just before I hit the ground and there I was, trapped in his big strong arms, staring up into his big blue eyes. I just melted. So you see I succumb to the cute meet. I've got to break the cycle and these romantic notions I have about love and marriage and dating and men. But I can't do it if I go around meeting cute. There's no way I can let you rescue me if you're not married."

The woman, Brody decided, was officially bonkers.

"Sorry." He shrugged. "I'm divorced."

She grimaced. "Oh, no."

"But this isn't a cute meet."

She glanced over at the fiberglass billboard lips, then peered down at her paint-spotted wedding dress and finally drilled him with almond-shaped green eyes, the only exotic thing about her.

The rest of her was round and smooth and welcoming, from her cherubic cheeks to her petite curves to the full bow of her supple pink mouth. She was as soft-focus as a Monet. Just looking at her made him think of springtime and flowers and fuzzy baby chicks.

Except for those disconcerting bedroom eyes. They called up unwanted X-rated images in his mind.

"I dunno," she said, "this seems dangerously cute to me."

"It can't be a cute meet," he explained, struggling to follow her disjointed train of thought, "because we've already met."

She tilted her head. "We have?"

"Yep."

"I thought you looked familiar."

"So no cute meet. Now give me your hand."

Reluctantly, she placed her hand in his. "Where did we meet?"

"Right here in Valentine." He spoke with a soothing voice. Her hand was warm and damp with perspiration. He drew her toward him.

She didn't resist. She was tired and emotionally exhausted.

"That's it," he coaxed.

"You do look familiar."

"Watch your head," he said as he led her underneath the billboard, toward the ladder.

She paused at the ladder and stared at the ground. "It's a long way down."

Tell me about it.

"I'm here, I'll go first. I'll be there to catch you if you lose your balance."

"Will you keep your hand on my waist? To steady me?"

"Sure," he promised recklessly, placing chivalry over common sense.

He started down the ladder ahead of her, found secure footing, wrapped his left hand around the rung, and reached up to hold on to her waist with his right hand as she started down.

Touching her brought an unexpected knot of emotion to his chest. Half desire, half tenderness, he didn't know what to call it, but he knew one thing. The feeling was damned dangerous.

"I'm scared," she whimpered.

"You're doing great." He guided her down until her sweet little rump was directly in his face. Any other time he would have enjoyed this position, but not under these circumstances.

"I'm going down another couple of steps," he explained. "I'm going to have to let go of you for a minute, so hold on tight."

The long train of her wedding veil floated in the air between them, a gauzy pain in the ass. In order to see where he was going, he had to keep batting it back. He took up his position several rungs below her and called to her to come down. As he'd promised, he put a hand at her waist to guide her.

They went on like that, painstaking step by painstaking step, until they were past the gap, off the billboard, and onto the collapsible aluminum ladder. In that regard, coming down was much easier than going up.

"You're certain I already know you?" she asked. "Because seriously, this has all the makings of a meet cute."

"You know me."

"How?"

"I'm from Valentine, just like you. Moved away, came back," he said.

Only four feet off the ground now. His legs felt flimsy as spindly garden sprouts.

"Oh my gosh," she gasped and whipped her head around quickly.

Too quickly.

Somehow, in the breeze and the movement, the infernal wedding veil wrapped around his prosthetic leg. He tried to kick it off but the material clung stubbornly.

"I know who you are," she said and then right there on the ladder, she turned around to glare at him. "You're Brody Carlton."

He didn't have a chance to answer. The ladder swayed and the veil snatched his leg out from under him.

He lost his balance.

The next thing he knew, he was lying on his back on the ground, and Rachael Henderson, his one-time next-door-neighbor-turned-jilted-psycho-bride, was on top of him. They were both breathing hard and trembling.

Her eyes locked on his.

His eyes locked on her lips.

Brody should have been thinking about his leg. He was surprised he wasn't thinking about his leg. What he was thinking about was the fact that he was being straddled by a woman in a wedding dress and it was the closest he'd come to having sex in over two years.

"You! You're the one."

"The one?" he asked.

"You're the root cause of all my problems," she exclaimed, fire in her eyes, at the same time Brody found himself thinking, *Where have you been all my life?*

But that was not what he said.

What he said was, "Rachael Renee Henderson, you have the right to remain silent..."

Chapter 2

Kelvin Wentworth was so steamed he couldn't enjoy his crullers. He tossed the half-eaten pastry to Marianne and dusted his sticky fingers against this thigh. The bullmastiff snarfed it up with a smack of her lips, and then eyed him to see if more was forthcoming. When she realized it wasn't, she settled back down on her plush pillow.

"Dammit, Marianne," he complained. "This couldn't have happened at a worse time. You should see what that foolish Henderson girl did to our billboard."

The dog made a huffing noise and covered her nose with her paws.

"I know!" Kelvin pushed himself up out of his chair and paced the generous length of the study that had been his daddy's and his granddaddy's and his great-granddaddy's before that.

Three generations of Wentworths had been born and raised in this house. All their portraits and photographs of their accomplishments hung on the wall. There was Great-Granddaddy, Kelvin Wentworth I, covered in crude oil and grinning like an opossum as his first well came in. Next was a snapshot of Granddaddy Kelvin Wentworth II breaking ground on Wentworth Novelties. Beside that was a picture of Kelvin's daddy, Kelvin Wentworth III, shaking hands with LBJ at the dedication of his man-made, heart-shaped Lake Valentine.

A wall of fame. An illustrious heritage.

"Maybe I should've gotten married," he mused. "Had kids."

Marianne didn't offer an opinion.

"I had plenty of chances. I just never expected to get this old, this quick. I always thought I'd have time. Sow some wild oats before I settled down. Then again, how could I get married when I had a town to run? Valentine depended on me. Needed me. Especially after Daddy died."

He stopped pacing in front of his own photograph in the lineup. In the picture he was being hoisted up on the shoulders of his teammates, all the while tightly clutching the Texas State High School Championship football trophy. Back then he'd had a full head of hair, a lean body, and a thousand-watt smile. "Where'd the years go?"

Marianne sighed.

"This Amusement Corp deal is the only legacy I have to leave behind," he said. "Other than the championship win. It's gotta go through. The Amusement Corp representatives can't show up in town on Wednesday and see that billboard in the shape it's in."

Marianne barked.

"You're right. I'm probably overreacting about the billboard. I can get it cleaned up in time. But it's not just the billboard. It's that damned Giada Vito and the back-to-nature concepts she's kicking up. What the hell is wrong with the woman? She has no idea what's best for this town. She's a foreigner for crissake."

But Kelvin knew what was best. His family had founded Valentine.

He walked over to the pool table in the center of the room that held a mock-up of his vision for Valentine's future. His plans had been a decade in the making and were finally coming to fruition.

Squatting down to eye level, he admired the replica of a theme park the likes of which had never before been conceived. Valentine Land. The ultimate destination for fun-loving honeymooners. He flicked a switch on the plywood foundation and everything sprang to life.

The *Gone With the Wind* roller coaster started up the incline. The *My Fair Lady* Tilt-a-Whirl twirled. The *Pride and Prejudice* waterslide gurgled. Strobe lights flashed in the *It Happened One Night* Tunnel of Love while the *Camelot* Carousel went round and round.

And along with the theme park would come the Wentworth Airport, Wentworth Resort Hotels, and Wentworth Restaurants.

Excitement coursed through Kelvin's veins. Great-Granddaddy had found oil and built this house. Granddaddy had constructed Wentworth Novelties and groomed it into the world's largest supplier of Valentine's Day novelties outside of China. Daddy had created Valentine Lake and started the annual Fish-A-Thon tournament to supply the local food bank.

And now it was his turn.

Kelvin was going down in history as the man who brought true prosperity to Valentine. He had Walt Disney dreams, and with Amusement Corp's backing, he could make it happen.

The telephone rang.

Irritated at being interrupted, Kelvin straightened and

went for the phone. The caller ID told him it was the sheriff. "What you want, Carlton?" he grunted.

"Are you really serious about pressing charges against Rachael Henderson?"

"Hell, yes, I am." He had to nip her insurrection in the bud. He couldn't have anti-romance sentiment floating round while trying to sell the town on Valentine Land.

"Couldn't she just agree to clean it up and let it go at that? There's no reason to take this to court."

"My sign was vandalized, Sheriff. Do your job."

"Judge Pruitt is out of town until tomorrow. If you insist on pressing charges, Rachael is going to have to spend the night in jail."

"Boo hoo. Tough luck. She should have thought about that before she went and painted up my billboard."

"You're being a hard-ass for no reason."

"She defaced a local landmark."

"It's not like it's the first time someone's taken a pot-shot at the sign."

"She's a negative influence. I'd think you'd be more concerned about her disrespect for our hometown."

"Okay, Mayor, you have every legal right to press charges, but I want to go on record here. I think you're being a jackass."

"Thanks for your opinion. Now why don't you take it and a buck fifty and head on over to Higgy's Diner and buy yourself a cup of coffee. I'll drop by to file an official complaint right after church."

Brody slammed the phone down on his desk and muttered an oath under his breath.

His only full-time deputy Zeke Frisco's wife had given birth last night to their first child. The baby was five weeks early, putting Brody at a disadvantage. His two part-time deputies had taken their summer vacations together in order to be off when Zeke went on paternity leave. The dispatcher, Jamie Johnston, was a single mom who worked nine to three Monday through Friday so she could take her kids to school and pick them up afterward without having to hire a babysitter.

Damn Kelvin and his insistence on pressing charges. If the Wentworths hadn't owned the land where the sign was erected, he would have told the mayor he could stuff it.

As it was, he'd had no choice but to arrest Rachael.

Hands down, the hardest part of his job was putting up with the mayor. There wasn't much crime in Valentine. Occasionally one of the regulars at Leroy's Bar on the outskirts of town would kick up a fuss and Brody would have to lock him in the drunk tank overnight. Or he'd have to haul someone in on a warrant for child support violations or unpaid traffic tickets. Once in a rare while there would be a few petty thefts or shoplifting incidents or he'd catch some high school kid selling weed from the trunk of his car. But most of the time things were pretty peaceful in his hometown and that's the way he liked it. He'd had enough excitement in Iraq to last a lifetime.

Kelvin was the only thing that got under his skin. That and his insecurities over his leg. He was determined to be a good sheriff in spite of his handicap.

Don't let Wentworth get to you.

Good advice. Now if he could just heed it.

Of course, the real source of his problem was the woman in the wedding gown sitting in lockup.

Inexplicably, his gut tightened as he remembered just how good it had felt to have her firm thighs wrapped around his waist. He still couldn't believe she was the same kid who used to live next door to him all those years ago.

Nor could he believe the way his body had responded to her. He hadn't felt much in the way of sexual interest since Belinda had taken off with another man. It had been over two years and while he'd gotten over her betrayal, he knew he still wasn't ready to lay his heart open again.

Lay your heart open? Hell, you're just horny. That's all it is.

But deep down inside, he feared that wasn't true. He was lonely and he missed the good parts about being married. The long talks, the intimacy, the fun times.

Love's not worth the risk.

He took a deep breath and pushed his hands through his hair. If he tilted his head, he could see through his open door to the jail beyond. Rachael sat behind bars, her head cradled in her palms.

Sympathy kicked him. He hated this but he had no choice. He had to go tell her she'd be spending the night in jail.

"How you holding up?"

Rachael sat on the cement jail slab amid the billowy taffeta of her paint-smeared wedding dress. She raised her chin to see Brody Carlton walk over to stand in front of her jail cell, his leather shoes creaking against the cement, his hands on his hips just above the holster of his gun. He looked amused.

"You think this is funny?" she snapped.

"I didn't say that."

"You're smirking."

"I'm not smirking."

"You are."

"Okay, maybe I am a little," he said, "but you've got to admit, it's sort of funny."

She glared. "It's not the least bit funny."

He wiped the smile from his mouth, but not from his eyes. "Can't say I've ever seen a bride behind bars."

"What's the matter with you," she scolded, "enjoying the tragedy of another?"

"You call this a tragedy?" he growled, the expression in his eyes suddenly flashing from teasing tolerance to borderline anger. "Princess, come down out of your ivory tower. You have no idea what real tragedy is."

She remembered something her mother had told her about him in passing. Brody had been sent to Iraq. He'd been wounded and won some kind of medal for bravery. But that's all she knew about him. She hadn't even known he was the new sheriff. She hadn't paid much attention to Selina's gossip about Valentine in the years after she'd moved away. She'd been too busy repeatedly falling in love with all the wrong guys. And she hadn't been back home for a long time. Usually her parents came to see her in Houston, or they all gathered at her younger sister's home in San Antonio. Hannah was married and had two babies.

Humiliation burned in her chest over what she'd just said to him. The man was a war hero. He'd seen real tragedy.

Oh God, she was so selfish.

"You're right," Rachael admitted, shamefaced. "It was a stupid thing to say. I was just feeling sorry for myself. I know this is a problem of my own making."

"You're upset."

He'd come closer and was now leaning against the bars with his hands on his hips, elbows thrust out, studying her like an anthropologist in the Outback. As if she were some curious creature who'd caught his attention. But it was a clinical, controlled interest devoid of personal feelings.

He's learned how to step outside himself, she realized. To detach from whatever emotionally chaotic situation he found going on around him. A handy skill. One she'd do well to emulate.

But instead of emulating his calm, cool manner, she found herself remembering what it had felt like straddling his hard, muscular body after they'd fallen from the ladder together. She recalled the tumble and the disconcerting thrill that had shot through her. The same thrill that—whenever she experienced it—had always signaled potential romance.

She'd managed to ignore it at the time, to thrust it from her mind. But now, looking at Brody's hard, lean frame, she was finding it very difficult to forget. He reminded her of the actor Matthew Fox. He played the character of Jack Shepard on the television show *Lost*: moral, principled, self-contained, not to mention a stone-cold hottie.

Rachael couldn't stop her gaze from drifting over him. She could smell his scent from here. Manly—all leather and gunpowder overlaying the aroma of clean soap. Stupidly, she found herself wondering if he tasted as masculine as he smelled. He possessed a strong, stubborn jaw and dark enigmatic eyes. The look he gave her seemed to say, *I know all your secrets; you can't hide anything from me.*

Rachael gulped. Not that she'd ever been any good at hiding her feelings.

He was tall. Well over six feet. A tower compared to her own five-foot-three inches. His dark brown hair was clipped short. Not quite a military cut, but not much longer. His tan uniform fit him to perfection. The sleeves of his shirt and the creases of his pants were crisply starched. Even in the muted jail lighting, the badge on his chest gleamed smartly. Give the man a black mask and a white horse, and he could pass for the Lone Ranger.

Involuntarily, Rachael licked her lips.

He was as tempting to her as a double scotch on the rocks was to a boozehound. Just looking at him had her spinning happily-ever-after daydreams.

Stop it!

She had a very serious problem. Fantasizing about a new guy the day after the old guy had stood her up at the altar.

Warped. She was warped.

Brody's not new. He's the very first guy you ever spun romantic fantasies about.

Yeah, and look where that had gotten her.

"Um," she said, "I need to use the bathroom and I have the most awful feeling that hole in the floor is where I'm expected to go."

A look of pity crossed his face. That irritated her more than his amusement. She didn't need his pity.

"I'll let you use my private restroom," he said, taking the jail keys from his pocket and opening the door. "And I've brought you a sandwich from Higgy's."

Her mouth watered but she wasn't going to let him know she appreciated his kindness. "Don't do me any favors," she muttered.

He arched an eyebrow. "You want to use the hole?"

"No, no."

The amusement was back on his lips.

Okay, he was officially making it easy for her to swear off men forever.

"This way." He took her elbow and guided her out of the cell. His fingers were calloused. His grip strong. Rachael felt something twist inside her. Something she couldn't name curled against the wall of her chest. She caught her breath, suddenly afraid to breathe.

Brody led her through the main lobby and back into his office. His shoulder brushed against hers. Rachael's skin tingled beneath his touch. Unnerved by the sensation, she felt her muscles coil up tight. This was ridiculous.

He shut the door behind them, indicated a second door on the other side of the room. "Don't get any ideas about escaping."

"You think I could shimmy out a window in this getup?" she asked, fluffing the skirts of her wedding gown.

"You climbed up on a billboard in it."

"You've got a point," she said and went into the bathroom.

A few minutes later, she emerged to find him lounging against the desk, arms folded across his chest. The thought that he'd overheard her in the bathroom made her cheeks burn.

"Eat your sandwich," he said, kicking a rolling chair over for her.

Rachael sat down on the other side of his desk, grateful for the ham-and-cheese sandwich on a plate covered with plastic wrap, along with a pickle and a scoop of potato salad. There was also a plastic glass filled to the brim with ice-cold sweet tea.

She was starving. She couldn't remember the last time she'd eaten. After Trace had left her at the altar, she'd taken off without thinking, without changing clothes, without even stopping for food. She'd hopped in her VW Bug and driven the four hundred miles from Houston to Valentine through the dark of night—with only a slight detour to Wal-Mart for the black paint—bent on annihilating that damned billboard because it represented a decade of bad dates, broken hearts, and shattered dreams.

She tore into the sandwich and Brody sat down opposite her. "So," she said between bites, "how long you been sheriff?"

"A few months. Ever since Mel Hartly got sick and I was elected his replacement."

"Aren't you kind of young to be a sheriff?"

He shrugged.

"It's the war vet thing, right?"

"I don't like to talk about it."

She studied him over the rim of her glass. "I heard you got some kind of a medal."

"That's talking about it."

"It might help if you discussed it."

"Does talking about getting dumped at the altar help you?"

He had her there. "No."

"Glad we settled that."

Rachael polished off the rest of her sandwich. "Hey, you remember that time we climbed the chinaberry tree in your front yard and I got stuck and you had to help me down?"

"Vaguely," he said.

"Seems like you're making a habit of helping me climb down when I get myself up a tree. I wanted to say thanks for getting me off that billboard in one piece. Thanks for the chinaberry tree, too."

He grinned. "Don't mention it."

She dusted off her fingertips. "So when can I get out of here?"

"Not until tomorrow morning. Judge Abigail's out of town. She'll be back to arraign you at ten."

Panic took hold of her then. "What? I'm going to have to spend the night here? Just for painting the billboard?"

"I couldn't talk the mayor out of pressing charges."

Her eyes stung. She swallowed hard. "Don't I get a phone call?"

"You do."

"Can I make it now?"

He nodded, plucked the receiver from the phone on his desk, and extended it toward her.

Rachael started to reach for the phone, but stopped midway. Who was she going to call? She was furious at her parents. Trace was on his way to Chicago. She certainly wasn't going to alarm her sister, Hannah. Immediately, she thought of her three best friends, all of whom had been at the wedding: Delaney, Tish, and Jillian. But Delaney and Tish both had little kids. She couldn't ask them to drive four hundred miles to bail her out of jail. And Jillian, well, much as she loved her, Jillian was such a cynic when it came to love she would probably get a huge kick out of the whole thing.

But what choice did she have? It was either Jillian or her parents and she wasn't speaking to them.

Taking in a deep breath, she spun around in the swivel chair until her back was to Brody and placed the call, all the while extremely aware of the heat of his gaze burning the nape of her neck.

"Samuels." Jillian answered the phone on the second ring in her usual clipped, no-nonsense style.

"Jilly?" She was alarmed to hear her voice sounding so shaky. "It's Rachael."

"Rach! Where are you? Everyone is worried sick. You

just took off without a word to anyone. Your parents are frantic. Have you called them?"

"No! And don't you tell them that I called you."

"Rachael," Jillian chided gently. "It's not like you to be so inconsiderate."

Well, it wasn't like Jillian—who often wore steel-toed army boots when it came to other people's feelings—to scold Rachael for being insensitive. That hurt.

"I'm sick of it, Jilly. My parents, my town, the media, advertising. Force-feeding me romance for twenty-six years when it's all just a load of bull..." Rachael paused to take a deep breath.

"Hey, you'll get no argument from me. I'm anti-romance. Always have been, always will be."

"I used to think you were coldhearted when it came to male-female relationships," Rachael said. "But I see now you were right and everyone else is off their rocker."

"I wouldn't go that far."

"Men suck."

Behind her, Brody cleared his throat.

Well, too darn bad if he got his feelings hurt. Men did suck. They pursued you like gangbusters, promising you the moon and the stars and happily-ever-after. Promises they had absolutely no intention of keeping once you succumbed to their pursuit and gave them your heart. Cruel bastards. Every last one of them.

"Listen, Jilly, I desperately need your help."

"Anything; you know that."

"I need you to come bail me out of the Jeff Davis County Jail."

"What?" Jillian sounded stunned. "You? You're in jail?"

"I got arrested."

"What for?"

"Vandalizing gigantic lips."

"Excuse me?"

"You'll see what I'm talking about when you get here."

"Get where? Where is Jeff Davis County?"

"Valentine."

"Your hometown?"

"Yes."

"Where is that, exactly?"

"This is the part that makes the favor really huge. Valentine is seriously in the middle of nowhere. Over four hundred miles from Houston. It's the only town in Jeff Davis County. We don't have a real airport, just a private airstrip. You'll have to drive. I'm being arraigned at ten in the morning."

Her friend hesitated but only for a fraction of a second. "I'll have to rearrange my schedule, but I'll be there. It sounds like you could use a good lawyer." Jillian was an ace Houston prosecutor. She'd rip the mayor's case to shreds and have Rachael out of there in no time.

"Thank you so much; you have no idea how much I appreciate this. I know what an imposition it—"

"Hush. What are friends for?"

"You're the best," she whispered.

"Now, are you sure you don't want me to let your parents at least know you're okay?"

Rachael paused, guilt warring with anger. "You can tell them you heard from me and that I'm all right, but please, Jilly, whatever you do, don't tell them I'm in Valentine. Don't tell them I got arrested. I need time to think this all through and figure out what I'm going to do next."

"I can respect that."

"Thank you," Rachael whispered.

"I'll be there in time for your court appearance," Jillian replied, then said good-bye and hung up.

Rachael cradled the telephone receiver then turned in the swivel chair to meet Brody's eyes. He was watching her the way a cat would watch a caged bird. Did they teach those unnerving looks in sheriff school? Or was this something he'd picked up on his own? A dubious gift from Baghdad, perhaps?

His gaze drilled into hers and a radiant wave of energy zapped from him to her. Fanciful, she told herself, struggling to deny the heat simmering inside her. She'd had these feelings before, mistaken them for something more than sexual attraction. She wasn't going to make that mistake again. She would admit it. She was sexually attracted to him.

Big deal. That's all it was. Hormones. Chemistry. It meant absolutely nothing. She was not going to start imagining the cute little cottage and the white picket fence and two kids in the yard.

She'd be much better served to imagine them naked, rolling around in his bed, having hot, sweaty sex. After that, she'd visualize herself getting up, getting dressed, and walking away without a backward glance.

While Rachael was cooling her heels in the Jeff Davis County Jail, Selina Henderson paced her hotel room at the Houston Four Seasons, trying for the fiftieth time to contact her daughter's cell phone. But just as it had the other forty-nine times, the call went to voice mail. Instead of issuing yet another plea for Rachael to call her back, Selina hung up and threw the phone across the room.

"Dammit all," she screamed and knotted her fingernails into her palms.

Anger had replaced guilt and concern. She was mad. Furious, in fact. Yes, Rachael had been hurt. She understood that. But this refusal to answer her phone or call her mother back was bordering on childishness.

However, the real object of Selina's fury wasn't her erstwhile daughter, but rather her soon-to-be ex-husband. She gritted her teeth. How could Michael have let it slip that they were getting divorced not ten minutes before that ridiculous Trace Hoolihan ran out on his wedding to Rachael?

She and Michael had driven to Houston together, agreeing not to tell Rachael about their split until she'd returned from her honeymoon. Agreeing for this one day to put up a united front. Selina had been so disgusted with Michael for going back on their agreement that she hadn't even been able to talk to him about their daughter.

So here she was on the verge of ending a twenty-seven-year marriage. All alone in a hotel room in a big city where she knew no one, and she had absolutely no idea where her daughter might have gone after being dumped at the altar on her wedding day.

Love, romance, marriage. Bah—*fucking*—humbug.

She flung herself across the bed she hadn't slept in. She'd been awake all night, thinking, planning, worrying, regretting, hating, loving, and hurting. The urge to cry was there, but honestly, she was cried out. Exhaustion permeated her bones. She was tired of fighting. Tired of pretending. Tired of trying to convince herself there was such a thing as happily-ever-after.

It was a myth.

Selina stared up at the ceiling textured with arty swirls. Forty-five years old, almost single and starting all over again. How had this happened? Once upon a time she'd loved Michael with an emotion so strong and fierce and true it scared her. Where had that foolish, lovesick girl gone?

It was a rhetorical question. She knew the answer.

The first tiny piece of doubt had taken root on her own wedding day when she'd discovered that her new husband had spent the night before their wedding with another woman. Her flaw had been that she'd loved him so much she'd chosen to believe his story that nothing had happened. That he'd gone out with his high school sweetheart, Vivian Cole, for old time's sake and nothing more.

God, she'd been such an idiot.

Selina closed her eyes. The swirly ceiling patterns were making her dizzy. Purposefully, she pushed away thoughts of Michael and the failure of her marriage. Her time had come and gone. This was about Rachael. What was she going to do about her daughter?

She wished she could hold Rachael in her arms and tell her not to grieve too hard over losing Trace. Tell her she'd been lucky to dodge a bullet. But she knew none of that would comfort her. As much as she might want to protect her daughter, she knew this was ultimately something she had to work out for herself.

And that thought left Selina feeling lonelier than ever.

Her stomach grumbled and she realized she hadn't eaten anything since the morning before. Food might be the last thing on her mind, but the hunger pains were annoying.

She reached for the telephone to call room service, but simply didn't have the energy to punch the button. Slumping back against the pillow, she pondered her next move.

Where did she go from here?

She'd been born and raised in Valentine. She was a

small-town girl with roots that stretched across the Texas-Mexico border. She was simple, earthy. She'd liked gardening and raising her babies and cooking hearty comfort foods and taking care of Michael.

Scratch that last part.

Michael was no longer her concern.

And her kids were grown. No one to cook for anymore.

A sudden, frightening realization took hold of Selina. She didn't know who she was, now that she was no longer the mother of young children or the wife of one of Valentine's most prominent and wealthiest citizens. She had no purpose.

It was a horrifying feeling, this sense of uselessness.

A tiny terrified part of her whispered, *Go back to Michael, tell him you made a mistake. Tell him you forgive him for Vivian.*

But that would be so easy to do. She'd been tamping it down, denying her feelings, denying the truth of twenty-seven years. She simply couldn't do it any longer.

So these were her choices? Continue to live a lie or fade away into old age all alone?

No!

Another part of her, a stronger part of her, the part of her she'd hidden away the day she married Michael, protested. Enough was enough. She would find a way out of this. She was only forty-five. There was still time left to decide who she was going to be for the rest of her life.

She was on the verge of something monumental. She could feel it. The only thing holding her back right now was Rachael. Once she knew where her daughter was, that she was safe and going to be okay, then Selina could let go.

Until then, her daughter was her main concern.

After that, all bets were off.

The thought made her feel better. *Deal with Rachael first, pick up the pieces of my life second.* It sounded like a plan. Selina liked plans.

There was a knock at the door.

Startled, Selina sat up in bed. "Who is it?" she called out.

"Room Service."

"I didn't order room service."

"This is room 321."

"Yes, but I didn't order room service."

"Someone ordered it for you."

Oh bother, Selina thought and got out of bed. She padded to the door and looked out through the peephole at the young man in a Four Seasons uniform, holding something clutched behind his back. She put the chain on and opened the door. "What is it? What are you holding behind your back?"

"These, ma'am." The young man revealed a slender vase filled with three pink roses in full bloom.

Immediately, she knew who they were from. She didn't want to take them, but the kid was already thrusting them at her.

From the time they were married, whenever Michael sent her flowers—which had been surprisingly often—he sent three pink roses in full bloom, never buds. Pink, he said, for the purity of her soul. Three because it was his lucky number and she was the luckiest thing that had ever happened to him. Full bloom to show how full his heart was with love for her.

She used to find the gesture exceedingly romantic. Now, in light of everything that had happened between them, she found it hopelessly corny and manipulative.

Even so, she couldn't seem to stop herself from taking

the chain off the door and reaching for the flowers. The young man scooted away and Selina took the roses inside her room. She shut the door, set the roses on the table, and perched on a chair beside them.

She stared at the roses. The cloying scent filled her nostrils and caused her head to ache. She thought about her husband and how she'd suppressed her fears, doubts, and emotions. Recalled how foolish she'd been over the years. Remembered all the dumb things she had taught her daughters about love and romance.

Then slowly, petal by petal, Selina disassembled the roses and ate them.

Chapter 3

From the CD player, the Rolling Stones were telling Michael Henderson that he couldn't always get what he wanted as he drove the Porsche he'd purchased that morning down the lonely stretch of highway leading west toward Valentine. Michael certainly didn't need Mick Jagger's advice on that score. Not only had he not gotten what he thought he wanted, he'd screwed up the thing he needed most.

His marriage.

He'd lost Selina for good.

After Vivian had shown up at Rachael's wedding yesterday, he was certain he had no chance of winning his wife back. Selina hadn't acknowledged the roses he'd sent to her hotel room that morning. But he really hadn't expected her to. Over the years, the romantic gestures he'd doled out had impressed her less and less. It seemed there was nothing he could do to convince his wife he loved her. Had always loved her. In spite of the fact he could be a stupid ass sometimes.

So why are you going home? Why not stay in Houston and fight for her? whispered a voice at the back of his mind.

"Because sometimes a man just gets tired of being discounted and disregarded," Michael muttered. No matter how hard he tried to make up for the past, it never seemed to be enough for Selina.

After twenty-seven years of marriage, was he finally done trying to please her?

The thought caused his heart to skip a couple of beats. No, he wasn't ready to throw in the towel. He just needed a break. Needed some time to think, to adopt a whole new life strategy.

Just as his daughter did.

He knew Rachael was okay. She was just pissed off at him and her mother and hurt over Trace Hoolihan's betrayal. He understood. She needed her space. Selina, on the other hand, didn't get it.

Overall, Michael wasn't a worrier, and while Rachael wasn't particularly sensible, she was a good girl. Other than her numerous failed love relationships, she'd never given him and Selina a moment's worry.

Michael tightened his fingers around the steering wheel and pressed harder on the accelerator. When had he first begun losing his wife?

After Rachael was born he'd noticed a change. From wife to mother, he'd told himself. It was inevitable. Hadn't his own father warned him that's what happened to a marriage? Kids took over.

He'd tried his damnedest to keep the romance going. Flowers sent simply because he loved her. Jewelry slipped unexpectedly into the pocket of her housecoat. He'd arranged impromptu getaways just for the two of them. Nannies hired, housekeepers retained, all to cut down on her workload so they'd have more time together. He'd given her an unlimited expense account, encouraged her to pamper herself with spa dates and nights out with her friends. But no matter how hard he tried, she hadn't seemed to appreciate a bit of it. In fact, the more he gave her, the more distant she became.

He'd thought things would improve when the girls went off to college, when the nest was empty and they had the house to themselves. He imagined them golfing together, taking a trip around the world, maybe even building a get-away cottage on the Gulf of Mexico. But that wasn't the way it turned out.

She hated golfing, didn't want to travel, and she was afraid of hurricanes. No matter what he suggested, she nixed it. Gradually, he ended up hanging out with his friends and she hung out with hers, until it seemed there wasn't any point in staying married. Except he still loved her desperately.

Truth was he'd been lonely. Starved for attention from his wife and hungry for her company. Was it any wonder that he'd answered flirtatious Vivian's e-mail in kind the fateful day it appeared in his in-box?

From the corner of his eye he caught a flash of red in his rearview mirror. A low-slung crimson Jaguar came out of nowhere, zipping into the passing lane.

In this part of the country it was rare enough to see an expensive foreign-made sports car. Most of the vehicles on the road to Valentine were farm trucks or pickups, with an occasional SUV, minivan, or compact car thrown into the mix. There was Giada Vito's green Fiat, but this powerful machine was no Fiat.

Jeff Davis County was not a particularly wealthy part of Texas, although once upon a time, in his granddaddy's day, there'd been a cache of oil hidden in the ground. But those days were long gone. There were only a handful of people in town who could afford an expensive sports car, and thanks to his granddaddy's planning, foresight, and wise investing, and the fact that they'd found plenty of Texas crude beneath the Hendersons' peanut farm, Michael was one of them.

The Jaguar pulled alongside the Porsche.

His masculine competitive streak had Michael speeding up for no good reason other than that he liked the singing strum of adrenaline racing through his veins.

The Jaguar sped up, too.

He peered into the driver's-side mirror, trying to see the face of his challenger, but the windows were tinted so darkly he couldn't even make out if the driver was young or old, male or female.

It's probably some other middle-aged fart going through a life crisis.

The Jag blew past him and eased back into the lane in front of him, jauntily tooting its horn in the process.

"Oh, so that's how it's going to be." He jammed his right foot all the way to the floor.

The Porsche, happy to be given the gas, leaped forward so fast Michael's head thumped back against the headrest.

The race was on.

His heart pumped faster than it had pumped in years. His pulse throbbed in his throat. In his ears. In his groin. His gaze was glued to the Jag's taillights as he slipped into the passing lane.

"Upstart," he yelled, shooting past the Jag.

On the radio, "You Can't Always Get What You Want" had reached a crescendo. The guitars were wailing and Mick was singing and Michael was driving like he'd never driven before.

He felt utterly, completely alive.

And the Valentine city limits lay just ahead.

His hometown. The place where he'd been born, grown up, married the love of his life, raised two daughters. The place where he would most likely die.

The bleakness of that thought hit him all at once and he suddenly felt like the oldest fool on the planet. What the hell was he doing drag-racing a stranger on the highway? Someone could get hurt. Killed.

He let off the accelerator.

The Jag passed him again.

Michael let it go, his attention snagged by the WEL-COME TO VALENTINE, TEXAS, ROMANCE CAPITAL OF THE USA sign. The sign that had been erected back in the 1950s after the oil had dried up and the town was desperate for revenue. Turning Valentine into a tourist destination had seemed foolhardy to many at the time, but it had been the brainchild of Kelvin Wentworth II and his scheme had unexpectedly saved the town.

But what socked Michael in the gut was the sight of those bright scarlet lips—they had dominated the Valentine landscape for his entire life—gone all dark and gothic black.

His mouth dangled open in shock. He slowed the Porsche to a crawl. What the hell? During his three-day absence in Houston, someone had vandalized the Valentine sign.

He hadn't expected to feel personally insulted, but he did.

By the time he drove down Main Street, he'd almost forgotten about the Jag. Until he spied it parked at the Exxon pumps.

He pulled in next to it.

The Jag's door opened and out stepped Vivian Cole,

dressed all in black and looking like she'd walked off
the pages of the glossy New York fashion magazine she
edited. Still thin, still attractive, still hotter than a fire-
cracker in July, even after twenty-seven years.

Blood pumping, engine running, radio blaring, Michael
slung open his door, stood up, and looked over the hood of
the Porsche at her.

Vivian slipped off her designer sunglasses and nailed
him with a brilliant, seductive smile. "Hello, Michael."

"V...V...Vivian," he stammered. "What in the hell
are you doing here?"

"Why, didn't I get a chance to tell you at Rachael's
wedding?" She smiled slyly and shifted her weight so that
her breasts thrust out prominently. "The divorce is final.
I'm moving back home to Valentine."

Michael's heart skipped three beats this time and his
mouth went stone-cold dry as one last time Mick Jagger
assured him emphatically that while he might not be able
to get what he wanted, if he tried hard enough, he just
might be able to get what he needed.

Brody watched Rachael over the surveillance camera as
she sat huddled on the cement bench, arms clasped to her
chest. She looked so forlorn.

*Stop feeling sorry for her. She got herself into this
mess.*

That's what his head told him, but his heart said something else entirely. He knew all too well how losing the
person you loved most could make you do crazy things.
Hadn't he volunteered to go to Fallujah for a second tour
after he'd learned Belinda had left him? He closed his
eyes briefly, remembering how that mistake had ended in
a bloody battle where he'd lost his leg.

He shook his head. The past was over. He lived in the now.

It was almost six p.m. and he'd been on the job since six a.m. And because it was Sunday and Judge Pruitt was out of town, Rachael was stuck in jail overnight.

There was no way around it. He couldn't leave her locked up here alone. He was going to have to spend the night in the jail.

Unless...

He took her home with him.

Right. And Kelvin would have his hide if she ran off in the middle of the night.

You could always handcuff her to your bed.

Unexpected erotic images bloomed in his mind. A freeze-frame montage of Rachael splayed out naked across his bed, her wrists cuffed to the headboard, her blonde hair fanned over his white sheets, her almond-shaped green eyes drilling him with a "come hither" gaze.

Ridiculously, Brody felt sweat bead his brow and his groin tightened.

Now this was just plain wrong.

It's only because you haven't had sex in going on three years. That's all. Don't read any more into it than that.

Maybe he shouldn't, but the images were disturbing as hell and he couldn't seem to shake them. It was as if he had X-ray vision and could see right through that wedding gown. In his mind's eye she had on a lacy white bustier, white lace thong panties, thigh-high stockings ringed with blue flowered garters. He imagined himself undressing her with his teeth.

Dammit. What was it about her that stirred the heaviness in his loins? How was she different from any of the other women he met in the course of his day? Why her? Why now?

As if Rachael Henderson, great-granddaughter of one of Valentine's founding fathers, daughter of the wealthiest man in town, would have anything to do with a gimp. She'd been engaged to a football player for the Chicago Bears. How was he supposed to compete with that?

Good God, why would you even want to compete for her? The woman is a head case, not to mention a royal pain in the ass.

But a very cute pain in the ass.

He thought about the chinaberry tree incident when they were kids and it brought up a few other memories. He recalled one summer when their families had celebrated the Fourth of July together. They'd shot off bottle rockets together. He and Rachael; his sister, Deana; and her sister, Hannah. As the memory drifted over him he could smell the gunpowdery scent of exploded Black Cats, taste watermelon on his tongue, see Rachael's face grinning in the glow of the porch light. How innocent and carefree they'd both been, unaware of the twists and turns the future held.

"Make your move, Carlton," Brody mumbled under his breath. "The past is past. Either take her home with you or call Deana and have her bring over a cot."

He weighed his options. Smart money said he should just stay here.

As he watched the monitor, Rachael reached up to swipe away a tear sliding down her cheek. His heart knotted up. Damn. He couldn't leave her in the cell overnight.

What a sap.

He might be a sap but he'd seen too many cruel and hurtful things. After he'd left Iraq he'd sworn to himself he'd do his best to ameliorate suffering whenever he had the chance. Cooling one's heels in the Jeff Davis County slammer might not be a big deal to him, but it was to her.

And that's what mattered. Even if he didn't trust himself around her.

Brody got up and headed back into the holding cell. He'd left her alone most of the afternoon to think things through. The minute he appeared in the doorway, she straightened, sniffled, and blinked hard, trying to hide the fact she'd been crying.

"You ready to go?"

Rachael hopped off the bench, her eyes hopeful, her fingers laced together. "You're letting me out? What about the mayor? I thought he was pressing charges."

"He is and I can't turn you loose until tomorrow when Judge Pruitt arraigns you, but that doesn't mean I can't put you under house arrest."

"You mean wear one of those little tracking monitor thingies on my leg?"

"I don't think that will be necessary in light of the fact the county doesn't own one of those devices."

"Oh," she said. "Are you just going to let me go home and come back tomorrow? Because in all honesty I'd rather stay here than go to my parents' house."

"Really?" He eyed her.

She waved a hand. "Long, miserable story."

"Actually," he said, "I was thinking I'd take you home with me. It's either that or I spend the night here with you."

"You don't have to stay with me. I'll be fine. Go home."

"Can't. My deputy's wife had her baby earlier than planned and both my jailers are off on vacation. I can't leave you locked up in here alone. What if there's a fire?"

"Good point."

"Besides, you look like you could use a home-cooked meal and a change of clothes."

"You're going to cook for me?" She sounded skeptical.

"Not that I couldn't," he said. "But we'll leave the cooking to my sister, Deana. She and her six-year-old daughter, Maisy, are living with me for a while."

"I see. So we won't be all alone at your house."

Brody had the strangest feeling Rachael was disappointed by the news, but he had no idea as to why that would be the case. *You're imagining things. You're wanting her to want you because you want her.*

"No," he said, denying his thoughts out loud as much as answering her question.

He opened the cell door and Rachael thrust out both arms toward him, wrists pressed together.

"What's that all about?" he asked.

"Aren't you going to cuff me?"

"I don't think that's necessary. It's not like you wouldn't be easy to track in that getup and I live just down the block."

"Like it's even necessary for you to arrest me in the first place."

"Seriously, Rachael, did you think you could just waltz into town, deface the most beloved icon in Valentine, and waltz back out again without any consequences?"

She shrugged.

"What does that mean?"

"I wasn't thinking."

"Clearly not."

"I suppose you're always rational and in complete control of your actions," she said.

"I try."

"Have you ever had your heart broken, Brody Carlton?"

He paused a long moment. "As a matter of fact, I have."

"Didn't anger and grief ever make you do something totally stupid?" she asked.

He thought of his ex-wife and swallowed hard. "We're not talking about me," he said, shutting the cell door behind her. "I'm not the one who gave the Valentine sign an unflattering makeover."

"So what did you do?" She tilted her head up at him. "When you got your heart broken?"

"I joined the Army."

"What was her name?"

"9/11," he said, not knowing why he was telling her this. He never talked about it. Was it to make her feel better about her life? Or to make himself look like a hero in her eyes? He didn't like the thought of that last motivation. He needed to get out of this conversation ASAP. He'd made a big mistake bringing it up.

She looked puzzled. "9/11?"

"I was in the Twin Towers that day."

She gasped. "Oh, no, Brody."

"Oh, yes."

"Wh . . . what were you doing there?"

"I was going to school at NYU, working on a degree in political science; my roommate and I were there on a class project."

"I can't imagine how horrible that must have been."

"There's no words. I lost my best friend."

"Your roommate died?"

He nodded. "Joe was trapped under a collapsed rafter. I stayed with him until the cops arrived, but his injuries were too great. He didn't survive."

Rachael shuddered. "I can't imagine the horror of it."

"Be grateful for that. I quit college and joined the Army. My life had changed forever and I knew I would never be the same again."

The sudden silence was as significant as a gunshot.

"Oh, Brody," she whispered. "I didn't know."

"Why would you?" he said, latching his fingers around her elbow and guiding her toward the front door, turning out lights along the way. "I don't tell many people. My family hadn't lived in Valentine for years and my paternal grandparents had already passed away by then."

She reached up and touched his shoulder. Gently, he shook her off. "Come on, let's go."

Rachael must have seen something in his eyes that warned her off because she didn't press for more details and she injected a teasing note into her voice. "You broke my heart, you know."

Brody let go of her elbow in the foyer to activate the alarm system, then he ushered her over the threshold and locked the door behind them. "When did I do that?"

"The very first time my heart got broken, you were the culprit."

"You're kidding."

"No."

He stared at her. "What are you talking about?"

"I was seven, you were twelve. I gave you a Valentine card on Valentine's Day. Not only did you not give me one in return, but you called me a baby, tore up the card, and told me to go away."

Her words took him aback. "I did that?"

"You did."

"I don't remember it."

"Of course not. I meant nothing to you."

He didn't know why he was feeling guilty for something he didn't even remember. "For crying out loud, Rachael, cut me some slack. I was a kid. Kids do dumb things."

"Well, I did make the mistake of giving you the Valentine

in front of your buddies," she admitted. "In retrospect it was thoughtless of me."

All at once, the memory came rushing at him. He and his buddies had been in his driveway shooting hoops when pigtailed, gap-toothed Rachael had cut across her lawn, clutching a big pink heart-shaped envelope in her hands. He'd barely noticed her until she came to stand underneath the basket, her green-eyed gaze fixed on him, her hand outstretched with her little fingers wrapped around the card. His name was written on it in a childish scrawl of blue crayon.

"Hey, Brody," one of his buddies had said. "I think you've got a secret admirer."

He didn't know why that comment had embarrassed him, but he felt it again now as he had then, the blaze of heat rising to his cheeks, the knot of denial that had the same one-two punch as anger.

"For you," Rachael had said, smiling. "Be my Valentine."

"Brody's got a girlfriend," his other buddy had chanted.

"Brody and Rachael sitting in a tree..." singsonged his first friend. "K...I...S...S...I...N...G..."

Shamefully, he recalled snatching the envelope from her hand, ripping it into two pieces, and handing it back to her. "I don't take Valentine cards from babies," he'd said gruffly, even as his guilty heart had nosedived into his stomach at the shattered expression on her face. "Go home."

She burst into tears as she turned and ran sobbing back to her house. If Brody listened hard enough to the past, he could still hear the sound of her front door slamming.

"Bet I can shoot a free throw from across the street," he'd said to his friends, using bragging and action to douse the bad feelings over what he'd said to hurt the sweet little girl next door. The truth was he liked Rachael and he had a Valentine for her up in his room, but he was horrified to think that his friends might discover his secret.

He considered telling her about the Valentine's Day card he'd made for her. Thought about apologizing for his behavior all those years ago, but what would be the point? Most likely, she wouldn't believe him anyway.

"Let's go," he said.

"Where to?"

"White house on the right at the end of the street."

"You bought the old McClusky place," she said.

"I did."

"When was that?"

"Two and a half years ago, when I got back from Iraq."

"I heard you got injured over there," she said as he hustled her down the sidewalk. Neighbors were standing on their porches and on their lawns gawking at the sight of Brody escorting a woman decked out in full wedding regalia toward his house.

"I'm sorry," she said, her voice full of sympathy. "For all your suffering."

Her kindness triggered his anger. "Don't," he growled.

"Don't what?"

"Don't you dare feel sorry for me. I don't need your pity."

Her muscles tensed beneath his fingers and Rachael fell silent.

Brody glanced over. Her head was tossed back, shoulders straight, jaw clenched, gaze beaded straight ahead. But she was blinking rapidly as if trying to hold back tears.

Aw, hell. What was the matter with him? Why was he lashing out at her?

They'd reached his house. The screen door flew open and his niece, Maisy, came barreling headlong down the front steps.

"Unca Brody, Unca Brody," she cried, but stopped abruptly when she saw he wasn't alone. She looked at Rachael the way only one female jealous of another could look. "Who are you?"

"My name's Rachael. What's yours?" she asked.

Maisy scowled at Rachael then swung her gaze to Brody. "What's she doing here?"

Rachael winced and he could see the hurt in her eyes. This weekend was clearly not good for her ego. Jilted at the altar, arrested for vandalizing the town's icon, and disrespected by a six-year-old.

"Rachael's going to be spending the night with us," he explained.

Maisy sank her hands onto her hips and glowered at Rachael. "Why?"

"Because I'm your uncle's prisoner," Rachael said.

Brody hadn't planned on telling Maisy that.

"Prisoner?" Maisy's eyes widened with increased interest. "Did you rob a bank?"

"No."

"Whadya do?"

"I put black lipstick on the Valentine billboard."

Maisy turned to Brody. "That's bad?"

"According to your uncle, it is," Rachael supplied before he could answer.

"How come you're wearing a wedding dress?" Maisy looked her up and down. Brody could just see his niece's little six-year-old brain cogs whirling and turning as she tried to figure this all out.

"I was at a wedding," Rachael explained.

"Were you the one on top of the cake?"

Rachael smiled. "Something like that."

Maisy's gaze shifted to Brody and she looked alarmed. "Is he the boy on top of the cake?"

"No, no," Rachael assured her. "The boy on top of the cake ran away."

"How come?"

"He decided he didn't want to get married after all."

"He didn't like you anymore?" Maisy asked.

"Not so much." Rachael shook her head and the wedding veil bobbed like a field of white butterflies.

"Let's go inside," Brody said, out of his element with this conversation. He could feel the pressure of the neighbors' gazes, knew they were being stared at. "What are we having for dinner?"

"It's taco night," Maisy said and slipped her little palm into his to lead him up the porch.

They went inside, Maisy pulling him by the hand, Brody tugging Rachael along by the elbow. The smell of chili powder, garlic, and onions hung in the air. From the kitchen, they could hear Deana humming a Faith Hill tune.

"Dee," he called out as Maisy escorted them into the kitchen. "We're here."

Deana turned from the stove, wiping her hands on a cup towel. She took one look at Rachael and her mouth dropped open.

It was then that Brody realized he should have given his sister a heads-up that he was bringing a prisoner home for dinner. And not just any prisoner, but a wilted bride-that-wasn't.

"What's all this, then, baby brother? If you tell me that you eloped, I'll clobber you." Menacingly, she waved a spatula.

"Rachael's in custody," Brody explained. "Zeke's with Mia and the baby and my jailers are out of town. I couldn't leave her locked up alone."

"You," Deana said to Rachael. "You're the one who defaced the Valentine billboard."

"Guilty as charged," Rachael said proudly.

"The whole town's buzzing about it. Some old-timers even want to hang you, but I want to shake your hand." Deana thrust out her palm to Rachael. "I've wanted to take an ax to that damned billboard for years. You go, girl. Down with romance."

Brody noticed Rachael's checks flushed pink with pleasure as she shook his sister's hand.

"Don't encourage her," Brody growled to Deana. "She broke the law."

Deana eyed Rachael's wedding dress. "I'm guessing there were extenuating circumstances."

"Dumped at the altar," Rachael said.

"Hey, consider yourself blessed you narrowly escaped," Deana said. "I'm going through a wicked divorce and Maisy's the only good thing to have come out of that mess."

"I'm sorry to hear about your divorce," Rachael said. "My parents are getting divorced. After twenty-seven years."

"You're Michael and Selina Henderson's daughter, right? You used to live next door to us on Downey Street," Deana said. "I babysat you and your sister, Hannah, a time or two before we moved to Midland."

"Uh-huh." Rachael nodded.

"You wanna get out of that dress?"

"I don't have anything else to put on. I left Houston without my bags."

"Don't worry," Deana said. "We're about the same size. I've probably got something you can wear."

"That'd be wonderful."

"Here." Deana shoved the spatula into Brody's hand. "Don't let the hamburger meat burn."

He stepped to the stove to scramble the browning hamburger meat around in the pan as Deana took Rachael's arm and led her from the kitchen, Maisy trailing in their wake.

Fifteen minutes later, they trooped back downstairs. Brody had already set the taco meat in the middle of the dining room table along with toasted corn tortilla shells, diced tomatoes, shredded lettuce, and grated cheese.

He looked up to see Rachael dressed in a pair of his sister's skintight blue-jean shorts, a skimpy, navel-baring sleeveless T-shirt, and a pair of white mules that showed off her toenails, painted a racy shade of scarlet. He could tell from the way she was tugging at the hem of the shorts that she wasn't accustomed to wearing the sort of daring clothes Deana preferred. His sister didn't own anything conservative and Rachael was stuck with the sexy outfit. And right now, Brody was glad. Rachael had also brushed her hair and it lay in smooth, gentle curls around her shoulders.

Wow! His libido lunged like a pit bull on a chain, desperate to be unleashed. Just looking at her was an exquisite form of torment.

She caught his eye and her cheeks pinked. That's when Brody realized he'd been staring. Openly. Hungrily.

Quickly, she looked away.

He sank down at the head of the dinner table and Rachael sat at the opposite end. He said grace, and everyone ducked their heads, except Brody. He didn't look down and he didn't close his eyes. Irreverently, he watched Rachael when his mind should have been on the prayer.

In the wedding dress, she'd been safe, untouchable—a bride on her wedding day. He'd felt the first burst of sexual attraction when she'd ended up straddling him at the bottom of the ladder, but mostly his feelings had alternated between pity, amusement, and minor irritation.

But what he was feeling now was a horse of a different color.

Her arms were bare and her legs were bare, her creamy skin exposed. He saw too much sweet flesh. The blood surging through his body told him this was a dangerous thing.

So was the sudden fire burning inside his groin as he watched her tilt her head, lift a taco to her mouth, and crunch into it with ladylike gusto.

The sight of her sweet, pink tongue unraveled something inside him. Something he'd kept wound up tight for a very long time. Something he feared he might never feel again.

Flaming hot lust.

Brody didn't like what he was feeling, but it was too damned strong to deny.

Chapter 4

Giada Vito was taking her evening power walk around Valentine Lake with one-pound dumbbells clutched in her hands when a man stepped out of the shadows of a hundred-year-old pecan tree.

"Aren't you skinny enough?"

She startled at the sound of the deep, threatening masculine voice that accompanied the hulking figure suddenly looming on the path in front of her. The weights could double as a weapon and she had pepper spray clipped to her belt. She'd lived in Valentine for fifteen years, but she'd been born in Rome, Italy. You'd never catch Giada leaving her doors unlocked or her keys in the car or her pepper spray in a drawer.

Raising her left hand, she cocked the dumbbell, ready to fling it if he gave her cause. Dropping the weight in her right hand, she went for the pepper spray on her hip, like a gunslinger at the O.K. Corral going for his six-gun.

He was the size of a bodybuilder, big and menacing, with an oversized cowboy hat tilted back on his slick, shaved head and a shark's deadly blue-eyed stare. He was dressed in a blue seersucker suit and he stood with the arrogant air of the privileged.

She recognized him then, but that didn't make her lower the weight or put the pepper spray back into her belt: Kelvin Wentworth in all his cocky, strutting glory.

"You shouldn't push yourself so hard. Anyone ever tell you that men like women with a few curves?"

"Anyone ever tell you to go screw yourself?" she replied tartly.

Kelvin laughed.

"What are you doing here?" She sniffed, pretending a courage she didn't feel. "You don't look like you've taken up power walking."

"I came to see you." He smiled and the smile scared her more than a frown.

"What for?" she asked suspiciously.

"Wanna set that weight down? I have a feeling you're just waiting for an excuse to bean me."

"My mother always said to trust your instincts," she replied. "And my instincts are telling me you're up to something."

He laughed again. "Sharp cookie. That's one thing I like about you, Vito."

"Hmm," she said. "Too bad that I don't like anything about you, Wentworth."

"How did this feud between us ever get started?"

"Feud?" She feigned ignorance.

"Come on. We both know you're only running for mayor to piss me off. What I don't know is why."

"Is it working?" She batted her eyelashes. "Am I pissing you off?"

"I find you . . ." His gaze raked over her body in a look so intimidating, Giada almost shivered. "Amusing."

"Would this little visit have anything to do with the fact that I am beating the pants off you in the polls?"

She arched an eyebrow and wondered why she was having trouble catching her breath. She could walk a mile in twelve minutes. Her lung capacity was that of a highly trained marathon runner. She had no reason to feel breathless.

"Beating my pants off? Only in your dreams."

Fury burned her cheeks.

"Come on. Let's sit down and have a civilized discussion." Kelvin reached out and took hold of her arm, pulling her toward a wrought-iron picnic bench positioned beneath the pecan tree.

"Hands off," Giada exclaimed and swung at him with the dumbbell.

But Kelvin ducked and the weight swished harmlessly through the air. The big man was quicker than he looked. He clamped a hand around her wrist and wrenched the dumbbell away from her. "Settle down a minute, Spitfire."

"Hmph. I show you spitfire," she said, struggling against him, the English she'd perfected slipping in the heat of the moment.

"I just wanna talk." He maneuvered her toward the picnic bench. "And if you depress the nozzle on that pepper spray, believe me, you're going to live to regret it. But be a good girl and maybe you and I can cut a deal."

She stopped fighting and slid a glance at him from the corner of her eye. Her interest was piqued. This sounded like a man on the ropes and desperate to get back on his feet before the bell rang. Curiosity got the better of her and she followed him to the bench.

He dusted leaves and errant pecan hulls off the seat with a sweep of his hand. She hadn't expected such a chivalrous gesture, but then he had to go and ruin it all by commanding, "Sit."

The contrary part of her wanted to argue, but common sense told her to pick her battles. She sat.

"Now isn't this much better?" he said, plopping down beside her. "Two politicians sitting down for a nice chat."

"A scenario that strikes terror in the hearts of voters," Giada observed archly.

He grinned. "Water?" He surprised her by pulling a small bottle of Evian out of his jacket pocket. "It's important to stay well-hydrated."

"I have my own," she said, determined not to take anything from him. She fished an identical bottle of water from her fanny pack.

He held his water bottle up and nodded.

In unison they twisted off the tops of their respective water bottles and drank. It was almost like a perverse toast. She found the idea unsettling.

To be honest, she found Kelvin Wentworth unsettling.

"So Giada…" He paused. "Is it okay if I call you Giada?"

"I prefer Ms. Vito." She straightened her back. It wouldn't do to let him get too familiar.

"Of course you do, Giada," he continued, his eyes narrowing. "Just what in the hell is your beef with me?"

"Other than the fact you're a narcissistic drama king who thinks the entire town revolves around him?"

"That wounds me deeply," he said, and splayed a hand over his chest, but the expression on his face told her he had the hide of a rhino. "Everything I do is for the benefit of this town."

"Ah," she said. "A self-delusional, narcissistic drama king."

Kelvin surprised her by throwing back his head and letting out a roar of laughter.

"What's so damned funny?" She glared.

"You," he said. "You look so feisty with your hands cocked and your knees bent like you're gonna take a swing at me."

"That's funny?"

"I'm more than twice your size."

"And that's something to brag about? You should look into Lean Cuisine. The baked chicken is quite tasty."

"I'm big all over." He wriggled his eyebrows, his innuendo clear.

Refusing to rise to the bait, Giada bit down on her tongue.

"You know," he said, "you and I could become friends."

"Not in this lifetime."

"Or we could skip the friendship and go straight to lovers." His eyes drilled into hers. There was no missing the sexual interest.

"I'd rather poke my eyes out with a rusty knife."

"You say that now," he said, getting to his feet, "but that's only because I haven't kissed you yet."

He moved toward her.

Giada reached for the pepper spray again but was dismayed to find it was not housed in the clip at her waist.

"Looking for this?" He waggled the small spray can in front of her.

"Bastard," she said through gritted teeth.

"You're going to have to do a lot better than that if you're hoping to rile me up," he said.

Giada glared and tried to stare him down, but he wasn't going along with it. Instead, he was grinning at her like one of her unruly students. His gaze slid over her warm as hot fudge over homemade vanilla ice cream.

An edgy warm sensation, thrilling and unexpected,

rolled through her. She snatched the pepper spray from his hand, stuffed it into the clip, grabbed up her dumbbells, and walked away as fast as she could, while the sound of his wickedly sexual chuckle rang in her ears.

Following a dinner filled with an undercurrent of sexual tension that Rachael hoped no one else could detect, she helped Deana wash dishes. Brody was a handsome man, no doubt. But she wasn't in any position to be thinking romantic thoughts. In fact, ridiculous romantic thoughts were the very things that had landed her in this mess.

Once she and Deana had finished cleaning the kitchen, Maisy begged the three adults to play Chutes and Ladders with her at the dining room table.

When she had been Maisy's age, Chutes and Ladders had been Rachael's favorite board game. Her parents had dubbed Sunday family game night when she and her sister, Hannah, were growing up. It was a tradition she'd hoped to continue with her own children. The children she'd dreamed of having with Trace.

Dreams died hard.

Misery pushed into Rachael's throat and she swallowed back the bitter taste of it as her game piece ended up on a chute and she slid all the way down, landing at the beginning square.

"Ha!" Maisy gloated. "Start over!"

"Maisy," her mother chided. "Don't be rude."

"What?" The child shrugged and tried to look innocent, but ultimately, she was unable to hide her mischievous grin.

"It's not nice to take joy in the misfortune of others, Missy. Next turn you might be right at the bottom of the chute alongside Rachael."

That's me, bottom of the chute. Starting over yet again.

Roll the dice. Take a chance. End up right back where you started. Story of her life. From now on she was finished with rolling the dice, taking chances, starting over. She was tired, discouraged, and fed up with romance.

"Your turn," Brody said.

"Huh?" She was so wrapped up in thinking about how sexy his forearms looked with the sleeves of his shirt rolled up she hadn't heard what he said.

She felt the heat of his gaze on her face and her cheeks heated. She rolled the dice without looking over at him, but her cheeks stayed strangely warm. One thing you could say about being back at the beginning, you couldn't fall down any more chutes. Not until you ventured out from home base, put your heart on the line all over again.

But she was done with putting her heart on the line. It hurt too damned much to have your hopes dashed again and again.

Maisy ended up winning the game. Brody came in second, Deana third, and Rachael a distant fourth. But of course. She'd landed on twice as many chutes as ladders.

Maisy interlaced her fingers, raised her arms, and walked around the room shaking her clasped hands over her head like a cocky, triumphant prizefighter.

Deana rolled her eyes. "Sorry for the poor sportsman-like conduct," she apologized to Rachael. "When it comes to competition, Maisy takes after her father."

"No need to apologize. She's just passionate about the game," Rachael said.

"Let's play again." Maisy hopped up and down beside the table.

"No way," her mother replied and tickled her under the rib cage. "The competition is too stiff."

Maisy giggled.

"Come on, Muffin." Deana ruffled her daughter's hair. "It's time for bed."

"Aw, Mom, can we please play just one more game?" Maisy pleaded.

"Well," Brody said and stretched out his long arms. "I've had enough ladder climbing for one day."

Rachael raised her head.

He caught her eye and winked. An inside joke. He was sharing an inside joke with her. A clutch of something dangerous hooked somewhere in the general vicinity of her heart.

Stop it.

But no matter how much she scolded herself, Rachael couldn't prevent her gaze from taking him in. Brody Carlton wasn't a man you could easily ignore. She was so busy staring at him, in fact, she barely noticed when Maisy said good night as Deana led her upstairs for her bedtime rituals.

Brody was still dressed in his sheriff's uniform, looking every inch the public servant, except for the turned-up sleeves. He watched her. She could see him sizing her up in that calculating, sheriff-y way of his.

A shaft of light slanting in from the kitchen threw a shadow over his profile. His hair was the color of maple syrup, his eyes equally as dark. He looked serious, dutiful, manly. On alert, forever on guard.

Rachael's heart fluttered and she had to dig her fingernails into her palms to remind herself where she was and how she'd gotten here.

He consulted his watch. "It's nine-thirty. You ready for bed?"

Those words, spoken in his rich, deep, masculine voice,

sent perilous mental pictures clicking through her brain. She imagined him leading her upstairs to his bedroom and kissing her with those hot, firm lips as his nimble fingers undressed her. She thought about peeling his shirt over his head, exposing his bare chest, running her fingers along the taut muscular ridges.

"Who, me?" she squeaked.

"It's a little early, I know," he said. "But I get up at five every morning."

"So go on to bed." She waved a hand. "I'm a night owl."

"That's not going to work. You're my prisoner."

"And that means…"

"You sleep when I sleep, wake up when I wake up."

"You've gotta be kidding me."

"Not at all."

"Seriously?"

"Yep." He gave her a look that sent all the blood rushing to her pelvis.

"Where will I be sleeping?"

"In my bed."

"What?" The word flew out of Rachael's mouth in a breathless gasp.

"Don't look so panic-stricken." An amused smile curled his lips. He was enjoying teasing her. "I'll be sleeping on the floor."

She felt her heart slip and slide right down into her shoes. "No. No way."

"Those are the rules," he said. "You're in my custody. Unless you'd rather go back to the jail."

"I can't let you sleep on the floor in your own home," she said. "I'll take the floor."

"Hey, when I was in Iraq I dreamed of sleeping on my own floor. It's a privilege."

Was he teasing her again?

Part of her—the stupid, starry-eyed part—almost told him they could share the bed *It Happened One Night*–style. Just the thought of reenacting the classic movie made her heart race with romantic notions. Rachael pressed a hand to her forehead. God, she was a hard case. Totally brainwashed by fairy tales and lippy billboards and the fanciful mush of moonlight and violins and grand gestures.

Lies. It was all a pack of lies.

And yet, she yearned for those fairy tales.

What she needed was a support group. Like alcoholics had. Or overeaters or gamblers. She needed help to talk herself out of these crazy romantic cravings.

Brody got up from the table, moving a little stiffly. "My bedroom's downstairs. You can use the adjoining bathroom. I'll put out one of my T-shirts for you to sleep in and I keep a new toothbrush in the middle drawer, just in case of unexpected visitors."

Rachael wondered what that meant. Did he have a lot of unexpected, overnight guests?

What do you care?

Right. She didn't care. His overnight guests were none of her business.

Thirty minutes later, she emerged from his bathroom, scrubbed clean after her unsavory day in jail. Tomorrow was a new day, an opportunity for a fresh start.

While she'd been in the shower, Brody had made a pallet on the floor near the door, boxing her in. If she had the urge to make an escape, she'd have to do it through the window. But she had no inclination to run. She might as well be here as anywhere. She'd vandalized the sign. She'd take whatever lumps the judge dished out when she was arraigned. She just hoped Jillian would get to Valentine in time to stand in as her lawyer. She didn't mind facing the music. She just didn't want to do it alone.

Brody was sitting up with his back against the door. Apparently he'd used another bathroom. His hair looked slightly damp from his shower and he had on a pair of pajamas that thankfully revealed very little of the hard body she knew lurked beneath. Knew because she'd felt his muscles when she'd straddled him after they'd fallen off the ladder together.

She was standing in the doorway between the bedroom and the bathroom wearing his University of Texas T-shirt, the hem skimming just above her knees. She watched his gaze drift slowly over her and she realized the light from the bathroom was shining through the material of the thin cotton shirt. He could see straight through it to the outline of her body beneath.

He moistened his lips.

Rachael gulped. Quickly, she reached back and flipped off the bathroom light. Brody let out an audible breath.

The bedcovers were turned back. He'd done that.

For her.

The thought made her go all soft and squishy inside.

Stop it!

She slid into bed, pulled the sheets up to her neck. Listened to the blood strumming through her ears.

"Lights out," he said and flicked off the overhead lamp, dousing them in darkness. In the silence, in the inky black of night, she could hear him breathing. It was a rough, deliciously masculine sound that sent chill bumps up her spine.

The bedside clock ticked, counting off the seconds until dawn. The pillow smelled of fabric softener, Egyptian cotton, and Brody. The mattress was neither too soft nor too firm. It was just right. She rolled over onto her side. The box springs squeaked.

Brody coughed.

Was he as aware of her as she was of him?

The silence elongated. Awareness stretched from her to him and back again. Then quietly, unexpectedly, he said, "I have a question for you."

"What's that?"

She couldn't help wondering if he was going to ask her about Trace. Why she'd been foolish enough to get engaged to a man who obviously did not love her. She hoped he didn't ask that. She didn't have an answer for it other than she'd been swept away on fairy-tale promises and foolish romantic ideals.

"How'd you get on top of the billboard?"

"Oh, that." Rachael laughed, relieved he hadn't asked her about Trace. "I climbed on top of the boxcar."

"How'd you get on top of the boxcar?"

"I climbed on the roof of my VW."

"The boxcar is parked that close to the sign?"

"I had to do a bit of jumping," she admitted.

"In a wedding dress?"

"I was pretty determined," she said.

"Carrying a can of black paint?"

"The paint can was on the ground attached to a rope. I had the other end of the rope in my hand. When I got to the billboard, I just hauled the paint up."

"You'd thought it out."

"I had a four-hundred-mile drive to put it all together."

"You were determined." Was that admiration she heard in his voice?

"That sign represents all that's wrong with Valentine." She rolled onto her back again, tucked her palms underneath her head, and stared up at the ceiling. "It symbolizes the wreck I've made of my life due to all the wrong values and starry-eyed beliefs this town instilled in me."

"You sure this isn't just a stress reaction to getting dumped and finding out your parents are getting divorced?"

"It's more than that."

"How are you feeling about your parents' divorce?"

Rachael took a deep breath. Good question. What was she feeling? She lay there letting the emotions flow over her—betrayal, sadness, guilt. Yes, guilt. She couldn't help thinking that somehow this was all her fault. She should have recognized that all was not right in her parents' marriage. She should have done something, said something. She should have been more aware of what was going on, not been so self-absorbed.

"Don't you think you're throwing the baby out with the bathwater?" Brody asked. "Romance is what kept this town alive after the oil dried up. There wouldn't be a Valentine without it."

"It might have been a bit rash," she admitted. "But a bold statement needed to be made. Someone has to take a stand. A balance must be struck."

"Is this the argument you're going to present to Judge Pruitt in the morning?"

"Yes."

"Good luck with that."

"What do you mean?"

"Judge Pruitt is as much in love with Valentine as Kelvin Wentworth. She's going to throw the book at you."

That provoked a knot of worry inside her. "Exactly what does having the book thrown at you entail?"

"Hours of community service."

"Seriously?" The thought panicked her. "How am I

going to do hours of community service? I live in Houston. Or at least I did. Before I gave up my apartment to move in with Trace."

"Plus you'll be expected to repair the damage you did to the sign. And there will probably be a hefty fine."

"How hefty?" Maybe she should have given a bit more thought to her vandalism spree.

"Depends on what kind of mood the judge is in. You better hope she had a good vacation."

Rachael blew out her breath in relief. "I've got a sharp lawyer on the way."

"That's good."

They fell silent again.

"Brody," she said after a long moment.

"Uh-huh?"

"Thank you."

"For what?"

"This."

"This what?"

"Bringing me home with you. Not leaving me in jail. I know you're probably violating all kinds of rules and regulations."

"Not too many. Besides, I'm the sheriff. Up to a point I can bend the rules," he said.

"I had fun tonight, eating tacos and playing Chutes and Ladders with you and Deana and Maisy."

She'd forgotten how much fun it was, spending time with a loving family. She thought of her parents and bit down on her bottom lip. She still couldn't believe they were getting divorced. Were all the memories of her happy childhood really such a lie? Had she romanticized even that?

"Hey," Brody said, interrupting her thoughts. "Don't

thank me. My motives were purely selfish. I didn't want to sleep on a cot in the jail."

"It couldn't be any worse than the floor."

"The floor's not so bad."

"You could get up on the bed. It's king-sized and I don't thrash around much." She didn't make the offer out of some movieland fantasy. She simply asked because he'd been so nice and she hated the thought of him waking up in the morning all stiff and achy simply because of her.

"I'm good right here," he said.

"Well," she said, "just in case you wake up in the middle of the night and change your mind, the offer stands. I trust you to be a gentleman."

Then Brody said something that took her totally by surprise. "Rachael, you've got to stop trusting people so easily."

Brody lay on the pallet for hours, listening to the sound of her soft breathing and imagining himself doing all kinds of unprofessional things. Talk about breaking rules and regulations. If a man could be locked up for his sexy thoughts, he'd be in prison for the rest of his life.

Finally, just when he'd managed to stop thinking about how damned much he wanted to kiss her, touch her, make love to her, and was almost asleep, Rachael bolted upright in bed.

"Brody, get up!"

His soldier's training kicked in and he was instantly alert. "What is it? What's wrong?" He grappled for his bionic leg in the dark, feeling intensely vulnerable without it on.

"You have to take me back to the jail right this minute."

He fumbled with the leg attachment. All he could see of her in the dark bedroom was the pale glow of the white

T-shirt she wore. He wanted to get the leg back on before she turned on the light. "What for?"

"This can't be happening."

"Tell me what's happening so I can fix it."

"You can't fix it. *You're* what's happening."

Was she talking in her sleep? Puzzled, Brody got his Power Knee in place and hoisted himself to his feet. "Rachael, are you awake?"

"Wide awake. I haven't been asleep."

Me, either.

The clock on the bedside table read 11:57. Almost midnight.

He snapped on the lamp next to the clock and sat down on the mattress beside her. It was all he could do to keep from taking her in his arms. What was with this illogical protectiveness? Sure, his natural male instinct prompted him to take care of a woman in need. But this was something different. Something more.

He was a sheriff; she'd been booked on vandalism. He could not allow himself to touch her in any way except in the course of duty. Cradling her to vanquish night terrors didn't come under that heading.

But dammit, he wanted to touch her. He wanted her to rest her head on his shoulder. He longed to trace his fingers over her throat, then trail lower to the curve of her breast and the flat of her belly and that soft, sweet spot between her legs.

Silently, he cursed himself. Good old-fashioned chemistry had knocked the wind out of him with this one.

She stared at him.

Brody saw panic in her eyes.

"I gotta get out of here," she said, throwing back the covers.

"Shh, settle down. Tell me what's wrong."

"You. You're what's wrong."

"I'm not following your reasoning."

"You. Me. This."

"Is it that meeting cute thing again?"

"No, no." She shook her head. "This is much worse. This is the romantic equation."

"Romantic equation?" Could people talk in their sleep with their eyes open?

"You know. It's like in *Sleepless in Seattle* where Sam has lost his beloved wife and he believes lightning doesn't strike twice. That he'll never love again. Meanwhile Annie is looking for lightning. It's the romantic equation between the two of them. They both lack something that only the other can provide. They balance each other out. Meg Ryan's character can give Tom Hanks's character back his belief in love and Tom can give Meg the lightning she's been searching for."

"I didn't see the movie."

Rachael looked at him as if he'd suddenly sprouted a second nose. "You never saw *Sleepless in Seattle*?"

"Is that a sin?"

"It's just the best romantic movie ever made. I've seen it twenty-seven times," she said.

He struggled not to notice that her nipples were poking right through the thin fabric of her T-shirt. Or how much she smelled like his sandalwood soap and minty toothpaste. "I can tell."

"Omigod." She splayed a palm to her forehead. "I'm doing it again, aren't I? Acting as if movie romances are real."

"Yep."

She took a deep breath and met his eyes. "I'm sorry I panicked and woke you up over something as silly as a romantic equation. You're right. We don't have a romantic equation. How could we? That's the movies, this is real life. Right?"

"You're thinking we have one of these romantic equations?"

"No. Not anymore. You set me straight. Thanks."

"So theoretically, if we were in a movie and we did have one of these romantic equations, what would ours be?" It was a dumb thing to ask, but he couldn't seem to stop himself.

"I'm lacking a hero in my life and you're a real hero. While you, on the other hand, are lacking a romantic soul and I'm romantic clean through to my bones."

"I suppose you had a romantic equation with those other guys who left you at the altar." It bothered Brody to think about those other guys.

"Actually, no. Maybe that's what was wrong with my other relationships. Maybe they were Bellamys."

"What are Bellamys?"

"In the romantic comedies of the forties and fifties there was an actor named Ralph Bellamy. He seemed like the right guy for the heroine. At least on the surface. But really he wasn't a match for her and she couldn't see it until the hero came into her life."

"You're doing it again," he said.

"Doing what?"

"Mixing up movies with real life."

Rachael looked chagrined. "I am, aren't I."

"You have no worries where I'm concerned," Brody said. "I'm not your man. I'm a complete cynic when it comes to love. Now go back to sleep. You've got a judge to face in the morning."

Then just as he had settled back down on his pallet, he heard her whisper, "But Brody, what if being a cynic is your half of our romantic equation?"

Chapter 5

By six the next morning, Rachael was back in her jail cell and in her paint-stained wedding gown waiting for her audience with the judge. Brody had cooked them fried-egg sandwiches for breakfast while Deana and Maisy slept.

He never brought up what they'd discussed in the middle of the night. For that, she was grateful and she prayed he hadn't heard that extra little bit she'd whispered to him in the dark.

The wedding veil lay folded neatly on the cement-slab bench beside her. Lightly, she picked up the fragile veil and fingered it, remembering the day she and her three friends had found it in that strange little consignment shop in Houston.

It was a floor-length mantilla style made of delicate rose pointe lace that had captivated Delaney. She'd been on the verge of marrying the wrong man when she found it. Both Tish and Jillian had been skeptical of the veil. But Rachael had been as enraptured by its romantic legend as Delaney.

According to the lore, long ago in Ireland there had lived a beautiful young witch named Morag who possessed a great talent for tatting incredible lace. People came from far and wide to buy the lovely wedding veils she created, but there were other women in the community who were envious of Morag's beauty and talent.

These women lied and told the magistrate that Morag was casting spells on the men of the village. The magistrate arrested Morag, but found himself falling madly in love with her. Convinced that she must have cast a spell upon him as well, he moved to have her tried for practicing witchcraft. If found guilty, she would be burned at the stake. But in the end, the magistrate could not resist the power of true love.

On the eve before Morag was to stand trial, he kidnapped her from the jail in the dead of night and spirited her away to America, giving up everything he knew for her. To prove that she had not cast a spell over him, Morag promised never to use magic again. As her final act of witchcraft, she made one last wedding veil, investing it with the power to grant the deepest wish of the wearer's soul. She wore the veil on her own wedding day, wishing for true and lasting love. Morag and the magistrate were blessed with many children and much happiness. They lived to a ripe old age and died in each other's arms.

"Baloney, rubbish, crap," Rachael muttered underneath her breath, although her heart still ached to believe in the magic of the wedding veil.

Delaney had wished on the veil to get out of marrying the wrong man and in the end, she'd found her heart's desire in her soul mate, Nick Vinetti.

Then Delaney had passed the veil on to Tish.

Tish wished to get out of debt, and the granting of that wish had brought her back together with the husband she'd lost but had never stopped loving.

And Tish had passed the veil on to Rachael.

And there, the fairy tales had ended.

On Saturday, the day she was to marry Trace Hoolihan, Rachael hadn't wished on the veil because she thought she didn't need it. Everything was already perfect. She'd been such an idiot.

She snorted and glared at the veil. Look how things had turned out. The very opposite of perfection. A punch of sorrow and regret pummeled her stomach and she drew her knees up to her chest. Not only had the day been horrible, but her life had gone distinctly downhill ever since.

Now, here she was, all alone, awaiting criminal mischief charges, and she was guilty as sin.

Tears welled up in her eyes. She dropped her forehead in her hands. She would not cry. She refused to cry. Trace was not worth her tears.

Her fingers tingled against the lace. What if she were to wish on the veil? Would anything happen?

Resolutely, she swung her legs off the bench, sat up straight, and settled the veil over her head. "I wish," she murmured, "to be cured of my need for romance. I wish to stop believing in true love and soul mates and happily-ever-after. I want a calm life free of the exciting adrenaline rush of first lust. I want to stop having crushes and spinning fantasies. I wish this love monkey off my back."

The minute she made the wish, something strange happened. Her scalp tingled until her entire head throbbed with a vibrant, pulsating energy.

Her pulse quickened. Her breath hung in her lungs. Her vision suddenly blurred.

Whoa!

And then there he was in the doorway of the holding cell. Gun strapped on his hip, badge glistening in the harsh fluorescent lighting, Stetson cocked back on his head. He looked strong and big and in control. The kind of man you could count on in an emergency. A guy who wouldn't run away at the first sign of trouble.

Brody Carlton.

"Rachael," Brody called her name and broke the spell.

The tingling in her head vanished, leaving her breathless and gawking at him as if he were a stalwart knight lifted from the pages of *Grimm's Fairy Tales*.

There you go with the romantic fantasies. Knock it off.

Clearly, the stupid wedding veil had malfunctioned.

"Yes?" she said, startled to find that her voice came out little more than a whisper.

"You have visitors."

She jumped off the bench, ran to the bars. "Visitors?"

"One of them says she's your lawyer."

"There's more than one?" Her hopes soared.

"Three to be exact and they aren't real happy with me."

Relief and happiness and a sweet sense of belonging washed over her. All three of her friends had come. She had true friends. Why on earth had she ever thought she needed a man?

"Against my better judgment," he said, "I'm going to let them all come back to see you. Mainly because your lawyer keeps making threats."

"You'll have to forgive Jillian," Rachael said. "She's a bit intense."

"A bit?"

"Okay, a lot intense. But she has a heart of gold."

He looked like he wasn't going to take her word on that. He left the room and returned moments later with Delaney, Tish, and Jillian following behind him.

"Oh, you guys," Rachael said as Brody unlocked the

cell door and let them inside. The bars clanged closed behind her friends and Brody stepped back into his office to give them privacy. "Thank you so much for coming to my rescue. I love you all!"

"The first time our sweet little Rachael gets into real trouble?" Tish said and enveloped her in a hug. "I wouldn't miss it for the world."

"How's Shane and the baby?" Rachael asked about Tish's husband and new infant son.

"Fine, fine." Tish nodded and tucked a dark auburn corkscrew curl behind an ear studded with multiple earrings. She was dressed in a bohemian-style peasant blouse and stonewashed blue jeans. "Max is cutting his first tooth and Shane sends his love."

Delaney hugged her next, her baby bump pressing into Rachael's side as she squeezed her so tightly it almost took her breath. "Sweetie, we know you're hurting. We're here for you."

"How are Nick and Audra?" Rachael asked, changing the subject by referring to Delaney's police detective husband and their toddler daughter.

"Great. Although Audra's deep into the terrible twos." Delaney turned to Tish. "Just wait until Max gets there. You'll think a demon has possessed your darling child."

"Do you know what sex the new baby is?" Rachael asked.

Delaney encircled her belly with her arms and her eyes lit up. "It's twin boys."

"Twins!" Tish exclaimed. "You didn't tell me that."

"We just found out on Friday. Twins run in Nick's family," Delaney explained.

Delaney and Tish started talking about babies. Rachael looked past them to see Jillian standing to one side, cool and slightly aloof as always. Watching everyone closely, not missing a beat.

Jillian possessed exotic looks with her ebony hair and dark eyes. She had the kind of curvy body that drove men wild and a Mensa IQ. She was dressed in an expensively tailored business suit and three-inch stilettos that sent her towering to over six feet. In her hands she held a leather briefcase. No doubt about it. Jillian was a force to be reckoned with.

As far as Rachael knew, Jillian had never had a serious romantic relationship. She'd snared every man she'd ever set her sights on, but then she dumped them just as easily as she collected them.

The four friends had all met at Rice University where they'd been sorority suitemates. Over the years, Rachael and Jillian had had their differences. A natural clash of romantic versus cynic. But now, for the first time, Rachael totally *got* where Jillian was coming from. And amid the bubbly new mothers, they had a new alliance. Women who weren't besotted by babies.

Plus, while she appreciated both Delaney and Tish for leaving their families to come all this way to show their support, Jillian was the only one who could really help her.

"We saw the billboard," Tish said.

"We still can't believe you did that," Delaney added. "You? Miss Romantic?"

"Not anymore," Rachael muttered. "I'm done with romance. Jillian had it right all along. Love stinks."

Delaney and Tish shared that knowing look of women lucky enough to have found true love. Then they glanced at Rachael with pity in their eyes.

A tinge of envy, mixed with anger, took hold of her.

Why couldn't she have found that kind of happiness, too? And so what if she never found true love? She could still have a happy, productive, fulfilling life. She didn't need a man for that. Look at Jillian.

"Could you guys give us a moment alone?" Jillian asked Delaney and Tish. "I need to go over her defense."

"I don't need a defense," Rachael said. "I'm guilty."

Jillian shook her fingers. "Not so fast. I'm going to prove there were extenuating circumstances that drove you to rash action."

"That's certainly true."

"Sheriff," Jillian called out to Brody. "Could you please open the door?"

Brody returned to let Delaney and Tish out and he escorted them back to his office, leaving Jillian alone with Rachael.

Jillian took Rachael's hand and pulled her down on the cement bench. "Tell me everything."

Rachael told her what had happened from the moment she'd fled the chapel in her wedding dress and driven straight to Valentine, stopping only to buy the bucket of black paint.

"You were pushed to the limits of your endurance," Jillian said.

"Uh-huh."

"You snapped."

Rachael nodded.

"Anyone who's ever been in love and been dumped will sympathize with what you've been through."

"Judge Pruitt married her high school sweetheart. The only man she ever loved," Rachael said.

"You forget, I live for challenges." Jillian's eyes gleamed. "First order of business, we've got to get you out of that wedding dress. The evidence against you is smeared all over it."

"I've got nothing to wear. My wedding trousseau is in the trunk of Trace's car."

"Trust you to say trousseau." Jillian shook her head. "Only a die-hard romantic."

"Hey," Rachael said. "I'm through with being a romantic. Painting the Valentine sign was my emancipation proclamation."

"Don't worry about the clothes. I've got you covered." Jillian snapped open her briefcase and took out a simple blue suit skirt with matching jacket and white silk blouse.

The conservative outfit was as far a cry from Rachael's style as Deana's flashy clothes. She preferred flowing, feminine garments in floral prints and pastels, dresses to pants, empire waistlines to form-fitting sheaths. But she accepted the suit without comment. Beggars couldn't be choosers and after all, Jillian knew what she was doing.

"Thank you," Rachael said. She reached over to pick up the wedding veil lying beside her on the bench and handed it to her friend. "I want you to have this."

Jillian shook her head. "I have no use for that thing."

"Delaney and Tish don't need it anymore and it didn't work for me. You might as well have it."

Jillian took the wedding veil, holding it gingerly, as if she feared it might give her some dread virus. "I'll hang on to it for you," she said and slid it into her briefcase. "Just in case you change your mind."

"I won't be needing it," Rachael said stubbornly. "I'm finished with romance."

"You say that now—"

"This time I mean it."

"Rachael, a leopard doesn't change its spots. You are

who you are. You can't change by graffitiing a billboard with black paint and declaring you're done with love. You're a starry-eyed romantic optimist. It's your essential nature. It's one of the things we love most about you."

"You're wrong," she said fiercely, struggling to deny that Jillian was right. "I can change and I will. I'm going to become a hard-boiled cynic, just like you."

"No, Rachael, no," Jillian whispered. "You don't want to be just like me."

"Yes, I do. You're smart and successful and you don't kowtow to anyone. You don't lose your focus when a man comes into your life. You're strong and powerful and brave."

"And lonely. Don't forget lonely."

Rachael blinked. "You're lonely?"

Jillian's nod was almost imperceptible.

"But you have Delaney and Tish and me."

"And you were all in love, all involved with your men." Jillian held up a hand. "Don't get me wrong. I'm not complaining. My work is rewarding. It's just sort of sad to have nothing but a briefcase to curl up with on a cold, winter night."

"Curling up with someone is overrated," Rachael muttered, trying to convince herself. She needed Jillian's cynicism to keep her on track. To prevent her from embracing her romanticism and letting it drag her down.

"This from a person who's never gone without someone to curl up next to," Jillian observed.

It was true. From the time she was sixteen years old, Rachael had always had a boyfriend. Whenever she was briefly without one, she felt lost, adrift, as if she had no real purpose, no identity if she wasn't part of a happy couple. This grasping need for romance had stunted her emotional growth, held her back.

How could she have shortchanged herself for so long? How could she have been so blind?

"Take the veil," she insisted, pushing it toward her friend. "I don't want it."

Jillian pushed the veil back toward her. "Neither do I."

"Then just take it and get rid of it for me, please? Sell it on eBay and keep the money. Give it to a bum on the street. I don't care, just make it disappear." *Before I change my mind.*

"You're sure?"

"Absolutely."

Jillian nodded. "Okay, I'll take it, but it's not for me. I'm holding on to it for your wedding."

"I'm never getting engaged again."

"You say that now—"

"I mean it!" she shouted.

She shouldn't have shouted. She knew that, but she was denying it out loud to convince herself as much as Jillian. This was tough. Battling lifetime indoctrination in the myth of Prince Charming and happily-ever-after. She was tired of wearing glass slippers.

It was way past time to lace up the combat boots.

Brody leaned against the wall of his office, sipping a cup of black coffee while Rachael used his restroom to change into her court outfit. She'd been in there for about fifteen minutes with the water running full blast. To hide the sound of her tears? He hated to think she was crying. Or—his cop instincts couldn't help wondering—the sound of her escaping out the window?

He discounted the idea as soon as it popped into his head. One, Rachael had never resisted taking responsibility for the consequences of her actions. As sheriff he'd learned most of those he arrested couldn't wait to blame someone else for their predicament, but not Rachael. And two, the window was really small. Even someone as petite as Rachael was bound to get stuck if they tried to shimmy out of it.

Belinda would have tried to go out the window.

The thought gouged him. Belinda's modus operandi was to run away or to blame her problems on other people. He hadn't known that about her before they married. They'd gotten engaged two weeks before September 11, 2001, because she'd thought she was pregnant. She'd been against his enlisting in the Army and initially, she'd wanted to back out of the engagement. He should have let her. But under the circumstances, he'd lobbied hard for the marriage and in the end they'd moved up the wedding and got hitched the day before he shipped overseas.

The same day she got her period.

Brody was almost grateful when the cell phone in his back pocket buzzed, breaking into his glum thoughts. He pulled it out, flipped it open. "Carlton here."

"Brody, it's Audie Gaston."

"What's up?"

"Someone broke into my store last night and stole a couple of gallons of black paint."

"They take anything else?"

Audie paused. Brody could almost see him looking around his cluttered hardware store.

"I'll have to double-check."

"How'd they get in?"

"Jimmied the back lock."

"Your alarm didn't go off?"

"I didn't switch it on." Audie sounded sheepish.

Why would someone steal black paint? He thought of

the billboard, but he knew it wasn't Rachael. Not only had she been in custody since yesterday morning, but when he'd processed her, he'd found the Wal-Mart receipt for a gallon of black paint in her purse. What he feared was that her desecration of the billboard had spurred a copycat vandal.

Great. That was all he needed. People going all over town painting anti-romance slogans.

Maybe this has nothing to do with that. Maybe it's just a coincidence.

Except that Brody didn't believe in coincidences. "I've got to go to court this morning," he told Audie, "but I'll be over there as soon as I can."

"Thanks." Audie grunted. "See you then."

Brody hung up, then rapped on the bathroom door. "Come on, Rachael. Get a move on. Justice waits for no one."

Judge Abigail Pruitt was not only the first African American to sit on the bench in Jeff Davis County. She was also the first woman. That made her something of a local legend.

"If you work hard and stay out of trouble you could be the next Abigail Pruitt," Valentine mothers told their daughters. "If she can be a judge, you can, too."

What they often failed to take into account was Abigail's razor-sharp mind, keen observation skills, and a dogged determination to excel, no matter how tough things got. Most people, whether male or female, simply weren't made of such stern stuff.

Judge Pruitt was closing in on sixty. She had a short shock of kinky gray hair, dark intelligent eyes, and a habit of stroking her chin with her thumb and index finger when she was deep in thought. She also possessed an ironclad sense of right and wrong and once she'd made a decision, she was not inclined to change her mind.

At nine a.m. on the nose, Brody led Rachael into the one-hundred-year-old courtroom, Jillian right at their heels. Delaney and Tish followed at a safe distance before slipping into the gallery seating.

Brody pushed through the swinging door separating the gallery from the bench. The aged wooden floors creaked beneath his feet. The building smelled musty and punitive. Rachael found herself wondering how many lives had been forever altered here. She knew hers was about to be one of them and she welcomed the change with open arms.

Judge Pruitt was already behind the bench. She set aside the papers she was reviewing, slid her reading glasses down on her nose, and stared unblinkingly at Rachael over the top of them.

Rachael tried a smile, but the judge remained stony-faced. No charming this woman. She wasn't accustomed to people ignoring her smile and it unsettled her.

"Intimidation tactics," Jillian whispered in her ear, anticipating Rachael's anxiety. "Let it roll right off your back."

Easy for her to say. Jillian was used to swimming in the shark-infested waters of the state legal system.

On the complainant's side of the courtroom, Mayor Wentworth stood with Jeff Davis County's lone full-time prosecutor, Purdy Maculroy. Brody guided Rachael to the defense stand and then stepped back to let Jillian take his place beside Rachael. The minute Brody's body heat was gone, she missed him. Something about his unflappable presence calmed her.

He gave her an encouraging wink that lifted her spirits. Why hadn't she met him before Trace?

You did. He rejected you.

He was twelve. She was seven. It didn't count.

Stop it! You're about to be sentenced in a court of law and you're going gaga over some guy?

But quitting just wasn't that easy. Looking for love in all the wrong places had unwittingly become her modus operandi.

The judge went through the usual housekeeping of proper courtroom procedure, and then she fixed Rachael with a strict glare. "You're charged with vandalizing the Valentine billboard."

"I'm an eyewitness, Judge," Kelvin Wentworth said, "to the destruction of our beloved town landmark."

Judge Pruitt addressed Purdy Maculroy. "Counselor, please remind your client he cannot speak out of turn in my courtroom."

"Yes, Your Honor." Maculroy nudged Kelvin in the ribs.

Everyone in town knew the one thing Judge Pruitt and Kelvin Wentworth had in common was their mutual adoration of Valentine. Other than that, they pretty well hated each other's guts. He was from the good-old-boy network and Judge Pruitt was anything but a good old boy.

"How do you plead, Miss Henderson?" Judge Pruitt asked.

"Guilty as charged," Rachael sang out.

Jillian stepped forward. "With extenuating circumstances, Your Honor."

Judge Pruitt steepled her fingers. "I'm listening, Ms. …."

"Samuels. And I intend to show how the town of Valentine drove my client to her rash and unlawful actions."

"Valentine made her do it?" Judge Pruitt arched a skeptical eyebrow. "That's your defense?"

"In a manner of speaking. If Your Honor would just hear me out," Jillian pressed.

Judge Pruitt waved a hand. "You may proceed."

"By nature, my client, Miss Rachael Henderson, is prone to fanciful romantic ideations."

"Meaning?" Judge Pruitt asked.

"She sees the world through rose-colored glasses, and she's easily swayed by love."

Gosh, when Jillian put it like that she sounded like a ditzy nutcase. Rachael sneaked a glance over at Brody to see how he was responding to this evaluation of her character, but the man was a rock, revealing nothing.

He must have been an exemplary soldier, to control his feelings so well. She tilted her head, studied his profile, but he gave away nothing. His eyes were focused on Judge Pruitt. He stood with a straight stance. She could see the preparedness in the way his hand rested on his hip just above his duty weapon. A hero. The other half of her romantic equation.

If she were in the market for another love—

You're not! Jeez, what are you? A glutton for punishment?

"Is that true?" Judge Pruitt asked.

Chagrined, Rachael realized her mind had wandered as her gaze had slid to Brody's rump and she hadn't heard the question. "Ma'am?"

"If you'd quit staring at Sheriff Carlton's butt long enough to discuss your fate, I'd appreciate it."

At Judge Pruitt's comment, Brody swung his gaze her way and their eyes met.

Rachael's cheeks flamed and she ducked her head. How embarrassing to be caught ogling Brody's backside. "Yes, ma'am."

"I asked if your lawyer's assertions were true. Did you learn that your parents were divorcing on the same day your fiancé jilted you at the altar?"

"Yes, Your Honor, that's true."

"Those are extenuating circumstances."

"Objection!" Kelvin shouted. "She's just trying to weasel out of what she did to our sign."

"You don't get to object." Judge Pruitt scowled at the mayor. "Please control yourself or I'll have you escorted from the courtroom." The judge swung her gaze back to Rachael. "Miss Henderson, I'm a firm believer the punishment should fit the crime. You have pled guilty. Your lawyer has laid out the extenuating circumstances that led to your lapse in judgment and I have taken that into consideration. A lapse that I trust was temporary."

"Yes, Your Honor." As satisfying as painting those lips had been, it wasn't worth this.

"Then I sentence you to clean the graffiti from Mr. Wentworth's sign, to commit one hundred and sixty hours of community service to the town of Valentine, and to pay two thousand dollars in restitution." Judge Pruitt banged her gavel.

"One hundred and sixty hours!" Jillian exclaimed. "Your Honor, that is excessive. My client lives in Houston. How can she be expected to spend a month out of her life working for Valentine?"

"She should have thought about that before she painted the sign," Judge Pruitt said archly.

"She has a job, a—"

"She's a kindergarten teacher. It's summer. School's out. Her parents live here in town. The sentence stands." Judge Pruitt banged her gavel again for emphasis. "You can make arrangements to pay your fine with Becky, the county clerk. And see Sheriff Carlton about scheduling your community service hours."

"Yes, ma'am," Rachael mumbled.

"Come on, let's get the hell out of this kangaroo court." Jillian hustled her out the heavy wooden doors. They stepped into the hot July morning. Rachael blinked against the blinding sunlight. Her eyes hadn't even adjusted before someone shoved a microphone in her face.

"Leesie Stringer, KRTE News, Del Rio," the woman said in a crisp, professional manner. Del Rio was the closest town with a television station. Beside the reporter, a cameraman was filming Rachael as she descended the courthouse steps. "Are you the woman that the Chicago Bears' new wide receiver, Trace Hoolihan, jilted at the altar?"

It was the ultimate humiliation. Ambushed by the media after being sentenced for something she'd done in reaction to being dumped on her wedding day. Rachael opened her mouth to respond but no words came out.

Jillian raised an arm to shield her face from the camera. "My client has no comment."

"Miss, miss," the reporter insisted, staying right at her elbow, keeping the microphone thrust in Rachael's face. "How does it feel to be thrown over for a professional football team?"

Rachael was about to offer a smart-assed retort, something completely unsuitable for the noon news, when suddenly Brody was there, getting between her and the reporter.

"You heard the lawyer. Miss Henderson has no comment and if you don't stop harassing her, I'll be happy to show you the inside of the Jeff Davis County Jail, Ms. Stringer."

The next thing she knew, Brody's arm was around Rachael's waist and he was escorting her to his patrol car.

"Miss Henderson, Miss Henderson," the reporter called out as Brody opened the door and helped Rachael into the passenger seat. "Did you know Trace Hoolihan is giving an interview to *Entertainment Weekly* and he's going to discuss why he jilted you at the altar?"

After Brody dropped Rachael off at Higgy's Diner for lunch with her friends, he drove to Audie's Hardware, which was just down the block. He parked in the alley and went in through the back entrance so he could get a look at the jimmied door.

He squatted to examine the pry marks. Big flat-head screwdriver, he surmised. The kind that was in every tool box in the county.

Audie must have heard him because he came to the back, winding his way past shelves of merchandise. "What do you think?"

Brody stood and pushed his sunglasses up on his head. "I think you need to start setting your alarm."

"You wanna see where they took the cans?"

"Sure." Brody followed Audie over to the paint section where he kept the premixed colors. They stood staring at the shelf where two cans of paint used to sit.

"You gonna dust for prints?"

Audie had been watching too much *CSI*. "I'll dust the back door for prints, but this is a public place. And I know the local builders come to your back door. Plus, these shelves are littered with fingerprints. There'll be no way of knowing who was the thief and who was thumbing through the paint cans or coming through your back door."

"I guess you got a point." Audie stuffed his hands in his pockets. "Oh, by the way, after I talked to you, I discovered something else was missing."

"What's that?"

"A pipe cutter."

"Hmm," Brody mused, stroking his chin with his thumb and index finger as he puzzled out what a thief would want with two gallons of black paint and a pipe cutter. Criminal mischief was clearly in the offing.

"You suppose this has got anything to do with Rachael Henderson vandalizing the billboard?"

"Maybe." Brody was staying tight-lipped. He didn't want any rumors getting started.

"You know that paint is for outdoor use. Oil-based. It don't come off easy."

"I'm sure that's what your thief was angling for. If he or she wants to make a statement, they'll want something that's hard to remove."

Audie sighed. "Thanks for coming by."

"No problem. And remember to turn on the alarm."

"Will do. Hey, I was just headed over to Higgy's for the blue plate special. You wanna join me?"

Brody shook his head. "With Zeke out, Jamie is the only one at the station," he said. "Enjoy your lunch."

After he dusted the back door for prints and came up with more than two dozen possible suspects, he knew he didn't have much chance of solving the break-in until the thief used the paint or he happened upon another clue. As Brody headed back to his office to file the police report, he couldn't help thinking that Rachael's little Valentine insurrection was already having unintended consequences.

And he had a sneaking suspicion things were just gearing up.

Chapter 6

Rachael and her friends were inside Higgy's Diner, seated at a pink vinyl booth with heart-shaped seat backs and a matching pink Formica tabletop. The waitress, a bosomy woman named April Tritt who'd altered her uniform to show both more leg and cleavage, handed them heart-shaped menus.

Rachael didn't need a menu. She knew Higgy's food offerings by heart. She'd worked here for two summers when she was in high school. At the time, she'd thought it was the sweetest job in the world. It had been ten years since she'd schlepped meat loaf on thick blue glassware plates, but the menu hadn't changed.

"Wow," Tish said. "Is this place for real? I feel like I've stepped into a thirteen-year-old girl's romantic fantasies."

Rachael glanced around the diner, seeing it through her friends' eyes. On the back wall was an elaborate mural of unicorns and rainbows along with the slogan ALL YOU NEED IS LOVE written in spindly neon pink script. The mural on the right side was a field of sunflowers, butterflies, and bumblebees. This slogan read: LOVE BLOOMS IN VALENTINE, TEXAS. The tackiest mural was the one on the wall where they sat. It featured hearts painted with a 3-D optical illusion effect that made the hearts appear as if they were beating. The slogan: WITHOUT LOVE THE HEART DOESN'T BEAT.

The remaining wall was filled with movie posters from such romantic classics as *It Happened One Night, Tootsie, Dirty Dancing, The Big Easy, While You Were Sleeping,* and *When Harry Met Sally.* And of course, Rachael's all-time favorite, *Sleepless in Seattle,* was also featured.

Shelves running along the wall were chock-full of romance-oriented memorabilia: motion-sensitive, dancing flowers that twirled and played "I Can't Help Myself" whenever anyone walked past; heart-shaped, rhinestone-studded, Elton John–style sunglasses circa 1974; velvet, heart-shaped ring boxes. Teddy bears embracing. Magnetic, lip-locking Raggedy Ann and Andy. Nesting white turtledoves. Scarlet, heart-shaped Mardi Gras beads. Pink feather boas. Heart-shaped candles in various sizes and colors. A figurine of a sloe-eyed girl with her arms stretched out as wide as she could open them and on the base were carved the words: *I Love You This Much.* Everything was manufactured by Wentworth Novelties.

For the first time, Rachael saw the truth. What she'd always thought of as kitschy, cute, and sweetly romantic was corny, cheesy, and incredibly tasteless.

What a load of hooey.

"Or," Tish went on, "the die-hard romantic's version of the Hard Rock Café. They should rename this place Hard-Core Romance Café."

"Um, the ambience is certainly original," said Delaney, always the diplomatic one.

"It looks like the creators of Hello Kitty dropped acid in here," Jillian observed, shrugging out of her jacket.

"Girls, girls," Delaney chided. "Rachael needs our support, not our criticism of her hometown."

"Seriously, though." Tish reached across the table to lay her hand on Rachael's. "I see why you snapped and went after that lippy billboard."

"You think this is bad?" Rachael waved a hand at their surroundings. "You should see the rest of the town."

"It's all like this?" Delaney sounded horrified in spite of herself.

"You didn't notice the heart-shaped parking meters when we drove up?" Jillian asked. "Or the heart and arrow in the cement sidewalk outside with 'Bill + Laurie 4 Ever' carved into it when we came through the front door?"

"There are hearts and names of prominent local couples on every sidewalk square on Main Street," Rachael explained. "Like the Hollywood Walk of Fame. Except they call it the Valentine Walk of Flames."

"Seriously?" Tish arched an eyebrow.

"I saw the 'Bill + Laurie' one," Delaney said. "But I didn't realize it was a pattern."

Rachael shrugged apologetically. "It's for the tourists. Tourism is Valentine's main industry."

"I did you a grave disservice, Rachael," Jillian said. "I should have argued more stringently with Judge Pruitt. I understand you so much better now. Clearly, you have been brainwashed from birth."

"You think?" Tish said, but it wasn't a question.

"One hundred and sixty community hours and two thousand dollars is too much to pay when you've been set up your whole life to take a fall."

"Two thousand dollars." Rachael moaned. "Where am I going to get two thousand dollars, much less the money to pay Jillian's fee and court costs?"

"Don't be silly," Jillian said. "You're not paying me a penny. We're friends. And don't worry about coming up with the money all at once. They'll let you make arrangements to pay it off. Which, by the way, we need to go see the county clerk about after lunch."

Rachael placed a hand against her stomach to soothe the twisting ache of anxiety. "I have six hundred and thirty-seven dollars in my savings account. How am I ever going to pay it all?"

"We'll find a way," Jillian said. "You interested in suing Trace for breach of contract?"

"Can I do that?" Rachael asked.

"Y'all ready to order?" April Tritt had wandered back over to their table with four glasses of ice water and set them down on the table.

Jillian frowned at the menu. "You have anything that isn't too heavy or deep-fried?"

"Nope," April said cheerfully. "We specialize in home-style country cooking."

"Take my advice," Rachael said. "At Higgy's, stick with the blue plate special."

"I don't like meat loaf," Jillian said.

"Menu surf at your own risk," Rachael warned.

"Blue plate," Tish ordered quickly.

"Me as well," Delaney said. "Meat loaf sounds like a nice comfort food."

"This fish you have on the menu…" Jillian pointed.

"The fried catfish fillets?"

"Could you ask the cook to blacken it?"

"Sure." April took their menus and sashayed off, rolling her generous hips for the benefit of the men in the diner.

"I hope," Rachael said, "the cook knows to prepare

your fish with blackened seasoning at a high heat and doesn't literally blacken it in the deep fryer."

Jillian looked alarmed. "Is that a possibility?"

Rachael shrugged. "Look around. This is Valentine."

"Excuse me, miss." Jillian hopped up and scurried after the waitress. "I've changed my mind. I'll have the blue plate special."

Tish giggled. "You were yanking her chain, right?"

Rachael smiled. "Sometimes Jillian needs to come down off her high horse a little."

Ten miles outside of Valentine, Selina had to pull over to have a good long cry. Early that morning Jillian had called to tell her Rachael had been arrested for vandalizing the Valentine billboard. On top of everything else, it was almost more than Selina could bear.

But she was first and foremost a mom. Rachael needed her—even if she might believe she didn't want to see her—and Selina was determined to be there for her. She'd lost her marriage; she'd be damned if she was going to lose her daughter as well.

She'd driven fifteen miles over the speed limit to make the drive from Houston to Valentine, at a personal record of four hours and forty-seven minutes. Rachael was supposed to have been arraigned at ten this morning, so she knew she was too late for that, but she wasn't too late to help her pick up the pieces of her life.

However, now that she was within hugging range of her eldest daughter, her composure flew out the window. After a hard, five-minute cry, she wiped her face, blew her nose on a Kleenex, and reapplied her makeup.

"Stiff upper lip," she told herself and got back on the highway.

A few minutes later, she rolled past the WELCOME TO VALENTINE, TEXAS, ROMANCE CAPITAL OF THE USA billboard.

Seeing the lips painted startlingly black and knowing her daughter was responsible caused her to feel both shocked and irreverently amused. The child had more spunk than Selina had given her credit for.

More spunk than me.

Good. It was wonderful that Rachael was fighting back. If Selina had stood up for herself twenty-seven years ago, she wouldn't be in this mess now.

She took a deep breath. Okay, maybe she was twenty-seven years too late, but she'd finally worked up her gumption. She was filing for divorce, moving out of Michael's ancestral family home. She'd already rented a furnished house in town and her friend Giada Vito had already promised her a job as a teacher's aide.

But now that she was here, where was she supposed to go? What should she do first?

Find Rachael.

She thought about calling her daughter's cell phone, but she'd been doing that for two days. Rachael wasn't taking her calls or returning her messages. It was eleven-thirty and she seriously doubted Rachael would still be at the courthouse, especially since her friends were in town. Selina didn't want to go home and deal with Michael, although he was probably at the country club playing golf.

Home.

The second-biggest house in town—Mayor Kelvin Wentworth owned the biggest—was no longer her home. Selina was going to have to get used to the idea. It shouldn't be too hard. Not when she was feeling so betrayed. Not when she'd already rented a house in town.

Honestly, it had never really seemed like her home.

She remembered arriving there as a new bride, filled with silly ideas of happily-ever-after, awed by her wealthy young husband, slavishly in love with him, but terrified he'd married her only because of the new life growing in her womb. It had been tough, living there with his parents. After the girls were born she'd convinced him to buy a quiet modest house in the middle of town. They'd lived there ten years before Michael's father had a stroke and they'd been forced to move back into the mansion. She couldn't help thinking those ten years had been the best of her life.

Fresh tears hovered at the back of her eyelids, but resolutely she shoved them away. What was done was done. She couldn't rewrite history.

"Great, now you're giving yourself pep talks with platitudes," she muttered. "You have lived in Valentine too long."

What she needed was a plan. And first on her list was finding her daughter. It was almost lunchtime. The chances of her being at Higgy's Diner were good.

As was usual for the Monday blue plate lunch special— meat loaf, garlic mashed potatoes, garden-harvested corn on the cob, buttered biscuits, sweet tea, and peach cobbler; all for just six dollars and ninety-five cents—the parking spaces up and down both sides of Main Street were filled to capacity.

Hoping someone was only running a fast errand inside the Mercantile Bank and would be pulling out soon, Selina steered the Caddy around the next block. And just happened to glance down the alley behind Higgy's.

Two people, a man and a woman, were sneaking out the back door like illicit lovers. The woman went left, the man went right, headed in Selina's direction.

She did a double take and slammed on the brakes.

The man was Michael.

And the woman was that hussy Vivian Cole.

Anger and hurt and the aching need for vengeance slapped her like a wet rubber glove across the face. It was one thing to suspect your husband was having an affair with his high school prom-queen ex-sweetheart.

It was quite another to have it so blatantly confirmed.

Twenty-seven years of doubts about a marriage she'd pretended was perfect coalesced into one stunning moment of utter betrayal. Her deepest, darkest fear had just come to pass.

Michael had never truly loved her. He'd just married her because she was pregnant with Rachael. And he'd spent almost three decades lying and pretending. Before she had time to fully think her actions through, Selina shoved the Caddy into reverse and stomped the accelerator. The tires squealed like mating bobcats as she whipped the car around.

Michael spotted her. He stood frozen in the middle of the alley, eyes wide, mouth falling open in disbelief.

Vivian was long gone.

Selina glowered through the windshield at her husband.

Michael raised his palms.

Twenty-seven years of loving him with all her heart, fearing, dreading that he did not love her the way she loved him, robbed her of any rational thought.

Without a moment's hesitation, Selina gunned the engine and aimed her Cadillac straight toward her rat bastard, soon-to-be ex-husband.

The four friends were deep into their meat loaf when a loud, booming impact sounded behind the diner and shook the building.

Rachael's head jerked up, her fork halfway to her mouth. *What was that?*

It sounded like a car wreck.

Immediately half the people in the diner were on their feet and headed for the rear entrance. The first one out the door was Audie Gaston.

"What's going on?" Delaney asked.

Rachael tensed as a weird feeling of impending doom came over her. "I don't know."

"Hey!" Audie yelled. "Someone call 911. Selina Henderson just smacked the hell out of Higgy's Dumpster with her Caddy and she's bleeding all over the air bag."

Heart thumping so fast he thought it might pound right out of his chest, Michael yanked open the passenger-side door of his wife's car. A minute ago, she had been aiming to run him down, but at the last second she'd swerved and demolished Higgy's Dumpster.

The air bags had deployed and he couldn't get to her via that route, so he pivoted and wrenched open the back door. He crawled in and leaned over the seat. "Selina, sweetheart, speak to me!"

From behind the wheel of the crunched Caddy, Selina could barely turn her head to look at him. "Fuck off, Michael."

Startled, he drew back. Never once in twenty-seven years had he heard his wife use such language.

Okay, she was seriously mad. He could respect that but he wasn't going to let her anger stop him from checking on her.

"Are you hurt?" he asked.

"That's none of your damned business."

She had a cut on her forehead and blood was slowly

oozing down the left side of her face. People came pouring out of Higgy's Diner, but Michael had eyes only for his wife. He reached out a hand.

"Touch me," she said, "and the next time I try to run you down, I won't swerve."

"You don't mean that."

"You think I'm blind?" she shrieked. "I saw you with Vivian."

"It's not what you think."

"That's what you said on our wedding day. And you know what? I believe it is *exactly* what I thought it was. I think you've been lying to me for twenty-seven years." She grimaced.

He didn't know how badly she'd injured herself in the accident, but he knew her real pain was emotional. And he knew he was the cause. What in the hell was wrong with him? Why had he been having lunch with Vivian?

In public, in front of the whole town.

Well, because it was in front of the whole town. No one would think they were having an affair if they were out in broad daylight together.

We aren't having an affair.

Maybe not yet, but his thoughts had been running along dangerous lines. Why else had he sneaked out the back door when he realized Rachael and her friends had come into the restaurant?

He'd been hiding from his daughter.

Shame flamed in Michael's chest. What in the hell had he been thinking? He'd had a great marriage, an unbelievably wonderful wife, and he'd pissed it all away by flirting with Vivian in those damnable e-mails she'd sent him after she'd separated from her husband. It was stupid. It was a middle-aged man looking back down the road of his life, wondering what might have been. And it had been a grave mistake.

Fool. He was an utter fool.

"Selina, honey," he said, his voice cracking with emotion. "You're bleeding."

He tried to reach for her again, but Audie Gaston was wrenching open the driver's-side door and diner patrons were spilling out of Higgy's and encircling the car. The squealing sound of the siren atop what passed as an ambulance in Valentine—a refurbished old World War II Red Cross vehicle—vibrated the air.

And then he saw Rachael in the crowd, pushing forward to get to her mother.

"Let me through, let me through," she said.

Michael backed out of the car.

"Daddy?" Rachael's eyes widened when she spotted him. "What happened?"

"Your mother..." He shook his head, unable to trust his voice.

"Tried to run down your father." Selina finished his sentence just as the ambulance pulled into the alley behind them.

The EMT rushed forward.

"I'm okay, I'm all right. I don't need an ambulance." Selina struggled to get out of the car around the air bag. Audie was holding out a hand to help her up and Rachael was standing beside her, nervously shifting from foot to foot.

Michael ducked his head back into the car. "Honey, you hit your head. You need stitches."

"You don't get to call me honey," Selina snapped and got to her feet.

"Mom," Rachael cautioned. "Be careful."

"I'm okay, I'm fine, really—"

Selina swayed and her knees buckled. The EMT caught her before she hit the ground. Michael raced around the back of the Caddy to help the man get her onto the gurney, but Audie Gaston was already there, filling in his role.

"I'm riding in the ambulance with you," Michael said as Audie and the EMT loaded her into the back of the ambulance.

"No, you're not," Selina said. "You gave up your right to do that when you took up with Vivian again."

"I didn't take up with her, I—"

"Daddy," Rachael said, muscling past him to get to her mother and shooting him a darkly accusing glance. "I think you've done enough damage for one day."

"Me? I…I…" he stammered, trying to think up a defense but realizing he had none.

Rachael climbed into the ambulance beside her mother and the EMT shut the doors.

Hurt and bewildered, Michael stood there watching his family drive away, and it hit him like a sucker punch to the jaw. Selina was serious. She wasn't going to try to work things out. There would be no counseling, no couples therapy, no relationship-enhancing retreat.

Clearly, in her mind, their marriage was over.

Valentine Hospital boasted only twenty beds, fifteen full-time nurses, one under-equipped operating room, and two doctors on staff: Dr. John Edison Sr. and Dr. John Edison Jr. The ambulance pulled up outside the emergency room—such as it was—at the same time as the sheriff's cruiser.

The minute Rachael spied Brody she felt both relieved and anxious. Her heart punched strangely against her chest. She was so happy to have him here. She didn't know how to handle the fact that her mother had tried to run her father down.

"What are you doing here?" she asked as he came over to help the EMT unload the gurney.

"Checking on your mother."

She raised a hand to her heart and wondered what it meant that he was checking on her mother. *He's the sheriff. Your mother smacked her car into a Dumpster. He's just doing his job. It's got nothing to do with you.*

"Are you all right?" he asked.

Rachael shrugged and tried to appear nonchalant. "Sure, fine, why wouldn't I be?"

"You've had an eventful weekend." His eyes darkened with concern.

"Hello, Brody." Selina smiled at him. "You look handsome today."

"You flirting with me, Mrs. Henderson?" he asked, pushing his Stetson back on his forehead as he and the EMT wheeled her into the emergency room.

"Well, if my daughter won't do it..." she said. "You know I'm single now."

"So I heard."

"Mother!"

"Settle down, Rachael. Brody knows I'm just teasing." Her mother said his name like they were the best of friends.

Brody's gaze met Rachael's, his eyes crinkled up at the corners. A slight smile tipped his lips. It was a knowing smile, a smug smile, and for some reason it bugged the hell out of her. She didn't like what his smile insinuated.

Why did it feel as if he knew her mother better than she did?

She'd been so clueless about her parents' marital problems. Probably the entire town of Valentine knew more than she did. She'd believed they were so happy and now she'd found out they'd been miserable enough to consider divorce. How was that possible? It made her reconsider everything she'd always believed about her family, and that tore her up inside. She felt betrayed by her own expectations and foolish to have accepted a fantasy as reality.

"Mom's going to be okay," Rachael said, struggling to fight her attraction to the man standing beside her. "So you can go now."

"I'll stick around," he said. "I don't have anything else to do. Besides, it'll give us a chance to set up your community service hours while the doctor examines your mother."

"Community service?" Selina asked. "What's he talking about?"

"I'll explain later," she said to her mother.

A nurse came into the room. "Hey, Selina, is it true you tried to run Michael over?"

"I tried," her mother said. "But I chickened out at the last minute and swerved."

"Didn't want to get blood on the Caddy's grille?" the nurse joked.

"Something like that."

Rachael hated hearing her mother talk this way. "Mom…"

"Brody," her mother said, "would you take Rachael out to the waiting room?"

Brody put a hand on her shoulder, but she twisted away from him. "I'd rather stay."

"Well, I would rather you would have stayed in Houston and talked things out with me," Selina said. "But you didn't."

Guilt grabbed hold of her and shook hard. This was all her fault. If she hadn't gotten so upset, hadn't run away, maybe her mother wouldn't have tried to run her father down. Rachael raised her palms. "Okay, fine. I'll be outside if you need me."

"Take care of her, Brody. She's fragile right now."

"I'm not fragile," Rachael muttered. And she damn well didn't need any man looking out for her, especially one as tempting as Brody. She gave in to temptation way too easily and her emotional wounds were raw. Her mother was right. She *was* fragile.

Crap.

"Can I offer you some advice?" Brody asked when they were sitting side by side in the waiting room.

"No."

"Don't blame what's going on in your own life on your parents," he said.

"You don't listen so well, do you?"

His grin widened. "I have a hard time keeping quiet when I see someone headed for trouble."

"I'm not headed for trouble."

"You're letting your emotions color your perspective. You can't make rational decisions when you're under the influence of powerful emotions."

"I'm beginning to get that. Thanks for your sage advice." She stepped away from him. Who was he to tell her how to run her life?

Brody trod closer, closing the gap of space she'd just opened, his gaze assessing her. The corners of his mouth curled up, his arms crossed over his chest. He was close. Too close. If she raised her hand, she would graze his upper arm.

He had such broad, straight shoulders. His uniform

fit like it had been tailor-made and Department of Public Safety tan was definitely his color. He looked sharp, smart, and in control.

Not to mention his mouth. Her gaze hung on his lips. He looked like he would be a great kisser. His mouth was just the right size. Not too large, not too small. And to think that she'd slept in the same room with this potent, masculine male. Involuntarily, she swallowed against the memory. She'd also acted a little irrational and she didn't want to remember that, either.

"Do you want to talk about your community service schedule?"

"No."

"It's court ordered. Plus, you've got to scrub down the Valentine sign and repaint it. That's not going to be a cakewalk."

"I'll get started on it tomorrow. That soon enough for you?"

"Why are you mad at me?"

Because, she thought. *You epitomize everything I've ever wanted in a man and I know I can't have you. I shouldn't even want you, after all I've been through. And yet I do. And I know it's all just a symptom of my affliction.*

She had a serious problem. She couldn't stay away from thoughts of romance no matter how hard she tried.

Rachael didn't answer him. Instead, she plopped down in an uncomfortable metal chair and picked up a well-thumbed copy of *Texas Monthly*. Brody settled in beside her.

She heard a faint whirring sound. Like gears turning. "What's that noise?"

He paused a long moment, then said, "My leg."

"Your leg?"

"It's computerized."

"Your leg has a computer chip in it?"

"My prosthesis, to be exact."

"Your prosthesis?" She sounded like a parrot.

He looked at her. "You didn't know?"

"I knew you were hurt in Iraq. I didn't know you'd…" She dropped her gaze to his knees.

"Lost a leg." He said it so matter-of-factly.

"But how? I mean…you climbed a ladder after me yesterday."

"Courtesy of the Power Knee. It's state-of-the-art. I'm part of a special test group. I couldn't afford the thing otherwise."

"I didn't see it when I slept in your room. Even when you got up in the middle of the night to reassure me."

"Because I didn't want you to see it."

"Are you ashamed?"

"No."

"Self-conscious?"

"A little, maybe. I don't want people thinking I can't do my job just because I'm an amputee. I don't want people judging me, lauding me. Or feeling sorry for me because of it."

"It must have been horrible. In Iraq." She shuddered. She could not imagine the awful things he'd seen, done.

"After the Twin Towers, it was nothing. It was what I had to do in order to justify what happened to Joe."

"Joe was your friend that got killed?"

"Yeah."

"But going to Iraq cost you your leg."

"Small price to pay for freedom."

A strange feeling came over her. Sadness, wistfulness,

and an odd aching sensation that made no sense. She didn't know what else to say to him, so she said nothing at all.

She was supposed to be in Fiji on her honeymoon sipping mai tais and making love to Trace. Not sitting here in the hospital emergency waiting room in Valentine, Texas, beside a sexy Iraq War vet with an artificial computerized leg, waiting for her mother to get stitches after a car smashup in which she'd tried to run down Rachael's father.

So much for best-laid plans.

A laundry cart laden with freshly folded sheets squeaked as a member of the housekeeping staff wheeled it from the laundry room; the smell of bleach, fabric softener, and the slightly singed odor of overheated cotton trailing the corridor.

"Is that why you're divorced?" she dared to ask. "Did your wife leave because of the leg?"

He got up without answering, heading for the coffeepot and Styrofoam cups on a stand in the corner. "You want a cup of coffee?"

She shrugged, but inside she felt weirdly disturbed. Was he still so hung up on his ex-wife he couldn't even talk about her? "Sure."

"How do you take it?"

"Lots of cream and three sugars."

"Sweet tooth," he commented, tapping three packets of sugar into the coffee and two spoonfuls of creamer. He dropped a red plastic stir stick into her cup and handed it to her. He sat back down, took a long sip of the coffee, and then said, "Belinda left before the leg. While I was still stationed in Iraq."

It took a second before she realized he was finally answering her question.

"Another man?"

He nodded.

"That sucks."

"Can't argue."

"At one time, were you guys ever truly madly in love?"

"I'm not exactly known for my romantic soul."

She sat up straighter, took a sip of her coffee. Perfect. Exactly how she liked it. "Really? Why not?"

"Couple of reasons, I suppose." He stared off into space.

"So what are the reasons?" she prompted.

"Huh?"

That's when she realized he'd been staring at her legs. The way she was sitting—still wearing the suit Jillian had brought her—the skirt had risen up high on her thighs. She lifted her butt off the seat, tugged the skirt hem down.

"Aw," he complained. "I was enjoying the view. You've got world-class legs."

That made her feel pleased, and feeling pleased made her feel put out with herself. "I thought you said you didn't have a romantic soul."

"Peaches," he said, his grin wolfish, "what the sight of your legs stirs in my soul is anything but romantic."

"Peaches?" she asked, latching on to anything to keep the excitement jumping inside her at bay. "What does that mean?"

He shook his head. "I have peach trees. You remind me of the peaches. Ripe and rounded and sun-kissed and juicy."

She didn't know what to say to that. One part of her wanted to enjoy the compliments, another part wanted to accuse him of sexual harassment. But she'd started this whole line of conversation.

"Rachael?"

Startled, she looked up to see Dr. Edison Jr. standing in the doorway. Her pulse quickened. She got to her feet. "Yes?"

"Your mother is going to be just fine. I had to give her a couple of stitches for the wound on her forehead but it shouldn't leave much of a scar."

Rachael splayed a palm to her chest and let out a pent-up breath. "Oh, thank heavens."

"She'll be ready to go in just a minute."

"Thank you, Doctor."

The junior Edison had no sooner disappeared than Selina came around the corner. Her color was pale and she had a small rectangular bandage taped just above her eye, but other than that she looked fine.

"Rachael," she said. "Take me home."

Rachael hesitated. "You mean take you home to Daddy's house?"

"No," she said. "Take me to my new home."

"You have a new home?"

"I moved in last week."

Distressed, Rachael sank her hands onto her hips. "Why didn't you tell me?"

"You were so busy getting ready for your wedding, I didn't want to spoil your big day."

"No worries there," she said. "Trace is the one who spoiled it."

"Along with your father and I. He shouldn't have sprung the news of our separation on you like that."

"It's okay. I'll adjust," Rachael said coolly, even though she was feeling anything but cool. She had a million questions for her mother about the divorce, yet she had no idea where to start. "Where are you staying?"

"Didn't Brody tell you?" Selina looked over at Brody, who'd also gotten to his feet.

"Tell me what?"

"I'm renting Mrs. Potter's place. She broke her hip and had to move into Shady Hills Manor and her son's letting me stay there while it's on the market."

Mrs. Potter had been the old high school principal before Giada Vito took over the job. The very same Mrs. Potter who lived right across the street from Brody.

"Hey," Brody said. "I can give you a lift home."

Chapter 7

Rachael called Delaney, Tish, and Jillian to let them know what was going on. She'd been so unnerved, she'd forgotten about her friends. They rallied around and came over to offer moral support as she got Selina ensconced in her new place.

Not long after her friends arrived, the local florist's delivery driver showed up with a bouquet of twenty-seven pink roses in full bloom. "Delivery for Selina Henderson," he said when Rachael answered the door.

Rachael tipped the guy and took the bouquet into the living room where Selina was propped up on the couch, watching the evening news and drinking a glass of Shiraz. Jillian had shown up with the bottle of wine and a corkscrew. Delaney, being pregnant, was the designated driver back to Houston. Everyone else was having a glass to take the edge off the day.

Selina took one look at the roses and waved them away. "Get rid of them."

"What?" Rachael stared at her mother.

"Throw them in the trash."

"Don't you want to know who they're from?" Rachael

held up the little white envelope that had come with the flowers.

"I know who they're from. Pink. In full bloom. How many are there? Twenty-seven, I'm guessing. For the number of years we've been married. Plus it's nine bouquets of three. I'm sure your father enjoyed the symmetry. Pitch them."

"It might not be from Daddy. Would you like for me to read the card?"

"No." Selina hardened her cheek and acted as if she were paying extra attention to the television sportscaster.

Rachael read the card anyway. "Selina, my darling, words cannot express the depth of my sorrow and shame for the hurt I've caused you. Please forgive me. Love, Michael."

"I told you not to read it."

"Aw, Mom. Come on, it sounds like he's really sorry. Can't you give him another chance?"

Selina raised her hand. "This is between me and your father. He thinks roses and an apology can fix everything. Well, it can't. I've spent twenty-seven years trying to convince myself romance was enough, but it's not. What matters is real intimacy. And that's the one thing he's never given me."

Rachael didn't know what to say. Deep down inside she kept thinking it was all her fault. If her mother hadn't gotten pregnant with her, her parents wouldn't have gotten married. Her father would have gone to Harvard the way his family had wanted. Her mother could have followed her dreams of being a chef. Instead she'd been stuck. Forced into pretending she was happy because she was a mom and had no choice. Guilt gnawed on Rachael. She hated thinking she'd held her parents back from what they had truly wanted in life.

"Please." Selina's voice was brittle, fragile. "Just get the flowers out of the house."

"We'll take them with us when we leave," Delaney said.

"Thank you," Selina whispered.

Just then Rachael's cell phone rang from inside her purse, lying on the floor beside the front door. She put the roses on the coffee table and noticed that her mother turned her head away so she couldn't see them. She went for her phone.

Her father's number flashed on the caller ID. She didn't want to take the call in front of Selina, so she ducked into the kitchen. "Hello, Daddy."

"Rach, are you with your mother?"

"Yes."

"Did she get the flowers?"

"She got them."

"Did she read the card?"

"I read it to her."

"What'd she say?"

"She's not impressed."

He blew out his breath. Rachael could almost see the dejected expression in his eyes. He was probably pulling a palm down his face the way he did whenever he felt defeated. "Have I lost her for good?"

"I've never seen her like this, Daddy. She looks so hopeless." Rachael wanted to ask her father what had happened between them to cause such a rift. She didn't dare ask if he'd had an affair. She couldn't bear to hear the answer. If her father couldn't be true to the woman he loved, how could she ever hope to find a man that could stay faithful to her?

Forget about finding a man. Find yourself.

"I love her so much…" His voice tightened and he paused.

Was her father crying?

Gut wrenching, Rachael found her own eyes tearing up and her throat constricting. Were all her happy childhood memories really a lie? She thought about the family vacations. The adventures the four of them had together. The kisses their parents had bestowed upon her and Hannah. The love they'd shown each other. It couldn't all be a lie. Could it?

She remembered waking up early one Christmas morning to find her parents sitting in the middle of the living room floor putting together a pink bicycle. Selina would read the instructions, then pass her father the appropriate tools. They'd worked as a precision team, except for when they'd taken a break to smooch and giggle. Surely, that gentle moment had been real.

Rachael thought of other happy moments and her chest knotted with emotion. Playing Marco Polo in the pool at Corpus Christi during spring break when she was nine. She on Daddy's shoulders, Hannah on Mom's. Getting lost on a trip to Carlsbad Caverns, Selina saving the day by having four Mars Bars and a pocket compass stashed in her fanny pack. Watching her parents dance together at Hannah's wedding to "Can't Help Falling in Love," her mother's head resting on her father's shoulder.

Sadness, regret, nostalgia, tenderness, and a flicker of hope mingled inside her. There was love there. Something like that couldn't be faked. Clearly, her parents had just lost their way. They could find their way back to each other. She desperately needed to believe that.

"How are you holding up, Princess?" he asked, his tone stronger.

She sniffled. "I'm okay."

"I should have smashed Hoolihan's teeth in and made him marry you."

That made her smile briefly. "I don't want a man who doesn't want me."

"Who wouldn't want you, Princess? You're smart and gorgeous and kind—"

"And something of a flake."

"No, you're not. But sometimes your trusting nature and your need to be liked lead you astray. You got that from me."

Her father had always been her hero. She'd had an idyllic childhood. Or at least she'd perceived it that way. Parents who loved each other. A younger sister she happily squabbled with over Barbies. A great hometown. She'd had everything she'd ever needed. The Henderson name opened a lot of doors. She'd been privileged and pampered, but never spoiled.

She had so many wonderful memories of her father. She remembered how he would perch on the edge of his daughters' little girl–sized chairs, his knees bent up to his chin, and pretend to sip imaginary tea when she and Hannah invited him to their tea parties. She remembered the piggyback rides and the bedtime stories and the way he would wrap ice in a cup towel and smash it with a hammer to make ice chips for her when she was home from school sick with the flu. She thought of how he would sneak her copies of teenybopper magazines her mother didn't want her to read. How he taught her to whistle and play chess and fish.

He was a good man. A kind man. He was Rachael's blueprint for the way a man was supposed to be. What did her mother mean when she said their marriage had been empty of real intimacy? That picture conflicted with everything she knew about her dad.

No one knows what goes on inside a marriage except the two people who are in it. She'd heard that somewhere and she supposed it was true, but she found it unsettling to think the romantic front her parents had presented all these years had been a façade. So what had gone on? What was she missing? How could she be so misguided? Why couldn't she shake this need for happily-ever-after, not just in regard to herself, but to her parents as well?

Confusion clouded her mind, misery churned her stomach. She didn't know what to think.

"Are you going to stay there with your mother?" her father asked.

"Yes."

"That's good. Thank you."

"Maybe you just need to give her some time, Daddy. Stop sending flowers. Stop trying to win her back."

"You really think that's the best move?" He sounded unconvinced.

"Just a little breathing room. That might be all she needs. Can you give her that?"

"I'm afraid if I back off, I'll lose her forever."

"I'm afraid if you keep on trying to woo her with romantic gestures, you'll lose her."

"I don't know what to do."

Stay away from Vivian Cole, she wanted to say, but she didn't have the guts to voice the words.

"Rachael," Tish called from the living room, her tone urgent. "You gotta get in here. You've gotta see this."

"I have to go, Daddy," she said. "But hang in there. I'll see if I can talk to Mom."

"I love you, Rachael."

"I love you, too."

She hung up the phone and stepped into the living room. What she saw made her jaw drop.

Deana and Maisy were watching *Entertainment Tonight* when Brody walked into the house. He passed by the television set just as Deana flipped the channel.

"Hey, look," she said. "It's Rachael's ex-fiancé, Trace Hoolihan, being interviewed by Kimberly Quick."

Brody stopped halfway to the kitchen and backed up. Hoolihan was good-looking in a pretty-boy way. All blond hair and straight teeth. Although Brody thought he smiled like a horse. Involuntarily, he fisted his hands.

"Turn it up," he told Deana.

"So, Trace," asked *ET*'s newest coanchor. "Rumor has it that you left the chapel in the middle of your wedding when your agent interrupted the ceremony to tell you the Chicago Bears had picked up your contract. Is that true?"

"Kim." Trace eyed the reporter as if she were a juicy T-bone steak. He leaned forward, placed a hand on her wrist and lowered his voice. "May I call you Kim?"

The anchorwoman giggled. "Of course."

"Hey, hey," Deana protested and snapped her fingers at the television screen. "None of that nonsense, girly. Giggling isn't professional."

"He's putting the moves on the *ET* anchorwoman two days after he dumped Rach at the altar," Brody growled. "Jerkwad."

"Little pitchers." Deana covered Maisy's ears and glared at Brody.

"What's a jerkwad?" Maisy asked, pushing her mother's hands away.

"Never mind. And don't go around saying it."

"Kim, don't believe everything you hear," Trace continued. "Those reports are greatly exaggerated."

Brody crossed his arms over his chest and glowered at the television. "What a prince."

"I'd already decided to break off the engagement before I heard about the offer from the Bears," Trace went on.

Brody wanted to punch him on principle.

"And why is that?" Kim, the glossy, giggly anchorwoman asked.

"I'd come to realize my fiancée was simply too needy. She had the most unrealistic notions about love and marriage and romance," Trace said.

"For example..." Kim led him to his next comments.

"She expected me to call her three or four times a day to reassure her I loved her." Hoolihan was looking straight into the camera now. "She was always sending me these goofy little cards and gifts. And she liked for us to wear matching outfits. Can you believe that? Whenever we went out, I felt like Ken and Barbie."

Kim clicked her tongue in sympathy and stroked Trace's forearm. "So tell us how it feels to get picked up by the Chicago Bears after the Houston Texans cut you last season."

"Aw, hell," Brody muttered. He sure hoped Rachael wasn't watching this. But Valentine being the small town it was, he knew someone was bound to call and tell her to turn on the TV.

He headed for the front door.

"Hey," Deana said, "where you going? I'll have dinner on the table in twenty minutes."

"When I drove in I noticed the peaches on the Alberta needed picking. I'll be back inside in time for dinner."

"Tell Rachael Trace Hoolihan is a bonehead," she called after him.

Was he that transparent? How had she known he planned on going across the street?

He plucked a bushel of ripe peaches off his tree, then carried them across the street. Brody didn't know what motivated him to do it other than the fact that he'd seen enough suffering to last a lifetime. He understood first-hand the cruelties man could inflict on his fellow human beings. When he'd returned from Iraq, he'd vowed when-ever an opportunity presented itself to help someone, he'd make the effort.

Yeah, whispered a voice in the back of his head. *Keep telling yourself that's the reason you're going over there.*

Of course it was the reason he was here. Why else would he be on Mrs. Potter's front porch, ringing the bell, wondering what he was going to say when Rachael answered the door?

Except Rachael didn't answer the door. Rather, it was her sharp-eyed lawyer. "What do you want?" Jillian greeted him.

"I brought Rachael some peaches," he said.

"Thank you." She held out her hands. "I'll take them."

"I'd like to give them to her myself if you don't mind."

"Look, Sheriff," she said. "You seem like a decent enough guy and all, but Rachael really isn't interested in talking to anyone of the masculine persuasion right this minute. Could you come back later?" She started to shut the door, but he stuck his Power Knee inside before she could get it all the way closed.

"You're not getting rid of me that easily, Counselor," Brody said, giving the woman his most determined stare. "I'm not leaving until I see Rachael."

Jillian studied him a long moment, then she squared her shoulders, tossed her head, and came to a decision.

"Okay, hang on. I'll ask her if she'll see you. But she's very vulnerable right now, so don't give her any crap about community service."

"This isn't about that."

"What's it about?"

"Anyone ever call you a bulldog?" he asked.

Jillian beamed. "Why, thank you, Sheriff. I will accept that as a compliment."

He allowed her to shut the door this time and he was left standing there with a basket of peaches in his arms, wondering why he'd felt the need to challenge Jillian. If Rachael didn't want to see anyone, why was he insisting?

Because his gut told him this was the right thing to do and he'd made a policy of always listening to his instincts. His gut had saved the lives of his men in Iraq. He wasn't ignoring it now.

He set the peaches beside the welcome mat. A minute later Rachael appeared. She stepped out onto the front porch, pulled the door closed behind her, and crossed her arms over her chest. She wore a simple white cotton V-neck T-shirt, thin blue cotton drawstring pants, and a pair of white crew socks. Her hair was pulled up off her neck in a breezy ponytail and her face was scrubbed free of makeup.

He'd seen her in other outfits over the past couple of days. From her spectacular wedding gown and white ballet slippers to the skimpy shorts set and mules she'd borrowed from his sister to the no-nonsense business suit and stilettos she'd worn in court today. But this outfit appealed to him most. Simple, honest, straightforward. She looked like the girl next door.

She is the girl next door, you bonehead.

Suddenly, he was hit with a memory. He and Rachael

sitting on the curb on a hot summer afternoon, quarters clutched in their hands, waiting for the ice cream truck to come around the corner. He could hear the music chiming: "Pop Goes the Weasel." They'd been in her backyard swimming pool. He'd probably been about ten and he'd only gone over to their house to get cool. She couldn't have been more than five, sitting there in her bathing suit, blonde hair plastered to her head, grinning at him like he was the most wonderful thing on earth. She'd made him feel like a hero when she'd pressed her quarter into his palm and whispered through the gap in her front teeth, "Peese buy me a peach push-up."

Rachael smelled like the girl next door, too. Like olive oil and honey. Soothing and sweet.

"What is it?" she asked, crossing her arms tighter. Holding herself in or blocking him out, Brody didn't know which, but he could read the body language loud and clear—*Keep your distance, buster.*

"I'm sorry," he said. "I know that was brutal to hear on national television."

"You saw *Entertainment Tonight.*" Rachael hit him with her vulnerable green-eyed gaze and his heart stumbled.

"Deana was watching. By the way, she sends her sympathy and a few negative comments about your ex."

That got a small grin out of her. The sight of her smile lightened his spirits. If she could find the humor in the situation, she was going to be all right.

Rachael blew out her breath, ducked her head, studied her socks. "You must think I'm a kook."

"When I look at you, 'kook' is not the word that comes to mind." The suggestive innuendo in his voice took Brody by surprise.

"No?" She raised her head, shot him a look, then quickly dropped her gaze again. "What word comes to mind?"

"Caring, expressive, a little overly passionate, maybe, but that's not a bad thing."

"It isn't?"

"No." He didn't know why, or what he intended to do when he got there, but Brody took a step toward her.

Rachael took two steps back, bumping her butt against the door. Her breathing quickened. He couldn't help noticing the rapid rise and fall of her breasts beneath the T-shirt. "Not even when that misplaced passion lands a girl in jail?"

His gut was telling him something else now. Something he needed to ignore no matter how much he ached to act on it. He had to be careful.

Kiss her.

Without meaning to, Brody propped one forearm against the doorframe above her, leaned in, and lowered his head. He heard her sharp inhalation of air, smelled the fruity scent of wine on her breath.

The sexual tension was so electric he could almost hear it snapping. Gut pulling him forward, he dipped his mouth lower.

And damn if Rachael didn't pucker her lips and close her eyes. She wanted him to kiss her!

Walk away. Your gut is losing it. Don't do something you'll regret. She's vulnerable. You're horny. It's a terrible combination.

Plus, there was the not-so-insignificant fact that he hadn't gotten naked with a woman since he'd lost his leg. He was the one who was vulnerable.

Common sense prevailed. He took his arm from the

door, stepped back, struggled to get his breathing—and other bodily functions—under control.

Slowly, Rachael opened her eyes and lost the pucker. She looked wounded.

Aw, crap.

"For what it's worth," he said, trying to make amends, "I think Trace Hoolihan is a giant jackass and that's the polite way of putting it. Why were you engaged to this guy?"

"He didn't always act like an ass. He was pretty humble and contrite after he'd been dumped by the Houston Texans. He was charming. Very charming. And romantic. Gifts. Candlelight dinners. Long walks in the park holding my hand. Plus I jumped in too quickly. He asked me to marry him three weeks after we met. He had me snowed. He's great at being whatever he thinks people want him to be." Rachael shrugged. "And I fell for it. Story of my life."

"Hey, at least you dodged a bullet," Brody said, then cringed inwardly. He wanted to make her feel better, but he realized he was doing a terrible job of it. What he really wanted was to take her into his arms and kiss her so hard she forgot Trace Hoolihan ever existed.

"Yeah," she said forlornly, "there is that."

"Look, Rachael." He raised a hand as impulse spurred him to reach out, cup her chin, and force her to meet his gaze, but he knew that would be overstepping boundaries. He craved feeling the curve of her soft cheek against his palm and he had to fist his hand at his side to keep from reaching out. "There's a million guys who would give anything to be with you."

And damn if I'm not one of them.

But of course he didn't say that. He couldn't say that. It was stupid to say that now and probably not even really true. He'd just been too long without sex and she was the first woman who'd stirred him this strongly in years.

"That's the problem."

"What?"

She lifted her head again and met his gaze, and this time didn't look away. "I've been putting my hopes and dreams and plans on a guy. Why? What's a guy going to give me that I don't have already?"

Brody arched an eyebrow. "I can think of one thing."

She raised a palm. "Okay, sex maybe, but I don't need a relationship for sex. I could trot on down to Leroy's Bar right now and get all the sex I wanted without any of the grief of a relationship."

Alarm spread through him. The thought of Rachael waltzing into Leroy's and picking up some random guy made him want to go right down there and suspend Leroy's liquor license. "You're not going to do it. Right?"

She didn't say anything, but a speculative look came into her eye as if she was honestly considering it.

"Right?" He ground out the word.

"Would it bother you if I did?"

Oh, hell yeah.

Back off. Calm down. Don't let her rattle you with idle threats. She doesn't mean it. She's just hurting. You of all people should understand that. "You can't let this Hooli-han character cause you to throw away your values."

"Why not?" she dared, anger sparking in her sea green eyes. "Where have my values gotten me? Alone. Dumped on my wedding day. Again. Arrested in my hometown. Humiliated on national TV."

"You're just angry."

"Damn right I'm angry," Rachael said. "And I have every right to be."

"Granted. Just don't go jumping into something you'll regret later," he said, still worried like hell she was going to saunter on down to Leroy's and make good her threat.

"I appreciate your concern, Sheriff. I really do, but I've been listening to men's advice just a little bit too long." She nodded fiercely and narrowed her eyes at him. "Now if you'll excuse me, I have company."

She turned to go inside.

"Rachael?"

She hesitated, hand on the doorknob, and slightly turned back to him. "Yes?"

"Don't forget your peaches." He handed her the basket.

She rewarded him with a smile that lit him up inside. She clutched the basket of sweet-smelling peaches to her chest. "Thank you."

"You will get through this," he said. "I promise."

"You're right." She lifted her chin proudly and tossed her head. "In fact, I've already got a plan."

"Please tell me it doesn't have anything to do with Leroy's Bar."

"Sheriff Carlton," she said, "I'm a big girl and I don't owe you any explanation."

And with that, she turned and went back inside the house. Leaving him feeling frustrated, irritated, and worried like hell she was setting herself up for big trouble.

Rachael went back into the house with the basket of peaches to find her mother and her friends all staring at her.

"So what's up with the sheriff?" Jillian asked. "Anything I should know as your lawyer?"

"Honey?" her mother said. "Are you all right? You look pale."

"There's nothing going on with the sheriff. He just

wanted to talk about scheduling my community service," she said, not knowing why she lied, other than the fact she didn't want to talk about what had happened on the porch.

What had happened on the porch?

She thought about the way he'd crowded her personal space, forcing her back against the door. How the look in his eyes had set her heart to thumping. How her stomach had gone all quivery with excitement. How she'd crazily, dizzily wished he'd kiss her until she couldn't breathe.

Dear God, she'd actually puckered her lips. For a moment, she'd been certain he was going to kiss her. She'd practically dared him to kiss her.

But he hadn't and she'd been sorely disappointed. And that disappointment disappointed her. What was wrong with her that she saw every handsome man as a potential love match? Why was she so desperate for love?

It was a question Rachael should have asked herself a long time ago.

"Ooh," Delaney said. "Peaches."

"Why don't you take some with you on your trip back to Houston?" Rachael offered.

"Thanks, we will. And speaking of heading back to Houston, it's almost a six-hour drive. You guys ready to hit the road?" Delaney asked Tish and Jillian. "I'd like to get home before midnight."

Rachael saw her friends out to their car and hugged them all before they left. It was good to see them again and she really appreciated the moral support, but it was tough having them witness her falling apart. Tish and Delaney had everything she'd ever wanted and she had to admit she was a little envious. Jillian, on the other hand, was an exemplary role model of a woman who didn't need a man to be a success in life. She should be more like Jillian.

Waving good-bye until their car disappeared from sight, she then turned and headed back inside the house, feeling even lonelier than she had before they'd arrived.

She found her mother at the kitchen sink, industriously peeling peaches. "What's up?"

"I needed something to keep my mind busy and these peaches are so ripe they'll go bad in a couple of days. We need to put them up. Would you go down to the cellar and get some of Mrs. Potter's Mason jars?"

"You're going to can them tonight?"

"*We're* going to can them. You need something to keep your mind off your problems, too." Her mother tossed her a red gingham apron. "Put this on."

Rachael retrieved the Mason jars from the cellar and washed them in the sink. She watched as her mother's fingers expertly skinned the peaches with a paring knife. Drying her hands on her apron, she reached for a plump, rosy peach and bit into it.

A burst of juicy peach flavor exploded in her mouth. "Mmm. Oh, this is so good," Rachael said. "If romance had a flavor, it would taste just like this. Sweet and lush and perfect."

"Romance," her mother scoffed, tossing pitted peaches into a large mixing bowl. "There's a reason it's sweet and lush and perfect. It isn't real."

Rachael grabbed a paper towel and dabbed at the peach juice dribbling down her chin.

"Romance is a fantasy. An ideal that doesn't exist." Selina took a potato masher from a drawer and started systematically smashing the pieces into pulp. "This is what happens to romance. This is what marriage does to you. Smashes and mashes until you're just flattened and there's nothing left of that sweet promise except carnage."

Whoa.

Rachael backed away from the peach nectar flying up from Selina's potato masher. "Mom? Are you okay?"

"Romance. It's just like this peach. It looks good at first. All tempting and tasty, but inside there might be worms or you could poke your gum with the sharp edge of the pit. And when peach juice gets on you, it leaves a permanent stain."

"Mom?" Tentatively, Rachael reached out to touch her mother's shoulder. Fear, concern, and genuine disaster gripped her. She'd never seen her mother so upset and she had no idea how to comfort her or what she could say to make things better.

Selina tossed the potato masher, dripping with mashed, stain-producing peach pulp, into the sink, dropped her face into her hands, and began to sob.

"It's going to be okay." Rachael slipped her arm around her mother's waist. "Daddy still loves you, I know that he does." The words sounded empty, but she knew they were true. How could she convince her? Was love enough? She used to think so, but now she had no clue.

Selina raised her head, swiped at her eyes with both hands. "Rachael, please don't end up like me. Living your life for one man. You put everything into Trace and see how he treated you? Don't let that happen again. Be your own woman. Believe in yourself. Don't make romance the be-all, end-all of your existence. Promise me that."

The look in her mother's eyes rattled Rachael to the core. All the values and beliefs she'd held dear for twenty-six years were in question. "Okay. I promise."

"I think I better go to bed now." She touched her bandaged forehead. "My head is throbbing."

Rachael got her mother some aspirin and helped her to bed, then went back to the kitchen to clean up the peach mess. As she washed and wiped, she reflected on the events of the past few days. She thought about all the mistakes she'd made. All the old sweethearts, the crushed dreams, the broken hearts. She thought about Robert, the first fiancé who'd dumped her at the altar. Correction. Robert hadn't dumped her, he'd just never shown up. Cold feet, he'd told her later when he'd called to apologize. And then he'd gone on to tell her he wasn't good enough for her. That she deserved someone who could love her as much as she should be loved. The sentiment had sounded right and she'd agreed with him. She thought she'd found that someone with Trace. How wrong she'd been.

She recalled how Trace had just made a fool of her during his *Entertainment Tonight* interview. She thought about how her anger had landed her in jail and then into community service that would force her to stay in Valentine for the remainder of the summer.

And, she thought about her parents and the turbulence they were going through even if she didn't understand what it was all about. Her stomach ached for them. Tearing the fabric of twenty-seven years woven together couldn't be easy. Sorrow clogged her throat and she clenched her fists against the sadness of it all.

Her mother was right. Romance wasn't real. It was just an illusion, a nice fantasy but nothing more. She'd let the pursuit of a fantasy run her life.

No. Not just run her life, but dominate it.

She simply had to change.

But what had happened with Brody on the porch this evening told her it wouldn't be easy. She couldn't trust herself. She couldn't do this alone.

She needed help. She needed a twelve-step program. But nothing like that existed. They had programs for sex addicts, but she wasn't addicted to sex. When she went after a man, sex wasn't her main goal. It was flowers and gifts and long walks in the park holding hands. It was the fairy tale she wanted. The knight in shining armor. The feeling of being Cinderella at the ball. The lovely promise of happily-ever-after.

Life just didn't work that way, no matter what growing up in Valentine had promised. But how did she stop yearning for it? How did she put an end to her cravings when there was no support group for romanceaholics?

The answer came to her as clearly as if someone had spoken into her ear.

Start your own.

Chapter 8

Early the next morning, Rachael was atop the Valentine billboard again, this time with turpentine and a scrub broom in her hands instead of a paintbrush. Cleaning up the sign wasn't as much fun as vandalizing it had been, but in a Zen-like way, it was almost as therapeutic.

As she mindlessly scoured the sign, her thoughts were on her new endeavor. The more she thought about Romanceaholics Anonymous, the more excited she got. This was her new mission in life. She'd seen the error of her ways and she was a convert. Now, to get other people on board.

She'd been working about an hour and she was already starting to sweat, even though it wasn't yet nine o'clock. The day promised to be another scorcher. Just when she was beginning to realize she should have brought water and sunscreen, Brody's Crown Vic motored by.

When he pulled to a stop on the shoulder of the road beneath the billboard, Rachael's heart started pounding erratically.

Looking resplendent in his uniform and sunglasses, he got out of the car.

Rachael set down the scrub broom and pushed back a strand of hair that had fallen from her ponytail and was trailing across her face. She glanced down at him.

Brody held a white paper sack in his hand. "Had breakfast yet?"

"Cereal bar this morning," she called back down. "But I've worked up an appetite."

He waggled the bag. "Come on down. You deserve a break."

He didn't have to ask twice. As fast as her legs could carry her, she was off the billboard and in the passenger seat of his car.

"Besides breakfast," he said, "I thought you might need a few other supplies." He handed her a second, bigger sack containing sunscreen, bottled water, a battery-powered fan, a straw hat, and a collapsible umbrella.

Something strange tugged inside her at his considerate gesture. "How did you know I needed all this?"

"I drove by earlier," he admitted. "I figured you'd forgotten how hot it can get in Valentine in late July."

He was right, she had forgotten.

"Egg McMuffin," he said, taking a breakfast sandwich wrapped in yellow paper from the other sack and passing it to her. "Hash browns and orange juice."

"Thanks so much." She hadn't known she was so ravenous until tempted with the aroma of food. She dug into the sandwich. They sat in the car, air conditioner running, eating in companionable silence.

They were halfway through breakfast when Brody's radio crackled.

"Sheriff?" came the young female voice over the bandwidth. "We've got trouble."

Brody stuck his Egg McMuffin back in the sack, dusted

his hands on a napkin, and then reached for the radio. "What's up, Jamie?"

"You better get over to the courthouse. Mayor Wentworth is raisin' a ruckus."

Brody rolled his eyes and Rachael suppressed a giggle. "What's he got his shorts in a bunch over this time?"

"He's pitchin' such a bitch I'm not really sure, but he keeps saying something about parking meters."

"I'll check it out, Jamie. Thanks." Brody settled the radio back in place.

"I better get out"—Rachael reached for the door handle—"and let you do your job."

"Stay put," he said. "Finish your breakfast. This shouldn't take too long."

He put the patrol car in gear and headed over to the courthouse. They arrived to find Kelvin pacing the courthouse lawn, face florid, mopping his brow with a handkerchief, letting loose with a string of colorful curse words.

That's when Rachael saw the parking meters. She sucked in her breath as a mix of emotions surged through her. Shock, disbelief, and an odd, heady sense of glee.

She wasn't the only one in town disgruntled by Valentine's gaudy attachment to romantic symbolism. Someone else had taken a stand.

Because every last one of the sixteen heart-shaped parking meters in front of the courthouse had been neatly beheaded.

"Calm down, Kelvin," Brody soothed.

"I will not calm down. Not only has this town been disrespected twice in one week, but you're consorting with the perpetrator." Kelvin glared at Rachael, who'd gotten out of the patrol car behind him. "She's the cause of it all. I want her arrested again."

Brody cast a glance at the parking meter heads that had been arranged in the middle of the courthouse lawn to form the letters "F.U." The poles stood impotently bare, no longer capable of extracting parking fees from courthouse patrons. The message was pretty succinct. Brody couldn't help wondering if Kelvin was the target of this latest vandalism and they were using Rachael's billboard scandal as a dodge. Or maybe it was just someone tired of paying to park.

"Rachael didn't cut the heads off the parking meters."

"How do you know?" Kelvin demanded.

"For one thing, I asked her and Rachael doesn't lie. For another thing, Rachael was in custody the night someone stole pipe cutters from Audie's Hardware."

"Yeah, but where was she last night?"

Brody looked at Rachael.

"I was at home with my mother," she said.

"There you go." Brody spread his palms.

"That doesn't mean she doesn't have an accomplice, and you're assuming someone used pipe cutters and that they were the same ones stolen from Audie's store. Hell, they could have used a Sawzall."

"Examined the tool marks." Brody waved at the markings on the posts. "It's a pipe cutter. Besides, a reciprocating saw would have made too much noise. Someone did this under cover of darkness and it took them most of the night."

"That's what I mean. It's someone with an anti-romance agenda like your girl there. It's a plot." Kelvin glowered.

"A plot?" Brody couldn't keep the amusement from his voice.

"And she's behind it." Kelvin jerked a thumb in Rachael's direction.

"So we're talking conspiracy theories here?" Brody pressed his lips together to keep from laughing. "Do you know how paranoid that sounds, Kelvin?"

"Someone's trying to sabotage my business deal. I have investors coming in tomorrow and someone is trying to make Valentine look bad."

Brody paused to consider what Kelvin was saying. The mayor was overly dramatic, it was true. But if Kelvin did have investors coming to town, there might be something to his paranoia. "What kind of investors?"

"I'm not prepared to discuss it with you."

"Then how am I supposed to explore your theory?"

"Just do your job and catch whoever did this."

"That's what I'm trying to do," Brody explained patiently.

Kelvin chuffed out his breath and ran a hand over the top of his bald pate. "How am I going to explain this to my investors? It's going to look bad."

"It doesn't have to."

Kelvin eyed him. "What do you mean?"

"You can say removing the parking meters was your idea. Wasn't it your daddy that got them installed in the first place? Free parking in front of the courthouse is a gesture of goodwill toward the town. It couldn't hurt you in the election."

Kelvin perked up. "That's not a bad idea, Carlton. Now get that woman back to the billboard so she can clean up her mess."

Brody snorted, knowing it was the best he could expect from the mayor. "So you don't want me to file a report. I mean, if you're having the parking meters removed, that's what you'd want appearing in the paper. Not that someone beheaded the parking meters in the middle of the night in the police blotter."

"Right, right."

Crisis averted.

Brody headed back to the car satisfied that he'd solved Kelvin's PR problem, but he couldn't help thinking this act of vandalism was just the start of something that could easily get out of hand.

And when he slid a glance over at Rachael, who was standing beside the patrol car looking so sweet and innocent, he couldn't help thinking that she was going to get caught in the cross fire.

"This is a call to order for the first ever meeting of Romanceaholics Anonymous. My name is Rachael Henderson, founder of the group, and I'm a romanceaholic."

The small group assembled in the meeting room of the Valentine Public Library consisted of her mother, Deana Carlton, Rex Brownleigh, Audie Gaston, and two old-maiden sisters, Enid and Astrid Pope, who were notorious for attending any and every social event in town. They all just blinked at her.

"You're supposed to say, 'Hello, Rachael,'" she schooled them from the podium. After spending two weeks boning up on twelve-step programs—in between serving some of her community service hours—she'd learned the basics. But tonight, their first time, they would be flying blind.

"Hello, Rachael," they greeted her in unison.

She beamed at them. "Very good."

They beamed back.

"Everything we say in here is confidential. It's like

Vegas. What happens in Romanceaholics Anonymous stays in Romanceaholics Anonymous. Does everyone agree?"

Heads bobbed.

"The first step," she said, "is for us to admit we are powerless over romance and that our lives have become unmanageable because of our romantic ideations. I'll go first and tell you what led me to start this group."

Even though Rachael was fairly certain everyone in the room had already heard her story through the Valentine grapevine, she told it anyway. "After my ex-fiancé Trace Hoolihan appeared on *Entertainment Tonight*," she said, leaving out the part that minutes later she'd been on the verge of kissing Brody Carlton, "I realized I had a problem and I couldn't conquer my addiction alone. And being back in Valentine, with all its emphasis on romance, I realized other people might have the same problem. So who would like to go first? You don't have to share if you don't want to, but the sooner you admit you have a problem, the quicker you'll get on the road to clearheaded thinking."

Deana's hand shot up.

"Come on up, Deana," Rachael said and took a seat while Brody's sister claimed the podium.

"My name is Deana Carlton, and I'm a romanceaholic," she said.

"Hello, Deana," the group greeted her.

"As many of you may know, romantic notions about happily ever after led me into an ill-fated marriage to a guy who turned out to be a con man. Because we had a daughter together, I stayed with him for seven years, pretending that everything was all right. My craving for the romantic gestures he dealt out when things were flush— lavish gifts, love notes pinned to my pillow, impromptu vacations—kept me hanging on. I never once questioned where he got the money for the extravagant gestures. I didn't want to know. Until government agents showed up on our doorstep to haul everything away."

Deana's voice cracked. She sniffled and a tear rolled down her cheek. Rachael hopped up to offer her a Kleenex. She was proud that she'd remembered to buy a brand-new box specifically for the meeting.

A murmur of sympathy ran through the collective.

"That's not even the worst of it," Deana said. "The bad part is that two days ago he called me and begged me to meet him in Costa Rica where he'd fled, but he said I'd have to leave Maisy behind." Deana cringed. "I'm ashamed to admit I actually bought the ticket. But then I heard about Rachael's meeting from the flyer she posted in the window at Higgy's and I knew I couldn't do this alone. I need help. To think I'd be willing to leave my child behind and go back to this guy because he made romantic promises I couldn't resist." She shuddered.

"Do you have the airplane ticket with you?" Rachael asked.

Deana nodded.

Rachael looked her in the eye. "I know this is hard for you, but I want you to tear that ticket up, right now."

Nervously, Deana licked her lips.

"You can do it," Rex Brownleigh called out.

Deana directed a shaky smile at the audience, reached in her purse, and took out the ticket. She tore it into little shreds.

"It's an e-ticket," Selina pointed out. "What's to keep her from going online and printing out another one?"

"The desire to get better," Rachael said. "Plus, Rex has his laptop with him. He can cancel Deana's ticket right now."

Rex opened his laptop.

"Do you want him to cancel the ticket, Deana?"

Deana, looking pale and shaky, nodded.

"Go sit beside Rex," Rachael instructed. "And give him the information so he can cancel the ticket for you."

Deana did as she was asked.

"What's to keep her from ordering another one when she gets home?" Enid Pope asked.

"We will."

"How's that?" asked her sister, Astrid. "Steal her computer? Lock her in leg irons?"

"We do it by offering her emotional support. Deana, whenever you feel tempted to fall back under the spell of your ex-husband, I want you to give any one of us a call. We'll talk you through it." She looked at Deana. "Okay?"

Deana nodded.

Rachael looked at her watch. "We've got time for one more declaration tonight. Anyone else want to admit that their life has become unmanageable because of romantic ideations?"

Rex raised his hand and Rachael waved him to the podium. He declared he was a romanceaholic and he was powerless to keep off Internet dating sites.

"I keep meeting women, falling in love with them, pouring my heart and soul into the relationship, and they walk all over me," he said. "I've had my car stolen, my identity ripped off, and I contracted a nasty computer virus all because I can't say no to women." His deep voice boomed in the confines of the tiny room. "Growing up in Valentine a guy is taught to be chivalrous and help damsels in distress. It all sounds so romantic, but what happens is that when you're sweet to a woman, she thinks you're a wimp and walks all over you."

"That's not necessarily true," Rachael said. She loved it when men were sweet to her. Problem was, she fell for sweet talkers who never really meant their declarations of love. "I think this is the hardest thing about being a romanceaholic, knowing the difference between mere romance and true love. That's why we need each other. To help us sort it all out. Do we need a guest speaker on the topic?"

"Yes!" the group said in unison.

"Okay, then. For our next meeting I'll see if I can find a psychologist willing to tell us how to recognize if it's true love or if it's just romance."

Her mother raised her hand.

"Yes, Mom?"

"By saying true love, aren't you playing into the romantic myth that there is only one love out there for us?"

"You're right. Thanks for pointing that out. I need help just as much as everyone else. That's why I started the group. Okay, we won't use the terms 'true love,' 'soul mates,' or anything else that indicates fanciful, romantic thinking. Does anyone else have anything they'd like to contribute?"

No one else offered to speak.

"All right, then, the meeting is adjourned. Same time next week. Remember, if you have the urge to do or believe something romantic, give one of your fellow romanceaholics a call. I have handouts with the list of names and phone numbers. There's coffee and cookies on the table in the back if anyone would like to stay and chat."

As Rachael headed for the coffeepot, feeling as if the first meeting had gone quite well, Rex Brownleigh sauntered over.

"I gotta tell you, Rachael," he said, "I'm really impressed

by your initiative. It took guts not only to graffiti the Valentine billboard but to start this group. You're being pro-active, taking charge of your life."

"So are you, Rex." She smiled. "By coming here."

"I was wondering…" Rex paused, ducked his head, shuffled his feet.

Omigosh, she thought, *he's going to ask me out.* How was she going to handle it? She should have expected something like this to happen in a group of romanceaholics, but she wasn't prepared.

Gulping, she felt the smile leave her face. "Um…yes?"

He raised her head, met her gaze. "If you'd be interested in getting even with Trace Hoolihan."

That took her by surprise.

"He shouldn't get away with treating you so badly," Rex said.

Revenge, Rachael knew, was never an honorable motive, but it was a very human one. Temptation took hold of her. It wasn't the normal temptation of romance. It was a different kind of thrill. One she'd never experienced before.

Well, she rationalized, if revenge could release her attachment to Trace, ultimately wouldn't that be a good thing, even if her motives were less than pure? He certainly hadn't been thinking pure thoughts when he'd said those unkind things about her on national television.

Politely tell Rex no and walk away, said her principled side, but her all-too-human side won and instead she said, "What do you have in mind?"

Rex grinned. "YouTube."

"Pardon?"

"You know, the Web site on the Internet where people upload videos—"

"I know what YouTube is," she interrupted. "What I don't get is how that's going to help me get even with Trace."

"We show your side of the story."

Rachael shook her head. "I don't really see the point."

"Vindication."

She had to admit, she wanted it.

"And," he said, "it'd be a great forum for Romanceaholics Anonymous. The more people you reach with the message, the more people you help."

She wanted that even more. "What exactly do you have in mind?"

Two weeks had passed since the parking meter incident and Amusement Corp's visit to Valentine to see the town and review Kelvin's proposal. Nervously, he waited for a call back. They'd promised to contact him by the end of the previous week. Now it was Wednesday and there was still no word. The time lapse made him realize exactly how much he wanted this deal to go through. Not just for himself, but for the good of his hometown.

"Any messages?" he asked Rex when he returned from lunch, noticing a blob of Higgy's chili pie on his tie.

"Amusement Corp didn't call," Rex said.

He was tired of playing cat and mouse. Tired of being in the "depend" role. He was going to take the bull by the horns. "Get Amusement Corp on the phone for me," he said and stepped over to grab a paper napkin off Rex's desk.

In the process, he dislodged a trifold brochure that fluttered to the floor. Kelvin bent to pick it up, barely glancing at it as he laid it back on Rex's desk. He was halfway to his office door before he did a double take, backpedaled, and snatched up the brochure.

Has Romance Made Your Life Unmanageable? Take Charge of Your Future Today. Join Romanceaholics Anonymous.

"What in the hell is this?" he asked Rex.

Hand poised over the telephone, Rex shrugged as if he had no idea what Kelvin was talking about, but he looked sheepish.

"Romanceaholics Anonymous." Kelvin flipped the brochure over. "They meet at the public library every Tuesday night. Who ever heard of Romanceaholics Anonymous?"

"It's a new twelve-step program."

"I get that," Kelvin snapped. "What I don't get is what this brochure is doing on your desk."

"Um." Rex shifted uncomfortably. "I went to the first meeting last night."

Kelvin narrowed his eyes. "Who's behind this?" His first thought was Giada Vito.

"Rachael Henderson."

"That meddlesome woman? What's her problem?"

"She thinks Valentine pushes an unrealistic view of romance," Rex said. "There's a lot of people in town who agree with her."

Kelvin snorted. "Are you really that clueless?"

"What do you mean?"

"Without that supposedly unrealistic view of romance, this town wouldn't even exist."

The phone picked that moment to ring.

They both jumped. Rex looked grateful as he reached for it. "Mayor's office, Rex Brownleigh speaking."

He pressed the hold button and shot Kelvin a look. "It's Amusement Corp."

Kelvin did a jig all the way into his office. He closed

the door, counted to ten, and then picked up the extension. "Mayor Wentworth here."

"Mayor, Jackson Traynor, Amusement Corp."

"Jack. How are things?"

"Just fine. I want to apologize for not getting back to you sooner."

"I've been so busy I hadn't noticed," Kelvin lied smoothly. "I hope you're calling with good news for Valentine."

"Um, that's the reason for my delay."

Jackson Traynor's tone of voice had Kelvin's testicles drawing up tight.

"We ran your proposal past our research team and there were some concerns."

"What kind of concerns?" Kelvin had spent ten years preparing that proposal. It was spotless.

"Are you aware that Valentine's town charter prevents the construction of a project of this size without seventy-five percent approval from the taxpayers?"

"Is that what has you worried?" Relief pushed out his fear.

"Frankly, yes. We loved your proposal, but your remote location is a strike against you and we can't commit to this project until you have a bond election."

"I can guarantee the votes. My family brought tourism to this town. The constituents will do whatever I want."

"We did a straw poll while we were in town and you don't have as much of a lock on the town as you might think you do."

"Meaning?"

"Your approval rating is only forty percent. Apparently a lot of people in Valentine are thinking about voting for your opponent."

Giada Vito. Kelvin narrowed his eyes. "I'll get those votes. I'll get that bond election passed."

"I really hope that you do, Mayor, because we're gung ho on your project. But we're looking at another property site outside Tyler and we can't finance both. You have until November to pass this bond," Traynor said. "Otherwise you lose out."

Kelvin hung up the phone feeling at once elated and belligerent. Between them, Giada Vito and Rachael Henderson were trying to hijack his town and he'd be damned if he was going to let them get away with it.

Rachael got a copy of her wedding video from Tish, who'd taped the ceremony. In between dishing up meals at the senior citizen center as part of her community service, she spent her spare time at Rex's house creating her YouTube montage.

Making the video was a painful experience, but useful in helping her overcome any lingering attachment she had to Trace—and hopefully to romantic love. Every time she watched the moment where her supposedly idyllic life crumbled, her resolve to forsake romance strengthened.

Idealizing men and marriage was not the road to happiness.

There she was in her wedding dress walking down the aisle on her father's arm. A traditional church wedding with all the trimmings. She'd planned it since she was a child. Making scrapbooks of it and gathering items for her hope chest. Doves and candles. Orchids and white roses. A soprano soloist warbling "A Forever Kind of Love." Six bridesmaids. Her sister Hannah's adorable three-year-old daughter as flower girl. The works.

It was the most perfect of wedding ceremonies.

Until the critical moment when the pastor asked, "Does anyone have any objections to the union of this man to this woman?"

It must have been cosmic timing.

In the hushed momentary silence of the church came the distinctive ringing of a cell phone.

With a clutch in her throat, Rachael recalled the fateful moment. The irritation she'd felt over the sheer rudeness of the guest who hadn't thought to silence their cell phone before entering the chapel.

"Speak now," the pastor said on the video. "Or forever hold your peace."

Rachael remembered beaming up at Trace, wishing the minister would hurry up and get to the good part. The part where he pronounced them husband and wife and they would walk hand in hand into their happily-ever-after.

But that moment never came.

"Here it comes," Rex said, timing the sequence of events for the video. "Wait for it, wait for it...three... two...one..."

"Since no one has any obj—"

"Stop the wedding," Trace Hoolihan's agent, Bob Boscoe, said, shooting to his feet.

Every single time Rachael saw it, a sick feeling rose inside her. Hand to her stomach, she took a deep breath and forced herself to watch, even though she desperately wanted to close her eyes. Aversion therapy.

The minister looked startled. Every gaze in the place turned to stare at Boscoe.

Except for Rachael's.

As if caught in a surreal dream, the on-camera Rachael just kept smiling—denying reality, determined that she was going to live the dream even if no one else was cooperating.

It was scary sad.

Rachael cringed and squirmed in Rex's rolling swivel chair, parked beside the bank of computers lining his living room wall. Rex was at the keyboard, making adjustments to the color, sounds, dimensions. Enhancing and enlarging. Splicing and merging. He clicked the mouse, zooming in on Boscoe's face.

"What is the nature of your objection?" asked the minister.

"Trace," Boscoe said, pushing aside the guests as he headed toward the altar waving his cell phone. "You've just had an offer from the Chicago Bears. They want you in as first-string wide receiver."

Rachael saw it happen all over again as, deep in her soul, she felt the moment she'd lost him. The pure joy on Trace's face as he let out a whoop, stepped away from Rachael and into Boscoe's embrace.

A heartbeat passed.

She relived the taste of bile spilling into her mouth. Experienced all over again the bone-crunching disbelief of shattered dreams. She smelled the cloying scent of too many flowers. Heard the shocked intake of the spectators' collective breaths.

"Trace?" Rachael's trembling on-camera voice whispered tentatively. Her eyes were wide, the smile on her face slipping. "What's going on?"

She was so pathetic.

Self-loathing took hold of her and she had to close her eyes and breathe deeply to fight off the nausea. She'd seen the video six times since the wedding and every single time it still clipped her hard.

"I'm going to Chicago," Trace crowed.

Not *we're* going to Chicago, but *I'm* going to Chicago.

"But what does this mean?" Her voice rose. On-screen she was blinking rapidly, swallowing repeatedly.

"I'm sorry, Rachael," Trace said, looking contrite. "But this is a once-in-a-lifetime chance to get back into the game. The wedding is off."

The church had erupted. People scrambled to their feet, surging the altar, most of them rushing to congratulate Trace.

And there she stood in the midst of it all, buffeted around like foam on the ocean. She saw Delaney step forward to wrap an arm around her shoulder. On-camera, her face went deathly white and she looked as if she was going to faint.

It wasn't the anger or disappointment or hurt that upset Rachael the most. Rather it was her wimpy reaction that made her want to reach out and slap her own silly face.

How could she have been so gullible, so naive, so trusting?

"Idiot," she muttered.

"Fool for love," Rex said.

"Just plain fool. I can't believe the way I twisted myself around for his affection."

Awkwardly, Rex patted her shoulder. "It's okay. This is therapeutic. You've got the proof of your mistake right in front of you and we can all learn something from it."

He was right.

"Hey," Rex said. "Look what I did since the last time you were here. This ought to make you feel better."

With a few finger strokes to the keyboard, Trace's head morphed into that of a jackass. He turned to the camera and brayed.

Rachael burst out laughing.

"Thatta girl." Rex chuckled along with her. "It gets better. Watch this."

He changed computer monitors and switched from her actual wedding video to the one he'd created for YouTube. The music began. It wasn't the music from her wedding, but rather "Love Stinks" by the J. Geils Band.

"Once upon a time," came Rex's deep-throated voice-over, "there was a beautiful young girl from Valentine, Texas, born on Valentine's Day, who'd been taught to believe truly, madly, deeply in the romantic myth of finding her Prince Charming and living happily ever after."

On-screen, Rachael appeared on her father's arm walking through the door of the chapel, looking radiant in her wedding gown, beaming brightly, the beautiful floral bouquet clutched in her hand. The picture of dreams come true.

"She thought she'd found the perfect man."

The shot cut to Trace standing at the altar looking ultracool and impossibly gorgeous with his thick mane of blond hair swept back off his forehead and his lantern jaw thrust forward. The traditional black tuxedo fit him like a fantasy, the pink rosebud boutonniere at his lapel a promise of everlasting love.

"Ha!" came Rex's voice-over.

"Love stinks!" shouted the J. Geils Band.

A camera shot showed the packed church. On the front pew Rachael's mother sat beside her father, both looking grim-faced, just moments before Rachael's entire world fell in. She should have seen the signs that her parents' marriage was on rocky ground. Why hadn't she seen the signs?

"Rose-colored glasses hide a lot of flaws," Rex's voice-over said.

The camera swung back to Rachael coming up the aisle, her gaze fixed on Trace's face. A rose-colored lens covered everything with a soft, dreamy filter. The shot dissolved with clueless Rachael stepping up to the altar.

"And then she was betrayed by the thing she held most dear," Rex's taped voice continued.

"Love stinks."

The sound of a beating heart galloping faster and faster as she watched the painful scene again of Bob Boscoe jumping up to announce the deal with the Chicago Bears.

Trace had known all along Boscoe was working on the deal. He had to have known. She'd been his backup plan if the Chicago Bears hadn't picked up his contract. It was only then that it occurred to Rachael that Trace might have been marrying her for her daddy's money.

She didn't know why it hadn't occurred to her before. Maybe because money didn't matter much to her. She'd been born and raised with it and she supposed she took it for granted. What she valued was love and romance.

"Dodged a bullet," Rex said and turned down the volume on the video.

"Huh?" Rachael blinked.

"You've got that 'woe-is-me' look in your eyes," he said. "Just imagine if the Chicago Bears hadn't done you a huge favor and lured Trace away. How long would it have been before you realized what a huge mistake you'd made?"

"Twenty-seven years?" She posed the question thinking of her parents' marriage.

The J. Geils Band kept right on singing.

On-screen, Trace was breaking her heart all over again, and then literally turning into a jackass compliments of Rex's moviemaker program. He'd also spliced in a clip of Trace's *Entertainment Tonight* interview, proving most everything he'd told the reporter about Rachael was a bald-faced lie.

Then came the pitch for Romanceaholics Anonymous.

"Single, lonely, looking for love in all the wrong places?" Rex asked on the audio. "Has an addiction to romance caused your life to spiral out of control? Don't make the same mistakes Rachael did. Keep your heart safe. Stop spending your life on a roller coaster of expectation looking for Mr. or Ms. Right. Stay sane. Get help now. Join Romanceaholics Anonymous. For more information, call…" And then Rachael's cell phone number flashed across the screen.

Rex pushed back in his chair and slid her a look. "What do you think? You ready to upload it to YouTube?"

He was right. It was the perfect revenge.

"Upload it," she said.

"There's no going back."

"I know. That's the point. I need to seal the deal, because even after all he's put me through, if Trace were to call up, apologize, and beg me to take him back, I can't promise that I wouldn't."

"Stay strong," Rex said. He did his magic with the keyboard and the next thing Rachael knew, it was too late to turn back. There her video was on the YouTube queue. *Trace Hoolihan Ditches Bride at the Altar.*

"Wanna watch it again?"

"Sure."

Rex clicked the button straight from YouTube.

As the video clip played out, and Rachael realized that hundreds, possibly thousands of people would see this and know the truth, something strange happened to her. She didn't feel scared or nervous or as if she wanted to take it all back. Gone were any doubts or uncertainties she might have had about her inner motives.

She felt empowered. She felt as if she was finally taking charge of her life. She felt as if she owned the world.

Chapter 9

July melted into the dog days of August. With the increased heat came an increase in crime. The fistfights at Leroy's grew more frequent. Brody's dinner was interrupted twice to mediate domestic disputes at the Love Line trailer court. And three times, Enid and Astrid Pope had called him over to their house the next block over because someone kept peeling the red glitter hearts off their white picket fence.

Brody had to consider whether it was the same culprit who'd vandalized the parking meters, but then he found Maisy playing with the glitter hearts in question and he made her take them back to the elderly ladies and apologize.

The rise in crime was a yearly pattern, but even so, the normally quiet town had seemed edgier and more restless since Rachael had come home to Valentine and started Romanceaholics Anonymous. From the patrons at Higgy's Diner to the customers at Audie's Hardware to the old men who played checkers in Bristo Park, the town was buzzing with both gossip and opinions.

Kelvin's "decision" to remove the parking meters

around the courthouse went over big with his constituents, just as Brody had predicted. Brody had analyzed the tool markings and he'd been correct: A pipe cutter the same diameter as the one stolen from Audie's Hardware had been used to behead the meters, but he wasn't any closer to discovering who'd done the deed than he had been the day it happened. He was hoping the vandal was satisfied with beheading the parking meters and he or she was done with their crime spree.

Brody was sitting in his office ordering supplies when Jamie called to him from the dispatch desk.

"Sheriff, come here. You gotta see this."

He got up and sauntered into the next room to find Jamie's eyes glued to the computer screen, listening to the sound of the J. Geils Band singing "Love Stinks."

"What are you looking at?"

Jamie crooked a finger at him. "YouTube."

Curious, he moved behind the dispatcher to see what had so captivated her attention. What he saw simultaneously stirred his sympathy, amused him, and concerned him. There was Rachael getting dumped on her wedding day,

Damn it, Rachael, what are you thinking?

Here she was stirring up trouble again. While he couldn't blame her for wanting to get even with the jerk who'd dumped her at the altar, she didn't seem to realize the problems she was making for herself. *Put the woman in a cage with a sleeping lion and she'd poke it with a stick.*

"I love it," Jamie said. "Down with romance. I think I'm going to attend the next meeting of Romanceaholics Anonymous and show her my support."

Brody groaned. Things were getting way out of hand.

He had to go talk to her, ask her to take the video off You-Tube before lookie-loos and reporters started showing up in Valentine.

He was halfway to the front door when the call came through.

"Sheriff's office," Jamie answered over the speaker phone. "How may I direct your call?"

"It's Selina Henderson. Tell Sheriff Carlton someone's vandalized my daughter's car right in our driveway."

Brody's eyes met Jamie's. "Tell her I'm on my way."

Five minutes later, he pulled onto Market Street and caught sight of Rachael's jaunty pink VW Bug, now savagely graffitied with militant slogans in angry black paint. VALENTINE—LOVE IT OR LEAVE IT. ROMANCE ISN'T THE PROBLEM, YOU ARE. But the one that chilled his blood was GET OUT OF TOWN, BITCH, OR SUFFER THE CONSEQUENCES.

Rachael stood there, arms wrapped around her chest, cradling herself. She looked so damned vulnerable. A feeling he'd never felt before and couldn't identify pressed down on him. A strange sensation tingled his upper lip and a sudden heaviness pulled at the back of his spine.

He got out of the car, his hand riding near the gun at his hip. He realized with a start he'd willingly shoot anyone who tried to hurt her.

She took one look at him and relief flooded her face. "Brody," she said simply, and the sound of his name on her tongue unraveled something inside him.

"Are you all right?" he asked, resisting the urge to reach out and touch her. He was here on official business. His inappropriate impulses had no place in this conversation.

"I'm fine," she whispered.

He fisted his hands to keep from touching her. God, how he wanted to touch her.

"Do you have any idea when this could have happened?" he asked.

She shook her head. "I came outside to get the newspaper and saw it. I suppose I should have expected something like this. A lot of people don't want to see Valentine change. The nail that sticks up is the one that gets hit."

Selina came over to wrap her arm around Rachael's shoulders. "It's okay, sweetheart. You have as many supporters as you do detractors. We're not going to let some small-minded individual terrorize us. Brody will find out who did this."

In order to hold his emotions in check, Brody kept his expression neutral and his mind on the job. He stepped closer to examine the VW Bug. He could have the paint analyzed to see if it matched the paint stolen from Audie's Hardware. But it would take time and funds to confirm what he suspected. That the person or persons who had stolen the paint and the pipe cutter had cut the heads off the parking meters and graffitied Rachael's car.

Except his theory didn't parse. The person who'd beheaded the parking meters appeared to be sending an anti-romance message. Whoever had graffitied Rachael's car seemed pro-romance.

Unless...

The intention wasn't to take a stand on either side of the issue, but rather to pit the townsfolk against one another.

But who? And why?

It was something to consider. He had more investigating to do. And that included interviewing Kelvin again.

Brody turned, not realizing Rachael had come to stand directly behind him, and his arm collided with her shoulder. The protective instinct rushed over him again.

"Sorry," she mumbled and stepped back.

"Hold still."

"What for?"

"I said hold still," he said more gruffly than he intended. He was still upset over the crude messages on her car. "You've got black paint on your cheek."

She seemed so tiny next to his bulk and he could feel heat emanating off her compact body. She stood stock-still, staring at the buttons of his uniform as if she were afraid to meet his gaze. He reached over with a thumb and tried to smear the paint away but it wouldn't budge. Just as he suspected. Oil-based.

Then he had an arresting thought. Rachael had bought black oil-based paint to use on the billboard. How did he know she hadn't vandalized her own car to stir up sympathy?

He hated that his cop's mind even went there. Hated to think she would do such a thing and the minute the thought was in his head he knew it couldn't be true. She was trembling, for Pete's sake. She was truly scared.

"Are they…do you think they'll…." She swallowed. "Could this turn violent?"

"Don't worry," he promised, knowing he was starting down a slippery slope but sliding headfirst anyway. "I won't let anyone hurt you."

By the fourth meeting of Rachael's Romanceaholics Anonymous group, Selina was surprised to find attendance had quadrupled. And even more surprised to find many had driven in from neighboring counties. Word had gotten out.

The pleased expression on her daughter's face did Selina a world of good. She'd been down in the dumps ever since she'd wrecked the Caddy.

And she was tired of being idealistic. She needed an intervention herself.

Selina was here to support Rachael's cause, but deep inside she feared she would never stop loving Michael, no matter how hard she tried.

And he'd been making her life miserable by sending flowers and chocolates over every day, along with cute little cards declaring his abiding love for her. The delivery boy seemed to enjoy it when she thrust the roses and Godiva truffles at him and said, "Give them to your girlfriend."

Then she would methodically shred the cards, gritting her teeth against the tears. She stuck the pieces in an envelope and mailed them back to him.

He wrote her more love letters, begging her forgiveness.

She sent him the bill for the Caddy's repair.

He paid it.

She ran up his charge card, buying hip, stylish clothes for her slender new figure. She'd dropped twelve pounds since she'd left him. Misery had some small benefits.

Without a whimper, he'd paid that, too.

Who was she kidding? Selina wasn't just there for Rachael. She was here for moral support. She needed help to keep from forgiving Michael, packing her bags, and moving back home.

Because she missed him something terrible. Twenty-seven years she'd lain next to him, bore his children, cooked his meals, been his constant companion.

And all this time, he'd carried a torch for Vivian Cole.

Pain and resentment crowded out nostalgia and longing. She deserved better than finishing second place in her husband's heart. Knotting her hands into fists, Selina determinedly held on tightly to her resolve.

People kept piling into the room, looking for places to

sit. Her face flushed with pride, Rachael had the librarian bring in more chairs. The sound of metal folding chairs being dragged across the linoleum floor mingled with the buzz of voices as they made room for the newcomers. The air smelled of books and strong coffee.

Audie Gaston winked at Selina. "You can scoot over next to me."

She knew Audie was halfway sweet on her. He gave her a ten percent discount at his hardware store. His wife had died years earlier and he'd grieved for a long time. He wasn't a particularly good-looking man, but neither was he ugly. He was tall, thin, balding, and wore owlish Harry Potter glasses. But he had a nice smile.

And a nice butt.

Selina smiled back and scooted her chair closer to him. *Take that, Michael.*

Rachael was at the podium. She looked so brave, standing up there in her simple floral-print sleeveless cotton blouse, wheat-colored Capri slacks, and beaded summer sandals. Her daughter hadn't worn a hint of her signature pink since she'd come back home. Pink, she'd told Selina, was for romantic fools and little girls and she was no longer either one. While Selina was proud of her for facing her character flaw and putting a plan into action for overcoming it, she couldn't help feeling a little sad that she was giving up on romance entirely. Selina couldn't help wishing something would develop between her eldest daughter and Sheriff Brody. Hypocritical, maybe, but ultimately all she wanted was for Rachael to be happy.

Brody was the kind of man Rachael needed. Strong, capable, empathetic, but not a pushover. Unfortunately, he hadn't been back across the street since the day Rachael's car had been vandalized.

It was probably for the best, she told herself. Any romance Rachael entered into now was bound to flop. Her eldest daughter was on the rebound. She simply wasn't ready, and the last thing Selina wanted was to see her get hurt again.

The meeting continued as person after person got up and told stories of woe brought on by romance. They were heartbreaking. Then a third of the way through the meeting, the door opened, creaking loudly on its hinges. Everyone turned to stare.

Michael lumbered in.

Selina's heart did the crazy swoon it always did whenever she unexpectedly caught sight of him in a crowd. But then it slid uneasily into the pit of her stomach.

His hair was rumpled, his eyes bloodshot, his gait unsteady. He'd been drinking.

Selina was shocked. Michael rarely drank. A New Year's toast, an occasional beer with a business associate to be social, but that was it. In fact, she'd only seen him completely drunk once, on the night before their wedding. The night he'd been with Vivian.

From her place at the podium, Rachael stopped speaking. Every eye in the place swung toward the doorway. "Daddy?"

In that moment, she sounded ten years old and it broke Selina's heart. What in the hell was wrong with Michael?

"Hey, sweetheart," he slurred and wriggled his fingers at Rachael. "Looks like you've attracted a nice-sized crowd."

Rachael cringed as if she wanted to crawl underneath the podium and cower there until everyone went away. Selina's heart wrenched. Her daughter was trying so hard, not only to hold it together after everything that had happened, but to recover and ultimately thrive.

"What are you doing here?" Rachael asked her father.

"I'm here for the meeting." He swayed.

"Hey, Michael," someone in the audience called out. "AA is meeting across town at Riverside Baptist church."

The comment drew a nervous laugh from the crowd. Anyone in the room who was from Valentine knew what was going on with the Hendersons. It was a small town and along with Kelvin, the Hendersons were the biggest fish in it.

Selina wanted to grab Michael by the throat with both hands and throttle him. How dare he spoil what Rachael was trying to do here just to get even with her?

"If you're going to stay, Daddy, then please take a seat," Rachael said.

"Rightee-o," he said, sounding like some misplaced Brit. Selina used to think his little catchphrase was cute. Now it sounded utterly ridiculous. Michael nodded and swung his gaze around the room looking for an empty chair.

But there wasn't one.

His gaze lit on Selina sitting next to Audie.

"I'll have someone get you a chair," Rachael said.

"I've got it," Michael said, making his way toward Selina. "I'll just have a seat right here." He plopped down on the floor between her and Audie and drew his knees to his chest to keep his feet from colliding with the chain of a lady sitting in the row in front of them.

Rachael hesitated. Clearly, she didn't know what to do. Selina watched the emotions war on her daughter's face—uncertainty, embarrassment, nervousness, self-doubt, all mixed with a tinge of anger. The audience watched her with interest, trying to anticipate how she would handle this turn of events. It was a lot of pressure and Selina's urge to throttle her husband escalated. She could smell the beer on his breath and it was all she could do to keep from kicking him.

It was much easier feeling angry at him for hurting their daughter than for hurting her.

Selina studied the top of his head and for the first time noticed a spot that was starting to thin. *What happened to the guy I married? Where is the kind and considerate man who'd got down on one knee and excitedly proposed the minute I'd told him I was pregnant?*

Honestly, though, wasn't that when all the trouble had started? The doubts and fears she'd had thinking he was marrying her simply because of the baby? Why else would a handsome, wealthy man like him marry the daughter of simple restaurant owners?

Rachael was talking again, inviting people to come up to the podium and share their stories of romance gone wrong.

Selina dipped her head and leaned over to whisper, "You shouldn't have come here."

Michael swung his gaze up to meet hers. He was clothed in white dress slacks and an oversized Hawaiian shirt, looking like the privileged son he was on vacation in the tropics. But his gaze was sharp in spite of the alcohol.

"Maybe if you'd answered my phone calls I wouldn't have had to resort to this."

"You could have come by the house," she said as sternly as she could at whisper pitch.

"I tried. You didn't answer the door."

"That's because I didn't want to see you. I still don't want to see you." Selina glared.

Who was this man? After twenty-seven years he remained a mystery to her. Shouldn't she know him inside and out by now? But she did not. Maybe that was the problem. On the surface, Michael was an affable, charming guy. But underneath it all ran a current of something deeper, darker. There was a part of him that he'd never revealed to her and his secrecy hurt as much as his betrayal with Vivian.

Blinking back the tears she was terrified were going to fall and give her away, Selina bit down hard on her bottom lip.

"I'd like to speak," Michael said and got to his feet.

Every eye in the place was back on him again.

"Sit down," Selina hissed.

"Since this is your first meeting, maybe you'd prefer to just listen tonight, Daddy," Rachael offered, a hint of panic in her voice.

"Nope. I wanna talk."

Rachael's gaze met Selina's. She looked as desperate as Selina felt. Michael started toward the podium. How tempting to stick out her foot and trip him.

"Let him go," Audie whispered to her. "Let him make a fool of himself."

And of me.

Miraculously, Michael reached the podium without stumbling. Rachael stepped aside with another *Help me!* glance at Selina. But her soon-to-be ex-husband already had the microphone in his hand.

"My name is Michael Henderson," he said, "and I'm a romanceaholic."

"Hello, Michael," chimed the crowd.

"Just look at what romance has reduced me to," he said. "A public drunk."

A ripple of sympathy went through the crowd as they made noises of condolence.

Irritation grated Selina. They were feeling sorry for him? He was the jerk who had broken her heart. He was the one who'd made a mockery of their marriage, not her. Why were they on his side?

"Most of you here know me. Nearly all of my entire adult life I've been a faithful husband—"

"Ha!" Selina interjected.

"To one woman," he continued as if she hadn't said a word. "I could have cheated. Right, Evangeline?" He winked at the flirty, curvaceous Rite Aid clerk sitting in the front row who blushed a blistering shade of crimson. "But I did not."

Michael looked out at the audience, but his eyes were focused on Selina and she knew he was speaking only to her. "What can I say? I'm a romantic guy. I showered my wife with gifts and trips. I put in a pool so she wouldn't swelter away in the Valentine summers. For her forty-second birthday I sent her to Tuscany so she could take gourmet cooking lessons from a famed Italian chef—and by the way, how do I know she didn't have an affair while she was there?"

The crowd was watching the action as if it were a prime-time soap opera, raptly shifting their gazes from Selina to Michael and back again.

Selina couldn't take anymore. She shot to her feet. "That was uncalled for. Francesco was nothing more than my teacher."

"Ah," Michael said, green eyes that same color as Rachael's snapping in anger. "But what exactly was he teaching you?"

The sound of the door opening and then quietly closing ratcheted the emotional tension in the room. Selina, along with everyone else, looked to see who'd come inside.

It was Brody Carlton. In uniform.

He surveyed the crowd, taking it all in, and seemed to

size up the situation almost instantly. He doffed his Stetson and moved to stand with his back against the wall.

"How do I know what Selina was doing at the country club when she was supposed to be taking tennis lessons from Gunther?" Michael continued. "I never accused her of an affair. I never entertained the idea. I trusted her. I loved her that much. But you can sure as hell believe I'm entertaining the idea now."

Selina's heart pounded and her ears rang and her breath left her body in one whoosh of pent-up air. She jumped to her feet, chest heaving. "Not once in twenty-seven years did I even glance at another man because I was so stupidly in love with you, but I'm beginning to think I should have had flings all over town. No one would blame me. You're always waving money in my face, bragging about how well you provided for me, expecting a pat on the back. Give him a hand, folks." Selina clapped. "Third-generation oil money who never had to work a day in his privileged life buys his poor little Mexican wife expensive baubles and expects to be lauded for lifting her out of poverty."

"So that's what this is all about," Michael said. "You're the one who feels inferior about your heritage, not me. I didn't marry you for your tamale-making abilities."

"Then why the hell did you marry me, when you were still in love with your high school sweetheart?"

"You're forcing me to say it?"

Selina sank her hands onto her hips, thrust out her jaw. "Go on, I dare you."

"You want me to say? I'll say it."

She'd never seen him looking so angry, but she was determined not to flinch. She grit her teeth, knotted her fists.

"I married you because you were knocked up."

A collective gasp went up from the crowd at Michael's confession and then everyone fell completely silent, waiting to see what would happen next.

Selina felt as if she'd been kicked in the gut. This was it. He'd finally admitted it. Finally voiced her greatest fear. In a weird way, she felt strangely exhilarated. Finally, they were communicating.

She heard Rachael make a soft noise of distress, and from the corner of her eye she saw Brody step forward. "Mr. Henderson," he said firmly, his hand hovering above the gun holstered at his hip, looking like Wyatt Earp swooping in to save the day. "Your Porsche is hanging out in the middle of the road and blocking traffic. It needs to be moved."

Michael's jaw set in the resolute line Selina knew too well. He realized Brody was taller, bigger, and had the weight of the badge behind him, but he was Valentine's favored son. He was accustomed to getting his way, even with law enforcement officers.

Brody took his handcuffs from his pocket and started for the podium, looking equally resolute.

"That's enough!" Rachael exploded. "I've had enough of this from all of you."

Everyone's attention volleyed to Rachael.

Selina had never heard her sweet-natured, accommodating daughter sound so authoritative. It both shocked and pleased her.

"Brody," she said to the sheriff, "back off. Someone will move my father's car in just a minute. Dad, have a seat on the stage." She pointed to the chair she'd just vacated. "Mom, come up here."

To Selina's surprise they all obeyed her. Brody stepped

out of the aisle. Michael sank down in the chair and Selina went to the front of the room.

Once she and Michael were on the stage together, Rachael paced in front of them, hands clasped behind her back, a frown of supreme disappointment on her face. She looked like a harried mom with two squabbling toddlers and she wasn't quite sure how to discipline them. Selina squirmed.

"For twenty-seven years," she said at last, "you two have allowed a pie-in-the-sky fantasy of what you think marriage is supposed to be rule your lives."

"Your mother certainly has," Michael said at the same moment Selina said, "Your father is the unrealistic one."

"Excuse me, but I'm talking here."

They shut up.

"Do you two want to stop romanticizing marriage and love?" she asked, looking so serious it was all Selina could do not to laugh. As if Rachael had any clue what marriage was really like.

"I don't romanticize—"

Rachael cut her off with a raised palm and a shushing noise. "You do. Most of the citizens of Valentine do. People," she said, shifting her gaze to the audience, "we've bought into the hype we've been promoting to lure tourists to our town. Marriage is not a piece of cake. It does not solve all our problems. If it did, would my parents be up here acting like spoiled brats?"

Spoiled brats?

Selina had gone to work in her family's Mexican food restaurant when she was nine years old. The middle child of seven, she'd grown up never having owned a new pair of shoes. Until she'd met Michael her life had been about hard work and sacrifice. No one had ever accused her of being a spoiled brat.

Michael, on the other hand, was the epitome of a spoiled brat. The only child of the town's second-most- prominent family, he'd had every possible advantage. Tennis lessons, swim coaches, golf clubs. He'd been the high school quarterback, the prom king, the class president. His first car had been a Mustang Cobra. He'd even gotten into Harvard, although he hadn't gone. All because she'd gotten pregnant.

His family had never let her hear the end of it.

"It's time to stop acting like spoiled brats and figure out what you really want for the rest of your lives. It's time to split the sheets, go your own way, and once and for all stop pretending you're Cinderella and Prince Charming."

Rachael's words carved an empty hole inside Selina. It was true. For twenty-seven years she'd pretended she was living a fairy tale but deep inside, she'd secretly been waiting for the castle walls to come crashing down.

The fairy tale was over.

The realization made her want to cry. She didn't want to let it go.

"It's tough, I know," Rachael said, her voice heavy with sympathy. "For all of you. But it's time to stop the hurt. It is possible to have a normal, healthy, loving relationship without all the game playing and the drama and the fantasy."

"Yeah," someone called out, "but where's the fun in that?"

"The fun," she said, glowering at the group, "is freeing yourself from a toxic pleasure-pain cycle. Peace is what you're really looking for. You're using excitement to fill the void. Real love isn't loud or flashy or grand or hurtful. It's calm and quict and tender and honest. Until you can be honest with yourselves, you'll never find the happiness that keeps eluding you."

Selina blinked, amazed by her daughter's strength, courage, and perceptiveness. Rachael was going to be okay. She wasn't going to end up like her mother and her father—married twenty-seven years without ever really knowing each other.

"Dad," Rachael said. "Go home. Leave Mom alone. She's done with the marriage."

Michael blinked as if he'd been poleaxed.

"And Mom, let go of your anger. There's no point in staying mad at him. You can't move on as long as you keep holding on to your anger."

Selina's heart sank and she recognized something important. She'd kept fanning the flame of her anger, because she knew if she let it go out, the last shred of her love for Michael would go with it.

Brody waited for Rachael as the romanceaholics filed out of the library. The flinty gleam in her green eyes was at odds with the soft roundness of her rosy cheeks. She looked like a kitten that had just unleashed her tiny but exceedingly sharp claws.

Brody suppressed a grin. Normally, he wasn't attracted to cute, cuddly women but from the first moment he'd spied her dangling from the Valentine lips, nothing about his feelings for her had been normal.

Or for that matter even rational.

His gaze drifted over the lush curves of her breasts sexily sheathed in a blue floral blouse. What was it about her that had so captivated him? How did she manage to wield such power with those startling green eyes?

No matter how much he tried to deny the attraction, every evening when he came home from work, he found himself gazing out the living room window hoping for a glimpse of her sitting out on the porch swing in the gathering dusk. Or watering Mrs. Potter's flower garden.

"Great meeting," Brody said when the last person had left the room.

Rachael cut him a razor-sharp glance. "I could do without the sarcasm, Carlton."

"I'm not being sarcastic," he said. "You did a great job."

She slumped down into a chair. That's when he realized her legs were trembling. "It was a nightmare."

"You didn't pull any punches. You told your parents exactly what they needed to hear."

"I wasn't thinking of them," she confessed. "I was hurt and mad and lashing out."

"It didn't come across that way at all."

"Really?"

"You sounded calm and sensible and full of wisdom far beyond your years."

"*Real*-ly?" Rachael asked, putting extra emphasis on the first syllable.

"Really."

"I was just fed up." She glowered and crossed her arms over her chest, ruining his view of her terrific cleavage.

"Remind me never to make you mad," Brody said, resisting the urge to lean over and kiss her frown away. "I loved the way you busted the whole Cinderella, Prince Charming thing."

"You don't think I'm turning into one of those bitter, men-hating women, do you?" she asked pensively. "I want to give up my romantic notions, but I don't want to give up on the opposite sex."

"Neither do I," he murmured, his gaze glued to the flutter of pulse at the blue vein in the hollow of her throat.

"You think I was out of line, don't you? Butting into my parents' marriage and offering them advice like I knew what I was talking about," she said.

"You're projecting your self-doubts onto me," he said, fascinated by her neck. God, she was gorgeous.

And passionate.

"Be honest. You think I'm an emotional mess."

"I never said that."

He didn't really think she was an emotional mess. A little overly focused on her emotions, but that was part of her charm and he was jealous of her ability to express her feelings. Brody had spent so many years holding himself in check he hadn't even been able to work up a good head of steam over Belinda. He'd just let her go. No fear of fairy tales in that relationship.

Or of real love, either.

"I know I'm an emotional mess, that's why I'm here. Doing this." She swept her hand at the empty room.

"You're not a mess," he said, wishing he'd led with that. Compelled by a force he couldn't explain, Brody stepped closer. "You're hurting and looking for a way to salve the pain. There's nothing wrong with that. You're human."

"It was crazy," she said. "The way I grew up."

"Uh-huh." He made sympathy noises, but his nose was filled with the smell of her watermelon-scented shampoo.

"It was like living in a fantasy land."

"That's a bad thing?"

"Yes," she said adamantly. "It doesn't prepare you for the real world. There's nothing quite as shocking as when happily-ever-after goes kaput."

"You're confusing shattered illusions with real tragedy," he said, hating that she'd made him think of Iraq. He'd been enjoying the fantasies dancing around in his head, fantasies of Rachael naked in his bed. Now he was thinking of war.

"Why do people do it?" she asked. "Why do they get

married? Why do they make promises they have no intention of keeping?"

He thought of his own marriage and winced inwardly. He'd made a mistake with Belinda and he was leery of making another one. "Most people don't intend to break their promise when they get married. Most people don't count on divorce."

"You're talking about your own marriage."

"I guess."

"So what went wrong?"

"My wife said I wasn't romantic enough. Plus there was the whole cheating on me thing."

"There you go," Rachael said.

"There I go where?" He didn't know if it was her screwy logic confusing him or the sight of her sweet peach-colored lips. Peach lips, watermelon-scented hair, grape green eyes. The woman was a virtual fruit salad and suddenly he wanted a taste of her.

"Romance, messing up a perfectly good relationship."

"It wasn't a perfectly good relationship," he said.

"No?"

"No."

"Then why'd you marry her?"

Brody shifted. He didn't like talking about his biggest failure. "She thought she was pregnant."

"You slept with her, even though you didn't love her?"

"Yeah," he admitted. "Not particularly admirable, but there you go."

"So you know how to separate sex from love."

He shrugged. "Biology is biology. Love is..."

"What?"

He swallowed, feeling the heat of her inquisitive gaze on his face. "I don't know what love is."

She tilted her head. Her gaze warmed his face. "How do you do it?"

"Do what?"

"That separating sex from love thingy." She wriggled two fingers. "I can't do it. I fall in love with every guy I sleep with."

The thought of Rachael sleeping with other guys poked a fist through his gut. "It's because you romanticize them."

"Exactly."

"Maybe next time instead of focusing on their good qualities you should focus on their flaws."

"There's not going to be a next time," she said, a staunch expression on her face.

"You're going to stay celibate for the rest of your life? You're only what? Twenty-five?"

"I'm twenty-six." Rachael nibbled her bottom lip and looked hesitant. "Okay, clearly I haven't thought this thing through."

"You're the founder of Romanceaholics Anonymous. Maybe it's something you should think through." Although, he quite liked the idea that if she wasn't going to be sleeping with him, at least she wouldn't be sleeping with anyone else.

What is wrong with you, Carlton? The woman is in emotional upheaval. A smart man would stay as far away from her as possible.

Sound advice, but somehow, he couldn't seem to take it.

"What I need," Rachael mused, "is hot sex with no strings attached."

Sex.

The word was a lightning rod, attracting sparks, zapping their gazes together.

"I need," she said, the gloss of her lips glistening in the glow from the overhead lamp, "mind-blowing sex."

Me, too.

She was calling to him with her eyes and with her mouth, but her body stayed rooted to the spot, and she had her arms folded tightly underneath her chest. She wanted him in theory, but in reality she still clung to her dreams of happily-ever-after. Tigers couldn't change their stripes. And no matter how much she might fight it, Rachael was a dyed-in-the-wool romantic.

Her lips parted, inviting him to kiss her. But she tightened her arms, hugging herself.

He leaned closer.

Her eyes widened.

He gave her his most formidable law enforcement stare, just to see how easily he could scare her off.

Rachael did not drop her gaze. She tilted her chin upward, hardening it stubbornly.

Surprising him.

Brody had expected her to turn and run for the door. He took a step forward, closing the short gap between them. Desire pulsed in his loins. He couldn't be around her and not want her. But even stronger than the desire was the need to hold her, comfort her, protect her.

She didn't move. Didn't flinch.

Not even when he raised his hand and reached out to trace her jaw with his thumb. The smell of books hung in the air, along with her fruit salad fragrance and the aroma of something more—something darker, muskier. It was the intense scent of sexual yearning.

He felt the tremor run through her body, but she held her ground. A corresponding shiver ran through him, down his spine, lodged in his groin.

What in the hell are you doing?

Why was he encroaching on her space? Was he trying to make her run or...*or what?* Take a stand?

The intelligent spark in her fascinating green eyes told him she just might be onto him.

He cupped her chin with his palm, tilted her face up even higher. Held her gaze with the power of superglue. He rested his other hand on her waist. Her flesh felt so soft underneath the thin material of her blouse.

She sucked in air at his touch, but she did not back up or look away. She just kept staring up at him, waiting.

The tension built.

Brody grew harder. There was no hiding his desire now. He flicked his gaze down the length of her throat, to her bodice. Her arms were still folded underneath her breasts, accentuating her cleavage. Her nipples were knotted so taut they pointed through the fabric of her bra.

"Rachael," he murmured and looked back at her face.

Her eyelashes fluttered. Her teeth parted. She wanted this kiss as much as he did.

He was barely breathing.

She swayed closer. "Brody."

His gaze fixed on her lush little mouth and he wondered what she was going to taste like. The fruit salad? Or the lust? Or a heady, wild combination of both?

Sweat pooled along his collarbone and his groin weighed thick and heavy.

Rachael pressed the tip of her tongue to her upper lip and Brody just about came undone.

The verdant spring in her eyes darkened to deep summer moss. He pushed his palm up the length of her jaw, splaying his fingers until they caught in the tangle of curls at the nape of her neck.

He dipped his head.

She made a hungry noise of approval.

His lips closed softly over hers.

She tasted a hundred times more delicious than he'd imagined. He savored the full flush of fruit salad—raspberries and melon and pineapple and peaches—mingled with the earthiness of longing need. And underneath all those layers of flavors, he tasted a heady dose of bravery and a yearning for experimentation.

A primitive, wholly masculine urge overtook him. He wanted to take her right there on the small stage in the back room of the Valentine Public Library among the smell of binding glue and inked pages and knowledge.

Carnal knowledge.

He wanted to undress her with leisurely fingers, and press burning kisses along the smooth creamy curve of her throat, to partake of her body and give her as much pleasure as he intended on taking.

Rachael molded her body to him. Lifting her arms up, wrapping them around his shoulders, pulling him closer. He cradled the back of her head in his palm and made a low, feral noise of need.

Brody deepened the kiss, slipping his tongue between her parted lips. He'd been aching to do this for weeks.

Chapter 10

Rachael gasped with pleasure, the strength of her need taking her by surprise.

She drank from Brody's lips, not caring that they were in a back room of the public library and anyone could walk in on them at any minute. She was as moist for him as a woman could get and growing damper by the minute. Her pulse rate spiked like a motorcycle kick-starting on high throttle and it sent a rush of hot, restless blood spilling into her heated pelvis.

Any doubts she might have had about what they were doing vanished in the hazy magic of his mouth. She forgot that she'd sworn off romance. Forgot that Brody was the very first man to ever break her schoolgirl heart. Forgot everything except the exquisite feel of his tongue against hers.

Rachael was devoured by a need so essential it surpassed everything else. She felt it to her very core, this crippling want. She'd never experienced any kiss quite like this and she'd experienced a lot of kisses.

Uh-oh, watch out, romantic fantasy alert, whispered the voice at the back of her mind, but his kiss drowned out the sound.

He made her feel so womanly, so desired.

Don't they all?

Actually, no, they did not. She'd just thought they did. This thing. This was different.

Yeah, right. Have many times have you told yourself that?

A dozen? More?

"Rachael," he murmured into her mouth. "You taste so damned good."

Could he be feeling it, too? she wondered hopefully.

Stop it, stop it, you're falling for a fantasy. Haven't you learned one damned thing?

Maybe, she told herself, maybe this could be just sex.

It was a lovely thought, but she had no idea how to create those boundaries. How to separate and compartmentalize love and sex. If she did, she wouldn't be here.

Could she learn? Could Brody be her teacher?

She'd been so gullible for so long, she wasn't sure she had the strength to overcome it. Especially with the man she'd had her first crush on. Her heart was so ready to get involved. She was a powder keg and he was a lit match. It was a stupid, stupid notion.

But here she was, seriously entertaining it.

Because who could resist lips like these? Her body burned wherever his mouth touched—her cheek, her chin, her forehead, her eyelids.

Unable to resist him, she just shut down her mind and let herself feel.

Blindly, without purposeful thought, Rachael lightly ran her tongue along the pounding pulse at the juncture of his throat and collarbone. He tasted salty. His rugged skin tightened beneath her mouth and a masculine groan escaped his lips.

Her mouth crept from his neck to his chest, her fingers working the buttons of his uniform, escalating the intimacy between them and sending her libido reeling into the stratosphere.

The air smelled of charged electrical ions rampant with sexual need.

She was acutely aware of something important shifting between them. But she didn't know if the shift was a good thing or a bad thing. The question was, did she really want to find out?

He stared deeply into her eyes, with something akin to desperation on his face. Brody took her by the shoulders, pulled her back. "Don't," he said, closing his hand around the fingers working at his buttons. "Not here, not now, not like this."

"Why not?"

"You deserve so much more. You deserve the true love you've spent your life looking for." He looked her in the eyes, desperation etched on his face.

She felt it all at once.

Passion was like a tornado destroying everything in its path. Yearning hormones. Whirling desire. Neediness and loneliness. Appetites and melancholia and hope. Always, ridiculous hope. The emotions collapsed in on her, heavy and warm and overwhelming.

Here we go again.

His gaze was a maelstrom. An obliterating cyclone.

They both stood motionless, his shirt half-undone, her lips puffy from his kiss, hair tousled, heart thumping.

He traced a finger over her cheek, his eyes lasering into hers.

Rachael's body stiffened. Wanting him, but terrified of where it would lead.

Heartbreak.

Brody dropped his hand, took two steps away from her.

Don't go, her treacherous heart whimpered.

Obliged by the same force that had caused her to make one romantic mistake after another, Rachael went after him.

"Your shirt," she said by way of an excuse, and reached up with shaky fingers to twist closed the buttons that she'd undone.

He stood stony as a statue, unmoving, unblinking.

What did she want from him? Rachael swallowed, moistened her lips.

Please?

His eyes darkened, lips tightened. He was fighting his impulses. It was like watching an epic battle unfold. She could see the interplay between common sense and temptation in the way his expression changed. Full of desire one minute, closed off the next. Behind it all she spied something startling.

He was afraid of the way she made him feel.

Her blood surged, thick as the mounting tension stretching from him to her and back again.

The second kiss was wilder than she had ever dreamed it would be, hot and hard, a restless driving force to taste and smell and feel. To consume. An opportunity to conquer, to plunder, to possess. The demanding flick of his tongue against hers brought a famished response so intense, she felt weak, as if all her energy had been drained.

Brody groaned and locked his fingers in her hair. Kissed her harder, deeper, and wilder still.

The taste of him!

He tasted like power and peppermint and Valentine's Day all rolled into one. Fanciful, romantic, idiotic.

But she could not stop. She inhaled him.

While the world shrank down into the minute width of mouths, she opened herself up to possibilities as yet undreamed. She was completely disarmed. With any other man the quick intimacy and astonishing sensuality would have appalled her, but with Brody everything was different.

Was it a difference she could trust? Or was it all an illusion of her own making?

Her lips shuddered against his mouth and her body molded to his. In Brody's arms, she felt cherished.

The sensation scared her.

She could not let this happen. Not again. She could have sex with him, but not until she learned how to stop spinning these silly romantic fantasies.

But she wanted so badly to believe in the dream.

Rachael vacillated, ensnared between who she was and who she really wanted to be. She did not appreciate this emotional tug-of-war. For years, she'd been living in a daydream, buying into a fairy tale that did not exist, pretending that someday some man would sweep her off her feet and make her life perfect.

That was never going to happen. She'd learned that only she was in charge of her life. Only she could change the future. Only she could alter her world.

"I'm sorry. This was wrong. I shouldn't have done that." She splayed a hand against his chest and pushed him away.

"Me, either," he said. "This was a bad idea."

"Awful."

"Terrible."

"Illogical."

"Irrational."

"Insane."

They stared at each other, both breathing hard.

One minute she was staring deep into his whirlpool brown eyes and the next second she was pressed against his chest again. His mouth closed in for a third kiss.

Third time charmed.

His tongue delivered thrills so hot Rachael feared she'd burst into flames. He sucked the oxygen right out of her lungs. Her head spun, the back of her knees wavered. If she died now, she'd have nothing to complain about.

Then he just let her go and stepped back.

Rachael stumbled against the podium.

"Good night, Rachael," he murmured and walked out the door.

What was going on here? Was he taking himself out of the running for her heart because he was a nice guy?

Kelvin stood in his underwear eating cold fried chicken over the sink. He'd just gotten back from his Elks Lodge meeting and he couldn't stop thinking about what he'd seen when he'd driven past the library.

Vehicles.

Lots of vehicles. So many cars and pickup trucks and SUVs that they couldn't all fit in the parking lot. They were parked in the vacant lot next door and overfilled even that. They were parked along both sides of the street. Michael Henderson's Porsche had been blocking the driveway, his fender sticking out into the road. And Brody Carlton's Crown Vic had squatted up on the curb.

Among the conglomeration of vehicles, Kelvin had spotted Rex's red Ford quarter-ton. What was up? If there had been a place to park, Kelvin would have gone in to see for himself.

He'd had dinner at the Elks Lodge, but curiosity dug into his belly like hunger pains and leftover Colonel Sanders made for a nice snack. But after he finished the chicken, he was still famished for information.

Kelvin tossed the thigh bone to Marianne, wiped the grease from his fingers on a paper towel, and picked the cordless phone from its base on the counter beside the microwave. Plopping down at the kitchen table, he propped his feet on the seat of the chair opposite him and punched in Rex's number.

"Brownleigh," he barked when Rex answered. "What the hell's going on at the library?"

"Um...I don't know what you mean," Rex hedged.

"Don't give me that crap. I saw your pickup in the parking lot."

Rex cleared his throat. "It was a Romanceaholics Anonymous meeting."

Kelvin was floored. How had the Henderson girl attracted a crowd that size? "That many people?"

"Standing room only. Over half the attendees came from another county."

"No shit?"

"None, sir."

"But how did people find out about it?"

"Viral video."

"Viral video?" Kelvin repeated and pressed a palm to the back of his neck. "What's that?"

"Rachael put a clip of her wedding video on the Web. Within two days it was the twentieth-most-downloaded video clip on YouTube."

"YouTube?"

"Dude, seriously, you gotta get on your computer more."

"I'm going to right now and you're going to talk me through this thing." Kelvin got up and headed for his study. Marianne plodded behind him.

"I'm in the middle of an IM session with a girl."

"I don't know what that is," Kelvin said, turning on his computer. "If you're trying to stop being romantic, should you be doing anything with a girl?"

"No." Rex sounded sheepish.

"Then consider yourself saved. Hang up with her or do whatever you have to do to get out of an IM session and talk me through this. I'm getting on AOL right now." He thought about bitching the boy out for being a traitor to his town and everything Valentine stood for by attending Rachael Henderson's anti-romance twelve-step program, but for now, it suited his purpose to have Rex fixed on Kelvin's needs.

Under Rex's tutelage, he went to YouTube, found Rachael's video, and watched it. The second it ended his stomach soured and his mouth went dry. "How many people do you think have seen this?"

"Oh, hundreds of thousands all over the world."

"What!" Kelvin jumped up from his chair and almost dropped the phone. "That many people know about her and this romanceaholics mess?"

"She's been bombarded with phone calls and e-mails. It's amazing how many people out there are victims of romance."

"Victims…victims…" Kelvin sputtered. "I'm the victim here. Valentine is the victim. The Henderson girl is going to quash the Amusement Corp deal and Tyler is going to end up with my theme park. I have to shut her down."

"What do you mean?" Rex asked.

"Never mind," Kelvin said and hung up.

He tossed the cordless phone on the leather couch and paced the study. The pictures of his ancestors looked down on him. The replica of Valentine Land mocked him.

You just thought you had the town in a lock.

Rachael Henderson was on a campaign to stomp out romance. He had to find a way to stop her before she ruined everything.

By the time she'd come home from the Romanceaholics meeting, her mother was already in bed.

Rachael had decided to take a calming hot bath but it wasn't working. She sat slumped in Mrs. Potter's claw-footed bathtub with pineapple-and-coconut-scented bath bead bubbles foaming up to her chin. Her stomach was in turmoil, still trying to digest what had happened at the library tonight.

Brody Carlton had kissed her.

Closing her eyes, Rachael leaned her head against the inflatable bath pillow and pulled in a slow, deep breath, trying to calm her racing mind.

She turned on the faucet with her foot, displacing the cooling waters with a fresh blast of hot liquid. She caught sight of her reflection in the shiny chrome fixtures. Her hair was disheveled, her mouth swollen from Brody's kisses, her eyes murky with concern.

Who was she?

Rachael no longer recognized herself.

Who was she becoming?

On the outside, Rachael was putting on a good front, acting as if she'd conquered her belief in happily-ever-after, but inside, she was still a mess. Distorted by her long-held values and beliefs that resisted change, distorted by the filters life in Valentine had placed on her sense of identity.

What was she if she wasn't part of a couple?

Where did she fit?

Who was she deep down inside?

Unable to answer these disturbing questions, Rachael blocked them out and submersed her head under water, trying to drown out the annoying voice in the back of her brain.

She held her breath as long as she could, listening to the sound of her own blood pounding against her eardrums, beating out a tune of deafening underwater silence. But no amount of breath holding could drown her disappointment. Finally, stripped of oxygen, she surfaced, gasping.

Demoralized, she climbed from the tub, wrapped her robe around her, blew her hair dry, and then climbed into bed. But her thoughts kept returning to Brody and what had happened at the library.

Impulsively, she picked up the cordless phone from its docking station, dialed information, got Brody's number, and called him before she realized it was almost midnight.

"Hello?" His dusky voice, which held the same smooth bite as one-hundred-year-old scotch, filled her ear.

Rachael swallowed hard. If she weren't fairly certain he had caller ID, she would have hung up.

"Hello?" he repeated, demanding that she respond.

Why had she called him?

Oh yeah, to tell him that his kiss had meant absolutely nothing to her. That she was totally immune to his charms. That she had no intention of falling off the wagon and into his arms.

"Rachael?"

Clearly, he did have caller ID.

"Um, yes."

"What's wrong? Why are you calling so late? Has something happened?"

She could just see him, immediately on alert, reaching for his gun, ready to do battle with bad guys.

"No, no, nothing's wrong. I'm sorry to call so late. I just couldn't sleep without clearing the air. Can you talk?"

"Hang on," he said. "I left the bathwater running."

"You take baths?" she asked. She'd never known a man who took baths.

"Helps me think. Hang on."

What did he need to think about? Had their kiss impacted him as strongly as it had impacted her?

She heard him settle the phone against what sounded like a hard surface. His dresser maybe? She could imagine him standing in his bedroom. Was he dressed? In his underwear? Or maybe even naked? Her pulse rate stoked as her mind's eye imprinted a daring picture of him. Bare-chested and bare-assed.

In a second, he was back. "What's up?"

Besides her core body temperature? "I thought...I couldn't sleep..." She heard him take a deep breath and the rough masculine sound sent a shiver through her. "We need to talk."

"What about?" he asked.

She heard the creak of bedsprings. Rachael closed her eyes and licked her lips. She could see his chest, ripped with muscles, minimal chest hair. His washboard stomach was flat and his...

Stop imagining him naked, dammit.

But she couldn't stop.

Oh, this was horrible, awful. She wanted him the way a child wanted a slice of birthday cake. A child didn't care if she gained weight or ruined her dinner or rotted her teeth. A kid spied a piece of cake and she just went for it, full out, no hesitation.

Exactly the same way Rachael had been going after men her entire life—grasping, needy, without discernment.

Except that she'd never before felt cravings this intense.

She ached to consume him in one greedy bite and lick the frosting from her fingers afterward. She hungered for him without any consideration for the consequences. She wanted to inhale his scent, taste his flavor, hear his voice as he groaned her name in the throes of passion.

To heck with one slice, she wanted the whole cake.

Did she have the strength to fight for what she needed? Or was she going to give in to the pull of romance as she'd done countless times before?

Just hang up!

"Rachael? You still there?"

"Uh-huh." She felt dazed, like she'd been in the dentist's chair breathing nitrous oxide.

"Are you all right? You sound...odd."

Not odd, horny.

"Um, fine, just fine," she lied, struggling to keep her mind on the reason she'd called him. She settled back against the headboard and drew her knees to her chest.

"Where are you?" he asked.

"At my mother's house."

"I know that," he said. "Whereabouts in the house are you?"

"In bed."

"Hmm." His voice cracked.

It suddenly occurred to Rachael that he might be having a few late-night fantasies of his own. Stunned, she sucked in her breath as chill bumps spread over her arms.

"So what are you wearing?" he asked in a deep, throaty voice.

Omigod, clearly he had mistaken the meaning of her call. Time to slice things off before they went too far.

"Or are you wearing anything at all?" he asked.

Rachael's cheeks blazed hot. She glanced down at her white cotton T-shirt with the faded Hard Rock Café logo. Sexy as granny pj's.

I am not playing this game, she told herself, but said, "A Victoria's Secret negligee."

From the other end of the phone line, she heard an audible gulp. She pulled a pillow over her head as her face flamed hotter.

"What color?" he asked.

"Black," she improvised, pressing a palm to her feverish neck. "With red satin ribbons."

He hissed in his breath as if he'd walked across hot coals.

She could see him in her mind, his big hand clasping tight to the receiver, his long muscular body stretched across his bed, naked as the day he came into the world.

"And black fishnet stockings," she added, feeling devilishly out of control.

He growled.

"Scarlet stilettos," she went on, enjoying his reaction.

"Stop!" he commanded in his law enforcement voice.

Her fingertips, which had somehow walked from the nape of her neck to the waistband of her panties, froze.

"And tasseled pasties." She kept going, unable to resist.

"Uncle," he croaked. "I give. You win."

Remorse fisted inside her. "I'm sorry," she apologized. "Phone sex was *not* the reason I called."

Brody chuckled, a rough, regretful sound that sent fresh chills slipping down her spine. "Listen…"

Rachael sat up straight. "Yes?"

"I'm actually glad you called."

"You are?"

"I wanted to talk to you about what happened at the library tonight."

"You mean between my parents?"

"I mean between us."

"Um, there is no us. You're you and I'm me and we're separate as separate can be. Separate and single and..." she chattered inanely. *Good Lord, woman, shut up.*

"Rachael," he said.

"Uh-huh?"

"Hush a minute and let me get a word in edgewise."

"Okay." Rachael held her breath.

"I'm not going to pretend I don't feel something for you," Brody said, "because I do."

"You do?" she squeaked.

"Yes, but I'm not the kind of guy who beats around the bush. The timing is off for us. You're in a bad place emotionally."

My sentiments exactly.

"And I'm just now getting over what happened in Iraq and my wife leaving me for another man. Trust isn't my strong suit and you can't build a relationship without trust."

"Okay." Where was he headed with this?

"You've got this whole anti-romance thing going on."

"Yes?"

"I know you feel the chemistry, too. Your kiss said it all. But you also told me you had trouble separating love from sex, so sex is out of the question, because the last thing I want is for you to get hurt again."

"Excuse me?" Was he putting out feelers in a round-about way to see if she could handle a casual fling?

"Isn't that why you called?" He sounded confused.

So why had she called him? "No!"

"Okay, but you were the one who mentioned Victoria's Secret and tasseled pasties."

Guilty as charged. And she was regretting her faux pas more with each passing second. "You thought I called to proposition you?"

"Did you?"

"No. . . . No . . . absolutely not," Rachael sputtered. "And I can't believe your arrogance. Why on earth would you think I would have an affair with you?"

"You said you wanted to learn how to separate love from sex. I thought—"

"Think again, Sheriff Egotistical."

He laughed.

Laughed!

Rachael's blood boiled. "I wouldn't have an affair with you if you were the last man on earth."

"That's too bad," he said, "because I think we could have great sex together."

After her ill-fated midnight phone call to Brody, Rachael's life went from bad to worse.

Her cell phone kept ringing with inquiries from people wanting to know how to join Romanceaholics Anonymous and/or praising her for the YouTube video. Rex called, all excited, to tell her that *Trace Hoolihan Ditches Bride* was officially the twentieth most internationally downloaded video of the day, but then he couldn't understand why the news did not make her happy.

"Great," Rachael muttered darkly. "Now I'm an *international* laughingstock."

"You're an international celebrity is what you are," Rex said.

Rachael snorted. She didn't want to be a star. She just wanted to stop falling blindly in love. And she wanted to go back to Houston and get on with her life. She had a week left on her community service sentence and then she was headed home. School restarted in two weeks and she'd have to start searching for a new apartment since she'd given hers up when she and Trace got engaged. Jillian had already told Rachael she could come and stay with her until she found somewhere suitable to live.

By the end of her day delivering meals on wheels she pulled her VW Bug—which she'd had repainted after the graffiti incident—into Mrs. Potter's driveway, and told herself she was not going to look across the street to see if Brody was home.

She looked.

And there he was.

Outside. Shirtless. Pushing his lawn mower across the plush Saint Augustine.

Their eyes met.

Brody raised a hand.

Rachael ducked her head and raced inside the house. *I told you not to look*, she scolded herself, but that didn't stop her heart from beating too fast. Good thing she was leaving town soon.

She found Selina in the kitchen making enchiladas. That was a positive sign. Her mother hadn't been eating.

"Smells good," she said, coming over to drop a kiss on her mother's cheek.

"Someone from Country Day called while you were out," Selina said. "I wrote the contact information on the notepad." She pointed with the tip of her paring knife to the message center by the phone.

Rachael bustled over to look at the note. *Mr. Sears called, he'd like a call back ASAP.* A cell phone number followed. Mr. Sears was the principal of Country Day where Rachael was employed as a kindergarten teacher.

"Must be something about the upcoming school year," Rachael said, picking up the phone and simultaneously kicking off her sandals.

She punched in the numbers, listened to it ring.

"Hello, Mr. Sears?" she said when the man answered. "This is Rachael Henderson."

"Rachael," Mr. Sears said, his voice sounding clipped and serious. "We need to talk."

Something about the principal's tone sent up warning flags. "Yes, sir."

"There was an emergency meeting of the school board last night," he said.

"Emergency meeting?"

"It's come to our attention that you've encountered a bit of controversy over the summer."

"Controversy?" she echoed, feeling blindsided. "The emergency school board meeting was about me?"

"Well, more specifically, about that video you posted on YouTube," Mr. Sears said.

"Yes?"

"The board feels that it's not only inappropriate for one of our faculty members to produce such content, but we're afraid the attention will be detrimental to Country Day."

"Are you asking me to pull the video from YouTube?" Honestly, after all the crank phone calls she kept getting, she was ready to have Rex yank it off the Internet.

"I'm afraid it's gone beyond that. Someone from your hometown notified us that you'd been arrested for vandalism."

Rachael felt a harsh stab of betrayal. Could it have been Brody? But why would he do that? Why would anyone? "Someone from Valentine called you?"

"Yes. Is it true?"

"The charges were a misdemeanor, and I—"

"Nevertheless, in light of your behavior," Mr. Sears interrupted, "the school board has decided to cancel your contract for the upcoming school year."

She felt at once both furious and terrified. A trickle of sweat ran down Rachael's neck and dropped cold into her cleavage. She'd just lost her job because someone in her hometown didn't like what she was doing. "You have no legal right to cancel my contract."

"Read your contract, Miss Henderson. We have every right to protect the students from a teacher with a criminal record."

Criminal record! All she'd done was paint a sign black.

"Mr. Sears, surely there's something I can do to change the school board's mind. You simply can't fire me. I love those kids, I love my job, I love—"

"You should have thought about that before you vandalized a billboard," the principal said, cutting her off. "I'm sorry, Rachael, but the decision is irrevocable."

Across town, Kelvin Wentworth received a phone call.

"It's done," said the voice on the other end of the line. "She's been fired from her job."

Kelvin smiled. "Good work."

"Are you sure it was such a smart move? I mean, now that she's out of a job, she's free to stay in town and devote all her time to stirring up anti-Valentine sentiment. And causing problems for your reelection campaign."

Kelvin snorted.

"Don't underestimate her. She's already done a lot of damage."

"You've knocked the pins out from under her with this one," Kelvin assured the man he'd coerced into doing his dirty work. "She'll have to concentrate on finding a job. In the meantime, I'll be winning the election."

Plus sealing the deal with Amusement Corp.

Kelvin smiled. At last everything was falling into place, and he wasn't about to let some snippet of a girl with starry-eyed dreams stand in his way.

Michael Henderson hung up the phone feeling dirtier than he'd ever felt in his life. He'd just betrayed his daughter to his lifelong rival. He was a complete and utter bastard. No wonder Selina had left him.

"But it's for the best," he told himself. Sometimes a father had to hurt his children in order to ultimately save them. He had to do this for Rachael's sake. He'd had no other choice.

Remorse ate him. *Did you have any other choice?*

No, he didn't. Agreeing to help Kelvin was the only way he could get Rachael to stop her anti-romance campaign. And dropping the romance campaign was the only way she was ever going to find the love she truly deserved. And it was the only way he could win his wife back. Besides, Country Day would have found out about her arrest for vandalism sooner or later and it was better that Rachael lose her job before school started rather than after.

You did the right thing.

Still, he couldn't help feeling devious and under-handed. He was so terribly, terribly ashamed of what he'd done but his motivation came from the heart. This was what he must do to help her. It was a father's cross to bear. Like when he'd had to hold her down for an injection when she was a screaming four-year-old with an appendix that had burst and she needed emergency surgery. Watching her suffer had been like cutting off his right arm. He felt exactly the same way now.

What's Selina going to think when she finds out you got Rachael fired?

"She's not going to find out," he muttered under his breath. "And neither is Rachael."

Because if Selina found out what he'd done, he knew she wouldn't understand. And she wouldn't forgive.

Before he had time to brood over that, the doorbell rang.

Michael frowned. He wasn't expecting anyone.

He walked to the front door, his footsteps echoing loudly in the house, which now felt so empty without Selina in it. He squinted through the peephole and saw Vivian standing on the doorstep in a raincoat.

Immediately, he knew what was beneath that raincoat.

Absolutely nothing.

It was a game they'd played when they were in high school. She'd wait until his parents were gone and come to this very door in her raincoat. She'd ring the bell and say—

"Girl Scout cookies. Get your sweet treats here," Vivian called out.

Michael gulped, closed his eyes, and shrank back from the door. What had he done?

She rang the bell again.

Go away.

The bell chimed a third time.

What the hell, Henderson, are you a man or a mouse? Open the door and tell her you're not interested.

But what if Selina didn't take him back? What if there really was no hope of repairing his ripped marriage? Didn't he deserve something good in his life?

Vivian is not good and you know it. You've been down this road with her before. Sure, she's sexy as hell, but she's nothing but trouble.

He had to take a stand. He'd cruised by for so many years on his money and his looks. He'd taken Selina for granted and he'd hurt her, and instead of being contrite about answering Vivian's e-mail, he'd been defensive. He'd accused her of being jealous and petty. He'd been in the wrong. And he'd wanted her back more than he wanted to breathe. That was the only reason he'd done what he'd done to Rachael. To repair his damaged family.

Michael took a deep breath, opened his eyes, and went for the door. Then quietly, emotionlessly, he told Vivian what he should have told her when she'd sent him that e-mail three months ago: "The only sweet treats I'm interested in belong to my wife."

Chapter 11

Faced with no job and an uncertain future, Rachael spent the rest of the next month trying to decide what she was going to do with her life. The heat of August ebbed into the slightly less-scorching heat of September. Football season started and along with it, a constant reminder of how well Trace was doing with the Chicago Bears while she was languishing jobless in Valentine.

Rachael had completed her court-ordered community service shortly after losing her job. She'd done her best to avoid Brody, and for the most part she'd succeeded. He'd raise a hand in greeting now and then if he spied her from across the street, or when he saw her in town. And she would wave back, but that was as far as things went.

The one area of her life where things were going well was with Romanceaholics Anonymous. Due to the popular demand generated by the YouTube video, Rex had helped her start her own Web site, and she'd created a blog devoted to debunking romantic myths. She'd also started several Romanceaholics chapters in surrounding towns.

But while it was emotionally satisfying, her anti-romance crusade wasn't generating any income. Selina had told her not to worry about money, that she'd take care of Rachael's expenses while she went through her metamorphosis, but the truth was she needed something to bolster her self-esteem.

Then one bright afternoon in late September, she came home from setting up a new chapter of Romanceaholics Anonymous in a neighboring town to find a black Lincoln Town Car parked outside Mrs. Potter's house.

Something bad has happened.

The thought seized hold of her and wouldn't let go. Her legs felt leaden as she trod up the sidewalk to the front door. Her heart flipped up into her throat. What else could go wrong?

She found her mother in the living room having coffee with a sharply dressed woman in her late thirties. The visitor wore a tailored suit that hadn't come off any department store rack, drop-dead stilettos, and an expensive, big-city coif. She looked decidedly out of place perched on an aged sofa with a hand-crocheted afghan stretched across the back.

"Here she is," her mother said brightly. It looked as if she'd been having trouble holding up her end of the conversation with the sleek creature on the sofa.

The woman settled her cup and saucer onto the scarred coffee table and rose to her feet, her right hand extended. "Hello, I'm Maggie Lawford. The entertainment editor for *Texas Monthly*."

"Rachael Henderson," she said.

"I know." Maggie Lawford's eyes sparkled.

"What are you doing in Valentine?"

"I'm here to see you. You're the talk of the Internet. My guess is that you're averaging ten thousand blog hits a day. Is that number in the ballpark?"

"I don't know. I'd have to ask my Web guy." Rachael tucked her bottom lip up between her front teeth. "Really? I'm actually on your radar?"

"Not just on my radar, but in my magazine."

"Excuse me?"

Maggie smiled. "I'm here to offer you a job."

"You drove all the way from Austin to offer me a job?"

"That," Maggie said, "and to see Valentine for myself. It's everything you describe in your blog and more."

Rachael's trepidation vanished and she felt a sense of anticipation that equaled the thrill she experienced whenever she encountered a potential love interest. She hadn't known that anything other than romance could make her feel this way—giddy, breathless, hopeful.

"It's so exciting," Selina said.

Rachael agreed with her mother, but facing her romanceaholism had taught her a few things. Just as she shouldn't romanticize a man, she had no business romanticizing a job, either. "Exactly what would the position entail?"

"Why don't we have a seat?" Maggie invited, settling onto the sofa again and crossing her chic legs. She patted the cushion. "Relax."

Rachael eased down beside the other woman and tried to restrain the surge of enthusiasm pushing against her chest. *Don't look too eager.* "What kind of job?"

"We'd like for you to write a monthly column."

It took everything she had inside her not to squeal out loud. She wanted to say, *Yes, yes, a thousand times yes.* But those were the words she'd used when Trace asked her to marry him. She was done impulsively riding the wave of excitement. She amazed herself by saying, "A monthly column is quite a commitment."

Brody, she thought, would be so proud of her. Immediately, she wondered why she was thinking about him.

"You'd be well compensated," Maggie said smoothly. She named a figure that was almost twice Rachael's salary at Country Day.

It was all she could do to keep from breaking out in a grin. "I'd have to relocate to Austin?"

"Actually, we want you to stay right here in Valentine. Keep your finger on the pulse of America's heartbeat. We can do everything through e-mail."

Hmm, something to think about. She wasn't sure she wanted to stay in Valentine. "What would the column be about?"

"Same thing you're doing on your blog. Raising questions about love and romance. Debunking romantic myths. Highlighting examples of what real love is. Show how movies, music, and the media create false illusions when it comes to courtship and marriage. Draw on stories from Romanceaholics Anonymous."

"Those stories are confidential," Rachael said.

"Fictionalize them," Maggie said smoothly. "Or convince people to go on the record."

Rachael frowned. "Wouldn't that be taking advantage of people's foibles and vulnerabilities?"

"Aren't you already doing that with your Web site?"

"Not specifically. So far, I've only skewered myself and my ex-fiancé."

"Ah, yes." Maggie smiled. "Trace Hoolihan."

Something unpleasant occurred to her. "That's why you're offering me this job, isn't it? Not because of my Web site, but because Trace is high-profile and that will bring readers to my column."

"That's part of the reason, I won't deny it. But you

underestimate yourself, Rachael. You're quite the writer. We admire your creativity and your spunk. You didn't take rejection lying down. You fought back. Painted that billboard. Posted that video on YouTube. Plus you know how to hit right at the center of your readers' emotions."

Stroke to the old ego. She had to hand it to Maggie Lawford. The woman was a good persuader.

"I do?"

"Come on. You know you're special."

It was flattery, but she fell for it, hook, line, and sinker. "If I decide to do this, I won't use stories from the people in my Romanceaholics meetings. Even fictionalized. It's unethical. They've put their trust in me and I won't betray them."

"That's fine," Maggie said without missing a beat. "Do the stories of the people whose names are on the Walk of Flames sidewalk on Main Street. Not all of them could have had a happily-ever-after ending."

Rachael looked to Selina to get her take on this. Her mother lifted her shoulders, held up her hands in a whatever-you-think-is-best gesture. "You only want to tell the stories of romances that have gone bad?"

"Conflict sells," Maggie said. "Happily-ever-after might be sweet to live, but romance without any bumps in the road is boring to read. Start with the love-gone-wrong tales. When you run out of those, we'll reevaluate."

Rachael considered it. "What are you thinking of calling the column?"

"We've been tossing around a couple of titles. 'Don't Let the Stars Get in Your Eyes' got the most votes."

Not bad. She liked it.

"Although 'Happily Never After' is still in the running."

Rachael didn't like that one so much. It was too negative. As if romantic love wasn't possible at all.

Maybe it's not.

"So may I call my editor-in-chief and give him the good news that you'll be writing for us?" Maggie asked, drawing her cell phone from her purse.

Rachael paused, knowing she was on the verge of a monumental opportunity. Her mouth was dry, her stomach in knots. Writing for such an acclaimed regional magazine would stretch her creative skills beyond anything she'd ever dared. It was a dream she'd never even thought to dream.

But this wasn't strictly about her. There was something else to think about. What would the column do to her hometown?

It could put it on the map, but it could also hurt a lot of people. Good, decent people who were just trying to make their way in life. Did she have any right to shine a floodlight on her community without the permission of its citizens?

On the other hand, she couldn't be held responsible for the way some people might react to her column. She'd spent her life as a people pleaser. It was time for her to do what she thought best.

Chin up, she met Maggie Lawford's eye. "Tell your editor I'm on board."

"That's wonderful." Maggie smiled. "Now, there's just one more thing."

What now? Rachael's muscles tensed. "Yes?"

"We're planning a big romance exposé edition for Valentine's Day and we want you to lead the charge. To quickly build you a following, we want to get your column started as soon as possible. The November issue will be going to press in three weeks and we want 'Don't Let the Stars Get in Your Eyes' to be in it. With that deadline in mind, we'll need your first column by the end of the week. Can you handle it?"

It didn't give her much time to take a breath, much less think this through. She'd already gone this far out on the limb. What was a couple more feet? "I can handle it."

"Excellent." Maggie Lawford got to her feet and extended her hand to Rachael again. "It's great to have you on board."

It felt great, too.

Except for the sinking feeling deep in the pit of her stomach that she had no idea what to write about that wasn't going to step on a lot of toes in Valentine.

The pressure was on.

An hour after she'd accepted Maggie Lawford's offer, Rachael sat in Bristo Park across from the courthouse, laptop resting on her thighs, the cursor blinking accusatorily at her from the blank Word document. She hadn't a single idea in her head.

What was she going to write about?

Think, think.

Nothing.

She shifted on the park bench, ran her tongue around the inside of her mouth, twisted a curl of hair around her index finger. Hmm. What could she say that she hadn't already said on her Web site?

The emptiness inside her brain was excruciating. She wasn't a writer. She was a kindergarten teacher. Why had she agreed to write that column? It had been a momentary lapse of sanity.

Pursing her lips, she gazed out across the clipped green

lawn for inspiration and saw nothing the least bit inspiring. A flush of red chrysanthemums encircled the tree. Maybe she could rant about the practice of romanticizing football homecoming games with high school football mums.

It was something.

She typed "Mums." Then paused to nibble her bottom lip. She thought about her own high school football mums and her heart went all melty remembering the boys who'd given them to her.

Snap out of it!

But the mums brought back such happy memories. Why would she want to bash the practice? Why deny other young girls the fun simply because she'd had rotten luck with romance? It felt like sour grapes.

Come on, come on, you're getting soft on me. You're in danger of falling off the wagon. Remember why you painted that billboard in the first place. You said you wanted to get your message out about the folly of buying into the myth of romance. Here's your chance.

Except she just couldn't seem to work up the requisite anger. At least not in reference to homecoming mums.

She backspaced, erasing "Mums."

Great. Blowing out her breath, she cruised her gaze around the courthouse square.

And spied Mayor Wentworth hustling down the steps of City Hall, his white Stetson jammed down on his head. Where was he off to in such a hurry?

Rachael narrowed her eyes. Probably heading out to cook up some new way to bolster his standing in the polls. She thought about the way he'd acted toward her ever since she'd begun her anti-romance campaign and suddenly an idea came to her.

It was perfect in its simplicity.

Lay the blame on Valentine's obsession with romance squarely where it belonged. On the shoulders of the man perpetuating the myth in order to hold on to his job.

And the sweet thing was, she was in tight with the mayor's assistant.

Smiling, Rachael stowed her laptop in its carrying case, then got up and walked across the park to interview Rex for her scathing exposé on Kelvin Wentworth.

Rachael paced Mrs. Potter's living room. Two days had passed since she'd e-mailed Maggie Lawford her column. Maggie had sent a terse reply, saying she'd call her today. Rachael had been waiting by the phone since eight a.m.

"Honey," Selina said. "You're getting yourself all worked up over this. Come on, what's the worst that can happen?"

"Maggie could pull the plug on the column."

"And you wouldn't be any worse off than before."

Good point, but Rachael wasn't in the mood to listen to common sense. She couldn't explain it, but it felt as if her entire future lay in Maggie Lawford's manicured hands. She'd given up being a starry-eyed romantic to become an eagle-eyed journalist. She was ready to fully embrace this identity and her newfound philosophy on love. The column was a validation of her progress.

Selina looked at her watch. "It's almost six o'clock. She's probably left for the day. I imagine she hasn't even had a chance to read your article, much less—"

The ringing phone cut off her mother's words. "Texas Monthly" scrolled across the caller ID screen.

Palms sweating, Rachael snatched up the cordless phone. "Hello?"

"Rachael," the editor said in her cool, clipped tones. "Maggie Lawford here. Your article..."

"Yes," she whispered and held her breath. In the space of time it took Maggie to answer, Rachael's heart skipped two beats.

"Brilliant. Absolutely brilliant. This is exactly what we were looking for from you."

Relief turned her knees to rubber and she dropped down on the sofa beside her mother. Selina raised a quizzical eyebrow. Rachael covered the mouthpiece with a hand and murmured, "She loves it."

"Yes!" Selina mouthed silently and showed her support by raising her fisted hands over her head in a triumphant gesture.

"I've got to warn you about something, however," Maggie said.

The mindless fear was back, grabbing at her belly and squeezing hard. "What is it?"

"There's going to be fallout from this column when it hits the newsstands next month."

"What do you mean...fallout?"

"The Wentworth name carries a lot of clout. Are you sure of your facts?"

"Absolutely. I have a source inside the mayor's office."

"Okay, then," Maggie said. "But I want you to be prepared."

Rachael ran a hand through her hair. "Prepared for what?"

"This little story is going to set off one hell of a firestorm."

"You're serious? The one article?"

"Rachael, don't you realize what you've done?"

Apprehension tickled her bones. "Um, no."

"Why, honey, you've fired the opening salvo in what I predict will become a protracted civil war between cynics and romantics. And not just in your hometown, but all across Texas."

"What are you going to do about this business?" Kelvin demanded, slapping a slick new copy of *Texas Monthly* on Brody's desk.

It was more than three weeks until Halloween, but Kelvin looked like he was already gearing up to attend the annual harvest bash as the Incredible Hulk. His blue eyes flashed fire, twin veins at his temples bulged, and his big neck was overflowing the top of his starched white collar.

Brody cocked back on the legs of his chair, interlaced his fingers, cradled his head in his palms, and leveled the mayor with a steady gaze. "Do about what?"

"You haven't seen this?" Kelvin thumped the magazine with a meaty thumb. "Your little girlfriend is making a mockery of our entire town."

"First off, Rachael is not my girlfriend," Brody said evenly. "Second, it seems to me she's making a mockery of you and your ancestors, not Valentine."

"It's the same damn thing," Kelvin roared.

"Ah, but you see, it's not. That's where I think the problem lies, and actually it's what Rachael's article is all about."

"She's going to cause me to lose the election."

"*You're* going to cause you to lose the election. Not Rachael, not Giada Vito. Your own behavior."

"Listen to this." Kelvin grabbed up the magazine and flipped the pages until he found what he was searching for. "The Wentworth family has molded the town of Valentine into an image that benefits them financially. Since the nineteen fifties, they've perpetuated harmful romantic myths, not out of any real belief in the lasting power of love, but simply to make their fortunes. Valentine isn't so much a town as it is a tourist trap, with its romantic novelties and a man-made, heart-shaped lake. And Mayor Wentworth, who, by the way, has never been married, is the ringmaster of this romantic circus."

Kelvin flung the magazine across the room.

"Any part of that untrue?" Brody asked.

"She makes it sound like I don't care about this town and the people in it. She's unpatriotic, un-American, un-Valentinian. What's the matter with her? Everyone believes in true love."

"Even you?"

Kelvin snorted. "Of course I do."

"Then why haven't you ever been married?"

"Because I never found the right woman. You have any idea what it's like to live in a town saturated with romance? To grow up indoctrinated in the family business of making Valentine's Day novelties, while all around you people are falling in love, but you never find that special someone?"

"Wow," Brody said. "You're sounding dangerously close to believing what you're saying."

Kelvin's eyes flashed in anger. "I have supporters. People in this town loved my father, my family. They love me and everything I've done for Valentine. This is going to cause a heap of trouble. Are you prepared for an uprising?"

"There you go being all dramatic again."

"And there you go, not taking this seriously."

Truth was, Brody was struggling not to smirk. "I can't arrest her for having an opinion, Kelvin."

"It's Mayor Wentworth," Kelvin said, pulling rank.

Brody couldn't resist. A smiled curled his lips. "Enjoy the title while it lasts...*Mayor*."

Kelvin whipped his head around to drill Brody with a glare. "What does that mean?"

"Rachael's got her supporters, too. And I happen to be one of them. I think the Wentworths have made this town look foolish for too long."

Kelvin stared at Brody as if he'd kicked him in the family jewels. A pained expression pulled his mouth downward. "I supported you for sheriff."

"You did."

"And this is the thanks I get?"

Brody spread his hands. "It's just an article. It'll blow over if you don't make a big deal of it. Show the town you have a sense of humor. Show them that—"

But he didn't get any farther. Kelvin stormed out the door, flipping Brody the bird as he went.

Brody shook his head and let out a breath of air. From the way things were stacking up, it was going to be a long few weeks until the election.

Rachael wasn't having any better a day than Mayor Wentworth. The phone had been ringing off the wall with citizens calling to read her the riot act over her column in *Texas Monthly*.

She'd been called a traitor, a communist, a bitter jilted old maid, and much worse. People she'd known her entire life snubbed her on the streets. Her hairdresser canceled her appointment, saying that under the circumstances she felt it would be hypocritical of her to cut Rachael's hair when Rachael hated the town so much.

That one really stung.

Maggie had warned her, but she still hadn't been prepared for the vitriol.

Sure, she had her supporters—the folks from her romanceaholics group, her mother, her father, and her sister, Hannah. Even Delaney, Tish, and Jillian had called to offer moral support. But she really hadn't expected the onslaught of hatred. Perhaps she was naive, but she'd thought people would appreciate her shedding light on Valentine's flaws. She'd mistakenly believed they would want to change the things holding the town back.

What had happened to her life?

Unbidden, her gaze slid over to Brody's house. She saw the patrol car parked in the driveway. He was home. Deana's car was gone, however.

He was home alone.

Rachael remembered the last time she'd been alone with him and her heart knocked. She saw his gate was open. She could hear the faint sounds of music coming from his backyard. It was a Chris Isaak tune about not wanting to fall in love.

The haunting melody drew her across the street.

Before she could stop herself, her hand was pushing his honeysuckle-covered gate open wider and she was walking into his backyard.

She rounded the corner of the house, his name on her lips, but the word died on her tongue when she saw him standing beside the patio table in his swim trunks, his tanned body glistening wet from a dip in the hot tub.

His back was to her and he was drying off his shoulders with a fluffy white bath towel. Her gaze slid down the well-defined muscles of his shoulder blades to the waistband of his shorts. Her mouth went dry. She could smell the scent of chlorine and redwood decking mingled with the fragrance of honeysuckle flourishing all along the fence, blocking the neighbors' view of his backyard. She heard the sound of the hot tub jets churning, Chris Isaak's mournful lyrics, and the soft, brisk, whisking noise of the towel rubbing vigorously against his skin.

He ducked his head, toweled his hair.

Then her gaze dropped from the view of his wet swimsuit cupping his firm butt to his thigh.

Her breath left her body in an exclamation of air as she saw the rounded stump below his knee where his right leg had been. The stab of hurt and sadness that she felt inside her heart for him was so powerful, she took a step backward.

And she bumped into a metal patio chair.

It screeched across the cement.

Brody lifted his head, looked toward her.

Rachael froze, her gaze riveted on his damaged leg.

"What are you doing here," he demanded, his voice harsh. He dropped the end of the towel to hide his leg. "Get out of here."

"Brody...I...I..."

"Go on." His face was a mask. She couldn't tell what he was thinking.

"I'm sorry," she said, feeling compelled to hold her ground. If she ran away now, he would think it was because the sight of his leg disgusted her. It did not, but she realized he was prepared to believe that.

For the first time, she spied the prosthetic leg propped against the hot tub decking. It looked bionic. Futuristic. Fascinating.

She took a step forward.

"Get out," he said harshly.

"I'm not afraid of you."

He was throwing daggers at her with his eyes. "You damn well should be."

"Why?" She raised her chin.

He hardened his jaw, pointed a finger in the direction of her house. "Go."

"There's nothing to be ashamed of."

"You're trespassing."

"Your gate was open."

"Maisy must have forgotten to close it." His dark, damp hair fell across his forehead. He looked so vulnerable standing there trying hard not to look vulnerable. He was embarrassed that she'd caught him in a moment of weakness. Her heartstrings tugged.

"Brody." Her voice came out lower and softer than she'd intended. The sound of his name hovered between them like the wings of a butterfly, soft and fluttery.

His jaw clenched tighter, as if he were holding back words or emotions he didn't dare let escape.

"Brody," she whispered again and crossed the patio between them, until she was directly in front of him, the thin towel the only barrier separating him from her.

Rachael shouldn't have done what she did next. She knew it as she was doing it, but she couldn't stop herself, didn't want to stop. Brody needed to know that he wasn't repulsive or disgusting or half a man. He needed to know that she found him sexy and virile and very attractive.

Her eyes didn't leave his face. She stared at him, stared into him, telegraphing with her eyes how much she admired and respected and desired him.

God, how she desired him.

He dropped the towel. She didn't see it fall because her gaze was transfixed on his, but she felt the terry cloth brush against her ankles as it landed on the cement. She didn't look down. For her there was nothing to see but his beautiful face.

"Rachael," he murmured.

His hand—fingertips, actually—brushed her hair from her forehead, then dropped down to feather her cheek-bone, his calloused palm curving against her soft skin. She stared into chocolate brown eyes glittering with an emotion she couldn't decipher. Sexual hunger? Yes, lust was certainly a component, but there was much more lurking in the shadowy depths of his gaze. She saw tenderness and concern and worry and apprehension as well.

You're romanticizing him. Stop romanticizing him.

But damn her, she could not stop.

Inside his manly features she could still see the boy next door who'd been her childhood crush. Older, damaged to be sure, life settled hard onto his broad shoulders. He was tough and scarred and changed, but some small part of him was still the same. The small-town boy who believed in the goodness of humankind, in spite of all the atrocious things he'd experienced. He was a ruggedly handsome man in green-and-orange Hawaiian-print swim trunks, the lingering smell of chlorine clinging to his bare, hard-muscled chest.

Her stomach contracted. She looked at him and she was seven years old again, besotted, silly with adoration.

"Rachael," he said her name again. It sounded half like a prayer, half like a curse of defeat.

He dipped his head.

She met him halfway, going up on tiptoe, leaning into him.

He cupped her face in his hands.

She slipped her hands around his waist, pressed her body against his. She'd wanted to do this from the moment they'd tumbled from the ladder underneath the Valentine billboard.

His erection was hard and unmistakable beneath his thin, wet swim trunks. He wanted her as much as she wanted him.

Joyous blood strummed through her veins as Brody's lips closed over hers and she felt his power drill straight into her bones.

Her ears sang with the sound of the humming hot tub and murmuring music. Her nose twitched with the sharp, chlorine-tinged smell of his skin. Her arms tingled against the tight skin of his taut muscles. She closed her eyes to deepen the minty taste of him against her tongue.

It was as if an invisible fist reached into her body, curled strong fingers around her heart, and squeezed. Emotions spattered inside her like shed blood. Desire and attraction. Hope and craving. Fear and thrill and nervous energy. Feelings toppled in on her, hard and sudden and scary as hell.

She was doing it again. Falling for the wrong man at the wrong time in the wrong place. Following her reckless, unrestrained heart when she should be listening to her head. She knew the dangers of this headlong feeling. She'd been here before. Many times. And each and every time, she'd come away singed.

Pull away, run, get out of here while you still can.

But romance addict that she was, Rachael could not obey her own admonition.

His kiss was hot. A searing brand.

His lips made her body quiver.

She made a soft mewling sound. He pushed his inquisitive tongue past her teeth, wrapped his arms around her, and drew her up tight against the expanse of his chest.

Rachael was surprised by his equilibrium, but she shouldn't have been. She already knew he was a steady, sturdy man. Built for endurance. Strong and reliable. Centered. Objective. Balanced.

In the past she'd been drawn to showy, charming men with unusual careers and big personalities. She'd been dazzled by flash and brash when what she'd really needed was substance. She'd never been with a man like him.

You're not with him now. He's not your boyfriend or your lover. He's just the guy who lives across the street.

A guy who took her home with him so she wouldn't have to spend the night in jail. A guy who brought her peaches when she was feeling down. A guy who seemed to understand her sometimes crazy, illogical behavior without judging her.

He threaded both hands through her hair, cradled her head in his palms. Holding her in place while he explored her mouth as if he was determined to unearth every secret she'd ever kept.

She melted. Just turned to butter right there in his backyard, beside the churning whirlpool. Melted and morphed and melded into him.

"Aw," he murmured against her lips, "you taste like peaches."

"Your peaches," she whispered right back.

That made him chuckle as his mouth took possession of hers all over again.

Her pulse swirled. Light, airy, floaty. Swept away.

This second kiss was fiercer than the first. Demanding, urgent, skipping beyond subtleties to unveil the hungry animal lurking inside the controlled man. A beast yanking at its chain. This kiss told her Brody Carlton was not as restrained as he seemed.

The thought scared her.

And excited her even more.

The insistent probing of his tongue against hers conveyed an urgency she'd never guessed prowled inside him. The commanding pressure of his lips induced a helpless response from her so intense it felt as if time and space vanished and she was left dangling over a bottomless abyss by a thread as thin as a spider's web.

He sucked the breath right out of her body, leaving her weak-kneed and giddy. Her mind spun ridiculous fantasies. She saw them standing at a wedding chapel, a preacher pronouncing them man and wife. She saw herself giving birth to his babies, watched him smile at her as if she'd given him the most prized gift in the world. She envisioned them growing old together, holding hands as they strolled along Valentine Lake every evening at sunset.

Brody kissed her harder and deeper, holding on to her as if he couldn't get enough. He made her feel powerful and cherished and terrified.

Rachael teetered. Caught on the twin horns of hope and fear. Oh, this was crazy. Wishing for something that did not exist. Unable to separate fantasy from reality. Seeking, always seeking the refuge of romance when it had done nothing but rob her of her vision to see life clearly. To see men clearly.

Brody was not some brave, stalwart knight who could slay all her dragons. He had no magical powers to wipe away her troubles. She would not find the answers she needed in his kisses. Falling in love with him would not solve all her problems. He was just a decent guy, with his flaws and fears like anybody else.

She had to stop this and she had to stop it now. Rachael jerked back. Ending the kiss. Ending the daydream.

Immediately, he let her go. He did not try to hang on. He did not cling.

She spun away and, head down, ran for the back gate. She never looked behind her. She couldn't bear looking behind her because she knew what she would see.

Dear, battle-scarred Brody, standing there on his one strong leg, looking hurt and confused and angry and sad and vulnerable. She couldn't bear knowing that she had led him on, made reckless promises with her lips.

Promises she dared not keep.

Chapter 12

Across town, Giada Vito sat in her office reading the *Texas Monthly* article. A huge smile broke across her face and she realized she had an important ally she'd been overlooking.

With the article, Rachael Henderson had given her a helpful gift, considering that Kelvin's recent standing in the polls had spiked with the addition of the bond election for Valentine Land.

Giada gritted her teeth.

Theme parks. Fantasy lands. Artifice. Bah!

A theme park might bring in jobs, but at what cost to the town? The last thing Giada wanted was to see her adopted hamlet turned into another Anaheim or Kissimmee with tons of traffic and congestion as tourism crowded out what was real and true and honest about Valentine.

According to *Texas Monthly*, Rachael wasn't the only one who disdained misguided romanticism and oversold commercialism.

She had to talk to Rachael and convince her to join her campaign. It was going to take a lot of scraping to win against the man whose thumb was pressed firmly on the town's jugular. And Rachael—with her contingency of recovering romanceaholics—could be her ace in the hole.

Deciding to skip her late-afternoon walk around Valentine Lake, Giada hopped into her Fiat, left the schoolgrounds, and headed for Rachael's house. Five minutes later, she turned down the tree-shrouded street at the same time she saw Kelvin Wentworth's Cadillac approaching from the opposite end of the block.

What was the irritating man doing here?

She parked at the curb to the left of Rachael's home at the same time Kelvin pulled up on the right. Simultaneously, they hopped out of their cars. He had a copy of *Texas Monthly* rolled up like he was going to whack something with it. Giada's copy was sticking out of the handbag she had slung across her shoulder.

"Vito," Kelvin said in a tone that was half-sneer, half-amusement. The sneer she understood. The amusement part irritated her.

"Wentworth," she countered, disdain in her voice. She hurried up the sidewalk, trying to get ahead of him, but she was wearing stilettos and Kelvin's long legs ate up the ground until they were rushing shoulder to shoulder onto the front porch.

She rang the bell. Kelvin hammered on the wooden door.

"You oaf," she said. "You'll scare the poor woman to death with your clumsy pumping."

"No one's ever complained about my pumping before," Kelvin said, a wolfish gleam in his eyes.

Giada frowned, and then she caught the sexual innuendo. She'd meant to say pounding, not pumping. Although she'd been raised from childhood with English as her second language, it was still a complicated and confusing tongue. And she'd left herself wide open to Wentworth's smirk. She made a face at him and rang the bell again.

She tried not to notice how good he smelled. He wore a spicy-scented cologne that enticed her nose. Kelvin laughed; the sound was rich and deep. It sent strange prickles up her spine. Prickles she did not enjoy.

"You're here to join forces with her," Kelvin said flatly.

Giada didn't answer. She didn't owe him an explanation. The air was thick and laced with the fragrance of the rust-colored chrysanthemums flourishing in the flower box underneath the window. She poked the doorbell again. In spite of the pink Volkswagen sitting in the driveway, she was beginning to suspect Rachael wasn't home.

Kelvin stepped closer, crowding her space.

The tiny hairs at the nape of her neck lifted. *Step aside. Move back.*

And let him win?

No way.

She didn't have to dither long. Kelvin was the first to move. He took her elbow, spun her around to face him.

A thrill of alarm buzzed through her. Her heart reeled recklessly against her rib cage. She turned her head, unable to meet his gaze, reaching for the doorbell again. *Please be home, Rachael. Answer the door.*

But there was no salvation. No rescue.

Kelvin dropped the magazine he'd been holding. It hit the welcome mat with a soft plop and his arms went around her waist. Her breath left her body in one abrupt whoosh. Her knees turned to noodles as his big hands settled on her hips.

His body heat seeped through the fabric of her silk skirt, past the lace of her thong panties, and into her quivering flesh. Liquid heat rolled through her, licking like flames. He splayed his hands, covering her buttocks with his big fingers. The sensation spreading out through her nerve endings was more provocative than if he'd actually stroked her bare flesh.

He bent his head.

Giada's heart lodged in her throat. *He's going to kiss me.*

What scared her most was that she didn't even try to get away. Her mace lay forgotten in the bottom of her purse. Her good sense was addled by the fragrance of his cologne mingled with the scent of fall flowers. His warm breath feathered the fine hairs at her forehead. His hands were still splayed across her buttocks. He pulled her up flush against him.

What was she doing? This was a small town and she had no doubt that at least one nosy neighbor was peeping from behind mini-blind slats.

His mouth covered hers and the first thing she thought was, *He tastes just like licorice.*

Licorice had been her father's favorite flavor of chewing gum. He'd always carried a pack in his front pocket. When she was particularly successful—bringing home good grades, coming in first at dance recital, winning first place in the science fair—he'd reward her with a stick of gum. Giada associated licorice with reward.

Kelvin's kiss sucked all the air from her body. Sucked common sense right out of her head. She would never have guessed a man like Kelvin Wentworth—born and reared in a small town that he'd never left—could kiss like this!

He kissed as if the sun rose and fell on her lips. As if the earth spun on its axis because of her. His kiss was dizzying and demented and utterly unforgettable.

What shocked Giada most of all was her uninhibited response.

She'd often thought he was egotistical and opinionated and thickheaded. A Neanderthal who'd once run a football so fast and far that he'd bamboozled the town for all eternity.

But she wasn't thinking those things now.

What she thought now was a lyrical throwback to her Italian girlhood. She remembered a story her grandmother had told her about the magic of a kiss and the power of true love. Her father had pooh-poohed the stories from her mother's side of the family. Romance, he'd taught her, would lead her down the wrong path. If she wanted to make it in the world, she needed a solid grounding in math and science and a firm, sensible head on her shoulders.

Instinct urged her to wrap her arms around Kelvin's neck, pull his head down closer, deepen their connection, extend the kiss.

And if Rachael Henderson hadn't chosen exactly that moment to come barreling up the sidewalk, Giada had little doubt that's exactly what she would have done.

Kelvin broke the kiss, stepped away from her. In unison, they turned to see Rachael standing on the bottom step, eyes wide, breathing heavy. Her lips looked swollen. Giada pressed the back of her hand against her own mouth, still moist from Kelvin's.

"What do you want?" Rachael cried, the panicky note in her voice out of step with any misgivings she might have felt by finding the mayor kissing the high school principal on her doorstep. Something else was going on with her. "Why are you here?"

She and Kelvin both spoke at once, drowning each other out.

Rachael raised a hand, climbed up the steps. "Please," she said. "Get out of my way. I have no desire to speak to either one of you." Shouldering them aside, she pushed into the house and slammed the door behind her.

Kelvin turned to Giada. He gave a shrug. "I guess we caught her at a bad time."

"It appears that is the case."

"I'll just come back later," he said.

"Me also."

Neither one of them made a move to leave.

"What you're doing is a mistake," he said.

"What is? Trying to stop you from turning this town into a theme park?" Giada asked.

"It's the only thing that's going to save Valentine."

"Says you."

"Yeah," he said, narrowing his eyes. "Says me."

"The town should be allowed to hear both sides, to make an informed decision. It's time you stopped treating Valentine as if it's your child and you're Big Daddy who knows best."

He arched an eyebrow. "Spoken like a foreigner who came strolling into town without any sense of history, determined to muck things up and ruin our traditions with dangerous ideas."

Giada sank her hands onto her hips, her mouth burning with regret. She'd been an idiot to let him kiss her. If she'd had some Scope, she'd gargle and spit right here. "I am a United States citizen. I have lived in this town for fifteen years and in this country for twenty. I belong in Valentine just as much as you do."

Kelvin snorted.

Giada's blood boiled.

She spun on her heels and scurried down the stairs, her

knees stiff with anger, her movements jerky. Egotistical bastard.

It wasn't until she was speeding away in her Fiat that she realized he'd won. He'd chased her off.

She stopped at the red light in front of the Dairy Queen and slapped the steering wheel with both hands, imagining just how pumped up and pleased with himself he was feeling right now. Giada glowered at her reflection in the rearview mirror. Kelvin might have won that little skirmish, but she was determined to win the war.

Leg quivering, Brody plopped down into the lawn chair, his skin suddenly slick with sweat. He saw the hem of Rachael's skirt swish as she jerked the tall wooden gate closed behind her. He heard the latch click firmly in the lock.

His stomach churned. His lips burned. His heart knocked like a jalopy. He needed much more than a kiss. Wanted much more than just her body. The depth of his desire rippled wide as shock waves.

Rattled, he shoved his hands through his hair and stared at the beach towel lying on the ground to one side of his Power Knee.

She'd seen him without his leg. And she hadn't turned away in disgust. In fact, she'd made the first move, covering the ground between them, her eyes daring him to kiss her.

He'd never been able to resist a dare.

What if she was only doing it because she feels sorry for you?

He hated the thought of it. Clenching his jaw, he tried to harden his heart against soft emotions. Tried not to feel the things he was feeling.

But what if it wasn't just pity? What if she'd honestly wanted him as much as he'd wanted her?

Brody grunted. What was this strange hold she seemed to have over him? She made him think stupid, romantic thoughts. Thoughts he knew better than to entertain. He'd witnessed firsthand just how much damage romantic love could do to a man, to a woman, to a family. He didn't want any part of it.

Love?

Come on, he wasn't falling in love with her. He liked her spunk. He admired her courage. He thought she was gorgeous as all get out and that body of hers...

Recalling the way her hot, curvy body had felt pressed against his, he hissed in a breath and his own body responded to the remembered stimulus. His fingers tingled from the feel of her silky hair. His ears pricked at the echo of her soft sighs. His mouth watered at the ghost of her taste, so sweet and rich and feminine.

All he could think about was getting his hands up underneath her skirt and pulling off her panties, then laying her down in the grass beneath the pergola and making love to her.

His erection stiffened.

It had been so damned long since he'd been with a woman and he wanted her so badly it made him ache all over.

But Rachael wasn't just any woman. She was special. Thinking about her made him smile. A crystal clear picture of her rose in his mind—that cascade of wavy blonde hair tumbling helter-skelter over her slender shoulders, the excited light in her almond-shaped green eyes, the sweet, honeyed flavor of her lips.

Truth was, she'd gotten to him. Slipped past his guard

with her earnest beliefs and heartfelt desire to reinvent their hometown. He'd spent so many years on alert, in tight control of his emotions, holding himself back, keeping his feelings in check. He was stunned to discover how little self-control he really possessed when it came to Rachael.

Lose control. It's okay. Just let go.

Easy to think, much harder to do. She wanted him as much as he wanted her. He'd tasted it on her. Her need. His hunger.

So go after her. Seduce her.

Brody fisted his hands. He couldn't, he wouldn't. But his dick was so hard he could barely draw in air. Dammit, how he wanted her.

She'd done this to him. Made him desire her in a way he'd never desired another. Miserable. He felt mindlessly miserable.

He tried to think of his ex-wife, tried to remember if she'd ever affected him like this. But for one blind moment, he couldn't even remember her name. All he could think about was Rachael.

Sassy, delightful Rachael, who'd turned both him and his hometown inside out.

His hand strayed to the laces of his swim trunks, his fingers fumbled as his breath came hard and fast. He imagined it was Rachael provoking him, stroking him.

Her fantasy touch caused every nerve ending in his body to jolt with electrical awareness as he recalled the feel of her soft arms entwining around his waist. He visualized her long silken curls tickling his bare skin. He saw her full, peach-colored lips tip up in a beatific smile.

Daydream mingled with memory as his imagination escalated the scenario playing out in his head. His cock

throbbed. His pulse raced. His brain hung on one thought
and one thought only.

Rachael.

Stop, stop. You've got to stop this.

But it was too late for that. His self-control was shot
to shit. He was lost. Overcome by lust and need and too
much deprivation.

He stripped off his swim trunks and palmed his penis.
His rhythm was frantic, desperate. He felt in equal parts
embarrassment and inevitability and determination. He
had to do something to alleviate the weighted need that
had settled in him like granite from the moment he'd first
spied her dangling from the Valentine sign.

Just get it over with. Quick. Empty out the testosterone.
Get your brain back.

He closed his eyes, took in a deep breath, did what he
had to do to reclaim his sanity.

Rachael.

A groan, half-pleasure, half-despair, slipped past his lips.
How he wished she were here with him. Doing this to him.

The lawn chair screeched against the cement, but he
didn't care. There was no stopping now. He was caught.
God, what had she reduced him to?

And then the orgasm was upon him.

Rachael.

Clenching his jaw, he shuddered as hot ribbons of
milky white ejaculate shot up and spilled over his fist.

In that moment of weakness, Brody realized something
deadly profound. No matter how much he wanted to deny
the dangerous pull, he *was* falling in love with her and he
had absolutely no idea how to stop himself.

"Rachael," Brody muttered, feeling more confused
than ever. "Dammit, woman, you've ruined me for good."

*   *   *

Kelvin scooped up his copy of *Texas Monthly* from Rachael's porch. He thought about ringing the doorbell to see if she'd open up, but his heart wasn't in it. What he needed was someone to talk to. His gaze swung across the street to Brody Carlton's house.

He walked over and knocked on Brody's door.

It took a while for the sheriff to answer. He was wearing swim trunks and nothing else. It wasn't often he had his prosthesis on display and it was something of a shock to see the bionic leg. Brody hid his injury so well, three-fourths of the time Kelvin forgot he was an amputee. The sheriff looked both breathless and irritated.

"Can I come in?" Kelvin asked.

"Can I say no?"

Kelvin didn't bother to reply, he just stepped over the threshold. "You alone?"

"Yes."

"Where's your sister? She coming home soon?"

"She's taken Maisy to see our aunt in Del Rio. They won't be home until Sunday night."

"Good." Kelvin sank down on Brody's couch. He picked up the remote control and flicked on the TV to ESPN.

"Come right in, make yourself at home."

"Thanks."

Brody sat down in the chair across from him. "What's the matter, Mayor? You look like you've been sacked in the end zone. Did you just find out Giada's kicking your ass in the polls?"

Kelvin tensed. "What did you hear?"

"Nothing." Brody frowned. "Seriously, Kelvin, are you okay?"

"Women. They screw with your head."

"Not going to argue with you there. Any woman in particular got you twisted up inside?"

"I'm forty-seven years old, Carlton. Forty-seven and I've never felt like this." Kelvin sprawled his arms across the back of the couch.

"Are you saying you're in love?"

"No." Kelvin rasped in a breath, but that was exactly what he was afraid of. "Not love, but something…"

"So who's the woman?"

Kelvin scowled. "You promise you won't laugh."

"I won't laugh."

"It's Vito."

Brody laughed.

Kelvin slapped a palm against his forehead. "I know; it's fucking hysterical."

"Hey," Brody said. "I've got problems of my own."

"She's going to win this election," Kelvin said gloomily, "and I'm going to be left with nothing."

"Maybe not. I mean, come on, the Wentworth name founded this town."

"That doesn't seem to matter much anymore. People want a change. There's a restlessness going around. Nobody wants to believe in love anymore, or traditional hometown values."

"Do you really think a theme park reflects hometown values?"

Kelvin shrugged. He didn't know what he believed. "I can't even think straight anymore."

"If Giada ever figures out that she's got you running scared, you're seriously screwed."

"Tell me about it. Thing is, I can't stop thinking about her. A smart politician would drag her through the muck, doing whatever it took to win, but…hell, I just can't.

There's something about her that's dug into me itchy as a chigger. It's weird. I feel as if it's more important for her to win this election than for me. I don't want to fight her anymore." Kelvin leaned forward and propped both elbows on his thighs, wishing he hadn't said all this to Brody.

"Okay." Brody raised his palms and gave Kelvin a shaky grin. "You've officially got me scared. You want me to make an appointment with Doc Edison for you?"

"Hey, look," Kelvin said, turning off the mute button on the television. "Roy Firestone is interviewing Trace Hoolihan."

Quickly, Brody turned his attention to the TV.

Kelvin sank back against the couch again and tossed the remote onto the coffee table. His gaze was fixed on the screen, but his mind was hanging on to Giada. Initially, he'd been attracted to her smoking-hot body, then her square-shouldered moxie. The woman possessed more passion and determination than most men he knew and Kelvin respected her for those qualities.

Except that when he'd kissed her, he'd discovered something else beneath that tough, competitive outer shell. He'd found a rival who could just as easily become a friend. There was a tender, generous woman hidden underneath those layers and he couldn't help wondering just what he would find if he could peel them all away to expose the real Giada Vito.

Was he kidding himself? Was it possible to fall in love at forty-seven? Was he falling prey to his own PR hype? Or deep down inside was this really his last chance at finding true happiness?

By the time the doorbell rang two hours later, Rachael had managed to pull herself together after what had happened in Brody's backyard. Her mother had gone quilting with a group of friends and Rachael was alone in the house, the remains of a Lean Cuisine chicken scaloppini frozen dinner still resting on the TV tray in front of her.

The doorbell rang.

Brody.

She hopped up off the couch, ran to the door, and peeked through the peephole.

Giada Vito stood on her front porch. Her head was held high, her shoulders ruler straight. She looked determined.

Disappointment pushed air from Rachael's lungs on a long sigh. Reluctantly, she opened the door. "What do you want?"

"May I come in?" Giada asked in impeccable English. Except for the faint hint of an Italian accent, no one would ever guess she hadn't been born and raised in Valentine.

Rachael stood aside.

Giada swept into the room.

"Have a seat." Rachael waved at the couch.

Giada perched on the edge of the cushion. She wore a silky peach-colored blouse cut in an Empire style, slim-legged black slacks, black-and-peach sandal stilettos, and pearl earrings. Her hair was pulled back from her face in an elegant twist and anchored to her head with a fat brown barrette. She held her black-and-peach Coach handbag in her lap and crossed her legs at the ankles, the epitome of culture and cool. The woman possessed an efficient kind of beauty that made Rachael feel like a slacker in her gray sweatpants, faded blue cotton T-shirt with the slogan I HEART VALENTINE on it, and slouch socks with a hole in one toe.

"I want you to join my campaign," Giada said.

"That's straight and to the point," Rachael said. "I'm not very political."

"You don't have to be political. You just do what you do."

"Meaning?"

Giada leaned forward, her expression intent. "We've got to shake this town up. They've been putting too much emphasis on romance. Education takes a back burner and that concerns me. When I asked my students about their life goals, fully three-quarters of the high school girls said they want to get married and have babies. Can you imagine? No ambition."

Rachael could imagine. Once upon a time she'd been one of those girls. Could still be one if she let herself give in to temptation. She thought of Brody, then pushed the thought aside. Too much temptation.

"I've already stirred up trouble." Rachael nodded to the copy of *Texas Monthly* resting on the coffee table beside the Lean Cuisine tray.

"Exactly," Giada said. "That is precisely the reason I want you on my campaign. You have started a passionate dialogue in this town the likes of which has never been seen. For the first time people are examining what this town stands for and they're beginning to realize they've sold out their inner values and beliefs for the sake of tourism."

"Tourism *is* Valentine's economy."

"It doesn't have to be," Giada said. "I know a way we can turn this town around."

"Oh?"

Giada lowered her voice. "I don't want to tip my hand. I have to know if you're a confederate before I let you in on my secret weapon."

Rachael ran her tongue over her lips and shifted uncomfortably. A couple of months ago, caught up in the heat of anger from being jilted, hung up on the fact that her parents were divorcing, she would have jumped at Giada's offer, anxious to get her message out. But now, in the fallout from the article, with her lips still achy from Brody's kisses, she wasn't so sure.

"You're addicted to it," Giada said.

"Addicted?" Rachael asked, trying to play innocent, but she heard the stress in her own voice.

"To romance. It's why you started Romanceaholics Anonymous. Why you wrote the article."

Silently, she nodded.

"This is why it's so important to do something about it before more young girls become addicted to the fairy-tale belief of true love and happily-ever-after."

"I know," Rachael croaked.

Giada reached over and put a hand on hers. "What are you so afraid of? I'm throwing you a life preserver. Grab hold, Rachael. Hold on for dear life. Save yourself."

She thought of Brody. Of how much she wanted to romanticize their relationship. Of how badly she yearned to fall madly in love with him. Already she imagined herself moving into his house, wearing his ring, having his babies. Making the same old mistakes. Leaving her heart open for more pain and disappointment. She had to nip these feelings in the bud.

Thoughts whirling, she met Giada's eyes. "Okay," she said. "I'll do it. I'll join your campaign."

For days Rachael's article in *Texas Monthly* and speculation over the upcoming political debate between Giada and Kelvin buzzed through the Valentine grapevine like wildfire through a timber drought. The restless edginess over romance that had started the day Rachael desecrated the billboard escalated as the town took sides. Divisions split friendships and families and love relationships.

Brody's wariness grew. With everyone stirred up, something unpleasant was bound to happen. The vandal hadn't struck again—not since graffitiing Rachael's car, but Brody hadn't stopped investigating. He had the field narrowed to a handful of suspects—most of them mischievous high school boys—but he had no proof. All he could do was wait for the vandal or vandals to strike again.

And Rachael was a prime target.

He kept a close eye on her house, watching her comings and goings across the street with a pair of high-powered field binoculars. He told himself it was protective surveillance, but more than once his gaze had lingered inappropriately on the sensuous curves of her fine body and his mind would wander to that day in his backyard.

As he watched her, Brody was sorry that his family had moved away when he was twelve. That he hadn't lived next door to Rachael during her teenage years. That he hadn't been there to watch her blossom from gangly kid into gorgeous young woman. Why did he feel as if he'd missed out on so much?

The Friday before the political debate, Brody performed his new bedtime ritual. He took the binoculars from the drawer in his bedside table, pushed back the curtains, and trained his sights on Rachael's driveway. It was just after ten, and while the VW Bug sat parked in the driveway, Selina's Cadillac wasn't there.

Rachael was alone.

The realization raised the hairs on the back of his neck as he imagined her all alone in that house, maybe stepping out of the shower naked, toweling herself dry....

That's when he spied a figure dressed in black ducking through the shrubbery surrounding the house.

"Sonofabitch," he said, flinging the binoculars on the bed and reaching for his pants.

Minutes later he was across the street, pulse thumping, gun drawn. A neighborhood dog barked. Crickets chirped. He could hear the gentle whirring of his Power Knee as he crouched and scanned the darkness.

He spied movement at the back of the house. Was it a tree in the breeze or something far more sinister?

And then Rachael screamed.

Chapter 13

Brody's appearance at her back door was almost as startling as the face she'd seen—distorted by a stocking—peeking in her kitchen window.

She caught her breath at the sight of the sheriff. An angry frown furrowed his brow and he held a gun clutched in both hands. "What is it? What's happened?"

Stunned, she waved at the window and managed to squeak out, "Peeping Tom."

"I'll be right back," he said. "Lock the door behind me."

He disappeared as quickly as he'd come, leaving Rachael feeling shaky and unsettled. She locked the door, then sank down at the kitchen table, the glass of milk she'd come downstairs for completely forgotten.

She'd managed to drag in a couple of deep calming breaths by the time Brody tapped on the back glass. She got up to let him in. He closed and locked the kitchen door behind him and laid his gun down on the counter.

"Whoever it was got away. But there's footprints in the dirt underneath your window. I'll make an imprint. See if I can discover what kind of shoes the Peeping Tom was wearing. Was it a man?"

"I think so." His eyes met hers and Rachael realized she was trembling.

"Peaches," he said, calling her by the sweet little nickname. "Are you all right?"

Helplessly, inexplicably, she burst into tears.

"Aw, hell, Peaches." He reached for her, pulling her into his arms.

It felt so good here in the circle of his embrace. So safe.

"Don't cry." His voice was raw and scratchy and he smelled of minty toothpaste and cotton pajamas. He was wearing his pajamas.

"You were in bed," she said.

"On my way there."

"How did you get over here so quickly? I barely had time to scream and there you were."

"I saw someone creeping around your house."

"You were watching my house?"

"I was."

"Watching over me?"

"You've stirred up a lot of trouble in town. I wanted to make sure you were all right."

"Thank you," she whispered.

Brody squeezed her tight. More tightly than he should. She felt so familiar in his arms. As if she'd always belonged there. It was a dangerous feeling but he could not shake it. Her body was so soft and warm and supple pressed against his. The scents of roses and lavender emanated from her smooth, creamy skin. Tears clung to her eyelashes and he had an irresistible urge to kiss them away.

This was what he'd been so afraid of, from the very moment he'd fetched her down off the billboard. That she would somehow worm her way into his heart. And now he was holding her as if both their lives depended on this hug and his heart was pounding so hard he feared it might explode.

At some point Brody realized he was rocking her like a child and smoothing her hair with his palm. And he had another flash of memory from their childhood. She'd gotten skates for Christmas one year and she'd fallen in her driveway and skinned her knee. He'd been out shooting hoops and had seen her fall. He'd gone over and scooped her up, holding her then much as he was holding her now. Seeking to comfort her. Make everything okay in her world.

He hadn't recalled any of this stuff in well over a decade, but now his head was flooded with memories of her: Rachael coming over to show him the blue ribbon she'd won in the second-grade spelling bee; Rachael, pigtails flying, running down the street to catch up with him as they walked home from school; Rachael, dressed as Cinderella, trick-or-treating on his front door step.

The treasure trove of memories tucked away in the far recesses of his mind amazed him. But he shouldn't have been surprised. How could he forget anything about Rachael?

With a quiet sniff, she pushed from his arms. "Sorry I wussed out on you. I don't know why I started crying."

"You've been under a lot of stress and it's damned scary to look out your window and see a face staring back in the middle of the night. And then I barged in here waving a gun around."

She smiled bravely. "You're just being kind. You don't have to keep propping me up."

"Listen," he said, "I'm right across the street. If you need anything—"

"I appreciate the offer," she interrupted, "but I can't go around depending on you. I created this monster. I have to learn how to deal with it."

"I'm afraid things are going to get worse before they get better. Tempers are running high."

"It's all my fault," she said.

He hadn't intended to make her feel responsible for what was happening. "You might have stirred up some controversy, but you do not deserve having your car vandalized or your privacy violated. I'm going to find out who's doing this and hold them accountable."

"Do you think it could be the same person who graffitied my car?"

"Maybe. But that was several weeks ago, so maybe not."

"I have unwittingly made a lot of enemies."

"Hopefully," he said, "that'll all be settled after the election is over."

"A lot can happen between now and then."

He nodded. "I'm worried about the debate. I wish you wouldn't speak."

"I have to."

He stroked her cheek with the back of his index finger. "I know."

"Thank you for understanding." She looked at him with such admiration it stole the air right out of his lungs. The urge to make love to her was so strong that if Selina hadn't picked that moment to arive home, Brody might have done just that.

In Brody's two years as sheriff of Valentine, a need for crowd control had never arisen. Until the bond election debate.

The political rally was scheduled for noon, but by

ten-thirty Main Street was already jammed with people coming out for the free hot dogs, soft drinks, and ideology the politicians were giving away. One look at the throng of people headed toward Bristo Park, where the grandstand had been constructed, and the steady stream of cars rolling in off the highway, and Brody could smell trouble in the air.

That many out-of-towners could mean only one thing. Word about the town's conflict had gotten out in a big way. And people wanted front-row seating for the fireworks.

He spied a white van wrapped with the logo of the Del Rio television station. The media were here. Not good. He pushed his Stetson down on his head and adjusted his firearm at his hip.

The crowd was moody. People carried signs and banners declaring which side of the fence they were on. ROMANCE IS A LOAD OF HOOEY versus ALL YOU NEED IS LOVE. They toted camp chairs and Igloo coolers as if they were heading for a tailgate party.

He heard grumbling in the crowd, caught snatches of conversations as people walked by.

"—trying to ruin our community."

"Giada's right, we don't have our priorities straight."

"Why don't she just go back to Italy where she came from? We don't need no foreigners telling us how to run our town."

"Unrealistic expectations about love wrecked my marriage."

"I'm telling you, the real culprit is that Rachael Henderson. Just because she can't hold on to a man she thinks everyone else has a problem with romance."

At the mention of Rachael's name, Brody's gut tensed. He whipped his head around to see who was running her down and spotted the dour-faced woman who owned the local bridal shop. She was carrying a sign that read: KEEP VALENTINE IN LOVE WITH LOVE. VOTE WENTWORTH FOR MAYOR.

Brody unclipped the two-way radio from his belt. "Zeke," he said, depressing the button on the handset as he spoke into it. "Get the crowd-control barricades over to the park ASAP."

"Um, Chief…" Zeke came back. "Do we even *have* crowd-control barriers?"

Good question. He had no idea.

"Go down to Audie's, get a dozen sawhorses and a couple of cans of Day-Glo orange spray paint. And hurry."

"How am I supposed to pay for it?"

"Tell Audie to put it on my account."

"You really think there's going to be a riot?" Zeke sounded both apprehensive and excited.

"I hope not, but I intend to be prepared. Now go."

"Will do."

By ten minutes to noon the crowd had swelled so large the park could barely contain them. The sawhorses, now spray-painted bright orange, were arranged in a circle around the grandstand.

Zeke was positioned at the entrance to the parking lot to escort Giada in when she arrived. Brody had called in his two part-time deputies to help with crowd control, but he couldn't help thinking they were seriously undermanned. If things turned unpleasant…

Think positive. This is Valentine, hometown of eternal love. How bad could it get?

A good fifty percent of the crowd booed as Zeke escorted Giada and Rachael up the steps of the grandstand, while the remaining fifty percent cheered, clapped, and glared at the other half.

Brody moved toward the grandstand and his eyes met Rachael's. He inclined his head toward the crowd. She smiled and winked.

At him.

Brody experienced a strange tickling sensation deep in the center of his chest and the air seemed suddenly thin. She was so damned kissable in the black silk dress she wore, thick with a pattern of red roses. With her hair tumbling down her shoulders, she looked as if she'd stepped from the pages of one of the fairy-tale stories his mother used to read to him and Deana when they were kids, stories about stalwart knights slaying dragons to rescue beautiful damsels in distress. Brody pictured himself as one of those brave knights. Scaling steep tower walls to claim a kiss. Driven by chivalry and a desire to be near such a compelling woman.

He was tempted to go up onstage and tell her to get out while the getting was good. He was worried for her safety. But another part of him was proud of her for taking a stand. She was fighting for what she believed in, even if it meant being a lightning rod for the town's anger.

Resisting the urge to go onstage, he curled his hands into fists and surveyed the crowd. Not all of the faces were friendly and his concern escalated.

A few minutes after Giada and Rachael arrived, Kelvin appeared, looking like the Fourth of July in a navy blue suit with a red-and-white-striped shirt and red and white boutonnieres in his lapel. The guy knew how to put on a show; Brody would give him that.

Kelvin received the same fifty-fifty mixed greeting Giada and Rachael had collected.

The debate began with Judge Pruitt acting as moderator. As the incumbent, Kelvin went first, grandstanding as usual. He had Purdy Maculroy set up the small-scale mock-up of Valentine Land on the table beside the stage. He invited people up to have a look. Brody cringed as the crowd pushed forward, oohing and aahing.

"Valentine Land will change lives," Kelvin waxed. "And in a big way. Today, young people leave Valentine because they don't have any opportunities for a vibrant future. Valentine Land will bring jobs to our community and stop the exodus of our youth."

"Yeah," someone in the crowd shouted. "But they'll be minimum-wage jobs."

Kelvin ignored the salvo, instead bragging about his accomplishments as mayor. Since the town hadn't changed much in fifty years, he took credit for the things his ancestors had done, especially emphasizing how the Wentworths had saved Valentine after the oil had dried up.

"Somehow, Kelvin, I don't see you as much of a knight in shining armor," another voice from the crowd catcalled. "We're not your kids and you're not our savior."

Kelvin's face darkened, but he let that comment slide as well. "I have with me Jackson Traynor from Amusement Corp. If you'll just give him a listen, I think you'll see why voting yes in the bond election will spell more money in your pockets."

While some of the citizens of Valentine felt free to razz Kelvin, they were considerate when it came to visitors and they heard Jackson Traynor out when he took the microphone and painted a prosperous picture of how Amusement Corp could put their town on the map in a big way. The man was good at his job. By the time he was done, Brody was halfway convinced Valentine Land was a good thing.

"Now," Judge Pruitt said after Jackson Traynor had finished his pitch, "it's Giada's turn for rebuttal."

Giada tossed her sleek auburn hair as she stepped up to the microphone and sent Kelvin a dirty look. The mayor grinned at her. Giada glared at him fiercely. "Mayor Wentworth and Mr. Traynor would have you believe that Valentine Land is going to put money in your pockets. Yes, maybe the theme park would generate additional tourist dollars, but at what cost?" Giada fixed the crowd with a steady gaze. "As a wise person in the audience already pointed out, most of these will be minimum-wage jobs."

"Any job is better than no job," called out a man whom Brody recognized as an unemployed regular at Leroy's.

"But a bond election is going to cost you money long before you ever see a return," Giada pointed out. "And the person who's really going to be getting rich is sitting right here." She pointed at Kelvin. "I say Mayor Wentworth is wealthy enough."

"Yeah!" shouted a small collective near the stage.

"Here's something else to consider," she continued. "Valentine Land is going to change the whole flavor of our community. The small-town atmosphere will be gone forever."

"You can't stand in the way of progress," Enid Pope yelled.

"Don't listen to my sister," Astrid Pope chimed in. "Enid's always gone for newfangled ways and look what happened to her when she got a computer. Fell for one of those Internet spam scams and lost twenty grand of our savings to some Nigerian scoundrel."

"You weren't supposed to tell anyone about that," Enid huffed at her sister.

"Yes, well, I told you to buy those cute little Rath sausages for the sauerkraut at the church potluck, but oh, no, you had to go buy those big old thick Polish kielbasas they inject with red dye. No one likes a giant red wiener in their sauerkraut."

"Speak for yourself," Enid retorted hotly. "Personally I love big red wieners. With or without sauerkraut."

Brody edged through the crowd, determined to get to the two elderly sisters before they started pushing and shoving. *It's come to this. Two old-maid sisters going at it over sausages.*

"Thank you, ladies, for your input," Giada said, "but let's get back on track. I believe if good-paying jobs are an issue for our town, there's another, less-destructive industry we can woo to Valentine."

"What's that?" someone asked.

"The goat weed that grows wild around Valentine is used in a popular herbal remedy. I've already been in talks with companies that manufacture them. We could start farming goat weed and everyone who had a chunk of land could have a piece of the pie, not just Mayor Wentworth and his Amusement Corp cronies."

That caused a ripple of conversation to run through the group.

"And," Giada added, pacing back and forth onstage, "my third objection to Valentine Land is just as important as low-paying jobs and changing the complexion of the place we love so much. Rachael Henderson has been instrumental in calling our attention to it. I'm going to let Rachael speak to you about it."

Giada handed the microphone to Rachael. Brody watched her square her shoulders and take center stage.

"As most of you know," Rachael said, "I started Romanceaholics Anonymous to counter the unrealistic romantic expectations living in this town engenders.

Valentine Land will only serve to perpetuate these dangerous values and misguided beliefs."

"Oh, can it, Rachael. You're just pissy because you got left at the altar," a man at the back of the crowd shouted.

"Yeah," said a woman near the front. "It's just sour grapes on your part because you can't hold on to a man."

Rachael's face paled and she clenched her jaw.

Anger, unexpected and hot, blasted through Brody. He had an overwhelming urge to track down the hecklers and either punch them or arrest them. Or maybe both.

Whoa. What the hell was wrong with him?

Rachael.

That was what.

Rachael of the wheat-blonde hair and exotic green eyes that caused his heart to skip beats. Rachael of the fruit-flavored lips that made a man ache to sin. Rachael of the tight, compact body that stirred his flesh.

She wasn't letting the detractors affect her. She was still talking about how Valentine had impacted her life in a negative way. How she'd made repeated mistakes in love because of the screwy values the town had instilled in her. She talked about how she'd spent her life chasing rainbows and unicorns and the myth of happily-ever-after that promised all would be well if she just found that one right guy, that perfect mate.

As he listened, Brody found his muscles tensing, his mind growing restless. He hated that she'd been hurt, but what he hated even more was that she'd lost her faith in love.

Why should that bother you? You don't have faith in love.

The thought struck him from out of the blue. While he might not have faith, some small part of him secretly had hoped that he was wrong, that you could find and hold on to great love without it destroying you.

The realization was a total surprise. How long had he been holding on to hope?

And then he realized something else.

He wanted to believe. In her. In love. In happily-ever-after. How ridiculous was that?

Brody was so distracted by his thoughts that it took him a split second longer than it should have to recognize something was going on in the crowd. A ripple in the sea of bodies. A hum that told him the mood was changing. He didn't know if the change was for Rachael or against her. He just sensed something was about to happen.

Instinctively, his hand went to the gun at his hip. He did not draw it, but his gaze was beaded on the thick of the crowd. Tensed and on alert, he waited.

Just as Rachael was talking about being left at the altar by Trace Hoolihan, a man from the opposite side of the grandstand rushed the stage. He was dressed all in black and held something clutched tightly in his hand.

Was it a weapon? Not a gun. It was too big for that.

However, Brody wasn't taking any chances. Not when it came to Rachael's safety. He was on the move, headed for the podium, his pistol drawn.

The crowd gasped, parted.

"Rachael, get down!" he shouted. "Duck!"

But his warning came too late.

"Duck!"

Rachael turned toward the sound of Brody's voice just in time to see a pie sail through the air.

It caught her full in the face.

The shock of it left her gasping—and tasting rich, chocolaty French Silk.

Her vision was gone, obscured by pudding and Cool Whip and graham cracker crust, but she heard the crowd erupt in a chaos of concerned exclamations, stunned murmurs, and nervous laughter. She reached up with the fingers of both hands, scooped globs of pie filling from her eyes and blinked, but still she could not see. She tried to take a deep breath, but pie went up her nose.

Sputtering, she shook her head. Panic gripped her. She couldn't breathe. And then she felt strong, calming arms go around her.

"It's okay, I've got you. You're safe."

Brody.

Immediately, the panic subsided.

He lifted her up, carrying her in his arms, walking down the steps of the grandstand. Barking out orders. Telling Mayor Wentworth to get back up to the microphone and end the rally. Directing Zeke to disperse the crowd. Instructing one of his other deputies to find out who'd thrown the pie.

Rachael wrapped her arms around his neck, holding on for dear life.

My hero.

No, no, that was dangerous thinking. She didn't need a hero. She was perfectly capable of saving herself.

But as she looked up at him, past the blur of French Silk clinging to her eyelashes, she couldn't deny the crazy emotions squeezing her heart. Safe, protected, cared for. But that wasn't all. She also felt nervous, giddy, surprised, curious, and underneath it all, a not-so-small dollop of fear.

She was scared, and not because someone had smacked

her in the face with a pie. She was terrified, yet secretly thrilled. Where was he taking her? What was going to happen next?

Still cradling her in his arms, he marched across the town square toward the sheriff's office. And darn her, she didn't resist. Didn't tell him to put her down. Didn't even try to wriggle out of his embrace. Rachael felt rather than saw the crowd jumping aside to let him pass.

Without putting her down, Brody pushed through the door into his office. He didn't let her go until he'd deposited her in the rolling swivel chair.

"Sit," he commanded, and she didn't dare move.

He stepped into the bathroom that adjoined his office and came back with a stack of paper towels. "Are you all right? Are you hurt? Injured?"

She shook her head and a blob of pie filling fell from her chin. It hit the floor with a soft plop. Suddenly, unexpectedly, she felt like crying, but she had no idea why.

Brody knelt beside her and tenderly wiped pie goop from her eyes with the wet paper towel. It was barely discernible, but she realized his hand was shaking.

Reaching out, she grabbed onto his wrist and stared him in the eyes. "Brody, are *you* all right?"

"Hell, Rachael, I thought . . ." He paused, swallowed.

"Yes?"

"I thought the pie-throwing guy had a weapon. I thought . . ."

He didn't finish the thought. He was breathing hard and staring at her.

"It was just a pie," she said.

"But it could have easily been a weapon. You could have been killed."

She laughed. "Over my anti-romance politics?"

"It's not a laughing matter. I've seen people killed over a lot less. I've seen..."

He had been in the Twin Towers on 9/11 and lost his best friend there. He'd been a soldier in Iraq. She could not even begin to imagine what he'd seen. Her stomach knotted up. "Brody," she whispered.

"Rachael."

Their gazes fused.

She let go of his wrist.

He dropped the damp paper towels, doffed his Stetson and sailed it across the room.

They both moved at once. Her arms went around his neck. His hand slipped around her waist. Neither of them cared that pie smeared her face.

He didn't hesitate. His mouth crushed hers.

Rachael tasted chocolate and whipped cream and graham crackers and delicious, delectable Brody.

The sensible, liberated part of her that had learned the dangers of falling in love indiscriminately wanted to struggle, to resist. But the part of her that was addicted to romance, the weakness that seemed inborn in her, totally capitulated.

He moved his hands up to cradle her head in both his palms, pinning her in place while he ravaged her lips, sweet with pie.

A searing blast of heat burned through her. Blistering her tongue, her throat, her chest and beyond until she was sizzling from the inside out with the power of his kiss.

She'd been kissed a lot in her pursuit of romance. She'd had her fair share of boyfriends. But nothing, no one, compared to this.

Brody was raw and real. He was both primal and patient. An odd combination that escalated her desire. They meshed liked peaches and cream. But what was happening here was far more serious than any sweet indulgence. Uh-oh, she was getting herself in deep all over again.

I should call someone. Mom, Jillian, Delaney, Tish, Deana, Rex, someone, anyone from Romanceaholics.

But his tongue stole all rational thought.

God help her, she was lost.

She whimpered.

He groaned.

The next thing Rachael knew Brody had pulled her out of the chair, rolling her atop him as he curled his back against the floor. Pie filling was between them, on them, everywhere—sweet and sticky and glorious.

She was astride him, legs anchored on either side of his waist, the tile cool against her knees.

He pulled her down to him and planted a series of hot, openmouthed kisses from her cheeks to her chin to her jaw to the vulnerable hollow of her throat.

Heaven.

While she'd always been a romantic, had loved kissing and holding hands and gentle cuddling, Rachael had never considered herself particularly passionate in bed. She liked sex well enough, and always tried to keep her man's needs in mind, but when it came to orgasms—well, hers were few and far between and generated mostly by battery-operated sex toys. Really, all she'd ever wanted was emotional intimacy. The physical part she could take or leave.

Until now.

Until Brody.

A couple of well-executed kisses from him and she blazed with a craving so hot it hurt. In his arms, she felt so alive. Fluid and free.

This man would never leave her at the altar. Never intentionally break her heart. She knew this about him, even though she could not say why or how. She just knew it as surely as she knew he'd willingly take a bullet for her. And her certainty pushed her headlong into perilous territory.

Greedily, she worked the buttons of his uniform shirt, frantic to get at him, desperate to expose his muscular chest, hungry to lick the salt from his bare skin.

Her breathing came hard and fast as she finally got the last button undone and recklessly stripped his shirttail from the waistband of his pants. She could feel his erection through his trousers. She grinned at his burgeoning hardness.

"Rachael." The sound of her name, wrenched from his throat in a harsh exhalation, had her muscles tensing tighter. He was as needy as she! His fingers were doing to her dress what she'd just done to his shirt.

When her blouse was open and he caught sight of the pink bra she wore underneath, he sucked in a fresh breath on a hiss of air. The sound—wholly masculine and appreciative, caused her womb to contract in response.

He reached up to thread his hands through her hair and pulled her head down to his once more. He stared into her eyes, never looking away, letting her see deep inside him.

She thought of how she must look, covered in French Silk pie, and she laughed.

He laughed, too, robust and raw.

And she started giggling and couldn't stop. She tumbled off him, landing on her fanny on the tile. Brody sat up, pushing a strand of hair back off his forehead, grinning broadly.

"This…is…this is…" She was laughing too hard to finish her thought.

"Are you laughing at me?"

For one brief second, he looked so vulnerable it hurt her heart, but just as quickly as it came, the expression vanished from his face. She shook her head. "Not... you..."

"The situation?"

She hiccuped. Nodded. She felt at once silly and giddy and profound. Everything made a weird kind of nonsensical sense. How had she gotten to this point in her life? Kissing the sheriff on the floor of his office, covered in pie, both loving it and fearing it and completely out of control?

And then, without warning, she started to cry. She had no idea why she was crying. One minute she was laughing and the next minute salty tears were streaming down her face, mingling with the sticky chocolate on her cheeks.

Alarm lit Brody's face, but then he pulled her into his lap and pressed her cheek against his chest as he wrapped her tightly in his arms. She could hear the steady strum of his heart, feel the heat of his body radiating through her.

"I... don't... know—" She broke off as a sob escaped her throat. "Why... I'm... crying."

"Shh," he whispered and pressed his lips to the top of her head. "It's too much, too soon. That's all."

She nodded against him, smearing a thin residue of chocolate over his pecs. He didn't seem to mind.

"You must think I'm an emotional mess."

"I think you've been through a lot over the last few months. Getting jilted at the altar. Finding out your parents are getting divorced. Losing your job. Incurring the wrath of fifty percent of your hometown. I'm amazed just how damn well you've held up, Rachael."

"I didn't mean to start this," she said.

"You didn't start it."

"Don't take the blame. I'm the one who started undressing you," she said.

"I kissed you first."

"I didn't stop you."

"I didn't want you to stop me."

She pulled back from his chest because she wanted to see his face. He looked down at her with the gentlest eyes she'd ever seen. How could a soldier have such gentle eyes?

"What are we going to do about this?" she wailed. "I can't get involved with you. I want to and that's the problem. I've never been without a boyfriend in my entire life, until the last couple of months. I don't trust myself. I don't trust these feelings I have for you."

"That's okay," he said. "I understand."

With the saddest look in his eyes, he took her by the shoulders and put her away from him, and then he slowly, tenderly buttoned up her dress.

Leaving Rachael more confused than ever.

Two days after the rally Rachael was at home working on her next article for *Texas Monthly* when Deana knocked on her door.

"I gotta talk to you," Deana said, breezing over the threshold. "I'm in trouble."

"Trouble?" Rachael blinked, her head still in the article. She forced herself to focus on Deana, who plopped down on the couch.

"Big trouble."

"Oh dear." Rachael perched on the arm of the couch beside her. "How can I help?"

"I need an intervention."

Rachael clucked her tongue. "Are you romanticizing a relationship?"

"More than that," Deana moaned. "All this time I've been going to the Romanceaholic meetings, pretending I'm clean and clearheaded, when I've been secretly sneaking around with someone."

Rachael placed a reassuring hand on Deana's shoulder. "It's okay. We all slip up," she said, thinking about Brody. "The main thing is to get back on track."

"How do I do that?"

"You're going to have to back away from this relationship. Give it some time to cool off. Then you can look at it objectively and see if there's a real future for the two of you as a couple or if what you're feeling is all hormones and daydreams."

"I'm afraid it's too late," Deana said. "He's in my blood. I'm addicted."

Rachael blew out her breath. "You've got to stop using language like that. He's not in your blood, you're not addicted to him. Do you want to end up in another relationship like the one you left?"

Anxiously, Deana rubbed her palms together. "He's nothing like my ex-husband."

"How can you be so sure?"

"He's just not."

"Is he charming?"

Deana laughed. "Not in the least. At least not in the way I used to describe charming. He's something of a dork. He's a computer geek. But I find his dorkiness charmingly refreshing. It makes me want to take care of him, but here's the weird part: he takes care of me. Other than Brody, no man has ever looked after me. He's sweet and smart and Maisy adores him."

Rachael sighed. "You are romanticizing him."

"I know," Deana said. "But how can you tell the difference between romantic notions and real love?"

Rachael had to think about that one. Honestly, she wasn't sure she knew the answer. "Time."

"But if time is the determining factor, how come things fell apart for your parents?"

Good question. She didn't have a ready answer. "I'm not sure what happened with my parents."

"Basically, you're saying we can never be sure about love."

"Yeah," Rachael said. "I guess that is what I'm saying."

"He makes me laugh," Deana said. "And he's got the sexiest voice."

"Where did you meet him?"

Deana looked shamefaced. "At a Romanceaholics meeting."

"Deana!"

"I know." Deana groaned, tilted her head, pressed her knees together and turned her feet inward.

"You simply can't get involved with another romanceaholic. You're both playing into the same addiction. He's romanticizing you. You're romanticizing him. It's a disaster waiting to happen."

"Well," Deana said, "as long as we have the same fantasy, what's the harm?"

"You have a daughter. You have to live in the real world for her. She's your top priority."

It sounded strange hearing that advice come out of her own mouth. When had she become the voice of reason when it came to romantic relationships? Honestly, who was she to tell anyone how to run their romantic life? She'd made a mess of hers from the moment she'd started dating.

"Let's get real for a minute," Rachael said, feeling like Dr. Phil. "Tell me the negatives about this guy. Is he employed?"

"He has a very good job."

"What kind of job?"

"If I tell you, you'll figure out who he is."

"That's a red flag statement. Why don't you want me to know who he is?"

Deana blew out her breath. "I'm afraid you'll think he's too young for me."

"How much younger is he?"

Deana gritted her teeth, then admitted, "Eight years."

Computer geek. Smart. Dorky. Sweet. Romanceaholic. Eight years younger than Deana. Rachael put it all together. "Omigosh, you're seeing Rex Brownleigh."

Chapter 14

Brody was having a crappy week. Ever since the rally, Valentine had become even more divided, with the romantics on one side of the fence and the cynics on the other, arguing the pros and cons of Valentine Land, and Kelvin Wentworth versus Giada Vito.

Brody and Zeke had been called out to break up more than one liquor-soaked debate at Leroy's that had deteriorated into fisticuffs over the difference between sex, romance, and true love. A local B&B on the banks of Valentine Lake, renowned throughout the state for its romantic getaway packages, had all ten of their bicycles-built-for-two vandalized. Someone had cut them completely in half.

With a pipe cutter.

This was the last straw for Brody. He was determined to catch the vandal before the election. For weeks he'd been trying to figure out who was behind these acts with no luck. It was time to set a trap. What he needed was something tempting the vandal couldn't resist vandalizing. But what?

At the request of its listeners, Valentine's radio station

KVAL—which had once played only upbeat romantic tunes—had taken to giving equal airtime to anti-love songs like "Love Stinks," "Heartbreak Hotel," and "Fifty Ways to Leave Your Lover."

But the greatest cause for concern was the number of couples who'd filed for separation or divorce. At just fifteen percent, the divorce rate in Valentine had been far below the national average. This past week, the rate had jumped to forty-five percent.

Added to the chaos were his chairman duties on the Fish-A-Thon for Love committee. The fishing tournament was a charity event held the last Saturday in October. The money raised from entry fees went to supply the coffers of the local food bank and to buy Christmas gifts and clothing for the needy children of Jeff Davis County. For years, Judge Pruitt had hosted the event Kelvin's father had created. All the town's prominent citizens and business leaders were expected to attend.

At least the tournament was a way to bring the town together for a day at an event that had nothing to do with romance.

Brody hadn't spoken to Rachael since that day in his office. Mainly because he knew if he got around her he was going to have to touch her and he wasn't real sure how to deal with that. The Friday afternoon before Saturday's fishing tournament, he walked into Higgy's Diner for a late lunch. The blue plate special was chicken and dumplings.

The restaurant was practically empty, save for a couple of the waitresses taking their lunch break. At the table in the corner a foursome of old-timers played dominoes. The hearty smell of roasted chicken and yeast bread filled the air.

Me, too.

"The whole love-versus-romance thing?"

"I realize I've been a poor example. Those kisses we shared..." She swallowed. He could see the longing on her face because he felt a corresponding longing deep inside him. "Let's just say I have to keep myself on a tighter leash. If I can't control my urges, how can I expect my Romanceaholics Anonymous members to control theirs?"

"You do realize you just issued me a challenge."

"I didn't."

"You did."

They stared at each other.

"Brody Carlton, I swear, if you try to kiss me again, I'll—" She broke off the sentiment.

"You'll what?" he dared.

"I'll...I'll move away from Valentine," she said, and with that, turned and flounced out the door.

Brody's chicken and dumplings arrived but he couldn't eat. His hunger for food had been replaced by a different kind of hunger: He had to have her and that's all there was to it. He'd told himself he wouldn't ever get involved in a grand love affair because great love destroyed lives, but he knew down deep in his soul she was the love of his life. And he had to convince her that she could have her happily-ever-after. The first step was to get her into his bed. He'd worry about the happily-ever-after part later.

It was time to take action.

Determinedly, he took out his cell phone and put a call in to Judge Pruitt.

"Hello, Brody," Abigail Pruitt said when her secretary had routed him through to her. "Is everything in order for the tournament tomorrow?"

"It is."

"I heard there's been a lot of trouble lately over this anti-romance nonsense stirred up by Rachael Henderson."

"Rachael's entitled to her opinion."

"True, true." The judge must have realized she was rubbing him the wrong way because she injected a soothing lilt into her voice. "But she's misguided. Getting dumped at the altar, along with the situation with her parents, has unfavorably changed her views."

"I think it's other people's reactions to her opinion that's the issue here."

"We can't have any problems. This charity is important. Not only to me, but to the underprivileged children of Jeff Davis County. And it's not just the tournament that concerns me. I'm tired of seeing my hometown divided into two opposing camps."

"My thoughts exactly," he said. "That is in fact the reason I'm calling."

"I'm listening."

"Although you and I might not see eye-to-eye on this matter, I think we both want what's best for the town."

"Agreed."

"I want to mend the rift."

"How?"

"By making the key players in this rift kiss and make up," Brody said.

"Excuse me?"

"I have a plan, Judge, but I need your help."

Selina didn't want to go to the fishing tournament. As Michael's wife, she'd been obligated to attend the event for the past twenty-seven years. Now that she was free, she'd planned on spending the last Saturday in October curled up in bed reading the latest Karen Rose thriller. But Giada had ruined all that by insisting all the teachers enroll in the tournament.

So here she was standing around the marina with the rest of the town, wearing layered flannel shirts, wool pants, wading boots, and a water-resistant peacoat. The air smelled of fish, fog, and wood smoke. She thought of the warm, cozy bed she'd left, sighed, and looked over at her daughter.

Rachael was busy scribbling in a composition book, jotting down notes on the tournament for her next *Texas Monthly* article. She looked serious, dedicated. Selina had to admit writing the column had done her a world of good.

Pride lumped in her chest. Her daughter had gone from a starry-eyed romantic who always had to have a man in her life to a clear-sighted, strong, independent woman who was making her own way in the world. Selina wished she'd had such bravery at Rachael's age. If she had, maybe she could have confronted Michael before it was too late.

Michael.

Involuntarily, she swung her gaze through the crowd, searching for him, and found him clustered with his cronies at the end of the dock, surveying the row of fishing boats.

Michael must have sensed her stare, because he glanced up. In that moment he looked as handsome as on their wedding day, a dimpled grin carved into his right cheek, his dark eyes sparkling, his hair ruffled by the breeze.

Selina's heart squeezed and her pulse galloped. No matter what had happened between them, the mere sight of him still weakened her knees. Stupid, foolish, yes, but how did you stop yourself from loving someone?

He caught her gaze and his smile disappeared.

Quickly, she ducked her head, studied the tips of her bright yellow wading boots.

"Mom?" Rachael said. "Are you okay?"

She met her daughter's eyes, forced a smile. "Fine. I just wish they'd get this show on the road."

"They should be drawing the names any minute." Rachael pointed to the redwood gazebo positioned at the head of the dock where the scales were located, alongside a microphone stand and a large circular lottery cage on a spindle filled with numbered ping-pong balls. It was the same equipment St. Jerome's Church used to call bingo every Friday night. "Here comes Judge Pruitt."

Selina noticed her daughter didn't comment on the fact Brody Carlton was escorting the judge to the gazebo. To be perfectly honest, it looked as if Rachael was struggling hard to avoid catching his eye. Just as Selina was avoiding Michael's.

Was her daughter falling for the sheriff?

Before Selina had time to consider this further, Judge Pruitt stepped up to the microphone. Posted on the wall behind her was a grease board grafted with the names of the contestants. After a microphone check, she began her welcome speech. She talked about the importance of the charity and then explained the rules. It was hardly necessary. Each year it was the same collection of faces who showed up.

The fishing boats went out in teams and the teams were selected by lottery—hence the caged ping-pong balls. You had no say in the matching process. You were stuck with whomever the lottery dealt.

The team who bagged the most fish during the course of the day won a trophy, Angler of the Year bragging rights, and the honor of being the largest contributor to the local food bank's freezers for the coming year. Michael was the reigning champion, having won it the last five years in a row. Her husband would probably win it this year as well.

Correction. Her soon-to-be ex-husband.

She felt suddenly hollow inside. The divorce papers had arrived in the mail last week and they were still sitting unsigned on Selina's bedroom dresser. All she had to do was write her name down and mail the papers back to the court and it would all be over.

Twenty-seven years down the drain. Kaput.

But she hadn't been able to bring herself to sign them.

Helplessly, she looked back toward Michael as Judge Pruitt picked a ping-pong ball from the hopper. "Michael Henderson," she called out.

"Yo!" Michael raised his hand.

"You're in boat #1 and your teammate will be..." Brody spun the cage. When it came to a stop Judge Pruitt stuck her hand in and came up with another ball. "Contestant #13." The judge turned to look at the board behind her. "That would be your wife, Selina."

"What are the odds?" Kelvin asked, whacking Michael on the back. "Getting teamed up in the tournament with your ex-wife."

"We're not divorced," Michael murmured. "Not yet."

"You could try asking Judge Pruitt for another teammate," Kelvin suggested.

"I don't want another teammate. She's the only teammate I've ever wanted."

Kelvin studied Michael. "You're still in love with her."

"I am."

"After all she's put you through?"

Michael nodded. "Especially after all she's put me through."

That made no sense to Kelvin. "I don't get it."

Michael made an odd noise. "Maybe someday, if you're lucky, you'll understand what real love is all about."

"If your love is so damned real," Kelvin said, feeling irritated, "how come you're getting a divorce?"

"Because I've been a blind, ignorant ass. Now if you'll excuse me, here comes my teammate." Michael turned away and headed for Selina, who was coming down the dock toward him.

Kelvin stood watching them, feeling half-jealous, half-smug that he'd never fallen in love.

"Kelvin Wentworth," Judge Pruitt's microphoned voice rang out across the water.

"Yes?"

"You're in boat #2."

He nodded.

The lottery cage spun, spit out another ping-pong ball. "And your partner is contestant #32."

Cupping his hands around his mouth to carry over the buzzing crowd, he called out, "Who's that?"

The judge looked at the board. "Contestant #32 is Giada Vito."

The minute Kelvin heard the woman's name, a spike of anger hammered straight through his temple. He'd rather eat arsenic with a smile than be stuck in a fishing boat with that woman.

"Oh, hell, no," he said, pushing his way through the crowd on the dock, headed for the gazebo. He thundered up to Judge Pruitt. "Get me another teammate. I refuse to fish with that woman."

Unflinchingly, Judge Pruitt pulled herself up to her full five-foot-three-inch height and met his scowl with a judicial icy glare. "I'm running the show, Kelvin. Either accept your teammate and deal with it, or forfeit your entry fee and withdraw from the tournament."

Kelvin fisted his hands. He'd seen that stubborn expression on the judge's face before and he'd never won against it. The notion of just walking away was tempting.

But something kept him from storming off. He didn't know if it was the realization that if he left, Judge Pruitt would win, or if it was Giada, standing off to the side, arms crossed over her chest, with a look on her face that said she was enjoying his misery.

"What's the matter?" Giada taunted. "Chicken?"

"To be with you?" Kelvin snorted, trying to deny the sweat popping out along his shoulders in spite of the chilly morning breeze floating in off the water.

"After all, we're going to be out on the water all day. All alone in that tiny little boat," she goaded.

He knew what she was up to. Vito wanted him to quit and storm off so she could look like the bigger person, but he wasn't about to give her the satisfaction. He might be stuck with her, but she was equally stuck with him and he was determined to make her miserable.

"Fine with me," he said, taking some small measure of pleasure at the startled expression dipping her eyebrows inward. "Get your gear and let's go."

One by one, couple by couple, Judge Pruitt executed Brody's scheme. She'd rigged the event, pairing cynics with romantics, forcing ex-lovers together, and teaming up business rivals. Each time the names were drawn, matched emotions ripped through the air—anger, disappointment, frustration, surprise, concern, and hope—until the docks were thick with tension.

"We'll be lucky if someone doesn't end up getting

killed by the end of the day," Judge Pruitt muttered to Brody.

"You've gotta trust me on this," he said sagely. "I know what I'm doing."

Judge Pruitt looked at him with new respect. "Why, Brody Carlton," she said. "I think you're finally starting to believe in the magic of true love."

Brody's eyes found Rachael in the crowd. Maybe he was.

On and on she went, pulling names until all the slots were gone, all the ping-pong balls drawn, all the participants off in their boats, except for two—Brody and his teammate.

Rachael. The lone remaining contestant left standing on the dock.

He took one look at her standing there in her wading boots and blue jeans and his gut turned to mush. Judge Pruitt had turned the table on him. "You did this on purpose," he accused.

"But of course. You think I'm blind just because I'm pushing sixty." She winked. "I saved the best for last. Now go fishing. Everyone else has a head start on you."

"Judge . . ."

"Brody . . ." She leveled a stern glance at him.

"This isn't going to work."

"She needs you, and you need her."

"Clumsy attempt at matchmaking."

"Okay, look at it this way. The town needs you to tone her down. Show Rachael that what she knows in her heart is the truth, no matter how much she's been hurt."

"And what is that truth?"

The judge handed him a bucket of minnows. "Get out on that water and find out."

He went because he wanted to be with Rachael. He took the bucket and walked toward her. She waited, her smile growing brighter the closer he got.

"Looks like it's me and you, Peaches," he said, stopping a few feet from her. "Is that a problem?"

"Not for me," she murmured. "You?"

He shrugged, suddenly feeling like he was in fifth grade at his first coed party, his mother nudging, prompting him to ask a girl out onto the dance floor. His heart was thumping and his fingers felt strangely numb curled around the minnow bucket as he led Rachael toward the last remaining boat tied to the pier.

Brody climbed in first, set down the minnow bucket, then turned and offered his hand to help her into the boat.

She placed her palm in his.

And he felt Abigail Pruitt's Valentine magic.

It wrapped around his heart soft and sweet as Rachael's smile. Wrapped and twined and twisted until he was knotted up with it. Knotted up with her. The scent of her perfume curled in his nose. The feel of her skin against his ignited a fire deep inside him. The sight of her hair falling from the loose ponytail at the back of her neck had him itching to plunge his fingers through the silky strands.

He shook his head, trying to gain some measure of control over his senses. She sat down in the front of the boat with graceful movements. He focused his attention on starting the outboard motor and guiding the dinghy toward open waters.

Neither of them spoke. They passed several of the other fishing boats bobbing on the water. Brody was encouraged to see most people appeared to be getting along, casting lines in the water, pulling up bass and perch, crappie and catfish.

But his mind wasn't on his constituents or fishing. Only one thing held his interest and that was the woman beside him.

Rachael had her back to him, and she was gazing out over the water as he zipped along, headed for his secret fishing spot. Anxious to anchor so he could tell her all the things he'd wanted to tell her for the past month.

At last they arrived in the narrow slough hidden from the main branch of the lake by a copse of oak trees and surrounded by cattails and water lilies. He cut the engine and let the boat drift for a bit before he dropped anchor.

"You want this?" he asked, bending to pick up a rod and reel. "Or do you prefer a cane pole?"

He raised his head, saw she'd turned around and was now facing him. "I'd prefer it," she said saucily, "if you kissed me."

"What?" he asked, unsure if he'd heard her correctly.

She repeated herself.

He needed no more encouragement and he wasn't asking any questions. He dropped the fishing pole and reached for her.

She was in his arms before he could even kick the minnow bucket aside.

Needfully, he trailed his fingertips over the nape of her neck and leaned to kiss the throbbing pulse at the hollow of her throat. Her silky skin softened beneath his mouth and a tight little moan escaped her lips.

His hand crept from her neck and down the hollow of her throat to her breast, heaving with each inhalation of air—a simple but lingering touch that escalated the intimacy between them and felt extremely erotic.

The air smelled rich and earthy. The boat rocked on the water. Time hung suspended, their mouths fused in an endless forever. Brody did not completely understand the spell Rachael had woven over him. He could think of nothing but melding with her.

She wriggled in his lap, her fanny grinding against his thighs. Her quick intake of breath, low and excited in the vast openness of sky and water, detonated his own need, volleying him higher and higher.

She nibbled his chin. The rasp of her teeth against his beard stubble rocketed a searing blast through his nerve endings and he groaned. What a woman!

Brody's lips found hers again and as they kissed, he raised a hand to touch her breast.

Her nipple poked against the material of both her silky lace bra and her flannel top.

His thumb brushed against her hard little button and she responding by wrapping her legs around his and sliding her bottom against his upper thigh. When he bent his head to gently suckle at her nipple through the material of her clothes, she gasped and clutched his head to her.

No, no, it wasn't good enough. He had to touch her bare skin or go mad.

Sliding his hand up underneath her shirt, he unhooked her bra from behind and set her breasts free. She moved against him, mewling softly.

Any hesitation she might have been feeling was gone, replaced by a stark hunger that shoved his libido into overdrive. No way could he resist the mounting pleasure, nor the sweet little sound slipping past her lips.

"We've got to stop," he gasped, wrenching his mouth from hers. "Or we won't catch a single fish."

"Who cares," she panted.

"We can't show up empty-handed," he said. "This is for charity."

"Then Judge Pruitt shouldn't have paired us together."

"How do you know she paired us up on purpose?"

"For heaven's sake, Brody, I might be a blonde, but I'm not dumb. Statistically it would be extremely rare for Giada to end up paired with Kelvin and my mom paired with my dad at the same time you and I got put together. She's playing matchmaker."

"Actually," he said, "she was shooting for peacemaker. The theory was that if everyone who'd been feuding ended up in a small confined space for several hours, they'd work things out."

"Or kill each other."

He shrugged. "We considered that possibility. Judge Abigail felt like love would win out."

"So you were in on this all along?" She pushed her hair from her forehead and shot him an assessing gaze.

He just smiled.

"That's collusion."

"I knew about the others, but I didn't know she was going to pair us together."

"Um," Rachael said, wriggling away from him. Suddenly his lap felt very empty without her in it. "You can tell your buddy the judge I'm not dropping my anti-romance campaign just because she paired me with a pretty face. Seriously, does she think I'm that easy? Throw romance at Rachael and she'll cave?"

He feigned shock. "That's all I am? A pretty face?"

Grinning, she raked her gaze over him and said slyly, "Well, there is the hot body."

"I'm just a sex object to you." He shook his head and pretended to pout. He was teasing, but the joke didn't feel so funny. The idea that she wanted him strictly for sex bothered Brody more than he was willing to let on.

"All that kissing made me thirsty," she said. "You want some water?"

"Yeah," he said, his gaze tracking her body as she leaned over to open the Igloo cooler.

Her shirt rode up in the process, giving him a tantalizing glimpse of her bare waist. Straightening, she handed him a water bottle and twisted the lid off one of her own.

"As I was saying," she continued after taking a long swallow of water. Brody couldn't help watching. God, she even swallowed sexily. "I've been giving it a lot of thought. I'm ready to learn how to separate sex from love and I want you to teach me how to do it."

He stared at her. "What?"

"You. Me. Sex. No strings."

Brody was not prepared for the invisible blow that suddenly slammed in the general region of his heart. He'd never felt a pain quite like this one, because he'd always been able to detach from his feelings when the situation called for it.

But not now, not with Rachael.

It was as if the regulator valve on his emotions had broken off at the hilt and his feelings were spewing out full throttle.

"You game for a good time?" She slanted him a sexy glance with those exotic green eyes of hers.

His gut torqued tight. *Say yes,* prodded his penis.

He lowered his eyelids, crossed his arms over his chest, and leaned back in the boat. He sent her a pensive stare while his mind scrambled around trying to find just the right thing to say. "Keep talking," he said. "I'm listening."

"You're considering it?"

"Peaches," he rasped, "what man wouldn't consider taking you to bed?"

Her cheeks pinked at his comment and she looked flustered. "If we're going to have a fling, there's got to be ground rules."

"Such as?"

"No compliments."

"Come on, no compliments?"

"Compliments are romantic. I don't do romance. Never forget that." Rachael shook a finger at him.

He made a face, but agreed. "Okay, no compliments."

"And no pet names. You can't call me Peaches."

"But I like calling you Peaches," he protested. "You're so sweet and juicy and..."

"Uh-uh." She held up a hand, shook her head. "That's a compliment. It's not going to fly."

"You're tying me up here."

Her eyes sparkled impishly. "Now that's sexual. That's allowed."

"Oh?" He grinned. "Is this your way of hinting that you're into bondage games?"

"Don't know," she said. "I've never given it a whirl, but I gotta tell you when I see the outline of those handcuffs in your back pocket I heat up inside."

He was heating up just hearing her talk about it. He'd never given it a whirl, either, but it sounded like fun. Anything with her sounded like fun. Even if they kept their clothes on.

"Good to know," he said. "Too bad I'm off duty and my handcuffs are sitting on my bedside table at home."

"If you had them, you wouldn't actually use them on me out here." Her eyes widened. "Would you?"

The game they were playing was making him sweat. "I might," he said, keeping his tone low, suggestive.

"On the water?" She sounded breathless, her voice high and tight. "In a semipublic place?"

His grin widened and he held her gaze. He saw the shiver of excitement shimmy over her body, felt a corresponding shiver run down his own. Slowly, he nodded.

"But . . ." she said. "You're sworn to uphold the law."

"Law enforcement officers can have a bad boy side, too," he said.

"How bad?" she asked, flicking out her little pink tongue to run it along her full bottom lip.

The look he gave her was all about sex, not a hint of romance in it. "I could show you right now."

She leaned closer. "Yeah?"

"Yeah."

"Brody," she said in a husky voice that turned him inside out.

Not only could cops be bad boys, but they could also be very, very stupid. What he did next was on par with the antics shown on *America's Dumbest Criminals*. He wanted her and not just for sex. He had to have all of her—body, soul, heart, the lot. Because somehow, in some way that he couldn't fully articulate or even understand, she'd become his deliverance.

She was in his arms again and he was kissing her as if the world were about to end. His fingers were at the zipper of her pants and her hands were threading through his hair as he pushed her back onto the floor of the boat.

The minnow bucket was in the way. Blindly, he grabbed the thing and slung it overboard. He didn't care about anything except having her.

Oh yeah, he thought as her zipper sprang open to reveal the swatch of scarlet thong panties hiding underneath.

Helter-skelter, he pressed his lips to her bare skin—her belly, her hand, the inside of her thigh, stripping the pants down over her hips in a frantic free-for-all.

She helped him, kicking the material free until she was naked from the waist down except for her panties, and the boat was bucking crazily on the waves.

"I want you," she said. "Now."

Brody rocked back on his heels. He wanted her, too, but not like this. His daydreams had centered on his bedroom, where she had once spent the night. He'd pictured long, leisurely lovemaking sessions, with music on the stereo and a great meal in their bellies.

But that was a fantasy and this was reality, and he knew the only way he was going to get to her was through sex. Because of her disillusionment with love and romance their relationship would have to go ass backward. He had to make love to her first, charm her later.

He could do that.

Right?

He thought of his leg and his self-confidence vanished. He remembered why he daydreamed of making love to her in his bed. Why his fantasies hadn't been more creative. In his bed, in his house, he could be in control. Of the lighting, of how he positioned himself, of how he'd camouflage his damaged leg.

Out here, in the open, in a dinghy, in the harsh light of day, he had no control.

But looking down at her, seeing the desire for him reflected in her eyes, he decided that control was decidedly overrated and impossible to achieve anyway.

Go with the flow.

She made a soft noise of encouragement, egging him on, pleading with her eyes.

Forget about your damned leg. Think only of pleasing her.

His trembling fingers tugged at the thin scrap of dark red lace, but his eyes were on hers, deeply searching her face.

"Kiss me," she whispered.

He did. Capturing her mouth, spearing his tongue past her parted lips.

Her breathing grew choppy, urgent, and she fisted her fingers into his chest, balling the material of his shirt in her palms, pulled him down flush against her.

The boat bobbed violently.

Rolling on the water, eyes closed as he kissed her, gave Brody the sensation of falling.

Falling, hell. He'd already fallen and there was nothing he could do about it except find a way to convince Rachael this thing between them was worth taking a chance on.

God, he needed her in the worst way.

He braced his upper body, his forearms pressed on either side of her, holding up his own weight as he stared down at her. He could feel her bare legs against the material of his jeans. The hard metal of his bionic prosthesis rested between her knees.

That realization unnerved him and he moved his leg, repositioning himself. Dragging his mouth from her lips, scooting down, pushing up her shirt as he went, planting kisses down her soft abdomen until he reached those panties barely covering the curl of beautiful blonde hair at the apex of her lush thighs.

When he slid his calloused fingers under her lacy panties, she hissed in an edgy breath.

"Spread your legs," he murmured and she obeyed, sweetly parting her tender flesh for him.

He slid her panties down her thighs. She shuddered when he trailed his fingers over her silky curves and his breathing went perfectly still. "Ah, you're so wet…" He almost called her Peaches, but he bit back the word.

"You're the cause," she said in a strangled voice. "It's all your fault."

"I'll gladly take that blame."

"I want you, Brody."

He raised his head and met her eyes. "But just for sex."

"Yes."

That's what you think.

He bent his head, kissed her down there, where she was wet and soft and smelled so womanly. His fingers played with her slippery heat. She moaned softly and arched her pelvis against his mouth, showing him her rhythm.

But somehow, miraculously, he already knew it. It was as if he'd always known her and what she needed—how hard, how soft, when to use a light touch, when to be firm. Her hungry, gasping cries grew noisier as Brody wound her body tighter and tighter until she was begging for release.

Except he wasn't letting her off the hook that easily. He kept teasing her, increasing the pressure and pace but each time she was on the verge of coming, he'd back off, let the lull pull her back down. Up and down he went, his mouth learning the landscape of her most intimate terrain.

Finally, she splayed a palm against the back of his head, holding him in place, making him finish what he had started. Brody made a noise of approval low in his throat and in response, she fisted her fingers in his hair.

He licked and suckled, cajoled and kissed. And then all at once, she burst apart.

He felt the tremor roll through her as she exploded for him, over him, because of him.

Her breathing slowed and she lay limp on the bottom of the boat. He was slow to move his mouth from her and slower still to wipe away her moistness with his palm. The glorious taste of her stayed on his tongue. He felt more whole than he'd felt before he'd gone to Iraq.

She'd brought him back to himself again. To the man he'd once been.

A hard man, still horny for her. But his release could wait. They had time. This moment had been all about her. Gently he redressed her as she looked at him through sated, dozy eyes. He pulled up the scarlet panties, worked her legs into her wool pants. He smelled her in his nose, on his skin, all over—the imprint of her indelible.

Chapter 15

While Brody and Rachael were blissfully drifting with the current, Giada and Kelvin were out in the big middle of the lake, surrounded by fishermen. Kelvin was still pissed off about being paired with her. He had a sneaking suspicion Brody and Judge Pruitt had rigged the drawing simply to get under his skin.

If they were trying to rattle his cage, he had to admit their scheme had the desired effect. No one could irritate him faster or more completely than his fishing partner.

Judge Pruitt and the sheriff, he decided, could just look somewhere else for campaign donations the next time they came up for reelection.

Kelvin looked over at Giada. She looked so self-assured sitting there on her little folding camp chair in her tight jeans and snug red sweater, with that smug canary-swallowing grin on her feline face—because she did look like a cat with her mysterious watchful eyes and her lithe, controlled movements. And like a cat, it was impossible to knock her off balance. She landed on her feet every time.

She was facing away from him, knees crossed, swinging one leg as rhythmically as a calico swishing her tail.

She held the rod and reel loosely in her hands—casual, relaxed, a woman who had the world by the balls.

Who was he kidding? She had *him* by the balls.

Kelvin wished a big fish would swim along, take the bait, and snatch the pole right out of her hands.

"We could be friends, you know," she said, completely out of the blue.

"Huh?"

"There's no reason we have to be enemies."

"The fact you're gunning for my job is reason enough for me." He didn't like talking to the back of her head.

"Don't pout."

"I'm not pouting."

"Yes? So why's your bottom lip protruding?"

Kelvin sucked his bottom lip up against his teeth. She was looking out over the bow of the boat. He was behind her. How the hell could she tell he'd had his lip poked out?

Giada pulled back lightly on the pole and turned the reel half a turn, softly murmuring something in Italian. The seductive sound of her native tongue spoken on the crisp late-autumn air sent a spike of hot desire straight through his gut.

She uncrossed her legs and leaned forward on her camp chair, closely watching the ripples on the water. "That's it, my sweet, take the bait."

"You gotta nibble?"

"Shhtt." She held up a hand, silencing him.

Her abrupt gesture irritated him. Everything about the woman irritated him, while at the very same time she turned him on in a way he'd never been turned on before.

He hated it. He loved it. Confused by his feelings, he plowed a palm down the length of his face.

"Gotcha," she whispered in urgent victory, setting the

hook and tugging back on her pole as she dialed in the line on the reel.

Eyes narrowed, Kelvin watched her haul in what had to be a fifteen-pound catfish. He snorted.

She tossed him a saucy look over her shoulder. "Jealous?"

He scowled.

"You know," she said, expertly taking the catfish off the hook and slipping it onto a stringer, "you can sit there and be miserable, feeling sorry for yourself all day, or decide to get over your foul mood and make a competition of this."

That piqued his interest. Kelvin was nothing if not competitive. "A competition?"

"Whoever catches the most fish today cooks dinner for the other," she said, and the lilting sound of her voice raised hairs on his forearms.

"I have an even better idea."

"Yes?" She swung around to meet his gaze.

"If I catch more fish, you drop out of the election."

Giada's hearty laughter carried across the water. "I don't give up that easy."

"Stubborn woman."

"Pigheaded man," she tossed back.

He studied her for a long moment. "How about this. If I catch more fish than you, you'll give me a chance to prove to you that Valentine Land would be good for this town."

Giada paused, considering his proposal. "I suppose that wouldn't hurt. I am open-minded."

"Fair enough."

"And what do I get? " she asked, eyebrows cocked on her forehead. "If I win."

"That, Ms. Vito," Kelvin said with the confidence of

a man who'd never lost a competition in his life, "ain't gonna happen."

"Don't be so sure of that," Giada said, and held up the stringer with the flopping catfish. "I've already got a leg up."

On the opposite end of Lake Valentine, at the very apex of the heart, things were shaky for Selina and Michael.

Selina had told herself she would be the bigger person. That she could get through this day and come out on the other side exorcised from the ghost of her marriage. *Face your fears and all that jazz*, she told herself.

But that's not what happened.

She sat rigid, arms crossed over her chest, looking in the opposite direction as Michael guided the boat through the water. At this point, she was seriously regretting not kicking up more of a fuss on the dock, even getting into the boat with him. What had she been thinking?

Honestly, she'd been thinking this was her very last chance to work things out, to save her marriage. It seemed a foolish notion now. Michael hadn't even looked at her since they'd cast off.

He found a secluded spot near the shore, cut the engine, and dropped anchor. Without a word, he went about baiting the hooks of both fishing poles.

"You don't have to do that," she said. "I can take care of my own pole."

Michael raised his head to look at her. His face was cool, expressionless. "I never said you couldn't."

"You've always treated me as if I were helpless."

"Huh?" Now he looked genuinely confused.

"You never let me run my own household," she said. "You hired nannies and housekeepers and gardeners."

"Most women would appreciate those things."

"I know how to perform manual labor, Michael."

"I know you do."

"I'm not some hothouse orchid."

He shook his head. "Am I thick as a brick or is this some woman thing that I'm not getting?"

Her cheeks burned as hot as if he'd boxed them. "It's not a woman thing. It's a human being, self-worth thing," she snapped. "And yes, sometimes you're as thick as marble."

"What did I do?" he cried. "Just tell me what I did!"

"The fact that you don't know," she said, "is indictment enough."

"Selina." He put out a hand to touch her, but she drew back, raised her arms defensively.

"Don't," she said. "Just don't."

She turned her head, peered down at the water.

"Are you crying?"

"No." She sniffled.

"Honey," he whispered. "Are you all right?"

She raised her head, drilled him with her eyes. "Fine, I'm perfectly fine."

"You don't look fine."

"Well, I am."

She jerked her gaze away again, busied herself with casting her fishing pole.

"You're driving me crazy." He shoved a hand through his hair. "If you hate me so much, why don't you just sign the damn divorce papers and be done with it?"

"Is that what you really want?" she asked quietly.

"No, it's not. It was never what I wanted!" he shouted, the temple at his vein throbbing.

"Then why did you have an affair with Vivian?"

"How many times do I have to tell you? We didn't have an affair. Okay, I admit, I flirted with her through e-mail. Big deal. It was harmless. It meant nothing until you made something out of it."

His words stabbed her heart. The man truly did not get it. "I wasn't talking about now," she said quietly.

He blinked at her. The anger came out of him in one loud whoosh of air like an inflated balloon let go without being tied off. "Selina . . . it wasn't what you think."

"Please," she said, raising her palms to ward off his excuses. "Don't insult my intelligence by lying to me again. For once, stop denying the truth. Once and for all, come clean so I can forgive you."

Their eyes met and what she saw reflected there both surprised and puzzled her. Michael looked as if he was hurting more than she was. "Okay," he said and gulped. "You want to hear me say it?"

"I've been waiting twenty-seven years."

"You sure?"

"I already know the truth. You reeked of her perfume when you came stumbling in from your bachelor party that night."

His face contorted with pain and shame. "Okay, yes, yes. I had sex with Vivian on the night before our wedding."

The words fell like bricks, hard and rough. They echoed off the water, sending ripples of sorrow throughout Selina's body, even though she'd braced herself to hear them.

"Say it again," she said, keeping her face as emotionless as she could.

"Sel . . ." His eyes begged her forgiveness.

"Say it again."

"I had sex with Vivian on the night before our wedding," he repeated, his voice filled with contrition.

"I already knew."

"How did you know?" He looked haunted.

"I know you better than you know yourself. What I want to know is why," Selina said, sounding as clinical as a psychologist even to her own ears. "If you loved me the way you said you did, why did you have sex with the one woman who could kill my soul?"

"Because I was scared out of my skull, Selina. I was nineteen years old. I wasn't ready to be a husband and a father."

"You think I was ready? You think I wanted to give up *my* dreams of college?"

He looked stunned. "I thought…I thought being a mother was the most important thing in the world to you."

"It was. Is. But if I could have chosen, I would have waited ten years to have babies. But I loved you and—" She broke off that train of thought. "What I do want to know is the reason you had the affair. Was it because you thought I trapped you into marriage?"

"It was just one night!"

"One night that changed the whole trajectory of our marriage. All these years, have you been pining for Vivian?"

He reached across the boat and grabbed her wrist. "No! God, no."

The fire in his eyes sent blood rushing to her heart. She clenched her jaw. "It's okay to tell me the truth. I can take it."

"You've got to believe me. From the minute I first saw you, there was never anyone for me but you."

Selina furrowed her brow. "And yet you slept with your ex-girlfriend the night before our wedding."

"I was drunk," he admitted. "But it was no excuse. I was scared and..."

"Looking for a way out."

Michael grabbed her by the shoulders and stared her straight in the eyes. The look she saw there was so passionate a faint flicker of hope flared in her chest. "You were the one I loved," he declared. "The only one I've ever loved. And since we've been married I've never once cheated on you. Not even after you left me."

"You haven't"—Selina paused, appalled by how much hope was surging through her—"slept with Vivian since she came back to town?"

"No."

She knew this man inside and out. Knew when he was telling the honest truth and when he wasn't. His eyes did not lie. She swallowed, splayed a hand against her chest, felt her heart gallop.

They were breathing hard, staring at each other. Feeling things they hadn't felt in years. Anticipation, relief, tentative trust, and a brief, bright flash of joy.

For one lovely moment, she thought he might kiss her. He leaned in closer. She tilted up her chin, her mouth suddenly dry.

If he kissed her, she was gone.

Please let him kiss me. Please let everything be all right. Please let the last twenty-seven years of my life have meant something.

A noise from the shore disturbed the moment. It was the sound of an expensive sports car engine.

Selina looked from Michael to the bank. They were near a picnic area. Cement tables and chairs. Shade trees. A parking lot. The scarlet red Jaguar pulling up was impossible to miss.

And so was the sophisticated woman slipping from behind the wheel, dragging a wooden picnic basket done up with a red-and-white gingham bow along with her.

Vivian.

She walked to the water's edge, swinging the basket. She waved at the boat. "Yoo-hoo, Michael, I brought your lunch."

Disbelief squeezed out the hope. Suspicion squashed the relief. Betrayal stomped the tentative trust.

"What's she doing here?" Selina asked, hearing the ice in her voice. *I won't shout. I won't do it. I won't give that bitch the satisfaction of seeing me lose it.*

"Honestly, I don't know." Michael stood, the boat rocking beneath them. Selina stood up, too.

Michael had to have set up a rendezvous in this spot. He had to have known Vivian was coming. The woman was cunning, but there was no way she could have known where they'd be fishing if Michael hadn't already told her.

Selina crossed her arms over her chest. "Don't lie."

"Okay, okay." He raised his hands. "I might have told her where my favorite fishing spot was, but you have to believe me. I did not invite her out here."

"Really, Michael," she said. "I don't give a damn. You want to be with Vivian. Go be with Vivian."

Then Selina placed two palms against his chest and shoved him headlong into the chilly October waters of Lake Valentine.

Just before dusk, Rachael and Brody returned to the marina empty-handed. After Brody had done what he'd done to her, they'd spent the rest of the day kissing and canoodling and enjoying each other's company.

While other Fish-A-Thon entrants unloaded their catches,

she and Brody sat in the boat grinning at each other, waiting their turn to tie up at the docks. His gaze was on her. His eyes alight with a spark of sexual hunger so hot it caused a trickle of sweat to roll down her breastbone in spite of the cooling air.

The wake of arriving boats rocked their little craft like a cradle. Water splashed against fiberglass in rhythmic, soothing sound. The remaining rays of late-afternoon sunshine dappled off the lake in a glistening golden glow.

The combination of Brody's hungry gaze mixed with the pastoral tempo of the lake ignited a deep yearning inside her. It was all she could do not to reach across the boat and kiss him again, in a dizzying lullaby of love.

No, no, not love.

Lust.

She had to stop confusing the two. Would she ever learn to stop confusing the two? She was a terrible Romanceaholics sponsor, unable to control herself when faced with temptation. The embarrassing thing was, she wanted more.

Lots more.

As long as you acknowledge what you're feeling is lust instead of love, it's okay to want him. Just don't romanticize him and you're hunky-dory.

But if she slept with him, really slept with him, all night, in a bed, with full-on sexual contact, did she have a prayer of keeping her heart out of the fray?

There was the rub.

Her fingers itched to pull his shirt over his head and run her fingers across his bare chest. Her mouth—which was already achy from so much kissing—tingled to taste him again. Her ears pricked up, desperate to hear him murmur her name in the throes of the most intimate of embraces.

Anticipation tightened her spine. Sexual hunger narrowed her eyes. Tension curled her toes inside her wading boots. Would these stupid boats ever move along so they could get out of here?

By five o'clock, all the contestants had returned except for her parents' boat. Because they hadn't made it back in time, they were disqualified. If Rachael hadn't been so wrapped up in Brody, she might have wondered where her parents were. She might have spun fantasies about them getting back together. Instead, all she could think about was what Brody looked like naked.

Finally, it was their turn to dock and climb ashore.

Judge Pruitt was in the gazebo, weighing fish and tallying up the scores. Rachael was surprised to discover that not only did Kelvin Wentworth and Giada Vito win the competition, but they were eyeing each other like lovers instead of enemies—an odd turn of events that would have aroused her curiosity if she had not been so preoccupied with Brody.

"Well," Brody said, walking her to her car as the crowd dispersed into the gathering twilight.

Rachael pulled out her car keys. "Well," she echoed.

They both laughed, staring at each other as if no one else existed. It was a scary realization. Knowing they both wanted the same thing. Knowing how dangerous this step was.

Lust, lust, lust, Rachael told herself. *Just lust.*

"You wanna grab a bite to eat?" he asked.

She sniffed at her shoulder. "I smell like fish."

"You could come over to my house," he invited. "I whip up a mean omelet."

"Are Maisy and Deana there?"

"Yes. You'll be safe."

"What if safety was the farthest thing from my mind?"

He arched an eyebrow and his smile turned wolfish.
"How about your place?"

"Mom's there." She frowned, wondering where her
mother had gotten off to. "Or if she's not there she could
walk in at any moment."

He leaned in closer, lifted a finger to trace a strand of
hair curling against her chin. "We can't have that."

Her heart was a caged tiger clawing at the prison of her
breastbone.

He stepped toward her until there was barely room
between them and lowered his voice. "We could sneak off
somewhere. Finish what we started in that fishing boat.
Maybe drive over to the state park and rent a cabin for
the night, out of sight of the Valentine gossipmongers. We
could pick up some groceries along the way."

*Watch it. Slow down. Think things through. Are you
sure you really want to take this step?*

His body radiated heat. His gaze burned.

Her stomach quivered.

*Please don't let him ruin it by saying something roman-
tic. Please, please, please let this be strictly about sex.*

"I want you," he said, "in my bed."

"Oh, Brody," she murmured and sank against him. "I
thought you'd never ask."

After she'd pushed Michael overboard, Selina went to
Audie's hardware store and rented an electric jackhammer from the teenage clerk behind the counter. With most
everyone in town out on the lake for the Fish-A-Thon, she
didn't meet with any resistance as she dragged the heavy
equipment out onto Main Street and borrowed an electrical outlet from Higgy's Diner to plug in the thick orange
extension cord.

She counted off the concrete sidewalk tiles hand-carved with hearts and flowers and entwined doves. One, two, three, four steps away from Higgy's front door she found it.

Their square.

Michael Henderson loves Selina Hernandez forever and always, June 21st, 1981.

Tears clumped in her throat as she remembered the day he'd carved it for her. It was the same day she'd told him she was pregnant with Rachael. They'd been pouring the new sidewalk down Main Street and everyone who was in love had been rushing to grab the prime spots. He'd bribed Kelvin to guard a section in front of Higgy's until he could get over there to make his mark.

Selina's heart clutched as she recalled the way Michael had looked, on his knees, a Phillips-head screwdriver in his hand as he used a heart to dot the 'i' in her name. When he'd finished, he'd thrown her a boyish grin over his shoulder, his face flush with the excitement of young love. It made her heart clutch just thinking about it.

They'd both had such high expectations.

What had gone so wrong?

Her insecurities? His wealthy family? The kids? Vivian Cole? All of the above?

Or was it simply that those same high expectations that had initially sustained them, in the end became their downfall? No marriage could live up to the romantic fantasies they'd spun in their heads. Life just didn't work that way.

A tear trickled down her cheek, but she brutally swiped it away with the back of her hand. The romance was over. The ride at an end. It was time to move on. With this symbolic gesture, she was setting herself free.

Sucking in a deep breath, Selina positioned the jack-hammer's chisel tip at the apex of the heart. Forever and always was such a short time.

Bracing herself for the impact of the vibrating jack-hammer, Selina flicked the switch.

Nothing happened.

She flicked it again. Off, on, off, on, off.

Dismay, as sudden as it was overwhelming, washed over her. She'd worked up the courage to eradicate her past and fate was conspiring against her.

She laid down the jackhammer and stalked over to the electrical outlet set into Higgy's outside wall. Maybe she'd tripped the ground fault breaker. She switched outlets and punched the reset button, then resolutely walked back to take up the jackhammer again.

You chisel this up, you can't get it back.

That was the point. She needed to do something irrevo-cable to show her commitment to her new path. To prove to herself she was over Michael.

Ha! You'll never be over him. You can't even carve up the sidewalk with his name on it.

The hell she couldn't. Grimly, Selina grasped hold of the jackhammer and flicked the switch again.

It jumped to life in her hands.

The power of the jackhammer was unexpected. It jerked her around like a rag doll. Her top teeth slammed against her bottom teeth, rattling her head. Her boobs jiggled. Her entire body vibrated. She felt as if she were inside a food processor.

The force was so strong she couldn't hold it in place.

On the sidewalk, the chisel tip bounced across the sur-face of the cement, hopping adroitly over the letters she was trying to destroy, doing little more than kicking up dust. Purposefully, she gripped the jackhammer tighter. The tip made a loud *rat-tat-tat* noise as it bit shallowly into the cement. Yes, yes, it was working. She could do this.

But her triumph was short-lived when she realized the tip had moved so much she was no longer even on the same square. She was chiseling up someone else's heart-felt declaration of love.

Crap!

She tried to drag the jackhammer back to the right square but her arms felt like they'd been jerked from their sockets. Dirt flew into her mouth and she spat, only to taste a fresh round of grit. Her hair swung, slapped across her face. Her eyes watered. Her ears rang. She trembled from head to toe. Maybe she should have spent a few weeks pumping iron at the gym before tackling this project.

To hell with it.

Selina dropped the jackhammer. It snaked across the ground, vibrating impotently. Angered by her lack of results, she grabbed hold of the extension cord and tugged it out of the wall.

The jackhammer fell silent. Cement dust motes swirled in the suddenly still air, but her ears kept ringing.

She looked up. A small knot of old-timers had appeared in the doorway of Higgy's Diner. They stared owlishly at her. Nodding curtly, she picked up the jackhammer, ignored her throbbing arms, and dragged the damn thing the four blocks back to the hardware store.

"You gotta clean it if you want your deposit back," said the kid behind the counter. He had a stainless-steel spike in his chin and a tattoo of a snake trailing up one arm.

"Keep the deposit," she snarled.

"Dude," the kid said, raising his arms defensively. "I just work here."

Selina narrowed her eyes at the teen, who could have stepped right out of a *Beavis and Butt-Head* cartoon. "You ever been in love?"

"No," he said.

"You're smart." She pointed at him. "Stay away from love. Have sex if you want, but stay away from love. And for God's sake, use a condom. You're certainly in no position to care for a wife and children."

The kid looked stunned by her frankness for a fraction of a second, then he snorted a laugh as Selina turned and walked out of the store, feeling hurt and angry and defeated. She couldn't even do a simple thing like break up a chunk of concrete.

But there was something far more irrevocable than jackhammering up Main Street that she could do.

Selina went home and climbed the stairs to her bedroom. She plucked the divorce papers off the bureau, sat down at her desk, and signed them. Then she stuck the papers in an envelope, sealed the flap shut, and took it to the post office.

Chapter 16

It was pitch dark by the time they arrived at the rustic cabin deep in the heart of the state park. Brody's pickup truck was laden with supplies for their sexual tryst and Rachael's body was tense with anticipation. She'd been waiting for this from the moment he'd dragged her down off the billboard.

Brody had called Zeke and told him not to contact him for the remainder of the weekend unless it was for an extreme emergency. Rachael tried to phone her mother to tell her that she wouldn't be home until Monday morning, but Selina wasn't picking up, so she'd just left a voice mail. Deep inside she was hoping that her parents had mended fences and at this very moment were together rekindling old sparks. The thought made her happy.

And so did the fact that she was here with Brody.

A comfortable silence had descended over them and they didn't speak as they unloaded the truck and settled into the cabin. Brody started a fire while Rachael took a shower. Neither of them had wanted to go home for clean clothes or toothbrushes, so when they'd stopped off at Wal-Mart for the food, they'd each bought toiletries, a change of clothes, and a big box of condoms. They didn't want anything to mar the delicious momentum that had them traveling headlong into wilderness lust.

Lust, Rachael kept reminding herself, was all this was.

Rachael emerged from the shower feeling fresh and clean. She pulled on the sage green long-sleeved cotton top she'd bought and paired it with black Lycra lounge pants and fluffy avocado-colored socks. She brushed her hair until it shone and when she was finally ready, she took a deep breath and slipped into the main room of the cabin.

A crackling fire in the fireplace greeted her along with the aroma of grilling meat.

"Mmm," she said, coming up behind Brody, who was standing beside the indoor grill, tongs in hand. She slipped her arms around his waist. "He can start a fire and cook, too. What more could a girl ask for?"

"If you don't know," he said, reaching out to wrap his arm around her shoulder and draw her closer to his side, "I've got a lot to teach you."

Grinning, she went up on tiptoes to nibble his earlobe.

Immediately, his body tightened. "Woman," he said, "you're playing with fire."

"Nothing wrong with that."

"There is if you don't want your steak singed." He dipped his head and gave her a quick kiss. "Now behave and toss the salad. We have the rest of the night for dessert."

"Okay," she said. "I'll toss the salad and keep an eye on those T-bones while you grab a quick shower."

"Are you suggesting I stink?" He laughed.

"Hey, if the wading boot fits..." She grinned, feeling lighter-hearted than she'd felt in a very long time.

While Brody showered, Rachael tore romaine lettuce

with her fingers and grated fresh Parmesan cheese for
Caesar salad. She popped a loaf of French bread into the
oven to heat and flipped the steaks over.

A few minutes later, Brody came back into the room
toweling his wet hair, wearing pajama bottoms and a University of Texas T-shirt. Her gaze tracked the length of
his body. Broad shoulders, flat abs, lean hips. When she
reached his feet, her heart clutched.

He was barefooted and her eyes lingered on his artificial leg. Looking at it made her stomach hurt for him and
all that he'd suffered. She quickly looked up to see that
he'd followed her gaze and a somber expression had darkened his eyes.

"Scary, huh?" he said.

"No, no," she murmured. "Not scary. Not scary at all.
It's a symbol of your honor and bravery. The leg doesn't
bother me."

"Don't feel obligated to patronize me."

Her heart clutched for everything he'd lost. The skeptical expression on his face was just so darned vulnerable
she couldn't stand it. Anxious to make it clear that his
handicap didn't matter to her in the least, she crossed the
room, reached up to wrap her arms around his neck, and
pulled his head down for a long, heartfelt kiss.

"Hmm," he said, when they came up for air. "We better
check those steaks."

"Pull them off the grill. I'll set the table."

She set the table and took the bread from the oven. He
plated the steaks and opened a bottle of pinot noir. They
sat across from each other at the redwood table. The cozy
atmosphere, the smell of great food, the company of the
ruggedly handsome man stirred romantic feelings and her
mind immediately started to spin "what if?" scenarios,

but she realized what she was doing and stopped herself
before her fantasies spun completely out of control.

*Live in the moment. Forget about tomorrow. Forget
about everything except now.*

The thought freed her and she settled down at the table
across from Brody with an uncluttered mind.

"A toast." Brody held up his wine glass.

Rachael raised hers. "What are we toasting?"

"To living in the moment."

The hairs on her forearms stood at attention. He'd read
her mind. How eerie was that?

"To the moment," Rachael echoed and she clinked the
lip of her glass against his.

They ate without speaking. The silence was comfortable, anticipatory. She watched him watching her enjoy
the meal. The steak was cooked perfectly, the salad crisp
and fresh, the bread warm and hearty, the soothing wine
washed it all down. The fire crackled. The smell of pine
wood wafted on the air. She allowed herself to fully experience the moment without wondering what was going to
happen next.

Following the meal, they cleared off the table and
washed the dishes together. Brody poured them both a
second glass of wine, then took her by the hand and led
her gently to the sofa in front of the crackling fire.

He took her hands in his. Rachael realized she was
trembling.

"You're chilled," he said and she didn't contradict
him even though she wasn't cold. She was trembling in
anticipation.

"Brody," she murmured. "Brody."

He dipped his head until his mouth was almost touching hers. "Yes, Rachael?"

Time hung suspended as they stared deeply into each other's eyes, his lips so close she could already taste the pinot noir on him, his fingers kneading her knuckles. Her speeding pulse raced blood through her body.

"Rachael," he whispered, his breath warm against her skin.

"Brody."

Lightly, he squeezed her fingers, the pressure sweet and reassuring. But she wasn't looking for sweet. She wanted sex. Good, hard sex. No romantic trappings. No idealizing something that didn't need idealizing.

Brody was so different from any other man she'd ever known. He had a calm, unflappable exterior but inside he seethed with a smoldering intensity. He was brave, but vulnerable. Honorable, but wary of people. The contradictions in him were exciting. A complicated man full of surprises.

And carnal delights.

His tongue was doing crazy, thrilling things while at the same time his calloused palm was pushing up under the hem of her T-shirt, to discover she was not wearing a bra. He made an appreciative noise as his hot fingers gently grazed her bare breasts.

In the past, she'd always closed her eyes when being kissed. It helped her to romanticize the moment. Carried her away to some sweet dreamland. But she no longer wanted anything to do with fantasy. She wanted the real man. She wanted to experience every sensation now.

His eyes were open as well and he was looking into her as deeply as she was looking into him. His tongue dueled with hers and his fingers stroked her breasts. His gaze was a vortex, drawing her into him, holding her pinned gloriously to the spot, his body doing wild things to hers. His palms planed her skin, thumb and index fingers of both hands nimbly squeezing her nipples.

Rachael moaned and arched into him.

"I've gotta have you now," he said. "I've been wanting you for three months. I can't wait any longer."

He stood up then, holding his hands out to her. She got to her feet and he led her to the bed in the opposite corner of the room. Her heart fluttered as fast as hummingbird wings.

He tugged her shirt off and then she pulled his over his head. Their gazes fixed on each other as they simultaneously tossed the garments onto the floor.

"Aw, Peaches," he said when he saw her breasts. "Your breasts are even prettier than I imagined they were."

"Don't call me Peaches," she whispered.

"Oh, right," he said. "No romance. Just sex."

"That's right."

Sexual tension pulsed between them, an alluring, blistering force. At the look of red-hot desire in his eyes, Rachael felt her cheeks burn.

He went down on his left leg in front of her, splayed a hand at the small of her back and pulled her to him. His mouth was level with her lust-swollen breasts. And when his tongue flicked out to gently suckle one protruding nipple, she hissed in a sharp breath and planted both her palms on his head.

While his tongue slowly licked her heated flesh, his hand strayed to untie the drawstring of her pants. He edged them down her legs, fingers skimming her thighs as he went. The center of her throbbed at the memory of his lips, of what he'd done to her in the boat. Instantly, she felt herself grow wet for him all over again.

She was acutely aware of everything. His touch. His

scent. The sound of his breathing. The taste of her own desire burning on her tongue hot as cinnamon.

He inched her panties down as well until her clothes pooled at her feet. He buried his face in the triangle of hair between her thighs and breathed deep. "God, you smell great."

Feeling slightly embarrassed, she stepped away from him and out of her clothing. It wasn't fair. She was undressed and he still had his pants on.

She held out her hands to him. "On your feet, Carlton."

Brody glanced up at her and she could see the hesitation etched on his face. He'd been dragging this out, trying to avoid the moment when he had to get completely naked in front of her.

He was a little off-balance and he had to take hold of her hand to keep from falling over when he pushed up off the floor. When he was standing again, she reached for the waistband of his pajama bottoms that barely contained his erection.

Her eyes latched onto his.

He looked a bit panicky. The pulse at his throat jumped and he had his jaw clenched tight.

"I..." Brody cleared his throat. "Rachael...there's something you've got to know before we take this any farther."

"Shhh, there's nothing to tell," she said, running her hands underneath his waistband. His bare skin was so warm to her touch, his body so responsive.

"Listen to me." He grasped her by the shoulders, cupped her chin in his palm, and forced her to look him. The expression on his face was somber.

She straightened. "I'm listening."

"I haven't..." He hesitated, his dark eyes growing darker

still. He heaved in a deep breath. "I haven't been with a woman since..."

She waited. Didn't prompt him. Let him go at his own pace.

"Since I lost my leg."

At once she understood his fear. He was afraid of disappointing her in bed, worried that he couldn't measure up to a man with two good legs. Rachael laced her fingers together around his waist and didn't break his gaze.

"It's okay," she murmured. "It's all right. Everything is going to be just fine."

"What if I..." He swallowed. "Can't live up to my end of the bargain?"

"Brody," she said. "Being here with you is the bargain. Anything else that happens is just cream on the peaches."

The look of gratitude that came into his eyes humbled her. To think he held her in such high regard!

She kissed him then, like she'd never kissed him before. Poured her heart and soul into it. Showing him without having to tell him how special this moment was to her, what a unique man he was. She rained kisses on his mouth, his chin, his jaw, and down his throat.

It seemed as if he was the first man who'd ever really seen her. It was as if he saw straight to the essence of who she really was. Neither a romantic nor a cynic. Neither a kindergarten teacher nor a columnist for *Texas Monthly*. Neither a starry-eyed bride-to-be nor someone's jilted fiancée.

She was simply Rachael.

In that moment she experienced total serenity. As if the world had finally clicked into place and nothing could disturb her equanimity. All these years she'd been chasing happily-ever-after. Holding on to and intensifying romantic feelings through her active imagination. Tying herself up, holding herself down with unrealistic expectations.

But through Brody's eyes she glimpsed her authentic self.

It wasn't some romantic notion. It wasn't a flight of fancy. It had nothing to do with elaborate emotions or tender feelings or the intensity of intimate dreams. It was a tangible, unshakable knowledge. A deep-down abiding faith in him.

And it confused her deeply.

Slowly, he took off his pants and sank down on the bed. He gave her a wan smile. "This is me baring myself in front of you."

"Thank you," she said. "For trusting me."

Rachael's gaze strayed to his penis and she gulped back her amazement. God might have taken this man's leg, but he'd graced him in other ways.

He followed her gaze and chuckled. "Is that wide-eyed look for me?"

Mutely, she nodded.

"I promise to be gentle with you if you promise to be gentle with me," he teased, and she loved that he could joke about this. "Unless, of course, you're not into gentle."

"Gentle is good." Okay, so maybe earlier she'd wanted hard, pumping sex, but now that had given way to this perfect-pitch moment and she was going with the flow. Gentle sounded fabulous.

Brody lay back against the pillows without taking off his Power Knee. He reached for her and pulled her down beside him. Cradling her in the crook of his arm, he smiled into her eyes.

Feeling utterly treasured, she curled against him.

He kissed her with exquisite tenderness, while he stroked her skin with the back of his hand. Slowly, leisurely, they explored each other with all five of their senses. Massaging, caressing, licking, tasting, finding the spots that made each other sigh, moan, and whisper.

"Give me your hand," he said.

She placed her hand in his and he guided her palm to his chest. She felt his heart thundering underneath his breastbone as if he'd just completed a triathlon. Curiosity fused her hand to his skin. She couldn't pull away.

Mesmerized. They stared into each other.

Magic. It felt like total magic.

It hit her then, what she was doing. Going down the wrong path, romanticizing this moment. Romanticizing him. She knew better, but the slow tempo he'd set had drawn her into the magic of the moment. She had to break the spell.

Live in the moment. Stop thinking. Just be.

Good advice, but how could she do that when he was looking at her as if she was the most precious thing he'd ever seen? Only one way. Sex. Not love. Not tenderness. Not emotional intimacy. Just sex. Hard and hot and real. Powerful, orgasmic sex to blow away the mist of fantasy.

She removed her hand from his chest and pushed him back against the pillow with both hands. She captured his mouth with hers, pulled his bottom lip up between her teeth, and bit down lightly.

He groaned.

Yeah, this was the ticket.

She pulled away to slide her mouth down his neck one hot kiss at a time. She tracked a path from his throat down the middle of his chest—with a quick detour to his nipples—before resuming her trek over his muscled abdomen, past his navel, to his pelvis, and finally ending up at his most impressive erection.

He shuddered when her lips touched his hot moist tip.

"Mmm," she murmured. "You taste delicious."

"Hang on," he said. "Two can play at this game."

"What...?" she asked, pushing her hair back from her face.

But he already had his hands around her waist, maneuvering them around so that while she was licking him like a lollipop, he was angling his head toward her most sensitive spot.

She sucked in her breath as his tongue flicked at her inner cleft. To counter his surprise, she stretched her lips over the expansive width of his penis.

His tongue was hot and wet and so was hers.

She swirled. He licked.

Up and down, around and around until they were both moaning and writhing, consumed by mutual pleasure.

On and on they played. He on her, she on him. Licking, sucking, tasting. Glorious sensations rippled through her body, turning her inside out. They increased the tempo as the pressure built, rising to the inevitable crescendo.

Rachael mewled softly whenever he did something right, grunted when he made a wrong move. It didn't take him long to pick up her rhythms, learn what she liked and give her more of it.

She took him deeper until she felt him pressing against the back of her throat, juicy and slick. She rolled her lips back, stretching wider to accommodate his bigness. She wanted to swallow all of him.

Finally Brody broke away, pulling his mouth from her throbbing anxious clit. "I can't stand it anymore. I have to be inside you."

"Condoms," she gasped, so addled by passion she was impressed that she had remembered. Thank heavens she'd remembered.

"I'm on it," Brody said, stumbling from the bed. He returned in a matter of seconds, but she was already drifting down from the pinnacle.

"Hang on," he panted, ripping open the box with his teeth and sending packets of condoms flying around the room. One smacked Rachael on her belly.

"Let me." She laughed and peeled open the foil wrapping. He was already in bed again. The leg didn't slow him down one bit. Rachael popped the condom between her teeth and proceeded to roll it onto him.

He groaned, took her by the shoulders, and flipped her onto her back. He was trembling so hard he could barely mount her.

And then he was inside.

She'd never had a man so thick, filling her up until she feared she might not be able to take any more.

"Peaches, you're dripping wet for me."

"I am, Brody, I am."

He was so damned beautiful. Hard, lean, a fine spray of dark hair between his nipples. Her hips twitched against his, the muscles between her thighs clenching.

Their breathing changed, getting hoarser, raspier. Their coupling was primal now. Fierce and hungry. He plunged heedlessly into her, driving them closer and closer to the edge.

They were almost there. Both of them. Ready to come together. As one.

"Ah-ah-ah." Rachael made a noise, desperate, hungry.

He must have misinterpreted her sound of encouragement and thought she wanted him to hurry when she wanted the exact opposite. He began to pump faster, sliding in and out of her, quickening his rhythm.

Why was he speeding up when they'd been so in sync before? If he kept this up, he was going to go off without her. Half-cocked.

It had been too long for him. She feared he wasn't going to last.

And then Brody just stopped.

Rachael felt as if she'd been left hanging headfirst off a cliff. Bizarre sensation. Then she realized her shoulders and head had slipped off the bed and she was indeed dangling.

"You're falling off the bed." Brody slipped out of her and gently moved her back onto the pillows.

They looked at each other.

"I was going too fast," he said.

She nodded.

"Tell me these things. Don't let me be a bad lover," he pleaded and his vulnerability hit her straight in the heart.

She stroked him, but kept talking, low and soothing. "You're not a bad lover, not at all. You're just a surprise. It's okay if our first time together feels a little strange."

In the past, she would have taken any glitch in lovemaking as a sign they weren't meant to be. Now, that seemed incredibly shortsighted. They were just getting to know each other's bodies.

"I surprise you?" he asked.

"Sheriff," she said huskily, "you have no idea."

"How do we overcome this strangeness?"

"No way through it . . ." she started to say.

"Except to do it," he finished for her.

They smiled at each other.

And began anew.

He kept up the steady rocking, driving her deeper and deeper into the savage wanting that was changing everything she had ever known about herself and what she was capable of.

Brody thrust into her again and again. His entire being seemed to slide deeper and deeper into hers until she could not differentiate where her body stopped and his began.

Something earth-shattering happened. Something she'd never experienced before. It was as if his soul had leaped from his body and shot straight into hers along with his orgasm.

He cried out as his essence poured out of him, imbuing her with streaming currents of his masculine energy.

Together, they melted.

Nothing else existed.

Even the cabin was gone, disappearing in the laser-beam moment of blissful orgasmic feeling.

He cried out one last time and shoved himself as deep as he could go into her warmth.

The walls of her sucked at him, gripping, kneading, pulling this man into the very core of her.

Mystical, magical sparks of flesh and fire melded together. Shattering, scattering, torturing. Melting her heart from the inside out.

A second orgasm sprang up from inside her groin, flooded her body, drowning her brain. She was numb, wrung, spent.

Brody's body shuddered, then went limp.

They clung to each other, helpless, as wave after wave of energy rippled through them. Gasping, he rolled over, sinking onto his back and taking her with him. He held her close as her chest heaved and quivered.

She slipped her arms around his powerful neck,

squeezing him tight as tears flowed warm and free down her cheeks. His strength pinched her chest and stole her breath.

And she had the most terrifying feeling that he had given her his heart for safekeeping and she had tucked it irrevocably inside her soul.

Rachael woke in the night to find Brody snuggled up behind her. His thick forearm was thrown around her waist, her butt tucked against his pelvis. In that brief moment of hazy half-sleep, Rachael allowed herself to dream.

Mine.

Joy flooded her heart. Weightlessness lifted her mind. Her toes curled inside her socks and a grin spread across her face. But just as quickly as her joy came, it was immediately replaced with crippling fear.

Her smiled vanished. Her toes straightened. Reality stomped around inside her head like a stevedore in hobnailed boots. The joy drained from her heart, swirled away into the darkness of the quiet cabin.

She'd been here before. Thought the same romantic thoughts. Found out later she was wrong. She'd promised herself she wasn't going to romanticize any man ever again and she'd gone and done that very thing with Brody.

Sadly, the poor guy had no clue what he'd let himself in for and she had a horrible feeling he was falling in love with her.

Hope flickered again, a desperate flame struggling to take hold. Ruthlessly, Rachael snubbed it out. No. She was not doing this again.

He stirred in his sleep, pulling her tighter against him.

Panic flapped inside her rib cage. She wriggled out from under his arm and sat up. She had to distance herself.

"Rachael?" he mumbled drowsily. "Are you okay?"

"Fine, go back to sleep, just heading for the bathroom."

"Hurry back," he said and patted the spot beside him. "It's lonesome without you."

Lonesome without you.

Oh! She so wanted to rhapsodize that comment. Instead, she dug her fingernails into her palms and padded to the bathroom.

She stayed in the bathroom for at least fifteen minutes, giving him time to fall back asleep. Finally, after her butt grew numb from sitting so long on the toilet, she headed back to bed.

And the minute she sank down onto the mattress, his arm was around her again, drawing her flush against him as if they were spoons in a drawer.

Wistfulness mingled with regret inside her. Why couldn't she have met him before Trace and Robert and all the others?

Wait. She had met him first. He was her first unrequited love. He'd had his chance and he blew it.

Come on. You were seven. He was twelve. It was a childhood crush. What did you expect from him?

The heat from his body warmed her. The reassuring sound of his steady breathing made her feel safe. The smell of him was in her nose, rich and masculine and so utterly . . . Brody.

"What's the matter, Peaches?"

Peaches. His pet name for her. Oh gosh, she was going to have to hurt him.

"Nothing," she mumbled.

"Can't sleep?"

She didn't answer.

"Would you like to talk about it?" he asked.

Now was as good a time as any, she supposed, to get it over with.

"I ..." she started. "I have a feeling you want more than I can give you."

He responded by pushing her hair aside and kissing the nape of her neck. "I have no expectations."

"Honestly?" She turned, faced him.

"Honestly."

"Um ... why not?"

"Why not what?"

"Why are you satisfied with what you can get? Don't you want the fairy tale? Great love, kids, happily-ever-after."

"The fairy tale is a myth," he said. "You know that."

"What about great love?"

"Great love scares the hell out of me."

"Really? How come? I was under the impression nothing scared you."

He didn't say anything for the longest time and she figured he wasn't going to tell her, then he said, "I saw great love destroy my parents."

She rested her chin on his chest and looked into his eyes. It was too dark to see any more than a glimmer. His body was a rock-solid layer of muscle beneath his skin, hard and warm.

"Love destroyed them? How?"

He shifted. She felt his breathing quicken.

"My parents were always that couple you see holding hands at the shopping mall. The couple who give each other knowing looks across a crowded room, even after they've been married for years. You never saw one without the other. They were always together."

"That's how my parents were. It was nice," Rachael whispered.

"Mom got sick," Brody continued. "She needed an operation but we didn't have any insurance because my dad was self-employed. Her surgery was going to cost double my dad's annual salary. This was during the first Gulf War and oil companies were paying huge amounts of money for people to rebuild Kuwait. My dad signed up to go in order to earn money for my mother's surgery. That's why we left Valentine when I was twelve. To go live with my mother's parents in Midland while my dad was away."

He told the story matter-of-factly, but Rachael heard the underlying pain in his voice.

"Six months later, my dad died in an oil-rig accident in Kuwait." Brody loosened his grip on her. "My mother was devastated."

Silence filled the cabin. An ember from the fireplace glowed dark red.

"The company had taken out life insurance on him, but by the time all the legal rigmarole was over and the money arrived, my mother was dead."

"Oh no." Rachael hissed in a breath.

"Not from her illness. If she'd held on, the operation would have had a good chance of curing her, but out of grief over losing my father. Without him, she didn't want to live. Not even for Deana and me."

"I'm so sorry, Brody."

He grunted. "So was I. But losing my parents at such a young age taught me a lot. It taught me how to stand on my own two feet and not depend on anyone to rescue me. It taught me life was damned hard. And, it taught me to stay away from great love."

"So," she said. "You've spent your life avoiding great love. That's why you married a woman you didn't really love. Because it was safe."

"Something along those lines."

Tears for everything he had suffered welled up inside her. She wanted to tell him great love was worth taking a chance on, but she didn't know that. She'd taken chance after chance and she'd never found the kind of great love his parents had shared.

"You see, Peaches, you've got nothing to be scared of where I'm concerned. So you can relax. The last thing I'm looking for is a great love."

Chapter 17

Long after Rachael had gone back to sleep, Brody lay in bed listening to the gentle sounds of her soft breathing and thinking about how he'd lied to her.

He'd told her he wasn't looking for a great love. The truth was, he'd already found it.

In her.

But he knew if he'd said that, if he'd given her the slightest inkling that he was stone-cold in love with her, she would run for the hills, afraid of her own feelings, afraid to take one last gamble on love.

He realized the only way to convince her was to not convince her. He couldn't romance her, no badly how he might want to. Romantic gestures would make her skeptical. She'd learned to see right through flowers and candy and long moonlit walks. The woman needed substance. A man she could believe in.

And he was determined to be that man. No matter how hard it was to keep his distance.

She was staunch in her anti-romance stance and he applauded her for her convictions. She'd grown a great deal in the past few months. She had gone from starry-eyed innocent, ready to believe any man who murmured the words "I love you," to a self-confident woman who refused to let anyone define who and what she was capable of becoming. He admired her for that, even though it made things harder for him.

He also had to admit he liked the challenge. And when he won her, it would be for all the marbles—a ring, marriage, commitment, kids, happily-ever-after, a forever kind of love.

Because Rachael wasn't the only one who had changed, and he hadn't fully realized it until tonight, until he'd been inside her, made love to her, fused with her.

He'd been wrong about his parents, about great love. He understood now that he was experiencing it. Great love didn't destroy. It made you whole in a way nothing else ever could. Rachael made him feel that way. Whole again.

And for a man who'd lost his leg, feeling whole again had seemed impossible.

He loved her not just for what she was—which in itself was significant with her beauty, her spontaneity, and her profound passion for life—but for what he was when he was with her.

Rachael's honesty about her emotions and inner struggles helped him face his own feelings. Feelings he'd kept buried for a long time, feelings that needed to be examined and then released. Her playful charm made him feel like a kid again, unburdened and free. And her supportive compassion had him trying his best to live up to the ideal of the man he saw in her eyes.

He loved her not for what she had made of herself— turning from a jilted bride dependent on a man for her self-worth into a sharp woman in charge of her own life—but for what she was turning him into, a man who was no longer afraid to put his heart on the line.

And that was the thing, wasn't it? He was no longer afraid, but she was. Ironic, really.

Brody smiled into the darkness, smiled and smiled and smiled because he knew she didn't have a chance. One way or the other, he was going to have her heart. And he could wait until she was ready because Rachael was worth waiting for.

Brody had a plan for trapping the vandal. His time with Rachael had unleashed his creativity and he realized what he could do to put a stop to the shenanigans that had been disrupting his town.

The Monday after the fishing tournament and his rendezvous with Rachael, he strode into Kelvin's office. "I want to borrow your mock-up replica of Valentine Land and put it on display in the town square."

Kelvin leaned back in his chair, feet propped on his desk. "Now why in the hell do you think I would agree to that? The model was ten years in the making."

"To catch the vandal and up your chances of getting the bond election passed."

That got the mayor's attention. He sat up straight, dropped his feet to the floor and leaned forward, fingers steepled. "I'm listening."

Michael had spent the weekend trying to get hold of Selina but she didn't answer her phone or come to the door. They'd been close to something out there on the lake before Vivian had shown up and ruined it all.

He hung around Higgy's Diner hoping Selina would show up in town. Audie Gaston took great delight in telling the story of how Selina had rented a jackhammer to break up their heart on the Walk of Flames. Michael's heart had slid uneasily in his chest. He'd gone right out and counted out the squares. One, two, three, four. There it was, scuffed but still intact. He'd inhaled a hungry lungful of air and it was only then that he realized he'd been holding his breath.

On the following Monday Michael walked the quarter mile down their driveway to the heart-shaped mailbox in his boxer shorts and bathrobe. On the stroll, he'd been thinking about ways to win Selina back. Romantic gestures hadn't worked. Neither had Rachael's advice to leave her alone. He knew there had to be some way to get through to her; he just didn't know what that was.

He popped open the mailbox lid, took out the bills and circulars and the ubiquitous credit card applications, and then he saw it.

The yellow envelope from Purdy Maculroy.

Michael's heart pinched painfully. He slipped a finger underneath the flap and got a nasty paper cut, but he barely felt it. His heart was what hurt as he took out the divorce papers, flipped to the back, and saw Selina's signature.

The pain in his chest intensified, shot up his shoulder, down his back, through his arm. The cut on his index finger was leaving dabs of blood on the divorce papers. His vision blurred. Sweat popped out on his forehead. He sat down hard on the ground, clutching his left arm. His mouth went dry. His body shook.

His heart!

He'd never felt such pain.

Later the doctors told him that if Brody Carlton hadn't driven by when he did, Michael wouldn't have survived the heart attack.

*   *   *

Selina and Rachael arrived at the hospital together and raced to Michael's bedside. The minute Selina saw her husband lying in the hospital bed hooked up to tubes and machinery she wanted to burst into tears. She was heartsick for the man she'd loved for as long as she could remember.

She expected Michael to say something to her but he did not. Instead he looked at Rachael. "Sweetheart, tell your mother to sit down. She looks like she's about to faint."

What? He wasn't even going to speak to her directly? Selina swayed on her feet. If Michael wouldn't talk to her after a heart attack it truly meant things were over for them. The thought hit her in the belly like a solid punch. She'd lost him forever.

"Mom?"

Rachael's voice sounded far away. She felt her daughter's hand on her shoulder, pushing her down onto the plastic chair at Michael's bedside. Selina swallowed back the tears. Even when she'd been so angry over Vivian she'd never stopped loving him. She'd simply been hoping against hope that he would prove to her she truly was the one he loved. That she hadn't made a mistake all those years ago.

Now those hopes were shattered.

But he was still the father of her children and she cared about him, even if he didn't care about her.

Michael didn't meet her gaze. "Rachael, could you run down to the cafeteria and get me a soda from the Coke machine?"

"You're not supposed to have..." Selina started, then bit down on her bottom lip.

"Sure, Daddy." Rachael headed for the door.

"Why don't you go ahead and have breakfast while you're down there," he said. "The nurse told me they have an omelet station until ten."

Was he sending Rachael away on purpose? Hope lifted her heart.

"You want to be alone with Mom?"

A muscle ticked at her husband's eye. He nodded, but did not smile. An ominous feeling twisted inside Selina and her hopes nosedived.

"She looks stretched thin," he commented as the door shut behind their daughter.

"Rachael's got a lot on her mind. She's divided the town and it's eating her alive. She wants what she wants but she doesn't want anyone else to get hurt in the process."

"I know how she feels," Michael murmured.

He looked so pale beneath his tan. Selina knotted her fingers together, dropped her hands into her lap, and stared down at her interlaced digits as if they belonged to someone else.

Then he reached out and placed a hand on her arm. She lifted her head.

He gazed at her and the steady light in his eyes stirred up memories of how gentle he'd been with her on the first night they'd slept together. The night she'd given him her virginity on a pallet under a carpet of stars at Lake Valentine. She thought about how his eyes had sparked with happiness when she'd told him she was pregnant with Rachael. She hadn't imagined it. He *had* wanted that child. What she'd never been certain of was if he'd really wanted her.

As he squeezed her elbow and his eyes darkened with sadness, Selina realized how quick she'd been to assume the worst, to doubt his love. She'd needed far too much proof. Why had she been so insecure? Could her insecurity be the very thing that had pushed him away?

He took her hand in his, raised it to his lips, and gently kissed her knuckles. His lips were cool against her skin. His expression was serious.

"I'm so glad you came, Selina."

"You're my husband," she said. "You had a heart attack. Why wouldn't I come?"

"Because you won't speak to me. Because you signed the divorce papers. Because ... I hurt you."

"No more than I hurt you," she admitted.

He looked at her and the expression in his eyes was so intensely remorseful she felt as if she'd been struck across the face. "I want ..." He swallowed.

"Yes?" She leaned in close, breath bated. The hope was back, stronger than ever.

He frowned, but didn't continue.

Her heart skipped a beat. "Michael," she said at the same time he said, "Selina."

Her name on his lips sounded like a prayer. A shiver went through her, stark and anxious.

"Don't die on me," she whispered. "We need to get this worked out. Need to get beyond this."

"I'm not going to die."

"You promise?" She could no longer contain the tears pressing against the back of her eyes. They seeped out, rolling down her cheeks.

"Aw, sweetheart." He reached up to flick away her tears with his thumbs. "Don't cry."

"I've been so stupid."

"No," he said. "I was the stupid one. Looking back to the past, trying to recapture my youth."

"You don't"—Selina hesitated, gulped back the tears— "want Vivian?"

Michael's harsh laugh sounded hollow inside the room. "I never wanted Vivian. It was foolish. I just wanted the way she made me feel. Like a young, virile stud."

"And I don't make you feel like that," she said flatly. "Marriage ruins the fantasy."

"It's a ridiculous fantasy," he said. "And I was looking like exactly what I was, a silly old fart trying to hang on to his youth. What I didn't realize was how selfish I'd been. All these years I kept holding on to the thought of what I might have been if you hadn't gotten pregnant. If I'd married Vivian. If I'd gone to Harvard."

Selina sucked in her breath, knotted her hands into fists. She'd known it. For twenty-seven years Michael had wondered what it would have been like to have a different life, a different wife. All the time he was sending her flowers and cards and showering her with gifts, he'd just been trying to convince himself he'd done the right thing. Married the right woman.

"You're free to go to her now," Selina said. "I won't hold you back. I'm sorry you've felt chained to me for so long." She tried to pull away from his grasp but Michael wouldn't let go.

"No, no; you made me see the light. It wasn't until you left me that I finally understood. I belong here in Valentine. I would never have been happy on the East Coast. Texas is in my blood. And I'm sure if I'd married Vivian we wouldn't have lasted a year."

The depth of emotion in his voice touched Selina profoundly. Finally, he was letting go of the past and getting in touch with the part of himself he'd let get pushed aside while he chased a fantasy.

"I'm sorry for the hurt I put you through."

"It's okay. It's all right."

"It's not. I'm to blame for what went wrong between us."

"No one is one hundred percent wrong," she said, finally realizing she had been laying one hundred percent of the blame on him. "I was too ready to imagine the worst of you."

Was it her imagination? Was it his near death experience? Or was that a deeply compassionate look in his eyes she'd never seen before?

"Why was that, Selina?" He stroked the back of her knuckles with his thumb. "Why couldn't you believe I really loved you?"

Selina swallowed. "I never felt good enough for you. A Mexican girl whose family owned the local taco restaurant. You a hilltop Henderson. Everyone knew you were marrying me because I was pregnant."

"That's not true," he said. "I'd been carrying your engagement ring around in my pocket for weeks before you told me about the baby, trying to work up the courage to ask you to be my wife. Ask Kelvin. He knew how nervous I was that you'd turn me down flat."

Selina sat up straight. "How come you never told me that?"

A sheepish expression crossed his face, making him appear incredibly boyish for his forty-six years. "I was afraid you wouldn't believe me."

She opened her mouth to protest, but then shut it. He was right. She wouldn't have believed him.

For a long moment, she just sat there studying him, thinking about the past and all they'd been through together. The ups and the downs. The highs and the lows. How far they'd come together. How much farther they had to go.

Michael toyed with her engagement ring and wedding band. "You're still wearing my rings."

She met his gaze. "Yes."

"I'm sorry, Selina," he said, his voice choked with husky emotion. "It was never my intention to hurt you. Since you've been gone I've realized how much I need you. How much a part of my life you are. Ever since you walked out, it's like my right arm has been amputated. Selina, I love you more now than the day we got married. I've never stopped loving you in spite of having acted like a damned fool. Please come home. I . . ."

His words trailed off. She was shocked to see a mist of tears in his eyes. She'd never seen her husband cry. Not even when he lost his parents. Not even when their children were born.

He held his arms out to her and she came to him, gingerly resting her head on his chest as he held her. Emotions fluttered inside her. Such a mix of feelings, misting her own eyes, filling her heart. He wrapped both arms around her and kissed the top of her head.

"Selina," he murmured. "My sweet, sweet Selina."

She tilted her face up to look at him. He brushed his lips against hers. "I wish," he said, "I wasn't hooked up to all this tomfoolery. I'd show you exactly how happy I am to have you in my arms again."

"Shh." She placed an index finger against his lips. "There will be time enough for that as soon as you get well."

"Sexual healing is the best medicine," he said.

"That's all going to have to wait until I get you home."

Home.

It sounded so good.

* * *

In the days leading up to the election, Brody tried his best to stick to his plan of not romancing Rachael, no matter how much he longed to do exactly that. Instead, he treated her like his oldest and dearest friend, and when he thought about it, that was precisely what she was.

They'd been kids in the sandbox together, living side by side until his family had moved away when he was twelve. He went through old scrapbooks and family photo albums and found pictures of them at backyard barbecues, swimming pool get-togethers, and neighborhood block parties. When he'd first started the project, he wasn't sure what he was looking for. Maybe some inkling of a spark between them, even back then.

What he discovered was the magical childhood they'd both had until life had intervened and taken him from the gentle cocoon of Valentine, Texas.

And then he found it.

What he hadn't really known he was looking for.

A Valentine card. Dulled with age, but made by hand from construction paper and dime-store lace. Intended for the girl next door, whose birthday just happened to fall on Valentine's Day. The edges had curled, the lace yellowed, the block-letter printing faded, but the sentiment was still there—young and so heartfelt.

When he lifted the card from the keepsake box he found among his mother's things, his chest tightened and his pulse quickened. Gingerly, he thumbed the card open.

Dear Rachael, I made ya this Valentine card for your birthday. Hope you like it. Your friend, Brody.

He remembered sitting in his room, cutting out the red construction paper, gluing on the lace, setting it aside to dry when his friends had come to the front door bouncing a basketball. He'd been twelve and easily distracted. He'd gone outside to play basketball and that's when Rachael had come over.

He still remembered the stark terror that had gripped him when she'd given him a slick, store-bought card and his friends had starting chanting, "Brody and Rachael sitting in a tree..."

Humiliated in front of the guys, he hadn't even thought of her feelings, he'd just ripped the card up and shoved it back at her. Memories came rushing back as he recalled how her cute little heart-shaped face had instantly dissolved into tears. How he'd hardened his heart, desperate to look tough around his friends.

What a jerk he'd been.

Okay, he'd been an embarrassed teenager, stuck with feelings he hadn't known how to deal with, but he shouldn't have treated her so callously. You'd think his behavior would have been enough to sour her on love right there. But no, Rachael, the eternal optimist, had kept searching and getting hurt until she'd finally had enough of romance, just at the time he was learning to open up his heart and take a chance on love.

Ironic as hell.

Bide your time. Hold out. Give her a chance to break down.

Good advice, but could he do it?

Brody glanced out his bedroom window toward the house across the street. Rachael now lived alone in Mrs. Potter's old house since Selina had moved back in with Michael following his heart attack and their reconciliation.

The jaunty pink VW Bug, repainted after the graffiti incident, had just pulled into the driveway. Rachael got out with a handful of plastic grocery bags and headed toward the front door.

Mesmerized, he watched her hip-swaying walk and his heart reeled drunkenly in his chest.

I love you.

It took every ounce of control he possessed not to streak across the street after her. He stood breathing heavily, curtains parted, eyes fixed on her house long after she went inside. And if Maisy hadn't come upstairs to tell him Zeke was on the phone, Brody couldn't say how long he would have waited there for another fleeting but soul-sustaining glimpse of her.

"Vandal struck last night," Zeke said when Brody picked up the receiver. "Your trap worked. He smashed Kelvin's tiny Valentine Land to smithereens. What now?"

Brody smiled. *Gotcha.* "You and I get busy hooking black lights up to the voting booths."

By election day the black lights had been installed in all the voting booths in town and volunteers had been first tested, then given instructions to call Brody as soon as they'd identified the suspect.

The polls hadn't been open an hour when Enid Pope, who was volunteering at precinct three, located in the First Methodist Church across the street from the court-house, called Brody. "Omigoodness, Sheriff," Enid said, excitement causing her voice to come out high and reedy. "It's just like you said. Purdy Maculroy is glowing green."

"Care to tell me why you smashed Kelvin's replica to smithereens?" Brody asked Purdy as he led him to the jail cell.

"I have the right to remain silent," Purdy said.

"True, true." Brody nodded.

"These charges aren't going to stick, you know." The lawyer glared. "It's entrapment."

"You wouldn't have gotten phosphorescent paint sprayed all over you if you hadn't been vandalizing mini Valentine Land."

"How'd you know I'd vote?" Purdy asked, as good as admitting he was the culprit.

"I didn't." Brody shrugged. "I just took a chance that whoever was behind the vandalism had a political agenda."

Purdy scowled.

"You went one step too far when you graffitied Rachael's car and peeped in her window. That made it personal for me."

At that moment Kelvin came bursting through the door of the sheriff's office. "I heard you caught the bastard." He skipped to a halt in the hallway outside the jail. "Purdy?"

Kelvin jerked his head toward Brody. "It's Purdy?"

"He's the one glowing green." Brody waved a black light in front of Purdy and he lit up like a Christmas tree.

"I thought we were friends," Kelvin said. "We play golf together."

"And I always have to let you win," Purdy spit out.

"You cut the heads off the parking meters."

Purdy didn't answer.

"You cut those bicycles-built-for-two in two."

Purdy made a face.

"But why?"

"He's not talking," Brody said.

"I know why." Jamie popped out from behind the dispatcher desk. "I just got the rundown on Purdy's finances."

"Hey," Purdy said. "You have no right..."

"You've been charged with felony criminal mischief," Brody said. "Your records are up for grabs. I had Jamie contact the bank."

Jamie passed him the documents she held in her hand.

"What's this?" Brody asked. "Fifty thousand dollars was deposited into your account the morning after Rachael vandalized the billboard. And the deposit came from the town of Tyler."

"Tyler's in the running against us with Amusement Corp. You traitor!" Kelvin lunged at the bars.

Purdy backed up.

"You sold out your hometown for fifty grand." Kelvin raised a fist.

"Calm down." Brody slung an arm around Kelvin's shoulders. "The vandal's behind bars and it's election day. You've got other things to worry about."

It was the biggest election in the town's history. Main Street was lined with red, white, and blue banners. Voters packed the polling locations, many waiting in line as long as an hour to cast their ballot. A first for Valentine.

The high school gymnasium was Giada's campaign headquarters, while Kelvin's supporters collected at the courthouse. The air hummed with conversation and controversy as people argued, weighing the pros and cons of the theme park bond, the mayoral candidates, and the scandal of Purdy Maculroy.

A festive atmosphere prevailed. Higgy's Diner offered an election day–themed blue plate special menu including Pork Barrel barbecued spare ribs, Hanging Chad coleslaw, Polling Place potato salad, and Ballot baked beans. The high school marching band took several laps around the town square, tooting out a heartfelt rendition of "Stars and Stripes Forever." The two retirement homes in town made a party out of it, bringing in their voter-eligible residents in shuttle vans, most of them hopped up on Geritol, wearing slogan buttons, waving palm-sized Texas flags, and talking about back in the day when Kelvin's grandpappy had been mayor.

By the time the polls closed at seven, Giada was so nervous she briefly considered taking the Xanax that Lila Smerny, the high school librarian and her campaign manager, offered her. In the end, she waved it away. If she lost, she lost. She didn't need pharmaceuticals to cushion the blow.

The first results that came in were mixed. While Giada was excited to learn she was leading Kelvin with a two percent margin, a large majority of the voters were saying yes to the theme park bond.

"They're so misguided," she moaned to Lila. "They have no idea what this thing is going to do to our lovely little town."

"And if you win, you're going to have to handle the fallout."

Giada blew out her breath. "Thanks for reminding me."

By eight o'clock, three-quarters of the votes had been counted. Giada was leading Kelvin 564 votes to 523. There were 854 votes for Valentine Land versus 233 against. Amusement Corp had obtained the seventy-five percent approval they needed to proceed with the project.

A camera crew from Del Rio was there, covering the story on a town divided, rehashing details about Rachael and Romanceaholics Anonymous. The media presence only served to escalate Giada's anxiety.

"The Xanax is in my pocket with your name on it," Lila whispered as the reporter headed Giada's way.

"Thanks, but I can handle it."

"Ms. Vito," the reporter said. "We've just confirmed Mayor Wentworth is throwing in the towel. He's on his way over here to concede the election."

"What?" Giada hadn't expected this. Kelvin was the type to go down swinging.

At that moment, the mayor, surrounded by hangers-on, strode through the door of the gymnasium. A camera crew was trying to get to him, but Brody Carlton and his deputy Zeke were acting as bodyguards.

Giada gulped.

Kelvin stopped in front of her. "Ms. Vito."

"Mayor Wentworth."

"I concede the election." He held out his hand. "You ran a good, clean campaign. Congratulations."

She took his hand and looked into his eyes but she could not read what he was feeling. He wasn't acting like himself. No grandstanding. No "look at me" behavior. He nodded, said a few words to the reporter, and then strode out of the building as quickly as he'd arrived.

Giada stood openmouthed, watching him go, her hand still tingling from his touch. *He's hurting and he's trying to salvage his pride.*

People were coming over, slapping her on the back, pumping her hand. Other supporters were throwing confetti into the air and blowing on celebratory kazoos. Someone wheeled in a big cake that had been waiting in the wings. The red velvet cake with cream cheese icing and neon blue frosting proclaimed: *Congratulations, Mayor Vito.*

She thought about calling her parents but it was the middle of the night in Italy. So she smiled and smiled and smiled and felt empty. Champagne corks popped. Someone pressed a chilled champagne flute in her hand. She had a sip but tasted nothing. Her mouth was dry, her head muddled.

She had won.

Yet she did not feel triumphant. For one thing, she'd lost her fight against the bond election. The Valentine Land proposition had passed.

And all she could think about was the sound of utter decimation in Kelvin's voice when he'd congratulated her.

Cell phones had been ringing nonstop. Everyone wanted to talk to her, but she had nothing to say. Since the day she'd declared her candidacy, she'd thought of nothing else but winning the election, besting Kelvin. Putting the arrogant mayor in his place. But now that she'd achieved her goal, the victory felt surprisingly hollow.

The hubbub in the gym grated on her nerves. She needed to get out of here, needed to isolate and identify the feeling gnawing at her. If she could identify it, she could quell it.

Without telling anyone where she was going, she slipped out the side door, got into her Fiat, and just started driving.

Twenty minutes later, she ended up at Lake Valentine. She parked at Lookout Point and got out of the car. There was a chill in the early November air and she hugged her sweater tighter around her. She could see the lights of Valentine spread out below.

She was the new mayor. This was her town now.

Giada knew she should be feeling overjoyed, but she was not. She leaned against the hood of the Fiat and drew in a deep breath. It hit her all at once.

She was lonely.

It washed over her in a wave as she thought of all she'd sacrificed to be a success. No husband. No kids. Her family still in Italy.

A sound of a snapping twig echoed behind her.

She wasn't alone!

The hairs on her arms rose and she realized she'd left her purse inside the car—her designer handbag with Mace in the side pocket. Heart pounding, Giada whirled around and spied a tall figure lurking in the shadows of the trees.

The world dropped away.

Kelvin stepped into the clearing, his big body clad in a gray wool suit with a jaunty canary yellow shirt and a brown bolo tie. He looked like the king of the jungle and she'd robbed him of his crown.

She had the strangest urge to fling herself into his arms at the same time she felt a desperate need to jump into the Fiat and peel rubber. She was alone in the dark with her archrival. He could kill her, weigh her down, dump her body in the lake, and no one would be the wiser.

Her knees turned to Jell-O. Her toes went numb. What was he doing here? Had he followed her?

The mossy smell of damp lake breeze made her shiver. His dark, wicked smile sent her pulse thumping. The hairs at the nape of her neck stood up. This wasn't a man who took defeat in stride.

Her head spun.

"Hello, *Mayor*." Kelvin's dark voice slid over her, inky black as the night.

Giada took a step back, teetered on her high heels.

He reached out a hand to steady her. His grip was hot, firm. She felt as if she'd been branded.

She tried to twist away. He didn't let go.

Her head spun. The evening air crowded her lungs, heavy with the noise of croaking frogs and thickening mist.

"I hope you know what you're doing," he said.

"Pardon?" Her voice came out in a whisper.

His hand moved from her elbow to touch her suit jacket, stiff with shoulder pads.

Breathing hard, she wrenched away from him. "You're not going to intimidate me to keep your stranglehold on this town," she said. "You lost the election fair and square, Wentworth. Now step off."

"You don't know what you're getting into—"

"No," she interrupted. "You don't realize how the Wentworth dynasty has been holding this town back."

"I was just thinking about you."

"Ha!" Her short bark of forced laughter echoed eerily out over the water.

"I was hoping," he said quietly, "you'd take a chance on me. On us."

"Bullshit," she said. "You just don't want to relinquish your position. You're thinking if you can date me, you can influence me into doing your bidding. Well, you've met your match, Kelvin Wentworth. You can't manipulate me like everyone else in this town."

"What are you so afraid of?"

You. I'm afraid of you.

He tracked his hand from her shoulder to her cheek and Giada suppressed a shudder. She was determined not to let him know how much he affected her.

She raised her chin, met his eyes with a stony stare. "I'm not afraid of anything."

"Except for not being in control."

"Don't you dare project your fears onto me."

He ran the pad of his thumb over her cheekbone. "Why'd you come after me?"

"I didn't come after you," she cried indignantly.

"You ran for office, you took my job. What was that all about if you weren't trying to get my attention?"

"You egotistical bastard." She shoved his hand away. Fury snapped her jaw closed.

"What drives you, Giada? What is it you really want?"

"I want you to piss off."

He threw back his head and laughed, a big rolling sound that sucked the energy right out of her bones.

"What's so damned funny?" Glowering, she sank her hands onto her hips.

"We're just alike, you and me."

"We are *nothing* alike."

"I know exactly what drives you, woman. You have to be the best at what you do. There's no such thing as second place. You're either a winner or a loser." He paused and she hoped he was finished. She wanted out of here, but he was blocking her way to the driver's-side door. She had a feeling if she tried to go around him that he'd just step into her path. "But sometimes winning isn't everything," he said, lowering his voice. "Sometimes you've just got to know you tried your best and that was enough."

"Oh, that's rich, coming from a scoundrel like you."

"If you're not worried," he said, "then why are you out here by yourself when you should be down at Leroy's Bar celebrating your victory?"

"I don't drink." She sniffed.

"You know what I mean."

"Why are you here?" She turned the tables on him. "Why aren't you down at Leroy's drowning your sorrows?"

"Because I was worried about you."

Giada snorted. "Please, you expect me to believe that? Why should you be worried about me?"

He stepped closer. Giada sucked in her breath. Gently, Kelvin slipped his fingers through her hair and raised her face up to meet his gaze. "Because I know how lonely it is at the top."

Deep inside she felt something splinter, slip.

"I know what it's like to need someone but be too afraid of being vulnerable to ask for what you really need."

It was as if he totally got her. As if he'd peeled off the top of her head and stared straight down into her mind. He saw past her tough façade to the girl who'd constantly striven to win her father's love and had failed time and again.

"You don't have to be afraid with me," he said. "I know you, Giada Vito, because I'm just like you."

"You're not," she cried, suddenly terrified. "We're not anything alike. You're just saying all this because you can't admit the truth. I won and you lost."

"Are you sure of that?" he asked.

Confused, she blinked at him. What did he mean by his comment? Was he going to challenge her win? Demand a recount? She fully expected it. "I won fair and square."

His eyes darkened in the moonlight. "I guess that all depends on what you mean by winning."

Chapter 18

The Monday after the election, Kelvin Wentworth flew to Austin to meet with Jackson Traynor. He had the speech rehearsed in his head, but he still couldn't believe he was going to deliver it. After all the lobbying he'd done to get them to consider Valentine for a theme park, he was going in there to tell them the deal was off. The whole deal with Amusement Corp had been contingent on his putting in an airport and hotels and restaurants. He was withdrawing his end of the bargain.

What was wrong with him?

Giada Vito. That was what. She had him so tied up in knots Kelvin didn't know who he was anymore.

The knots twisted even tighter when he walked into the conference room and spied Giada sitting there in a gray tweed suit, purple blouse, and a sharp new hairstyle shot through with streaks of auburn. He'd always been a sucker for redheads.

One look into her enigmatic brown eyes kicked his pulse up and he felt strangely breathless.

"What's she doing here?" Kelvin asked Mr. Traynor. He was so unnerved at the sight of Giada he went on the defensive, tightening his shoulders, narrowing his eyes, and curling his hands into fists.

"Mayor-elect Vito is the one who called this meeting," Traynor said.

"Could I see you in the hallway for a moment, Ms. Vito?" Kelvin asked, not sure what he was going to do with her once he got her out there, but his hands were just itching to hold her.

"If you'll excuse us, gentlemen." Giada smiled at the men collected around the conference table. "We'll be right back."

She followed Kelvin into the corridor. Once the door snapped closed behind them, he turned to face her. "What are you doing here?"

"I could ask you the same question."

"I came to tell them to back off Valentine Land," Kelvin said.

"And I came to give them my complete support."

"Why?" they asked each other in unison, and then both said, "Because you were right."

They looked at each other and laughed.

"Are we friends now?" he asked.

"Better than friends," she said, a seductive look coming into her eyes.

Kelvin felt his body respond. He couldn't take not touching her one minute longer. He slung an arm around her waist and tugged her to him, caveman-style.

Giada wrapped herself around him as if she'd been yearning for him to do just that. Her enthusiasm caught him off-balance and he had to tighten his grip on her to keep from stumbling.

He'd heard about hot-blooded Italian women; was he about to get the scoop firsthand?

"I can't believe you traveled here to give up your dream for me," she said.

"Ditto."

Her eyes rounded. "So what does this mean?"

"You tell me."

"I think it means you like me." She lowered her eyelids, sent him a sultry glance. "A lot."

He snorted. " 'Like' isn't the word for it."

"Why, Mayor, what are you saying?"

"I'm not the mayor anymore. You are."

"Not until January." She studied his face. "Is this going to be an issue for us?"

"Us?" he echoed.

"As in you and me. Or is that too forward? Too much of an assumption?"

"I've been a bachelor all my life."

"I know," she said, her gaze never leaving his face. "I've never been married, either."

"Too hard to get along with?" he teased.

"No harder than you."

"I'm pretty hard right now."

"I can tell." Her laugh was throaty.

"I think I just might be falling in love with you."

"You sure of that?"

"Okay, I'll admit it. I'm head over heels," he said, looking at her as intently as she was looking at him. "How do you feel about me?"

"I fell for you hook, line, and sinker."

"So you'd marry me if I asked?"

"Are you asking?"

"Of course not. I'm a die-hard romantic. If I were asking you to marry me, I would make a Valentine-sized production out of it."

"That's good," she said, "because I've come to expect big productions out of you."

"In case you haven't noticed, I'm not a subtle guy."

"Subtlety is overrated. Besides, you have the ability to change." She reached up to run a finger over his cheek. It was all he could do not to shudder with desire at her light touch. "I still can't believe you came here to turn down Amusement Corp's offer."

"I had a mistake to correct. You were absolutely right. I was letting my ego get in the way of what was best for Valentine. You know I love that town."

"It's one of the things I love most about you," she murmured.

He heard only respect and admiration in her voice and it made him love her all the more.

"You know," she said, "I'm a novice when it comes to public office. I was hoping you might give me some pointers."

"You mean it?"

"I'm not as confident as I appear. In fact"—she lowered her voice—"I'm scared to death. I mean, I'm responsible for running an entire town. A little guidance would be much appreciated."

He narrowed his eyes. "You're not just saying that to stroke my ego."

She shook her head. "I'm being honest here. For the first time in my life I feel like I can admit when I'm over-whelmed and it's all because you make me feel secure enough in my insecurity."

"Woman," he said, "I am so turned on by you right now."

He pulled his car keys from his pocket. "You want to drive to the airport or shall I, after we tell Amusement

Corp Tyler can have the theme park? If they want it badly enough to hire Purdy Maculroy to vandalize his home-town, they can have it, problems and all."

"You can drive this time," she said. "I'll drive home from the airport."

"Deal," Kelvin said and then he kissed her, knowing he'd made the best move for Valentine he'd ever made in his life.

Rachael was keeping the faith as best she could. It was hard since she was living at Mrs. Potter's alone now that her mother had moved back home. Her parents were doing well. Her dad was healing and her mother was radiant in a way Rachael had never seen before.

She decorated the house for Christmas and wrote her column for *Texas Monthly*. She'd upped her attendance at Romanceaholics meetings from once a week to twice a week, then to three times a week, until she was attending a meeting somewhere almost every day—often driving as far away as Del Rio to find a session.

But no matter how many meetings she attended, she couldn't get Brody out of her head. He was always there, a constant in the back of her mind. No matter what else she was doing, she thought of him. Attending meetings, run-ning errands, giving speeches, or writing her column. He was with her, his name a silent prayer.

Brody, Brody, Brody.

She kept waiting for him to make a move. To convince her that romance *was* all that it was cracked up to be. She had a speech prepared to shoot down his arguments. She kept it tucked in her purse.

He did not make a move.

That rattled her.

Why didn't he make a move?

You don't want him to make a move. This was supposed to be casual sex, remember. You lived in the moment. The moment is over. Live in this current moment.

But by contrast, this moment without him in it felt lonely and dull.

You're romanticizing him again.

It was harder living here without her mother for distraction. She called her friends several times a day. Delaney and Tish, with their babies to attend to, sounded distracted and rushed. Jillian was the only one who would patiently listen to her talk about Brody and then tell her to stay strong.

It was hard to do when he was quietly, secretly doing nice things for her.

Every morning since that night in the cabin, she found the *Valentine Gazette* sitting on her front welcome mat instead of in the shrubbery where it usually landed. After a cold snap blew through one morning, covering the cars in a sheet of ice, she toddled outside, wearing three layers of clothing and armed with an ice scraper, only to discover that her windshield was already scraped clean.

When the flood lamp over the driveway went out, Rachael arrived home one evening to find the light shining brightly and Brody Carlton standing on his front porch in the dark, watching until she was safely inside.

She'd raised a hand to thank him.

He'd waved back.

That had been the extent of their exchange.

But he was quietly, steadfastly showing her what real love was. She was just so scared to trust. To believe again.

The fact that he wasn't tempting her tempted her all the more. She found excuses to go across the street.

Borrow a cup of sugar from Deana. Invite Maisy over to make Christmas cookies. Christmas caroling with her Romanceaholics Anonymous group.

None of those brief encounters satisfied.

Then on Christmas Eve, as she was wrapping presents, the doorbell rang. Her mind leaped to one conclusion.

Brody!

Excited by the notion that the sheriff was on the front porch standing underneath the mistletoe she'd hung up, she raced downstairs and flung the door open without first checking to see who it was.

Trace Hoolihan stood there holding a gigantic bouquet of pink roses.

"What do you want?" she snapped.

"I came to see you," Trace murmured, his voice coming out thick and husky.

"Me?" She narrowed her eyes. "What for?"

Trace took a deep breath. He was just as handsome as ever. Too handsome, actually, with his slicked-back, stylishly long blond hair, perfect nose, tanned skin, and big, white, straight smile. He looked as if he'd stepped off the cover of *GQ* in his tailored suit, cranberry silk tie, expensive Italian shoes, and camel-colored cashmere coat.

She couldn't help comparing him to Brody.

Rugged, good-looking Brody with his dark, precision-cut hair, crooked nose, and lopsided smile. If he were to be on the cover of anything, it would be *Outdoor* magazine or *Texas Highways,* in his Stetson, cowboy boots, and faded blue jeans.

She thought of how easy life had been for Trace, a banker's son, and how hard Brody had had it. Losing both parents by the time he was fifteen, being in the Twin Towers when tragedy struck, leaving behind a piece of himself in Iraq. How had she ever preferred the softness of someone like Trace to the substance of a man like Brody?

"You look so beautiful," Trace said.

She crossed her arms over her chest and glared. "What do you want?"

"I came to tell you how sorry I am for the way I treated you."

Then before Rachael had time to react, Trace tossed the bouquet onto the porch swing, pulled her into his arms, and kissed her underneath the mistletoe.

Brody was cruising down the street in his Crown Vic, returning from picking up nutmeg at the grocery store. Deana was whipping up eggnog for Kelvin's annual Christmas party that evening. He'd been wondering if Rachael would be attending when he saw her standing on her front porch kissing some guy. One look at the red Corvette with the Illinois plates in the driveway, the Chicago Bears parking pass sticker on the back windshield, and a huge bouquet of pink roses sitting on the porch swing, and he knew the guy in question was most likely her old flame Trace Hoolihan trying to weasel his way back into her good graces.

The realization hit him like a sledgehammer.

Rachael was getting back together with her ex.

You blew it, buddy-boy. Holding back was not the way to go. As much as Rachael denies she wants romance, that's exactly what she wants.

His gut soured and sweat beaded at his collar. His caveman instincts had him wanting to slam the car in park right there in the middle of the street, get out, and challenge Hoolihan to a good old-fashioned fistfight, winner take Rachael.

But he couldn't give in to his natural inclinations for

three reasons. One, he was an officer of the law and he didn't take his duty lightly. Two, after Iraq, he'd sworn off violence. Three, Rachael wasn't a possession men could fight over. She was a human being with a mind of her own. He couldn't treat her like an object. If Trace was the man she wanted, it would do no good to get angry. Never mind that she was tearing him apart inside. That was his cross to bear. He loved her, even if she didn't love him back.

Wincing, he turned into his driveway and got out of the car, just in time to see Rachael let Trace Hoolihan into her house.

And with that, the tender hope for the future Brody had been nurturing for weeks was snuffed right out.

"The Bears are headed for the play-offs and I'm first-string running back," Trace said. He peeled off his cashmere coat and hung it on the rack by the door while Rachael trailed into the kitchen scouting for a vase for the roses.

She'd let him in only to get him off the porch, and she prayed none of the neighbors had seen him. She knew how quickly gossip spread through Valentine.

Her lips were still damp from Trace's wet, sloppy kiss. How had she ever convinced herself that she liked his kisses? She wiped her mouth with the back of a hand and finally just stuck the roses in a Mason jar.

"Don't you have a vase for those?" Trace asked, coming into the kitchen behind her.

"This is as sophisticated as it gets," she said, feeling irritated.

"Are you still mad at me?"

"Let's see. You ran out on our wedding to join the Chicago Bears and then you disrespected me on national television. Why on earth would I be mad at you?"

Trace hung his head, looking chagrined. "Not two of my finer moments. I'm truly sorry for that. But you got back at me," he pointed out, "with the whole YouTube thing."

"You saw that?"

"I was the laughingstock of the locker room for weeks."

"You deserved it."

"I did."

Rachael turned to face him. "Why are you here, Trace?"

"I missed you, Rach."

She snorted indelicately. "Come on. You've been the star of the Chicago Bears since September. I know you've got more groupies than you can handle."

"I don't want groupies, I want you. I've come to realize all the groupies in the world can't offer me what you were so willing to give," he said.

"And what's that?"

"Your support, your loyalty, your love."

"You had your chance with me."

"I was a fool."

"Yes," she agreed, "you were." She could forgive him because she'd grown beyond the petty need for revenge.

"I want to spend the rest of my life making it up to you," he said. Then he sank down on one knee and reached for her hand.

Her stomach pitched. Her pulse raced. Panic swept through her. No, no.

He withdrew a small black-velvet box from his pocket. It sprang open with a sharp cracking sound to reveal a three-carat diamond sparkler. "Marry me, Rachael. I really mean it this time. I can't make it without you in my life. I thought fame and fortune were what I wanted but I found out it doesn't mean a damn thing if you don't have anyone to share it with."

Once upon a time, after a speech like that, Rachael would have forgiven him anything. Back before she'd learned all that glitters isn't gold. Once upon a time, she would have been impressed with the appearance of things, with the trappings of romance—the roses, the diamond, the going-down-on-one-knee thing. Once upon a time, she would have accepted his proposal, terrified that she might never get another one. But that was before she'd learned she was worth something in her own right. That she didn't need a man or romance to define her.

Rachael pulled her hand away from him and stepped back. "Get real. I'm not about to marry a man who treats me the way you treated me."

"I won't take no for an answer," he said, rising to his feet. "I'm pursuing you with my last dime. I'll send flowers every day. I'll buy you gifts and spoil you with vacations and spa treatments."

"I don't want those things anymore, Trace. You were the one who helped me realize that I was living a false life. I was happier with fantasies and illusions than I was in the real world. That's no way to live."

"I don't get it." He looked truly puzzled. "You prefer to live alone in a crappy little house in this dried-up town rather than marry me, move to Chicago, and live in the lap of luxury."

"Yep," she said. "I do."

"You're breaking my heart here. What am I going to do without you, Rachael?"

"If you're lucky, you'll do the same thing I did when you broke my heart. You'll find the real Trace hiding inside." Using her knuckles, she tapped his chest at his heart.

Bewildered, he stared at her. "You've changed."

"Thank you." She smiled.

He shook his head. "I don't know how I'm going to get through the Super Bowl without you."

"Face it. That's the real reason you're here," she said.

"Huh?" His look was blank. Trace had no idea what his true motives were, but she understood him better than he understood himself. Somewhere along the way she'd learned to look past outer appearance to the truth that lay beyond.

"You're stressed out about the Super Bowl and you need a woman around that you can trust to prop you up. Groupies can't do that for you, but you knew I could."

He blinked. "I don't get it."

"You don't really love me, Trace. You loved what I did for you. I was there to hold your hand when things got tough. Remember, you proposed to me on the day the Houston Texans cut you from the team. And the minute things got better you ditched me. I'm nothing more than a security blanket."

"That's not true," he denied, but she saw it in his eyes. It was totally true.

"Trace," she said. "You don't need me. Honestly, you're a big boy. It's time to toss out the security blanket. You can handle this all on your own. You won't choke during the Super Bowl. You're going to be fabulous. Now go back to Chicago where you belong."

Kelvin Wentworth's party was in full swing by the time Rachael arrived. Elvis Presley was on the stereo, dreaming of a "White Christmas." Festive twinkle lights were strung around the room. The Christmas tree was oversized and spinning gently on a rotating stand. Giada was at the refreshment table, ladling up cups of spiced eggnog and gazing adoringly at Kelvin, who was playing Santa to a group of children.

The outgoing mayor's bullmastiff, Marianne, wearing antlers and a crocheted red-and-green doggie sweater, weaved her way through the crowd, picking up dropped tidbits of food like a high-suction Hoover. The incoming mayor's cat, Hercules, curled up on the window ledge, watching the proceedings with yellow-eyed disdain.

Rachael hung up her coat, deposited the presents she'd brought with her on the long table laden with gifts, and slipped away from the main room. She was still a bit off-balance after Trace's visit that morning and his ensuing marriage proposal, but she was feeling liberated in a way that she'd never felt before.

She had closure. She could let go of the remaining vestiges of her past and move on.

That's when she saw Brody, looking dashing in a pair of black Dockers and a red-and-green-striped, button-down Western shirt—a cowboy's version of Christmas attire.

Standing under the mistletoe.

It was all she could do to keep from going over there and kissing him. Just when she'd decided, *Aw, to hell with it, I'm going to kiss him anyway,* April Tritt, dressed as one of Santa's elves in a skirt so short you could practically see Australia, beat her to it.

The kiss April planted on him was not a light peck on the cheek. As the oversexed woman pulled Brody's head down to hers, jealousy chewed off a big chunk of Rachael's heart.

April finally let go of him and stepped back.

Brody raised his head, saw Rachael.

Their eyes met.

Brody stepped past April and came toward her.

Suddenly feeling self-conscious, she ducked her head and turned toward the refreshment table, her green jingle bell earrings jangling merrily. She heard the scrape of Brody's boots on the polished hardwood floor, but she didn't look up.

"Merry Christmas, Peaches," he murmured.

Rachael looked up.

His eyes were dark, enigmatic.

"Brody." His name came out of her like a sigh.

"Rachael."

"You've got lipstick..." She made a motion toward the corner of his mouth.

He swiped it away with the back of his hand. "That business with April—"

"No need to explain." She held up a palm.

He reached for two cups, raised his eyebrow at her. "Eggnog?"

She shrugged. "Sure."

He dipped them both a cup and passed one to her. She curled the cup in her hand.

"How you been?" He was staring straight at her. No, that wasn't right. He was staring *into* her.

"Fine. You?"

"Good."

She blew out her breath.

He shifted his weight. Brought the glass of eggnog to his lips, but she saw that he didn't swallow.

"That bad?"

"What?" He looked startled.

She nodded at his glass. "The eggnog. Is it so bad you're just pretending to drink it?"

"It's spiked with rum and I'm driving."

"So why even take it?"

"Something to do with my hands, I guess."

"Oh." She looked away again, unable to bear the heat of his scrutiny. Unable to say all the things she desperately wanted to tell him.

"I saw you," he said.

"You saw me?"

"This morning. On your front porch. With Trace Hoolihan."

Rachael remembered the kiss Trace had given her. "That's the trouble with mistletoe." She glanced over his shoulder at April, who was glaring at her from across the room. "It can cause a kiss to look like something it's not."

"Hey." He shrugged. "More power to you."

"You don't care that I was kissing Trace?" She could hear the dismay in her voice and she knew he heard it, too.

"We agreed, no strings attached, just sex. Exactly how you wanted it."

"You said you wanted it that way, too, remember? You said great love destroys."

"Maybe I was wrong."

She hissed in a breath through clenched teeth. "Yesss?"

He nodded at Giada and Kelvin, who were gazing into each other's eyes. "What about those two?"

"First blush of romantic love. It'll wear off."

"And then look at your parents. They were able to find their way back to each other."

"After my dad almost died."

"Sometimes it takes the threat of losing the thing you love most to give you a wake-up call." And with that, he turned and walked away, leaving Rachael shaken to her very core.

Chapter 19

On Christmas morning, Rachael awoke alone to a throbbing headache from the three glasses of spiked eggnog she'd downed at Kelvin's party after Brody had run off. She glanced at the clock and shot out of bed. She was due at her parents' house for brunch.

Fifteen minutes later her mother greeted her with a hug. Her father looked fantastic for someone who'd had a heart attack six weeks earlier. Hannah chattered while her daughters played chase around the kitchen table, and her husband carved prime rib for the brunch buffet as the rest of the guests arrived. It seemed almost half the town was at the celebration, including Deana and Maisy and Rex Brownleigh. Deana and Rex kept exchanging moony-eyed glances.

Rachael cornered her mother in the kitchen as she flipped crepes onto a warming plate. "Did you invite Brody?"

"Of course I did. He said he was working so Zeke could have Christmas Day off with his family."

"Oh." Then to show she wasn't asking about him specifically, she added, "Did you invite Kelvin and Giada?"

"They had private plans."

"Sounds like things are heating up between those two."

Selina lowered her voice. "Giada told me they're moving in together."

"No kidding."

"I'm happy for her."

She touched her mother's arm. "How are things with you and Daddy?"

Selina's face dissolved into a beatific smile. "I haven't been this happy in years. Oh, Rachael, I love him so much. I've always loved him, but nothing like this. We finally opened up to each other and talked about things we should have discussed years ago. He's stopped cloaking his true feelings with romantic gestures and we have real intimacy at last."

"I'm so glad." She gave her mother a squeeze.

Selina smiled as tears misted her eyes. "Here." She handed her daughter a jar of peach preserves. "Put these on the table to go with the crepes."

As everyone gathered around the buffet table filling their plates, Rachael opened the peach preserves and spooned a dollop onto her crepes. She found a seat in the corner of the kitchen, out of the general fray, settled in, and took a bite of crepe draped in peach preserves.

It tasted as if summer exploded in her mouth—rich and ripe and full and as juicy as the fresh peaches plucked from Brody's tree. Each bite brought back memories of the day he'd brought that bushel of peaches across the street.

She thought about peaches and romance. She thought about her parents and what they'd been through. She remembered her mother, upset and hurting, smashing the peaches, decrying love and marriage. She thought of Kelvin and Giada, middle-aged and never married and yet still finding each other, willing to risk, to take a chance on love. She thought about Deana and her new romance with Rex.

But most of all she thought about Brody. How steady he was. How honest and straight and true. He hadn't given her flowers. Hadn't wined and dined. No grand romantic gestures from him. But he'd given her something much better. He had given her his summer peaches on the day she'd faced her greatest humiliation. He'd been there for her when her father had had his heart attack. He'd made love to her. And just last night, he'd told her he loved her more than anyone else on earth could ever love her.

Tears tracked down her face as she ate. Her epiphany grew brighter, stronger with each bite of peaches. Yes, the first flush of romantic love was like a beautiful, perfectly ripe peach. And like her mother had said, life could knock you around. Smash the romance right out of you.

But this was what she realized: In order to have these delicious peach preserves in the winter, the peaches had to be smashed up, boiled down, condensed, distilled. That sweet little romance of summer had to disappear in order for the rich, sustaining preserves to exist.

One spoonful of preserves was ten times sweeter than the freshest peach.

Her chest pinched and her breath went shallow. This, then, was the difference between romance and love.

Romance was fun and light and frivolous. You could enjoy it, have a good time with it, but it did not sustain you for long. Only the preserves could do that. Only true love.

With that understanding, Rachael knew what she had to do.

*   *   *

The last thing Brody Carlton expected to find when he wheeled his Crown Vic past the Valentine library was Rachael's pink VW Bug parked in the middle of the street and the lights on inside the building.

But there weren't any cars in the parking lot.

Was she hosting a Romanceaholics meeting tonight and the members had yet to show up? Had she forgotten to set her VW's parking brake and the car had rolled back into the street?

Brody pulled his cruiser into the parking lot and got out. He heard the sound of music in the air but it wasn't Christmas music. Instead, it was Bonnie Tyler's "Holding Out for a Hero." Every time he heard that song he thought of Maisy's favorite movie, *Shrek*.

Smiling, Brody went up the steps to the side door of the library where the Romanceaholics usually entered. He stepped inside and saw a big banner stretched across the empty room that read: JUST PEACHY? OR DOES YOUR LOVER HAVE WHAT IT TAKES TO BECOME PEACH PRESERVES?

What the hell?

"Rachael?" he called out. "You in here?"

His voice echoed back to him over the sound of Bonnie Tyler emanating from the boom box on the stage.

"Brody?" Rachael's head popped out from the closet behind the stage.

"Yep."

She came out of the closet holding what appeared to be a giant papier-mâché peach.

"What's that?"

"Prop for the Peach Festival," she said, as if that explained everything, and sat it down on the stage next to the podium.

"Oh."

"You're too early. You're not supposed to be here yet."

He cocked his head and grinned. He'd grown accustomed to her seemingly nonsensical conversations. He'd learned how to read and interpret her. "When was I supposed to be here?"

"I'd imagined you coming in during the middle of the meeting while—" She raised a hand to cover her mouth. "I'm doing it, aren't I? Projecting a romantic fantasy. I should just let reality happen the way it's going to happen. You're here now. It'll do."

"Okay," he said, knowing if he waited she'd explain herself.

She wore a green-and-red festive Christmas dress that made her eyes look even greener than usual and her cheeks were flushed. She smelled sweet and fresh, just like summer, even in the dead of winter. She sank her top teeth into her bottom lip and then she told him her theory about peaches, peach preserves, and love.

"What do you think?" she asked and anxiously knotted her fingers together.

"Sounds like a solid hypothesis to me." He went toward her, pulling off his leather jacket and Stetson as he went. When he was close enough, he put them on the lectern. "The peach analogy appeals to me."

Her eyes were wide. They were only a couple of feet apart. He wanted to touch her so badly his hands stung. He wanted to push his fingers through her hair, dip his head, and kiss her with all the passion he'd been holding back.

"It's what I'm going to tell the Romanceaholics."

"Is it, now." He wanted her to come to him, to bury her face against his neck and tell him how much she wanted to be with him. Instead, she swayed there, just staring into his eyes.

"I've come to realize everyone is entitled to a little romance in their lives, just as long as they don't mistake it for the real thing."

"What's that?"

"Great love," she said on a whispered sigh.

"Rachael," he replied, and then he couldn't say another word because his chest was so knotted up.

"Brody, I said you were just casual sex to me, but that was a lie. From the moment you risked life and limb to haul me down off that billboard, I knew you were a true hero. A good man. A man who wouldn't leave me standing at the altar while my bouquet wilted. I knew you were the kind of man who fought for what you believed in. I knew you'd never pick a sports team over me."

"What took us so long to get here?"

She moistened her lips. "I was so scared of making another mistake that I couldn't trust what I knew about you deep down inside." She knotted a fist and placed it against her belly. "I was terrified of getting hurt again."

"I was pretty terrified, too," he admitted. "I'd convinced myself it was better to stay away from great love than to take a chance on losing it. But ever since I came back to Valentine I've felt like I've just been waiting for something big to happen to direct the rest of my life. I think that big thing was you."

Rachael brought both hands up to cover her mouth. Her heart was pounding and her eyes burned with unshed tears of joy.

"Hang on," he said. "I've got something for you. I was saving it for Valentine's Day but the time feels right."

He left her standing there and sprinted out the door.

She felt off-balance and scared. Did he have a ring? Was he going to ask her to marry him?

Don't romanticize it. Just let the moment happen the way it's going to happen. Be present. Get out of the castle in your mind.

And there he was, back inside the library, breathless, his hair mussed, his cheeks reddened from the cold night air.

"It's early," Brody said, extending the envelope toward her. She noticed his hand was trembling. "No, it's late. In fact, it's almost twenty years overdue. I know it doesn't make up for not giving it to you all those years ago, but here I am, asking you to be my Valentine."

She took the envelope, yellowed with age, opened the flap, and slipped out the handmade card. It was a red construction-paper heart with lace—faded yellow like the envelope—glued around it. In the handwriting of a twelve-year-old the card read:

Dear Rachael, I made ya this Valentine card for your birthday. Hope you like it. Your friend, Brody.

She jerked her gaze up to his face. "You made me this? When you were a kid?"

He nodded. "I found it in one of my mother's keepsake boxes."

"You saved it. Why would you save it?"

"I'd like to take credit for that, but it was my mother's doing. I'm glad she was a packrat."

"Oh, Brody." She sighed. To think the first boy she'd ever loved had been the right one all along.

"You were my great love even back then," he said. "I just didn't realize it."

"I'm sorry it's taken me so long to understand the difference between show and substance."

"I've missed you," he said, wrapping his big, strong

sheriff-y arms around her and lifting her off the ground. He squeezed her tight and kissed her hard. She could feel the strength of his love, every inch of it, as he let her slide gently back down the length of his hard body until her feet were firmly on the ground.

"Is this the happily-ever-after?" she asked.

"Nope."

"It's not?"

"Nope."

"I dunno," she teased, "it feels dangerously like happily-ever-after to me."

"Can't be," he said.

"Why not?"

"This is the happily-ever-before."

"Before what?"

He put his forehead against hers and she stared deeply into those delicious brown eyes she knew so well. "Before the greatest adventure of our lives. Full of ups and downs. Laughter and tears. Romance and sorrow. Joy and pain. And love. Always, forever, love."

The door opened just then and several of her group members appeared in the room.

"Meeting's canceled, folks," Brody called out to them. "Your fearless leader has learned the true meaning of love. She'll let you in on it at your next meeting."

Then he swept Rachael off her feet, and to the sound of the romanceaholics clapping and cheering, and Bonnie Tyler singing about a hero, he carried her out of the library and into their newfound love.

Epilogue

On Valentine's Day, Brody and Rachael got married where they'd met cute: underneath the Valentine billboard. Yes, it was nostalgic and romantic, but Rachael didn't care. It might not have been the wedding she'd dreamed of since she was six years old, but it was absolutely perfect in spite of the chilly breeze and the big fat rain clouds bunching up overhead.

Brody looked handsome as all get-out in a Texas tuxedo and a black Stetson. The man took her breath away.

Rachael wore a brand-new wedding gown and the magical wedding veil, which in the end had granted the deepest wish of her heart, if not the actual wish she'd made that day on the cement bench in the Valentine jail. She hadn't exactly gotten that love monkey off her back. What she'd gotten instead was a new, liberating view of love, romance, and all the myriad emotions in between.

Judge Pruitt presided over the proceedings and almost the entire population of Valentine was there, including Kelvin and his bride, Giada, who, according to rumors down at Higgy's Diner, was already pregnant. Delaney and Tish and their husbands and babies, along with Jillian, had driven from Houston. Selina served as Rachael's matron of honor, wearing the same silk, peach-colored dress she'd worn when she and Michael had renewed their wedding vows the week before. Her father stood up as Brody's best man in a Texas tuxedo of his own.

"If anyone knows any reason these two should not be wed, speak now or forever hold your peace."

Silence fell over the congregation and then Rex, who was standing with Deana and Maisy, said, "Hell, Judge, marry them already. Everyone in town knows these two were meant for each other."

The crowd laughed.

Rachael passed her bouquet to her mother, then turned back to Brody. He took her hands in his and stared deeply into her eyes with a love so strong and true it took her breath away. This, then, was real love. Friendship, sexual attraction, steadiness, community. Rachael felt herself enveloped in the power of it.

"I now pronounce you man and wife."

And with that, Rachael and Brody were married. The romantic equation was completed. She'd at long last found her hero and he'd found his romantic heart.

And everything, Rachael realized, was just peachy.

All of Me

*Michele Bidelspach—the most insightful,
understanding editor I have ever worked with.
Thank you for the Gilmore Girls.
May you find that grand love of your very own.*

Acknowledgments

Thanks to Lou Ann King for showing me around her quaint little Colorado lake town. I love you like a sister. Thanks to legal eagles and fellow writers Dorien Kelley and Jamie Denton for all their help with the legal mumbo jumbo. Any mistakes are solely my own. You guys rock!

Jillian's Story

Chapter 1

Houston deputy district attorney Jillian Samuels did not believe in magic.

She didn't throw pennies into wishing wells, didn't pluck four-leaf clovers from springtime meadows, didn't blow out birthday-cake candles, and didn't wish on falling stars.

For Jillian, the Tooth Fairy and the Easter Bunny had always been myths. And as for Santa Claus, even thinking about the jolly fat guy in the red suit knotted her stomach. She'd tried believing in him once, and all she'd gotten in the pink stocking she'd hung on the mantel were two chunks of Kingsford's charcoal—the kind without lighter fluid.

Later, she'd realized her stepmother put the coal in her stocking, but on that Christmas morning, while the other kids rode bicycles, tossed footballs, and combed Barbie's hair, Jillian received her message loud and clear.

You're a very bad girl.

No, Jillian didn't believe in magic or fairy tales or happily-ever-afters, even though her three best friends, Delaney, Tish, and Rachael, had supposedly found their true loves after wishing on what they claimed was a magic wedding veil. Her friends had even dared to pass the damnable veil along to her, telling Jillian it would grant her heart's greatest desire. But she wasn't falling for such nonsense. She snorted whenever she thought of the three-hundred-year-old lace wedding veil shoved away in a cedar chest along with her winter cashmere sweaters.

When it came to romance, Jillian was of the same mind as Hemingway: *When two people love each other, there can be no happy ending.* Clearly, Hemingway knew what he was talking about.

Not that Jillian could claim she'd ever been in love. She'd decided a long time ago love was best avoided. She liked her life tidy, and from what she'd seen of it, love was sprawling and messy and complicated. Besides, love required trust, and trust wasn't her strong suit.

Jillian did not believe in magic, but she did believe in hard work, success, productivity, and justice. The closest she ever came to magic were those glorious courtroom moments when a judge in a black robe read the jury's guilty verdict.

This morning in late September, dressed in a no-nonsense navy-blue pin-striped Ralph Lauren suit, a cream-colored silk blouse, and Jimmy Choo stilettos to show off the shapely curve of her calves and add three inches to her already imposing five-foot-ten-inch height, Jillian stood at attention waiting for the verdict to be read.

On the outside, she looked like a dream prosecutor—statuesque, gorgeous, young, and smart. But underneath the clothes and the makeup and her cool, unshakeable countenance, Jillian Samuels was still that same little girl who hadn't rated a Christmas present from Santa.

"Ladies and gentlemen of the jury, have you reached a verdict in this case?" Judge Atwood asked.

"We have, Your Honor," answered the foreman, a big slab of a guy with carrot-colored hair and freckled skin.

"Please hand your decision to the bailiff," the judge directed.

Jillian drew a breath, curling her fingernails into her palms. Before the reading of every verdict, she felt slightly sick to her stomach.

The bailiff, a gangly, bulldog-faced middle-aged man with a Magnum P.I. mustache, walked the piece of paper across the courtroom to the judge's bench. Judge Atwood opened it, read it, and then glared at the defendant over the top of his reading glasses.

Twenty-three-year-old Randal Petry had shot Gladys Webelow, an eighty-two-year-old great-grandmother, in the upper thigh while robbing a Dash and Go last Christmas Eve. Gladys had been buying a bottle of Correctol and a quart of 2 percent milk. He'd made off with forty-seven dollars from the cash register, a fistful of Slim Jims, and a twenty-four pack of Old Milwaukee.

"Will the defendant please rise?" Atwood handed the verdict back to the bailiff, who gave it to the jury foreman to read aloud.

Head held high, Petry got to his feet. The man was a scumbag, but Jillian had to admire his defiance.

"Randal LeRoy Petry, on the count of armed robbery, you are found guilty as charged," the foreman announced. As the foreman kept reading the verdicts on the other charges leveled against Petry, Jillian waited for the victorious wash of relief she always experienced when the word *guilty* was spoken. Waited for the happy sag to her shoulders, the warm satisfaction in her belly, the skip of victory in her pulse.

But the triumph did not come.

Instead, she felt numb, lifeless, and very detached as if she were standing at the far end of some distant tunnel.

Waiting…waiting…

For what, she didn't know.

People in the gallery were getting up, heading for the door. The court-appointed defense attorney collected his papers and stuffed them into his scuffed briefcase. The guards were hauling Petry off to jail. Judge Atwood left the bench.

And Jillian just kept standing.

Waiting.

It scared her. This nonfeeling. This emptiness. Her fingernails bit into the flesh of her palms, but she couldn't feel that either.

"You gonna stand there all day, Samuels, or what? You won. Go knock back a shot of Jose Cuervo."

Jillian jerked her head around. Saw Keith Whippet, the prosecutor on the next case, waiting to take his place at her table. Whippet was as lean as his name, with mean eyes and a cheap suit.

"Chop, chop." He slammed his briefcase down on the desk. "I got people to fry."

"Yes," Jillian said, but she could barely hear herself. She was a bright kite who'd broken loose from its tether, flying high into a cloudless blue sky. Up, up, and away, higher and higher, smaller and smaller. Soon she would disappear, a speck in the air.

What was happening to her?

She looked at Whippet, a weasly guy who'd asked her out on numerous occasions, and she'd shattered his hopes every single time until he'd finally given up. Now he was just rude. Whippet made shooing motions.

Jillian blinked, grabbed her briefcase, and darted from the courtroom.

Blake.

She had to talk to her mentor, District Attorney Blake Townsend. He would know what to do. He'd tell her this feeling was completely normal. That it was okay if the joy was gone. She would survive.

Except it wasn't okay, because her job was the only thing that gave her joy. If she'd lost the ability to derive pleasure from putting the bad guys behind bars, what did that leave her?

The thing was, she couldn't feel happy about jailing Petry, because she knew there were thousands more like him. She knew the prisons were overcrowded, and they would let Petry out of jail on good behavior after he'd served only a fraction of his sentence to make room for a new batch of Petrys.

The realization wasn't new. What was startlingly fresh was the idea that her work didn't matter. She was insignificant. The justice system was a turnstile, and her arms were growing weary of holding open the revolving door.

She was so unsettled by the thought that she found it difficult to catch her breath.

Blake. She needed to speak to Blake.

Anxiety rushed her from the courthouse to the district attorney's office across the street, her heels clicking a rapid rhythm against the sidewalk that matched the elevated tempo of her pulse.

By the time she stepped into the DA's office, she was breathing hard and sweating. She caught a glimpse of her reflection in a window and saw that her sleek dark hair, usually pulled back in a loose chignon, had slumped from the clasp and was tumbling about her shoulders.

What was happening to her?

The whole room went suddenly silent, and everyone stared in her direction.

"Is Blake in his office?" she asked the DA's executive assistant, Francine Weathers.

Francine blinked, and it was only then that Jillian noticed her reddened eyes. The woman had been crying. She stepped closer, the anxiety she'd been feeling morphed into real fear.

She stood there for a moment, panting, terrified, heart rapidly pounding, staring at Francine's round, middle-aged face. She knew something bad had happened before she ever asked the question.

"What's wrong?"

The secretary dabbed at her eyes with a Kleenex. "You haven't heard?"

A hot rush of apprehension raised the hairs on the nape of her neck. "Heard what? I've been in court. The Petry case."

"I..." Francine sniffed. "He..."

Jillian stepped closer and awkwardly put a hand on the older woman's shoulder. "Are you okay?"

Francine shook her head and burst into a fresh round of tears. Jillian dropped her hand. She'd never been very good at comforting people. She was the pit bull who went after the accused. Gentleness was foreign.

"This morning, Blake...he..."

Jillian's blood pumped faster. "Yes?"

"It's terrible, unthinkable."

"What?"

"Such a shame. He was only fifty-six."

Jillian grit her teeth to keep from taking the woman by the shoulders and shaking her. "Just tell me. What's happened?"

Francine hiccoughed, sniffled into a tissue, and then finally whispered,

"Blake dropped dead this morning in the middle of Starbucks while ordering a grande soy latte."

The next few days passed in a fog. Jillian went about her work and attended her cases, but it felt as if someone else was in her body performing the tasks while her mind shut down, disconnected from her emotions. She'd never experienced such hollow emptiness. But she could not cry. The tears stuffed up her head, made her temples throb, but no matter how much she wanted to sob, she simply could not.

Francine had learned from Blake's doctor that he'd had an inoperable brain tumor he'd told no one about. That new knowledge cut Jillian to the quick. He hadn't trusted her enough to tell her he was dying.

The morning of Blake's memorial service dawned unseasonably cold for the end of September in Texas. Thick gray clouds matted the sky, threatening rain. The wind gusted out of the north at twenty-five miles an hour, blowing shivers up Jillian's black wool skirt.

She still couldn't believe Blake was gone. Speculation about who would be appointed to take his place swirled through the office, but, grief-stricken, Jillian didn't give the issue much consideration. Blake was gone, and no one could ever replace him in her heart.

Learning of her mentor's death compounded the feelings of edge-of-the-world desolation that had overcome her during Petry's trial. She'd met Blake when he'd been a guest lecturer in her summer-school class on criminal law at the University of Houston. He'd found her questions insightful, and she'd thought he was one of the smartest men she'd ever met.

Their attraction was strictly mental. They admired each other's brains. Plus, Jillian had lost a father, and Blake had let a daughter slip away. When Blake had been elected district attorney about the same time Jillian graduated from law school, his offer of a job in the DA's office was automatic.

Jillian didn't question if it was the right step for her. Blake was there. She went. Other than Delaney, Tish, and Rachael, Blake was the closest thing to family she could claim.

The memorial service was held in an empty courtroom at the Harris County Courthouse. Law was Blake's religion. Saying farewell in a church didn't seem fitting. Francine had made all the arrangements. The room was jam-packed with colleagues, opponents, allies, and adversaries. But there was no family present. Blake had been as alone in the world as Jillian.

A poster-sized photograph of Blake sat perched on the judge's bench. Beside it was the urn that held his ashes. The smell of stargazer lilies and chrysanthemums permeated the courtroom. Jillian took a seat in the back row of the gallery. Her head hurt from all the tears she'd been unable to shed. Her throat was tight. Her heart scraped the ground.

Suddenly a memory flashed into her head. One night, four months earlier, she'd gone over to Blake's house for dinner to celebrate putting a cop killer on death row. She'd expected Blake to be in a good mood. He was supposed to be cooking her favorite meal, spaghetti and meatballs. She'd brought a bottle of Chianti for the occasion. Instead, after he'd invited her in, he told her he'd ordered takeout Chinese and then he'd gone to sit in the bay window alcove overlooking the lake behind his property, a wistful expression on his face.

She sat beside him, waiting for him to tell her what had happened, but he did not. Finally, after several minutes of watching him watch the birds landing on the lake for the evening, she'd asked, "Blake? Is something wrong?"

He tilted his gray head at her. He looked so tired, and he gave her a slight smile. "You should get married," he'd murmured.

"Huh?" She'd blinked.

"You shouldn't be here hanging out with an old man. You should be dating, forming relationships, finding a good guy, getting married."

She hadn't expected the hit to her gut that his words inflicted. "You know I'm not a big believer in marriage."

Blake had looked away from her then, his eyes back on the birds and the lake. "You deserve love, Jillian."

She had no answer for that. "Marriage didn't work out so well for you."

"Because I screwed it up. God, if only I could go back in time…" He let his words trail off.

"Did something happen?"

He glanced at her again, and for just a second she saw the starkest regret in his eyes. Regret tinged with fear. The look vanished as quickly as it had appeared, and she convinced herself she must have imagined it.

"Nah." He waved a hand. "Just an old man getting maudlin."

The doorbell had rang then. The delivery driver with their kung pao chicken and steamed pork dumplings. The rest of the evening Blake had been his usual self, but now, looking back on the moment, Jillian couldn't help wondering if that was the day he'd been diagnosed with the brain tumor.

She blinked back the memory. Her nose burned. *Oh,*

Blake, why didn't you tell me you were dying? He'd worked up until the last minute of his life and then died so tritely in Starbucks.

Jillian's heart lurched. She felt inadequate, useless. And guilty that she hadn't seen the signs. She remembered how his vision seemed to be getting worse. How lately he'd been making beginner mistakes when they played chess. She thought they were close friends, and yet he hadn't told her about his illness. Hell, she might as well admit it. She felt a little excluded. He hadn't trusted her with his darkest secret.

Just before the service began, the doors opened one last time and Mayor Newsom swept inside with Judge Alex Fredericks, followed by Alex's beautiful young wife with a towheaded toddler on her hip. The minute Jillian spied Alex and his family, she felt the color drain from her face.

Nausea gripped her.

The last time she'd seen Mrs. Fredericks had been on Christmas Eve of the previous year. At the same time Randal Petry had been shooting Gladys Webelow at the Dash and Go, Jillian had been ringing Alex Frederick's doorbell in the Woodlands, dressed only in a denim duster and knee-high cowboy boots. Learning for the first time that her new lover was married with a family.

Jillian sank down in her seat and prayed neither Alex nor his wife spied her. Newsom ushered them to the front of the room, where they sat side by side in three empty folding chairs. The service lasted over an hour as one person after another took the microphone to remember and honor Blake. Jillian had prepared a speech, but when the officiating minister asked for any final farewell words, she stayed seated. She couldn't bear standing up there in front of Alex.

He had been the biggest mistake of her life.

Her friends urged Jillian to open herself up to a relationship. They'd made her start to hope that she could find love, that there *was* a man out there for her.

And hope was such a dangerous thing.

Alex was handsome and charming and at just thirty-six already a criminal court judge. They looked good together, both tall and athletic. Her friends were all falling giggly in love, and Jillian dared to think, *Why not take a chance*? For the first time in her twenty-nine years on the planet, she'd put her fears aside, opened herself up, and let a man into her heart.

And then she'd found out about Mrs. Fredericks.

Idiot.

She should have known better. No matter what anyone said, there was no such thing as magic. No happily-ever-after. Not for her anyway.

"If there's anyone else who'd like to say something about Blake, please come forward now," the minister said. "If not, Mayor Newsom has an announcement he would like to make, and then we'll conclude the service with a closing prayer."

The minister stepped away from the microphone and the mayor took his place. Newsom shuffled his notes, cleared his throat, and then launched in.

"We've lost a great man in Blake Townsend. He's irreplaceable. But life goes on, and Blake wouldn't want us standing in the way of justice," Newsom said as if he had a clue what Blake wanted. "Since all his friends and colleagues are gathered here in one place, it seems the best time to announce the appointment of our new DA before my formal press conference this afternoon."

A murmur rippled through the crowd.

It was crass and inconsiderate, announcing Blake's successor at his memorial service, but classic Mayor Newsom. The guy had the class of a garden trowel. Jillian caught her breath and bit her bottom lip. She sensed what was coming and dreaded hearing it.

"Judge Alex Fredericks will be the new Harris County district attorney." Newsom turned to Fredericks. "Alex, would you like to say a few words?"

Anger grabbed her throat and shook hard. No, no! It could not be true.

Jillian would not sit still and listen to this. Bile rising in her throat, she charged for the door. Reality settled on her shoulders, even as she tried to outrun the inevitable. She hurried across the polished black marble floor of the courthouse, rushing out into the blowing drizzle, gulping in cold, damp air.

She didn't see the Tom Thumb delivery truck. She just stepped off the curb and into its path.

A horn blared. Tires squealed.

Jillian froze.

The truck's bumper stopped just inches short of her kneecaps.

She stared through the windshield at the driver, and he promptly flipped her the bird. She smiled at him. Smiled and laughed and then couldn't stop.

The driver rolled down the window. "Get out of the road you crazy bitch."

Great, terrific, you almost get run over and you're laughing about it. The guy's right. You are crazy.

She wandered the streets, not paying any attention to where she was going and ending up walking the path through the city park she and Blake had walked many times together, engaged in friendly legal debates. She wondered what he'd think of Alex as his replacement. Blake hadn't known about her relationship with Alex. She'd been too ashamed to tell him.

Her mind kept going back to the memory of the night Blake had told her she should get married, and the more she thought about it, the more convinced she became that had to have been the day he'd gotten his diagnosis. The death sentence he'd shared with no one.

The rain pelted her, and Jillian realized she'd been walking in a big circle for the last thirty minutes. Ducking her head against the quickening rain, she hurried to her office. The place was empty. Everyone else had probably gone to lunch after the services were over. She shrugged out of her coat, dropped down at her desk, and closed her eyes.

"Blake," Jillian whispered out loud. "What am I going to do without you?"

All her girlfriends were married now, getting pregnant, having babies, living lives so very different from her own. She'd used Blake to fill the void. Every Thursday night, they'd played chess together. He'd make dinner, because Jillian didn't cook, or they'd go out to eat, her treat. He was the one she called when she had trouble with a case, and she was the escort he took to political functions. Many assumed they were having an affair. But she'd never felt any of those kinds of feelings for Blake, nor he for her. He'd always been like the dad she'd never really had.

Except now he was gone.

"Ms. Samuels?"

She opened her eyes to see Alex Fredericks standing in the doorway.

His gaze was enigmatic, his stance intimidating.

Jillian thrust out her chin, refusing to let her distress show. "Yes?"

"I want to see you in my office."

She stared. Was the bastard about to fire her? Ever since she'd ended their affair, whenever she appeared in Alex's courtroom, their relationship had been adversarial. She'd lost more than one case she might have won if there'd been another judge on the bench.

"Don't you mean Blake's office?"

"I'm the new DA," he said. "It's my office now, and I want to see you in there immediately."

Jillian wanted to tell him to go to hell, but she held her tongue and got up.

Other employees were filtering into the building. She followed Alex into Blake's office. A fresh surge of anger pushed through her as he commandeered her mentor's chair.

Alex was a very handsome man, with just enough flecks of gray in his black hair to make him looked distinguished. He possessed glacier-blue eyes and a dimpled chin. His shoulders were presidential, his waist lean. He nodded at a chair across from the desk. "Sit down."

"I'd rather stand."

"Suit yourself."

She crossed her arms. His smirk irked the hell out of her. "What do you want?"

"Aren't you going to congratulate me on my new position?"

"No."

He leaned forward, rested his elbows on the desk, and pressed the tips of his fingers together. "You know, things don't have to be this way between us."

She glared.

This was the scumbag who'd bruised her ego and usurped her mentor's place. It wasn't so much that he'd lied to her about his wife. If she was honest with herself, she'd admit she wasn't even that upset over losing him. What really hurt was his betrayal. Just when she'd decided to finally trust a man and put her heart on the line. She'd taken a chance and it had blown up in her face. Plus, he'd made her an unwitting partner in his adultery. She couldn't forgive him for that.

The bastard.

Shame. That's what she felt when she looked at Alex Fredericks. Shame and remorse and self-loathing.

"I'd like to give you the benefit of the doubt, Jillian. We can start over fresh, you and I." Alex raked his gaze over her, his eyes lingering on her breasts.

Her fingers twitched to reach across that desk and smack his smug face. "Give *me* the benefit of the doubt?"

"I'm merely saying there are ways we can repair our tattered relationship." Alex got up and came around the corner of the desk toward her. Surely he was not suggesting what she feared he was suggesting. Was he hinting about resuming their affair?

Jillian held her ground. She was not about to let him make her back up, but she hated being this close to him. Hated the familiar smell of his cologne in her nostrils. Hated that she'd ever thought he was worthy of her caring.

He stood right in front of her, his eyes predatory.

"I've missed you, Jillian," he said.

She snorted.

"It's true."

"Does your wife know how much you've missed me?"

Alex shifted his weight. "My wife and I...we have an understanding."

"What? You screw around and she doesn't understand?"

"I've especially missed that sarcastic wit." He reached out and stroked the back of his hand across her cheek.

"Don't." Jillian grabbed his wrist and flung his hand away from her. "Don't you ever touch me again."

"I *am* your boss."

"And this is sexual harassment. I can file charges."

Alex's expression was hooded, inscrutable. He was too good of a politician to acknowledge her accusation. He didn't move.

Jillian sank her hands on her hips and stepped forward until their noses almost touched. She'd seen this man naked, done intimate things with him that she now sorely regretted. She couldn't believe she'd slept with him and even stupidly imagined having a future with him. She felt like a complete idiot. She'd been right all along—love was for suckers and fools.

He blinked and she saw a flicker of contrition in his eyes, but the whisper of humanity was gone as quickly as it appeared. "Ms. Samuels," he said coldly.

"Yes?"

"I wouldn't recommend that course of action. It would be my word against yours, and I could make your life here quite miserable, indeed."

He was right and she knew it. Blake was gone, and even before that she'd been feeling a strong sense of unease. Now with Fredericks in charge, it was too much to bear.

She experienced that end-of-the-tunnel sensation again she'd been feeling ever since that day in court with Randal Petry. The same day Blake died.

"I don't have to put up with this," Jillian said, injecting her voice with steel as cold as his.

"What do you intend on doing about it?" He drew up his shoulders, puffed out his chest.

"You're a real ass, and I can't believe I slept with you."

"As I recall, we didn't do much sleeping. I miss you,

Jillian. Your fire and your guts and your passion. Seriously, I'd really hate to demote you."

That did it. She wasn't going to put up with his threats. She'd had enough. "You know what, Alex? Shove this job up your ass. I quit."

Chapter 2

Back in her own office, Jillian opened her desk drawers and chucked her belongings into a cardboard box. She thought about calling Delaney or Tish or maybe even Rachael, who was living in the isolated terrain of southwest Texas.

But Jillian did not pick up the phone. Her friends all had their own lives, loves, husbands, and children.

They would listen to her, of course. And sympathize. But they couldn't really understand. They could never know what it was like to grow up the way she'd grown up. They'd try to get her to laugh and tell her everything was going to be all right. But she knew that wasn't true. Nothing was ever going to be the same again.

Blake was really gone.

It hit her then. That she really didn't have anyone. She was alone and it was her own fault. She'd wanted to stay unattached. Her job had been her excuse, but in truth, intimacy of any form scared the hell out of her.

Maybe in the back of her mind, she'd always known Alex was unobtainable. He was too good-looking and accomplished to be single, plus she'd never come right out and asked him if he was married. Why not?

You've got to stop this line of thinking. You can't let yourself get dragged down.

She feared that if the dark cloud chasing her ever caught up with her, the depression would swallow her whole. She had to do something. She had to get away from her life, think this thing through, formulate an action plan.

Two security guards appeared in her doorway. "DA Fredericks sent us. We're here to escort you off the premises, Ms. Samuels," the tallest one said sheepishly.

"Fine." Jillian snapped her briefcase closed and straightened.

"I'll carry that box for you," said the second security guard.

"Thank you."

They escorted her down the corridor, past the curious eyes of her colleagues. Jillian held her head high. A few minutes later, hands shaking, she slid behind the wheel of her red Sebring convertible, the cardboard box stowed in the back behind her, her briefcase stashed on the passenger seat. With trembling fingers, she tried to stab the key into the ignition. After several fumbling attempts, she finally got the engine started.

Were all men cheating bastards? Lying pigs? Even Blake had cheated on his wife. He'd told her his infidelity was what had destroyed his marriage. He regretted it. He was ashamed of what he'd done, but he'd done it. If a good guy like Blake couldn't keep his pants zipped...

I'd like to give you the benefit of the doubt, Jillian. We can start over fresh, you and I. Alex's words rang in her head.

Jillian gritted her teeth. Had he honestly thought she'd jump at the chance to resume their affair? God, how she regretted sleeping with the man, but even more, she regretted feeling as if they'd had something special.

Fool. In your heart you knew better.

It was her own fault for daring to think she deserved the same kind of happiness her friends had found. They'd all wished on the wedding veil. All met the loves of their lives. They'd told her it was worth the risk. That she could find love too. So she'd dared to take a chance.

And it had exploded in her face. Dammit, she'd known better.

Blake dropped dead in Starbucks of the brain tumor he'd hidden from me.

He had abandoned her as well. The only man she'd ever really trusted. Jillian stared unseeingly through the windshield as she drove from the parking lot, her mind numb. Losing Blake hurt so damned much.

Tears, hot and unexpected, burned the back of her eyelids, but she refused to let them fall. She sucked in air, sucked up the pain, closed off her heart. Never again. She'd been hurt too many times by men to ever truly trust one.

It didn't matter that her three best friends had found true love and happily-ever-after. They were different from her. They believed in magic.

No matter how hard she tried, Jillian couldn't believe.

Without even knowing how she got there, numb from everything that had happened in the past week, Jillian drove to the condo she rented in a trendy area of Houston not far from downtown. Her lease was up at the end of the month; she'd planned on renewing it, but now she realized there was nothing holding her here. She'd lost everything. Her mentor, her job, her self-respect.

She wanted to curl into a tight ball and howl from the pain. She hated herself like this. Vulnerable, taken advantage of, used, disregarded. She'd spent her life trying to rise above the victim mentality, to prove she deserved better than the way she'd been treated by her stepmother.

But now she felt stupid, deceived, cheated. And worst of all, the defensive mechanism that had kept her safe all these years, the guard she kept around her heart, had failed her miserably.

She walked into her quiet, lonely house, aching to her very core. She didn't know what drove her, but she tossed her purse and her briefcase on the table and stalked to the bedroom. She went to the cedar chest at the end of her bed, started yanking out sweaters and tossing them heedlessly about the room. At the bottom of the chest she found what she hadn't consciously known she was looking for.

The magical wedding veil.

Rachael had passed it on to her months earlier. It was a floor-length mantilla style made of Rosepoint lace. She remembered the day Delaney had found the veil in a consignment shop just before her wedding to the wrong man, and she remembered the fanciful story the store owner had told.

According to the lore, in long-ago Ireland, there had lived a beautiful young witch named Morag, who possessed a great talent for tatting incredible lace. People came from far and wide to buy the lovely wedding veils she created, but there were other women in the community who were envious of Morag's beauty and talent.

These women lied and told the magistrate that Morag was casting spells on the men of the village. The magistrate arrested Morag but found himself falling madly in love with her. Convinced that she must have cast a spell upon him as well, he moved to have her tried for practicing witchcraft. If found guilty, she would be burned at the stake. But in the end, the magistrate could not resist the power of true love.

On the eve before Morag was to stand trial, he kid-napped her from the jail in the dead of night and spir-ited her away to America, giving up everything he knew for her. To prove that she had not cast a spell over him, Morag promised never to use magic again.

As her final act of witchcraft, she made one last wed-ding veil, investing it with the power to grant the deepest wish of the wearer's soul. She wore the veil on her own wedding day, wishing for true and lasting love. Morag and the magistrate were blessed with many children and much happiness. They lived to a ripe old age and died in each other's arms.

Delaney had wished on the veil to get out of marrying the wrong man, and in the end, she'd found her heart's desire in her soul mate, Nick Vinetti.

Then Delaney had passed the veil on to Tish.

Tish had wished to get out of debt, and the granting of her wish had brought her back together with the husband she'd lost but never stopped loving.

And then Tish had passed the veil on to Rachael.

Rachael had wished to stop being so romantic, and she'd ended up marrying the hero of her dreams.

Jillian didn't believe in magic, but the wedding veil was all the hope she had left. She'd lost everything else.

"What a load of crap," she muttered, but even as she muttered it, she took the antique veil from its protective wrapping and settled it on her head. Compelled by a mys-terious force beyond her control, she stared at herself in the mirror.

"I wish," she muttered, "I wish I'd been born into a lov-ing, trusting, giving family. I wish…I wish…I wish…" Her words trailed off as she realized what it was she really wanted.

Finally, she whispered, "I wish I had a brand-new life."

The second the wish was out of her mouth, her scalp began to tingle and she felt her body grow suddenly heavy. With the wish on her lips, the veil on her head, and utter despair in her heart, Jillian curled up on the floor and fell into a deep, exhausted sleep.

Until two years ago, Tucker Manning had led a magical life.

People said he was charmed, and it was true. Born the youngest child and only son to James and Meredith Manning, he'd been spoiled by his parents and his three older sisters straight from the get-go. He'd possessed an easygoing personality and a bad-boy smile women simply couldn't resist.

And when he discovered he'd not only inherited the famed Manning carpentry skills, but that he had a natural flare for architecture as well, the world beat a path to his door. He had put himself through architectural school with his carpentry skills. For his senior class project, twenty-two-year-old Tuck had designed and constructed an innovative learning center for elementary schoolchildren. Then something amazing and bizarre happened.

The grade point average of every single child enrolled in Tuck's new learning center shot up.

Tuck brushed if off to coincidence. But educators seemed convinced it was the building. They claimed something about the lighting and the open-air blueprint stimulated learning. Other schools heard what had happened, and they commissioned Manning Learning Centers.

Tuck designed them. Each and every time, test scores rose and grade point averages shot up. Tuck figured it was a self-fulfilling prophecy. People thought their children would get smarter in his buildings, so they did.

Architectural Digest ran a feature story on him, dubbing him "Magic Man." He traveled the world building schools and getting rich.

Then he met Aimee Townsend in Albany, New York. A kindergarten teacher by trade. Beautiful girl. Petite. Honey-blond hair, big blue eyes, creamy porcelain complexion. Wearing a *Wizard of Oz* green sweater and a short brown wool skirt. Nice legs. No pantyhose. Wholesome and heartwarming.

Tuck had designed and built *that* classroom as if it was just for her.

Two months later, they were married and bought a loft in Manhattan. He loved city life, but Aimee was a small-town girl at heart, and she made him promise that when they were ready to start a family, they would move to the place where she'd spent her summer vacations as a kid before her parents got divorced. The place she loved most in the world.

Salvation, Colorado.

Tuck had said glibly, easily, "Sure. Why not?" Kids were a long way off.

Then Aimee got very sick with a deadly form of ovarian cancer. He took her from doctor to doctor. Private clinic to exclusive hospital. They consulted experts in Europe and Japan. They went through most of his money, but Tuck didn't care. All he wanted was to save his wife.

In the end, Aimee had whispered, "Take me to Colorado, Tuck. That's where I want to die. At the lake house. In Salvation."

And that was where the magic had run out.

Now Tuck hunkered alone in a small rowboat in the

middle of Salvation Lake in Salvation, Colorado. In spite of his down coat, the wind sliced through him, as cold as a ceramic blade. To warm himself, he took another swig from the bottle of Johnny Walker Red at his feet. The whiskey neatly seared the back of his throat.

"Look at the stars, Aimee," Tuck whispered into the midnight sky carpeted with a thousand points of starlight. "Brilliant as the night I asked you to marry me. Remember?"

The water stretched out around him, inky black and vast. He was a good fifty yards from shore, where the first snowfall of the season clung to the pine trees, looming up like ghostly giants.

"I know I didn't get started on renovating the lake house this year like I promised. A lot of things got in the way. Chick Halsey hired me to add a bedroom onto his house, because he and Addie are expecting another baby. Their fourth. And before that, Jessie Dolittle had me build a pole barn for some new mules. Then there were the special order cabinets for an older couple that just moved up here from Denver. Now the lake house will have to wait because of winter. I'm sorry to disappoint you again, babe. I'll get started on it come spring, I promise."

Another slug of the Johnny Walker and he was a regular furnace inside.

He could picture Aimee sitting across from him in the rowboat. Her long blond hair trailing down her back, her blue eyes aglow, looking the way she'd looked the night he proposed. Right here on this lake. It had been summer then, Fourth of July, actually. Fireworks going off all around the lake, a picnic basket of fried chicken sitting in the bottom of the boat between them. The taste of watermelon on their tongues as they'd kissed.

He'd slipped a four-carat diamond sparkler on her hand, and she'd said, "Yes, yes, yes. You just have to promise me one thing."

"Anything," he'd breathed.

"You can never, ever cheat on me the way my dad cheated on my mother. I won't stand for it. Promise you'll never break my heart."

"I promise," Tuck had sworn. It was an easy promise. He loved her so much, he'd never jeopardize what they had over another woman. His mistake, he realized now, was that he hadn't made her swear not to break his heart.

Tuck's breath frosted in the chilly air. "I miss you, babe. I miss you so damn much. I'm not worth shit without you."

If Aimee were here, she would have chided him for cursing. She was so sweet, so innocent. Too innocent for this sorry world.

Grief knotted his throat.

It was bad today.

Some days it was better. Some days he was almost his old self again, flirting innocently with the waitresses at the Bluebird Café, whistling while he sanded down cabinets or planed doors, smiling at people on the streets. Forgetting for hours at a stretch. Some days the sorrow didn't hit him until he was underneath the covers with the lights turned off, and the empty spot in the bed beside him stretched out as wide as the lake.

Then the grief would sledgehammer him. His beloved Aimee was gone, and he was alone.

Some days, like today, were so bad that the only thing that could dull the pain was good old Johnny W. He put the whiskey bottle to his lips. Took another sip and wondered if it was against the law to drink and row.

When the hell did it ever stop hurting? When would he wake up and not listen for the sound of her moving about the kitchen, cooking him egg-white omelets, which he despised but had eaten anyway to make her happy? She'd told him he had to watch his cholesterol, because she wanted him with her until they were stooped and gray. Tuck had eaten the loathsome egg-white omelets, but she'd been the one to break the pact. Aimee would never grow stooped and gray. She was forever twenty-five.

He threw back his head and howled at the starry sky. "Fuuuuck!"

The sound of his mournful curse carried on the crisp night air, echoing up and down the lake. The outburst made him feel a little better so he did it again.

"Fuuuuck!"

Wind rushed into his lungs, freezing the pipes the whiskey had previously warmed. He got to his feet, threw his arms wide, and embraced the icicle breeze. Bring it on, Mother Nature.

"Fuuuuck!"

The boat wobbled. Tuck stumbled. Johnny Walker played fast and loose with his balance. He tried to sit back down, but gravity already had him in a choke hold.

Next thing he knew, Tucker Manning, the former Magic Man of Manhattan, was tumbling headlong into Salvation Lake.

Evie Manning Red Deer was locking up the Bluebird Café when her husband, Ridley, came up the sidewalk and slipped his arms around her waist. He pressed his face into her hair and pulled her up flush against his body so she could feel his arousal pressing into her backside.

"Mmm," he murmured. "You smell like fry bread."

She turned in his arms. His shoulders were as broad as beams, his ebony hair longer than hers, and she slipped her arms around his neck, tilting her lips up for a kiss.

Ridley crushed his mouth against hers. Evie breathed him in. God, how she loved this man.

When she'd come to Salvation to be with her younger brother in his time of grief over losing his young wife, she could never have imagined that she would fall in love with a native, marry him, and end up running the Bluebird Café. She was a pastry chef who'd trained at Lenotre in Paris. She'd trotted the globe. Seen the world. Met royalty and movie stars. She'd had far more than her share of lovers. But Salvation, Colorado, was where she'd lost her heart, and she'd freely surrendered her old life to be with this man. Ridley Red Deer was everything Evie had never known she wanted.

Ridley was kind and generous, strong and understanding. While he was truly masculine, he had a tender heart as big as the sky. He grounded her, calmed her in a way no one else ever had.

He broke the kiss, nuzzled her neck, and slipped his hands up underneath her coat.

"Ridley." She giggled.

"Uh-huh?" He lowered his eyelids suggestively.

"We're out on the street for everyone to see. Save it for when we get home."

"Everyone knows how crazy I am about you." He ran his tongue along her neck, sending shivers of delight darting down her spine. "How I can't keep my hands off you."

Panting, she pulled away. "Down, boy."

He chuckled and let her go but reached out to take her hand. She looked at his profile in the lamplight. Proud Native American nose, ruddy skin, high cheekbones, intelligent dark eyes. Her heart did an instinctive little hopscotch the way it always did when she caught sight of him.

Ridley linked his fingers through hers, and they started down the street, swinging their arms in unison, heading for their house on the next block over. Every night, he came to walk her home from the café.

"So how was your day?"

"We cleared four hundred dollars."

"Not bad for a Thursday in down season."

"We had a caravan of recreational vehicles stop in, snowbirds on their way south for the winter. They'd seen the feature story on us in *RV Today*."

"That's great."

She could hear his pride for her in his voice. Evie leaned into him, inhaled his familiar scent. "So how was Tucker when you left him?"

"Um, I wasn't with Tuck tonight."

"What do you mean?" She punched her husband playfully on the upper arm. "Are you teasing me?"

"Dutch dropped by and we watched college basketball. UNLV trounced the hell out of USC."

Evie stopped walking and sank her hands on her hips. "Ridley, please don't tell me you forgot."

"Forgot what?"

Worry grabbed hold of her. "Rid, it's the second anniversary of Aimee's death. I told you this morning to go hang with Tuck when you got off work."

"You didn't tell me."

"I did." She heard her voice rise an octave.

"When did you tell me?"

"You were in the shower, and I was putting on my makeup, and I clearly told you—"

"If you told me when I was in the shower, then I didn't hear you. Running water and all that."

"Never mind." Evie spun on her heels and started walking in the opposite direction. She wrung her hands. "I can't believe you forgot the day Aimee died."

"You're overreacting," Ridley said, chasing after her. "Tuck's been a lot better lately."

She stopped and spun around. "Am I? What about last year?"

A sobering look passed over her husband's face. "That was last year. Tuck's come a long way since then."

"But it's the anniversary of her death."

Ridley pressed a hand to the nape of his neck. "Look, I'm sorry. I should have remembered."

"We've got to get over to the lake house. No telling what kind of shape he's in." She started running down the street, then cut across the town square, an odd sense of urgency pressing down on her. Tuck was in trouble; she just knew it.

"Evie, hang on," Ridley called out. "I'll go get the car."

Ten minutes later, they pulled up into the driveway of the lake house where Tuck had been living. All the lights were out, and the place was silent.

"It's dark," Evie said, anticipating the worst.

"It's nine-thirty. Is it possible he just went to bed early?"

Evie hopped out of the car, dashed up the front steps, and twisted the knob. The door sprang inward. No one locked their doors in Salvation except during tourist season. Evie flicked on the light in the foyer. "Tuck?"

Ridley came up behind her. "Tuck!"

"Tucker, are you here? It's me and Ridley."

No answer.

"Check the upstairs bedrooms; I'll check his workshop," Evie instructed her husband.

They split up and searched the house. Minutes later, they met up again in the kitchen. Ridley was shaking his head.

"He's gone and done something stupid again," Evie said. "I just know it."

"You don't know that." Ridley slid his big arm around her shoulder. "Don't jump to conclusions."

"We've got to check the dock."

"Why would he be on the dock? It's freezing cold out on the water."

Evie strode out onto the redwood dock, feeling the boards vibrate as Ridley came up behind her. She tried to imagine what she would feel like if something happened to her husband, but the thought was too horrible to bear.

"I see your brother's rowboat," Ridley said.

"Where?"

Her husband pointed out across the lake stretching as dark as midnight.

Evie squinted. She could barely make it out, but the boat looked empty. Her hand strayed to her throat.

Oh, little brother, what have you done?

The next thing she knew, Ridley was stripping off his coat, kicking off his shoes.

"What is it?"

"I see something. I see him. He's out there."

"Tuck's in the water?"

In answer to her question, Ridley dove in. Evie's blood thundered in her ears as she watched her husband disappear underneath the icy black water.

Chapter 3

Tuck coughed up a lungful of Salvation Lake.

He opened his eyes and looked up at his sister and brother-in-law. He was lying on his back on the dock, soaking wet, shivering so hard he could barely breathe.

"Thank God, he's alive." Evie burst into tears.

"Go start the car, crank the heater," Ridley instructed.

Evie ran ahead of them.

It was only then that Tuck realized his brother-in-law was as wet as he. Ridley slipped an arm underneath Tuck's shoulder and helped him to his feet. "Lean on me."

"Wh-wh-wh—" His teeth chattered so hard he could barely speak, so he just gave up trying and let Ridley half drag him to his Toyota 4Runner.

Evie had the engine running and the heater blasting by the time Ridley deposited Tuck in the backseat. She draped a blanket over her husband's shoulders and then folded another one around him.

She wrinkled her nose. "You smell like a brewery."

Tuck didn't defend himself. His sister was right. He smelled—and felt—like a skid-row bum.

Glowering, she hopped behind the wheel and drove to her house. They arrived and got out of the car.

"I can't believe you tried to drown yourself," she scolded, following along beside them as Ridley helped Tuck in the back door. His damned legs didn't want to bend.

"I...didn't." It was all Tuck could manage.

"No?" Evie worried her bottom lip with her teeth and sank her hands on her hips.

Tuck shook his head and slumped into the kitchen chair.

"Then what were you doing out on that lake?"

He didn't have the energy to answer.

Evie turned. "Rid, get out of those wet things and take Tuck with you. I'll have hot soup waiting when you get finished."

"I'm taking him to the sweat lodge," Ridley said.

She made a face. "He needs to get dry first."

"He needs more than that, and the sweat lodge will warm him up," his brother-in-law said firmly. "If ever a man has needed a vision quest to set him on the right path, it's your brother."

"He doesn't believe in that stuff. You know we were raised Roman Catholic."

"You're the one who doesn't believe," Ridley said.

Tuck knew Ridley used the sweat lodge as part of his religious practices, but he'd never been invited to take part. He'd been mildly interested and had asked a few questions, but Ridley and Tuck had the kind of relationship where you didn't pry.

"Your brother has an open mind," he continued. "You get Tuck some soup. I'm going to go start a fire in the sweat lodge."

"Not in those wet things you're not."

"Woman," Ridley growled. "I know you get bossy when you're upset, so I'm not going to fight with you. Heat your brother some soup. I'll be back in a minute."

Ridley disappeared out the back door, leaving Tuck alone with his second oldest sister. Evie turned her back on him, went to the refrigerator, pulled out a plastic container of homemade chicken noodle soup, and stuck it in the microwave to heat.

Tuck sat dripping water all over her kitchen floor and shivering into the blanket. "I'm sorry, Evie. It wasn't my intention to upset you. It was just…I couldn't stop…Aimee."

She shuddered and tears gleamed in her hazel eyes. "Tuck, I know you're still grieving, especially today, but I can't bear to think of what would have happened if we hadn't come along when we did. I don't mean to lecture, but it's been two years. At some point, you've got to let go of Aimee. You know she wouldn't want you to keep hanging on, jeopardizing your own life."

Tuck drew in a shaky breath as the gravity of the situation hit him. He *had* almost died tonight, and he didn't even know how he felt about it.

"You've been doing so well lately, and I'd thought you were finally healing and—" The microwave timer dinged, and Evie broke off what she was saying. She took out the soup, plucked a spoon from the silverware drawer, and slid the Tupperware bowl across the table toward him.

Grateful for the soup, Tuck reached out for it as Ridley came in the back door. "The sweat lodge is ready," he said. "You can bring the soup with you."

He got up, holding the bowl, and followed his brother-in-law into the backyard toward a white domed structure with a small hole in the roof. A thin plume of gray smoke swirled through the opening, sending the smell of mesquite into the air.

"Go in and take off all your clothes," Ridley instructed. "Sit down on the bearskin rug, and breathe in the smoke. Make your mind empty. Pick a word that resonates with you. A mantra like love, peace, serenity. Repeat it over and over as you breathe slow and deep. Stay in here until you have a vision."

"You're not coming in with me?" Tuck met his brother-in-law's eyes.

"This is your vision quest. You're the one who's searching for meaning, my friend."

"Umm...from what I can tell, there is no meaning."

"Exactly. Now go find it." Ridley gave him a shove. "I'm tired of your sister fretting about you. It's time you took responsibility for your own healing."

Anger crouched inside Tuck, a tiger ready to spring, but he knew Ridley was right. He'd worried Evie long enough. Who knew, maybe a vision quest was precisely what he needed. "I...How will I know if I'm doing it right?"

"Let whatever happens be okay," Ridley said cryptically. Then he turned and went back into the house.

Tuck ducked into the sweat lodge. There was a small fire in the middle of the room and radiant sauna stones circling the fire pit. Other than bearskin rugs, quilted blankets, and oversized throw pillows, the place was empty. But there were stereo speakers bolted to the walls, and they spilled low, steady sounds of Native American Indian drumming.

He stripped off the wet clothes. The temperature in the sweat lodge climbed. His primary objective was warmth and dryness. He didn't give a damn about a vision quest.

The bearskin rug tickled his naked butt. He sat cross-legged in front of the fire. Smoke swirled upward, funneling through the flue and out the hole in the roof.

Johnny Walker Red was still doing a number on his head. He closed his eyes. Took a deep breath.

Let whatever happens be okay.

He sipped the soup, feeling the liquid warm him up inside. He sat and sipped, inhaling smoke and listening to drum music and waiting for something to happen.

But nothing did.

Tuck thought of Aimee and how'd he'd promised to buy the lake house from her dad and renovate it. She believed the house held special spiritual powers. It had given her peace in her final days. She believed it could restore his inspiration, reignite the creative magic her illness had stolen from him if he'd give it the chance. But he'd lost his faith in magic.

"Fix it up, Tuck. Fix up the house and you'll see. It will come to full life again, just as you will in the process of rebuilding," she whispered to him on the day she'd died. "Promise me, please."

He'd promised, but he hadn't had the heart to follow through with it yet.

Tuck thought of his rowboat still out on Salvation Lake. He thought about Evie and Ridley and how they spent too much time worrying about him. Hell, Evie had moved to Salvation because she'd been so worried about him, and then she'd met Ridley and married him. He thought of how easy life used to be for him—the Magic Man.

But the magic was long gone. He'd used up his share.

He took a deep breath and felt a slow, languid heat snake through his body. His muscles relaxed. His head spun.

Dizzy. He felt dizzy.

Dreamily, Tuck set aside the cup of soup. It was hot in here, steamy, and getting hotter all the time. Sweat beaded his brow. Smoke grew thicker in the room. He coughed, blinked, and then he could have sworn he saw someone step out of the smoke.

It was a woman. High breasts, narrow waist, curvy hips, walking straight toward him, cloaked in shadows and smoke.

"Aimee?" he croaked.

She came closer and he could see it wasn't Aimee. His Aimee had been petite, small-boned, blond.

This woman was an Amazon. At least five-ten, maybe taller, black Cleopatra hair, chocolate brown eyes.

"Who are you?" he whispered, but she didn't answer.

Instead, she started to perform a slow, deliberate strip-tease, and it was only then that he realized she was clothed in veils. White veils. Wedding veils. She twirled in time to the drumming, peeling off a veil with each turn. The music got faster and so did she, whisking off veil after veil until she was a whirling dervish, spinning around the sweat lodge.

The music stopped.

And she spun to a halt in front of him.

All the veils were gone, strewn about the sweat lodge. She was totally naked.

Instantly, he got an erection.

God, she was a beauty. The cut of her shiny ebony hair accentuated her high cheekbones. Ivory skin smooth as glass. Full, crimson lips. The high thrust of her pert pink nipples. The flat of her belly. The springy dark triangle of hair above her thighs.

Her gaze was bold, but her eyes…her eyes…they were *lonely*. As lonely as Tuck's.

The music started again. A slow, thumping beat. Like the heart of an athlete.

Thud. Thud. Thud.

She sauntered toward him; she was as leggy as a runway model.

Was she real? Was he dreaming? It didn't feel like a dream. Was he on a vision quest? Was this supposed to be happening?

Let whatever happens be okay, Ridley had said.

What did that mean? Was he just supposed to go with it no matter what transpired? Have sex with a stranger?

She dropped to her knees in front of him, reached out, and walked her fingers up his forearm.

Tuck gulped.

If this was some kind of hallucination, it was a damned good one. She felt so real.

"Who are you?" he asked again.

A sly grin lifted her lips. "Don't you know?"

"No."

She laughed, a low sexy sound, and then she said the strangest thing. "Why, I'm the other side of you."

"Other side of me?'

"Uh-huh. Mirror image."

Her answer made no sense. He was just about to tell her that, when she leaned in close and ran her tongue along his lips. She tasted like dark chocolate—rich and sinful.

He hadn't been with a woman since Aimee, and he didn't want to be with this one, but his body had other ideas. His cock grew even harder.

She noticed. Purred. Touched him.

He was granite in her hands.

Shame shoved Tuck's heart into his stomach. He felt as if he was cheating on Aimee.

It's just a dream.

Was it?

And besides, Aimee's dead. You're not cheating on her. You're a young, healthy man. You're allowed to have sexual desires.

Where were these thoughts coming from? What was happening to him? This was a bad idea. He had to get out of the sweat lodge. He tried to get up, but the naked woman with the exotic brown eyes was throwing her legs around him, straddling his lap.

"No, no. I don't want you." He settled his hands around her waist to pull her off him, but her skin felt so warm and soft beneath his palms that he just held on.

"Shh," she murmured, like a mother soothing her baby. "Shh." She put her lips against his throat and kissed him so lightly that it felt as if she was tickling him with a feather. "It's okay. It's all right."

He closed his eyes, battling against his desire. "I'm not in a good place. I'm—"

"Shh." Her arms went around him, and she cradled his head to her breasts.

Tuck shifted, his resistance melting. He laid back against the bearskin rug and took a deep breath. Smoke swirled in his lungs. His head spun. The room was so hot. His body was drenched in sweat.

Lower and lower she kissed, heading for dangerous territory.

He threaded his fingers through her hair. "No, no," he protested weakly.

"Yes..." She kissed him. "Yes."

Another kiss.

Then her hand was on him. Stroking his throbbing

head. She laughed a smooth laugh that loosened something in his belly.

"It's just a dream anyway; it's not real," he muttered, all the fight gone out of him.

She closed her mouth over him, and overwhelmed, Tuck simply surrendered.

Jillian woke up from her naughty sex dream with a flushed face and a pounding heart. She shivered, remembering him. Tall and muscled, but not overtly so. Straight nose, strong chin, a trustworthy jaw ringed with a stubble of beard. His eyes had been the color of expensive whiskey. His hair like winter wheat.

He'd seemed so sad. As if he'd been carrying the weight of the world on his shoulders for a very long time and didn't possess the strength to take one more step.

And then she'd seduced him.

Gulping, Jillian shook her head to dispel the image and threw back the covers. And that's when the realization hit her. She had nowhere to go and nothing to do. In all her twenty-nine years on earth, it was a first.

She fell back against the pillows, staring at the ceiling, thinking of the sex dream. It had seemed so real that she wouldn't have been surprised to find the man beside her. Yet, while her body felt strangely electrified, the other side of the bed stretched empty.

What did surprise her, however, was the fact she still wore the mourning clothes she'd worn to Blake's funeral. And she still had that stupid wedding veil on her head.

Chagrined at having put the veil on in the first place and being desperate enough to make a wish, she yanked it off and sprang to her feet. She could have lingered in bed, tried to get back the wisp of the smoking hot dream, but

Jillian was not a woman who lingered, even when she had nowhere to go or nothing to do.

She folded the veil and stuffed it in the cedar chest, wanting it out of sight, out of mind. She stripped, leaving her clothes lying in the floor, and took a hot shower, washing away the last remnants of the haunting dream, the man with the whiskey eyes.

There. It's over. Forgotten.

But as she poured herself a cup of coffee from the automatic-drip coffeemaker on her kitchen cabinet—it was the only kitchen appliance she owned beyond the major ones that came with the place—she thought of him again.

He'd seemed so damned sad.

The guy wasn't real. Move on. It was just a dream.

God, but he'd had some kind of body.

Haven't you had enough of men after what Alex—

Enough.

Determined to stop thinking about the dream man, she took peanut butter—the smooth kind—from her pantry. She slathered it on a slice of wheat bread, folded it over, and called it breakfast. Balancing the peanut butter sandwich on her coffee cup, she opened the back door and walked out onto the stoop of her condo, where she liked to sit and watch the sunrise and eat her morning meal on the few days in Houston when the weather allowed such indulgences.

Jillian had just settled onto the first step and stuck the sandwich in her mouth when she saw him.

Hunkered in the corner behind the yaupon holly. Watching her like a fugitive. Correction. He wasn't watching her; he was watching the sandwich.

She took the peanut butter sandwich out of her mouth. "You hungry? You want this?"

He leapt from the shrubbery and trotted over.

Up close, she could see his mixed heritage—Lab, Doberman, collie, German shepherd, and with those ears, maybe even a bit of basset hound. He possessed big brown melancholy eyes, a sharp nose, and a tail that was too long for his body. He looked like a five-hundred-piece jigsaw puzzle put together by a three-year-old.

Nothing fit.

The mutt stopped at the bottom of the steps, nose twitching, oversized tail wagging. Jillian extended the sandwich, and he took it from her hand with surprising gentleness.

It was gone in two quick bites.

He looked hopeful.

"You still hungry?"

Of course he was still hungry. His flanks were so lean that she could count his ribs. His hair was matted, and she feared he had fleas and ticks, so she was leery of letting him into the condo.

"Hang on," she said. "I think I've got a can of chunked white albacore in the pantry."

He hung on.

She got the tuna. He scarfed it down as quickly as he'd disposed of the peanut butter sandwich. When he was done, he sat on his haunches and looked at her. She was not a pet person. Had never owned one. Not even a goldfish. Her stepmother wouldn't allow it, and she had no idea what to do with him.

You need to find his owner.

She knocked on her neighbors' doors. The dog followed. No one claimed him. After an hour of canvassing the neighborhood, she ended up back at her condo.

"Right back where we started."

The expression on his doggy face seemed to say, *Story of my life*.

She took him to the vet. She had nothing else to do, and it helped keep her mind off Blake and Alex and quitting her job and her crazy, wedding-veil-induced sex dream with a whiskey-eyed man in a sweat lodge.

"The dog's been neglected," the veterinarian told her. "He needs medicine."

"That's why I'm here."

"We'll give him shots, clean him up, check his blood work, and he needs to be neutered."

"I'm not going to keep him. I just want him healthy while I look for his owners."

"I seriously doubt he has an owner. If you keep him, look into the neutering thing."

"I'm not keeping him. I'm not a pet person. I don't do pets."

The vet prescribed medication. "Give him these pills once a month to prevent heartworms."

"Hello, not keeping him."

He pressed the prescription into her hand. "In case you change your mind."

She wasn't going to change her mind. She couldn't change it if she wanted to. Her condo didn't allow dogs.

When she got home, she called the *Houston Chronicle* and took out an ad. Then she went on the computer and posted on craigslist. *Lost dog.* She detailed his vital statistics and added her cell phone number.

"Now we wait," she told the mutt.

He gazed at Jillian as if she was the most impressive person on the face of the earth.

"Remember, Mutt, I'm not a pet person, so don't get attached. I'll just break your heart."

He looked as if he didn't believe her.

"I will. I'm mean that way. Ask anyone."

Her cell phone rang.

"Hey," she told Mutt. "This could be it. Your long-lost family." She flipped open her phone. "Hello?"

"Jillian Samuels?"

"Yes?" She hadn't put her name on the craigslist ad. The call couldn't be about the dog.

"This is Hamilton Green. I'm Blake Townsend's attorney," the man said.

At the mention of Blake's name, she curled her fingers tighter around the phone. "Yes?"

"I need to speak with you in person."

"What's this about?"

"Mr. Townsend has left you an inheritance and a sacred responsibility. May I have my secretary pencil you in for a three-thirty appointment on Tuesday?"

"How was the sweat lodge?" Ridley asked Tuck as they drove to the construction site on the other side of the mountain the following morning. They were both working as contract labor—Ridley hired as an electrician, Tuck as a carpenter for a new spec house going up.

Ridley was behind the wheel of his SUV. Tuck was ensconced in the passenger seat wishing he'd driven alone. But he'd woken up in the sweat lodge that morning, and Ridley had just assumed they'd carpool to the job site.

Tuck shrugged.

"Did you have a vision?"

"I don't want to talk about it."

"You sure? Because sometimes vision quests can be pretty intense."

"Mule deer in the bar ditch." Tuck pointed not so much

to warn his brother-in-law just in case the animal decided to dart into the road as deer often did in that part of the country, but to distract him from the conversation. That damn vision was imprinted on his brain. It made him feel horny and guilty as hell. He was afraid of his own subconscious, and the last thing he wanted was to have Ridley Red Deer analyze it.

His brother-in-law slowed.

The doe raised her head as they motored past, and she stared Tuck squarely in the eyes. The deer looked accusatory, as if she knew all about those shameful sweat lodge happenings.

You're losing your marbles. Snap out of it.

"You sure you don't want to talk about it?" Ridley asked. "It might help to powwow."

"I'm good, thanks."

"That bad?"

"We're not talking about this."

"So you *did* have a vision?"

"That constitutes talking."

"Gotcha. No talking about the vision quest."

"Thank you."

A long moment of silence stretched out. Tuck let out a relieved breath. Ridley was gonna drop it. He stared out the window, studying the fall scenery. This time of year, most of the leaves were gone. The snow on the ground was light, but there would soon be more.

"So how'd you end up in the lake last night?" Ridley ventured. Apparently, he just wasn't going to let it go.

"My sister put you up to this conversation, didn't she?" Tuck asked.

"How'd you know?"

"You're not usually so intrusive."

"Come on, dude. Throw me a bone. You know Evie. She'll gnaw my ear off with questions if I don't bring her something."

"Sort of like what you're doing to me?"

"So you can see how annoying it is."

"She's my sister. I know how annoying it can be."

"About the lake..."

Tuck sighed. "I was feeling sorry for myself. Took a boat ride on the second anniversary of my wife's death. That's not so crazy."

"In the middle of the night? In Colorado? In October?"

"Hey, at least it wasn't February."

"Valid point. Although if it had been February, you could have just skated out on the lake."

Ridley shut up again, but this time Tuck was afraid to count on the silence. *Note to self: Find another carpool buddy.*

"Your sister loves you. She worries."

"I know."

"We both care about you."

"I know that too."

"There is life after Aimee."

That one he wasn't so sure about it. He might be breathing, but it sure as hell wasn't much of a life. Walking around with only a small shred of heart left inside him.

"You should start dating again."

Tuck folded his arms over his chest and stared determinedly out the window. "I'm not ready."

"Evie and I could double-date with you. If that'd make it easier." Ridley stopped at an intersection behind a green garbage truck.

Tuck focused on an banana peel dangling from a crack in the truck's tailgate. "Not interested."

"How about Sissie Stratford?"

"Aimee didn't like her, and she's got that phony laugh."

"Too bad Lily Massey got engaged to Bill Chambers. Aimee liked her and she's really pretty."

"I'm sure Bill isn't thinking it's too bad Lily said yes to his proposal."

Ridley snapped his fingers. "I know. What about Lexi Kilgore? She's nice."

"She's older than I am."

"Please, by what? Three years? Evie's two years older than me, and it makes no difference at all."

"Lexi's nice enough, but there's just no spark there; besides, she talks too much."

"What about that new bartender at the Rusty Nail? Have you see her?"

"I haven't been at the Nail in weeks."

"She's cute. Blond. I know you have a thing for blondes. I think her name's Tiffany or Amber or…" Ridley snapped his fingers. "Brandi. It's Brandi. Her name is Brandi."

"How very bartendery of her."

"So, you want me to introduce you?"

"Rid," Tuck growled. "I appreciate the effort, I really do. But I'm just not interested."

"You do know what my cultural beliefs are in regard to the vision quest, right?"

Tuck shrugged. "You might want to make that a little clearer for me."

"When you're a young man entering adulthood, or you're at a crossroads in your life, my tribe believes the vision quest guides you on to the next phase in life. You, my friend, are at a serious crossroad."

He couldn't argue with that. "Okay."

"The dream you had in the sweat lodge is a harbinger of what's ahead," Ridley continued. "Not what's behind you."

Tuck pondered that one. A harbinger of what lay ahead. Hmm. So he was going to be sexually molested by a wedding veil–draped dervish? The thought made him both uncomfortable and excited.

The excitement disturbed him.

"So about this vision. Maybe you're confused by the symbolism and you need me to interpret—"

"I'm turning on the radio now. What program is it that you really hate?" Tuck reached for the radio dial and snapped it on. He didn't want to discuss this. "Yeah, here it is—*Rush Limbaugh*."

Ridley laughed. "Okay, I get it. Please spare me *Rush*. I'll shut up about the vision quest. But when you're ready to talk—"

"I know where to find you."

Chapter 4

All weekend long, no one called about the dog.

By Tuesday, Jillian was convinced no one was going to claim him. Poor baby. She knew what it was like to be unwanted. "I guess I'm stuck with you, Mutt."

The dog didn't seem to mind.

Jillian was starting not to mind so much either. Sure, he shed hair all over the place, so she had to vacuum every day, and he had the bad habit of chewing on her shoes, but she was surprised by how much the dog lifted her spirits.

It was a pity. She'd found someone worse off than she was and that cheered her up.

"I'm only keeping you around because you make me feel good about myself," she told him.

Mutt seemed cool with that too.

"Can you behave yourself while I'm off to see Blake's lawyer? No shoe chewing? Especially stay away from the Jimmy Choos. If I'm unemployed much longer, I might have to sell those suckers on eBay for some quick cash."

Mutt wagged his tail.

"Okay, I'm taking you at your word. But to be on the safe side, I'm shutting you out of the bedroom. And fair warning—if I'm keeping you, we *are* looking into that whole neutering thing."

The dog lowered his head. Amazing how he seemed to understand her. Who knew that dogs could be so cool?

At three-thirty on the nose, Jillian walked into Hamilton Green's office. She'd tried not to think too much about what Blake could have left her in his will. Thinking about it made it too real. She still wasn't ready to fully accept that he was gone.

Maybe he'd left her his marble chess set. She'd like to have that to remember him by. As she settled into the chair across from the lawyer in his plush scholarly looking office, the tears she'd yet to shed thickened behind her eyelids.

"Thank you for coming, Ms. Samuels, and please accept my condolences on the loss of your mentor." Hamilton Green had a broad flat face, a Jay Leno chin, and salt-and-pepper hair that gave way to male pattern baldness. You could tell he'd never been handsome, not even in youth.

"You knew Blake was my mentor?"

"We golfed together. He spoke of you often and with great fondness."

The pressure behind her eyes tightened. She realized she'd known Blake longer and more thoroughly than she'd known her own father.

The lawyer steepled his fingers. "I'm certain his fondness for you is the reason he appointed you as executor."

Her throat constricted. "He did?"

"Blake also left instructions in his will that you be the one to scatter his ashes over Salvation Lake."

The announcement took her by surprise. "Me?"

He nodded. "The will still has to be probated, of course,

and as executor, you'll be checking up on everything. But as it stands in Blake's current will, he left the bulk of his estate to legal aid charities. You were the only individual mentioned in his will. He had a new will drawn up the week after his daughter's death."

Jillian's nose burned. She bit down on her bottom lip. Honestly, while Blake had been her mentor and they'd been close, she hadn't truly realized she'd meant so much to him.

"He left you his property on Salvation Lake."

"Where is that?" Blake had never mentioned anything to her about owning lake property.

"Salvation, Colorado. It's a small tourist town north of Denver. The house was built in the sixties, and it has never been renovated. It's been vacant for years. I have no idea what condition it's in or even the approximate value of the property."

"Blake left me a lake house?" she repeated, still unable to believe it.

"He did at that."

"And he wants me to scatter his ashes on the lake?"

"Yes."

It was a lot to absorb. Emotion clotted her throat at the notion of scattering Blake's ashes. Alone. Suddenly, her world seemed very small, indeed. She had no experience with this sort of thing. She didn't even have anyone she could ask. Blake would have been the person she would have turned to for such advice.

"Here's a copy of his will and the keys to the house." Hamilton Green pushed a manila envelope across his desk toward her.

"The house is paid off?"

"Free and clear."

She took a deep breath, determined to do her duty firmly and without negligence. This is what Blake wanted. She would not disappoint him.

"And here are Blake's remains." The lawyer picked up an urn that had been sitting on the floor beside his desk and handed it to her.

At the weight of the urn, a tumult of emotions flipped through her. Sorrow and surprise, uncertainty and confusion, despair and yet at the same time, a small unexpected flicker of hope.

Blake had left her a lake house in Colorado.

It was almost as if he'd thrown her a life preserver in her moment of greatest need.

Salvation.

A fresh start. From the grave, Blake was offering her a fresh start. He'd given Jillian her first job; now he was giving Jillian her first home.

She stared at the urn and the manila envelope and the keys, and in that moment, she just knew what to do.

Accept Salvation.

Ridley Red Deer was worried about his wife's little brother.

He shouldn't have put Tuck in the sweat lodge. Clearly, from the way he had been acting, he hadn't been ready for whatever had happened in there. It had been like sticking a six-year-old on a Harley without a helmet and telling him to take off. A vision quest was heavy-duty mojo.

On the second anniversary of Aimee's death, Ridley had felt guided. He thought the spirit had spoken to him, telling him to shove a soaking wet, drunken Tuck into the sweat lodge to renew his ragged soul. But he could see that Tuck had been unsettled by whatever he'd experienced.

Doubt gnawed at Ridley. Evie had been right.

His wife was always right. It was damned aggravating.

Thing of it was, Ridley couldn't undo it. Tuck had already been initiated. He'd seen something. The only way Ridley could help him was to get him to discuss what he'd seen.

But Tuck was not inclined to talk.

Ridley picked up a six-pack of Michelob on his way home from work and dropped by the lake house. He found Tuck huddled on the dock in a deck chair, staring at the sunset with a University of Colorado blanket thrown over his lap.

"Are you remembering how cold the water is this time of year?" Ridley asked.

"Hey, buddy," Tuck greeted. "Have a seat."

Ridley dusted snow from the deck chair beside Tuck and plunked down. He twisted the top off a longneck bottle of Michelob and passed it to his brother-in-law before opening a second one for himself.

They said nothing for a long time. Just sipped and watched the sun slide down the sky. Finally, Ridley broke the silence. "You still planning on staying at the lake house?"

"Yes," Tuck said fiercely. "Starting next spring, I'm renovating the house the way I promised Aimee. I should have started it when Blake deeded the place to me four months ago, but I just couldn't summon the energy."

"It was pretty weird how Blake just deeded you the land out of the blue," Ridley said.

"I guess he felt guilty." Tuck's voice caught. "Blake never came back to Salvation after the divorce. I suppose he held on to the cottage simply because he planned on giving it to Aimee one day. She had her own key, and he'd given her permission to use it anytime, but their relationship was so strained that she didn't want him to know we were here. She wouldn't let me tell him that she was dying."

"That's hard-core."

"Aimee just couldn't forgive her father for cheating on her mother and busting up the family. I tried to talk to her about forgiving him, but as sweet as she was, forgiveness was not one of Aimee's virtues. If you ever got on her shit list, you were banned for life."

"That must have been really hard on her dad," Ridley mused. Thinking about becoming a parent was causing him to consider things in a different light. He wondered what he would do if he ever found himself in a situation like Blake Townsend's relationship with his daughter, and he couldn't fathom it.

"She never gave him a chance to make amends. She didn't want him to know about her cancer."

"Why?"

"She didn't want his pity. Nor did she want him to suddenly start trying to be a father when he hadn't been around all those years."

Ridley was still puzzling it out. "Aimee cheated her father out of precious time with her. Looking at it from her father's perspective, she was pretty cruel to the guy."

"I know." Tuck looked glum. "But she had her mind set, and I couldn't change it. Sometimes you've just gotta stay out of it."

Ridley nodded. "You have no desire to ever go back to architecture? No more Magic Man of Manhattan?"

Tuck snorted a harsh laugh. "I was so full of shit back then. It took something like losing Aimee to make me see what matters most in life. The people you love. Like you and Evie. Aimee's ashes are scattered on this lake. I'm not going anywhere. Salvation's home."

"Aw, dude, tell me you're not getting mushy. Here, have another beer."

"I'm thinking I should hold off."

"Probably wise." Ridley nodded and noticed that fresh snowflakes had started drifting from the sky.

After another long moment, Tuck spoke. "I saw a woman."

"Huh? Are you dating someone?"

"No, no. I saw a woman. In the sweat lodge. In my vision. At least I hope it was a vision."

Ridley tensed. His stomach knotted. A woman could be a good omen or a bad one. It depended on the circumstances. He prayed it wasn't a bad omen. Evie would skin him alive if Tuck had had a vision with a bad omen. He didn't want to push. He was afraid his brother-in-law would pull back in like a truculent turtle.

"It probably wasn't even a vision," Tuck continued. "Probably just some weird Johnny Walker dream."

"Yeah, you gotta stay away from that stuff."

"I know. Usually I do . . . it's just that . . . anniversaries hit me hard." Tuck exhaled audibly.

Ridley's butt was getting cold, but he knew Tuck was on the verge of opening up, and he didn't want to break the tenuous thread. "So this woman you saw. She wasn't Aimee?"

Tuck shook his head.

"That bothered you? Seeing a woman and it not being Aimee?" He rubbed his palms together to warm them. It was cold on the dock, yes, but that wasn't the only place the chill was coming from.

"Yeah."

"This woman, what'd she look like?"

"Dark hair, pale skin, tall. I mean, really tall. Close to six foot. Beautiful in a smart, high-class kind of way. Like Cleopatra."

Ridley grunted. Uh-oh, that didn't sound good. Not good at all. He took a swig of his beer, afraid to ask what needed to be asked next.

"And," Tuck added, "she was naked."

Ridley choked on his beer. He sputtered, coughed. His braid fell forward across his shoulder.

"You okay?"

Ridley couldn't stop coughing, and tears of strain misted his eyes.

Tuck pounded him on the back. "Rid? You need the Heimlich?"

He shook his head. Oh shit. Evie was gonna kill him dead. "I'm okay."

"You sure?"

"This woman you saw," Ridley croaked. "Was she an...um...a temptress?"

Tuck's head jerked up. "How did you know?"

"The temptress is quite common in folklore and mythology," he said, not wanting to tell Tuck what seeing a temptress in a vision quest really meant. His brother-in-law simply wasn't ready to hear about that. "Did she...um...did she tempt you?"

"It was a sex dream, if that's what you're asking."

"Were feathers involved?" Ridley asked hopefully. Feathers were a good omen. Maybe feathers could temper the ominous naked-temptress-sex-dream thing.

Tuck frowned. "No, not feathers."

"But something?" Ridley fisted his hands. This was getting worse by the minute. He should stop asking questions, but he couldn't. He had to know exactly how bad it was.

"Veils."

Uneasiness took hold of him. Ridley's blood thickened in his veins, and his breath went thin. Hurriedly, he took another swallow of beer. "What kind of veils?"

"Wedding veils. Lots and lots of white lace wedding veils." Tuck slapped a hand on Ridley's thigh. "So, Red Deer, you're the Native American here. What does the vision mean?"

"Mean?" Ridley asked, hearing the nervousness in his voice. "Who says it means anything?"

"It doesn't mean anything?" Tuck sounded oddly disappointed. "I thought by the way you were choking on your beer that it probably meant something."

"Naw, not really," he lied. "I just swallowed wrong."

"You're a lousy liar, Rid."

"Who says I'm lying?"

"Me. When you lie, your nose twitches. Word to the wise—stay away from poker."

"It does not." Ridley put a hand to his nose.

"Then why are you touching your nose?"

"Bastard."

"So what's the big woo-woo sweat lodge secret?"

"No secret."

"Then why'd you come sit out here with me in the cold if you weren't trying to get me to tell you about the vision?"

"Because I'm worried about you."

"Ease my troubled mind. Tell me what the damned vision means."

"I'm no expert," Ridley hedged. He was in over his head.

"What does being visited by this wedding-veil-wielding temptress portend for the Magic Man of Manhattan?"

"It probably doesn't mean a thing."

"But if it did mean something…"

Ridley rolled off a shaky laugh. No point in alarming Tuck when he didn't have any strong evidence that something untoward was going to happen. "Hang loose, dude. You're blowing this all out of proportion. Sometimes a cigar is just a cigar."

"We still can't believe you're moving to Colorado lock, stock, and barrel," Delaney Cartwright Vinetti told Jillian as they shut the door closed on the rented U-Haul trailer and tucked a lock of hair behind her ear. "And in October. Autumn doesn't seem like the prime time for a move to a mountainous state."

"It's the perfect time," Jillian assured her. "I've got nothing else to lose."

Delaney was a pretty brunette with a people-pleasing personality. She'd been the one to find the three-hundred-year-old wedding veil in a consignment shop, and she'd immediately fallen under its spell. She'd believed in the fantastical story that went with the veil. She'd wished on it just before she was about to marry the wrong man and ended up finding her true love. Nick Vinetti was a detective for the Houston PD. They had a daughter, Audra, three and a half, and one-year-old twin sons, Adam and Aidan.

"But Blake's will hasn't even been probated yet."

"I'm the executor; I have to go check out the property."

"But you're moving. Visiting I could understand, but you're moving to the place sight unseen."

Jillian shrugged. "The lease was up on my condo. I couldn't justify signing up for a second year."

"It seems so sudden," Tish Gallagher Tremont added. "You don't even know what you're getting into."

"Now, come on, Tish, you're supposed to be the adventurous one of the group. Don't tell me motherhood has changed you that much," Jillian said.

Tish was an auburn-haired beauty who was almost as tall as Jillian. Delaney had passed the wedding veil on to her, and Tish had reconnected with the love of her life, former secret service agent Shane Tremont. They had a son, Max, who just turned two, and a three-month-old daughter, Samantha.

"And you're not eligible to practice law in Colorado," Tish said.

Her friends might not realize it, but she'd thought this thing through. "Not yet. But I have some money saved, and I'll sit for the Colorado bar as soon as I can. In the meantime, I'll take a job as a law clerk. It won't hurt to brush up on the basics."

"Jilly, are you really sure this is what you want?" Rachael Henderson Carlton asked. "We're all going to miss you something terrible."

When Tish had remarried Shane, she gave the wedding veil to blond-haired, blue-eyed Rachael, who—after she'd started Romanceaholics Anonymous—ended up falling madly in love with Brody Carlton, the sheriff of her hometown of Valentine, Texas. Rachael was roundly and radiantly seven months pregnant with their first child due sometime around Christmas.

"I'm going to miss you guys, too, but come on, let's be honest. You've all got your own lives now. It's time I found my place in the world."

They'd been friends since they were suitemates at Rice University, and Jillian loved them all dearly, but they'd moved on with their lives, and she'd been the one left standing still. But the minute she'd told them she was going to Colorado, they'd organized a moving party and shown up, even pregnant Rachael, who lived four hundred miles away. They truly were special friends.

"You're going to be so far away from us," Tish bemoaned.

"We'll call each other every week. Plus, you can come visit me during the summer or during ski season. There's a ski resort on the other side of the mountain from Salvation."

Rachael's eyes misted with tears. She was the most emotional of the four and Jillian's polar opposite. "Oh, Jilly."

Jillian pointed at her. "Now, now, no waterworks, missy."

"B-but...you're going to be up there all alone. No friends, no family."

"Except for you guys, I haven't had a real family since I was five," Jillian said. "And besides, I've got Mutt now."

At the sound of his name, the dog trotted up, wagging his tail. He'd just come back from the vet after having his little snip-snip operation, and he wasn't his normal peppy self.

"And isn't he adorable," Tish cooed, and scratched Mutt under the chin. The dog ate up the attention.

"Where'd you get him?" Rachael asked.

"He just showed up the day after Blake's funeral," Jillian said.

"No kidding?" Tish looked uneasy.

"Oh my." Rachael sucked in her breath.

"Oh my, what?"

"The dog, it's Blake's way of sending you a message that he's okay," Rachael said as if she completely believed what she was saying and it made perfect sense.

"What?" Jillian frowned.

"You've never heard that?" Tish asked. "I've heard it."

"Heard what?"

"That if a dog shows up right after a loved one dies, it's the loved one communicating to you from beyond the grave. It's a sign telling you everything is okay," Delaney added.

"You too?"

"It's a common folklore," Rachael said. "Google it when you get a chance."

"You said the operative word. Folklore. As in fable, old wives' tale, blarney."

"She has such little faith." Rachael sighed to Tish. "What's it going to take to make a believer of her?"

Jillian looked at Delaney. "Speaking of folklore, I've got something for you."

"Oh?"

She stepped to her car, picked up the sealed garment bag, and handed it to Delaney.

"What's this?"

"The wedding veil. Please take it."

"No, no, Jilly. It's yours."

"I don't want it."

"How do you know? You're starting a new life. It might be exactly what you need."

"The bride thing?" Jillian splayed a hand over her chest. "So not me."

"Jillian…" Delaney made a you're-being-difficult sound in the back of her throat.

"Delaney…" She mimicked her friend's tone.

Delaney gave her the sweetly tolerant look a mother gives a willful child. "It's going to hit you one day; you *do* know that."

"What? A bus? A train? A milk truck? Should I up my life insurance?"

Delaney ignored her sarcasm. "Love. You can't out-run it."

"Not even in Nikes?"

Delaney smiled and shook her head. "Salvation's not going to know what hit them."

"Seriously, take the veil." Jillian thrust the bag toward her. "You bought it; it's yours."

"I don't need it anymore."

"I don't need it either."

"On the contrary. You've never needed anything more. You're at a crossroads in your life. Make the wish, Jilly."

"Too late, I already did and nothing happened."

Delaney exhaled and her eyes widened. "You? You wished on the veil?"

"Yep, and like I said, nada, zip, zero."

"I can't believe you wished on the veil. You swore you'd never wish on it."

"Like you said—crossroads, desperation. I had a moment of weakness. Lost my head."

"And..."

"And nothing."

Delaney's smile grew sly. "I get it. Something *did* happen, and it scared the underpants off you."

"Hey, hey." Jillian spread her arms. "Check it out. I'm completely clothed here, people."

But her underpants sure as hell hadn't been on in that dream. She wanted to fan herself just thinking about it, and she hoped the expression on her face didn't give her away.

Delaney giggled and clapped her hands. "It happened. You saw him."

"Did not." She heard the defensiveness in her voice.

"You saw your soul mate."

"Pfttt."

Rachael came around the side of the moving van to where Jillian and Delaney were standing. "What happened to you?"

"Jilly made a wish on the veil," Delaney said gleefully. "And she saw her guy."

Oh great, tell the romanceaholic.

"There was no guy. I saw no guy," Jillian lied.

Rachael rubbed her palms together. "So what did he look like? Handsome? Hot?"

"There's no guy."

"You put on the veil," Tish joined in. "Made the wish and absolutely *nothing* happened?"

Dammit. She knew she should have just thrown the stupid veil in the trash. "That's right. I just fell asleep."

"With the veil on?" Tish quizzed.

"Um…yeah. So what?"

Tish and Delaney and Rachael all exchanged meaningful glances as if they were party to something significant that Jillian could never understand.

"What?" Jillian demanded.

"Did you have some kind of dream?" Delaney raised her eyebrows.

"I don't remember," Jillian lied.

"She dreamed about him." Tish nodded her head knowingly. "She dreamed about him, and it scared the underpants off her."

"Why does everyone keep accusing me of losing my underpants?" Jillian sighed in exasperation. "I'm not Britney Spears."

"I bet it was a sex dream. Was it a sex dream, Jilly?"

Rachael leaned in closer. "Tell us all about your sex dream."

"Geez, you people..."

"It was a sex dream," Tish said.

Jillian rolled her eyes. "And you wonder why I'm moving a thousand miles away from you lunatics."

"Fourteen hundred away from me." Rachael made a sad face.

"We're just teasing you, Jilly." Delaney touched her forearm. "If you really don't want the veil, I'll take it."

"Good. Thank you." Jillian sighed again, this time with relief as Delaney accepted the bag. "It's all I ever wanted."

"That and the hot guy from your sexy dream." Rachael giggled, her eyes crinkling merrily.

Despite their good-natured ribbing about the veil, Jillian knew her friends truly cared about her. She was closing a chapter in her life. She could see the significance of it reflected in their faces, and she knew they could see it on hers. These three women were the closest thing she had to a family.

"I'm gonna miss you guys," she said earnestly.

"Group hug." Rachael held her arms open wide.

Normally, Rachael's insistence on group hugs got on Jillian's nerves, but this time, she let it happen and didn't even blink away the mist of tears.

Chapter 5

Two days later, at five forty-five in the morning, Jillian drove into Salvation.

She'd made poor time, what with the drag of the U-Haul on her Sebring's bumper hitch and having to make frequent pit stops for Mutt. But since no one was expecting her, the time of her arrival wasn't much of an issue. The weariness of two days on the road clouded her brain. Yellow asphalt stripes disappearing beneath strumming tires. Eighteen-wheelers jockeying for position. The dry flat taste of too-strong coffee. The sitting-too-long ache in her knees and tailbone.

Jillian rounded the last curve in the road, and there it lay dead ahead. Through the damp windshield, she watched the streetlamps wink off as the orange wash of morning scrubbed the horizon a hazy blue.

Salvation.

Small, sleepy, and so adorably cute she almost turned the car around and headed straight back to Houston. Jillian didn't do adorable or cute, but Rachael would have loved the place.

The first thing that came into view was the picturesque

town square. Decorated quaintly with festive pumpkins and hay bales and scarecrows. There was a faint dusting of snow on the ground mingling with the fallen autumn leaves—orange, yellow, red.

The architecture was a mix of Swiss Chalet, French farmhouse, and Queen Victoria. There were carved window boxes and wrought-iron streetlamps and quirkily painted wooden park benches positioned outside the shops—bookstore, green grocer, novelties and souvenirs, yarn and fabrics, drugstore and sundries.

On the corner was a diner dubbed the Bluebird Café. A clot of SUVs and pickup trucks were parked outside. Ninety percent of them American made. Smoke swirled from the chimney, filling the air with the scent of mesquite. She'd had breakfast on the interstate an hour earlier or she might have stopped, eaten some eggs, met a few of the residents.

Her new town.

Jillian drew in a deep breath. This was where she was going to be living. Salvation, Colorado. Population 876, according to the sign she'd just passed.

She'd never lived in a small town.

A warm gush of sudden panic swept aside her stubborn resolve. Anxiety hunkered on her shoulder. What in the hell was she doing? Yanking up her life to relocate to a place she'd never been. She was jumping the gun. Blake's will wasn't even probated yet, and she'd moved all her earthly possessions up here. She'd quit her job, given up her condo, and taken on a dog.

What if the townsfolk didn't like her? What if she didn't like them? Was she crazy? Was she having a midlife crisis twenty years early? Was this all just a knee-jerk reaction to losing Blake?

What's done is done. Make the best of it.

Resolutely, she shrugged off her doubts and reached for the hand-drawn map on the seat between she and Mutt. The map that she'd found in the envelope Hamilton Green had given her. According to the directions, Salvation Lake was a half mile outside of town. She would be there soon.

Butterflies fluttered in her stomach.

"This is it," she told Mutt. "Our new home. What do you think?"

The dog put his paws on the side of the door and licked his lips as they passed by the Bluebird Café. Apparently, whatever they were serving for breakfast smelled tastier than the kibble he'd just eaten.

The houses on the road to the lake were just as adorable as the buildings circling the town square. The place was a fairy-tale town. Like something from the books she'd read when she was a kid and dreamed about but was too afraid to hope such places really existed. Honestly, it was too perfect for words.

"I don't trust perfect," she muttered under her breath. "There's no such thing as perfect."

Mutt looked at her.

"I know what you're thinking. Okay, so I'm not the most trusting person in the world. Especially when it comes to men. Consider yourself very lucky I adopted you."

Mutt barked.

"You're welcome."

A garbage truck rumbled past. The driver waved.

Jillian didn't wave back.

Mutt's ears dipped.

"What? Don't look at me like that. I know what you're thinking. Get to know the garbageman, maybe he'll throw you a bone. But you don't know this guy. He could be a serial dog killer. He could throw you poisoned meat. Best motto—trust no one."

Okay, it was official. Too many days on the road with only a dog to talk to had made her nuts. Once she got settled in, she simply had to introduce herself around town.

And maybe see if she could hire someone to help her unload the U-Haul.

Off to the right, she spied the lake in between gaps in the pine trees, the deep blue of the water melding with the orange cream sky. The lush evergreens were dusted with powdered-sugar snow. The paralyzing beauty took her breath away, and she fell instantly in love.

"It's incredible," she murmured, and her earlier misgivings were swept away by the azure majesty of the early morning sun shimmering off the lake.

"Maybe we can go fishing in the spring," she told Mutt. "You'd like that. Lots of sitting in the sun."

One of the few memories she had of her father was when he'd taken her fishing. She'd been quite small, three or four at most, and all she could remember of the trip was the tiny pink plastic tackle box with yellow daisies on it and the way her little hand had felt in his big palm as they'd walked to the water.

"Oh, oh, here it is. Enchantment Lane." She made a right. "Is that a corny name or what?"

Mutt yawned.

"Are you bored already? But we're only three weeks into this relationship, buster." She carefully navigated the twisty one-lane road. "Hey, be on the lookout for number 1414."

Most of the summerhouses appeared shuttered and

locked for the winter season. She expected number 1414 to be boarded up as well.

It wasn't.

However, the hedges were long past the point of needing a trim, and the cottage begged for a fresh coat of paint. Several pickets in the wooden fence had rotted out, and the rainbow-hued wind sock on top of the house was tattered. Dead tree branches littered the yard, and the mailbox was dented and rusting.

Home sweet home.

Jillian let out her breath. When had Blake last visited here? She'd known him for eight years and had never heard him once talk about his summer house or even taking a vacation. And why hadn't he hired someone to see after the place?

"Looks like we've got our work cut out for us, Mutt. You up for it?"

Disappointment anchored her to the seat, car keys in her hand. She didn't know what she'd been hoping for. Hamilton Green had warned her the property wasn't in the best of shape.

"But, hey, let's look at the bright side. We've got a killer view."

Mutt whined.

"I know, I know, you gotta pee." Jillian sighed and shrugged off her disenchantment with the house on Enchantment Lane. "Let's go."

She got out and walked Mutt around the side of the house so he could take care of business. From this angle, Jillian could see the redwood dock leading down to the water. The sight of the lake cheered her up a bit. This was her place. She owned it. Or at least she would as soon as Blake's will was probated.

Home.

"Home," she said out loud. She'd never had a real home.

Yeah, okay, the place needed work, but she wasn't afraid of manual labor. On that score, her stepmother had trained her well. Who knew a childhood spent as an indentured servant had an upside? A coat of paint, trimmed hedges, new boards in the fence and the place would be good as new.

"In nice weather, we can have breakfast on the dock and watch the sun come up," she told Mutt. "Would you like that?"

The dog paid her no mind; he was too busy sniffing the ground, exploring his new surroundings.

"Gird your loins. It's time to see the inside." She tugged on Mutt's leash and led him up the cobblestone walkway to the front porch. There she found a porch swing with a busted chain, the back corner resting on the ground. "Add that to the list."

She took the key from her pocket and slipped it into the lock, but before she ever turned the key, the door eased opened.

"It wasn't locked," she murmured. "Why wasn't it locked?"

She hesitated, not sure if she should go in or not. Everything was unnervingly quiet, but Mutt didn't seem alarmed. Jillian wasn't a coward, but neither was she a fool. Should she call the sheriff? She didn't want to look like an idiot on her first day in town. Maybe some teens had broken into the place and were using it as a make-out spot.

That thought sunk her spirits. She had to investigate. If someone was inside, she had Mutt to raise the alarm. Tentatively, she pushed the door all the way open and stepped over the threshold.

Hamilton Green had told her the summerhouse was furnished, but she hadn't expected it to look as if someone was living here. A pair of men's muddy work boots sat on a newspaper in the tiled foyer. Mutt sniffed them. A brown all-weather men's coat hung on a hook above the boots. The small foyer table held a blue glass bowl filled with pocket change, car keys, and breath mints. Not to mention an inch of dust.

A sudden thought occurred to her. What if she had the wrong place?

Nervously, Jillian stepped back out on the porch to double-check the numbers on the house. Yep. 1414. This was it.

"Why do I feel like I'm suddenly in a Stephen King novel?" Jillian asked.

Tongue lolling, Mutt looked up at her.

"Right, I got it, you have no idea who Stephen King is. But let me assure you this is seriously spooky."

Jillian hauled Mutt back inside, shut the door, and unclipped the leash from his collar. Then she edged into the living room.

Water stains dotted the ceiling, letting her know the roof leaked, and she noticed the walls needed painting even worse than the outside of the house. The back of an over-sized brown leather couch faced the foyer. A red and white crocheted afghan was draped over it. Across the room sat a stone fireplace. There were a couple of flat-bottomed chairs, both heaped high with newspapers and magazines. An empty pizza box lay open on the coffee table.

Someone *was* living here.

Had Blake been renting the place out and neglected to inform Hamilton Green? Or had some vagrant wandered in and made himself at home?

She skirted the edge of the couch, looked down, and saw the most gorgeous naked male back she'd ever seen. Startled, Jillian slapped a hand over her mouth and jumped backward.

Her gaze focused on every minute detail. The tanned spine disappeared into the waistband of a pair of black briefs barely covering a firm gorgeous ass. The delineation of his taut musculature, the slope of the small of his back, the masculine thickness of his thighs all served to shove her libido into hyperdrive.

Mutt growled low in his throat, pricked up his ears, and cocked his head.

The guy snored, oblivious to the fact he had company.

Jillian's gaze tracked from the exquisite butt, up the curve of the small of his back, to his broad shoulders that barely fit on the couch, to the shaggy thatch of wheat-colored hair sticking out all over his head and back down again. His muscular calves were tangled in a blue quilt, and a pillow without a case lay on the floor beside the couch.

That was some kind of body.

A skitter of excitement ran through her. Once upon a time, she wouldn't have minded waking up to find a backside like that in her bed. But since Alex, she'd sworn off men. The creatures did nothing but cause misery and heartache.

She didn't know what to do. If he was a vagrant, she should call the police and have him evicted. If he'd rented the place, then she needed to wake him and tell him about Blake dying and leaving her the house.

Either way, he had to go.

But how to rouse him? If she tapped him on the shoulder, he was sure to turn over, and she really didn't want to see what was on the flip side.

Or did she?

Mutt was still growling at the guy in a low menacing tone she'd never heard the dog use.

Jillian cleared her throat. Loudly.

Nothing.

Apparently, the interloper could sleep through an avalanche.

Okay, she was going to try the tapping-on-the-shoulder thing. But first she had to cover him up so she would stop staring at him. She caught her bottom lip between her teeth, dropped her purse on the floor, and tiptoed toward the couch.

She leaned over, going for the red and white afghan, intent on tossing it over him, when a strong hand reached up and grabbed her wrist.

Jillian shrieked.

He had a vise grip like the Incredible Hulk.

In one fluid motion, he rolled off the couch onto the floor, taking Jillian with him. He made a guttural noise as his butt smacked against the rug.

The red afghan had fallen over Jillian's head, and she couldn't see a thing. All she could do was feel. Everything about him was hard. His grip, his chest, his thigh, his...his...oh God.

Jillian fought, shoving the afghan from her face, batting back the hair that had fallen into her eyes, and sputtering and struggling against him.

"Let go of me," she howled.

"Who in the hell are you? What do you want? Why are you in my house?" He peppered her with questions in a voice as deep as a scattergun blast.

Jillian was in his lap, and he wasn't letting go. She finally got her vision cleared and found herself peering straight into whiskey-colored eyes, fringed with long dark lashes. His silky, wheat-brown hair was rumpled, his jaw shadowed with beard stubble. His entire face bespoke bone-deep sadness.

His gaze met hers.

All the breath left her body. Her heart leapfrogged into her throat. Her stomach dropped to her knees, and her jaw unhinged. Panic bulleted through her veins.

Impossible. Unbelievable. This simply could not be happening.

It was him.

In the flesh.

The rugged, hunk of a man from her wedding veil–induced sex dream!

Tuck stared into the eyes of the woman from his vision quest and felt the earth shift beneath him.

This was impossible, illogical, but here she was.

Dream. Gotta be a dream.

But it sure as hell didn't feel like a dream with her warm, firm ass parked in his lap.

Was there such a thing as vision-quest flashbacks? He'd have to ask Ridley.

Her eyes were bright, her lips so temptingly close. He couldn't help but think about kissing her. He slid his arms around her waist and she—

Slapped him.

"Ouch!" He raised a hand to rub his stinging cheek.

Okay, neither a dream nor a flashback. If it was a flashback, she'd be kissing him, not smacking his face.

So if it wasn't a dream or a flashback, that meant...Holy shit, holy shit, holy shit, this was real.

There was a strange woman in his house—and not just

any strange woman but one whom he'd had sex with in a sweat lodge vision. And she was far more beautiful in real life than she'd been in the dream. Her hair was blacker, glossier. Her eyes more intelligent. Her skin creamier. Her scent spicier.

"Let go of me." She splayed a palm against his bare chest and shoved him.

Hard.

Tuck tipped backward and his head hit the floor.

Her stare fixed on his lower anatomy, and she let out a squeak of surprise at the sight of his cock burgeoning against the seams of his undershorts.

Quickly he grabbed the afghan and flung it over his lap. Just as quickly, she jumped to her feet and ran to the opposite side of the room. He secured the afghan around his waist with his fingers and scrambled onto the couch, placing a pillow strategically over his lap.

They were both breathing like marathon runners at the twenty-fifth-mile marker.

"Who the hell are you?" they asked in unison.

"I'm Jillian Samuels," she said.

At the very same time, he said, "Tucker Manning."

And then they both said, "What are you doing here?"

It was a very strange moment. It wasn't every day that a man met his fantasy woman.

She's not your fantasy woman. You just had a dream about her.

Except that apparently hadn't been just a run-of-the-mill dream but a portentous vision, just as Ridley had claimed. Flippin' freaky.

"This simultaneous talking isn't getting us anywhere. You go first, Jillian," he said, being polite. "You're the visitor here."

"Actually, Tucker..."

"Call me Tuck. Everyone calls me Tuck."

"Actually, Tuck..." She drew herself up to her full height, which had to be close to six foot. She was almost as tall as he was. "I'm not."

"Excuse me?"

Her expression grew somber and her voice softened. "I'm sorry to be the one to tell you this..." She hesitated, drawing in a deep breath.

He couldn't help noticing her chest rise with the inhalation. If the vision he'd had of her was in any way accurate, she had a great pair of breasts underneath that fluffy red sweater. "Yeah?"

"Why are you staring at me like that?" she snapped.

"Like what?" Tucker forced his eyes off her breasts and onto her face. She was the kind of woman who made a man think about midnight skies and four-poster beds. And for a guy who hadn't thought about any woman like that since his wife, it was damned disconcerting.

"Like you know what I look like without any clothes on."

"Sorry, nasty male habit." He wasn't about to let her know about his sweat lodge vision. If he did, he had no doubt she'd slap him again. Probably even harder this time and he would deserve it for the lascivious thoughts circling his brain.

"Well, knock it off and pay attention. I'm delivering bad news here," Jillian said.

"Oh." He straightened on the couch, stabbing his fingers through his mussed hair. "I'm listening. Whatcha got?"

"There's no other way to break the news than to just say it. Blake Townsend's dead."

"Huh?" Her words didn't register.

"Blake's dead." Tears glimmered in her eyes.

"Blake's dead?" he repeated, hearing his own words come out hollow and strange. Her words still weren't registering. "How..." Tucker's chest tightened and his brain fogged. "When?"

"Two weeks ago."

"What happened?"

Jillian sank down on the fireplace hearth. He saw her bottom lip was trembling, and he realized she'd cared deeply about Blake. "It was all so trite. One minute Blake was mundanely ordering a grande soy latte at Starbucks just like it was any other morning, and the next minute he was on the floor dead from a brain tumor. Turns out he'd had it for months. Inoperable. He never told anyone."

The pain written on her face told him that Blake keeping his illness a secret hurt her deeply. "That's awful. How come..." Tuck broke off, unsure of what he was feeling. He swallowed past the lump in his throat and tried again. "Why didn't someone tell me?"

"No one knew you were living here. Blake's lawyer thought the place was vacant. He told me the place hadn't been occupied in years. Who are you, by the way?"

"I'm his son-in-law."

Jillian sucked in her breath. "Aimee's husband."

"Yeah."

"I...I'm sorry for your loss," she said. Their eyes met and damn if Tuck didn't see empathy in her gaze. That pissed him off. She had no right to look as if she understood his pain. "I know what it's like. Blake was...We were close."

"Ah..." So *that* was the lay of the land.

"Not *ah*." She glowered. "There's no 'ah.'"

"You and Blake were lovers."

"God no!" she exclaimed as if the thought horrified her. "We were friends. He was my mentor. A father figure."

"Lucky you." His turn for sarcasm. This woman had usurped Aimee's father.

"Don't get angry," she said. "It's not my fault that Blake and Aimee had a tumultuous relationship."

Tuck scowled. He didn't like hearing her speak Aimee's name. He sat there in his underwear feeling pretty damned exposed when he spied the dog for the first time. Or what passed for a dog. Apparently it had been snooping around the house, making itself at home, before coming over to plop down at Jillian's feet.

"What's that?" he asked.

"That's Mutt."

"Aptly named."

"Thank you. I thought of it all on my own."

He grinned. "Hey, folks, who knew? She's beautiful and imaginative too."

"Yep, the total package, that's me. Like DIRECTV."

Their banter must have struck her as inappropriate at the same time it occurred to him how out of place it was, and they simultaneously glanced away.

She gazed down at her hands. "So, anyway, Blake left me the lake house in his will."

"What?"

"The lake house. It's mine."

He jumped to his feet, barely hanging on to the afghan, fighting the rage pushing at him. He thought about dropping the blanket simply to intimidate her, but something told him this woman did not intimidate easily, and he'd end up being the one feeling embarrassed if he exposed himself.

She stood up as well, looking calm and cool and completely emotionless. In that moment, Tuck hated her.

"Listen," she said. "I don't know the understanding you had with Blake—why he was letting you live here—and it's really none of my business. But the house is mine now, and this is your official eviction notice. I'd appreciate it if you could be out of the house by the end of the week."

And with that, she turned, whistled to her dog, and walked out.

Chapter 6

Jillian made it to her car before Tuck caught up with her. He was hopping around on one booted foot while trying to jam his other foot in the remaining boot. He'd pulled on a pair of faded jeans, the fly unzipped, and he'd thrust his arms though a blue flannel jacket, but he didn't have a shirt on underneath.

"Whoa, wait just a damn minute there, sister!" he shouted.

She turned to face him.

He got his boot on and zipped up his jeans. His cheeks were flushed, his scruffy hair mussed, his eyes flashing fire. He slammed a palm against her car door just as she reached for the handle to jerk it open.

"Take your hand off my car," she demanded as calmly as she could in the face of her rising ire. She'd had a rough few weeks, and her nerve endings dangled on a precarious thread.

"Not until you hear what I have to say," he growled.

Tuck stepped closer, crowding her space, but Jillian knew all about those kinds of intimidation tactics and she didn't budge.

Sinking her hands on her hips, she glared. "Fine. Speak your piece."

"You don't own this lake house."

"Maybe not technically. Not until Blake's will is probated, but he left it to me."

"No, he didn't."

"Are you deaf?" She reached in her purse and pulled out the will. "I have it right here."

"When was that will drawn up?"

She told him.

The anger in his eyes deepened. "The week after Aimee died," he muttered, seemingly more to himself than to her.

"Yes."

"You can't inherit the lake house."

Jillian drew in a deep breath. She realized he was still hurting from the loss of his wife. It was written all over him. She didn't know what his relationship with his father-in-law had been like, but she supposed it wasn't good. Blake had only mentioned him a time or two, and he'd only referred to him as "Aimee's husband," never by name. "Look, I'm not heartless. I understand you're still recovering from your wife's death and—"

"Don't"—he shook a finger at her—"don't you dare pretend you know anything about me or what I'm going through."

Something in his tone had Jillian raising her hands in surrender. "Okay, all right. I did just spring this on you. You need time to process. I'll give you two weeks to find someplace else to live."

"You're not listening to me," he said. "You can't inherit the lake house, because Blake deeded the place to me four months ago."

His words yanked the air right out of her lungs. "What?"

"You heard me."

Four months ago. About the same time Jillian suspected Blake had been diagnosed with the brain tumor. But if he'd deeded the lake house to Tuck, why hadn't he changed his will?

Maybe he forgot. He did have a brain tumor.

Or maybe Tucker Manning was lying his ass off.

"Impossible."

"Au contraire. Not only is it possible, but it's also true."

Jillian narrowed her eyes. "I'd like to see the deed. I am the executor of Blake's estate."

"I . . . um . . . don't have it."

"Imagine that." Jillian snorted. "Did you really think you could pull one over on me, Manning? I am a criminal prosecutor."

Tuck looked mad enough to spit nails. "I'm not a liar. Blake deeded me the house."

"Easy enough to prove. Simply produce the deed."

"It's with my attorney."

Was he seriously trying to con her? She tilted her head, studying him. He seemed sincere. And pissed off.

Just then Jillian's cell phone rang.

Tuck turned and headed back for the house.

"Where are you going?" she called after him.

"To see my attorney."

"It's Sunday." Her phone rang again.

"Take care of your own business." He tossed the comment over his shoulder as he disappeared into the house.

Glowering, Jillian flipped open her phone, saw from the caller ID that it was Delaney, and put a pleasant tone in her voice. "Hey."

"Hi, Jilly, did you get there yet?"

"Yes, I arrived in Salvation safe and sound."

"Oh…wonderful…glad…there."

The cell phone reception was spotty in the mountains, plus Delaney's kids were hollering in the background. With her index finger, Jillian plugged up the ear that wasn't pressed to the phone. "Huh? What did you say?"

"Let me close the door to the playroom," Delaney shouted.

Static crackled. A few seconds passed.

"There, is that any better?"

"Some, yeah. Sounds like the natives are restless."

"That's life with three little kids under the age of four," Delaney said cheerfully.

"How do you make it through the day?"

"Turn them over to their father the minute he comes home from work." She chuckled. "So how was the trip?"

"Good. Although it took longer to get here than I expected," Jillian said, wondering what Tuck was doing.

"How's the house?"

Jillian wasn't ready to tell Delaney about the snafu she'd just encountered. She didn't know for sure that Tuck's claim to the lake house was true. "Do you remember that movie with Tom Hanks and Shelley Long?"

"*The Money Pit*?"

"That's the one. That's my house."

"I'm sorry."

"Yeah, well, life's a grand adventure or it's nothing, right?"

"Like having three toddlers."

"I'll take the money pit. Listen…"

"Yes?"

"About that veil."

"You want it back. I knew you'd change your mind."

Jillian leaned back against the passenger seat and propped her booted feet on the dashboard. "I don't want it back."

"Jilly, you still there?"

"I'm here."

Jillian watched Tucker come back out of the house, raise the door to the garage, get into a red four-wheel-drive extended-cab pickup truck, and burn rubber out of the driveway. He didn't even glance over at her as he shot past.

"Bat out of hell," she muttered.

"What?"

"Not you, Laney."

"What's wrong?" Delaney snapped her fingers. "Hey, hey, Audra, quit whacking your brothers with SpongeBob."

"I thought you shut the door."

Delaney sighed. "They opened it. Bunch of little Houdinis the Vinetti offspring."

"Doesn't Nick have extra handcuffs lying around?"

"They're locked on my bedposts." Delaney giggled.

"Okay, that classifies as way too much information. Anyway, about this veil . . ."

"Uh-huh?"

"As you know, I had a sex dream when I fell asleep with it on," Jillian said.

"You wished on the veil, right?"

"I did."

"What did you wish for?"

"A new life."

"And it's coming true." Delaney sounded positively giddy. "The veil is never wrong."

"That's not the half of it."

"What's the whole of it?"

"You're not going to believe this, but when I got here, there was this nearly naked guy asleep on the couch in my house."

"Excuse me?"

"He was in his underwear."

"Seriously?"

"We're talking heart attack material. He's that good-looking."

"That cute, huh?"

"There's more."

"More?"

"Laney, he's the guy from my sex dream."

"Jilly, I just got chill bumps."

Jillian plucked at a loose thread on her sweater. "I'm wigged out."

"And you didn't believe in the veil."

"I still don't."

"So how do you explain the guy?"

Jillian sighed. She'd been asking herself the same question. "There's got to be some kind of logical, rational—"

"There is. The veil's magic."

Jillian faked a cough. "Ahem, let's not go down that road."

"Face it. You're fated. He's your soul mate."

"That's so bogus."

"What about me and Nick?"

"Right place, right time."

"I saw Nick's face when I wished on the veil. Saw him before I ever met him."

"Self-fulfilling prophecy."

"And what about Tish and Shane and Rachael and Brody?" Delaney asked.

"Mass hypnosis. Maybe mass psychosis."

Delaney laughed. "Deny it all you want. This man is your destiny, and there's nothing you can do about it, so you might as well accept it."

Jillian blew out her breath to keep from saying something to Delaney that could damage their friendship. "Tucker Manning is *not* my destiny."

"Tucker? That's his name?"

In the background, Jillian heard one of Delaney's kids wail. "Oops, sounds like they're reenacting the story of Cain and Abel. You better get a jump on it."

"You're just trying to get out of this discussion... Aidan, you take that toilet paper out of your mouth right this minute."

"Bye, Laney."

"Tucker's your destiny."

"He is *not*."

"Oh ye of little faith."

"Crazy woman."

"Skeptic."

"I'm hanging up now."

"Don't run away from love, Jilly. The wedding veil is waiting right here for you when you need it."

"This reception is really bad. You're cutting out. Gotta go." Jillian turned off her cell phone and blew out her breath. She looked over at Mutt. "Coming here was a very big mistake."

Tucker stalked into the Bluebird Café looking for his brother-in-law. On Sunday morning, the place was packed with the before-church breakfast crowd. He paused a moment to scrape his boots on the welcome mat.

"Hey, honey," Evie called out from behind the counter

when she spied him. "What'll you have? Chocolate-chip waffles are on the special."

"Where's Rid?"

"He's playing fry cook."

Tuck went around the counter and headed for the kitchen.

"Put on a hairnet if you're going in there." His sister was such a stickler for hygiene.

"I'm just gonna stand in the door and talk to your husband. I won't be hanging over the food."

"Don't distract him. He'll burn himself."

Tuck stuck his head in the kitchen and saw Ridley flipping bacon on the griddle. The smell was enticing. His stomach grumbled, but his mind was too preoccupied to think about food right now. "I gotta talk to you and it won't wait."

"Sure, what about?"

"Can we go outside?"

Ridley raised his head. "You sound serious."

"I am serious."

"Dutch," Ridley said to the sad-faced, fortysomething prep cook with a prison tattoo on his forearm. "Flip the bacon for me, will ya? I'm taking a quick break."

Dutch grunted.

Ridley slid an anxious gaze toward the front counter. "Let's make it snappy. Your sister's on the warpath."

"What'd you do?"

"I didn't do anything. Honest. Those fertility drugs she's taking make her like she's got a triple dose of PMS."

"Yeesh."

"You better believe yeesh." Ridley led Tuck out the back door into the alley, yanking off his hairnet as he went.

"I grew up with three sisters. I have a clear picture. You have my sympathy."

"So what's up?" Ridley fished a single cigarette from his shirt pocket and lit it up.

"I thought you quit."

"I'm trying. It's not working. Don't tell Evie." Ridley took a deep puff.

Tuck paced the alley. "Listen, about this vision I had in the sweat lodge. The temptress."

"Yeah?"

"She's here."

Ridley frowned. "Whaddya mean she's here?"

"I mean she's in Salvation."

"Your temptress is here? In Salvation? In the flesh?"

"That's what I'm telling you."

"Can't be. A vision isn't real, Tuck. It's a prophecy. A metaphor for the future."

"Well, this metaphor is real, and she's got legs that won't quit. She walked into my house this morning and found me sleeping in my BVDs on the couch."

"You mean you dreamed about her walking into your house."

"No, I mean she literally walked into my house." He told Ridley about Jillian and then he told him about Blake.

"Blake died?"

"Yeah. Explains why he deeded me the lake house out of the blue. Guess he knew he was dying. What I can't figure out is why he left the house to the temptress in his will."

"The temptress has claims on your house?"

"Looks like it. But my deed postdates her will."

Ridley splayed a palm to the back of his neck and looked worried. "For real?"

"For real."

"No shit." Ridley whistled.

"No shit."

"How come you were sleeping on the couch?" Ridley took another hit off his cigarette. "You've got a king-sized bed."

Tuck threaded his hand through his hair. "I can't sleep in there. It's too big. Too empty."

"Without Aimee."

"Yeah," he admitted. "So I had a vision about this temptress woman, and now she shows up at my house claiming it's her house. I'm thinking it means something important. What does it mean, Rid?"

"Um…" His brother-in-law avoided his eyes. "I better get back in there. Evie's gonna come looking for me." He crushed the cigarette butt under his boot and turned to leave.

Tuck put out a hand to stop him. "Tell me."

"Tell you what?"

"The prophecy."

Ridley laughed, but it was a hollow sound. "You don't believe in any of that stuff, remember?"

"Having her show up has made a serious believer out of me. What does it mean?"

Ridley looked uneasy.

"Is it bad?"

His brother-in-law shrugged, but he looked alarmed. "I'm no expert."

"You can tell me. I can handle it. How much worse can it be than losing your wife to ovarian cancer when she's only twenty-five?"

"I guess there's going to be a legal battle over the lake house."

"Looks that way."

"But you've got the deed, right?"

Tuck swallowed. "Sutter Godfrey's got it. He was supposed to file the damned thing, but then he broke his hip...."

"Sutter never filed the deed?"

"I don't think so. I wasn't paying that much attention."

"That sucks. You could lose your house."

"Tell me. In the meantime, I think she's planning on moving in. She's pulling a U-Haul."

Ridley hissed in a breath. "Where you gonna go? This time of year there's not a lot of places for lease in Salvation."

"I don't know. This whole thing caught me off guard."

"You could come stay with me and Evie."

Tuck shook his head. "You guys are trying for a baby. I'd cramp your style."

"Family's family. We'd make do."

"Why should I be the one to leave? She's the interloper." Tuck stuck his fingers through his belt loops. "So are you going to tell me what it means to have a vision about a temptress?"

Ridley swallowed audibly. "Having a vision about a temptress is bad luck."

"I'd already sort of figured that out."

"The temptress signifies broken plans, broken hearts, broken dreams. But seeing a temptress in real life that you've already had a vision about..." He shook his head. "Out of my sphere of expertisc, but I'm betting it ain't good. The woman is bad luck. A jinx."

Tuck looked him squarely in the eyes. "You're telling me."

*   *   *

After Jillian got off the phone with Delaney, she decided to take inventory of the house. She was the executor of Blake's will, after all. It was her job. She had the right.

By lunchtime, Jillian had a list as long as her arm of things that needed repairing in the house, and she'd only made it through the downstairs kitchen, living area, and bathroom. She hadn't even ventured into the bedrooms upstairs.

Feeling overwhelmed, she plunked down onto the couch and stared glumly at her surroundings. What had she gotten herself into?

This behavior wasn't like her. She wasn't impulsive or spontaneous. So why had she thrown everything away and just moved up here on a whim? In retrospect, it was quite stupid. Especially since she might not even have a legal claim to the house. What in God's name had she been thinking?

What? Why? Because her life in Houston had stopped working. She'd needed a change and needed it badly. But she hadn't bargained on feeling so…so…What did she feel?

Jillian sighed. Well, there was nothing to do but make the best of the situation. She'd clean the house, that was a first step. And she'd start by throwing away the piles and piles of magazines and newspapers stacked all around the living room. Apparently Tucker Manning was something of a pack rat.

She rummaged through the kitchen, found black plastic garbage bags, and returned to the living room. She picked up a stack of magazines. *Architectural Digest* mostly. She tossed them into the garbage bag and then reached for another handful.

Her gaze fell on the cover. There was a picture of Tuck

looking quite debonair in a tuxedo. He was winking, arms folded across his chest, biceps bulging at the seams of his suit, a sly grin on his face.

The caption read MANNING MAGIC.

This was the scruffy naked bum she'd found sleeping on the couch in her house?

Unbelievable.

Correction. It's not officially your house yet.

Fascinated to uncover this new information, she sat cross-legged on the floor and flipped to the page with the article about the brilliant young architect the media had dubbed the "Magic Man." He designed classrooms so conducive to learning that test scores and grades shot up in students who attended classes in a Manning school.

The article heaped praise on his talent, citing him as one of the most influential young architects of his generation. There were detailed photographs of the learning centers he designed and pictures of his exclusive Manhattan loft. According to the piece, he dated starlets and heiresses and traveled the world.

Why had he given it all up to live like a vagrant in Blake's summerhouse? Yes, he'd lost a wife, but that was two years ago. Why hadn't he gone back to his former life?

Jillian flipped back to the cover and saw the magazine had come out four years earlier.

"Wow, you're a lot more complicated than appearances led me to believe, Tucker Manning," she muttered.

"And you're a lot snoopier than you look," growled Tuck from the living room archway.

Startled, Jillian let out an "Eeep" and tossed the magazine in the air.

Glowering, Tuck "Magic Man" Manning marched across the living room and scooped up the magazine from the fireplace hearth where it had landed. "Mind your own damn business. And keep your hands off my magazines."

"Why are you so testy?"

"Um...let's see. I have some strange woman claiming to have inherited my house. You think that has anything to do with my sour mood?"

"So get another place and leave this one to me. According to that magazine, you're rolling in dough."

"Not anymore," he snapped.

"Went bankrupt, did you?"

"What part of 'mind your own business' do you not understand?"

"So you're the Magic Man."

"Don't go there."

"Imagine," she teased. "I've seen the Magic Man in his BVDs."

He snorted. "Only because you were breaking and entering."

"Door was open, no breaking involved. I was merely entering. And in case you've forgotten, I was operating on the assumption that it was my house."

"As if you'd let me forget that."

"What happened to the tux?"

"Huh?"

"The tux you were wearing on the magazine cover. What happened to it?" she asked.

"I sent it out to have it cleaned along with my Rolls-Royce."

"What would *Architectural Digest* say if they knew how truly crabby the Magic Man could be. Not so magical after all."

He chuffed out his breath. "I'm not that guy anymore, so can we just drop the whole thing?"

"Aw, but we were just getting to know each other."

"You're a smart-ass, aren't you?"

She batted her eyelashes. "Thanks for noticing."

"Hmm," he said.

"Hmm what?" She canted her head.

"I can see why you're not married."

Ouch, that was a low blow. Clearly he was getting even with her for the Magic Man teasing. "How do you know I'm not married."

"Are you?"

"No." She looked away so she wouldn't have to meet his eyes, and she saw how badly the corners needed dusting. There were so many cobwebs that John Carpenter could set a horror flick in here.

"Okay, then, let's go."

"Excuse me?"

"Let's go."

"Go where?"

"To the Bluebird."

"Bluebird?"

"What are you? An echo? It's a café."

"What for?"

"For one thing, it's lunchtime," he said. "And I know you haven't eaten, because there's no food in the house."

"But plenty of beer in the fridge," she noted.

"You've been going through my things."

Jillian hazarded another glance at him. That blue flannel against his olive complexion...*well*...totally breathtaking. "Hey, you were the one who took off."

"The second reason we're going to the Bluebird is to see Sutter Godfrey. He has lunch there every Sunday."

"Sutter Godfrey?"

"My lawyer."

"We're not bothering the man on his day off, especially when he's eating a meal. It'll keep until tomorrow."

"No." Tuck's eyes flashed darkly. "No, it won't. I want this thing settled right now. I have a feeling you don't believe me about the deed."

He was right, she didn't.

"Let's go," he repeated.

Jillian shrugged into her jacket. "Just to be clear, I'm not going with you because you ordered me to go. I'm hungry."

"Don't worry, I didn't mistake you for someone who took directions well," he said.

"As long as that's settled." She flipped her hair out from under the collar of her jacket where it had gotten caught. "What kind of food do they serve at the Bluebird?"

"It's a café. They serve café food."

"Now who's the smart-ass?"

Silence fell and she instantly had a flashback and saw the firm shape of his bare back as it disappeared into the waistband of his undies. Briefly, she closed her eyes and willed the image away.

"You with me?"

She opened her eyes and shot him a surreptitious glance. He had long, extravagant eyelashes that were in sharp contrast to the rest of his thoroughly masculine face. Those lashes kept his rugged looks from being too harsh. His lips were full but angular. Her gaze just hung there. Spellbound, she wondered if his lips tasted as good in person as they had in her dream.

"Are we taking separate cars?" she asked.

He pulled his keys from his pocket. "I'm driving. You've got a U-Haul attached to your Sebring."

"Oh yeah." She'd forgotten about that.

"What should I do with Mutt?"

"Bring him along. The Bluebird keeps a leash clip chained to a pole outside for four-legged visitors, along with a water bowl and complimentary dog biscuits."

"Wow, imagine. Pet pampering in the wilds of Colorado."

"It's not Antarctica."

"The cell phone reception *is* pretty bad."

"Mountains. They're tall."

"Ooh, there's that smart mouth again."

They reached his pickup truck, and he walked around to the passenger side to hold the door open for her. It felt weird, and she realized she couldn't remember a guy ever opening the car door for her. Surely someone had, but the memory escaped her. A funny, unexpected feeling she couldn't define swooped through her.

Hell, he impressed you.

No, no, she wasn't impressed; she was just…just what?

He opened the back of the extended cab and whistled for Mutt, and the dog hopped inside.

"So," she said when they were in the car together and headed up Enchantment Lane. "What happened with the big, splashy architectural career?"

"The topic isn't open for discussion."

"Ooookay. How do you make a living these days?"

He paused for so long that she thought he wasn't going to answer the question, and then finally he said, "Carpenter."

"Seriously?"

"Is that so hard to believe?"

"From the shape the lake house is in? Yeah. How come you didn't fix it up, if as you claim, Blake deeded the place to you?"

"I was getting around to it."

"Ah," she said.

"Ah, what?"

"The Round-to-It. Bane of homeowners everywhere."

Tuck grunted and ignored that comment, but his eyes were on her. She tried not to notice, but she couldn't help seeing the interest there. His tousled hair fell sexily over his forehead. Just like in her dream. Nervously, she fingered the bracelet on her wrist.

Stop looking at him. Stop thinking about him. Find something else to occupy your mind.

Jillian thought about all that work that needed doing on the house. Thought of his carpentry skills. He couldn't be all bad. He'd opened the car door for her and brought her dog along on their outing.

And he'd given her one hell of an orgasm in her dreams. Two orgasms if she was being technical.

That was reason enough to stay as far away from him as she could manage. But how was she going to do that while he was living in the house she'd inherited?

Except for the fact that maybe she hadn't inherited it after all.

As Tuck pulled into the parking lot of the Bluebird, Jillian had the sudden realization that moving to Colorado might have been one of the dumbest mistakes of her life— even dumber than her ill-fated affair with Alex Fredericks.

Chapter 7

Evie watched Tuck return to the café with Jillian in tow. One look at the woman and she thought, *Uh-oh*.

She didn't understand the uneasiness in her stomach or her sudden mother-bear need to protect her little brother at all costs. All she knew was the interloper looked like Warrior Woman—with her tall imposing height, her sharp dark eyes, and the I-dare-you-to-cross-me set to her shoulders. She was a scrapper, and the last thing Tuck needed was a fight.

Who was she, and what was she doing with Evie's baby brother?

Wiping her hands on her apron, Evie came around the front counter, her gaze sizing up the Amazon.

The Amazon's return stare was cool and emotionless.

Evie narrowed her eyes. "Hey, Tuck. If you're looking for Ridley again, he went down to Fielder's Market. We ran out of eggs. Dutch had a mishap with the eggs Benedict."

"Nope, we're here to see Sutter."

We're here? As if they were a couple. Looking for the town's only lawyer. Something smelled fishy.

"He's in the back at his usual table with the usual suspects." The curiosity was killing her. Apparently Tuck wasn't going to introduce her. Evie pasted on her best hostess smile, even though she wasn't feeling the love, and thrust out her hand. "Hi," she said to the Amazon. "I'm Evie, Tuck's big sister."

The Amazon barely cracked a smile. "Jillian Samuels." She shook hands like a logger. Firm and strong and serious.

"Nice to meet you."

"Same here."

"You passing through town?"

"Evie, could you cut us some slack? We just want to see Sutter," Tuck said. "Then later we'll grab some lunch."

Evie's fingers tingled and she jammed her hand into her back pocket. "Is there a problem?"

"Nothing Sutter can't handle," he said, and turned for the back room, Jillian at his heels like a shadow.

Evie felt a stab of something closely akin to jealousy. For the last two years, she'd essentially been the only woman in her grief-stricken brother's life. She deserved more info than that. Blast it, she'd changed his diapers and pulled his first baby tooth and taught him how to whistle and snap his fingers. She trailed them to the door of the other room.

Tuck walked up to Sutter, who was surrounded by his cronies—the town elders—who kept counsel in the Bluebird most days of the week and introduced the old barrister to Jillian.

Evie cocked her head, trying to eavesdrop on the conversation, but the lunch crowd was booming. The diner hummed with the noise of buzzing voices and clanking silverware and the Hank Williams CD Dutch had stuck on, now playing "Hey, Good Lookin'."

She started to slip farther into the room, but a pair of masculine hands coming to rest on her shoulders stopped her in her tracks.

"Mind your own business, big sister," Ridley whispered into her ear.

Evie stiffened. "Tuck is my business."

"He's a grown man."

"A heartbroken grown man."

"Still..." Ridley turned her around and pointed her in the direction of the kitchen.

"Who's that woman he's with? Did you know he was seeing someone? How come you didn't tell me?"

"I don't know who she is for sure, but I imagine it's the temptress."

"The who?" Evie jerked her head to stare up at him as he guided her away from the group in the back room.

Ridley sighed. "Promise me you won't get upset."

"Upset? What's there to get upset about?" She twisted from Ridley's masculine grip.

"Remember the night I put him in the sweat lodge?"

Evie didn't like the sound of this. "Uh-huh...."

"Well, your brother had a vision."

"A vision, huh?"

"In the vision he was visited by a temptress."

"Meaning?"

Her big husband nodded his head toward the back room. "Meaning she's his destiny, and there's not a damn thing you can do to change it."

Sutter Godfrey was holding court.

The elderly lawyer sat in a wheelchair at the head of the table, dressed in a blue seersucker suit straight out of the 1940s, complete with a blue and white polka-dot bow tie.

He was a thin man, with a thick flush of white hair and a dapper Charlie Chaplin mustache. He had to be pushing eighty downhill. He was surrounded by five other men, four of whom were in his age group and dressed in the usual hunter regalia—camouflage clothes, down vests, and orange baseball caps. A couple of them looked to be of Native American ancestry. The fifth appeared to be a decade younger than the rest of the bunch. He had on jeans, a starched button-down white shirt, and a gray tweed jacket.

The minute Sutter spied Jillian, his pale blue eyes lit up. "Scoot over, Bonner, Carl, and let the young people have a seat."

She and Tuck took the quickly vacated positions to Sutter's right; "Sutter," Tuck said, "this is Jillian Samuels. Jillian, Sutter Godfrey."

"It's rare for Salvation to be graced with the charm and beauty of one so refined as you," Sutter drawled in a deep South Carolina accent.

Her bullshit meter clicked rapidly. "You have a gift for flattery, Mr. Godfrey. A handy talent for a lawyer."

"Let me introduce my associates." Sutter went around the table naming off the men. The guy in the tweed jacket was Salvation's only practicing physician, Dr. Bonner Couts. The two Native Americans, Tom Red Deer and Sam Soap, were the elders of their tribes. One was a retired mechanic, the other a still-practicing accountant. The remaining two men were Carl Fielder and Dub Bennet, town counsel members and local merchants. Carl owned Fielder's Market, and Dub ran a hunting and fishing guide service.

They might be fading into old age, but it was clear that this group still held a lot of power in the community.

"So what might I do for you and this lovely lady, Tucker?" Sutter took a sip of coffee, eying them over the rim of his cup as he waited.

"Could you please confirm for Ms. Samuels that Blake Townsend deeded me his lake house?"

Jillian clenched her hands in her lap. She didn't want to know why her throat suddenly squeezed so tight she could barely breathe.

Sutter pursed his lips and set down his cup. "I do recall having that conversation with Blake, yes, indeed."

Tuck exhaled audibly. "So you filed the deed?"

"Hmm." Sutter paused. "I do believe so, yes. But as you recall, that was about the time I took a nasty fall down the steps of the Peabody Mansion and broke my right hip."

"I recall."

Sutter nodded as if that explained everything.

"So you have a copy of the deed on file in your office?" Jillian asked.

"Most likely," Sutter drawled. The guy spoke as if a simple yes or no would kill him.

"I'm the executor of Blake's will. Is it possible to get a copy for the probate?"

"Surely, my dear." He smiled. "Anything for a beautiful lady."

"That would be helpful, thank you."

"Of course," he went on, "you'll have to go find it for yourself. I can no longer climb the stairs to my office."

"You don't have an assistant?"

"Sadly, my previous assistant took up with the wrong kind of fellow, found herself in a family way, and left town in shame."

"What about a computer? Don't you have electronic files?"

Sutter shook his head. "I never learned to use those infernal machines. My assistant had one, but I have no idea what she did on it."

Good grief, had she been jettisoned back to 1950? If she turned around, would she see Sheriff Andy Taylor and Deputy Barney Fife walk through the door? Would Aunt Bee come rushing in with a homemade apple pie? Would Opie tag along, fishing pole cocked over his shoulder?

Tuck leaned over to whisper, "Most people go to Boulder for their legal needs."

She shot him a why-the-hell-didn't-you? look, at the same time Sutter cleared his throat. Jillian glanced back to see the elderly lawyer was dangling a set of keys from his index finger. "If you plan on riffling through my office, you'll be needing these."

"Thank you, Sutter," Tuck said as he pushed to his feet. "We'll be back in a bit."

"I'll be here." He gave a wave of his hand.

Carl and Bonner resumed their seats while Sam broke out the dominoes. Yep, Andy, Barney, Bee, and Opie had to be around here somewhere.

The Peabody Mansion turned out to be the large turn-of-the-twentieth-century Victorian in the town square. Before they left the diner, Tuck got Evie to make them a sack lunch while Jillian retrieved Mutt from where he'd been attracting the attention of passersby on the sidewalk. He was eating up the strokes and scratches behind the ears with his usual extroverted glee.

They didn't bother taking Tuck's truck. It was a short walk from the Bluebird to the Peabody. The wind was brisk, and Jillian found herself wishing for a thicker sweater. She suppressed a shiver, but the next thing she knew, Tuck's flannel jacket was around her shoulders.

It smelled of him. Manly, comfortable.

"What—"

"You looked cold."

Disconcerted by Tuck's gentlemanly manners and the way his masculine scent disturbed her senses, she wanted to shrug off the jacket and give it back to him, but she was cold, so she drew it closer around her and managed a grudging, "Thank you."

"You're welcome."

An awkwardness settled between them as they mounted the steps of the Peabody. The once-stately manor had been converted into office space. Besides Sutter's office, the sign out front told her the place also housed the offices of two certified public accountants, a used bookstore, and a business specializing in flooring and window treatments.

She also noticed there were no parking meters. A town where you didn't have to pay to park? Too damned charming.

Tuck unlocked the front door and they stepped inside.

The house smelled nostalgically of old boards, old books, old wallpaper, and lavender potpourri. It was a get-comfy-snuggle-up kind of smell. Like rain on a winter's day. Like cedar chests and autumn leaves and thick cable sweaters. Between that and the lack of parking meters and the feel of Tuck's jacket on her shoulders, Jillian was about to overdose on quaint.

"Wanna have lunch down here before we tackle Sutter's office?" Tuck asked, pointing to seating in the bay window between the flooring store and the CPA's offices that overlooked the town square.

She wanted to get this over with, but her stomach rumbled. She was hungry. "Sure," she said, slipping off his jacket and handing it back to him.

Tuck pulled sandwiches from the white paper sack. "Tuna on rye or turkey on whole wheat?"

"Whichever one you don't want."

"Evie cut them in half; why don't we mix and match?"

It sounded too damn cozy, but he didn't wait for an answer, just started taking out the sandwiches. Mutt sat on the floor at their feet, thumping his tail and licking his lips.

"Okay," Tuck said. "I can see the sandwiches have got to be divided three ways. He broke off a chunk of his tuna on rye and passed it to Mutt.

Jillian didn't know why she found the gesture touching, but she did. *This town is making you feel sappy. Snap out of it.*

"Sit." Tuck patted the cushion beside him, then held out a wax-paper-wrapped section of turkey on wheat.

She sat beside him on the seat. "Just to be clear, I'm not sitting because you told me to."

"Gotcha. Independent, strong-minded, you don't need no stinkin' man telling you what to do."

When he said it like that, it made her sound like a stone-cold bitch. Did she really come off that way?

"As long as that's settled," she said, trying to act like she'd been teasing. "Are there any chips in that bag to go with the sandwich? I like the crunch."

"Yep, we've got the barbecued variety or salt and vinegar."

"Ooh, salt and vinegar, my favorite."

"Tart, I should have figured." He tossed her the bag of chips.

"Is there something you want to say to me?"

"Nope. Evie stuck some colas in the sack as well. You want one?"

She nodded and he popped open a Coke for her. Avoiding his gaze, Jillian unwrapped the sandwich, took a bite, swallowed. The turkey was succulent, roasted, hand carved. "Honestly, Tuck, I know we got off on the wrong foot, but thanks for lunch."

"You're welcome."

Silence fell and it wasn't the good kind.

Hurriedly, she ate the sandwich, giving Mutt the last few bites; then she dusted her fingers with a napkin and sipped her soda while she waited for Tuck to finish his meal. He seemed to be taking an extraordinary amount of time eating. Did he normally eat so slow, or was he trying to aggravate her?

"Look," she said, "I'm sorry about all this."

"Nothing to be sorry about," he said, dabbing mayonnaise from his bottom lip with a napkin. For some unfathomable reason, her gaze hung on his mouth, and she couldn't tear her eyes away. "It's my house, and we're going to find the document that proves it. You're the one who's going to be inconvenienced."

"If Sutter didn't file the deed, it's murky legal territory. The vague testimony of a doddering old man will not hold up in court. You need a proper legal document to lay claim to the lake house."

"I've got them."

"Do you?"

"I'll fight you on this," he said, his voice taking on a steely edge she'd never heard before.

She met his gaze. "I fully expect you to. But I have to tell you, back in Houston, I'm known as the Bulldog, because when I sink my teeth in, I never let go. I never give up. I never surrender."

"Is that a threat?"

"No," she said, alarmed by the sudden rapid pounding of her pulse. "It's a fact."

He held her gaze, turned it into a stare, didn't even blink. "You want a battle, I'll give you a battle. Just know before you get into this, Bulldog, that I've got the home-field advantage."

Tuck couldn't say why he'd challenged Jillian. The confrontation hadn't been a conscious decision. It had just come pouring out of him on an emotional current so strong it took his breath away. As if all the pent-up anger that had been lying dormant underneath his grief couldn't be stomped down any longer. He needed a target for his resentment and Jillian was it.

"Let's get this over with," he said, picking up the remains of their lunch and tossing it in the trashcan positioned inside the front door. "The sooner we find that deed, the sooner I'll get rid of you."

Jillian inhaled audibly.

Tuck turned to glance at her, and for the briefest of moments, he spied utter hurt in her eyes. Instantly, she wiped the emotion away, but he saw it and felt like a complete shit for having said what he did. Jillian Samuels was more vulnerable than she wanted anyone to know.

He should have realized that. Should have been more attuned to her feelings and what was going on with her. Aimee would have been ashamed of his behavior. Not only had Jillian's mentor just died, but she'd also packed up her belongings and moved to a place she'd never even visited. A lawyer, picking up lock, stock, and barrel when Blake's will hadn't been probated?

Something wasn't right. She did not seem the kind of woman who acted on whims. Something was driving her.

She was running away, and the lake house had been her refuge.

"I'm sorry," Tuck apologized. "I shouldn't have spoken so rudely to you."

"Never apologize for being honest," she said lightly, but he heard the brittle edge in her voice. She *was* in emotional pain.

Damn it all.

He couldn't deal with his own feelings, much less hers. Tuck pivoted on his heel and started up the carpet-lined staircase to Sutter's second-floor offices. Jillian and her dog followed.

The key fumbled in the lock, giving her time to catch up with him. Mutt was running the halls, entirely too cheerful. He tried not to be pissed off at the dog. It wasn't his fault Tuck's life was so screwed up.

He shoved the door inward. The hinges shrieked. The minute they stepped over the threshold, they both stopped in their tracks, mouths agape.

The phrase "looks like it's been hit by a tornado" was a serious cliché, but in all truthfulness, it was the only phrase that fit. Papers were strewn about the room; piles of manila folders lay in haphazard stacks. Musty old law tomes were spilling off the bookcase and shelved in the oddest places—cluttering the floor, the sofa, the top of the radiator. The drawers of the file cabinets were open, briefs and deeds and accident reports hanging from them willy-nilly.

But that wasn't the worst of it. In the middle of the floor was a murky puddle of foul-smelling water. Directly above the puddle was a serious water stain on the ceiling that also ran down one wall, and there were telltale signs of mold. No telling how long Sutter's roof had been leaking.

A sigh seeped out of Jillian.

"I hope you weren't in a hurry," Tuck said.

She laughed. A short, humorless sound full of weariness, disappointment, and defeat. "Sutter has no idea the place looks like this, does he?"

"I'm guessing not."

Jillian chuffed out her breath and crossed the room to sink into the leather desk chair. Dust rose up around her. She sneezed.

"Bless you," Tuck said automatically, before he remembered she was the enemy intent on kicking him out of his home.

"Thanks. I need all the blessings I can get."

"You're not the only one."

Her eyes met his. "We are in something of a pickle, aren't we?"

"It's not a good day," he agreed.

"This was supposed to be my fresh start," she said, her shoulders sagging in a dejected slump. She looked like a prizefighter going down for the last count.

Why did he have a sudden compulsion to make her feel better? It was a good thing she was feeling overwhelmed. She'd be all the more likely to get into her Sebring and head that U-Haul back to Houston. The thought made him feel a bit sad. He wanted her to stay and fight.

But why? Why would he feel that way?

"Look," he said. "You've had a long day. Let's just call it quits until tomorrow."

Another one of those rueful nonlaughs escaped her. "I don't even have anywhere to stay, and from the look of it, at this time of year, Salvation isn't exactly flush with lodging options."

She was right. In the summer, Salvation did a big

tourist trade. But come the end of September, the motels and B and Bs closed for the winter and didn't reopen until May. There was ski season, yes, but people preferred to stay on the slopes rather than an hour's drive down the mountain to Salvation.

He didn't know why he said it. He didn't mean to say it. But the next thing he knew, Tuck opened his mouth, and the words simply tumbled out. "You can stay at the lake house until we get this thing sorted out."

They went back to the lake house, Tuck built a fire, then quickly left her alone after mumbling something under his breath about meeting some friends of his. He didn't offer to let her tag along, but why would he? Just because she was alone in town and didn't know anyone. She'd usurped his home. He was bound to be upset.

Jillian sat on the couch staring into the fire, Mutt sleeping at her feet. She felt out of place and offtrack. What the hell was she doing here? She didn't belong in Colorado. She belonged...

Where did she belong?

That was the thing. She didn't belong anywhere, but Salvation was supposed to have been her new beginning. Her chance to find her place. To fit in. To finally achieve the love and belonging that had been so elusive for most of her life. She'd found it temporarily, in college, with her three friends. Then again, in Blake. But while she'd had their love, she'd never had that sense of community or permanence. Never lived in a place where everyone knew you and accepted you anyway.

Until this very moment, Jillian hadn't realized how much she wanted that. She shivered, even though she wasn't cold. Mutt raised his head from his place on the floor and looked up as if sensing her vulnerable mood. He sighed and rested his chin on her foot.

"Okay." She laughed, reaching down to scratch him behind the ears. "I'm not completely alone. I have you. We're in this together, Muttster. It's you and me, kid. Homeless wanderers."

He made a whining noise in the back of his throat.

"What's the matter, boy?" She kept scratching his ears. "I just took you outside, and it's too early for your supper."

He looked sad.

"You want me to stay and fight?"

His eyebrows went up. Who knew dogs had such expressive faces?

"You like it here, don't you? Much nicer than the city. Woods to run through. A lake to play in. Rabbits to chase."

He thumped his tail. His fur was soft beneath her fingers.

"I like it here too."

So fight for it.

"Do we have mental telepathy going on here, Muttster? Or am I cracking up?"

Another thump of his tail.

This was a damnable situation. She'd found out Blake had left her paradise, then in the same breath taken it away. Why would he do something like that? If he deeded the land to Tuck, why not change his will as well?

He wasn't thinking straight. He had a brain tumor.

Or . ..

An elusive thought chased through the back of her mind. It made her sit up straight, but before she could fully wrap her head around the notion nudging around, it was gone.

Oh well, perhaps it would occur to her later. In the meantime, she knew what she had to do next.

First thing tomorrow morning, she was calling Hamilton Green and getting to the bottom of the property dispute.

After building a fire in the fireplace to warm the house for Jillian, Tuck had taken off. He felt agitated, confused, guilty, sad, and aggravated with himself. He didn't know where to go, and he wasn't in the mood to talk to anyone about what he was feeling. The only person whose opinion mattered to him at the moment had been dead for two years, her ashes scattered over Salvation Lake.

He hadn't been on the water since the anniversary of Aimee's death, the night he'd fallen in, and he shouldn't be out on it now, but here he was, bobbing in the little red rowboat, wrapped in a parka, a wool blanket across his lap, his cheeks numb from the cold damp wind, staring listlessly at pine trees lining the dock and wondering where in the hell his life had gone.

It was just beginning to sink in that Blake was dead. Even though he'd never really known his father-in-law, he couldn't help feeling a deep, underlying sense of loss and regret. For what could have been. For what would never be. Fences would never be mended. Past hurts would never be forgiven. Misunderstandings would never be resolved.

It made his gut ache. More death, more sorrow.

And then there was Jillian.

Being around Jillian unsettled him, and it wasn't due to any of Ridley's bad-luck-temptress stuff. Well, all right, maybe it was a little, but there was more to his unexpected emotions than that.

He was attracted to Jillian, and that disturbed him because he hadn't been attracted to a woman since his wife. And then he'd gone and told her she could stay with him at the lake house.

How stupid was that?

Why?

He didn't really know why. Maybe it was because Jillian didn't look at him as if he was one of the walking wounded. Everyone else in town treated him as if he was an amputee. No one in Salvation—except for Evie—had known him before Aimee. It was nice, at least for a little while, not to be defined by his status as a widower. It felt good to flirt. To feel like his old self again. And that made him guiltier than ever.

Maybe it was because Jillian seemed to understand, being close to Blake and losing him. She had an underlying sadness in her eyes that tugged at something inside him.

Maybe it was because on some level he felt sorry for her. Apparently, she didn't have anyone else in her life. If she did, why would she have moved up here with all her worldly possessions without first coming to check the place out? Why didn't she have anyone with her, helping her move?

But maybe—and this is the one he really didn't want to admit—just maybe, a part of him wanted to explore the attraction.

Tuck studied the lake house. It was starting to look its age. It needed renovating, updating. On her deathbed, he promised his wife that he would rebuild it. He'd also promised her he would marry again and have the kids the two of them would never have together, but he'd lied about that too. For the life of him, Tuck couldn't imagine getting married again. No one could ever take Aimee's place in his heart.

"I can't believe your father left the lake house to *that woman*," he spoke out loud to Aimee. "And then he turned around and deeded it to me. Why would he do it? Why would he mess with our heads that way?"

If Aimee were here, she'd probably say, "That proves he's an asshole."

But if Aimee were here, this whole mess wouldn't be an issue. If she hadn't gotten sick...

If Aimee hadn't gotten sick, he wouldn't be in Salvation. He'd still be the Magic Man living their Manhattan lifestyle. It was only Aimee's illness that had brought him here. And it was his devotion to her and the small peace he'd found in this odd little town that rooted him.

Now everything was changing. Blake Townsend was dead, and Jillian Samuels had arrived laying claim to Aimee's beloved lake house.

What did it all mean for his future?

Blake deeded the place to you. Even if Sutter forgot to put through the paper work. He wanted you to have it.

But Jillian was a lawyer. She knew how to fight. She was a prosecuting attorney from Houston; she was accustomed to bare-knuckled brawling. She'd slice him to ribbons in a court of law. Unless he could find proof Blake had deeded him the property, he was going to lose the place that had meant so very much to his beloved Aimee.

One thing was clear—he had to get Jillian out of his house.

Chapter 8

Jillian and Mutt ended up bedding down in one of the upstairs bedrooms after the ten o'clock news. She'd heard Tuck come in around midnight, and she'd tried unsuccessfully not to picture him stripping off his clothes and tumbling onto the couch.

She'd seen him in the nude in her dream and then almost naked in real life, and the man certainly lived up to the fantasy. She'd heard him. Thought of him. And then she'd touched herself in the darkness and pretended it was his hand.

Jillian awoke at seven feeling unsettled and out of place, with the smell of fresh-brewed coffee luring her downstairs. She found Tuck in the kitchen fully dressed, making eggs. She felt oddly disappointed to see him in blue jeans and flannel instead of the way she'd pictured him in her mind.

It's official. You're a pervert.

"Coffee," she demanded.

"My, you're bright-eyed in the morning."

She just glared. "Coffee?"

Tuck chuckled, filled a cup, and pushed it gingerly toward her. "Cream? Sugar?"

"Do I look like a lightweight to you?"

"Black it is."

"Thank you."

"You're welcome."

"I need to take Mutt out," she mumbled after she'd had a few sips. "And give him some kibble."

"Already taken care of."

"That was nice of you."

He shrugged. "Mutt wouldn't leave me in peace until I did. How do you like your eggs?"

"You're cooking? For me?"

"Why not?" His grin dazzled.

All at once, she felt a little woozy, like she'd been running too hard and too long. She couldn't ever remember any man cooking for her, other than Blake.

Jillian plunked down on the barstool across from the stove and sipped her coffee. She couldn't help but notice Tuck's long, masculine fingers.

"Eggs?" he asked.

"Over easy."

Their eyes met; then Tuck looked away, but not before she caught the lingering glance he slid down her body. The look ignited the sparks shooting between them.

Suddenly she realized she was still in her pajamas, and her hair was mussed, and she just felt...*exposed*. Her hand trailed to her collar, and she fastened the top button.

"Are you cold? 'Cause I can crank up the heater."

"No, no. I'm fine." Sitting here, looking at him, she was the antithesis of cold. She was a bonfire.

He dished up the eggs on a blue Fiesta ware plate and slid them across the bar toward her.

"Gracias."

"You speak Spanish?"

"I'm a lawyer from South Texas. Even when you don't speak Spanish, you speak a little Spanish."

He put his eggs on a green plate, leaned his back against the counter, and ate standing up. Was he that reluctant to take the barstool next to her?

"So how come you're really here?"

She shrugged. "I thought I'd inherited this house."

"If that's the only reason you came here, why not just sell it through Blake's lawyer?"

"I'm the executor of his will. I came here to settle things."

"In a U-Haul?"

"Hey, you wouldn't tell me about the Magic Man thing. Why should I tell you my sob story?"

"Point taken."

"These are good eggs."

"Thanks. I added shredded cheddar."

They ate in a silence punctuated only by the clinking of forks against Fiesta ware.

"Now that you know the place isn't legally yours, what are you going to do?" he asked.

"I don't know that. I haven't seen this mysterious deed."

"You calling me a liar?"

"I'm just saying that in the eyes of the law, at this moment in time, you have no proof Blake deeded you the property, and I have a copy of his will that gives it to me."

"Okay," he said, tossing his plate in the sink and crossing his arms over his chest. "Let's play what if. What if we can't find the deed? What if you take me to court and win and the place is yours? Then what? You're seriously planning on living in Salvation?"

"Yes," she said mildly, although her muscles tensed, and she didn't know why.

"What are you going to do for work?" Tuck asked. "It's pretty hard to make a living up here, especially during the winter."

"You seem to manage."

"My needs are modest."

"Mine are too."

He raked his gaze over her and snorted. "Not if your hundred-dollar haircut is any indication."

Irritated, Jillian ran a hand through her hair and glared. "In answer to your earlier question, I'm setting up a law practice. I have to take the Colorado bar first, but until then, I have some money socked away."

Tuck's eyebrow raised in surprise. "You're going to open a law practice in Salvation?"

"Why not? Is that so far-fetched? If Sutter's the only lawyer, the town is in desperate need of competent legal counsel."

"Sutter's competent."

"The man's over eighty and healing from a broken hip."

"Most people go to Boulder for their legal needs."

"With me here, they won't have to."

"Listen," he said abruptly. "I've gotta get going. New job starting today."

"Um, okay. Thanks for breakfast."

"No big deal." He headed for the door, turned, paused.

"What?"

"Maybe you could find another place to stay. There's plenty of motels in Boulder, or you can try contacting Jefferson Baines. He's a local realtor. He'd know if there was anything for rent in Salvation at this time of year."

"Excuse me? Wasn't it just yesterday that you asked me to stay?" She tried to sound teasing, but damn if it didn't come out accusatory.

"I'm unaccustomed to roommates," he said gruffly. "Of course, you can stay until you find a place of your own. I'd just appreciate if it was sooner rather than later."

"I understand," she said, even though she was a bit confused by his about-face.

After Tuck left, Jillian took Mutt for a walk, then came back inside to wash the breakfast dishes before jumping into the shower. Showering was a bit tricky, since the faucet handle was broken off and she had to use a pair of pliers she found on the bathroom counter to adjust the water temperature.

"Totally brilliant, Jillian. If you really do end up inheriting this place, it's going to cost a small fortune to get it renovated." Maybe she should just let Tuck have the lake house and forget all about it.

And do what? Go where?

A sudden rush of grief washed over her, and she bowed her head against the flow of hot water, sucking in great sobs of air. Her entire body shook. She fisted her hands against the pain. She missed Blake so damned much.

She wished he were here. Wished she could ask him what he'd been trying to do by willing her the lake house in Colorado. Making her think it was the answer to her prayers, then getting here and discovering he'd given the place away to someone else.

It hurt.

Another betrayal in a lifetime of betrayals.

If he'd just bothered to change his will, she would never have gotten her hopes up, never had any expectations, never dared to start wanting something she'd always been afraid to want.

A place to call home.

Her throat constricted. Despair wasn't like her. She

was tough, she was resilient, she didn't wallow in self-pity. And she wasn't going to give up without a fight. All her life she had to scrap for everything she'd ever gotten. Why should this be any different?

Determination pushed out the grief. Tenacity dried her eyes. A sense of purpose stilled the echoes of past hurts and betrayals.

She got out of the shower, dressed, and found her cell phone. Steeling her jaw, she called the courthouse in Boulder and identified herself as the executor of Blake's will and asked if the lake house deed had been filed to Tucker Manning. Once she determined that it had not, she dialed Hamilton Green's number.

His secretary answered and put her on hold. Jillian paced the living room while she waited, palm splayed against her forehead.

Finally, Hamilton came on the line. "Miss Samuels?"

She didn't bother with pleasantries; she just launched right in and told him about Tuck and his claims on the house Blake had willed to her.

"But you said Mr. Manning doesn't have the document and his lawyer didn't file it."

"That's correct. He can't find the deed."

"If he doesn't have a deed, he doesn't have a case," Hamilton said. "The house is yours. Of course, you know he can choose to contest the will. My guess is that it's a shakedown."

"His lawyer backs him up."

"The lawyer could be in on it. Be careful, Jillian. People in small towns stick together, and they're distrustful of outsiders."

"I'm not getting that kind of vibe from him. Are you certain Blake never said a word to you about deeding the property to his son-in-law?"

"Never. I didn't even know Blake had a son-in-law. That's what makes me so suspicious. Why would Blake go through some small-town attorney to deed the property instead of coming directly to me? Why not then change his will?"

"That's what I keep asking myself."

"Are you certain this guy was Blake's son-in-law?" Hamilton asked. "Maybe he's an imposter. Stranger things have been known to happen where money and property are involved."

Was he? Jillian frowned. She remembered Blake telling her Aimee was married, but for the life of her, she couldn't remember him mentioning Tuck's name. Could Tuck just be some guy living in the lake house, pretending to be Aimee's husband?

She dismissed the idea as soon as it occurred. Something bizarro like that might happen in Houston, but not in Salvation. It was too small, too insular. Unless the whole town was in on the subterfuge, and that thought was too ridiculous to entertain for even a second.

"I'm sure he's Aimee's husband, and I imagine that he's telling the truth about the deed. It's probably buried somewhere in his lawyer's hellhole of an office," she said.

"Excuse me?"

Quickly, she explained about the ransacked condition of Sutter's place of business.

"Egads," Hamilton said. "Incompetence at its finest."

"The guy's old and recovering from a fractured hip," Jillian said, feeling an unexpected urge to stick up for Sutter. "And his secretary apparently plundered the place. There are extenuating circumstances."

"So he let you into his office carte blanche?"

"Yes."

"That doesn't sound very prudent."

"I was with Tucker at the time."

"Hmm."

"Hmm, what?"

"Nothing...just..."

"Just what?"

"If you had access to his office and he never actually filed the deed, you have the power to make sure it's never found."

"Are you suggesting I destroy the deed if I find it?" Jillian put steel in her voice, unable to believe what he was hinting at.

"No, no, of course not," Hamilton backtracked. "That would be unethical."

"Not to mention criminal."

"Right, right. Just pray you don't find the deed."

"And if I do?"

Hamilton paused. "When did this Manning say Blake deeded him the property?"

"About four months ago."

"That's about the same time Blake learned he had a brain tumor."

Jillian could see where Hamilton was headed with this. "You're going to claim Blake wasn't in his right mind when he deeded the lakehouse to Tuck."

"If he was in his right mind, why not go through me?"

"I can't answer that, but we both know Blake wasn't mentally impaired."

"Do we?"

She considered what Hamilton was saying. Blake had been forgetful before his death. Distracted. But who wouldn't be with a diagnosis of an inoperable brain tumor hanging over them?

"Honestly, Jillian, you're in the driver's seat. This man doesn't have a deed, and unless it's found, he has no legal claim on the house. And even if the deed is found, we can take him to court on the grounds Blake didn't know what he was doing when he deeded him the property. We stand a good chance of winning based on Blake's brain tumor and the fact that he, a lawyer, didn't draw up a new will to reflect the deed change. Question is, do you want to fight?"

Did she?

Jillian stopped her pacing and glanced out the window at the supreme beauty of the lake stretching out in front of her. Just looking at the calm water, the pine trees, the purple-blue of the snowcapped mountains instantly quieted her mind. Serene, peaceful, the place called to her soul in the way no place ever had.

Home.

"I want to fight."

"Then get in that house and set up camp there. You've got the power of the will on your side, and right now he's got nothing. Remember, possession is nine-tenths of the law."

After spending the remainder of the morning unloading her possessions from the U-Haul into the garage, Jillian drove to Boulder and dropped off the trailer as prearranged with the moving company.

Then she returned to the lake house, stopping to pick up a fast-food salad for her and a junior-sized hamburger for Mutt on the way. After finishing her lunch, she dressed in a gray wool suit, white silk blouse, red Hermès scarf, red and gray Jimmy Choos, and conservative gold jewelry. Perfect attire for winning over a jury. Hopefully it would have the same effect on Sutter Godfrey.

As Jillian motored up Enchanted Lane, heading toward town, it occurred to her that no one here knew her. She could become anyone she wanted. This was truly a fresh start. A clean slate. No one had to know about her past. A liberating thought.

Jillian parked in front of the Bluebird and went inside. It was almost two, but the place was still half full with customers, most of them over sixty. The minute she stepped through the door, every eye in the place was glued to her.

"Afternoon," several people called out. She noticed a bunch of old coots were giving her legs the once-over.

Note to self: In the future, wear pants.

She raised a hand. "Hi."

"You looking for Tucker?" asked Evie from behind the counter.

"Actually, I'm looking for Sutter. Is he here?"

"Always." Evie nodded toward the back room and the sound of dominoes being shuffled.

"Thanks."

She found Sutter Godfrey in exactly the same position he'd been in the previous day, surrounded by his cronies. The doctor was gone, but in his place sat another buddy. She wondered if Sutter ever moved from the spot.

Sutter glanced up at her, but the welcoming light that had been in his eyes when she was with Tucker had vanished.

"Hello, Mr. Godfrey."

"Miss Samuels." He played a domino, earned ten points.

Jillian shifted on her heels, suddenly feeling very awkward. "Might I have a few minutes of your time in private?"

He paused, and for the longest moment, she thought he was going to refuse. An unexplained panic grabbed hold of her, but she forced herself to remain calm on the outside. She'd had lots of practice cloaking her feelings.

"Fellas," he said to his companions, "can you give us some space?"

They all looked at her a bit suspiciously but got up from the table and headed into the main part of the café. She was beginning to feel like the business suit had been a huge miscalculation, clearly marking her as a foreigner in their community. Jillian took the vacant seat to Sutter's right.

Sutter steepled his fingers. "How might I help you, Miss Samuels?"

She forced a smile. "The question is, Mr. Godfrey, how can I help you?"

He shook his head.

"Did I say something wrong?"

"You don't need to pull any of those big-city sales tactics with me, young lady. Just tell me what you want."

Okay, so he wasn't going to be the pushover she'd imagined. That was fine. She lived for challenges. "I want to work for you."

"I'm not hiring."

"You're not even going to hear me out?"

He pressed his lips into a straight line and leaned back in his wheelchair. "Let's have it."

"You need an assistant."

"Maybe," he said grudgingly.

"No maybe to it. I saw the inside of your office yesterday with Tuck. It's in shambles."

"So Tucker told me."

"A man of your stature—"

He held up a hand. "Normally, I am a fan of flattery, but cut the bullshit. What do you want, and why?"

"I need a job, and I'm trained as a lawyer."

"Exactly. Why would you want a position as my assistant?"

"For one thing, I haven't taken the bar in Colorado. For another, I want to start a legal practice here in Salvation, and when I do, I think it would work out to both our advantages if you agreed to take me on as a partner and mentor me in family law, as opposed to me setting up a competing practice."

He laughed. "Sweetie, all it would take from me is one word, and no one would darken your door."

"Are you that sure of yourself?" she asked. "You're over eighty, in a wheelchair, and you never filed Tuck's deed. Some people—especially the young people—in this town just might think you're losing your touch."

"Spoken like a true lawyer." There was admiration in his voice.

"So you'll consider taking me on?"

He paused again. "Your scenario sounds all well and good in theory."

"What are your reservations?"

"Why do you want to set up a practice here?"

"I inherited a lake house."

"A lake house that's already been deeded to someone else."

Jillian blew out her breath. "Still haven't seen a deed yet."

"It's there."

"Then why not let me straighten out your office and find it?"

"What? Put a fox in the hen house?"

Jillian drew herself up straight. "I resent the implication. If the deed exists, I'll honor it."

"The deed exists."

"Your word isn't legal proof."

He cocked his head. "You want to work for me and yet you don't trust me."

"Trust isn't my strong suit," she said, figuring her answer was going to end the interview, but to her surprise, he nodded.

"I get that. You been kicked around a lot."

She didn't know how to respond to that, so she said instead, "I graduated top of my law school class. I've worked in the Harris County DA office ever since. I've—"

He held up a palm. "I don't doubt your credentials."

"No?"

"It's your motives I have issues with."

"Let me clear it up for you. I want a new start, in a new place, and even if the lake house isn't mine, I intend on staying—"

"Why?" Sutter interrupted.

"Salvation is quiet and serene and—"

"Exactly what are you running from?"

Jillian hardened her chin against his question. Was he insinuating she was a coward? "I'm not running from anything."

"Right."

"I'm not."

"High-powered assistant DA chucks it all to move to the mountains. You're running from something. What's his name?"

Damn! The old man was too good. "Who says it's a him?"

"Okay, then, what's her name?"

"It's a him," she admitted, not really knowing why she did. "His name is Alex Fredericks."

Sutter nodded. "I suspected as much."

Confused, Jillian blinked at him. "You know Alex?"

"I know he took over Blake's job. I also know Blake was worried about you after your affair with Fredericks went sour."

"Blake talked to you about me? Blake knew I had an affair with Alex?" The news completely ambushed her.

"He did."

Jillian recovered quickly. "So you should know he wanted me to have the lake house."

Sutter shrugged. "Maybe he wanted Tuck to have it more."

"Then why didn't he change his will?"

"I don't know. That's one for you to puzzle out on your own."

"So, you'll give me the job as your assistant, and when I pass the bar, you'll consider making me your partner?"

"You don't have to push so hard."

"Then you're considering it?"

"You're persistent," he mused. "Determined. Not one to give up even when it's clear you've made a huge mistake. I'm considering taking December tenth in the pool."

Jillian frowned. Just when she thought the old man was sharper than she thought, he said something completely off the wall. "Excuse me?"

"The town has a pool," he said.

"For swimming?"

He laughed. "For betting."

"I'm not following you."

"We're taking bets on how long it will take you to high-tail it back to Houston."

"Seriously? They're already taking bets on when I'll leave town?"

"Oops, that stubborn look in your eye means you'll last at least a couple of weeks longer. I'm putting twenty dollars on December twenty-fourth. Holidays get to the best of 'em."

"Think again—Christmas means nothing to me."

"Smart, fiery. I like that."

She slammed a hand on the table, making the dominoes jump. "Then hire me."

Sutter just sat there grinning at her like she was the best entertainment he'd had in weeks. It irritated the hell out of her. "I'm not getting tired of this town."

"You ever spend the winter in the Rockies?"

"No."

"I thought as much."

His smile took on a knowing quality that made her want to do something to rattle his smug certainty. "No, but I spent thirteen years being raised by a stepmother who treated me like her personal servant. I had a biological mother who abandoned me and a father who died when I was five. I put myself through college and law school, sometimes working three jobs to make ends meet. I'm not a spoiled, pampered rich kid, nor am I a weak-willed whiner. I'm tough and I'm strong, and when I make up my mind to do something, it gets done."

"Hmm," he said mildly. "I guess I better take February first."

"Dammit, I'm staying. From now on, Salvation is my home, and I have a lake house to prove it."

"You don't have the lake house yet."

"Then you prove that I don't. Oh wait, you can't because you can't get upstairs to your office." She was mad now and was past the point of caring if he gave her a job or not.

His laughter infuriated her. She jumped from the chair, grabbed her purse, and headed for the door.

"Wait," Sutter called.

With her pulse throbbing furiously in the hollow of her throat, Jillian turned. "Yes?"

"I'll tell you what, Miss Samuels. I can see you're quite earnest, and I admire industriousness. I'll pay you fifteen dollars an hour to get my office in order, and when you find Tuck's deed, we'll talk again about hiring you for real."

Chapter 9

With that one comment, Sutter had ensnared her in a catch-22. He would take her on as his protégé only if she found the deed that would spell her own downfall. With the deed, she'd have no lake house and no real reason to stay in Salvation. But without the deed, she'd have no entry into the town's business community.

She had a choice to make. Was she going to stay in Salvation no matter what happened with the lake house?

Sutter sat, arms crossed, awaiting her decision.

Either way, it wasn't going to hurt to take the temporary job. It would give her something to do and bring in a little money. Besides, she had nowhere else to go. "I accept," she said.

"All right." He motioned for his friends who were hanging around the door. "Carl, put me down for February first in the pool. This one's a scrapper. She'll outlast most."

Jillian couldn't help smiling as she left the Bluebird and headed across the street to Sutter's office in the Peabody Mansion. "You're going to lose that bet, you old goat. I'm not going anywhere."

The flooring store and the CPA offices were open when she walked through the front door. Before Jillian got to the staircase, a diminutive, bespectacled woman about Jillian's age, with light auburn hair and a nose dusted with freckles, popped up from behind the counter at the entrance to the flooring store.

She waved a plump hand at Jillian. "Come here, come here."

The woman sounded so excited that Jillian trotted over.

"Come around, come around, and kick your shoes off."

This was starting to feel a little weird, but she walked around the counter to see three different kinds of floor padding behind the counter. She noticed the woman was dressed in a bulky purple knit sweater with Holstein cows appliquéd on the front and a long denim skirt. She was also barefooted.

"The shoes, the shoes." The woman waved again.

Obediently, Jillian kicked off her shoes.

"Now, walk on all three samples and tell me which one feels the cushiest. I've been testing them out for so long that I've lost all objectivity."

"Um, okay." *That's not all you've lost.*

"Really get after it. March. Get the feel for how it's going to hold up under traffic."

Jillian stomped the floor padding. "Like this?"

"There you go." The woman whistled and picked up one of Jillian's stilettos. "Hey, are these Jimmy Choos?"

"Uh-huh."

"Classy." The woman eyed Jillian and handed her the shoe. "From head to toe, I might add."

"Thank you."

"You're new in town."

"How'd you know?"

"I know everyone in Salvation, and it's the wrong time of year for tourists." The woman shoved her bangs back off her forehead and extended a hand. "Lexi Kilgore, and you are..."

"Jillian Samuels."

"Nice ta meet ya, Jillian. So, what do you think?"

"About what?"

Lexi gazed at Jillian's feet.

Jillian glanced down. "Oh, the padding."

Lexi sank her hands on her hips. "Give it to me straight. Which is the softest? Number one, number two, or number three?"

Jillian considered the question for a moment. "Number three."

"Ah." Lexi raised a finger. "But is it too soft? Will it hold up to the demands of heavy foot traffic?"

"I don't know."

"Of course not. How would you? You're not in the flooring business." Lexi looked at her. "Are you?"

"No, no."

"Whew." Lexi splayed a hand across her chest and blew out her breath. "That's good, 'cause it's hard enough making a living in town without more competition."

"You're safe where I'm concerned. No interest in the field of flooring whatsoever."

"That's why I had to branch out into window treatments," Lexi went on. "Can't be too specialized in a town this small."

"I can appreciate that."

Behind the frames of her glasses, Lexi's eyes perked up. "So, Jillian, if you're new in town, do you think you might be needing new flooring? Or window treatments, maybe? I just changed suppliers, and he's got killer connections for Roman shades. Straight from Florence."

"I might be interested at that."

Lexi clapped. "Really? That's great. Where are you living?"

"I inherited a house on Enchantment Lane."

"Fantastic location. Which house?"

"Number 1414. It was owned by—"

"But that's Tuck and Aimee's place." Lexi looked confused.

"Tuck and Aimee," she repeated, fully realizing for the first time that in everyone's mind, Tuck was still linked with his late wife.

"Oh yeah. You didn't know?" Lexi touched her arm. "It's so sad. Tuck's wife died of cancer. She was only twenty-five, poor girl. Aimee was so sweet," Lexi went on. "Everyone loved her. She and her mother and father came here every summer from the time Aimee was small. Then after her parents got divorced when Aimee was thirteen, they just stopped coming."

"Sad," Jillian echoed, not knowing what else to say.

"But that lake house has been in the Townsend family for three generations. It sat empty for years, until Aimee got sick and Tuck brought her here. She'd made him promise that one day, when they were ready to have kids, they'd leave New York City and come home to Salvation and renovate the lake house. But Aimee died before Tuck could do that."

Jillian's chest tightened. "So tragic."

Tears misted Lexi's eyes. "But tragic in a romantic way. Like *Love Story* or *The Notebook*. Tuck is such a great guy." Lexi sighed. "He's having trouble letting go, moving on."

"I imagine it is difficult."

"So how'd you get the house?"

"Aimee's dad, Blake, was my mentor. He recently passed away and left it to me."

"Blake's dead?" Lexi wrung her hands. "I hadn't heard. Oh, that's such a shame. I imagine the fact he never reconciled with Aimee before she died took a toll on his health."

"I imagine."

"So what's going to happen to Tuck? Where's he gonna go?"

"Doesn't his sister live here?"

"Yes, but she and Ridley are trying for a baby. Tuck would never impose on them."

"Tuck doesn't have the money to buy his own place?"

Lexi shook her head. "Aimee's medical bills blew through his fortune. He took her to all kinds of specialists and alternative medicine doctors, looking for that last-ditch cure."

She considered telling Lexi about the missing deed and the erupting property dispute, but she decided against it. Word would get out soon enough.

"So what do you do for a living, Jillian?" Lexi changed the subject.

"I'm a lawyer. At least in Texas I am. I have to sit for the Colorado bar. Until then, I'm Sutter Godfrey's new assistant. And speaking of which"—Jillian waved at the upstairs—"I better get to work. His office is a disaster zone."

Lexi nodded. "His last secretary was a real piece of work. Took advantage of the poor old guy. Embezzled from him. Nasty business."

"He said she got pregnant and left town."

"That too. I'm happy to see Sutter's got a real professional helping him now."

"It's been nice chatting with you, Lexi, but I better get to work." Jillian made a motion for the door.

"Wait, wait, let's exchange cards." Lexi plucked a business card from a gold-plated holder on the counter. "For when you're ready to put new flooring in Aimee's place."

Jillian exchanged cards with her and wandered out into the hallway, Lexi still following her and talking ninety miles an hour. The CPAs were standing in their doorway, eying Jillian with curiosity. They were twins. Two men in their late thirties, dressed alike in matching long-sleeve burgundy polo shirts and black Dockers.

"Jillian, Bill and Will Chambers. Guys, this is Jillian Samuels. She's a lawyer, and she inherited Tuck and Aimee's place," Lexi chattered.

Seriously? Bill and Will?

Suddenly, Lexi burst out laughing.

"What?" Jillian asked.

Lexi splayed a hand over her mouth. "Oops, sorry. I just had a thought. Now we've got Bill, Will, and Jill all working under the same roof."

"I never go by Jill," she said.

"But it gets better." Lexi waved a hand. "Bill's getting married this Christmas at Thunder Mountain Lodge, and his fiancée is...drum roll please...named Lil."

"Come on, Lexi, you know Lily doesn't like to be called Lil," Bill said.

Lexi grinned impishly. "Maybe not, but it's fun to say. Bill and Lil, Will and Jill. Hey, Jill, are you single? Will's single."

"It's Jillian," she corrected.

"Aimee was such a sweet girl," Will said, quickly

changing the subject. "Bright as sunshine." The one she thought was Will shook his head, clearly ignoring Lexi's sidebar into rhyming names. "So sad what happened. And poor Tuck, two years later and he's still having trouble moving on."

"Everyone adored her." Bill sighed. "Such a tragic loss."

Yes, yes, Aimee the saint. Immediately Jillian felt bad about her uncharitable thoughts. What in the hell was wrong with her?

"So where are you from, Jillian?" Will asked.

"Houston."

Bill's gaze met Will's. "I've got dibs on Halloween."

Will eyed Jillian. "She'll last at least until Thanksgiving."

Jillian couldn't believe this. "You guys are betting on me too?"

"What bet?" Lexi asked.

"It seems the whole town is betting on when I'll leave, and I just got here yesterday."

"Ooh," Lexi said. "I want in. Who's running the pool?"

"Not you too!"

Lexi shrugged but didn't look the slightest chagrined. "Hey, not much happens in Salvation. We have to take our excitement where we can find it."

Jillian had to laugh. What else was there to do? "I've got to get to work, guys."

"See ya later." Lexi wriggled her fingers.

"If you need a good accountant," Will said, "please, keep us in mind."

"I will do that, thanks."

"And don't forget your flooring needs," Lexi sang out.

"Never fear, when I'm ready to retile, you're on my

speed dial." Finally Jillian escaped and climbed the stairs to the second floor.

The old wooden staircase creaked underneath her feet. Once she reached the second floor, it was easy to locate the frosted glass door with SUTTER GODFREY ESQUIRE stenciled on it in dramatic black script. She pulled his keys from her purse, but the door wasn't locked. She turned the handle and stepped inside to find a plastic drop cloth covering the floor and a blue-jean-clad man on a ladder. All she could see was from the waist down. The rest of him was sticking up through a pretty big hole in the ceiling.

His butt was at Jillian's eye level.

She'd seen that butt before. Jillian looked up at the same time Tuck looked down.

"This is your new job?" she asked, at the same time Tuck said, "Sutter hired me to repair his roof and the water damage to his office."

"I'm working for him too. As his assistant."

Tuck stared at Jillian, unable to believe his crappy luck. He was going to be stuck with Jillian at home and at work? "Found a job on your first day in town. That's a coup. Congratulations."

"How am I supposed to get anything done if you're hammering and running saws?" She sank her hands on her hips.

"How am I supposed to get anything done if you're underfoot?" he groused.

"This isn't going to work."

"You're telling me."

"Sheetrock dust."

"Clacking, clacking on the keyboard," he countered.

"What have you got against me?"

"Other than the fact that you've invaded my house?"

"It's not my fault. Besides, it's *my* house."

"Just until the deed turns up."

"I'm beginning to think there is no deed. I called the Boulder courthouse and learned a deed hasn't been filed in your name. I called Blake's attorney, and he says Blake never mentioned a word to him about deeding you the lake house. In fact, Blake never mentioned you at all." She sank her hands on her hips. "How do I know you and Sutter aren't in cahoots, trying to bilk me out of my inheritance? Believe me, if that deed does turn up, I'm going over it with a fine-tooth comb."

"*Your* inheritance?" Tuck gave an angry snort. "That house belonged to Blake's daughter, not some skank who wormed her way into Blake's bed." He folded his arms over his chest. He shouldn't have said that. The second the words left his mouth, he knew they were low and mean and untrue. He'd lashed out in pain and anger at the only target around.

Jillian clenched her jaw. She looked as hurt and angry as he felt. He felt like even a bigger butthead. "Excuse me, I did not sleep with Blake Townsend!"

He wanted to apologize, but he was entrenched in his position. "So you say."

"I'm so mad at you right now that I could grab this ladder and shake it until you fall off and break your stupid neck, but I won't because…" Her voice trailed off.

Tuck put a hand on the ladder just in case she decided to carry out her threat. In his other hand, he held the flashlight. "Because of what?"

She pursed her lips.

Tuck climbed down the ladder. "Because of what?"

Her dark eyes softened. "Because I don't want to go to

jail for manslaughter. The momentary sense of pleasure wouldn't be worth the consequences."

"That's not what you were going to say."

"It doesn't matter what I was going to say."

"I want to hear it. Spit it out."

She arched an eyebrow. "You sure you can take it?"

He jerked his chin upward. "I can handle whatever you can dish out."

"I'm overlooking your attitude because I know how much you're hurting over the loss of your wife."

That got him square in the gut. "I don't want or need your sympathy. I'm acting like a jerk because I'm a jerk, not because my wife died."

"You're not a jerk."

"You don't know me."

"I know you've been through a lot of pain."

He hated the way she was looking at him. Just like everyone else did. As if he was an emotional cripple. "No more than the next Joe."

"Losing a spouse is not trivial."

Anger rose in his chest. "Oh yeah, and you're so well versed on what it feels like to lose a spouse? Don't even try pulling that empathy crap on me. You don't have a clue what I've been going through."

Jillian recoiled as if he'd slapped her, and immediately Tuck wanted to kick his own ass. "You're absolutely right," she murmured. "I don't, but I do know what it's like to lose the only person who truly gets you."

"Blake."

She nodded and without another word, turned on her heels and stalked over to the desk he'd swathed in a plastic drop cloth to protect the papers from falling ceiling debris. She batted back the plastic.

"Here, let me help." He went toward her.

She picked up a letter opener off the desk and wielded it. "Back off. Don't do me any favors. I can take care of myself."

He raised both arms in a gesture of surrender and cocked her a grin. "Don't stab, I'm backing away slowly."

She giggled then, and it was such an odd sound coming from her that he laughed too. What an emotional roller coaster they were both on. Tuck didn't quite know what to make of her. She had this tough, no-nonsense way about her, but then unexpectedly, like now, he'd glimpse another side of her. A softer side he imagined she didn't often show.

Jillian put the letter opener down. "Sorry," she apologized. "I can get a little defensive."

"Yeah, well." He pulled a rag from his back pocket and wiped his hands on it. "Me too. I suppose."

She peered at him through lowered lashes.

"Truce." He stuck out his hand.

"Truce." She accepted it.

They shook hands.

The contact was electric. Tuck's head reeled, his body stiffened and his gut clenched in a wholly enjoyable way. Damn, damn, damn. She smelled like freshly laundered linen, crisp and clean and cozy. He thought immediately of a turned-down bed.

Her eyes widened. She dropped his hand like she'd just learned he had leprosy.

Tuck was just as shocked. He couldn't believe he was reacting this way, and he felt ashamed. *I'm sorry, Aimee.*

"Did you find somewhere else to stay?" Tuck ventured, praying she would say yes, especially after she'd just electrocuted his hand.

"I did."

Hallelujah, he could have his life back. "Boulder?"

"Right here in Salvation."

"Convenient for your new job. Jefferson Baines hook you up?"

"Nope."

From the way she was looking at him, he wasn't getting good vibes about this. "What's the address?"

Her gaze was steely. "Fourteen-fourteen Enchantment Lane."

Hell, he knew that's what she was going to say. "No, no."

"Yes, yes."

"You can't stay with me."

"From a legal standpoint, I can. Since I'm executor of Blake's will and he left the house to me—unless you produce documentation that says otherwise—I *can* stay in the house. I've unpacked my U-Haul. Like it or not, until you have that deed, I'm your new roommate."

Jillian held her breath as Tuck snorted, fisted his hands at his side, pivoted on his heel, and then stalked out of Sutter's office, slamming the door behind him.

In the wake of his obvious anger, she felt as if she were standing alone in the desert with a hot blast of sand pelting her as she stared at miles and miles of empty landscape.

What? You thought taking over a man's home was going to be easy?

No, but she hadn't expected to feel so…What was she feeling?

Jillian swallowed against the vacant, lost sensation surging inside her, and she flashed back to that day in court where the same emotions consumed her. Coming to

Salvation was supposed to fix this hollow feeling. It was supposed to make her whole. Fill her up.

Instead, she was adrift, unsure of herself, isolated. But that was no different than she'd been for most of her life. Maybe she should reconsider staying at the lake house.

And go where? Back to Houston? There was nothing left for her there.

She sucked her bottom lip between her top teeth and stared dismally at the shambles around her.

This is where you start. This is square one. This is your new beginning.

The sound of footsteps tromping on the roof drew her gaze upward. *Stomp, stomp, stomp.* Had to be Tuck and from the sound of it, he was still steamed.

Too bad.

It was time to take a stand. Sure, she could just pack up and drive away, but no matter where she went, she now realized things wouldn't be any different. She'd feel the same sense of loneliness. There was only one way to overcome it. Step from her aloofness. Entrench herself in a community. Make friends. She loved the town, loved the house, and by gosh, if she made an effort, she could love these people and they could come to love her.

Really? whispered the ugly little voice in the back of her head. *You really think that anyone is going to love you? Your own mother didn't love you. Why would these people?*

Jillian closed her eyes against the sudden rush of tears. She would not cry. She would not. Gulping, she sniffed, blinked.

No, she would not cry, but neither would she run. For better or worse, she'd made her decision. She'd come to Salvation to find a home, and that's what she was going to do. Come what may, she wasn't going to let Tuck Manning stop her.

Later that day, Tuck stalked into the lake house, planning on laying down the law and telling Jillian why she simply could not stay there. He had the arguments all prepped in his head when he heard her singing at the top of her lungs from the direction of the bathroom. The cheerful sound stopped him in his tracks.

He canted his head, listening to identify the tune over the sound of the shower running—"I Can See Clearly Now."

The tune reached out and smacked him. He sucked in his breath.

Aimee used to hum it when things were going badly. She'd told him once it was the song her father hummed just before he went into court for his final summation. She recalled sitting on the bed in her parents' bedroom, watching Blake knot up his tie in front of the mirror while belting out the old Johnny Nash tune.

Tuck had asked, "If it's a song favored by your dad, why do you sing it?"

"It gives me courage and hope."

"But you and your dad don't get along."

She shook her head and looked at him as if he were a naïve child. "I love my father with all my heart, Tuck. I just can't forgive him for destroying our family."

And that was Aimee's greatest flaw. Her inability to forgive if you'd wronged her. He'd never wronged her, so he'd never been on the receiving end of her unforgiving nature, but suddenly he had an unexpected empathy for Blake. And a deep sadness for Aimee, who'd been unable to let her father make amends.

Had Jillian picked up the song from her mentor? Did she, too, hum the tune when things were going badly? Was it the equivalent to whistling in the dark, pretending you weren't scared of the boogeyman?

The thought dissipated his anger.

And before he could move, the bathroom door opened and Jillian stepped into the hallway, wrapped in nothing but a beach towel while she busily dried her hair with a bath towel.

"Oh," they exclaimed simultaneously as their eyes met.

And for one long moment, time just hung.

Tuck stared at her, his throat muscles paralyzed. He couldn't speak or swallow.

She stared back, her dark eyes glimmering in the light from the hallway bulb, rich as cocoa beans dipped in Swiss chocolate.

Something inside Tuck slipped. An awareness that he'd never felt before. For the first time, he noticed the little imperfections on Jillian's face. The tiny half-moon- shaped scar in the center of her forehead. The way her eyelashes were so long they looked fake. How the hairline on her left side grew farther back than on the right side. Oddly, those imperfections served to make her more appealing.

Her cheeks were flushed pink from the hot water of her shower, contrasting sharply with her otherwise creamy white complexion. With that dramatic dark hair and her pale skin, she would have made a hell of a Goth girl if she'd wanted.

He expected her to duck into her bedroom for cover—Aimee would have under similar circumstances—but Jillian just stood there, appraising him with her best prosecuting attorney gaze. He forgot every word that had been in his head just minutes earlier.

"Your mouth is hanging open," she said coolly, rubbing her hair between the terry cloth fold of her towel.

"Um…" He grunted, unable to push anything resembling civilized conversation over his tongue.

"Is there something you wanted?"

You, I want you.

The thought raced through his mind and took him completely aback. "Um…"

"Yes?" She fluttered those dynamite lashes.

He cleared his throat. *Remember, you were going to lay down the law, tell her she had to hit the road.*

She waited.

Dammit, he couldn't help himself; his gaze dropped to where her towel was knotted just above her breasts. "Um…"

Droplets of water spattered the hardwood floor at her feet. His eyes tracked downward to her bare toes painted fire-engine red. He'd never seen anything more erotic.

"Tuck?"

His gaze shot back to her face. "Huh?"

"You were trying to say something to me?"

"Yeah, yeah." He nodded, trying to shake off the mental fog that had befallen him. "There's only one way this arrangement is going to work."

"If you move out?" Jillian asked with a hopeful tone in her voice.

"You wish," he said. "I'm not going anywhere."

"Well, neither am I. So if you want me gone, you better find that deed."

"Believe me, I'm on it. But in the meantime, since you're so determined to hang around where you're not wanted—"

Jillian tossed her head. Wet strands of hair slapped

lightly at her cheeks. "I'm determined to take possession of what's mine."

The hot look in Tuck's eyes sent a shiver of ice straight down her spine. "That's still in question."

"So until it's settled, we need to find a way to live together." Her heart was pounding. She was trying so hard to look cool, calm, and collected. She didn't want him guessing just how much courage she'd had to summon to stay here rooted to the spot in nothing but a beach towel when she wanted nothing more than to dart upstairs to the guest bedroom where she'd spent the previous night.

"Agreed."

Was it her imagination or did he sound as off center as she felt? "I could live upstairs; you take the downstairs."

It was official. She'd lost her marbles. She should either leave or throw him out, but here she was proposing a live-in relationship.

He eyed her. "You sure?"

"We're both adults. We can make this roommate thing work."

"Roommates, huh?"

He smiled and she saw he had a cosmically cute dimple in his right cheek. She could see why he'd been christened the Magic Man. There was something very compelling about that grin.

Mutt trotted over and sniffed at Tuck's shoes. The traitor.

Tuck leaned down to scratch the dog behind the ears, and Mutt sighed like he was in heaven. He'd won over her dog.

She didn't like that. "Let's get the ground rules straight."

"Yes, ma'am."

"Smart-ass."

"You started it."

"I hate getting up early in the morning," she said, ignoring his quip.

"That's good, because I'm an early bird. We can avoid each other."

"No bringing women back here. You want to make out, go to her place."

"You don't have to worry about that."

"Okay, then no bringing guys back here. You want to make out, go to his place."

"I'm not gay."

She could tell that, but she hadn't wanted to assume anything. "So you're what? Celibate?"

"Something like that. But the same goes for you. No bringing guys over."

"Agreed."

A dark look crossed his face. Abruptly, he turned. "I gotta go. I just remembered I have another job."

"After working on Sutter's place all day?"

"Carpentry never sleeps." He was shrugging into his coat, avoiding looking at her.

"What does that mean?"

"A man's work is never done?"

"Okay, so I'll see you when I see you."

"Yeah." He moved toward the door with purposeful strides, leaving her wondering exactly what she'd said to send him scurrying for freedom.

By Friday, the tension between Tuck and Jillian was so thick it would have given a chainsaw a run for its money.

She spent as much time as possible in the office, going through Sutter's files and pending cases, trying to make order out of chaos. It wasn't easy in the midst of Tuck's construction. She'd gotten the bulk of it tamed to manageable tasks, but she hadn't stumbled across the deed to the house on Enchantment Lane. Which was both a blessing and a curse.

Added to this, whenever she got home, Tuck would leave and come back long after she went to bed. He got up before she did, and he was out the door before her feet hit the floor.

It was more difficult avoiding him during office hours, although as long as he was patching the roof, she only saw him when he came down for lunch or to go to his truck for supplies. However, yesterday, he'd finished the roof and today he would move on to repairing the office ceiling.

Jillian realized she simply couldn't take it anymore. Not when she kept having fevered dreams about him. Not when she kept entertaining inappropriate sexual thoughts about a man who was emotionally unavailable. Today, she'd tell him that he had to go.

She walked into the office to find him on the ladder again, impressive butt on display as it was the first day. She tried to ignore him, but it was like ignoring a persistent toothache.

Apparently he was trying to ignore her as well, because he didn't say a word. Not even "good morning." Neither did she.

The room was deadly quiet.

The clock on the wall ticked loudly. Jillian cleared her throat.

"I'm going up into the attic," Tuck said. "Looks like Sutter's got termite infestation, and they're eating up the support beams."

"Thanks for the update but don't feel obligated to keep me apprised of your comings and goings."

"Just trying to be courteous," he said tightly.

"No need." She kept her gaze focused on her laptop even though she wasn't seeing a word of the codicil she was drawing up for Tom Red Deer's will.

He left the room, his boots clomping loudly, letting her know she irritated the hell out of him. Well, it cut both ways. He got on her nerves as much as she got on his.

Tuck climbed into the attic, his thoughts in turmoil over Jillian. Living with the woman for the past several days had been tough. He'd never lived with anyone other than Aimee, and it felt strange, unnatural.

He shone the flashlight through the attic and shook his head. It would take him forever to replace all the damaged timber. After he assessed the damage and started to work on the water-damaged Sheetrock, he poked his head through the hole in the ceiling and stared down at Jillian below.

Sitting there in her chair, attention homed in on the computer screen, she looked the epitome of an accomplished businesswoman. But he'd seen another side to her. Knew she wasn't near as tough as she wanted everyone to think. Jillian Samuels had a soft underbelly she struggled hard to hide. But Tuck wasn't fooled.

"How 'bout some tunes?" he said after a long minute of watching her.

"Huh?" Jillian raised her head and met his eyes, but immediately her gaze skittered off his like striking marbles. He fully understood her reluctance to make eye contact. He wasn't exactly thrilled with the jolt of awareness that passed through him every time their gazes met.

"Music," he said.

"Music?" she echoed.

He nodded toward the radio perched on the top of the bookshelf behind her.

"Oh, okay." She got up and turned on the radio. She played with the dial. Classical music poured from the speakers. She sat back down.

"You gotta be kidding me."

Jillian heaved an exaggerated sigh. "Something wrong?"

"You're seriously going to listen to that?"

"Mozart. It'll boost your IQ."

"Maybe I don't want my IQ boosted. Maybe I like being dumb."

"Clearly. What would you like to hear?"

"Country and western."

Jillian made gagging noises.

"What? You're from Texas. Aren't you required by law to like country and western?"

"Precisely why I don't like country-and-western music. Force-fed Merle Haggard and George Jones and Dolly Parton as a kid. Scarred me for life."

"All right, then. I'll settle for rock or pop or hip-hop. Anything but that mind-numbing Mozart."

"I can't listen to music with lyrics while I work. It messes with my concentration."

"Okay, so forget the tunes."

She snapped the radio off. "Go ahead, be culturally bereft. See if I care."

Tuck watched her go back to her laptop, his gaze trailing over the gentle slope of her ass.

Tell her the real reason you don't want to listen to Mozart. Tell her about all the times you took Aimee to the symphony. How she loved classical music and the sound of it reminds you too much of her.

"Jillian, I..."

"Yes?" She looked at him expectantly.

"Nothing," he mumbled. He didn't even know her. He couldn't tell her this private stuff.

She went back to her laptop.

Tuck tried to return to his work, but time and again, he found his eyes drawn to her. In spite of himself, he kept thinking about the vision he'd had of her in the sweat lodge. The temptress. It was damned eerie and unsettling.

She got up and made her way over to Sutter's filing cabinets. He couldn't help admiring the way her hips swayed when she moved.

After riffling through the top drawer a moment, she bent lower, going for the bottom drawer. Tuck canted his head, appreciating how the conservative gray wool skirt tightened over the curve of her ass.

Very nice.

He shifted for a better look.

His knee slipped off the support beam. He tried to right himself, but it was too late; his balance was compromised, and the Sheetrock was weakened from water damage. Tuck heard the ceiling crack ominously beneath his weight at the same time he felt it give away.

Next thing he knew, gravity had hold of him and it was all over.

Chapter 10

Tuck fell through the hole in the attic, slamming onto Sutter's office floor with a resounding *bang*.

Jillian let out a startled scream, sucked in a deep breath, and tasted Sheetrock dust. She spun around to find Tuck lying on his back at her feet.

"Tuck, Tuck, are you okay?" She squatted beside him.

His eyes were closed and his breathing shallow. He moaned softly when she touched him.

"Tuck, look at me."

He opened his eyes, peered up at her, and blinked.

Jillian raised her palm. "Tell me, how many fingers am I holding up?"

Groggily, he shook his head, grunted.

Oh dear, this wasn't good. "Speak to me."

He grinned up at her. "Hi."

"Hi? That's all you have to say? Hi?"

"You look worried. Why are you worried? You get the cutest little wrinkle line between your eyebrows when you frown."

Jillian pressed the pad of her thumb between her eyes

and stopped frowning. "Of course I look worried—you just came crashing through the ceiling."

"I did?"

"You don't remember?"

He reached up to finger her hair.

"What are you doing?"

"You have such pretty hair," he murmured. "Black like a raven's wing."

Alarm spread through her; his eyes looked glassy. Should she move him? Should she call an ambulance? Did they even have an ambulance in Salvation? She was unprepared.

Jillian wrung her hands. She might be a killer in the courtroom, but when it came to medical stuff, she was useless. She fainted at the sight of blood. Thank God he wasn't bleeding.

She plucked his hand from her hair. "Tuck, try to concentrate. Do you know what day it is?"

"You're a pretty temptress."

"Temptress?"

"Ridley says you're a jinx, but I don't believe it."

"Ridley? Who's Ridley?"

"Evie's husband and my best friend."

"Ridley's your brother-in-law?"

Tuck nodded. "That's it."

"Why does Ridley think I'm a jinx? He doesn't even know me."

"Shh." Tuck placed an index finger to his lips. "It's a secret."

"What's a secret?"

"You're the vision."

"Huh?"

"I know." Tuck winked and his voice took on a suggestive tone.

Startled, Jillian pulled back. "Know what?"

He grinned. "What you look like naked."

All at once, Jillian *felt* naked. Clearly the man was addled, and he had no idea what he was saying. Actually, neither did she. "You must have a concussion. We need to get you to a doctor. Can you stand?"

"And lips. The color of raspberries. Beautiful, beautiful lips."

"Tuck," she said sharply. "Listen to me. You've got to concentrate. You fell through the ceiling and hit your head. We have to get you to the doctor. Can you get to your feet?"

"Okay. Can do." He smiled at her like someone who'd had one drink too many.

"Here." She pulled his arm around her neck. "We're just going to stand you up."

"Hey," he said.

"What now?"

"You smell pretty too."

"Okay, I have pretty hair and lips, and I smell good too; we've established that," she said. "Can we please move on?"

"Absolutely." His jovialness scared her. He seemed far too happy under the circumstances.

"On the count of three. One, two, three..." She leveled him off the floor.

He muttered a string of curse words.

Ah, that was more like it. "What is it, what's wrong?"

"My foot."

"What about it?"

"Hurts."

"Can you bear weight on it?"

"Yeow!"

"Obviously not." Jillian sighed. "Can you hobble?"

The color drained from his face. "Hobbling's a good option."

"Lean on me."

He leaned into her, and Jillian became aware of exactly how big he was. She was plenty tall, but he was still a head taller, and his chest grazed against her breast. Through the material of both his flannel shirt and her silk blouse she could feel his hard, honed masculine muscles flexing, and she could feel her own nipples tightening at the contact. She slid an arm around his back.

She was so aware of him. His weight, his scent, his sinew and bones. She gulped, felt the movement slide all the way down her throat, leaving her feeling dry and breathless. She'd never been so acutely aware of a man's body before.

Or her own.

Her heart hammered. She moistened her lips, but the dryness hung on. Arid Colorado air.

And hot Colorado he-man.

Her thoughts were totally inappropriate.

Stop this. Stop thinking about his body. You're a perv. The man needs a doctor. Get your head out of the gutter and on your goal.

"Here we go," Jillian said. "You ready? Out the door and down the stairs."

"Stairs." He grunted.

"You can do this. I'll help you do this." Jillian looked at Tuck's face to make sure he was all right. He was staring at her as if she was the most fascinating thing he'd ever seen. He must have really whacked his head if the attraction was stronger than pain. His gaze drilled into her, as penetrating as a buzz-saw blade, slicing right through her, causing her nipples to strain even tighter against the lace of her bra.

Totally, completely inappropriate. Lusting after an injured man. *Concentrate on getting him down the stairs without too much jarring.* Without too much lusting.

They clumped down the stairs together, Tuck hanging on to the banister with one arm, his other arm slung over her shoulder, his leg bent to lessen the likelihood of him whacking his injured foot against the steps.

She was so close, his warm breath feathered the fine hairs on her neck, causing shivers to run down her spine.

"I damn well hate this," he grumbled.

"Hurting yourself?"

"Well that, but mostly I hate looking like a big pansy in front of you."

"You don't look like a pansy."

"Right. This is exactly what every woman wants, a big strong guy who has to lean on *her.*"

"Hey, you're not superman. Everyone needs someone to lean on now and again. I'm here. I'm tough and tall. It's okay to lean."

He grunted his disagreement, although he did say, "The tallness is a plus."

Jillian realized that with having a wife who'd had a long illness, Tuck had played the role of caretaker for so long he felt uncomfortable when he was in the position of needing someone to take care of him. Well, too bad, he could just get over his macho need to be the rescuer.

Before Jillian and Tuck reached the bottom of the stairs, Will and Bill, who must have heard the commotion, came running to help load Tuck into his pickup. She was relieved to step back and let the twins help out. Lexi came out of her store as well, fluttering anxiously about and asking a hundred questions.

"Is there a hospital in town?" Jillian asked.

"You'll have to take him to Boulder," Bill said.

"Just take me back to the house and call Dr. Couts," Tuck said. "I'll be okay."

"Forget it," Jillian barked. "You're going to the emergency room. End of discussion."

"You sure are bossy," Tuck said.

"Damn straight. You bust yourself up in front of me, you're stuck with me until you're officially patched up."

"I'll keep that in mind."

"See that you do."

Once Tuck was sitting in the passenger seat, relief washed over her. She'd gotten him past the first hurdle. She thanked the accountants and Lexi for their help and climbed in behind the wheel.

"Give me your keys," Jillian said to Tuck. "And the directions to the hospital."

"Can you drive a stick?"

"I can," she said. "I'm multitalented."

Tucker winced and lay his head back against the headrest.

"Does it hurt badly?"

"Not gonna be doing the Cotton-Eyed Joe anytime soon."

"How's your head?" She started the engine. "Still dizzy?"

"Better."

"That's good." She angled for the highway and promptly smacked a pothole.

Tuck sucked in his breath through clenched teeth.

"Sorry, sorry. I don't know where all the potholes in town are yet."

"S'okay, but talk. Distract me from the ankle."

"All right, all right. What should we talk about?"

"I dunno, what do you do for fun when you're not being a lawyer?"

"I go running. I've run a couple of marathons, do three or four ten-kilometer races a year."

"That's exercise, not fun. How do you relax?"

It was a legitimate question and one she didn't really have an answer for. "I do yoga occasionally."

"Again, exercise."

"Maybe I haven't yet conquered the concept of relaxing," she admitted.

"You're going to have a hard time acclimating to Salvation until you learn how to slow down."

"I'm getting that."

"You may never be able to reduce your speed. The slow lane might not be in your nature."

She shot a glance at him. "It's not going to work. You're not running me out of town."

"I have been thinking," Tuck said. "If that deed never turns up, how 'bout you sell me the lake house?"

"What? No."

"Why not?"

"For one thing, I'm not a quitter. For another thing, I need this change of pace. As you pointed out, I don't know how to relax."

"You can learn to relax anywhere. I've lived here two and a half years. It's where I..."

Lost my wife.

He didn't say the words, but she heard them just as clearly as if he had. She felt sorry for him, but she wasn't going to let him guilt her into leaving the lake house. The only way she was leaving was if he produced the deed. Blake had left the lake house to her. It was as if he'd known the place was exactly what she needed. She was rebuilding her life here in Salvation. She wanted a fresh start, and this was her chance.

"I'll pay you more than it's worth," Tuck enticed.

"Why would you offer that if you knew the place had been deeded to you?"

"I want it."

"Sorry." Jillian shook her head. "It's not for sale."

"The place needs major work. It's gonna cost you a mint to fix it up."

"Then why would you pay more than it was worth?"

"Because the place means that much to me. Sentimental value."

Guilt, that nagging emotion, knocked around her head. He certainly knew how to twist the knife. "It's got sentimental value to me as well. My mentor left it to me."

"He left it to me too."

"Which you can't prove. I feel for your situation, truly I do—"

"But you don't care."

"Look, I don't even really know you."

"And yet you're driving me to the hospital. What's that all about?"

"Common courtesy. You'd do the same for me."

"How can you be so sure?"

"You wouldn't?"

"Of course I would, but if the roles were reversed, I'd take your word for it about the deed and get out of the lake house."

"Easy for you to say—the roles aren't reversed."

"Why is it so important to you? It's gotta be more than the fact that Blake left you the house. If you were keeping it strictly for sentimental value, you would just have it as a summer place. You wouldn't have pulled up stakes, left your job in Houston as assistant district attorney."

"I don't owe you an explanation."

"Come on, we're living together. And besides, don't you want to help me take the focus off my pain?"

This was the longest conversation they'd had in a week of living under the same roof. "I was feeling burned out," she surprised herself by admitting.

"And?"

"There's no *and*."

"There's an *and*. I can hear it in your voice. What are you really running away from?"

"That's none of your business."

"Okay, fine, keep it bottled up inside." He shifted in the seat beside her and let out a small groan.

"It hurts a lot, doesn't it?"

"Of course it hurts a lot, and you won't even help distract me."

"Okay, all right, I'll distract you."

"You're a peach."

Jillian snorted. "I don't know why I'm telling you this. I could do something else to distract you."

"Oh yeah? Like what?"

She didn't miss the wicked tone of innuendo. "Sing 'Ninety-nine Bottles of Beer on the Wall.'"

"A favorite of yours?"

Jillian narrowed her eyes. "I should just let you suffer in silence."

"Please don't. We've got twenty miles of highway stretching in front of us," he said.

"I'm not even sure I like you. Why should I tell you my secrets?"

"It's a man," he guessed. "Broke your heart."

"More like bruised my ego," she admitted.

"What happened?"

She hesitated.

"Come on," he wheedled. "You can tell me. I won't judge."

She shrugged. "Really, it's nothing you want to hear about."

"How do you know unless you tell me?"

Drawing in a deep breath, Jillian realized she did want to tell him, even though she was afraid of what he might think of her. She felt awkward, self-conscious. She didn't know why she was telling him this except that he was a stranger, and she hadn't told anyone about Alex, and the dirty secret was burning her up. Finally, she just blurted it out.

"I had an affair with a married man." Furtively, Jillian angled a glance over at Tuck to see how he took the news.

His expression didn't change.

That encouraged her to go on. "I didn't know he was married," she continued, realizing that she sounded defensive. She felt defensive. No, that wasn't true. She felt guilty, ashamed. "But he was married just the same."

"That must have been a blow when you found out the truth."

"It was horrible." She shuddered. "Last year. Christmas Eve. I thought I'd surprise him. We'd been dating about a month, but we'd never gone to his place. That should have been a tip-off. I was dense. Or I didn't want to see the warning signs. I got his address from his employee file and went to his house. I dressed up. Victoria's Secret underneath a denim duster. I wore cowboy boots. I even had toy six-shooters strapped to my hips."

"Sounds sexy in a cowgirl kind of way."

"Thank you, it was."

"I would have liked to have seen you in it."

"You can't. I burned the outfit."

"Darn my luck."

He was sounding pretty damned chipper for a man with a busted ankle. "So anyway…I rang his doorbell…" She trailed off. Did she really want to go there?

"And?"

"A woman comes to the door. Younger than me. Hell, she barely even looked twenty-two. Beautiful, beautiful girl. Dressed in a sweet Christmas outfit. A vest with Santa faces on it. She had an infant on her hip, and she was smiling and smiling and smiling like I was bringing her a big fat Christmas present. In the background, I hear *his* voice. 'Who is it honey?' he asks her."

"Kick in the teeth."

"To say the least. 'Who are you?' his baby wife asks me. She's trying so hard to keep the smile on her face. Then *he* comes up behind her in the foyer. I'm tall. The baby wife isn't. Our eyes meet over wifey's head. His face goes pale, he knows he's busted. It hits me all at once. I am so stupid, so clueless."

"So what didja do?"

"What could I do? I'm feeling like I went fifteen rounds with Mike Tyson, but I figure there's no reason for two of us to feel that way. I didn't do it to protect him. Buzzards could peck his eyes out and I wouldn't shoo them away, but I couldn't bear to crush little Miss-Santa-Claus-Vest's heart, so I simply said, 'Sorry, wrong house.' I turned and ran back to my car."

"That was kind of you, sparing the wife's feelings."

"It was very uncharacteristic of me. My impulse was to cold-cock him right in front of her. I don't know why I didn't rat him out. Or maybe I do. I remember looking into her face and thinking, 'She believes she's got the world on a string. She thinks she's landed this great guy who's given her a great life, and she's in for a world of hurt when she finds out the truth.' But I couldn't be the one to knock the house of cards down on her. Yes, I'm tough. In the courtroom, I take no prisoners. But there, on that porch, I knew opening my mouth would be like kicking a puppy."

"The guy sounds like a complete prick. You're better off without him."

"Yeah."

"Why were you with him in the first place?"

"He was handsome and could be very charming and witty. I have a thing for witty men."

"I'll try to remember that. Were you in love with him?"

"I was trying to be in love with him."

"You can't try to be in love with someone," Tuck said. "You either are or you aren't."

"Okay, then, I wasn't. But I wanted to be."

"Why?"

"Because I've never been in love, and I just wanted to know what it felt like."

"You've never been in love?" He sounded incredulous. "Honest?"

"No. Not romantic love. I mean, I loved Blake, but in a daughterly kind of way."

"Why haven't you ever been in love?" he asked.

She shrugged. "I guess I never let myself. I had dreams—big dreams—and I wasn't going to get sidetracked."

"Not even a high school crush?"

She bit her lip. "Not that I can recall. I've always felt like an outcast because of it. Like there's something wrong with me because I didn't feel...this...this *thing* everyone else carries on about. But all my friends were falling in love, and they seemed so happy and I...I wanted that too. I wanted to be normal."

"That's understandable."

"It's pathetic. Trying to force myself to love someone."

"Jillian?"

"Yes?" She looked over at him again.

Tuck's smile was genuine, even though his eyes were tinged with the pain he was trying to hide. "It's okay. You didn't know he was married. You're not a terrible person."

"Yeah, well, it doesn't feel that way."

"You're not," he reiterated.

"Then Blake dies and the mayor appoints this same guy—the guy I had the affair with—as the new district attorney."

"Shit."

"You can say that again. How could I stay there and work for him?"

"You couldn't."

"I didn't. I quit. Then I find out about Blake's will, about this place, and I take it as a sign I'm supposed to be here."

There was an awkward pause in the conversation. Jillian sneaked a peek at Tuck from her peripheral vision. He had a faraway expression on his face. What was he thinking about? Probably how much his foot hurt.

"I had an affair with a married woman once," he admitted. "Except I knew she was married. She was separated, getting a divorce, but she was still married."

The scenery whizzed by the window. Mountains blue and majestic. Pine trees tall and green. Air so thin it made your heart hurt.

"What happened to the relationship?" she asked him. "With the married woman who was separated and getting divorced."

"She went back to her husband."

"Ah."

He shrugged. "It happens."

"How'd that make you feel?"

"Used."

"Exactly."

"It's not easy being the dirty little secret."

"I've never told anyone about Alex. Not even my best girlfriends," she confessed.

"I've never told anyone about Kay."

"I'm glad I told you." She smiled at him. "I do feel better."

He smiled back. "Me too."

Jillian felt something warm and melty inside of her. "Does this mean we're starting to become friends?"

"Do you want to be friends?"

"We *are* living together."

"But in a strictly platonic way," he hastened to add.

Message received loud and clear. Friendship was all he could offer her.

But that was good. That was fine. Splendid even. After Alex, she was taking a break from sexual relationships. "Friends would be nice. I need friends. I'm friendless in Salvation," she said.

"Not totally friendless," he said. "You have me."

"And Lexi who runs the flooring/window treatment store. She wants to be friends."

"Lexi's nice. And you'll make other friends. Salvation is a friendly place."

"I dunno. Everyone I've met seems really attached to Aimee and possessive of you." The minute she said his wife's name, Jillian could have bitten off her tongue.

Tuck said nothing.

She sneaked a look over at him. Noticed the strength of his profile. The firm jaw line, chiseled cheekbones, masculine nose. He was staring out the passenger side window, and his breathing was quick and shallow.

"I'm sorry," she apologized. "I shouldn't have said that."

"Nothing to be sorry for," he said lightly. "Turn here. The hospital is just up ahead."

Jillian slowed, but her heart was pounding. Why was her heart beating so fast? "How's the ankle?"

"Numb."

"Your boot's probably cutting off the circulation."

"Probably."

"Good thing we're here."

"Good thing," he echoed.

An odd feeling hit her then. One she couldn't name but didn't like. It made her feel all jumbled up inside, and she was afraid that if he saw her face, he would know exactly how much he'd unsettled her.

Art of the bluff.

She could hear Blake inside her head. He'd taught her a lot about hiding her feelings. She was a lawyer and a damned good one. Jillian put on her game face. She parked his pickup in the emergency room parking lot and looked over at him. "I'll be right back with a wheelchair."

"Relationship?" the emergency room clerk asked Jillian as she wheeled Tuck into an examination room. "Sister, girlfriend, wife?"

"Friend," Tuck said at the same time Jillian said, "Lawyer."

"So which is it?" asked the clerk, nervously giving Jillian the once-over.

"She's a lawyer and a friend," Tuck said. "But don't worry, we're not suing anyone. The accident was my own fault."

"Although the Peabody Mansion *is* falling apart." Jillian followed them into the examination room. "You could sue Sutter."

"That's not the way we do things in Salvation. Besides, he's your boss. Wouldn't suing him be a conflict of interest?"

"I'm just outlining your options. It's an unsafe work environment."

"I accepted the risks when I took the job." *And when I stared at your ass.* "I'm not suing."

He had to admire the way Jillian held it together. Getting him out of the mansion, calmly driving him to Boulder, throwing her weight around to get him seen as soon as possible.

Tuck tried to imagine Aimee handling a minor emergency like this, and he couldn't do it. One time he'd accidentally cut open his palm with a utility knife, and when Aimee had seen the blood, she'd passed out. He'd ended up getting her in bed and then calling a neighbor to come stay with her while he'd driven himself to the emergency room. It was kind of nice, he realized, having a woman who could hold her own in the face of an emergency.

That's not fair. Aimee was a trooper when it came to facing cancer. She was tough as hell, just in a different way.

True. Aimee had been a saint. Tuck bit the inside of his cheek and focused on the pain in his ankle. It wasn't hard to do. A doctor had come into the room and was working off his boot.

Jillian sat in the corner on a rolling stool, watching

while the young doctor, not long out of medical school, diagnosed a broken ankle. He sent Tuck for X-rays to confirm it; then he put him in a fiberglass walking cast and handed him crutches and a prescription for Vicodin.

The entire time, Jillian watched the doctor like a hawk—serious, watching for mistakes. The doctor told them he'd once been a ski bum but decided to go to medical school and specialize in emergency medicine after his best friend was killed on the slopes right in front of him. As he talked, the guy slid flirtatious glances at Jillian.

Tuck couldn't blame him, although he felt a sudden urge to tell the guy to keep his scintillating glances to himself. The woman was stunning. But maybe Tuck was being unfair, misreading the signals. Maybe the doctor was just worried because the clerk had told him Jillian was a lawyer, and he was terrified of being sued.

"He hit his head too," Jillian said, her eyes on Tuck's face, but her fingers were worrying the bracelet at her wrist. "Check him out for that. He didn't know where he was for a minute or two. He could have a concussion."

"Thank you for calling that to my attention." The doctor did a quick neurological exam, then turned to Jillian. "I think you're worried for nothing. Your friend checks out fine. No sign of a concussion."

"You're certain?" She narrowed her eyes at the doctor, and Tuck got a small whiff of what it would be like to face her in the courtroom. The effect was unsettling. She'd never get a chance to use those kind of interrogation skills in a place like Salvation.

"I...ca...could get a CAT scan if you like," the doctor stammered, and blinked.

"Do that."

For the first time, Tuck noticed how pale she looked,

how her forehead knitted in worry. She was really concerned about him. That was unexpected.

"I'm fine, Jillian," he said. "There's no need for an expensive CAT scan."

"You're sure?"

"I'm okay." Tuck didn't know what compelled him, but he snugged the crutches up under his arms and reached out to touch her shoulder. She looked startled, and a flush of sudden color rose to her cheeks.

A rush of emotion sledgehammered him. She put on one hell of a tough act, but inside she was a softie. He felt the heat rise in his own cheeks and he ducked his head to keep her from seeing him blush.

"So he's good to go, Doc?" she mumbled.

"Yes."

Jillian hopped up, grabbed her purse, and hurried ahead of him. "I'll bring the truck around."

Tuck watched her leave, wondering just why he was feeling so damned mixed up inside.

Chapter 11

Yₒu were right," Tuck told Ridley as he sank down next to him in a back booth at the Rusty Nail the day after his accident. He propped his crutches against the wall beside him. He'd had to get out of the house; he was going stir crazy with nothing to do but watch television and think about Jillian.

"Right about what?"

"The temptress is a jinx."

Ridley's eyes widened as someone put a Carrie Underwood tune on the jukebox. "What in the hell happened to you?"

"Jillian Samuels happened to me."

"Huh?"

"The temptress."

"Yeah, I get that, but how'd she jinx you?"

"I was so busy staring at her butt that I fell through the ceiling."

"Back up, back up, I'm not getting this."

Quickly, Tuck filled his brother-in-law in on what happened the previous morning at Sutter Godfrey's office and how he ended up at Boulder General Hospital with Jillian.

"You know," Ridley said, "if she hadn't been there, you'd have been in a real fix."

"You're not listening. I was in the fix because she was there. You were absolutely right. She's cursed."

"That seems a bit strong. I never said she was cursed. Plus, I might have been hasty in my interpretation of your vision," Ridley said.

"What do you mean?"

"I was talking to my uncle Tom about what you saw, and he said the temptress isn't necessarily a bad omen," Ridley explained.

"No?" Tuck swept a hand at his casted foot. "What do you call this?"

"Bad luck?"

"Isn't that the same thing as a jinx?"

"Not really."

Ridley waved at the passing waitress, and she stopped by their table.

"Hey, Rid." The petite blonde smiled.

"Hey, Brandi."

"What'll you have?"

"My *single* brother-in-law here would like...what?"

"Draft beer," Tuck said. "Whatever's on tap."

Brandi laid a napkin on the table in front of Tuck. "We've got Coors and—"

"It'll do."

Brandi's eyes widened.

"Don't mind his gruffness," Ridley apologized for him. "Tuck's wife died. He's a widower."

"Oh, you poor thing." Brandi sighed. "I'm so sorry. I'll be right back with your beer." She scurried off.

Tuck glared at his brother-in-law. "Why did you tell her that?"

"Sympathy date."

"I don't want to date her. She's a child."

"She works in a bar; she's at least twenty-one."

"Yes, and I'm almost thirty-one. If she'd be interested in me at all, it's because she's got eyes for my Social Security check."

"Aimee was younger."

"By only five years."

"So the temptress, is she younger?" Ridley took a sip of his beer.

"We're close to the same age. But you're right. She's a jinx. I've got to find that damned deed. Sutter claims it's in his office. Jillian's straightening the place up, but she hasn't run across it. Is the offer to bunk with you and Evie still open? I'm asking you because I know my sister will automatically say yes."

Ridley shifted in his seat. "Um…the doc has her on a different dose of fertility hormones, and it's made her voracious, if you catch my drift. Why do you think I'm hiding out here? I'm exhausted."

Tuck plugged up his ears. "That's my sister you're talking about. I don't need to hear any of this."

"Just letting you know what you're stepping into if you come stay with us."

"Okay, never mind, forget I asked. I'll sort out my living arrangements some other way."

Ridley's eyes lit up, and Tuck turned to see what he was looking at. Evie had come through the door. She spotted them and walked over to cozy up on the bench beside her husband.

"What happened to you?" she asked Tuck.

"Fell through Godfrey's attic and broke my ankle."

"The Peabody Mansion is a hazard. It should be

torn down." Evie reached for the bowl of peanuts on the table.

"Bite your tongue, woman." Ridley slipped his arm around her shoulders. "That house is the very foundation of Salvation."

"Then the town is on very shaky ground."

"She's right," Tuck added. "It's eaten up with termites."

"But it's the first house ever built in Salvation," Ridley protested.

Evie leaned across the table and whispered to Tuck, "He's such a sentimentalist."

"Not that I'm not happy to see you," Ridley said, "but who's manning the Bluebird?"

"Dutch." Evie crunched a peanut and leaned against her husband. "And before you get alarmed, beef stew is on the dinner special, so all he has to do is dish it up and make cornbread. Gives us plenty of time to go home for a quickie before the trivia tournament starts."

"I really do not want to know about this," Tuck said.

"Uh-oh." Ridley's eyes were fixed on the door.

"What? Am I wearing you out?" Evie chuckled and patted Ridley's chest. "Where's that famous Native American stamina you love to brag about?"

"Your jinx is here," Ridley told Tuck.

"What?" Evie asked.

"Tuck's new roommate."

"Oh, Jillian," Evie said. "I like her. She's sharp."

As a razor blade.

Tuck searched the crowded bar for Jillian and finally saw her standing next to the door. He couldn't help himself—his eyes clung to her. Her straight, symmetrical haircut swung about her shoulders like a swaying curtain as she moved, giving her a patrician appearance.

Her cheeks were windblown, and she had on a pair of black slacks, black boots, and a snug-fitting, white V-neck sweater that made him drool.

He felt like one of those cartoon characters whose eyes bug out of their heads when seeing a gorgeous woman. It was all he could do not to let loose with a wolf whistle. Oo-ga, oo-ga.

Queenie, he thought. *Mistress of all she surveys.*

He realized this was the first lustful interest he'd seriously entertained about a woman since Aimee. His libido had come kicking back to life—and in big way.

Great, this was exactly what he did not need.

Then stupidly, Tuck raised his hand and waved at her. *Dimwit.*

She smiled then, and it felt like the sun coming out after a long winter storm.

Tuck slid across the bench, making room for her at the booth. Evie raised an eyebrow and exchanged a look with Ridley. He shrugged.

Jillian sauntered over.

"Have a seat," Tuck patted the cushion beside him.

"Just for a second," Jillian said, sliding in beside him. "I'm waiting for someone."

A male someone? he wondered, then hated himself for wondering. What did he care if she had a date? It was nothing to him. He barely knew her.

"What'll you have?" Brandi asked Jillian and Evie as she brought Tuck his beer.

"Cherry Coke for me," Evie said.

"I'll have a glass of the house Chardonnay." Jillian folded her hands on the table and leaned forward, unwittingly exposing her cleavage.

Tuck ogled.

Jillian turned and caught him. She frowned and drew her shoulders back.

He grinned and lounged insouciantly against the booth. It felt good, feeling lusty again.

"Slow learner, huh?" she said.

"What?"

"Falling through the ceiling because you were paying more attention to my ass than what you were supposed to be doing didn't teach you anything?"

Evie hooted. "I like her." She reached across the table and shook Jillian's hand. "I like you."

Tuck scowled. "The women are ganging up on me, Rid. We guys gotta stick together. Help me out here."

Ridley held up his palms. "Hey, you're on your own, dude. I gotta go home with Evie."

"Smart man." Jillian grinned.

"I've got him trained." Evie plucked the cherry from the glass of Coke the waitress deposited in front of her and popped it into her mouth.

"No, no," Ridley disagreed. "I just let you think you have me trained."

"What difference does it make?" Evie asked. "As long as things work out the way I want them to?"

Ridley rolled his eyes. "Do you hear your sister?"

"Hey," Tuck said. "Don't look at me. I was stuck with her from birth. You married her."

"And it was the happiest day of my life." Ridley smiled.

Evie patted her husband's hand. "Did I mention he's a very smart man?"

On the jukebox, Carrie Underwood gave way to Merle Haggard and Jillian covered her ears.

"You want me to go fix it?" Tuck offered. "I can find

something to replace Merle, but I doubt I can scrounge up *A Little Night Music.*"

"You've been holding out on me," Jillian teased accusingly. "You are familiar with Mozart."

Tuck measured off an inch with his thumb and forefinger. "Never underestimate the Magic Man."

Evie groaned, but in a good-natured way. "Watch out, my little brother is feeling cocky."

"I for one am happy to see it," Ridley commented. "His eyes haven't had this much spark since . . ."

Ridley broke off as Tuck mentally filled in the blank. *Since Aimee got sick.*

Silence fell over the group.

"So this is the local watering hole." Jillian rushed to fill the emptiness and swung her gaze about the place.

Tuck appreciated the rescue at the same time he felt resentful. It wasn't her place to ease his emotional tension. Her hair flowed over her shoulders like water over rocks when she swiveled her hair. The cut was so stylish and artistic he had no doubt she'd forked over big bucks for it. For some reason, he resented that too. He shouldn't have. Back in the days when he was the Magic Man, he'd splurged on haircuts as well.

"Looks like half the town is here," she went on.

It was after five now, and people were stopping in for happy hour on their way home from work. It was the only saloon in town. Although the Rusty Nail also served sandwiches, hamburgers, and appetitzes, it was first and foremost a drinking establishment. Pool hall in the back. Video games, trivia tournaments, and eternal ESPN on the plasma-screen televisions throughout the front.

Tuck saw it through Jillian's eyes. Peered into the past to remember how the Rusty Nail had looked the first time he'd come here with Aimee one summer before they were married. In happier times. Before the ovarian cancer diagnosis.

Men dressed in jeans and flannel and down vests and hunting caps perched on stools at the bar. Women sat at tables with their girlfriends drinking rum toddies. A laughing couple fed each other nachos. A fistful of older guys hunkered over the pool tables. The air smelled of cheese and beer and French fries. The décor was standard Colorado neighborhood pub fare with rawhide lampshades, a roaring fireplace in the center of the room, and trophy deer heads on the wall.

Tuck knew without having to ask that the Rusty Nail was a long way from Jillian's Chardonnay-drinking, Mozart-listening, hundred-dollar-haircut world. Sooner or later, she was going to realize that as well and head back to the big city. Even if the deed Blake had signed over to him never turned up. All Tuck had to do was wait her out. The house meant nothing to her and yet it meant so much to him. It was his last connection to Aimee.

"Ooh," she said, and nudged Tuck with her elbow. "Who's that pretty blond woman with Bill?"

"That's his fiancée, Lily Massey. She teaches high school math."

"And the guy in the suit talking to Will?"

Tuck's eyes followed her gaze. Trust Jillian to find the only man in the room dressed in a three-piece suit and carrying a briefcase. His flank felt odd where her elbow had dug into him, and he caught a whiff of her hair, which smelled like cucumbers. "That's Jefferson Baines. Celebrity real estate agent."

Jillian shot a look at Tuck. "I take that to mean he's a real estate agent to celebrities looking for a mountain getaway and not a celebrity himself."

"He kisses a lot of asses. You figure it out."

Jillian glanced back at Jefferson, tilted her head, and studied his ass. "He looks like he's good at it. That's an Armani he's wearing."

"Jefferson is a legend in his own mind." Tuck snorted. "He conned Sylvester Stallone into a ninety-nine-year lease on a lodge in Crystal Ridge. And rumor has it he sold Carmen Electra a ski condo in Estes Park and slept with her. But I'm betting he started that rumor himself. At least the last part."

"Hmm, I don't know about that," she said. "The Rolex at his wrist looks real."

"The guy's a total poser. He lives in a one-bedroom apartment on Donner Avenue. The floors are made out of laminate. What kind of real estate agent worth his salt lives in a place with laminate flooring?" Tuck noticed Jillian was giving him the strangest look. "Laminate is an insult. Here he is a real estate agent and he's got a place with faux wood that ain't gonna last."

"I've heard the opposite. I heard laminate was more durable than hardwood," she said.

"Vicious lies spread by the makers of laminate flooring," Tuck replied sagely.

"Let me get this straight. Jefferson Baines has weak wood." Jillian nodded. "I see. That's very enlightening. Good to know in case I'm ever in the market for strong wood."

A Machiavellian smile lit up her face. This was how she looked in the courtroom, he realized. Manipulating language to suit her needs. He felt led on.

Jillian nodded at the twin CPAs. "So, what kind of wood do Bill and Will have?"

"They inherited their mother's place on State Street.

Soft wood in that area of town. Their floors are pine."
He eyed her, wondering what she was up to. "But Bill's
upgrading when he and Lily get married. They're going
for oak in the home they're having built."

"How do you know?"

"I've been commissioned to build their cabinets."

"What about that guy?" She pointed to an effeminate-
looking young man at the bar. "What kind of floor does
he have?"

"Bamboo. Exotic but green. Why the sudden interest in
flooring?"

"I've never given it much thought," she said. "But you
make it sound so fascinating."

"You can tell a lot about someone by their flooring
choices," Tuck said.

"Ah, I see." Jillian laughed and lowered her eyelashes.
"So if you were building your own place, what kind of
floors would you have, Tuck?"

He dropped his voice and met her eyes. "Mahogany all
the way, Queenie. It's thick and hard and lasts forever."

"What about Sutter Godfrey?" She nodded toward the
dapper old man as one of his cronies wheeled him through
the door of the Rusty Nail. "He's got mahogany in the
Peabody Mansion."

"Ah," Tuck said. "But it's very old wood. Termite riddled. Diseased wood can be very dangerous."

"Just for the record," Ridley said. "We've got tile
throughout our entire house."

"Poor us, we've got no wood at all," Evie said in a mock
mournful voice, and then grinned.

"Because you wore it out." Ridley tickled her lightly in
the ribs.

Evie giggled.

"I suspect we're not talking about flooring anymore," Jillian said.

"I'm up for a good flooring discussion. What's on the table? Hardwood, laminate, tile, natural stone, granite, carpet?" Lexi Kilgore sidled up to their booth. "I'm sorry I'm late, Jillian. Customer came in at the last minute."

"Granite's good," Tuck mused. "I'd forgotten about granite."

Jillian sent him a chiding glance, making him feel like a laggard. "We've moved on, Tuck. Keep up."

"Can I sit with you?" Lexi asked, wedging herself in next to Jillian, leaving her with no choice but to scoot closer to Tuck.

Her thigh settled against his, and he could feel her body heat radiating through the layer of their clothes, seeping into his skin. He liked the contact, and his body responded, stirring in a way it hadn't stirred in a long time. It bothered the hell out of him that he liked it.

"How's the ankle, Tuck?" Lexi asked. "You took a nasty spill. Your face was so white that when Bill and Will helped Jillian get you to the truck, I thought you were going to pass out."

Tuck lifted his mug. "I'm cruising. Thanks for asking."

Jillian frowned. "You shouldn't mix painkillers and alcohol."

"Nope, I stopped taking the Vicodin this morning."

"It could still be in your system."

"It's only one beer, and look, it's not even a third gone. I'm good to go."

"Uh-huh." She didn't looked convinced.

"I am," he said defensively. Damn, but the woman could set his back up quicker than anyone he'd ever met.

"When are you going to start renovating the lake

house?" Lexi asked. "You know I have to special-order that particular carpet she wanted—"

"I'll have to get back to you on that," Tuck interrupted, wishing she hadn't opened that can of worms.

"Carpet?" Jillian said. "You were planning on putting carpet in your own house?"

"That was before you showed up to contest my ownership."

"No granite? No wood at all?"

He glared. "Aimee's choice in flooring is off limits to you."

Silence engulfed the table. In the next room, pool balls clacked. On the jukebox, Shania Twain sang about feeling like a woman. Tuck felt like an asswipe.

Jillian downed her wine.

Lexi and Evie and Ridley all rushed to speak at once.

"Let's order," Ridley said. "I'm starving."

"You want another Chardonnay?" Evie asked Jillian. "I'm flagging down our waitress."

"Are you guys ready for the autumn festival?" Lexi chirped, and plastered a bubbly smile on her round face. "I can't believe it's next Saturday already. Where did the time go?"

Brandi trotted over and took the drink and food orders. Tuck tried to rouse some interest in her, but compared to the sharp, sleek woman beside him, the barmaid looked like a schoolgirl.

He thought about apologizing to Jillian for being so touchy. She'd simply been teasing him, and he'd bit her head off. Yes, he was still grieving his wife, but that didn't give him an excuse to be a rude jerk. He didn't know how to begin, so he busied himself with polishing off his beer and staring down the cleavage of her awesome fluffy white sweater.

"I probably should be getting home," Jillian said without looking at Tuck. "I'm still trying to plow my way through Sutter's open cases. It is a mess. I don't know how the man gets any business done."

"But we've got nachos coming," Ridley said. He could tell that his brother-in-law was trying to make up for Tuck's assholishness. "The Rusty Nail makes the best nachos in town."

Evie shot him a look and cleared her throat loudly.

"Besides the Bluebird, of course." He tightened his arm around her, clearly not interested in joining Tuck in the doghouse. "No one's a better cook than Evie."

Suck up, Tuck mouthed silently.

"I saw that, Tucker Manning." Evie shook a finger at him.

"Brandi." Ridley motioned when the waitress brought them the drinks and nachos. "Bring Tuck another beer. He needs some loosening up."

"No, no," Tuck said, but Brandi was already zooming off.

"Consider it, man," Ridley said. "She would wait on you hand and foot."

"Who would?" Jillian asked.

"Brandi the barmaid," Evie supplied. "Ridley's determined to play matchmaker for Tuck."

"Tuck's back on the market?" Lexi's eyes lit up. "I had no idea."

"It's been two years," Evie said. "He's only thirty. He needs to move on."

"Oh agreed, agreed." Lexi bounced in her seat.

Tuck groaned inwardly. He didn't want it getting out all over town that he might start dipping his toe in the dating pool again. Lexi was a sweet woman, but he wasn't the least bit interested in someone that damned bouncy. Was he really thinking about dipping his toe in the dating pool? He slid another glance at Jillian's exceptional cleavage.

Jillian cocked her head and studied Brandi as she took drink orders from a neighboring table. "She'd be perfect for you if you don't mind changing diapers."

"Hmm." Tuck sniffed the air. "Smells like jealousy in here to me."

"Please." Jillian laughed as if the idea was completely preposterous. "I have no romantic interest in you whatsoever."

"Really?" Lexi sounded hopeful and clasped her hands in her lap.

"Really," Jillian said emphatically.

God, how had he gotten himself into this conversation? Brandi came back and slid the beer across the table. She winked slyly at him. Tuck gulped and just dove right into the beer. Anything to keep from dealing with this.

Jillian crossed her leg underneath the table, and the tip of her shoe grazed his shin. He caught another whiff of her cucumber-scented hair and had the strangest urge for a garden salad. She smelled like lush, summer produce, and the thought of nibbling on her was making him hard.

"I think this is an exciting time," Evie said, leaning across the table. "Ridley and I are working on a baby. Jillian's just moved to town. Lexi's expanding her business to include window treatments, and my little brother Tuck has decided to come out of the shadows and return to the land of the living."

All eyes were on him. Tuck blew out his breath. It unnerved him. The thought of starting over, trying again.

He wasn't sure he was ready. Hell, he wasn't sure he'd ever be ready.

"A toast." Evie lifted her glass and looked at Tuck pointedly. "To new beginnings."

Everyone raised their glasses and echoed, "To new beginnings."

"Hey," Lexi said to Evie after they clinked glasses. "Have you thought about window treatments for the nursery?"

And they were off, Evie and Lexi talking about babies and curtains with circus animals on them that matched the receiving blankets Evie had already bought.

Clearly an outsider in the conversation, Jillian leaned back against the seat, and strands of her hair trailed along Tuck's shoulder. To keep from yanking her into his arms and stealing a kiss, he made himself think about work. How was he going to finish the job Sutter had hired him to do with a broken ankle?

But no matter how hard he tired, Tuck couldn't keep his mind, or his eyes, off Jillian. He was in serious trouble here. It wasn't just her cleavage or the tickling strands of her hair against his skin or the cucumber scent of her invading his nostrils. It wasn't the pucker of her rich raspberry lips when she took a sip of wine or the way her slender neck curved into her shoulders or the heat of her long, firm body radiating through his that clouded his brain.

Okay, so maybe it was all those things, but it was something more as well, and he had no idea what it was or what to do about it.

He squirmed in his seat.

She looked over at him. "Are you okay?"

"Um...I gotta move my legs. Kinda cramped up here."

"Oh," Jillian murmured, and leaned over to touch Lexi's arm. "Could you let us out, please? Tuck wants to stretch his legs."

Lexi let them out and Jillian got up, stumbling a little in the process. Tuck put out a hand to steady her. She'd had only two glasses of Chardonnay. He didn't know if she was a lightweight in the booze department or if it was those high-heeled boots giving her the trouble. You had to admire a woman who stood five-foot-ten and still wore heels.

"Thanks," she said breathlessly, and moved away from his hand. She reached for his crutches and passed them to him. "You know, I think I'm just going to call it a night."

"So soon?" Lexi said.

"Are you sure you should be driving?" Tuck asked.

She sized him up. "Like you could drive me home with a broken ankle?"

"We could walk. It's only a quarter of a mile."

"You're on crutches."

"I have tough underarms."

"It's downhill."

"I'm willing to risk it if you are."

"Hang out a little longer," Evie said. "We'll drop you off in a bit."

"You stay," she told Tuck. "Let Rid and Evie bring you home. I'll see you back at the house."

"You're not walking alone."

"What? Someone in Salvation is gonna mug me? You people don't even lock your doors."

"It's October. There still might be bears wandering about looking for some last-minute snacks before hibernating. I'd hate for you to be an appetizer."

Her eyes widened. "Oh. I hadn't thought of that. Okay, you can come." She retrieved her jacket from the coat rack, shrugged into it, then turned and headed for the door, her ass swaying seductively as she walked away.

Tuck hitched his crutches underneath his arms. *If she really is a jinx*, he thought, *I'm about to find out for sure.*

Chapter 12

All Jillian could figure out was that the house Chardonnay at the Rusty Nail had more kick to it than her usual label. She had no other excuse why her head was spinning sweetly and she was dumbly ambling down the road toward the lake house in the dark of night guided only by a sky filled with stars and Tucker Manning limping along beside her on crutches.

She'd had only two glasses. Why did she feel so unsteady?

Maybe it had nothing to do with the wine and everything to do with the delicious hunk of man beside you.

The air was crisp and clean, and she felt a little breathless. High altitude, she told herself, but whenever she sneaked a glance over at Tuck's profile, her pulse rate spiked. A shiver shot down her spine at the same time a moist heat rolled between her inner thighs.

Quick! Think about something else.

But her dumb, numb brain refused to cooperate. His scent hung in the air. Some kind of spicy cologne tinged with the yeasty aroma of beer and the musky fragrance of outdoor man. He was a far cry from the men she normally dated—smooth, polished, overly groomed men like Alex or the muscle-bound, pretty-boy himbos who looked good in a Speedo but didn't think too much.

Tuck was a guy's guy. Good-looking for sure, but in a rugged, tousled way. He didn't shave half the time, his hair was just a tad past the point of needing a trim, and she'd never seen him in anything other than flannel and denim.

Oh wait, there was that time when she'd walked in and found him on the couch in only his underwear.

Anyway, she'd never been with a guy like this. Unabashedly blue collar to the bone. Sure, he'd had his Magic Man phase. She'd seen the article on him in *Architectural Digest,* gussied up in a tuxedo. He could give Alex Fredericks a run for his money. But that had just been a lark for him. This Tuck, this guy here with the broken ankle and wind-blown hair and whiskey-colored eyes, he was the real deal. He could hunt and fish and start a fire with his bare hands. No wonder he'd settled in Salvation. No matter where he'd been born and raised, he was Colorado to the bone.

And without even trying, he turned her on like no man ever had.

"Here we are." Tuck stopped walking at the top of Enchantment Lane. The streetlamps ended at this point. They both stood looking to where the road dipped before it disappeared in the darkness.

"I think we should have taken that ride from Evie and Ridley," she said.

"They're still at the Rusty Nail. They play in the trivia tournament at eight on Thursday nights."

"Ah," she said.

"So, you and Lexi. Friends?"

"I'm new in town. I was looking for someone to hang out with."

"You've got me," he said. "I'll hang with you."

"Yeah, here's the deal. I'm thinking you wouldn't be so good at the girl talk."

"You never know; I might surprise you. I grew up with sisters."

"But what if you're the one I want to talk about?" She slapped a hand over her mouth. Why had she said that? Damnable Chardonnay.

"You want to talk about me to Lexi Kilgore?"

She made a derisive noise. "Noo…it was just an example of a topic we couldn't talk about. Should we do this thing now before we slowly start dying of exposure?" Jillian asked, vigorously rubbing her upper arms to stay warm.

"Ready as I'll ever be." To descend the hill, he bravely thrust his crutches out in front of him, anchored them on the asphalt, and swung his body through. He used his good foot to hold a new spot while Jillian followed behind him.

"This is a piece of German chocolate," he said.

She held her breath, just waiting for him to fall on his ass. What had they been thinking coming out here alone in the dark?

Tuck tried the maneuver again, succeeding a second time. "Look, ma, no leg."

"Don't get cocky, buster."

"We'll be just fine unless we run into a bear."

"Tell me you're making this whole bear thing up just to make me nervous."

"Nope," he said cheerfully. "Bears are very real, and they can get really cranky if you come between them and a hearty meal."

"I'll make a mental note to avoid that."

"Sound's like a plan."

Up ahead she could see the lake house, and relief pushed through her. "We're almost there."

"With the steepest part of the landscape to traverse," Tuck observed.

"Here, I'll lead the way." Jillian marched off in front of him.

"Jillian," he called.

"Yeah?" She swiveled her head as she stepped over a cross-tie timber that lined the lake property from the curvaceous Enchantment Lane.

"Watch out for—"

But she didn't hear the rest of the warning. The heel of her boot caught on something in the dark, and she found herself stumbling headlong toward the ground.

She put out her palms to catch herself. Her knees kissed the cool damp earth at the same moment she heard the clatter of Tuck's crutches as they tumbled to the dirt; then she felt his strong arm slide around her waist. "What are you doing? You're gonna fall if—"

Too late.

He was already slipping and taking her all the way down with him.

Somehow, Tuck ended up flat on his back in the pine needles with Jillian stretched out across the length of him, his arm still locked securely around her waist. His chest was so broad and firm. His eyes so dark. His breath so warm against her skin.

"Brilliant move, Einstein," she muttered.

"How do you know this move wasn't highly planned and calculated?" he asked.

"Too graceless. Then again, you're a guy…" She hitched in her breath. "*Was* it planned?"

He laughed. "Are you kidding? I couldn't do that on purpose if I tried. Besides, pratfalls just aren't my style. Face it, you weren't the only one imbibing tonight."

They stared into each other's eyes, and Jillian suspected he knew as well as she did that the situation they were in had nothing to do with alcohol. She scrambled off of him before she did something wholly inappropriate and exceedingly stupid. She turned toward the house, blood pounding in her ears.

"Hey," Tuck called out. "You just going to leave me here?"

"Huh?" Jillian blinked. She'd been so focused on getting away from the hard heat of his body that she'd forgotten he was lying there like a turtle, unable to hop up or flip over on his own. "Oh yeah. Sorry."

She hurried back to him, knelt beside him, and helped lever him off the ground. She reached for his crutches. Thrust them at him.

Wind rustled through the pine trees and sent a shiver over her skin. She didn't want him thinking she was shivering because she was so close to him, even though she was. "It's cold out here," she said. "Let's get inside."

"Let's," he echoed.

In the darkness, she could barely see the porch.

"Next time we go out drinking," she said, "we should remember to put the porch light on."

"Good idea. Next time."

They rounded the side of the house, their boots making hollow noises as soon as their feet hit the redwood deck. The moon, which had been playing peep-eye with the clouds, burst forth from its hiding place in that moment, bathing the dock in a silvery glow.

It was a beautiful shot of an autumn lake in moonlight.

She heard the sounds of the wind-blown water gently lapping the shore, a hoot of an owl from a nearby tree, a dog barking in the distance. She caught the scent of wood smoke in the air, along with the cool, crisp, languid odor of mountain water.

She stopped to suck in an awed breath. "This view is stunning."

"Yeah," he whispered. "It is."

Jillian didn't have to turn her head to know Tuck was looking at her and not the water. "It's romantic."

"That too."

"Did you and Aimee make love out here often?"

"A time or two," he surprised her by admitting. "But only in the summer. Aimee didn't like the cold much." His tone took on a wistful note.

"And yet she loved Colorado."

"In the summer mostly."

"You're lucky," she said.

"Lucky?" His voice sounded gravelly.

She swept her arm at his vista. "To have all this."

"What are you talking about? I have nothing. Not legally. Not until that deed turns up and I lost the most precious—" He broke off and maneuvered himself away from her.

She knew he was talking about his wife. She didn't mean to make him think about her, but she supposed when you love someone that much and lose them so young and tragically, you never really stop thinking about them. Jillian wondered what it would feel like to be so loved.

Jealousy bit into her, and she hated herself for being jealous of a dead woman. How pathetic was that?

"You've got a lot more than you think you do. You've got a great sister and brother-in-law who love you. You'll soon have a little niece or nephew on the way. You're doing a job you love. You're young and strong and gorgeous, and you have your whole life ahead of you if you could just let go of the past."

"Hey!" Tuck snapped. "You've got no right telling me what to do with my life."

Jillian held up her palms. Her heart was breaking for him and everything he'd lost, but the man was desperately in need of some tough love. "You did everything that was humanly possible to save her."

"Yes, I did." His tone was vicious.

"So let yourself off the hook. You're not the one who's dead, Tuck."

"It's so damned easy for you to say. You have no idea what it's like. You've never even been in love."

His accusation hurt, but it was true. "You're right. I'm the interloper, the stranger, the misfit. Story of my life. No one wants to hear what I have to say. I don't belong."

He drew an audible breath. "That's not what I meant."

She turned away from him, hugged herself in the cold, and walked out onto the dock. He was the damned Magic Man, and he didn't even realize it. Yeah, so life had taken his wife, kicked him hard in the balls, but he'd had something Jillian had never had.

Love.

A lump formed in her throat. No one had ever told Jillian that she was loved. At least not that she could remember. Not her mother, not her father, certainly not her stepmother, and there'd been no grandparents. No man had ever said the words to her. She told herself she didn't care, that it didn't matter, that she didn't need that kind of messy emotion in her life, but it was a lie. She wanted love more than anything. Wanted it so much that she kept putting herself in situations where she'd never get it, stacking the deck against herself in a self-fulfilling prophecy.

Stop feeling sorry for yourself. Suck it up. Get over it.

"Hey," he said.

Jillian did not turn around, but she heard him clopping across the wooden deck with his three-legged crutch walk. "Yeah?"

"Let's go inside. I'm freezing my ass off."

The petulant part of her wanted to tell him to go inside, that she didn't need him. She didn't need anybody. But she hadn't become a great prosecutor by holding on to resentment. The sensible part of her that knew how to make a plea bargain, the part of her that was shivering *her* ass off replied, "Okay."

They went inside together.

But once they were in the cottage with the door locked and the moonlight safely hidden behind the curtains, Jillian didn't know what to say or do next.

Tuck propped his crutches in the corner of the foyer and shrugged out of his coat. It was still early, Jillian realized as the Bavarian cuckoo clock mounted near the fireplace struck nine.

They looked at each other. The smell of wind and lake and pine trees flared in the short distance between them. She was looking at his lips and he was looking at hers and...

"You are not going to kiss me," she said.

"No." He leaned closer.

"It would be stupid."

"Agreed." Tuck was so close now that their lips were almost touching.

"We're strangers."

"But roommates."

"Strange roommates," she murmured.

"Very strange." He ran the back of his hand over her cheek.

"We're both in bad places in our lives."

"Terrible."

"We're embroiled in a property dispute." Jillian leaned toward him, closing the miniscule gap. "Kissing would be disastrous."

"Catastrophic." Tuck curled a lock of her hair around his index finger.

"I mean, where would we go from there?"

"Right."

"We're certainly not going to sleep together."

"Absolutely not."

"Never mind the sexual chemistry."

"Yeah, forget all about that." His palm was at the nape of her neck now, his fingers splayed through her hair.

Jillian kept telling herself, *No, no, no,* but all she could think about was that damned sex dream where Tuck had a starring role and how they'd been so ripe and hungry for each other.

God, it was hot in here. Like the frickin' Sahara Desert.

They were nose to nose. Her body was on fire, her blood boiling. Tuck's cheeks were flushed. Jillian suspected her own were as well.

"I'm going to step away from you right now," she said.

"Me too."

She didn't move.

Neither did he.

Their chests were pressed together. She felt her nipples harden beneath the lace of her bra. Damn her anyway. "I thought you were stepping off."

"I am."

"I'm waiting."

"I'm going." He didn't move.

Her breath was chugging through her lungs as if she was a ten-pack-a-day smoker. "Good-bye."

"See ya."

Then he snatched her into his arms and kissed her so hard her head spun. He speared his tongue past her lips, and she just let him. Not only let him, but parted her teeth and *encouraged* him to continue.

Dumb, dumb, dumb.

His flavor filled her mouth, enveloped her, flooded her.

Unbelievably, impossibly, he tasted exactly the way he had in her dream. Through his taste alone, she could have identified him blindfolded in a room filled with a hundred men. His fingers fisted in her hair, and he held her to him so tightly she couldn't move—didn't want to move.

Tuck plastered his other hand to her fanny, pulling her up flush against him and grinding his hips against hers, giving her full appreciation of his rock-hard erection.

Desire shot through her, stronger than before.

Break it off. Pull away. Stop this before it's too late.

Ah, but his kiss was drowning out that prudent voice, dissolving any last shred of resolve she might have. She nipped his bottom lip between her teeth.

He moaned low in his throat and maneuvered her against the wall, probably to keep himself from being thrown off balance. She wished she had something more than a wall to stabilize her.

Tuck pressed his body into hers. Excitement shot blood through her veins at an alarming rate, and she hissed in her breath as he branded her neck with his dangerously hot tongue.

The kiss was hard. Savage. Every muscle in her body

twitched in response. Jillian was so sure it would be gentle, tender. She didn't mind that the kiss wasn't what she expected. In fact, she liked the surprise.

His frantic tongue increased her desire for him. She cupped his face with both hands and kissed him back just as fiercely as he kissed her.

Tuck grunted, running his hand up underneath her shirt, his palm skimming her belly.

If Mutt hadn't picked that moment to come bounding in through the kitchen, a fast-food wrapper in his mouth, Jillian couldn't say what would have happened next.

But Mutt did come in and with his oversized tail wagging, wedged himself between Jillian and Tuck, breaking them apart.

"Someone's jealous," Tuck panted.

"Looks like that same someone's been rummaging in the trash," Jillian said breathlessly, her lips still tingling.

They stared at each other, and suddenly it all felt so wrong when seconds ago it had felt so right. She thought of all the reasons they couldn't be together, the least of which the fact that he was still hung up on his dead wife.

Tuck shoved a hand through his hair, looking sheepish. "About what just happened . . ."

"Big mistake." She rushed in to say it before he did.

"Huge."

"Gigantic."

"Monumental."

"Enormous."

"Epic."

Jillian stepped away from him, tugged down the hem of her sweater. "This can't happen again."

"Gotcha."

"I mean it."

He raised his palms. "Completely hands off."

She knelt to scratch Mutt's ears and willed her heart to stop pounding. She felt rather than saw Tuck hobble away.

She raised her head. "Tuck?"

He turned, looked at her. "Yeah?"

"It's nothing personal, you know. You're a great guy. I'm sure of it."

"You're not so bad yourself, Queenie."

"Why do you call me that?"

A smiled curled his lips. "Because you look so damned regal. So untouchable."

"The Ice Queen," she said, thinking about what her fellow lawyers said about her.

"Oh no, Queenie," he said. "You're regal as hell, but try as hard as you might to convince people otherwise, there ain't nothing cold about you."

"So Jillian is Tuck's temptress, huh?" Evie said to Ridley when they got home from the Rusty Nail just after ten o'clock.

"Yes, but don't tell him that I told you about his vision quest. He'd be upset. He didn't like telling me that he'd had a sexual fantasy about someone other than Aimee."

Evie unbuttoned her blouse. "I like her, but she's nothing like Aimee."

"Is that good or bad?" Ridley asked, trailing her from the kitchen into their bedroom.

"I'm just saying she's not Tuck's normal type." Evie stripped off her blue jeans and paraded over to the toilet.

It still threw Ridley for a loop when she went to the bathroom in front of him. It wasn't that he minded. He liked seeing her naked anytime he could. He'd just grown up in a family that was very private about their bodies.

When they'd first hooked up, the uninhibited way Evie shed her clothes both thrilled and shocked him. He wondered if they were going to have issues over nudity when they had kids or if becoming a mom would change her. Did he like the idea of her changing, or not? Honestly, the whole baby thing unnerved him. He wanted one, yeah, but the reality of it had him quaking in his boots.

Ridley stepped to the sink and wet his toothbrush. "Tuck believes she's a jinx."

"That's because you told him she was." Evie peeled off several squares of toilet paper.

"Hey, go easy on that stuff," he said. "With what the fertility treatments are costing us, we gotta cut every corner."

"Ridley, are you seriously suggesting that a couple of extra squares of toilet paper are going to put us in the poor house?" She flushed, then came over to elbow him away from the sink so she could wash her hands.

Sometimes it bugged him the way she encroached on his space, and he had to remind himself she grew up in the second position in a family with four kids, while it had been just him and his older brother. She was accustomed to having to jockey for everything she got in life, while Ridley, as the youngest of two, had pretty much had everything handed to him.

"You know, I was really prepared not to like her." Evie lathered her hands with peach-scented liquid soap. Little orange bubbles floated in the air between them. Ridley noticed how small and yet incredibly strong her fingers were—all that kneading and chopping and slicing. "And not because of all that jinx stuff. But you know what? I actually think she might be good for him."

"You're not worried he'll fall for her and she'll hurt

your brother?" Ridley mouthed around his toothbrush, and kept brushing long past the point he was ready to rinse, waiting for Evie to move away from the sink.

His wife dried her hands on a peach-colored towel. "Honestly, I don't think he could get any worse than falling into Salvation Lake on the anniversary of Aimee's death. And she is so not Tuck's type—he likes them petite and sweet. I don't think there's much danger he'll fall in love with Jillian."

Ridley spit and rinsed. "So you did see the sizzle. There's megawatt sexual tension between those two."

"Oh yeah, they've got chemistry, but that's good. Hot sex is all he needs right now. The man's been celibate for two years. He could do a lot worse than Jillian as his transitional woman, but I'd hate to see her get hurt."

"I don't know," Ridley mumbled, feeling decidedly uneasy. "From everything I know about vision quests, she's either a temptress whose going to be his ruination or she's his destiny."

"You're reading too much into that vision stuff."

"Don't discount what you can't understand."

Evie sank her hands on her hips. "Did you do a vision quest when you met me?"

Ridley shrugged. His wife had that pick-a-fight look on her face and a pugilistic set to her shoulders. "Did you lock the back door?" he hedged.

"You did!"

He shook his head.

She advanced on him.

Grinning, Ridley backed up until his butt hit the bathroom wall. She looked so beautiful all naked and fiery eyed. "Come on, tell me. What did you see?"

"I saw a woman with the most amazing red hair." He

reached out to twist a lock of her hair around his thumb. "And she was passionately whipping up a batch of the most delicious biscuits. I could taste them in the vision. Buttery, light, and flaky. I knew a woman who could make biscuits like that had to be an angel. I fell instantly in love."

"With me," she whispered.

"With the biscuits. You were just a side bonus."

"Ridley James Red Deer." She playfully swatted his shoulder. "What an awful thing to say to the woman who's going to be the mother of your children."

"Well, if that's the case, shouldn't we be working on making babies instead of standing here talking?" He snaked a hand around her waist and lifted her up into his arms.

"My big strong Indian brave." She sighed into his chest.

He took her mouth, kissing her firmly yet tenderly, letting her know just how much she meant to him. Things had been a little tense between them lately, and he wanted to sweep all that pressure away and just enjoy sex the way they used to before all the fertility treatments and ovulation charts.

Evie let loose a needy moan, and he carried her into their bedroom. His tongue swept her sweet, sweet mouth as he laid her down on the soft mattress. Blood rushed pell-mell to his cock, turning him to stone. God, he was hard for her.

She tasted so good. Better than the awesome biscuits she baked. He loved how petite she felt beside his bigness, how smooth she was to his roughness.

Two people couldn't be more opposite. He was a Native American man from the mountains. She was from an educated urban family. He'd gone to school on a reservation. She'd trained in Paris. While he was learning to hunt and fish and live off the land, she was speaking French and turning the simplest ingredients into elaborate meals. She was bossy; he was born to help. She was direct; he was oblique. She was fire. He was water.

And yet, in spite of their differences, they made it work. Who knew? Maybe it worked because of their differences. They had their ups and downs, sure, but they never got bored.

She wound her arms around his neck, and a shiver shot down his spine. His fiery woman made him burn. She peered into his eyes with a look that was pure Evie. "Take me, big man."

And so he did.

Thirty minutes later, they lay together, letting their ragged breathing return to normal. Evie rested her head on his chest. "Have you done a vision quest about our baby?"

Ridley hesitated, not wanting to get into this, but Evie was having none of his silence. She raised up on one elbow and looked down at him. "Rid?"

He sighed and put a hand over his eyes. "No."

"Why not?"

He cleared his throat and reached over to idly stroke her bare breast with the back of his finger, hoping to distract her, but she had the focus of a border collie herding sheep.

"Well?"

"I'm afraid of what I might see."

"Or not see." Her voice was serious.

"Yeah," he admitted.

"I want to go on a vision quest," she said.

Oh crap, what had he gotten himself into? "It's not that simple, Evie. You've got to believe in it for a vision quest to give you the guidance you're looking for. And it's not like magic. It doesn't make you psychic or foretell the future. You just see images, have dreams that guide you to make decisions."

"You sent Tuck on a vision quest without any hesitation."

"That was different. Tuck was desperate. And he had an open mind."

Evie sat up. "I'm desperate to know if we're going to have any children."

"Evie, we're gonna have kids, one way or another."

"What does that mean?"

"If we have to adopt, we will."

"I want my own kids," she whispered. "Our kids. I want to know what it feels like to be pregnant."

"Come on, you know you'd love an adopted child just as much as you'd love a biological one. You've got so much love to give, Evie."

"You're right, but still, I want to try. I want the full experience."

Ridley blew out his breath. "That's another reason I don't want you to go on a vision quest. I don't know if you could handle it if you didn't get the message you're searching for, and I can't bear seeing you hurt."

"I'm hurting now."

"I know."

"You're being stubborn about this."

"Maybe, but this is my spiritual practice, and you have to respect that. It's not a parlor trick." Glaring, he sat up. "You have to respect it."

"I can, I will, I promise, if you'll just go on a vision quest with me," she pleaded.

He hated to deny her, but it wasn't that simple. If she didn't see anything, she'd be disappointed. If she saw something that told her they couldn't have their own kids, she'd be crushed. He had to be the bad guy here, for her peace of mind. "I'm sorry, Evie. The answer is no."

"No?" Her voice quavered, full of tears. Damn those hormones that could change her mood so quickly.

"That's right," he said as calmly as he could. His inclination was to give in, but he had to stand his ground. "No."

"I'm not sure I can be around you right now."

"I accept your anger. It's healthy."

"Good, you can accept it on the couch." She shoved a pillow at him. He knew she was just reacting to her fears, but still a man had only so much patience. "Go sleep on the couch. And you can sleep there until you agree to guide me on a vision quest."

Ridley jerked back the covers, stormed to his feet, and jammed the pillow under his arm. "Fine, but I've got to tell you that banishing me to the couch is certainly not the way to get the babies you want."

He slammed the bedroom door behind him and heard her burst into tears.

It was in his nature to go back inside, wrap his arms around her, tell her that he was sorry and that he'd do what she wanted. But on this matter, he knew he couldn't give in.

Not just for his sake, but for Evie's as well.

Chapter 13

All right, all right, she was going to stop thinking about Tuck. Right here, right now. No more fantasies about him or that kiss.

Determinedly, Jillian sucked in her breath, dropped her purse into the bottom drawer of Sutter's antique desk, and plunked down into the rolling leather chair. She reached up to run her fingertips over her lips, trying to recapture the feel of Tuck's mouth on hers from the night before.

Great, you can't go two minutes without thinking about him.

Hell, she'd lain awake all night thinking about him.

Stop thinking about him. Now!

Right, right. Head in the game. Purposefully, she straightened the stack of papers in the in-box that didn't need straightening, looked up, and spied the ladder she'd moved to the corner yesterday while cleaning up the mess from Tuck's fall through the ceiling.

Immediately, she thought of Tuck and how he'd looked standing on that ladder.

Stop it.

She turned on her laptop and slid another glance at the

ladder. She could smell Tuck's scent in the room. Outdoorsy and masculine, mingling with the musty smell of old house and water-damaged Sheetrock.

It's just your imagination. You can't smell him.

All at once, the taste of him filled her mouth, and Jillian just *yearned* for him. His kiss had been such a heady combination of need and restraint, of tenderness and demand.

Knock it off. Get to work.

All right, all right. She cracked her knuckles, took a deep breath, and focused her attention on the computer screen.

But she knew the ladder was still there. Standing like a forgotten soldier. A constant reminder of the man she was struggling to forget.

"Dammit," she muttered, pushing back her chair.

Jillian headed for the ladder with the intention of stuffing it into the adjoining supply room, but before she reached it, the office door opened and a beautiful young blonde stepped over the threshold.

"Hi," she said. "You must be Jillian Samuels, the new lawyer everyone in town is buzzing about."

"I haven't taken the Colorado bar yet, but, yes, I suppose I am."

The woman stepped across the room, her hand extended. "Lily Massey."

"Ah," Jillian said, shaking her hand. "Bill's fiancée."

She beamed. "I am."

"What can I do for you, Lily?" Jillian asked. "Or did you just stop by to say hi?" She hadn't been in town long, but she'd quickly learned people liked to pop in to get a good look at her and satisfy their curiosity. Or size her up before making their bets in the guess-when-she's-gonna-leave-town pool.

"I need to speak to you about my prenuptial agreement."

A real client. Good, good.

"Have a seat," she invited with a wave at the chair positioned in front of Sutter's desk.

Lily glanced up and eyed the hole in the ceiling. "What happened?"

"Long story."

Lily kept staring upward. "Are we safe?"

That was a loaded question. As a lawyer, she knew safety was an illusion. At any moment, you could step off the curb in front of a Tom Thumb delivery truck and get run down. You could fall through the attic and break your neck. You could drop dead of a brain tumor in the middle of Starbucks. And yet, she was certain that was not the answer Lily Massey was looking for.

"As long as we don't go into the attic." Jillian sat in the rolling leather desk chair, and Lily tentatively eased down across from her. "So you want to draw up a prenup?"

"No," she said. "I want you to tear it up."

"Excuse me?"

Sighing, Lily leaned back against the chair. "My father made me get one. I'm from L.A. Everyone gets a prenup. Dad insisted when he came up for our engagement party. He thinks he's protecting me but..." She trailed off.

"But?"

"He doesn't understand."

"As a lawyer, I'm afraid I have to side with your father. Do you have significant assets?"

"I've got a small trust fund, yes. But Bill has money of his own. He's been saving for the right woman to come along."

"That's all very romantic but not terribly practical. This country's divorce rate is fifty percent."

"You're from a big city, too, aren't you?" Lily asked.

"Houston."

"You've never lived in a place like Salvation."

"That's true."

"You don't understand either. About small towns and people with integrity. When they give you their word, it's law."

"People in small towns don't have a lock on integrity. Proportionally, there's just as much greed and corruption in Salvation as there is in L.A."

Lily shook her head. "No, there's not. You'll see if you stay long enough. This is a special place. The people in it are special too."

Okay, so Lily was a bit delusional. She didn't seem to know the first thing about human nature.

"I'm guessing Bill is hassling you about the prenup?" Jillian ventured.

"No," she said. "Exactly the opposite. He cheerfully signed it."

"So what's the problem?"

"Bill didn't ask me to sign one."

"Why not?"

"He says what's his is mine. Don't you see?" Lily asked. "My prenup ruins everything."

Jillian leaned forward. "How so?"

"A prenuptial agreement says I expect the marriage to fail. I don't."

"It's just a legal document to protect you, worst-case scenario."

"I don't live my life that way." Lily shifted, crossing her legs at the knees. "Preparing for the worst and hoping for the best. I believe that if you prepare for the worst, then that's what you're going to get."

Jillian didn't expect Lily's comment to affect her like it did, but suddenly she experienced a yawning hollowness in the pit of her stomach. That's what she'd done her entire life. Prepare for the worst and hope for the best—that is, until she moved to Salvation. She hadn't prepared for anything. She'd broken her pattern and look where it had gotten her. Living in a house that in all likelihood she was going to lose, living with a man who made her feel things she didn't want to feel.

"Instead of destroying your prenup, why not just get Bill to draw one up of his own so you'll be on equal footing?"

Lily twirled the large marquis-cut diamond on the ring finger of her left hand. "He says he has faith in us, that he knows we're destined to be together. He's not afraid. He loves and trusts me."

"That's all well and good, but what's going to protect you if this marriage doesn't work out?"

"My faith will protect me. Faith in our love."

"You're basing this on emotions. Be practical. Think of your future," Jillian lobbied.

"Haven't you heard a word I've said?" Lily tilted her head. "I'm in this marriage for better or worse, for richer for poorer, in sickness and in health. Bill is the love of my life. Now, if you don't mind, would you please get the prenup? I'd like you to witness its destruction."

"If that's what you want." Jillian got up and headed for the file cabinet she'd spent the past week organizing.

"I'd also like you to attend our wedding so you can see for yourself that what Bill and I have is the real deal. It's on Christmas Eve at Thunder Mountain Lodge. The whole town's invited."

She's so naïve. "That's very kind of you, Lily."

"So you'll come? You will still be in Salvation by Christmas?"

Was this a challenge? Or was she just taking it that way? Why not go to the wedding? It wasn't like she had plans for Christmas Eve.

"We're doing it up big," Lily enticed. "A grand celebration for a big love."

"Sure, why not," Jillian accepted, her fingers walking through the files under the M, not really sure why she did.

"That's great. And, Jillian?"

"Yes?" She looked up, Lily's prenuptial agreement in her hand.

The young woman's smile was brilliant. "I hope someday you find *your* true love."

"I'm in a pickle, Aim, and I don't know how to get out of it," Tuck spoke out loud to his dead wife. "I need your advice on what to do about Jillian."

Dead silence.

Normally when he talked to Aimee, he experienced a comforting peace wrap around him. He knew it was probably all in his mind, but nevertheless, when he talked, he imagined she was listening, and that made him feel better.

Not today.

Today he felt emptier than he had since he'd fallen into the lake on the anniversary of her death. It was a rotten sensation, and he wanted to run away from it, but there was nowhere to go, and it had nothing to do with the fact that he was held captive by the cast on his right leg. He couldn't run from his hobbled mind.

"Aimee?" he tested.

Nothing.

His chest ached. Restlessly, he shifted on the couch. "Are you gone?" he whispered.

From his pallet in the corner beside the fireplace, Mutt lifted his head and gave him an expectant look.

"It's okay, Muttster, go back to sleep."

The dog lowered his head, and Tuck tasted something salty on the back of his tongue. He swallowed, blinked, picked up the remote control, and flipped through the television channels in search of a diversion but found none. He couldn't concentrate on mindless daytime TV prattle.

"I'm sorry, Aim. I didn't mean to kiss her. But you've been gone for so long, and I'm so lonely and I miss what we had so much. I want that again. You were right when you told me that I'd want it again, but I didn't believe you. I don't want to want another woman. But I do."

Dammit. The salty taste was back in his mouth again. He clenched his jaw and swiped at his eyes with his sleeve.

"Aimee?" he murmured, reaching desperately for something he knew was long gone.

Mutt whined.

"When you're right, dog, you're right. There's no one here but me and you. I gotta let go. I know, I know…but seriously, how the hell does a guy do that? And what woman's gonna want me with all my emotional baggage?"

Mutt barked.

A knock sounded on the door.

Tuck blinked, scrubbed at his eyes, and took a deep breath, struggling to tamp down his emotions and hoping whoever was at the front door would just go away. After the fifth knock, he heard the door handle jiggle open.

"Tuck, you in here?" Ridley called from the doorway.

"Come in," Tuck hollered, shifting on the couch to a sitting position. "What's up?"

Ridley came through the door, bringing with him the smell of Bluebird cheeseburgers. "Lunch's up."

"Dude, how'd you know I was starving?"

"Your sister is omnipotent."

"Gimme." Tuck reached for the brown paper bag in Ridley's right hand, then spied the stack of wood his brother-in-law had tucked under his left arm. "What's that?"

Ridley tossed him the sack and sat down beside him on the couch. "A special project for you while you're laid up."

Tuck's ears pricked up with interest as he opened the paper bag, and the smell of grilled onions wafted into the room. He loved the idea of something to do while he was recuperating. "Special project?"

Mutt whined loudly and licked his lips.

Ridley laid the maple wood on the coffee table, fished a dog biscuit from the front pocket of his shirt, and tossed it to the dog. "Evie's Christmas gift from me. I want you to make it."

"Yeah?" Tuck eyed the expensive maple as he bit into his cheeseburger.

"Music box."

Tuck nodded, swallowed. "I'm with you."

"Cradle on top of the box. Cradle that swings. Intricate detail. Not gonna be easy."

Excitement pushed out the loneliness he'd been feeling before Ridley had walked in. He's been an architect and a carpenter, but he'd never tackled a woodworking project like this. All his skills had been plied on houses, not delicate crafts. Eagerness had him putting down the cheeseburger and picking up the maple. He wanted this. Needed it. "Plays Brahm's Lullaby?"

"George Michael's 'Faith'."

Tuck grinned at Ridley. "Dude, I'm so there."

Two weeks passed with Jillian and Tuck tiptoeing around each other. Or rather Jillian tiptoed. Tuck sort of clumped about in his cast. Jillian made arrangements to take the Colorado bar exam and spent her spare time studying at Sutter's office or playing chess with Lexi. Tuck immersed himself in crafting Evie's music box. Neither one of them spoke again about the kiss they'd shared. In fact, they both did their best to avoid talking about anything personal.

They fell into the rhythm of roommates trying hard to give each other space. She got up at five-thirty each morning, went running with the dog, showered, and left the house before Tuck ever woke up. In the evenings, Tuck hung out at the Bluebird or at Evie and Ridley's.

The weekend before Halloween, Tuck finished the music box. He could see a hundred different ways he could have done it better, but he had to admit it wasn't half bad for his first attempt at crafting a music box. But once it was done, time weighed heavily on his hands. He wanted—needed—something else to occupy his mind while his ankle healed. That Saturday morning, when Jillian returned from her jog with Mutt, he announced, "I'm going stir-crazy. I need something to do. I'm going to strip the wallpaper off the kitchen, then texture and paint the walls."

"You can't do that," she said, toweling the perspiration from her neck. "Our property dispute hasn't been settled. Blake's will hasn't been probated."

"Look, the place needs renovating. Whether you end up living here or I end up with the place, it's got to be done. What's the harm in giving me something to do?"

"You'll want to decorate it your way, and if I end up with the place, I'll have to redo it."

"I tell you what, you can pick out the décor."

She narrowed her eyes. "Why would you do that? Is it because you know there really is no deed?"

"There's a deed."

"Then why?"

"You are the most distrustful woman I've ever met," he said. He tossed his head and his hair fell over his forehead. He needed a haircut, but she liked the rakish look longer hair gave him. "I'm bored and I'm desperate enough to let you paint the kitchen pink if that's what it takes."

"I won't paint the kitchen pink."

"I had no doubts. You're not a girly-girl."

"Fuchsia, maybe," she teased.

"So you wanna make a supply run to the hardware store in Boulder?" He smiled.

"Who pays for the material?"

"We split the cost."

"Again, why would you do that?"

"Occupational therapy. It's not any more expensive than material for some useless craft project."

He had a point. The charming grin—combined with the sexy hair—did her in. She ignored her prudent side, tossing caution out the window. It would be pretty damn nice to get rid of those ducks. "Yeah, okay. Let me get my purse."

By noon they'd only managed to steam off about a quarter of the mallard duck wallpaper. It was a painstaking process. Intrigued by the whole wallpaper peeling endeavor, Mutt kept getting underfoot, and they spent half their time shooing him away. Finally, Jillian got up and put the dog outside. "Go chase a squirrel or something."

She came back, and hands on hips, watched as Tuck meticulously steamed a section of aged yellow wallpaper. "Mallards in the kitchen. Imagine."

Tuck grunted. "It is a lake house."

"Who picked out that wallpaper?"

"Aimee's grandmother I imagine. This lake house was in the Townsend family for three generations."

Jillian pushed her bangs back off her forehead. "Then Blake goes and breaks the chain by leaving it to me."

"And then deeding it to me," he reminded her.

"Why would he do that?"

"There weren't any Townsends left to leave it to."

"No, I mean, seriously, why would he leave the place to me and then deed it to you? The brain tumor is the likely explanation, but I was with Blake the day before he died, and while he had been getting progressively forgetful, he didn't really seem impaired."

"I can't answer that."

"I mean, why didn't he just leave the place to you to begin with? Why drag me into it at all?"

"I don't know that either. Maybe because you were more like a daughter to him than his own daughter, and Aimee didn't have any kids to leave it to."

She stared at him. "How come you never had kids?"

"There wasn't time," he said sharply. "We wanted to, but Aimee..." He shook his head, didn't finish.

What in the hell was wrong with her? Why had she asked that? "I'm sorry. That was completely rude and none of my business. Would you like to break for a quick lunch?"

"Yeah." He straightened, turned off the steamer, and went to the sink to wash his hands, his cast thumping heavily against floor.

"You're limping less."

"It doesn't hurt as much as it did." Tuck wiped his hands on a cup towel. "I can sleep on my stomach again."

"That's good," Jillian murmured. Immediately, her mind went to the thought of him lying on the couch the way she'd found him that first morning almost a month earlier. She pushed the image from her mind and went to peer into the refrigerator. "We're out of groceries. You wanna just hit the Bluebird?"

"That'd take too much time. We have bread," Tuck said. "And sliced cheese. We could have grilled cheese sandwiches."

"Clearly, you haven't tasted my cooking."

"Don't worry, Queenie, I'll handle it."

Jillian tucked her fingers into the back pockets of her jeans. "I wish you wouldn't call me that."

"Why not?" He twisted the tie off a loaf of wheat bread. "It suits you."

"That's a depressing thought."

"How come?"

"Queenie makes me feel as if you think I think I'm better than everyone else. I'm reserved with people. I know that, but it doesn't mean I think I'm better."

"I don't think that at all." He turned the gas burner on low.

"What do you think?"

"A queen is a woman who's foremost among others. Plus, you said you played chess with Blake, right?"

"Yes, it's my favorite game."

He gave her a look that said, *There you go.* "And what's the most powerful piece on the chess board?"

"The queen."

"Exactly."

"So when you call me Queenie, you're saying I'm powerful?"

"Yup."

Jillian couldn't help smiling. "Powerful, huh?"

"Far more than you know."

"I think I like that."

"That's what I've been trying to tell you. Wear your crown with no misgivings, Queenie." He winked at her and melted butter in a nonstick skillet.

He finished cooking the sandwiches and served them up. They sat at the bistro table in the breakfast nook. They hadn't sat here together like this since the morning after the first night Jillian spent at the lake house. From this vantage point, they could look out the window and see a section of the lake stretching out frosty green beyond the snow-covered pine trees.

Soft rock music poured from the radio in the kitchen window. They'd found a station they could both agree on. Delbert McClinton was singing "Givin' It Up for Your Love." The song had come out the year Jillian was born. She knew because the audio tape *The Jealous Kind* had been among her father's music collection when he'd died. As a teenager, she'd listened to his tapes over and over, trying to make a connection to the man she barely remembered. She shook her head, shook off the past.

"This is the best grilled cheese sandwich I've ever eaten," she told Tuck, surprised at how tasty it was. "What'd you do to give it that extra zing?"

"Mustard."

"Hmm."

"And not just any mustard," he said. "Grey Poupon."

"Should we be eating this in a Rolls-Royce?"

"I'm in the mood to slum it, how 'bout you, Queenie?"

"I've been slumming it for a very long time, Magic Man. Rolls-Royces are a bit beyond my budget. I was a county employee."

Tuck leaned back in his chair, stretching his long legs out in front of him, his eyes lingering on her face. Jillian glanced away, looking out the window to see a few black-headed sparrows perched on the bird feeder on the deck, pecking at sunflower seeds.

On the radio, The Lovin' Spoonful was playing "Do You Believe in Magic?" No, Jillian didn't. But she wished she could.

"You really planning on staying in Salvation?" Tuck dusted bread crumbs from the table onto his empty plate. "Even when the deed turns up?"

She was already getting attached. She was quickly growing to love the house, the mountains, the lake, the town. The fact that everyone treated her as though she were transient was bothersome. It made her feel a little unwelcome, even though the community was friendly. They had not embraced her fully.

Or could it be you haven't fully embraced them, and they're picking up on your emotional reserve?

She lifted her chin. "Yes, I am."

"Wait until after you've weathered a Colorado winter and see if you still feel the same way."

"What's the deal?" she asked. "You in the local pool to see how soon I'll leave town?"

"You know about that?"

"You better change your bet. I'm not leaving."

"That stubborn, huh?"

"Partly," she admitted. She met his gaze, and he was studying her with half-lidded eyes. "But mostly because I need this chance at Salvation."

"Pun intended I'm guessing."

"All my life I was so focused on being a prosecutor. It's all I ever thought about, all I ever worked toward," she said.

The Lovin' Spoonful posed their question again. Do you believe in magic? Such a stupid song.

"So when all the other little girls were talking about being rock singers and movie stars and models, you said, hey, I wanna put the bad guys in jail?"

"Yes, yes, I did. I was quite enamored of *Law and Order,* but it went beyond that."

"In what way?"

"I was attracted to law because the roles are clear. I liked the responsibility and the authority. I'm a cards-on-the-table kind of gal. I like a career where preparation, caution, and constant questioning are valued. I like the fact that it's clear who the bad guys are and who the good guys are. I get off on the dangerous undercurrent inherent in criminal law. The courtroom is the only place where I felt like I truly belonged."

He smashed the bread crumbs on his plate with the pad of his thumb. "You're always thinking, aren't you? Trying to figure out everyone's angle."

"Always," she admitted.

"What's mine?"

"Huh?"

"If I was accused of a crime, how would you assess me?"

"I'm not sure this little analysis game is such a good idea," she said.

"Why?" He leaned closer, his eyes suddenly sharp, the languid expression completely disappearing. "Afraid you'll hurt my feelings?"

"Honestly? Yes."

"You think I'm that sensitive?"

"I value the friendship we've started to forge. I don't want to blow it."

"Like I almost blew it the night we walked home from the Rusty Nail."

"Yeah," she said. "Like that."

"I promise I won't get offended. I'd really like to know how I look through Queenie's eyes."

"Shouldn't we be getting back to the wallpaper?"

"We can steam and strip and talk all at the same time."

"Are you sure you really want to know?"

He raised his chin. "I do."

"No holds barred?"

His eyes glistened a challenge. "No holds barred."

"Even if it might sting?"

"That's what no holds barred means."

Jillian sucked in a breath. "Okay, here goes, but remember you asked for it."

Tuck stacked their plates in the kitchen sink, grabbed up the steamer, and went back to the wallpaper. "Go ahead, I'm listening."

Jillian took up a putty knife and came to stand beside him, prying off the paper he'd loosened with the steam. "In spite of having been the Magic Man," she said, "you're an underachiever."

"You've been talking to Evie."

"Yes, but I didn't have to talk to your sister to figure this out about you."

"No?"

"If you'd worked hard to become an architect, if designing those classrooms was so important, you wouldn't be here in Salvation, hiding out."

"Interesting theory, except maybe I don't view it as hiding out," he said.

"You don't. I get that, but it's part of what I'm basing my opinion on."

"So we're in agreement."

"You settle."

"What does that mean?"

"You settle for what's in front of you, because you don't want to tolerate the discomfort of desire."

"Now you sound exactly like Evie."

"Your sister has said something similar?" Jillian arched her eyebrows.

He moved to run the steamer over a different section of wallpaper. "Maybe."

"You remind me of an F. Scott Fitzgerald quote I read once."

"And what's that?" Warm steam rose up between them.

" 'The test of a first-rate intelligence is the ability to hold two opposed ideas in the mind at the same time and still retain the ability to function.' "

He turned and grinned at her as that irresistible lock of hair fell over his forehead again, making him look completely adorable. "Ah, Queenie, you're saying I'm smart?"

"I'm saying you straddle the fence."

"Not so."

"Please." She snorted. "Democrat or Republican?"

"What's that got to do with anything?"

"Just answer the question."

He shrugged. "I'm not married to either party. Depends on the candidate."

"My point exactly. You sway whichever way the wind blows." She peeled off a long strip of mallards.

"That's unfair."

"Paper or plastic?"

"No preference."

"Baseball or football?"

"I like them equally."

"Stem cell research—for or against?"

"I don't have all the facts. I can't make an informed decision without studying both sides of the issue."

"Aha!" Jillian crowed. "Beautifully proving F. Scott Fitzgerald's point."

"You're pretty competitive, aren't you?"

"You're the one who said you could take it."

"I might have been a bit hasty with that."

"You know why I think you quit being the Magic Man?"

"Um…because my wife got diagnosed with advanced ovarian cancer?"

"Aimee was just an excuse. I think you stopped being the Magic Man because you didn't know how to deal with being special," Jillian said, sliding the putty knife underneath a section of wallpaper and then peeling off the chunk. She dumped it in the big cardboard box they had sitting in the middle of the floor. "It was too much pressure. Being a star happened to you accidentally, right? You designed these classrooms and because of your designs, people learned better in your buildings. So there was this mystique about you and you weren't secure in your…"

Jillian stopped talking when she realized Tuck was frozen in place beside her and that he hadn't spoke or moved since she'd mentioned Aimee's name. And she knew then that somewhere, she'd crossed the line.

Nervously, her eyes flicked to his face.

His expression was pure stone.

"Tuck?"

"How dare you," he accused. "How dare you insinuate

that I used my wife's illness to run out on my career. You don't know me. You have no idea how much I loved her or what I would have done for her. She was my life, my soul, my heart. I didn't give a damn about my fucking career. All I cared about was Aimee. And you dare to stand here and blather about—" Tuck broke off abruptly, clenching his fists at his sides.

Jillian felt as if she'd been kicked in the gut by a horse. She'd been too glib, too insensitive. What in the hell was wrong with her? She'd known better than to bring up Aimee's name and yet she'd done it anyway.

"Tuck...I..." She reached out to him.

He raised his palms, took a step back. "You know what? I can't do this. I can't have this conversation with you."

She backed up, hurt by his pain, disturbed that she'd caused it. Saddened that no one had ever loved her the way he had loved his wife and convinced that no one ever would. Why would they when she had it in her to say such inconsiderate things?

Tuck threw down the steamer, picked up his car keys from the hook by the back door, hunched his shoulders, and limped out.

Leaving Jillian feeling utterly abandoned.

Chapter 14

Tuck tracked Ridley down at the Rusty Nail.

"I flipped out on Jillian," he said morosely, and peered into the beer he hadn't touched. "I flipped out and now I don't know how to go back and undo it."

"Do what I do—act like it never happened."

Tuck leaned back and gave his brother-in-law a long appraising glance. "And that works?"

"No, but it's my defense mechanism and I'm sticking to it."

"Even though it doesn't work."

Ridley took a slug off his longneck beer. "Yep."

"How long have you been sleeping on the couch?" Tuck asked.

"How did you know?"

"You've got that I-ain't-getting-any look about you."

"You should know."

"Point taken."

"Evie told you, huh?"

"Yep." Tuck took a sip of beer. "Why don't you just let her do this vision quest thing?"

"Yeah, because it turned out so well when you did it."

"Hey, you were right about Jillian. She is a jinx."

"No, I was wrong about that. She's not a jinx. I didn't know your psyche well enough to interpret your vision. Honestly," Ridley said. "I think Jillian is the best thing that could have ever happened to you. Since she's been in Salvation, you've come alive again."

Tuck made a dismissive noise.

"You have."

"This arrangement isn't working. I gotta find a new place to live," Tuck said. "I feel like I've been backed into a corner with no way out. I'm choking."

"You're going to give up the house? Aimee's house?"

Tuck briefly closed his eyes, fighting off the barrage of emotions like a bullfighter dancing around the bull. He'd never experienced such a mix of feelings—anger, sadness, hope, regret, shame, denial, expectancy, loss, fear. He pressed his lips together, then said, "That deed's never going to turn up. For all I know, Sutter's previous assistant ran it through the shredder."

"Or Jillian did."

He shook his head. "She wouldn't do that. She wants the house, but she's a straight shooter."

"I'd invite you to stay with us, but I have no idea how long I'll be needing the couch."

"It's all right. I can find somewhere else. I shouldn't abuse your hospitality," Tuck said.

"You oughta call Jefferson Baines. He might know who's got a place to rent on this side of the mountain."

Tuck snorted and took another swallow of beer. "That pinhead?"

"He's a pinhead, yes, but he does know the real estate market around here."

"All the high-priced places."

"You can afford it."

"Hello? I'm no longer pulling down high six figures. Self-employed, remember? Lousy health insurance. Aimee's illness put a huge dent in my savings."

"Still, I know you've got *some* tucked back."

Tuck tightened his jaw. "That's earmarked for renovating the house."

"You know . . . ," Ridley started.

Tuck held up a hand to halt him. "Stop right there. I know what you're going to say, and I don't want to hear it."

"Okay."

They sat there not talking, just drinking. Tuck found himself thinking about what Jillian had said. She'd been right about everything, and that was why he'd overreacted. A guy didn't really like having a mirror held up to his face so he could see his flaws. Plus, he'd asked for it and then hadn't been able to take it. He *had* pulled in his head like a turtle; he *had* turned his back on life.

Still, something had been made abundantly clear to him. He had to get out of there, and the sooner the better. Because if he stayed at the lake house, he feared he might not be able to keep his hands off her.

And that would be such a bad thing?

Yes, yes it would, because he was coming to treasure the friendship they were forging, and he didn't want to do anything to screw it up. Staying in that house with her, when they were so clearly attracted to each other, well, it was just plain stupid.

Come Monday, he'd go see Baines and ask him to be on the lookout for a place for him to rent.

In the meantime, Tuck had to make sure to keep his mouth shut and his hands to himself.

* * *

Jillian went to the Bluebird for dinner after spending the remainder of the day peeling off the kitchen wallpaper with only Mutt for company. Partially because there wasn't anything else to eat in the house besides lamb-flavored Eukanuba and partially because she was hoping to run into Tuck.

Disappointment washed over her when she discovered he wasn't there. She seated herself at the counter and was busy studying the menu when she felt someone come up behind her.

Tuck? His name immediately leapt into her mind.

Jillian turned, but it wasn't Tuck.

"Hello, we haven't met yet. My name's Jefferson Baines and you are…" The real estate agent extended his hand.

Jillian shook it. "Nice to meet you Jefferson. I'm Jillian Samuels."

"Jillian." He said her name like a used-car salesman and held it in his mouth for too long.

"Does anyone ever call you Jeff?"

"Only if they don't like breathing." He laughed heartily.

"Jefferson it is, then."

He leaned one elbow against the counter, slouching insouciantly, trying to look casual in spite of his Armani suit and Gucci loafers. "I've been seeing you around town."

"I just moved here a few weeks ago."

"I live halfway between Salvation and Thunder Mountain," he said. "Thunder Mountain is where all the action is, but Salvation does have its charms."

"It does."

"Word around town is that you're a lawyer."

"I am."

"You and I have something in common."

"We do?" He was the kind of guy the old Jillian might have been interested in once upon a time. Tall, handsome, career-focused, ambitious, well dressed.

"We're fellow Texans," he said. "I'm from Dallas. I hear you're from Houston."

She tilted her head so that her hair swung over her face. Not to be coy but to study him from behind her cloak of hair. He had cover-model good looks. You had to be careful of guys that gorgeous. Alex had taught her the truth of that lesson. "You heard correctly."

"It's quite a change," Jefferson went on. "From the big city to Salvation."

The guy couldn't claim scintillating conversationalist on his résumé. "Yes."

He leaned closer. "How are you adjusting to small-town life?"

"Just fine, thanks for asking."

"I also heard that you inherited the Townsend lake house."

"That's still in question."

"I heard Tucker Manning's laying claim to the place as well."

"You hear a lot."

"I keep my ear to the ground and my nose in the wind."

"You're quite the contortionist."

He laughed.

Jillian canted her head, trying to figure out his angle.

"You know," he said, "if it turns out the lake house really does belong to Tuck, I've got a gorgeous place I could show you up on Thunder Mountain."

Ah, so this was really why he'd come over to her. Somehow she immediately liked him better, because he was trying to sell her some property instead of getting into her pants.

"That's good to know. I'll keep that in mind, Jefferson. Thanks for the information." She sent him her friendliest, "you're dismissed" expression.

He gave her another thousand-watt smile. "There's something else I was wondering about..."

"Oh yeah?"

"I've heard...I mean, it's none of my business...but there's a rumor going around..."

Jillian straightened and met his eyes. "What do you want to ask me, Jefferson?"

"Tucker's living in the house with you?"

"Uh-huh."

"With you, with you?"

"Excuse me?"

"I mean.... umm...uh...do you two have a thing going on?"

"We're roommates."

"That's it?"

"We're friends."

"And...er...nothing else?"

Jillian thought about the kiss Tuck had given her, and she plastered a smile on her face. It had been fourteen days since she and Tuck had walked home from the Rusty Nail together. Fourteen days since he'd kissed her in the foyer of the lake house. Fourteen days since he'd set her blood to boiling and her head to reeling. And nothing else had happened since then. Until today. Until their fight.

She knew how many days it had been, because she'd counted every last one of them by the hour. "Nope, nothing else."

"Then the speculation around town that you two are an item is just speculation?"

The last thing Jillian wanted was to add to the Salvation rumor mill. "Total fabrication."

"I thought so," Jefferson said. "I mean, Tuck is so hung up on his late wife. Some say he'll never get over her."

"Do tell."

"Yeah, he brought her to Salvation and became a carpenter even though he was making big bucks as an architect, just because she used to enjoy spending summers here as a kid. He gave up everything for her and then she died anyway. Stupid move, if you ask me, derailing your career like that."

"I think it sounds incredibly sweet and loving."

"That's why they say he'll never get over her. No one can take Aimee's place."

"I see."

"So you're unattached?" Jefferson leaned against the counter, and his eyes brightened.

A twinge of emotion that she couldn't identify knotted up tight against her rib cage. Jillian wasn't much interested in going out with Jefferson Baines, but that emotion— whatever the hell it was—had her holding up her bare ring finger. "Free as a bird."

He let out an audible breath, and that was the first time Jillian realized Jefferson was nervous about chatting her up. She softened a bit toward him. She knew some men found her intimidating. Her height and what Tuck called her regal appearance were the culprits. She had donned her queenly armor when Jefferson approached. Giving him the silver-cool tone she used when offering plea-bargain deals to defense lawyers, and he'd managed to hold his ground.

She felt a little sorry for him then and understood he wasn't as slick and glossy as he wanted to appear. She asked him to sit down and join her for a cup of coffee. He readily agreed. Jillian tried to take the real estate agent seriously, but whenever she looked at him, all she could think was *faux wood*.

And then she immediately thought of Tuck and envisioned smooth, hard, rich mahogany.

"So, what do you say?" Jefferson asked.

It was only then that she realized he'd asked her a question, and she had been so busy thinking about Tuck's favorite hardwood she hadn't heard. His head was cocked to one side, and he was looking at her earnestly, waiting for an answer to his question.

"Sure," Jillian said, pretending she knew what he was talking about.

Jefferson beamed. "Great. That's really great."

Crap, apparently she'd just agreed to something. But what?

Jillian smiled so as not to hurt his feelings if he realized she hadn't heard a word he said. "So, to recap..."

"I'll pick you up at seven Friday night."

She nodded, keeping the smile going. Apparently she'd just accepted a date with him. Well, fine. It was a good thing. Clearly nothing was going to happen with Tuck, and that was fine. She didn't want anything to happen with Tuck. She didn't want anything to happen with Jefferson, either, for that matter, but it didn't hurt to get out of the house. Especially since she and Tuck were around each other constantly.

"Jillian?" Jefferson asked.

"Right. Seven o'clock, Friday night. It's a date."

*　　　*　　　*

Neither one of them mentioned what had happened on Saturday. They kept things light. Jillian spent what little time she hung around the house upstairs, while Tuck stayed downstairs. They barely saw each other. Which was perfect. Or so she told herself.

On Friday morning, Jillian got up earlier than usual, because Sutter actually had a new client coming into the office at seven-thirty to draft a will. She found Tuck at the bistro table eating scrambled eggs. He didn't offer to make her any.

She reached for a box of corn flakes from the cabinet, along with a spoon and a bowl, and came back to sit down across from him.

"Good morning," she said.

"Good morning." He didn't look up from the copy of *Sports Illustrated* he was reading.

She got up again to pour herself some coffee. "You want another cup?"

"I'm good."

"How's the ankle?" She sat back down, dismayed to see her corn flakes had already gone soggy.

"Couldn't be better."

"Did you let Mutt out?"

"Fed him too." He flipped the page of his magazine without ever looking up.

He looked so damned complacent that she had an irresistible urge to rattle his cage. "I'm meeting Jefferson Baines for dinner, so I won't be home until late."

Tuck's fork stopped halfway to his mouth, but he acted only mildly interested. "Oh yeah?"

"Yes." She couldn't quite meet his gaze. "He asked me out. We're going on a date."

"Have fun." He picked up his fork and went back to his eggs.

Disappointment curled inside her. "That's all you're going to say?"

"What? You want me to tell you not to go?"

"No, I just figured that you'd have something smart-ass to say about faux wood."

"I've already told you my opinion on Jefferson Baines. No need to repeat myself."

"So you don't care if I date him?" She left the bistro table to toss her soggy cornflakes into the sink.

"Why should I care? You're a grown woman. Date away."

"Fine. I will."

"Are you mad at me?"

"No, no." God, what was she saying? She was practically begging him to ask her not to go out with Jefferson. "Why would I be mad?"

"Great. Glad to hear it."

"Perfect, I'll just go, then."

"Have a good time."

"You can bet I will."

"Watch out for the Viagra."

"What?"

"Faux wood and all that." Tuck winked.

"You can be quite infuriating, you know that?"

"Right back at you," he said.

Jillian snatched up her purse and marched for the back door. Something, she didn't know what, told her to glance back over her shoulder.

She caught him, his eyes off the magazine and totally focused on her. What knocked her off guard was the way he was looking at her—as if a house he'd invested months in designing and building had just gone on the market.

* * *

Tuck couldn't believe Jillian was going out with Baines. If that's the kind of artificial show-off she went for, no wonder she'd never been in love.

"What do you care?" he growled under his breath as he pulled into the parking space at the Peabody Mansion. After he'd broken his ankle, he delayed the jobs that required going up on ladders. Sutter had told him to take his time getting back to repairing the old Victorian. His ankle wasn't a hundred percent, but Doc Couts had taken the cast off the day before, and he was healing well enough to get back to work. Especially since Ridley had promised to drop by and help him when he finished an electrical job he had on the other side of town. He was ready for this.

Or so he told himself. What he didn't admit was that he couldn't wait to be around Jillian again.

He went inside.

"Hey, Tuck, how's the ankle?" Lexi greeted him from the doorway of her flooring store.

"Much better, Lex, thanks." He looked at her, and she smiled at him kindly. Too kindly.

"I heard Jillian's going out with Jefferson," she said.

Ah, that explained the look on her face. She was feeling sorry for him. "Yeah," he said. "I heard the same thing."

"You're not jealous?" Lexi asked.

He shrugged. "Why would I be jealous?"

"Aren't you two sort of seeing each other?"

"No." He waved a hand. "Why? Did Jillian tell you that we were seeing each other?"

Lexi shook her head. "I just sort of assumed it. Since you were living together—"

"That's strictly by necessity," he rushed to interrupt

her before she got any further. He didn't want any rumors starting. "Until this property dispute is settled. We're just roommates. It's strictly platonic."

"Are you sure? Because the way she looks at you sometimes..."

That pulled him up short. "Huh? How does Jillian look at me?"

"Kind of wistful. And lusty. Like she wants to jump your bones but she's afraid to get too close."

"Naw. You've misinterpreted the look. She's not interested in me that way," he insisted. "We're just friends."

Friends, huh? More like adversaries who drive each other crazy with sexual chemistry.

"Are you sure?" Lexi prodded.

"Positive."

"So then you're free tomorrow night?"

That gave him pause. "Why, Lexi Kilgore, are you asking me out?"

"Well, maybe, kind of. You see, I have this gift card to Thunder Mountain Lodge, and it expires tomorrow if I don't use it, and there goes the fifty bucks for my last birthday from Gramma Louise. I really don't want to go alone. I was going to ask Jillian, but now she's going out with Jefferson."

"Is this a pity date?"

"Hey, you'll get a free meal."

Tuck looked at her. Lexi had always been nice to him. For three or four months after Aimee died, she had brought him casseroles once a week. She was a sweet woman with a bubbly personality, and if he hadn't been so broken up over losing his wife, they might have already gone out. Why not accept her invitation? Jillian was going out with Jefferson; he could have a date too.

"Lexi, I'd enjoy having dinner with you tomorrow night."

By the time Tuck got home from work, it was just after five o'clock. He and Ridley had spent the day replacing the Sheetrock in the ceiling of Sutter's office, but to his surprise, Jillian had left the building right after they'd started work, and she hadn't come back. So he was relieved to see her Sebring in the driveway when he arrived.

He walked in the door and heard the shower running. The sound of it—and the image that popped into his head of Jillian standing naked under the running water—caused his heart to thump loudly in his ears. The cottage had only one bathroom. He'd been planning on adding a second, but now he was glad he hadn't.

Sauntering into the hallway, he stripped off his shirt and tossed it into the built-in hamper. Okay, so it was an obvious move, but he wanted her to get an eyeful of his bare chest when she came out of the bathroom.

The water shut off.

A couple minutes later—while Tuck stood around trying to act like he'd just taken his shirt off—the bathroom door opened. Jillian emerged in a white bathrobe with her hair twisted up in a blue towel. In her hands, she held a pair of red silk thong panties.

She looked up, let out a little shriek, and fisted the panties in her hand. His groin tightened. "What the hell are you doing lurking in the hallway?"

"Had a dirty job today. I need a shower."

"That gives you the right to skulk?"

"It's my house. I can skulk if I want to."

"That's up for debate. It's been five weeks and still no deed. It's past time to get Blake's will probated."

"I wasn't skulking." He noticed her gaze skipped over his bare chest.

"Now you're a liar as well as a skulker." She seemed to just now remember she was holding the skimpy red panties. Quickly, she stuffed them in the pocket of her bathrobe.

"You wearing those for Jefferson Baines?" God, why had he said that? Now she was going to think that he was jealous. Which he was, but he didn't want her knowing it.

"What if I am?"

He stepped closer, blood racing, heart pounding so hard he was afraid she could hear it. He smelled the cucumbery scent of her shampoo. A droplet of water trailed down her neck. He watched it slide over her skin and disappear between her breasts. So far, he'd consciously avoided showering when she did. Usually, she showered in the mornings, and he took the evening. But tonight, she had a date, so she'd changed her routine. All to his advantage. She couldn't fault him. She was the one who'd gone off their schedule.

Jillian stood her ground. She wasn't easily intimidated. Her eyes met his, and she watched him warily as he walked toward the door.

And grazed her breast with his elbow.

She sucked in her breath. "Hey!"

"Sorry for the accidental boob graze."

"Accidental my ass—you did that on purpose."

"If you don't like getting your boob grazed, maybe you shouldn't stand in the hallway wearing nothing but a bathrobe."

"I don't get it," she said. "This morning you couldn't seem to care less that I was going out with Jefferson."

"I don't." He took in the haughty slope of her shoulders.

The regal way she held her head. How the hallway light reflected a soft glow off the creamy complexion of her skin. Damn, but she was beautiful and sexy as hell. He kept thinking about what she'd look like in that red thong and how he'd like to be the one to take her out of them.

"Then why are you here? You know I'm getting ready for a date. Why not go to the Bluebird or the Rusty Nail until I'm out of the house?"

"Because," he said. "I have a date as well."

Chapter 15

Jefferson told Jillian he'd made dinner reservations at Thunder Lodge on Thunder Mountain. It took almost an hour to drive the fifteen miles of winding mountain roads to the ski resort.

On the drive in his late-model black Lexus, Jefferson tried to engage Jillian in idle chitchat, which she didn't hear a word of because she kept thinking about Tuck and how he'd looked standing bare-chested in the hallway. It was the first time she'd seen him undressed since the morning she'd walked in and found him sleeping on the couch.

There was no doubt about it—the man had world-class pecs and biceps. He could be a swimsuit model if he so desired. She licked her lips, remembering how he'd looked standing there with the shadow of the bathroom door falling over him, the play of light delineating the striation of his muscles.

What in the hell had gotten into him? Was he jealous? She scarcely dared hope. Did he really have a date? Or had he made it all up?

When she thought about Tuck out on a date, *she* felt

jealous. The first time he dates since his wife's death and it wasn't with her. Why did she want it so badly to be her?

"Do you like the music?" Jefferson asked.

For the first time, Jillian realized Vivaldi was spilling one of his seasons out of the stereo system. Why did she have a sudden craving to hear the Lovin' Spoonful sing "Do You Believe in Magic?"

"Lexi told me you like classical," Jefferson confessed. "She suggested Vivaldi."

"How kind of you to play it for me and to think to ask Lexi what kind of music I like." She smiled. "That's very considerate."

"I do my research when I take a lady out."

God, he sounded so cheesy. What was taking them so damned long to get to Thunder Mountain? "Uh-huh."

"See that house up there?" Jefferson pointed to a sprawling split-level log cabin hidden in the mountains.

"Mmm-hmm."

"I sold it as a summer place to Wolfgang Puck's nephew," he said proudly.

"That must have been interesting."

"He gave me a gift certificate to Wolfgang's restaurant for the next time I'm in Vegas. Would you like to go to Vegas with me sometime? You know, what happens in Vegas..."

"Stays in Vegas," she finished for him. "Yes, I've heard the slogan."

Jefferson swiveled his head and winked at her. "So, what do you say about a trip to Sin City? We could stay at the MGM Grand. Catch Blue Man Group onstage?"

"Let's see how one date goes."

"Gotcha."

It was all Jillian could do to keep from rolling her eyes.

She shifted in the seat, angling her body away from his, and stared out the window to while away the time while Jefferson gave her a running commentary on who owned the houses they passed, how much the houses were worth, and who was likely or unlikely to have property on the market soon. The guy knew his business. She had to give him brownie points for that.

They rounded a curve, and in the rearview mirror, Jillian caught a glimpse of a pickup behind them that looked exactly like Tuck's. Her pulse accelerated. Was he following them?

But that was stupid. Tuck drove the number-one selling pickup truck in America. In silver, the most common color for vehicles. The chances of Tuck being behind them were very slim. So why did she feel a sudden burst of excitement?

Because you're starting to get hung up on the guy.

She wasn't. Was she?

She waited for the next curve to even out to see if she could catch another glimpse behind them, but the road just kept spiraling upward.

Be real. Why would Tuck be behind you?

Well, there was only one road up the mountain, and he'd said he had a date. It wasn't as if Salvation was flush with great first-date places. Most likely, anyone headed out for a date would go to either Boulder or up to Thunder Mountain, and the mountain had the better view.

"Almost there," Jefferson said, and reached across the car to touch her arm.

She drew back.

"Sorry," he apologized. "Did I overstep my boundaries?"

Jillian forced a smile. Honestly, he wasn't a bad guy,

just overeager and not at all her type. "I've just been a little tense lately."

"Well, tonight is your night to relax. Thunder Lodge is known for their excellent wine list and romantic ambiance."

"Good to know." The thought of getting snockered was appealing, but the last thing she wanted was to lose her edge around Jefferson. He hadn't tried anything funny yet, but he had said that stupid crap about Vegas.

"Lily Massey and Bill Chambers are getting married up here."

"So I've heard. I've been invited."

"Really? You wanna go together?"

"One date at a time, Jefferson."

"Gotcha."

They arrived at the restaurant at last. Jefferson tossed his keys to the valet and offered her his arm, trying his best to be a good date. But Jillian just wasn't in the mood to appreciate his efforts. As he escorted her into the building, she couldn't help glancing over her shoulder to see if Tuck's pickup had arrived.

"This way," Jefferson said, and ushered her inside before she had time to see who was coming up the mountain.

The restaurant was quite elegant. White linen tablecloths. The waitstaff attired in traditional black uniforms with white aprons. A maître d' who seated them right away at a spectacular table by the window overlooking the ski run. An impressive wine list just as Jefferson had promised.

There was night skiing at the resort, and from where they were seated, they could watch skiers sluice down the mountain. Fun classic rock from the fifties and sixties was being played on the slopes, and they could hear it inside the restaurant. It was a great place with the proper romantic atmosphere. The only trouble was, Jillian kept wishing she was there with someone else.

Tuck.

Just as the waiter arrived to take their drink orders, Jillian looked up from her menu to see Tuck and Lexi walk in. Her stomach lurched.

In his suit and tie, Tuck stole her breath away, and she had to admit Lexi looked quite lovely in a lavender skirt and blouse set. A waiter steered them toward the opposite side of the room, but Lexi headed their way. Tuck looked surprised and followed her over.

"Hello," Lexi greeted, sauntering up to their table. "Imagine running into you guys here."

Tuck clamped a hand on Jefferson's shoulder. "How you doing, buddy?"

"Tuck," Jefferson said. "I didn't know you and Lexi were dating."

Lexi beamed. "It's the first time we've gone out."

"Hey, why don't we all eat together?" Tuck suggested.

Jillian rummaged in her mind for an excuse why they should not share a table, but Lexi clapped her hands in that endearing way of hers and said, "Oh yes, that would be so fun."

Tuck was already pulling out Lexi's chair for her. Jillian shot him a withering glance. He grinned at her. She glared.

The waiter hovered.

"Instead of two glasses of cabernet," Jefferson instructed, "go ahead and bring us a bottle." Then he turned to Tuck. "This is our first date as well."

"Really?" Tuck popped open his linen napkin and spread it across his lap, all the while keeping his eyes trained on Jillian.

Lexi leaned over and whispered behind her palm to Jillian, "This is so much fun. Me being out with Tuck, you with Jefferson."

The excitement in her new friend's voice made Jillian glower at Tuck. What was he pulling? "Don't expect too much," Jillian whispered back, desperate to protect Lexi. "This is his first date since Aimee."

"Don't worry," Lexi whispered. "I know what I'm doing."

Jealousy, sharp and unexpected, sliced into her. From the ski slopes came the sound of "Do You Believe in Magic?"

"Hey," Tuck said. "They're playing our song."

Jillian stared at him. "Our song?"

"Your song?" Lexi raised an eyebrow.

"You have a song?" Jefferson asked.

"Yeah." Tuck held Jillian's gaze. "It was playing on the radio when we had our first fight. Remember?"

Oh, she remembered, all right. "That doesn't make it our song."

"It makes me think of our first fight. Doesn't that qualify as our song?"

"You can only have a song if you're a couple," Jillian said. "We're not a couple."

Several long minutes passed. Then the waiter returned with wine and took their food orders. Tuck and Jillian ordered filet mignon cooked medium. Jefferson and Lexi ordered the phcasant.

Jillian was sitting directly across from Tuck, and in spite of herself, she couldn't help noticing how sexy he looked freshly shaven and smelling of manly cologne. Jefferson's cologne had a floral undercurrent, but Tuck's was woodsy, earthy. She'd never seen him dressed in anything but flannel and jeans except for on the cover of *Architectural Digest.*

His eyes met hers across the table as if he could read her mind. He gave her a short, sly smile, and she felt as if she'd been lit on fire. White-hot embers of desire that had been burning inside her from the moment they had met sparked, flared.

When the bread basket came, Tuck and Jillian reached for it at the same time, and their hands touched. The heat of his hand short-circuited her hormones and she burned.

Yes. *Burned.*

For Tuck.

Blindly, she left the roll in the basket, drew her hand back, and reached for her wineglass instead. She took a big gulp, trying senselessly to put out the brushfire rolling through her.

"So tell us, Jefferson, what big real estate deals are you working on?" Tuck asked, smoothly buttering his bread, but the whole time he was talking and buttering, his gaze was on her. His whiskey-colored eyes were luminous, the pupils dilated in the candlelight. He parted his lush lips and very sensuously took a bite of bread.

"Well, Tuck…" Jefferson launched off on his latest project while Lexi asked eager questions.

But Jillian wasn't listening to Jefferson babble. All she could do was look at Tuck and think, *I want this man.*

Lexi fueled the conversation when talking houses turned into specifics and she got down to flooring and window treatments.

"What do you think of laminate flooring, Lexi?" Tuck asked, but he was still looking at Jillian.

She shot him a knock-it-off look.

Simultaneously, he slightly lifted his eyes and his shoulders.

"Laminate definitely has its place," Lexi said.

"Thank you." Jefferson raised his fork. "A lot of people look down their noses at laminate, but when you have three cats like I do, you appreciate something that, while looking like hardwood, is actually much more practical."

"Really?" Lexi's eyes widened. "I have three cats as well—Mandi, Andi, and Moe."

"Faux wood," Tuck mouthed to Jillian.

Jillian swung her foot and kicked Tuck under the table. "Ow!"

"Oops, sorry, clumsy me."

"Watch the pointy-toed shoes, Queenie. My ankle still isn't one hundred percent."

"Queenie?" Lexi asked.

"Her nickname," Tuck explained.

"It's not my nickname," Jillian said hotly. "It's the insult Tuck likes to irritate me with."

"It's not an insult. If I was insulting you, I'd call you a bathroom hog."

"I don't hog the bathroom."

"I disagree. When I went to shower for my date with Lexi, guess what—no hot water."

"So you had to take a cold shower. Poor baby."

"Bathroom hog."

"Cry baby."

"Um…my pheasant is delicious," Lexi said to Jefferson. "How's yours?"

"Wonderful. So with three cats, what kind of flooring do you have?" Jefferson asked.

Tuck was glaring at her. Was he mad? He's the one

who'd started this whole mess. Now here he was ruining dinner.

"Could you guys excuse me a minute? I need to make a phone call," Jillian said.

"Hurry back." Jefferson smiled.

Jillian darted to the alcove near the restroom; from here, she could see Tuck sitting at the table. She got out her cell phone and called his number.

He answered at the table.

"What in the hell are you doing?" she demanded.

"Hang on a minute." While she watched, he lowered the phone, said something to Lexi and Jefferson, then pushed back his chair, got up, and started sauntering toward her, all grin and swagger.

"Okay," he said into the phone, his eyes on her face across the length of the restaurant. "I'm back."

"What in the hell are you doing here?"

"Last time I checked, it's still a free country. You don't own Thunder Mountain." The closer he came to where she huddled in the alcove, the wider his grin grew.

"You asked Lexi out to make me jealous," Jillian accused.

"I did not," Tuck huffed. "Lexi asked me out."

"You are such a liar."

"She did. Go ask her. She had a birthday gift card to Thunder Lodge that was about to expire."

"You expect me to believe that coincidentally on the same day I was going out with Jefferson, Lexi had a gift card to the same restaurant where he was taking me?"

"It's the truth."

Was it? Tuck didn't seem the kind of guy who'd be unkind enough to ask Lexi out simply to use her as an excuse to spoil Jillian's date.

"Besides," he said, "you went out with Jefferson to make me jealous."

"I did not. I accidentally got roped into this."

"That might be true, but you sure went to a lot of trouble to make sure I knew all about it." Closer and closer he sauntered, those whiskey eyes drilling into her like lasers.

Jillian backed up. "Lexi's going to think you're interested in her."

"I'll make sure she knows we're just friends."

"Like we're just friends."

"Yeah." His voice was husky.

Tuck kept coming, looking at her as if he were stripping her clothes off with his eyes. What had happened to the man in mourning she'd been living with for the past several weeks?

Gone was the emotional barrier he'd erected. Hell, gone was any respect for her physical space as he walked right up to her, taking the cell phone from his ear and snapping it closed just as her butt bumped the wall behind her.

"You're being rude," she said. "Leaving your date alone."

"You left the table first. Your date is just as alone as mine." He was standing toe-to-toe with her, his mouth merely inches away. "And you kicked me. Now, that was rude."

She had an overwhelming urge to reach up, grab him by that expensive tie that looked like a holdover from his Magic Man days, tug him into the bathroom, and make out with him.

If it hadn't been for the waiter who came up behind Tuck, she might very well have done just that.

The waiter coughed.

Tuck swiveled his head but kept his body angled in Jillian's direction. "Yes?"

"Um, sir, the rest of your party left."

"Yeah?"

The waiter extended the check and cleared his throat. "They said you'd be paying the tab."

"So what happened last night?" Jillian asked Lexi the next morning. She stopped by the flooring store with Styrofoam cups filled with hot coffee and cream puffs from the Bluebird as a peace offering.

"Evie's cream puffs!" Lexi squealed and bit into one. "Oh, yummy. Thank you."

Jillian rested her hip against the edge of Lexi's counter and crossed her arms over her chest. "So, about last night…?"

Lexi giggled and wiped powdered sugar from the end of her nose with the back of her hand. "That was rude of Jefferson and me running out and leaving you with the check. I do apologize."

"No, no, it was rude of Tuck and me to go off and leave you guys at the table. Honestly, Lex, we didn't mean to hurt your feelings."

Lexi blinked at her. "What do you mean? My feelings weren't hurt."

"I thought you and Tuck…that you were interested in him."

Lexi laughed.

Puzzled, Jillian canted her head. "What's so funny?"

"I asked Tuck to take me to Thunder Mountain, because I was jealous of you dating Jefferson."

"You like Jefferson?"

"For ages. And in the two years he's lived on the mountain, he's never really noticed me. Sure, he comes in here and talks shop, but he's never seen me as anything more than a flooring supplier. Until last night." Her eyes sparkled.

"You don't have a crush on Tuck?"

"No."

"Really? I sort of thought you did."

"He's good-looking, sure, and very sexy but..." Lexi shook her head.

"But?"

"Tuck's a one-woman man."

"You mean he'll never get over Aimee?" An emotion she couldn't name burned Jillian's stomach.

"I mean he's a one-woman man," Lexi repeated. "I'm sorry you guys had a lousy time at dinner."

"We didn't have a lousy time."

"You two were fighting like cats and dogs."

"Fighting?" Jillian suppressed a laugh. Fighting was the last thing they'd been doing. Flirting like mad and having sex with their eyes across the table was more like it.

"Then when Jeff asked me—"

"Wait, wait, I thought he didn't let anyone call him Jeff."

"I told him that Jefferson was too stuffy. He looks like a big cuddly Jeff to me."

"Ookay." The man looked neither cuddly nor like a Jeff to Jillian, but there was no accounting for taste.

"Anyway, when Jeff asked me if I wanted to go back to his place and just let you guys fight it out, I couldn't resist. I hope you're not too upset about the tab thing. It was Jefferson's idea. And I have to admit, it felt kind of naughty." Lexi giggled again.

"No, no, no problem. We didn't mind paying. Tuck and I just...we were..."

"I know." Lexi nodded. "Embarrassed by your behavior."

That wasn't what she was going to say, but it would do.

"Guess what?" Lexi touched Jillian's forearm and lowered her voice. "Jeff and I had sex until dawn. I'm worn out, but I've never been happier."

After that night at Thunder Lodge, things between Tuck and Jillian shifted. Rather than avoiding each other as they had been doing, they started spending more time together as renovations on the lake house progressed.

While they worked, they talked about all kinds of things—politics, religion, celebrities, architecture, pet care, carpentry, and law. The only topics off limits were Tuck's marriage and Jillian's childhood. She'd never been comfortable discussing it. In fact, Blake was the only one who'd known the entire sordid story.

Through their discussions, Jillian and Tuck got to know each other better and found out they had a lot more in common than they'd ever suspected. They both loved water parks and Rocky Road ice cream. They agreed George W. Bush was the worst president ever to hold the title commander in chief and that Craig Ferguson was much funnier than Conan O'Brien. They admitted recycling was a great thing to do, but they were both a bit lazy about it.

They discovered they shared an obsession with Court TV, and they enjoyed amateur stargazing. They had each seen *Les Miserables* on Broadway six times and realized to their surprise, that on one occasion, they'd actually been at the same theater showing. Tuck told her stories about what it was like growing up with three older sisters, while Jillian regaled him with tales of law school. He took her shopping for some "decent"—as he put it—winter clothing, declaring none of the things she'd brought from Texas would hold up to a Colorado snowstorm.

Every passing evening as they painted and hammered and plastered and tiled and talked, the house slowly began to take shape. Then on the Sunday before Thanksgiving, Tuck issued an invitation.

"Evie's having our annual family Thanksgiving feast at her house and you're invited," he said as they were putting new baseboards up in the living room.

In truth, she hadn't thought much about the upcoming holiday or how she would spend it. Usually, she hung out with Delaney, Tish, and Rachael, but this year, they all had their own celebrations, and she was so far away that when they'd called to invite her, she'd turned them down.

"You can meet my entire family."

That both pleased and intimidated her. "I don't know...," she hedged.

"Come on," he said. "It'll be fun."

"You really want me there?"

"Not just me," he said. "Evie and Ridley too."

"Okay," she said, "I'll come."

Then Tuck rewarded her with a smile that lit up her heart, and she realized what a very dangerous thing that was.

Chapter 16

Tuck had to admit he was nervous about bringing Jillian to Thanksgiving dinner. He didn't want anyone reading anything into the gesture, other than the fact that he and Jillian were simply roommates and good friends who enjoyed spending time together.

He'd told her about Evie's invitation because he couldn't stand the thought of her being alone. At least that's what he told himself. The truth was, he wanted her there. Wanted her with him, but he wasn't ready to face the implications of that desire, so he blocked it out.

But when his big family got together, he knew they could be a bit overwhelming. He and Jillian stood on Evie's front porch. He had Evie's music box to give to Ridley wrapped up in newspaper. He'd held on to the box until he'd received the musical apparatus programmed to play "Faith" that he'd ordered online. He'd installed it the day before.

Jillian had two bottles of wine tucked under her arm. Her contribution to the festivities because, as she'd told him in the truck on the way over, she didn't cook and who could compete with Evie on that score anyway?

Tuck leaned over to ring the doorbell.

"Wait, wait." She placed a restraining hand on his wrist. "How do I look?"

His gaze trailed over her, and he couldn't help but think how breathtaking she was. "Fabulous."

"No, really." She smoothed out the front of her burgundy dress with her palm. "The neckline isn't too low, is it?"

"It's perfect. They're going to love you."

Nervously, Jillian flicked out her tongue to moisten her lips. "How can you be so sure?"

Tuck reached out to give her forearm a comforting squeeze. "You've put away some of the toughest felons in Texas, Queenie. I assure you that you can handle my family."

"Yes, but I wasn't worried about impressing the felons of Texas."

"You don't have to impress them. Just be yourself."

"Okay." She took a deep breath and tucked a strand of hair behind her ear. "Go ahead. Ring the bell. I'm ready to run the gauntlet."

He couldn't help but be touched that she cared so much about what his family thought of her that it affected her emotional equilibrium. He'd never seen her looking so vulnerable. It made him want to put his arm around her waist and protect her from any and everyone. The impulse surprised him.

"Jillian," he whispered as he heard the door open. "Don't worry, sweetheart. Whatever happens, I've got your back."

Had Tuck just called her sweetheart?

Jillian shook her head and blinked, unable to believe

her ears. Why had he called her sweetheart? Had he just slipped up? Or was there some hidden meaning to it?

But there was no time to ponder the questions. Ridley was greeting them at the door and ushering them over the threshold. Jillian stepped inside, and immediately her senses were assaulted with the sights, smells, and sounds of a large extended family gathered for a holiday celebration. Ridley took their coats and Jillian handed him the two bottles of Chardonnay she'd brought.

The dining room table was laden with food. Two gigantic turkeys. An industrial-size pan filled with cornbread stuffing, along with a serving tureen of giblet gravy. Side dishes galore—candied yams, fruit salads, vegetable casseroles, deviled eggs, mashed potatoes, macaroni and cheese, yeast rolls and cranberry sauce. And on the sideboard a bounty of desserts. Chocolate cake, peach cobbler, oatmeal cookies, and pies—apple, pumpkin, pecan, French silk, cherry, and rhubarb. There were soft drinks and lemonade for the kids. Wine, tea, and coffee for the adults.

The air was thick with the dizzying smells of sage and roasted turkey and cinnamon and nutmeg and onions and butter and garlic.

A half-dozen kids cavorted underfoot, giggling and running and playing tag. In the living room, the television was tuned to a college football game, and there were several men gathered around it.

Tuck took her by the elbow and introduced her. She met his father, James, who looked so much like Tuck it took her breath away. It was like having a snapshot into his future. Apparently at sixty, Tuck was still going to be a stunningly handsome man. She also said hello to Tuck's other brothers-in-law, Steve and Magnus. Steve, a native

New Yorker, was of stocky build and average height, and he was as dark as Swedish-born Magnus was blond.

Next, Tuck took her to the kitchen. She shook hands with his other two sisters, Desiree and Sabrina. They looked a lot like Evie, both slender with classic features. Tuck's mom, Meredith, insisted on giving her a hug.

"And this is Grandmother Fairfield," Tuck said, taking her over to meet the matriarch of the clan. "We just call her Gran."

The minute Jillian laid eyes on the older woman, she knew this was who she had to prove herself to. She had to be in her mid-eighties, but her eyes were still sharp even though her shoulders were stooped.

"Tuck," Ridley said from the doorway of the kitchen. "Can I borrow you a minute to help me set up the extra table for the kids?"

"Sure thing," Tuck said, and then abandoned Jillian to his womenfolk. So much for having her back.

Ridley furtively pulled Tuck into the garage and eyed the box nestled in the crook of his arm. "Is that it?"

"It is."

"Hang on." He locked the garage door so they wouldn't be interrupted by inquisitive nieces and nephews. He couldn't believe how nervous he was. The fact that Tuck had taken so long over the music box heightened his anxiety. He wanted this gift to be special. Tuck was a talented carpenter, but Ridley knew he'd never crafted anything like this before.

Tuck unwrapped the music box from the newspaper. Ridley held his breath.

"Your hands are shaking," Tuck said.

"Hell, I know." Ridley's voice was gruff.

"Don't drop it." Tuck settled the gleaming wooden box in his hands.

Ridley just stared. It far exceeded his expectations. The craftsmanship was exquisite, but more than that, it was as if Tuck had read his mind. Gently, he pushed his big thumb against the delicate cradle atop the music box. It swayed softly. A lump humped up in his throat. "Dude..."

"You like it?"

"Evie's gonna cry when she sees it."

"Is it what you wanted?"

"Dude...," he said again. There was nothing else he could say. Evie was going to love the music box, and hopefully she would understand what he was trying to tell her with it. He carefully opened the box, and the cradle rocked as it played "Faith."

Just then, someone rapped on the garage door. "Rid? You need some help out there?"

It was Steve. Ridley unlocked the door, let him into the garage, and locked it behind him.

"What are you guys doing out here so clandestinely? Sneaking a smoke?" He looked hopeful.

"Gave it up," Ridley said. "Supposedly it lowers your sperm count."

"Hey, what's that?" Steve homed in on the music box cradle.

"Evie's Christmas present. That's what we were doing out here."

"That's beautiful." Steve reached for it. "Do you mind?"

Ridley handed it to him.

Steve traced a finger over the intricate scroll carvings. "Where'd you get it? This is first-class woodwork."

Ridley jerked a thumb at Tuck.

Steve's eyes met Tuck's. "You did this?"

"I was laid up with a broken ankle."

"This is amazing. I mean, I knew you were a talented carpenter, but damn, Tuck, you could make a mint off these."

"It's not that big of a deal," Tuck said.

Ridley wanted to poke him and tell him not to be so modest.

"I'm serious," Steve said. "I know a guy. Owns a gallery in SoHo. This might not be his thing, but I'm sure he can refer you to someone who would know how to represent it."

"Hey," Ridley said to Tuck. "You could have a whole new career."

"Rid, you mind if I take this back to the city with me? Show it to my guy, see if he's interested?" Steve asked.

"You better ask Tuck if he's interested."

"Well?" Steve arched his eyebrows.

Tuck shrugged. "It's Ridley's box."

Steve looked at Ridley again.

Ridley didn't want to part with the box, but if Steve could help get Tuck back in the mainstream flow of life, he'd make the sacrifice. "Just make damn sure you get it back to me safe and sound so I can give it to Evie on Christmas."

"You guys are coming to New York for the holiday, right?"

"I don't know." He and Evie hadn't cemented their Christmas plans.

"That's what Meredith and Jim are planning."

"We'll play it by ear."

Steve slapped Tuck on the back. "Damn, man, I still can't believe how good you are. Mark my words, my friend is going to go ape over this. Looks like the old Manning magic is back."

"Can I do anything to help?" Jillian offered, feeling like the odd woman out in the kitchen filled with family members.

"You can make the poppy-seed dressing for the spinach salad," Evie said. "The recipe and the ingredients are on top of the microwave."

Happy to have a chore, she moved purposefully to the microwave and started making the poppy-seed dressing, only to become aware that Grandmother Fairfield was staring at her.

"So you're Tuck's roommate, huh?" the old lady asked.

"Yes, ma'am."

Gran snorted. "Roommates," she muttered. "In my day, we called it shacking up."

"Mrs. Fairfield," Jillian rushed to assure her. "Tuck and I really are just roommates and friends."

"Hmph," Gran said. "Who you trying to kid? I see the way he's looking at you."

Her comments startled Jillian. How did Tuck look at her? Had his grandmother already picked up on the sexual chemistry between them? To distract herself, she took the cap off the white-wine vinegar. "I can assure you our relationship is strictly platonic."

"Maybe for now . . ."

"Mom," Tuck's mother thankfully intervened, "would you like me to escort you to the table? Evie's just about ready to serve dinner."

"Sorry about Gran," Evie whispered as her mother took her grandmother into the other room. "She's got strong opinions."

"I understand," Jillian said, and busied herself with adding sugar and poppy seeds to the white-wine vinegar.

A few minutes later, everyone was seated at the table while Tuck's father said grace over their meal. Afterward, everyone dove in and started passing plates around the table. It was a warm and friendly atmosphere until Gran, who was eyeing Jillian from across the Thanksgiving spread, said, "You're nothing like Aimee, nothing at all."

"Mother!" Tuck's mom scolded, while several other people chided, "Gran!"

"Well, she's not."

Tuck reached for Jillian's hand under the table and gave it a squeeze. She was amazed at what that one gesture did to her heart.

"When are you and Ridley going to give us some grandbabies?" Meredith asked Evie, taking Jillian out of the hot seat and putting Tuck's sister squarely in it.

"We're working on it, Mom."

"You're thirty-five and the clock is ticking."

"We know, we know." Evie's smile was tight, strained.

Jillian immediately felt sorry for her and guessed that she hadn't told her family about her infertility issues.

"What's the problem?" Gran narrowed her eyes at Ridley. "You shootin' blanks?"

"Gran!" the entire room exclaimed.

"Everyone else tiptoes around the truth. I just call 'em like I see 'em. I'm eighty-five. I don't have the time or patience for hem-hawing."

"The turkey is delicious, Evie," Jillian said.

"Hem-hawer," Gran accused.

Jillian met the older woman's gaze. "You don't want me to hem-haw. Okay, I'm calling it like I see it. You're a rude old lady."

The entire collective gasped.

"Nope." Gran grinned mischievously. "She's not a thing like that goodie-two-shoes Aimee. So what's the deal between you two?" She wagged a wrinkled finger between Tuck and Jillian. "Is it true love or just sex?"

"Not that it's any of your business, Mrs. Fairfield, but I'm not having sex with your grandson."

"Must be true love, then."

"I don't believe in the concept of true love."

"You don't believe in true love?" Gran stared at Jillian as if she'd stepped off a spaceship from another planet.

Everyone else at the table was gaping at her as well.

"I think the concept of destined love is a myth perpetuated by fairy tales and greeting cards."

"Then stay far away from my grandson, missy. He's been kicked around by life enough in his short time on earth. He doesn't need to go falling for a woman who doesn't believe in true love."

"Well, if believing in true love makes a person as cranky and bitter as you are, then I'm happy to do without it," Jillian said.

The entire roomful of people fell silent, including the kids. Everyone looked at one another. Suddenly Jillian realized how rude she'd sounded.

Dear God, what had she done? What had she said? Why had she said it? She had no idea how to maneuver in a family. She had no right to be here. Chagrined, Jillian pulled her hand from Tuck's, jumped up from the table, grabbed her coat off the rack by the door, and ran outside as fast as her legs could carry her.

Humiliation tightened Jillian's face. She was a horrible, horrible person. Baiting an old lady.

She stood in Evie and Ridley's backyard, staring at the snow-covered mountains, breathing hard and trying to calm her racing heart. She could see the ski lodge from here. Thunder Mountain was a sprawling winter tourist destination, not far from Salvation as the crow flies, but a thousand miles difference in tone and flavor. Salvation did not possess the ubiquitous overpriced mountain gear shops or celebrity-owned boutiques or chain restaurants or sprawling condo expansions or new-age healing centers that had sprung up around the resort.

Jillian caught a glimpse of Tuck from her peripheral vision as he followed her out the back door. He stood behind her, two thermoses clasped in his gloved hands. She couldn't look at him.

She heard the snow crunch under his boots as he walked toward her, and she could feel the heat of his gaze stinging the back of her neck. She cringed at what he must be thinking of her right now.

The smell of Thanksgiving hung in the air, smoked turkeys and roasted chestnuts and cranberry sauce. Cornbread stuffing and green-bean casserole and glazed carrots. It smelled like home. It smelled like family. And it was more than clear that she didn't belong.

She thought about the way Tuck's family had looked at her, and she'd just known what they were thinking. *You can't replace Aimee.* What is this woman doing here? She's not one of us.

Jillian had never belonged.

Not with her mother. Not with her father and her stepfamily. Honestly, not even with her friends Delaney, Tish, and Rachael. Even with them, she'd held herself in reserve, never really fully letting down her guard. The only person she'd ever allowed herself to have a strong emotional connection with was Blake, and that was simply because he'd been as lonely as she was.

Jillian had thought she kept up her guard to protect herself from getting hurt. What she now realized was that she'd never let people in because she was afraid that if they knew who she really was deep down inside, they wouldn't want anything to do with her. She felt like such a fraud, dressed in festive clothes, pretending to be someone she was not. Pretending to be the kind of woman who could successfully navigate holiday family gatherings and be accepted.

What did Tuck see in her? Why did he want to be her friend?

"Jilly?" he murmured.

She turned. He extended a thermos toward her. A lump of emotion knotted her throat.

"Coffee. Black as pitch just the way you like it."

She took the warm thermos, clutched it in her hands, dipped her head, unable to meet his gaze. "I'm sorry for the way I behaved in there. I don't know what came over me. I can't imagine what your family must think of me...um...coming unhinged like that. I truly am sorry. I'm ashamed of myself."

"Jillian." Her name on his lips was a gentle reprimand. "Look at me."

She tilted her chin up and met his warm, unwavering gaze.

"You've got nothing to be ashamed of. For one thing, Gran had it coming. For another thing, you're as entitled to your opinion as anyone in that room. If anything, I'm ashamed of the way they behaved. I hope you'll forgive them. Normally they're really not like that. They're just all worried about me—"

"I know, I know. You lost the love of your life, but I feel sorry for whoever you end up marrying, Tuck, because she'll never be able to live up to the sainted Aimee."

Silence fell.

Jillian remembered the day of their first fight. It had been about Aimee. She gulped. "Tuck, I apologize. I shouldn't have said that."

"It's all right," he said, twisting open the top of his thermos and taking a sip. "Aimee wasn't perfect. She had her faults. It's easy to forget now that she's gone."

Jillian followed his lead and took a sip of her own. She hardly dared believe he was able to talk about Aimee without getting defensive. "Is it terrible of me to want to hear what her faults were?"

"Not terrible at all." He smiled, but it didn't reach his soulful whiskey eyes. "Simply human. Okay, here goes. Aimee stole the covers at night. I'd end up shivering on one side of the bed, and she'd have the blankets heaped on top of her and tumbling off over on the other side to the floor."

"A real blanket hog, huh?"

"And she had the most irritating habit of chomping the ice in her drink. Crunch, crunch, crunch. Drove me around the bend."

"Ice-chomping blanket hog. How did you stay out of divorce court?" Jillian dared to tease.

"And Aimee had this way of laughing that ended in a snorting sound. I thought it was cute when we were dating, but after a couple of years, it got a little annoying."

"You loved her terribly, didn't you?"

"Yeah," he admitted. "I did. But she's gone and I'm still here, and I gotta find a way to live with it. I don't want the next woman I marry to feel as if she has to compete with Aimee's memory."

"You're right. Whoever this woman is, she deserves all of you, Tuck, and I say this from my heart as your friend. You deserve to love again without fear of being hurt. Life hurts but you shouldn't avoid living to keep from feeling pain. For one thing, it doesn't work."

"No?" He never looked away, never even blinked.

"Hurt and pain will always find you. And secondly . . ."

"Yeah?"

"You gotta have the pain in order to appreciate the pleasure and the joy life has to offer. Life is filled with contrasts for a reason. Hate and love. Shadows and light. On and off. Up and down. It's the paradox of a dual universe."

"And you say you're not spiritual? You're sounding a lot like Deepak Chopra to me."

"Okay, so I've done some reading, some spiritual exploration."

"So what's your excuse, Jillian? Why aren't you out there doing the carpe diem thing when it comes to dating, romance, and love?"

"Because," she said, finally admitting it to herself as she admitted it to him. "I've been living so long in the shadows that I've lost the ability to see the light. I don't want you to get lost in the darkness, Tuck. I care about you too much to let that happen."

"You . . ." The expression in his eyes flared, but she couldn't really read the emotion there. "You care about me?"

"Of course I care about you. We're friends, right?"

"Yeah. That's right. Friends."

"Friends," she echoed.

"And you don't believe in true love."

She shook her head.

He nodded. "So if we're friends, how about going skiing with me on Saturday at Thunder Mountain?"

"Um…" Did she want to go?

"Friends have fun together. Correct?"

"I suppose they do."

"Then let's go have some fun. Just you and me."

"You sure your ankle is up to it?"

"It's been seven weeks since I broke it. No better time to find out what shape I'm really in."

The back door opened at that moment, and Evie came out on the steps, coatless, arms wrapped around her, turkey apron still tied at her waist. She was shivering against the wind. "Come inside, you guys. It's time for pie."

Chapter 17

I love the way Jillian lit into your grandmother." Ridley chuckled to Evie once all the guests were gone and they were cleaning up the kitchen together. Ridley was washing the dishes, Evie drying them. "The old gal has been allowed to run roughshod over your family for too long."

"I was mortified."

"For Jillian?"

"For you."

"For me?" He cast a glance at her. "What for?"

"That shooting-blanks comment."

"We both know that's not true."

"Yeah." Evie blew out her breath. "I'm the one with the problem."

"It's not a problem. We've only been trying for a year. We'll get there, honey. You're just putting too much pressure on yourself."

Evie didn't answer and instead industriously dried one of the turkey platters Ridley had just handed to her. She wished she shared his optimism. But she was going on thirty-six. Already, the days of her viable eggs were numbered.

"Jillian is one fiery pistol." Ridley chuckled. "I just

wonder how much longer she and Tuck can keep this platonic relationship going."

"Speaking of fiery pistols..." Evie tossed the cup towel aside and snaked her arms around Ridley's waist, babies burning on her brain. "What do you say we leave the dishes until tomorrow and call it a night?" She stood on tiptoes to take his earlobe between her teeth.

"Come on, honey." He loosened her arms. "I'm exhausted, and we've both got to get up early in the morning. We can go one night without sex."

"But I'm ovulating."

"We did it last night and twice the day before."

"Excuse me. I didn't realize having sex with me had become such a chore for you." She turned away.

"Evie..." He grabbed her arm and pulled her back toward him. "Don't get mad."

"Ridley, you just don't seem to grasp how important this is to me."

"And you don't seem to realize all the pressure you're putting on me to perform. I'm only human. It's taking all the fun out of our lovemaking."

"You want me to relax?"

"I do."

"Then guide me on a vision quest. Reassure me that I will get pregnant, that babies *are* in our future."

Ridley exhaled in exasperation. "I've told you before that a vision quest is not the answer for you."

"I think you're being mean not letting me do this."

"And I think you're being unrealistic."

"Tuck had a vision of Jillian and now here she is. That's pretty powerful mojo."

"Exactly. It's not something you mess around with if you're unprepared for it."

"I'm your wife. Don't you love me?"

"Of course I love you. That's precisely the reason I don't want you to do it."

Evie yanked away from him in frustration. Why was he so adamant she not go on a vision quest? Why was he denying her this peek into the future?

"Hey, hey." He chased after her. "Come here."

"What?"

His arms went around her, and he lowered his head to kiss her. Evie didn't kiss him back.

"You forget all about the vision quest and I'll make love to you every night until you get pregnant. How's that?"

Evie looked into the dark eyes of the man she loved more than life itself. "Okay, all right, but tonight, I get to be on top. I heard it increases your chances of having a boy."

The snow at the top of Thunder Mountain on Saturday morning was the finest skiing powder Jillian had ever seen. The day was perfect. Sun shining, no wind to speak of. The slopes smooth and tightly packed.

Below them on the black-diamond trails, expert skiers maneuvered over moguls, jumping and swishing in their colorful ski attire. A small flotilla of novice skiers followed an instructor down one of the easier, green-circle trails. And at the very bottom of the mountain, they could see the raw beginners snowplowing madly on the bunny slope. To their left, the ski lift deposited a new round of skiers and then circled back down for more.

Jillian wriggled her fingers into her ski gloves. *We're just here to have fun*, she kept telling herself. *It's nothing more than that. Not a date. Two friends out enjoying the mountain.*

"I'm tired of being a gaper. I'm ready for the milk run. Race you to the base." Tuck grinned and pulled his ski goggles down over his eyes. "Last one down buys lunch."

He took off.

Never one to resist a challenge, Jillian's competitive streak kicked in, and she shot after him.

He hopped over moguls like his ankle had never been compromised. Jillian's heart momentarily vaulted into her throat, but when she realized he could handle himself, she deftly maneuvered the mogul. Aha! She still had it.

Tuck had insisted she rent parabolic skis, and they were amazing. The hourglass shape gave her more speed and control, and they responded immediately to the slightest pressure. Technology had made great strides since the last time she'd been skiing in college during spring break with Delaney, Tish, and Rachael.

They raced, flying around trees, zipping down the hill, zigzagging over the granular surface soaring toward Thunder Lodge, the Chalet condos, the bank of metal lockers where skiers stashed their possessions. It felt decadent, this hedonistic, holiday, cold-weather dash, as if they'd shoplifted something money couldn't replace—time, a precious memory, happiness. They were still young, they were free, and Jillian basked in their very aliveness.

The snow was sugar, tempting and white. On their skis, Jillian and Tuck raced, breathless and hungry, muscles charged and blood pumped with adrenaline. It was a glorious game, and Jillian realized that she did not play nearly often enough.

On the skis, on the mountain, pulling in the cold, crisp morning air, Jillian felt like someone else. It was as if she'd stepped into the body of another Jillian, this one lighter, giddier, silly even. Gone was Queenie and in her place was...

Who?

She didn't know, but she liked this new woman, this new sensation wrapping around her, crowding out the cloak of loneliness she'd worn for twenty-nine years. Something happened to her on the top of that mountain as she played snow tag with Tuck. Something she could not explain. Something that filled her with hope and expectancy. Something that made her soul sing.

Jillian spurred her body onward, eager to win, determined to beat him. She dug her poles into the snow, pushing faster, aiming for a shortcut, even though it was steeper than the path Tuck had taken. Jillian had never been afraid to assume risk in order to claim her prize.

But even so, they arrived at the base at exactly the same moment. No winner, no loser.

Equals.

It was, Jillian decided, the perfect ending to the perfect ski run. Grinning, she took off her ski cap and shook her head.

Tuck sucked in his breath. Jillian's face was turned in profile to him as she looked back at where they'd come from, her gaze drinking in the pine trees, the snow, the mountain vista.

She ran her fingers through her hair, and the wind tossed the ebony strands over her shoulder. She looked mind-shatteringly beautiful in her powder-blue snow-bunny suit that snugged her athletic body like a leather glove, hugging her breasts and womanly hips, nipping in at her sculpted waist.

He pushed his goggles up on his forehead. Her cheeks were flushed, her eyes hidden behind the darkly tinted lenses of her sunshades. The bright morning light warmed their skin. She tilted her head back to catch the sun full on, briefly shut her eyes, inhaled deeply, and then looked at him.

"I love the smell of snow," she breathed.

Hypnotized by the sight of her, Tuck could only nod. White snow, black hair, ripe body in blue clothes.

She pointed at the ski lodge. "Break for lunch?"

"Guess it's Dutch treat," he said.

"I'll pay."

"It's not a date and I didn't win the bet. We're friends. It's Dutch treat."

"Unless," she said, "I pick up lunch and you can pick up the tab for the hot toddies after the last run of the day."

"I can go for that."

They skied to the lodge, shrugged out of their gear, locked up their skis, and went inside. They were a little early for lunch, and the place was fairly empty, so the waitress showed them to a table in the lounge area. The television at the bar was tuned to *The Price Is Right*, but the sound was muted.

The smell of hearty, winter food scented the air—chili, pot roast, hunter's stew, chicken pot pie. Tuck ordered the chili, and Jillian went for the chicken pot pie.

"How's the ankle?" she asked.

"Good as new."

"I'm having a good time." She smiled at him over the rim of her coffee cup while they waited for their food order. "Thanks for inviting me."

"No problem. I'm enjoying the view." Tuck looked at her instead of out the window at the majestic mountain, letting her know he wasn't speaking about the scenery. He was confused by his own statement. They were forging a

friendship. Why was he mucking things up with the insin-
uation that there could be more?

She briefly met his eyes, then quickly turned her gaze
out the big picture window. She looked unsure of herself.
He couldn't blame her. He was feeling as unsteady as a
toddler taking his first steps. "Yes, it is beautiful."

"Gorgeous." He never took his eyes off her face.

She fingered the bracelet at her wrist as if it were a tal-
isman she used to comfort herself when she was feeling
off balance. He'd watched her perform the gesture before.
She rubbed her fingers over it like a rosary. Whether she
knew it or not, the woman had faith in something. A
power beyond her.

A crackling fire in the fireplace near their table suddenly made a loud snapping noise and spilled a shower of
sparks into the grate. She jumped, slightly startled. Then
her gaze met Tuck's.

"Dry wood," he explained.

"Ah, we're back to the subject of wood again." Her eyes
twinkled, teasing him. "It's a favorite of yours. A regular
theme."

"What can I say? I'm a carpenter at heart." He chuckled. "Wood is my medium."

"Medium is fine with me. I've found that large is often
not all it's cracked up to be."

Desire churned Tuck's stomach as he caught her sexual
innuendo. He felt at once both concern and excitement. He
wanted her, yes, but he wanted her friendship even more.
The morning they'd just spent together convinced him of
that. He wasn't going to jeopardize the good thing they
had going.

Sex was sure to mess things up.

But the look in her eyes—the look that told him she

wanted him as much as he wanted her—cut like razor wire and made him think, *What if, what if, what if?*

He was sitting next to her so they could both view the mountain through the picture window. He could see the pulse at the hollow of her throat fluttering. His own heart was fluttering too. His gaze dropped to her wrist again, watching as she twirled the silver and turquoise filigree bracelet.

"Where'd you get the bracelet?" he asked.

"Blake. He gave it to me for my law school graduation."

Tuck snorted, shook his head.

Jillian's chocolate brown eyes narrowed. "What does that snort mean?"

"He was far more of a father to you than he ever was to Aimee," Tuck said.

"And you resent that."

"Yeah. I do."

"From what Blake told me, Aimee was the one who'd cut him out of her life," she said.

Anger sparked inside him. "Blake was a shitty father."

"Maybe. I wasn't there. But he was the closest thing to a father I ever had. I'm saying that whatever went on between him and Aimee, it was a two-way street. Aimee wasn't all sweetness and light."

"Excuse me, are you disrespecting my dead wife?"

"That's not what I meant, but you do idolize her memory. No living woman could live up to Saint Aimee."

Tuck couldn't believe she was going there. "Don't," he said through clenched teeth. "Don't you say a word against her."

Her jaw tightened and she turned her head to look out the window. Tuck was startled to see unshed tears glistening at the corner of her eyes. Immediately, he felt contrite. Reaching out, he put his hand on her forearm.

She stiffened.

"Jillian," he murmured. "I don't want to fight with you. We've had such a great day. I just wanted…"

He looked down at her wrist, at the bracelet that represented the wall between them. His love for Aimee, her loyalty to Blake. Ghosts sat in the two vacant chairs at the table. Ghosts of the past, mucking up the promise of a hopeful future.

"Don't try to figure me out, Tucker Manning," she said. "Save your efforts."

"I can't." Tuck lifted a hand and slowly traced the back of one finger down the side of her cheek and along her tensed jaw.

He was encouraged when she didn't pull away. In fact, she swiveled her head around to meet his gaze full on.

"You fascinate me, Jillian Samuels," he said.

The breath left her lungs in a small sigh.

He knew he shouldn't do it, but he couldn't seem to stop himself. She looked so hurt, and he felt so compelled to smooth things over between them. He brushed his lips against hers. A breezy, hardly there kiss.

The touch of their mouths sent a shudder clean through him.

She sighed a second time.

He lowered his head, slid his arm around her back, pulled her closer, and kissed her more firmly.

Jillian parted her lips, but she didn't lean into him, and she kept her arms stiffly in her lap. Tuck touched the tip of his tongue to hers, but she closed her mouth and drew back.

"No," she whispered.

Tuck pulled his head away. "I…I…" He didn't know what he wanted to say. Words seemed empty, useless tools with which to try and scale this…this…*thing* between them. "Are you okay?"

She nodded, but her eyes never left his. Her body radiated a bizarre combination of self-discipline, anger, desire, and fierce melancholia.

The waitress interrupted, depositing their food on the table. The earthy aroma of cumin-rich chili scented the air between them.

He looked at Jillian, at the regal set to her shoulders and the hooded expression in her dark eyes, and he felt so inadequate. His heart hammered and his gut twisted and his mind spun. *What in the hell am I going to do about this feeling?*

Just as he was pondering that question, he got a glimpse of the weather report on the television. At the same time he noticed the ominous weather pattern outline on screen, the bartender took it off mute. From the looks of the Doppler radar, the blizzard would be slamming into them within the next three to four hours. Luckily, Salvation was only an hour's drive away, but they needed to get a move on in order to get down the mountain safely.

"Hunker down, folks," the weather forecaster announced. "Because within the next three hours, the blizzard of the decade is headed for Thunder Mountain all the way down to Boulder."

All day long, the talk at the Bluebird had been of the coming blizzard. By the time Evie closed the café early, the snow swirled like heavy lace throughout the town. She got home to find Ridley had stocked them up on firewood and supplies in case they lost electricity.

"I got a bastard of a headache," he told her. "I'm going to bed early. You coming?"

Evie went with him, but her mind was so keyed up she couldn't sleep. She kept thinking about the blizzard, about Thanksgiving dinner, about the babies she wanted so desperately, about the vision quest Ridley refused her. The more she thought about that last part, the more irritated she got.

By midnight, she was still wide awake, and the blizzard hadn't yet hit. Evie made the decision she'd been on the verge of making for weeks. She tiptoed out of bed and slipped into the sweat lodge.

She'd only been inside it once, right after he built it. She had to admit the symbol of her husband's spirituality bothered her on a gut level. Intellectually, she didn't care. She told herself she liked that he practiced what he believed. But emotionally? It made her feel left out. She didn't have faith in things unseen the way he did, and his adherence to this custom she didn't know or understand was a wedge between them.

You have to get over this. You're hoping to have a baby with him. Ridley's going to want to share his beliefs with his child, and you can't deprive him of that. It's time you understood your husband's faith.

She started a fire in the fire pit with the piñon wood, turned on the gas-powered sauna and battery-powered MP3 player. The sound of low, steady drumbeats spilled from the speakers. In the dark of midnight, with only the flickering firelight for a guide, Evie took off her coat and her flannel pajamas in the sweat lodge. It exuded the musky, masculine smell of her husband. Stripped naked, she sat on the bearskin rug.

After peppering Tuck with questions about his vision quest, Evie tried to emulate the conditions. She crossed her legs in lotus position. She inhaled deeply of the piñon wood smoke. She hummed a mantra—*baby, baby, baby.*

The temperature in the lodge grew hotter. Sweat beaded Evie's brow, her upper lip, the flat space between her breasts.

Baby, baby, baby.

The bearskin rug felt luxuriously sensual against her bare butt. Smoke swirled upward, funneling through the flue and out the hole in the roof.

Baby, baby, baby.

She waited. Prayed. Minutes passed. Finally an hour. Nothing happened.

Her butt was growing numb, her entire body was now bathed in sweat, and the incessant drumbeating was getting on her nerves. What was she doing wrong?

You don't believe.

The thought came to her from the air, but it sounded exactly as if Ridley had said it. Startled, Evie looked toward the door. But it remained closed.

She thought of the baby she wanted. Wrapped her empty arms around her chest. She thought of her husband asleep in their king-sized bed. Tears pricked at the back of her eyelids.

You gotta have faith.

Evie took a deep, shuddering breath and let it out slowly. The languid, heated smoke snaked throughout her body. Her muscles relaxed; her head went comfortably numb.

Buzzy. She felt all warm and buzzy.

Smoke grew thicker inside the room. The smell of piñon wood was overpowering. And the drums, they just kept beating. *Pound, pound, pound.*

Baby, baby, baby.

Her eyelids drooped heavily. She coughed, blinked.

Then, in the haze of smoke, she saw something.

A baby.

Evie smiled immediately and joy contracted her stomach, but as she watched, a woman came and picked up the baby and disappeared into the cloud of smoke.

Then suddenly she was surrounded by children. Babies, toddlers, little boys and girls in Easter attire. They were standing on the lawn of the White House. It was the annual Easter Egg hunt. All the children had mothers who were carrying baskets heaped high with eggs.

And there was Evie, standing alone, watching the event take place all by herself. No child at her side, no baby in a stroller, no round pregnant belly like many of the young mothers. She realized suddenly that at thirty-five, she was the oldest woman on the White House lawn.

Tears spilled down her face, and a wrenching sob squeezed her throat. She looked down at the basket that she realized was looped over her right arm. Inside, atop the bright green artificial grass, were three tiny white eggs.

Evie threw back her head and howled with grief. The vision was clear enough. She did not have a lush full basket of eggs. There were no babies in her future, no children of her own flesh and blood to love. She was a failure as a woman.

The pain was horrible.

Evie drew her knees to her chest and let the tears flow. Ridley was right. She shouldn't have come in here. Shouldn't have seen what she'd just seen. Shouldn't have learned the truth this way. Alone. Without him to comfort her.

"Evie!"

She jerked her head toward the door. Saw her big man standing there with a deep frown cutting into his brow, anger tightening his jaw. With his wild, dark hair falling loose to his shoulders, he looked all the world like a surly black bear. Her heart galloped.

"What in the hell do you think you're doing in here?" Ridley growled.

In that moment, Evie knew she'd crossed the line and there was no way she could step back across.

Chapter 18

For three days, Jillian and Tuck were trapped inside the lake house together while the blizzard of the decade raged outside.

On the second day, the electricity went out. Tuck kept the fire in the fireplace roaring. They played chess by candlelight. Jillian beat him seventeen games in a row before he vowed never to play her again. They roasted marshmallows over the blaze and brewed up hot chocolate over the gas stove. They listened to the weather report on the radio. They made stew and cornbread. They drank pots of coffee and sat huddled under a blanket, watching *When Harry Met Sally* on Tuck's DVD player until the batteries gave out.

"Do you think men and women can simply be friends?" Jillian asked him when the movie was over. They were sitting side by side on the couch, Mutt sleeping at their feet.

Tuck shrugged. "Sure."

"You don't buy into Harry's philosophy, then?"

"Nope."

She turned to look at him in the firelight. "Are we friends?"

"I like to think we are."

"I don't know. I think Harry made a valid point."

"Women and men can't really be friends?"

"Exactly. The issue of sex is always there."

Tuck looked into her eyes.

Tension permeated the room. Sexual tension. Taut and hot. Jillian glanced away and stared into the fireplace, focused on the flames flicking the wood, the smell of mesquite.

But no matter how hard she tried to direct her attention elsewhere, every cell in her body was acutely aware of the man sitting next to her. The sexy man she was stranded with in a snowbound cabin.

She fisted her hands against the tops of her thighs. Her throat felt tight, the set of her shoulders even tighter. Restlessly, she wriggled her toes inside her thick woolen socks. Even way across the couch, Jillian could feel the heat emanating off Tuck's body. The room smelled of him—musky, manly, magnificent.

"Fear and stubborn pride kept Harry and Sally apart when they could have, should have, been together much sooner," she said.

"Yeah," he said. "Stupid Harry, stupid Sally."

"Or," she said, "I suppose you could look at it from the opposite angle. They let sex spoil a wonderful friendship."

"You can't have a great love relationship and a great friendship at the same time?" Tuck asked. Then before she could answer, he said, "No, wait, you're the woman who doesn't believe in true love at all."

"It's not that I don't believe in love," Jillian said. "It's just that I don't believe it's some magical, fairy-dust kind of thing. Seriously, do you?"

"I used to. Once upon a time."

"And now?"

"I'm not so naïve. I thought true love would save me from pain. What I found out is that it causes more pain than you can possibly believe."

"Yeah," she said. "I suppose there is that."

They looked into each other's eyes, there in front of the flickering firelight.

"Come here," he murmured.

"What?"

He reached out and ran his fingertips along her shoulder, and she moved closer to him, anxious to feel his breath on her neck, to feel the beating of his heart beneath her palm.

She was someone new. Different. No longer a legal eagle from Houston. No longer that stepchild on the outside looking in. No longer the dirty mistress, the judge's ugly little secret standing on the doorstep on Christmas Eve dressed like a Victoria's Secret cowgirl.

Tuck just held her in the circle of his arms. Held her and looked straight into her. "You've never been valued the way you deserve."

"I'm no Magic Woman."

"You are."

"I've told you, I don't believe in magic."

"David Copperfield would be so disappointed."

"He knows there's no such thing as magic. He makes a living faking people out."

"Why are you so afraid to believe?" Tuck asked.

Jillian wrinkled her nose. "I hate getting my hopes dashed."

"There is something out there, Queenie." He tightened his arms around her. "Something that can't be explained. I saw it in those learning centers I designed." And apparently in the music box he'd designed for Evie. It felt good, knowing the magic was back.

"Yeah, so why did you stop designing them?"

He drew in a deep breath. "You've got me there."

They sat there for a long time, snuggled up on the couch together, listening to the wind howl and Mutt snore.

Tuck played with a lock of her hair. She had such beautiful hair. Silky and straight. He had so many questions to ask her. They'd known each other almost two months, and he hadn't asked her the truly important things about her past.

"Tell me," he said. "Tell me about your pain. Tell me what makes it so hard for you to believe."

"It's a long sordid story," she said. "I'm sure you don't want to hear it."

He waved a hand at the bank of snow pressing heavily against the window. "It's not as if we're going anywhere. What was your childhood like? I've gotten the impression it wasn't good."

Jillian sighed, moved from the circle of his arms, and curled her legs underneath her. "I don't even remember my mother, and I barely remember my father."

"They're dead?"

"My father is. My mother..." She shrugged. "Who knows where she is?"

"You never tried to find out?"

"No."

"Why not?"

"She never wanted me."

He waited, not pressing, letting her tell her life story at her own pace.

She stared into the fire, seemingly hypnotized. When she spoke again, it was almost to herself. "My parents hooked up when they were quite young. My mother was eighteen, my father nineteen. From what I gleaned from my stepmother, they had a very tumultuous relationship. Then again, her version of things tends to get pretty skewed."

Tuck gave her his full attention.

Jillian pulled her knees to her chest and clasped her arms around her legs. The pensive look on her face told him she was leafing through her memories. "My dad was married to my stepmother when he got my mom pregnant. My mother didn't tell him about me. But having a baby didn't stop her from hanging out in bars and pool halls. She had an alcohol problem. I realize that now. I remember falling asleep on shuffle-board tables to the sound of Hank Williams and Merle Haggard on the jukebox and the smell of beer and cigarettes in the air. In the meantime, my dad had this whole other family I knew nothing about. Two other daughters. Legitimate daughters."

Tuck thought about his own stable, loving family. His parents who were still happily married after forty years. He'd been so lucky and he knew it.

"Then on Christmas Eve, when I was three years old, my mother left me on my father's porch with a letter of explanation pinned to my chest, rang the doorbell, and just drove away."

"Damn. That was cold-blooded."

"I don't remember that day, but I suppose in her mind she was doing the best thing for me."

"You must have felt so scared and lonely that you blocked it out." The thought of that three-year-old kid abandoned on a doorstep on Christmas Eve fisted anger inside him. What kind of person would do such a thing?

She blew out her breath, and that's all Tuck thought he

was going to get out of her. He said nothing further. If she didn't want to talk about it, she didn't want to talk about it.

But then a few minutes later, she surprised him by saying, "My stepmother was very unhappy to suddenly have a third daughter to raise. I don't think that marriage was a happy one. My stepmother wasn't the most stable person emotionally, and my dad threw himself into his work. He'd leave before I woke up in the mornings, and often he wouldn't return until long after I was in bed. Like I said, I was really little, and I don't remember that much about him. The one clear memory I have of him was this one time he took me fishing, and he bought me this little pink tackle box with yellow daisies on it. In a dumb way, that was one of the reasons I was so excited about inheriting a lake house. So I could go fishing."

The vision of a little black-haired girl clutching a pink tackle box with daisies and a kid-sized rod and reel caused something inside him to unravel. "Aw, hell, Queenie."

Jillian paused again and glanced over at him. The raw pain on her face was almost unbearable.

In that moment, he saw past her beauty, beyond the dark enigmatic eyes that were often hooded to hide her thoughts. Beyond the high, feminine cheekbones, the thick black eyelashes, the regal nose. He saw beyond the promise of her beautiful mouth and the chin she kept clenched so firmly, as if she feared it would give away too much of her heart if she relaxed her hold.

"My dad died in a car crash when I was five. His secretary was in the passenger seat. She died too. My stepmother claimed they were having an affair." She shrugged again. "Maybe they were."

"What happened to you?"

"My stepmother raised me, but she treated me differently

than her daughters. I suppose it's understandable under the circumstances, but a kid only knows she's being singled out, punished more often. Not long after my father died, my half sister Kaitlin and I were playing hair salon, and I whacked off Kaitlin's hair. My stepmother had a fit. It was Christmastime, and that year she put coal in my stocking. She told me I was a very bad girl and Santa didn't love me. Later on, she mellowed, or the doctor got her on the right medication, and she stopped being so mean, but those early years..." Jillian shook her head.

Quick anger pulsed through him that anyone could treat a child so cruelly. No wonder Jillian was locked up so tight and afraid to trust. She'd been betrayed in so many ways; he couldn't blame her.

"You're kidding me."

"I wish I were. One time when I was nine or ten, she just took off with her kids for the weekend and left me at home alone. During the day I was fine. In fact, I liked having the house to myself, even though I was supposed to clean the entire place while they were gone. But that night, a storm rolled in. I was in my bed upstairs, all alone. Not even a pet. My stepmother hated animals. Refused to let us have any. So I finally fall asleep, and in the middle of the night, I wake up and I'm sure I've heard a sound downstairs."

"You must have been terrified."

She nodded. "I lay there, not really knowing if I'd heard a sound or if it was something I dreamed. I held my breath, listening, hyper-alert to every creak of the house. My blood was strumming through my ears. Did I hear a noise or was it my imagination? But my mind was being so loud I couldn't hear. I didn't move, terrified that if someone was in the house, they'd hear me and come after me."

"That's horrible."

"There are lots of people in this world who had it worse. I know that. I had a roof over my head and food to eat. But I wanted out of there. I studied hard in school, luckily it came easy to me. I excelled. Got scholarships to college. Got my wish. Got the hell out of there. Graduated magna cum laude from law school."

It aroused something inside Tuck that she'd trusted him enough to tell him all this. He wanted to touch her, to comfort her for that long-ago pain, but he had no business, no right. Still, he couldn't just leave her with her shoulders tensed, her chin clenched, her mind ensnared in the past. He skimmed her forearm with his fingertips—briefly, lightly, just enough to let her know he cared.

"I'm sorry."

Tuck couldn't handle the swell of emotions flooding through him. He couldn't keep looking at Jillian. Instead, he got up and threw another log on the fire. When he turned, he saw tears reflected in her eyes.

It shook him. She was so strong, so brave. He didn't think of her as the sort who cried. Unlike Aimee, who had bawled at Hallmark commercials.

"Jillian." He went to the couch and put his arms around her.

She blinked. "I'm sorry. I don't usually do this. I don't even talk about it."

"Thank you for telling me."

"It was so long ago. I got over it. I survived."

Tuck squeezed her tighter. "You never get over something like that."

Jillian made a noise, half bravado, half sorrow. "Hey, we all have our crosses to bear. You lost someone very precious to you."

Every cell in his body ached. He knew what it was like

to suffer a great loss. She looked over at him. This shared intimacy forged a deeper understanding, a tighter bonding between them.

"Losing Aimee changed me forever, you know." He swallowed, unable to believe he was talking about his wife with her. "I'll never be the same."

"Right." She moved from him, dabbed at her eyes.

His arms felt strangely empty. He liked holding her, but he wasn't sure that he liked that he liked it.

"I think this calls for a stiff drink. You want something to drink?"

"I don't think we have anything stronger than Coke."

"Let me see." Tuck got up, grabbed the flashlight off the table, and rummaged around the kitchen. He thought there might be a beer or two in the fridge, but it was empty. He checked the kitchen cabinet. Nothing. Then he checked the cabinet over the stove.

Score!

"Look what I found," he said, coming to the archway between the kitchen and the living room and holding up a bottle of Baileys Irish Cream for her to see. "Irish coffee anyone?"

"Oh me, me." Jillian waved at him from the couch. "With this cold weather outside, I could use some warming up inside."

Tuck had to bite his tongue to keep from saying something raunchy and totally inappropriate. He concentrated on pouring the coffee and stirring in the Baileys and trying not to think about how much he wanted to kiss Jillian. He couldn't very well go back in there with a boner.

Think about carpentry.

Finger joint, butt hinge, tongue and groove.

Oh crap, that was only making things worse. He'd

never realized before what erotic terminology his profession employed.

"Hey," she said, sashaying into the kitchen. "Can I help? Need me to hold the flashlight?"

"Yeah," he said, and passed her the flashlight. "Thank God for battery-powered coffeemakers."

"Thank God," she echoed.

She was standing so close that he could smell her unique Jillian scent. He was in serious trouble here, and there was nowhere to run.

And at that moment, Tuck realized running was the last thing on his mind.

Two hours and three Irish coffees later, Jillian was giggling like a teenager. They'd been playing truth or dare, and Tuck had just dared her to stand on her head.

"Ten years of yoga," she said from her upside-down position, with her back against the wall beside the fireplace.

"You win, pretzel lady. Come down before you get a headache."

Jillian dropped her feet to the floor and sat upright, combing her fingers through her hair.

Tuck laughed. He was at his most alluring. Dark eyes filled with anticipation, his mouth quirked up at one corner, warm, inviting, sexy.

And Jillian was at her most suggestible. Tipsy and snowed in with a sexy man she'd been having erotic dreams about for quite some time. In a flash of sudden knowledge that almost knocked the breath from her body, she recognized she was falling for him.

It was more than friendship. She wanted sex from him and lots of it.

His masculinity aroused her, his cleverness intrigued, his intricacy provoked her. She admired his dedication to family, his loyalty to this town, his empathy to his friends.

She considered what he'd revealed by talking so intimately about Aimee. She sipped at the Irish coffee long past the point where she should have stopped drinking. Her head spun and her heart pounded and she felt warm all over.

Wings of panic fluttered against her rib cage. The new understanding that her feelings for him had strengthened, deepened, altered her reality. She wanted to make love to him.

Now and for a long time to come.

Jillian was scared, terrified that this glimmer of joy she was feeling would evaporate if she studied it too hard. How could she trust in this tenuous emotion? She'd let down her guard with Alex and look what happened.

But Tuck's not Alex and he isn't married.

No, he was worse. He was a widower still in love with his dead wife, and there was no way she could compete with a ghost.

Confusion wrapped her in its grasp, and the most she could manage was a simple, "Thank you."

Tuck said nothing, just sat there watching her in the firelight.

She didn't expect him to feel the same way about her. That was too much to hope for. But the hungry expression in his whiskey-colored eyes told her that at least he wanted her sexually. Wanted her quite badly, in fact. That was easy enough to read. His eyes roved over her body and his jaw tightened.

Jillian had spent her adult life telling herself sex was enough, but with Tuck, she didn't know if she could keep convincing herself that was true. She gulped, suddenly swallowed up by unexpected melancholia. Jillian shook her head, mentally warding off the sadness. She wanted him. She would take whatever she could get. If sex and friendship were all he had to offer, so be it. She didn't really believe in anything more than that.

"I...I need to go freshen up," she said, and set her mug down on the coffee table. "I'll be right back."

She rushed into the bathroom that Tuck had just finished renovating the week before. He'd textured the walls in Venetian plaster. The beautiful sage green color she'd picked out made her think of the prairie in springtime. Since the lights were out, they had candles going in every room, and the dancing flames enhanced the old-world look of the new décor.

Jillian washed up in the new copper sink he'd installed in the stylish yet rustic bathroom cabinetry he'd built himself. She splashed cold water over her face, trying to dampen the effects of the Baileys Irish Cream and snap herself out of the magical spell the blizzard seemed to have cast.

She stared at her reflection in the mirror and saw how wide and shiny her eyes looked. "I don't believe in magic," she told her reflection. "I don't, I don't, I don't."

But she did believe in great sex, and there was a handsome man out there, and it had been months since she'd had sex. There were condoms in her purse, and he seemed as interested as she, so why not take a gamble?

She left the bathroom and went to change from her sweater and jeans into a pair of silk sapphire blue lounging pajamas and a diaphanous matching bathrobe. She hesitated a moment when she remembered Alex had given her the pajamas and robe set, but then she thought, *What the hell?* They looked good on her no matter where she'd gotten them. The material flowed like water over her body, soft and fluid, and the neckline showed off just the right amount of cleavage.

Sexy but not blatantly so.

And that's when Jillian knew she was going to seduce him. She went back to the bathroom and brushed her teeth and then her hair. She put on just enough makeup to give her a fresh, dewy look—charcoal mascara, pink cream blush, cinnamon-flavored lip gloss—applying it as best she could in the restricted lighting. She peeled off the slouch socks she liked to wear around the house and went back to the bedroom in search of the blue feathered mules that matched the silk pajamas and robe.

Taking a deep breath, she affected her sexiest walk and sauntered back out into the living room, stopping long enough to open her purse, find the condoms, and slip them into the pocket of her robe.

Tuck didn't hear her approach. He was busy poking the red-hot embers and adding fresh logs to the grate. She paused a moment to admire him in the firelight.

Even in studious repose, the man exuded a rugged sexuality that took hold of Jillian and wouldn't let go. Maybe that was the very reason she wanted him so much. He brought a raw, primal realness into her world.

She ran her hands along the pajamas, the silky material rubbing against her body, the feel of it escalating her excitement. How she wanted him!

And how nervous she was that he might reject her.

Tentatively, she licked her lips, lowered her eyelashes, and stepped closer. She heard something clang to the floor, glanced over, and saw Tuck had dropped the poker, along with his jaw.

"Jesus, Jillian."

Startled, her hand flew to her throat. What? What had she done wrong? "Yes? What is it?"

He gulped. "It's just that...you look..."

"What?"

"So damned *hot*."

The gleam in his eyes sent a flush of pride pumping through her bloodstream. She couldn't ever remember a man making her feel quite this sexy. The air crackled with sexual tension.

They stared at each other.

Tuck smiled and closed the gap he'd opened when she'd taken him by surprise. "You never cease to amaze me."

"Is that a good thing or a bad thing?"

"Oh, trust me. It's a very good thing."

She ran her tongue over her lips.

"Are you as tipsy as I am?" he asked.

"No doubt."

Tuck splayed a palm to the nape of his neck. "I gotta admit, I'm feeling a little nervous."

"Me too."

"But excited."

"Same here."

"We don't have to do this."

"I know."

They never broke eye contact, just kept looking and looking and looking at each other.

She had started this, but Tuck was the one who crossed the line. He closed the remaining space between them, reaching out and pulling her up flush against him.

Jillian felt all the air leave her body in one long pent-up whoosh, and it was like she'd been holding her breath all her life, waiting, just waiting for this moment. Waiting for him.

Tuck kissed her with the enchantment only a magic man could deliver. Strong, confident, decisive, he made his move, boldly exploring her mouth with his hot tongue.

She felt a primal, dazzling need sewing her to him, strengthening her desire to see this thing through.

Their radiant energy grew, fused, swelled. She wrapped her arm around his neck, pulling him down closer. Her lips vibrated with receptiveness.

"You can say stop at any time and I'll pull the plug," he said. "I just want you to know that."

"Right back at you, but I don't want to pull the plug."

"Neither do I," he said. "But you need to know I haven't been with anyone since…"

Neither one of them wanted to say her name. Jillian nodded. "Yes, I understand."

"It's been over two years. I might not last five minutes."

"We're snowed in. We're not going anywhere."

He kissed her again. "Where shall we do this?"

"Let's start right here on the rug in front of the fire."

"Aw, you're just a big romantic at heart."

She smiled encouragingly.

Gently, Tuck ran his hand up under the hem of her top, his rough palm skimming her bare belly. With his other hand, he tilted her chin up and brought his mouth down on hers for another soul-searching kiss.

She melted into him.

Enveloped in each other, pasted together by contact at the shoulder, hand, leg, hip, and chest, Tuck and Jillian sealed their destiny and closed their fate.

She wrapped her arms around his waist, and he enfolded her to him. It felt as if their very cells were entwined. They were oblivious to everything on earth beyond themselves and this moment.

They had fallen down the well of each other. Tuck's energy filled Jillian with rapture. His masculine power rolled off every inch of her in glorious waves. He evoked in her a desire immeasurable, a thirst so vast all the oceans of the world evaporated in a single drop.

How was this possible? How could she have become so deliriously intoxicated with him?

Her emotions terrified her.

The air vibrated between them. One wrong move and they could fall off the earth. Their entire time together had been like this. A daring adventure, and now they were embarking on a dangerous affair.

At last Jillian understood why she'd hidden behind casual sex all these years. By keeping her affairs casual, she could gamble without risks. Feel without feeling.

But now all that had been stripped away. She was metaphorically naked. Fully exposed.

It felt glorious.

And scary as hell.

Chapter 19

Queenie." He smiled and pulled her closer, pressing his lips against the hollow of her throat. "You're so righteous and regal."

She was afraid then, in the circle of his arms. Afraid of losing this precious moment, of never getting it back. She wanted so much to hope for happily-ever-after, but she didn't believe in it.

He took her by the hand and led her upstairs to the bedroom. She meekly acquiesced. He seated her at the vanity, turning the chair around so she could watch him in the candlelight. She was supposed to be seducing him, but he was taking over, turning the tables on her.

While she watched, he stripped off his clothes. His bare, taut buttocks flexed as he moved, the pale skin contrasting the tan above his waist. She went breathless staring at his abs. Compelled, Jillian could not look away.

He was glorious. All biceps and triceps and glutes and hamstrings. Take that, Adonis. She couldn't ever remember having such a well-built lover. She would remember this body for a long time to come.

And his face!

Straight out of a fantasy. His jaw was square, his cheekbones prominent. His wheat-brown hair shining in the candlelight; the scruffy cut suited his dreamy, artistic nature. Architect, carpenter, a man who knew how to use his brains.

And his hands.

She got to her feet and slowly began to take off her clothes. She had performed lots of stripteases before, and she'd never been self-conscious. Not even the first time she'd tried it.

But now, she found herself hesitating, fumbling at her buttons, feeling unsure. What was wrong? What was different?

She rushed through the process, anxious to get it over with. He didn't seem to notice that he'd received the abbreviated version of her burlesque moves. Even the look of frank appreciation in his eyes when he saw her naked did nothing to allay her uneasiness.

He smiled tenderly.

"Tuck," she whispered, and he came across the room toward her and cupped her breasts in his warm palms. Her nipples became even harder beneath his hands, and he thumbed them ever so slightly.

They exhaled at the same time, breathing out each other's air.

She thought he was quivering, then realized it was her, shaking so hard her knees wobbled.

"Now," he said, "let's get comfortable."

He arranged the pillows on the bed, piling them high and then easing her down onto her back atop them. He lay on his side next to her and walked his fingers down her arm.

"How do you want to be touched right now?"

"Kid gloves," she whispered, and his eyes lit with such feverish delight she knew he understood. "Feather fine. Lots and lots and lots of foreplay."

"I can do that." He reached out and with an incredibly light caress, grazed the base of his palm over her collarbone.

Jillian shivered.

His hand was a silken glide, his lips delicious. He swirled his fingers over her navel. Softly and sweetly he kissed the leaping pulse at her neck. He dropped down the length of her throat and then took tiny succulent nibbles.

Then his tongue went traveling south to the peaks of her jutting breasts. His tongue flicked out to lick over one nipple while his thumb achingly rubbed the other straining bud, drawing it in to the extraordinary blaze of his mouth.

His thigh tightened against her leg, and his abdominal muscles hardened to pure, smooth steel.

"Tuck," she whispered his name on a sigh. She loved his name. It rhymed so nicely with a very naughty word. *Tuck, Tuck, Tuck.* "Tuck, that feels so good."

Her eyes flew open and she lifted her head up off the mattress. She had to see what he was doing to make her feel so good. Her gaze latched on his lips as she watched him drawing her nipple in and out of his mouth.

She let her head fall back against the pillows. "Go lower."

He dipped his head, trailing his tongue down the middle of her chest to the flat of her sternum before he veered off into other territory, her nipples responding to his touch.

While his lips were finding her breasts, his hand was

dancing around the juncture of her thighs. She parted her legs slightly, just enough to let him slip a finger or two between them.

He suckled first one nipple and then the other while strumming her clit lightly with an index finger.

She tilted her pelvis, arched her back. "More," she begged. "More."

And then his mouth and his fingers were in the same place, and he had moved around so that his head pointed south. His lips closed around the tiny throbbing head of her cleft while his fingers tickled the entrance of her womanhood.

His tongue laved her sensitive skin as he suckled her deeply. She writhed against him, trying to push her body into his, needing more. Barbed ribbons of fevered sensation unfurled straight to her throbbing sex. Her inner muscles contracted, rollicking with desire for him.

"Tuck," she whispered weakly. "Tuck."

"Yes, sweetheart. What do you want? Tell me what you need."

"I want it all. I want everything."

"Like this?"

"Yes," she hissed as he moved his mouth back and forth, his hair a silky glide beneath her fingers. "Yes, yes, yes."

Tuck worked his magic with his fingers while his tongue led her into uncharted territory. She was on sensory overload as he gently guided her to a paradise she'd only dreamed of before now.

But this wasn't a dream. The warm wetness of his mouth, the sweet taste of his kiss still lingering on her tongue, the earthy smell of his masculine scent, the sound of the wind roaring outside the window. This new awareness of him awoke something inside her, and all the old failures and disappointments fell away.

He was beyond good-looking to her. He was pure life, pure joy. His mouth moved over her without caution or fear. He pushed Jillian past her knowledge of herself. She had never before been so physically possessed. His movements shook her world. The walls of the room seemed to ripple. Could a blizzard cause an earthquake?

No. The ground did not tremor, only her body.

She rode the flow of emotions, navigating the swell of pleasure and desire and discovery with accomplished ease. His warmth enveloped her, and she experienced a sense of safety with him that she'd rarely felt before.

He was lifting her up to a place she'd never known existed. She loved the adventure of him and was fascinated by this aspect.

Then she was seized by a sudden bittersweet feeling. This moment could not last. She closed her eyes, determined to ignore the sadness. Besides, this was all she needed. This brief slice of delight. She wasn't a commitment kind of gal. No reason to be sad. She was having fun, and he was doing some very nice things to her with his tongue.

Tuck's feet were pressed against the headboard, his long masculine legs parallel to her face. His hard shaft poked into her ribs.

She had a wicked thought and turned toward him, curling her spine outward while at the same time shifting her pelvis closer to his mouth and dipping her chin so she could lick the head of his penis with her tongue.

He gave a yelp of pleased surprise. His mouth was on most her feminine lips while at the same time she stretched her own mouth over the expansive width of his penis.

His tongue was hot and wet. So was hers.

She swirled. He licked.

Up and down, around and around, they were both moaning and writhing, consumed by pleasure.

On and on they went. He on her, she on him. Licking, sucking, tasting. Glorious sensations rippled through her body, turning her inside out. They increased the tempo as the pressure built, rising to an inevitable crescendo.

Jillian mewled softly whenever he did something right, grunted when he made a wrong move. It didn't take him long to pick up her rhythms, to learn what she liked and give her more of it.

She took him deeper until she felt him pressing against the back of her throat, juicy and slick. She rolled her lips back, stretching wider to accommodate his bigness. She wanted to swallow all of him. She breathed in the heady smell of his sex.

He broke contact. "Jilly, I gotta have you now, but I don't have any condoms."

She moved around in bed to face him and looked into his proud face, reaching up to trace her finger along his cheek and feeling something monumental move inside her. It was an emotion unlike anything she'd ever felt before. She couldn't name it. She stopped trying to figure it out, just let it sweep her away.

"I have a condom," she said, "in the pocket of my pajama pants."

"I'll get it."

He retrieved it and hurried back. Then he was kissing her again. Her mouth, her nose, her eyelids, her ears. He was over her and around her and then, at long last, he was inside her.

"Jillian," he whispered her name, soft as an ocean

breeze, caressing her with sound as he rotated his hips from side to side, maintaining tight, intense contact.

Now, with him deep in her moist wetness, she felt every twitch of his muscle. He lit her up inside. She had no thoughts beyond wanting him deeper, thrust to the hilt inside of her.

She wrapped her legs around his waist and rocked him into her. Her fingers gripped his buttocks, pushing him farther. Her turn to own him. Her turn for control.

Frenzy.

Everything was urgent and desperate and frantic. She felt like her breath encompassed the entire world. Need. Such need. To find, to press, to hurt, to soothe, to fly free.

They came together, and it was like pouring gasoline onto a fire. Infused, she could not tell where he began and she ended. No separation. Their connection was one hundred percent, and it filled the world. There was no space for anything else. Their oneness banged through their whole bodies. No moment existed in which they were not part of it, of each other.

She bristled with joy. It felt strong and resilient. It rippled through her body, burning her to a crisp. She was warm and gooey and completely scorched, and she loved it.

When it was over and they were two once more and Jillian lay panting in his arms, the total obliteration of what had just happened scared her witless.

Lucid thought surrendered to utter emotion. The wipeout had been pure. Complete. Unadulterated lust had knocked her into a trance from which she feared there was no awakening.

Oh shit, what had he done?

Tuck stared at the ceiling, listening to Jillian's soft,

measured breathing beside him. He wasn't ready for this. Okay, so his body had been ready, but certainly not his mind, not his emotions.

You're just scared.

Hell, yes, he was scared. You bet your sweet ass he was scared.

It was the Baileys Irish Cream, the snow, the romance of the fireplace. It was *When Harry Met Sally*. It was her distractingly wonderful smell. It was the stew and the cornbread and the coziness of married life he missed. Tuck searched for something, anything to blame, except for the truth.

Himself.

They could put this behind them, he tried to convince himself. They could go back to being friends. This didn't have to get complicated or sticky. They were sophisticated adults.

It was a one-time thing. An error in judgment. It didn't have to define their relationship from here on out.

Except that Tuck yearned to reach across that bed, pull her to him, and make love to her all over again.

Don't do it; don't compound the mistake.

He had to get up. Get out of here. But there was nowhere to go. A blizzard wailed outside. They were stuck.

His hand reached across the bed and felt the warm, round shape of her underneath the quilts. He turned on his side, propped himself up on his elbow, and stared down at her.

The night-light cast a soft glow over her sleeping features. His breathing grew shallow, and his eyes drank her in. This slumbering mystery woman who enticed him enough to make him forget about Aimee.

Guilt clamped down on him then. Guilt and shame. He

didn't want to feel remorse, but there it was, doing battle with his desire.

And still, he couldn't stop wanting Jillian. She was so captivating, so alluring. She drew him in like a magnet. Any man would want to sleep with her. She was a temptress, and she didn't even try to be one. It was just innate in her DNA. Exotic and erotic.

He traced his gaze over her, comparing her long, leggy body to Aimee's. But there was no comparison. They were opposites in every way. Jillian dark and tall, Aimee blond and small. Jillian cynical and courageous. Aimee sweet and accepting.

He ran his hand along her body, learning the slope of her shoulders, memorizing the arc of her breast, the scoop of her waist, her taut, flat stomach.

"Tuck," she whispered his name like a prayer in the cold, dark of midnight. She was a warm beacon, opening her arms, welcoming him to her.

He was damned. He could not stay away from her heat, her vitality. He sought her lips and branded her with his kiss. She made a soft noise of approval low in her long, slender throat.

His hand found her nipple, and she shivered beneath his fingertips. She felt so good, so right, and yet he was so scared. Terrified of what he was getting into. It felt like quicksand. He was drowning, but he couldn't—wouldn't—turn back no matter how hard he tried.

Tuck tugged her to him, pressing his erection against her leg and running his hand down her spine, feeling each vertebra as his mouth trailed over her skin.

Jillian sighed and threaded her fingers through his hair.

Tuck slipped his hand down her back to the round smoothness of her butt. God, what a magnificent ass she possessed. Urgent need welled up in him, just as strong as before. Need he both regretted and longed for.

Kissing her hard, he stroked one hand along her buttocks, the other across her stomach, sending it lower until he slipped a palm between her thighs.

Her eyes were trained on his face. He could feel the heat of her gaze. He looked deeply into her, felt something slip inside him. Something brave and worrisome.

And then he found her sweet spot. She was warm and dripping wet for him. He groaned his approval.

Jillian whispered Tuck's name again and swallowed him up with her eyes.

He felt light-headed. He told himself it was the alcohol, but he knew it was not. Jillian that made him dizzy. His mind was filled with a hundred scenarios of how he wanted to make love to her next. Carry her into the bathroom, maybe bend her over the counter, let her watch in the mirror while he took her from behind. Or maybe hoist her legs on his shoulders and hang her head off the bed. Or perhaps stand on the floor, drag her to the edge of the mattress, tuck a pillow under her butt, and impale her completely. Or...

But before he could even finish imagining the next position, she was leaning over him, pushing him onto his back while she swung her leg over his waist and straddled him.

She bent her head and kissed him, spearing her tongue past lips that were parched for her. Hungrily, she ran her hands up his arms and pinned his wrists over his head, anchoring him to the bed. She eased her body down over his erect, throbbing shaft, and he sucked in his breath as her tongue stoked his passion.

The temptress moved over him, her flesh soft and moist

and hot. God, she was glorious, and he reveled in the feel of her.

He was lost, swept away in a vortex of lust. A part of him, the part he didn't want to recognize, admitted he'd never felt this kind of desire before. Not with any other woman. Not even with Aimee.

Immediately he felt disloyal, and he would have lost his erection if the temptress hadn't chosen that moment to squeeze him tightly with her inner muscles.

He laughed aloud and she laughed with him, and in that moment, the temptress disappeared and it was just Jillian. His friend. Who had tonight become his lover.

Her hair was a tumble about her shoulders. Her dark eyes glazed with lust as fierce as his own. Her mouth was swollen from his rough kisses. He'd worked her over as fully as she was working him.

Raw, primal sex consumed them, and they tumbled about the bed, slinging pillows, mussing sheets, grappling and groaning and doing wild, wonderful things to each other.

"You...are...amazing," he managed to say, and then he was atop her, pressing her into the mattress, kissing her again and again and again while outside the storm raged on a banshee bacchanal.

I want her. Not just now, but forever. Keep her always.

The thought rumbled in the back of his brain, but he was afraid to think it, to hope for it. He'd had magic once and he'd lost it. He was terrified to find it again in case it slipped through his fingers once more. He couldn't bear the pain of losing such a love again.

Not love, he tried to convince himself. Not love, just great sex. He refused to confuse the two.

He stopped moving, not knowing what to do. Trying to

banish his thoughts and just go with the feeling. He closed his eyes, not wanting her to see the war going on inside him. Not wanting her to suspect that he was falling. He didn't want to fall.

Not again.

She wasn't the one. She couldn't be the one. She wasn't bound to stay in Salvation. And she didn't believe in magic.

He had to stop this before it was too late. Before he was too far gone. Abruptly, he rolled out from under her.

"What . . . ," she gasped. "Where . . ."

"I'm thirsty," he said, not looking at her. "You want some water?"

She reached up, wrapped her arms around his waist, and pressed her lips to his back. "I want you."

He got up, pulled the covers over her so he wouldn't have to see how wonderful she looked naked in the bed he'd shared with Aimee. "I don't want you to get cold."

"Tuck?" She sounded small and lonely, and he felt like an utter bastard, but he couldn't make himself go back to her.

"You hungry? I could heat up some leftover stew."

"I'm hungry for you."

Like a coward, he left her there. He ran to the kitchen. He stuck a glass under the faucet and ran the water until it was overflowing.

And he never went back.

Jillian waited, wondering what had happened. When he didn't come back to bed after several long minutes, she got up and padded into the living room and found him sleeping on the couch.

She told herself she wasn't going to cry, and then she

burst into tears. Wretched bastard. What was going on? She went back to bed and reached for the phone. To her amazement, she got a dial tone in the middle of the storm. Choking back the sobs, she called Delaney.

"Hello?" Delaney asked in a drowsy voice.

"You were asleep."

"Jilly?"

For the first time, Jillian looked at the clock. It was eleven o'clock mountain time. That meant it was midnight in Houston. "I'm sorry. I didn't realize how late it was. Please go back to sleep."

"What's wrong?"

"Nothing's wrong...I..."

"Are you crying?" Delaney sounded incredulous.

"I'm not crying." Jillian sniffled.

"I've never seen you cry. What's wrong? How can I help?"

"Nothing, everything's fine. Go back to sleep. I'll call you tomorrow."

"If you hang up this phone, Jillian Samuels, I'm coming to Colorado to kick your butt."

"You were totally wrong, Delaney. Tuck is not my Mr. Right."

"Oh, Jilly, what happened?"

"I...we..."

"Yes?"

"There's a blizzard here. We got snowed in together."

"Ah, you slept together."

"Well...yes. Then he freaked. Completely. Left the bed in the middle."

"The middle of what?"

"Sex."

"He left in the middle of sex?"

"He said he was thirsty. He went into the kitchen and never came back. I went looking for him. He's asleep on the couch. This is bad. This is very, very bad. Has Nick ever got up in the middle . . . ?"

"No," Delaney said adamantly. "Never."

"See? I told you. Tuck is not Mr. Right. Mr. Right would not get up in the middle."

"Maybe he's just scared."

"Like I'm not? Now I'm scared and mad."

"So how was it? Before he left in the middle."

"It was great, fantastic, the best ever—that's what's so frustrating," Jillian said, wanting desperately for Delaney to tell her that Tuck absolutely was her destiny and that all she needed was to wait for him to realize they were meant to be.

Instead, Delaney said, "Well, maybe he isn't the one."

"I dreamed about him while wearing the veil."

"Could just be a coincidence."

"I dream about the guy and then I meet him in real life. That doesn't seem like a coincidence. I mean, if anything is fated, it would seem like that would be a clear sign."

"So he is the one?"

She sighed. "I don't know. If he is, he's not cooperating. How did you know for certain Nick was the one? Wedding-veil thing aside. What made you ditch Evan and everything you had planned for Nick?"

"He came after me to stop me from having myself kidnapped at the wedding. He wanted to be the one to kidnap me."

"That is romantic." Jillian sighed.

"You can't compare Nick to your guy. Apples and oranges, Jilly. Tuck's a widower. You have to cut him some extra slack."

"I can't compete with a dead woman, Laney, and I shouldn't have to."

"No, no, you're right."

"I'm going to tell him the sex was all a mistake," Jillian said.

"Was it?"

"Well, he left in the middle, so obviously he thinks so. I'll beat him to the punch. I'll just tell him it was all a huge mistake. I'll blame the blizzard. I'll blame the Baileys…"

In the background, Jillian could hear Nick's low throaty voice whisper something sexy.

"It's okay; it's all right," Jillian said, feeling dismally lonely.

"Jillian, no, this is important. Talk to me. I'm listening. I'm here for you," Delaney reassured her.

"I know that, but just go make love to your husband and give him a hug for me for being the kind of guy who doesn't run away in the middle."

Chapter 20

*D*umbass.

Tuck berated himself. He'd screwed up. Big-time.

He'd been snowed in a lake house mountain cabin for three days with an incredible woman who was his polar opposite in every way. Thing was, he'd just had the best sex of his life, and he felt guilty as sin. He'd loved Aimee with every bit of his heart, but making love to her had never been so...so...*all-consuming.* The way it was with Jillian.

And then he'd gotten up right in the middle of sex last night and just left her lying there. The sex was just too damn good. Impossibly good. Unbelievably good. That's what turned him inside out.

Jillian threw herself into lovemaking like it was a religion. She was fiercely devout. Dishing out wild, no-holds-barred sex with a fervency that stole the breath right out of his lungs. And yet at the same time, she tasted as sweet as cotton candy and as crisp as freshly laundered linen. An erotic combination of sultry-eyed temptress and honey-voiced waif. And the smell of her was all over him. Understated but persistent. Uniquely Jillian.

His Jillian.

Tuck groaned. No, no, he had to stop thinking like this. She wasn't his Jillian. Could never be his Jillian.

Why not? whispered a subversive part of him that wasn't playing by the rules. *Why not?*

He craved her. Ached for her. His body tensed and his mouth watered and he hungered to take her again and again and again. Nothing had ever had hold of him like that.

The bedroom door creaked opened, and he heard her pad into the living room. He should pretend to be asleep again like he'd done last night. It's what a smart man would have done.

But when was the last time he'd done anything smart?

He just lay there, staring at the ceiling, and when her head popped over the top of the couch, their eyes met. Glued.

She said nothing and neither did Tuck, but he was acutely aware of her eyes on his.

A long, uncomfortable pause ensued. The only sound between them was Mutt's doggy breathing as he slumbered on the floor in front of the fireplace.

Finally, Jillian drew in a deep breath. God, even the way she swallowed looked sexy. "How'd you sleep?"

"Fine, fine. You?"

"Peachy." She nodded.

She was lying and they both knew it. He'd heard her thrashing around all night, just as he'd been.

He swung his legs off the couch, sat up.

She sat down where his legs had just been. Her hair was mussed, and the sheet creases on her face shouldn't have made her look cute, but dammit, they did. She stared into the ashes of the spent fire, where a few coals smoldered, and dropped her hands into her lap. She wore the blue silk pajamas she'd worn last night. Even with that rumpled-no-makeup-just-rolled-out-of-bed thing she had going on, Jillian was stunning.

Her cheeks pinked under his scrutiny, and her eyelids lowered heavily. "About last night...," she started, then stopped.

"Yeah?"

"I understand completely why you did what you did."

"You do?" That was amazing because Tuck didn't know why he'd done what he'd done.

"It was a mistake."

"Mistake," he echoed.

"We both know that. We don't want it to ruin our friendship, so let's just pretend it never happened. Okay?"

"Okay."

"That is what you want, right?"

"Yes, yes. If that's what you want too."

She nodded rapidly. "Oh yes, exactly. Big mistake."

"Bad."

"Terrible."

"Worst ever."

They looked at each other and both managed to summon up a weak laugh.

"Promise me it won't ever happen again," she said, "please."

"I promise."

"We won't even speak of it." She folded her arms across her chest and looked resolute.

"Speak of what?"

"There, that's it. Perfect."

Neither one of them said another word. Mutt raised his head and looked at them as if their quietness had awakened him.

Tuck didn't rush to fill the silence, because he had no

idea what to say or how to make things right. He didn't even know if he wanted to make things right. One thing he did know—he couldn't stop visualizing her on his bed, in his arms, her body lithe and supple and naked. Passionate and hungry and alive. And she'd looked at him as if he was the center of her universe; that look had been his undoing. That's what had scared the hell out of him.

Tuck was so damned confused. On the one hand, it was as if she'd been made to order. Rush delivery sex mate. Long, shapely legs. Exotic eyes dark as Swiss chocolate. Raspberry-flavored mouth. Silky ebony hair. A devilish tongue that roused the caveman inside him.

And a sweet, moist, tight feminine box that drove him mad with desire.

He wished like hell he hadn't walked out on her in the middle of sex last night. He wished he could go back and fix it. Part of him wanted to gather her in his arms, haul her back to bed, and start all over again. But another part of him—the cowardly part that had run out on her in the first place—held him back.

"Jillian, I . . . ," he started, but had no idea what else he was going to say. *She regrets it. Let it go. You told her you'd let it go, so let it frickin' go.* He cleared his throat. "Jilly—"

"Shh!" She raised a hand.

"What is it?"

"Listen."

Tuck cocked his head, listening. "I don't hear anything."

"Exactly. No wind."

The blizzard was over.

It took all morning and part of the afternoon for Tuck and Jillian to dig out of the snow, but once they had a path cleared to the road, they donned cross-country skis and took off.

Jillian glided off to Fielder's Market with Mutt for groceries. Tuck headed for Evie's house to corner his brother-in-law. He desperately needed a guy's perspective on this whole situation.

After he'd promised Jillian they wouldn't talk about it again, Tuck thought of a hundred questions he wanted to ask. For instance, had *any* of it been good for her? Because things had been pretty darned fantastic for him until he'd made like Foghorn Leghorn and chickened out.

Maybe he shouldn't have bailed. If he'd stayed in the bed with her last night, maybe he would have gotten her out of his system. As it was, he was totally obsessed with her. Dammit. She was tougher than he was, putting all this behind them. Dusting her hands of their lovemaking as if it never happened.

Grumbling under his breath, Tuck pushed himself faster with the ski poles, not even noticing how appealing the town looked bunked under the snow. He hoped Ridley had beer in the house. He was in the mood to knock back a couple of brews. Never mind that it was only three o'clock in the afternoon. He'd been snowed in with Jillian for three days, and he needed a release.

Aimee, he should think of Aimee. Aimee would help him forget Jillian.

Okay, okay, what did he love most about Aimee?

Tuck wracked his brain, and in that panic-stricken moment, realized he couldn't call up his wife's face. Whenever he tried to imagine Aimee, he saw Jillian. Instead of Aimee's blond locks twining down her back in soft curls, he saw Jillian and her patrician Cleopatra haircut. Black and straight and angled to her shoulders. He tried to remember how Aimee had felt in his arms all soft and round and girly. But instead, his fingers were recalling the touch of Jillian's strong, lithe, athlete body.

Jillian was in his head. Not just in his head but on his skin. He could smell her. Taste her. She'd invaded his senses like a dictator taking over a country.

Thankfully, he'd finally reached Evie and Ridley's house. He kicked off his skis and whammed his fist against their door.

Ridley answered, his hair down around his shoulders, looking comfortable in sweatpants and a red flannel shirt. "Dude," he said. "You look like hell. What happened?"

"What happened?" Tuck said, shouldering past his brother-in-law. "I've been snowed in for three days with Jillian Samuels. That's what happened."

"The plot thickens."

Tuck raked his gaze over Evie. "How'd you guys weather the storm?"

Ridley shut the door behind him. "Your sister and I have been snowed in as well. It started out sketchy. Just before the storm hit, I caught Evie in my sweat lodge. She'd had a vision that really upset her, but then I convinced her the dream was a good omen, not a bad one, and we straightened everything out. If things went as good as I think they did, you might be an uncle in nine months. We stayed in bed the entire three days."

"Aw, come on, man." Tuck clamped his hands over his ears. "I don't want to hear that stuff about my sister."

Ridley grinned. "You're jealous because I got some and you didn't?"

"Well . . . ," Tuck said, trailing off.

"Huh?" Ridley blinked.

Tuck paced the tile floor of their living room in his ski boots. *Clump, clump, clump.* "It was the snow. The fireplace. The Baileys Irish Cream..."

"You and Jillian did it?" Ridley asked.

"Yes."

"Damn."

"What is it? What's wrong? Is it the jinx thing?"

Ridley laughed. "No. I was pretty well off base about the jinx thing. I owe your sister twenty bucks."

"Huh?"

"Evie bet me twenty bucks if you guys got snowed in together you'd end up in bed."

It was Tuck's turn to curse, but he said something a lot stronger than *damn*. "It was a mistake. A huge mistake."

"It was just sex, right? How big a mistake could it be? Unless you forgot to wear a condom."

"I wore a condom." He clenched his jaw and dropped down on the leather love seat. "It's not that."

"You want a beer?"

"Please."

Ridley retrieved the beer, popped the top, and pressed it into Tuck's hand, but after one swallow, Tuck didn't want it. His brother-in-law perched on the hearth, where he sat and just waited.

Tuck started talking. He told him everything. The kissing, the dancing, the watching of *When Harry Met Sally*, the downing of Baileys Irish Cream. The great sex. The really great sex that came after the sex. And the terrible sex where he got up in the middle of things and ran away.

"Wow," Ridley said after he'd finished. "You really screwed up."

"Tell me about it. Thing is, this morning, she wanted to forget all about it. Didn't even want to discuss it."

"Can you blame her?"

Misery crawled through him. He pulled a palm down his face. "What should I do?"

If anyone could help him think of a way through this sticky mess, it was Ridley. His brother-in-law could handle temperamental Evie when no one else on the planet seemed to be able to manage that trick. Tuck valued his opinion and his advice.

"Nothing," Ridley said sagely.

"Nothing?"

"Nothing."

"But I can't stop thinking about her, and I have to live with her, and how can I wake up every morning and see her and go to bed every night in a separate room and not touch her and..."

"Take a deep breath," Ridley advised.

"You, you're the one who caused all this. You put me in your sweat box—"

"Sweat lodge," he interrupted to correct Tuck.

"And you made me have this vision quest I wasn't even interested in having."

"You needed it."

"I have this pervy sex dream about her and then I meet her in the flesh. It's spooky. It's weird. The hairs on my arms go up every time I think about it. Then you tell me she's a jinx and to stay away from her. Then you come back and tell me you were wrong and that she's good for me, and and so I started thinking, maybe, *maybe*..." Tuck was getting light-headed from not pausing to breathe.

"Hey." Ridley shrugged. "I'm as fallible as the next guy."

"You could have told me that *before* I took your advice. Now she's looking at me as if I'm a leper, and I've ruined our friendship to boot."

Ridley got up, came across the room, and clamped a hand on Tuck's shoulder. "You, my friend, have a lot to learn about the fairer sex. I can't believe you were married for three years and never figured this stuff out."

"What do you mean?"

"Jillian's probably feeling exactly the same way you are. Worse maybe. You did get up and leave her in the middle of sex. What's she supposed to think? She's gotta be thinking she repulsed you somehow. So to save face this morning, she comes up with this let's-forget-all-about-it plan."

"You really think so?"

"Sure I do and—hey, are those *hickeys*?"

Tuck slapped a hand over his neck. "None of your business," he mumbled, remembering exactly when Jillian had stamped him with her love bites.

Ridley cocked his head and pretended to pout, but his eyes were twinkling with laughter. "Evie's never given me hickeys."

"Stop feeling jealous. If you want hickeys, ask her for hickeys."

"She says they're trashy."

"Then tell her to give you a hickey where no one can see it."

"Good idea."

"Could we get back to the issue at hand? What am I supposed to do about living with Jillian?"

Ridley pursed his lips and placed his hands on his hips. "Move out, I guess."

His brother-in-law said the words Tuck needed to hear. He knew he needed to hear them, but he still wished Ridley hadn't said it.

"You know, I've never seen you this affected by a woman since Aimee."

"I never…" Tuck paused, unable to believe what he was about to say. "I was torn in two when I lost Aimee. It was like I had my heart ripped out of my chest, but, Rid, when we were dating, I never felt this kind of torment. What Aimee and I had was quiet and calm and tender. This thing with Jillian—"

All teasing humor was gone in his brother-in-law's eyes. "Is true passion. That's why you walked out on her in the middle of sex—she scared the crap out of you."

A chill went straight through his bones. He didn't want to admit it. Didn't want to say it. Didn't want to feel it. He refused to betray Aimee's memory and what they'd shared.

"You were pretty young when you and Aimee got married," Ridley said.

"I loved her."

"I'm not saying you didn't love Aimee. I'm just saying there's more than one kind of love."

"I'm not in love with Jillian," Tuck insisted, but even as he said it, he felt something treacherous tighten his chest.

Ridley started humming 10cc's "I'm Not in Love."

"Knock it off." Tuck scowled.

He was not in love. He couldn't be in love. Aimee had been his soul mate. They'd both known it. You only get one soul mate. Right?

Ridley kept humming.

"I'm not in love," Tuck growled.

He wondered if Jillian believed in soul mates. She'd told him she didn't believe in magic, but what they'd shared last night—until he'd screwed things up—had been pretty damn magical, indeed.

And if he admitted it (which he didn't), then he'd have to confess (which he couldn't) that the sexual magic between them was stronger than what he'd shared with Aimee.

Tuck shoved the thought away. Jillian was just older, more experienced than Aimee had been. She knew tricks his sweet little bride had never dreamed of; that didn't mean anything except sex with Jillian had been great. No, beyond great. It had been...well...*magical*.

Jillian probably didn't think so. She'd been quick to deny it this morning. But what if Ridley was right? What if Jillian had just said those things to save face?

"Tuck?"

"Huh?"

"You might want to set that beer bottle down before you bust it in your hand," Ridley advised.

Tuck blinked at his brother-in-law. He'd zoned out, his mind caught in the past, worrying the dilemma. He'd forgotten he was at Ridley and Evie's house. He looked down and saw his hand was wrapped around the long-neck Michelob bottle so tightly his knuckles had blanched white. He forced himself to relax his grip and settle the bottle onto a coaster resting on the end table.

"You need to tell her."

"Who?"

"Jillian."

"Tell her what?"

"How you really feel."

"I don't know how I feel."

"You do. You just don't want to admit it."

"I'm glad you're so all-wise and all-knowing, Rid. Wanna tell me what I'm thinking right now?"

"You're thinking I should go screw myself."

"See, you *are* all-knowing."

Ridley shook a finger at him. "She got to you."

"I like her, sure. I'm not denying that. We're friends. Or we were. Now I don't know what we are." Longing mixed with despair, then did the tango with an odd combo of hope and resignation.

"Friendship's a great way to start a relationship."

"We didn't start out as friends. We started out as two people forced to share a space."

"No one forced you. You could have left the lake house at any time. You could have moved in with me and Evie. You had options. But you didn't choose to exercise them. There's a reason you didn't leave. Why?"

"I don't know, but whatever the reason, I can't stay there now."

"Granted. Not with the way you left things."

"We can't go back to being friends," he mused. "No matter how much we both might want to pretend this never happened. Harry was right."

"Harry? Who's Harry?"

"When Harry Met Sally."

"Oh right, I agree with Harry. You can't stay there and go back to the way things were. So make a move. Either take it a step further and embrace the sex, or forget the friendship and give up the lake house. The deed has never shown up anyway. Just let it all go."

"It means letting go of Aimee," Tuck whispered.

Ridley's eyes were kind. "I know."

Leave or stay? Did he want to embrace the sex? Yes. He wanted it a lot. Jillian had reconnected Tuck with the part of himself that had stopped living the day Aimee had died, but was he really ready for such a huge step? On the other hand, was he ready to walk away from Salvation? Say good-bye to his memories? Was he ready to let Aimee go?

"Whichever one you choose, just quit ruminating about it. You're driving me nutty. We're sitting here after a break in the blizzard gabbing like girls when we should be outside getting stuff done while the sun's shining. Pathetic."

Just then the phone rang.

"Good to see we still have communication with the outside world," Ridley said, and picked up the phone. "Hello?"

Tuck took a swallow of the beer he didn't want.

"It's for you." Ridley handed the phone to him.

"Jillian?" he asked stupidly, nonsensically. There was no reason for her to call him here.

"Steve."

"Steve?"

Ridley handed him the phone. Tuck put it to his ear.

"Yo, my man," Steve said. "I finally got through. We've been trying to call you guys for days. Rang your house first, got no answer, thought you might be here."

"Blizzard just broke, cabin fever," Tuck explained.

"Everyone good?"

"We made it through all right."

"Good. Listen, I've got some great news for you about that music box."

"Yeah?"

"I showed it to my friend, but it wasn't something he handled, so he passed it off to a dealer who specializes in handmade curios. She displayed it in her shop. Customers went nuts over the box. I knew they would. Anyway, she received offers upward of twelve hundred dollars."

Tuck was stunned. "For a music box?"

"There's no substitute for craftsmanship. The dealer said it was like everyone who picked it up fell under its spell. Get this, she took orders."

"On my behalf?" Tuck didn't know if he liked that or not.

"For customized boxes."

"Before asking my permission?"

"Don't get mad. She got thirty-five special orders at twelve hundred dollars a piece. She hasn't taken any money. She told them she didn't know if the artist could deliver that quickly, so you're not obligated. I'm telling you, that music box is bewitched. The Magic Man rides again."

"Huh?" Tuck couldn't believe it.

"Listen, here's the best part. Stella Bagby—that's the dealer's name—is going overseas for the winter. She's willing to let you stay in her place in Midtown while you make the boxes and she's scouting out wholesale deals for the wood to maximize your profits."

"You want me to come back to Manhattan?"

"Just for the winter. Just until you get this new business established."

"You've put in a lot of effort on my behalf."

"Hey, you gave me a job when I sorely needed one. Plus, Desiree and the kids would love to have you so close. We miss you. Ridley and Evie have had you long enough."

"I'll think about it."

"Just let me know soon. Stella wants to sublet if you're not interested, and she leaves for Europe next week."

"That's not much time."

"The stars are aligned; it's time to make a move."

"Yeah. Thanks, Steve."

"Don't mention it. Either way, you're coming up for Christmas with Evie and Ridley, right?"

"Right."

"You bringing Jillian?"

"No."

"Ah, that's a shame. Des and I really liked her."

Me too. "Listen," he said. "I gotta go. Lots of postblizzard things to do."

"Don't leave me hanging too long."

"I'll call you tomorrow."

"Bye." Steve hung up.

"Crossroads," Ridley said as Tuck handed the phone back to him.

"Yeah." He felt stunned, overwhelmed. One minute he was talking to Ridley about moving out and just giving Jillian the lake house, and then suddenly there was this opportunity to move back to Manhattan and start his old life all over again.

"Inevitable and necessary," Ridley said cryptically.

"Huh?"

"It's part of the vision quest."

"What is?"

"The crossroads. Which way are you going to go? Who are you going to be? The decision is now, my friend."

"I'm not ready."

"Doesn't matter. The universe is ready for you to commit. One path or the other. New York or Salvation. Hold on to the past or embrace the future. The choice is yours."

Tuck sank down in the kitchen chair, his head spinning.

Just as quickly as he'd turn cosmic, Ridley was back to his practical, laid-back self. He walked to the coat rack, took down his parka, and shrugged into it. "I'm going out to chop firewood. You coming or are you getting your period?"

"Asshole." Tuck grinned.

Ridley cheerfully flipped him the bird and headed out the back door.

Tuck realized that he had firewood of his own that needed chopping. He trooped out the back door behind Ridley and snapped his skis back on, his thoughts on Jillian. He had an option now. A place to go if he left Salvation. But what was he going to do about his feelings for Jillian?

She was so different from Aimee. The two women were night and day and not just in their appearance.

Aimee had loved cooking and sewing and housekeeping. A homebody. An earth mother. She didn't have strong opinions except in regard to her father and his infidelity that had wrecked their family, and she rarely offered her advice or input. Decision making put her in a dither.

It used to drive him crazy when he'd ask her where she wanted to go for dinner and she'd shrug and say, "Wherever you want to go." It was as if she was defined only by him and his work. When they were married, he'd thought it was great. Thinking back, it felt one-sided. He'd been in charge of their marriage, and Aimee had been along for the ride. Look up *agreeable* in the dictionary and the description fit Aimee to a T.

Jillian had no interest in domestic chores. She did what had to be done in the housekeeping realm, but that was it. She had a dazzling, brilliant mind, and she wasn't afraid to use it. She had so many opinions she could open an Opinions R' Us franchise. Jillian would never allow herself to be defined by any man, and he admired the hell out of her for having her own life, her own will. If he was told to pick one word to describe her, he couldn't do it, although *gumption* would be on the list, along with *strong, argumentative, bold,* and *sexy.*

Aimee had never ruffled his feathers. Jillian stimulated him in a hundred different ways. Some good, some irritating, none of them boring.

But was he ready for anything more than friendship and sex? Could he really put his heart on the line again? He was terrified that he could not.

And that was the deal. Jillian deserved someone who could give her his full love. Without reservation or hesitation. The fact he was hesitating said it all.

It was time to let go and walk away.

Manhattan was calling.

Chapter 21

Two days after the town dug out from the storm, Jillian came in the back door from work, set her briefcase on the kitchen table, and doffed her knit cap and gloves. "Hey, Tuck," she called out. "You'll never guess what happened today..."

Her words trailed off as she caught sight of him standing in the doorway, two big leather suitcases gripped in his hands.

"Tuck?" she asked tentatively. At the same time, it felt as if someone had smacked her in the back of the head with a two-by-four. "What's up?"

But she didn't have to ask. The look on his face, the set to his shoulders, she just *knew*.

"I'm moving out, Jillian." He set down the suitcases.

"Oh," she whispered, and felt something inside of her slide sideways. Things had been odd between them the past few days, but she'd put that down to the awkwardness of what had happened during the snowstorm. They still hadn't talked about it. She thought at some point they'd discuss it, define the new direction of their relationship. She'd been stepping back, giving him time. But clearly, there would be no talking. Tuck was moving out.

Her first impulse was to plead with him not to go, to ask what she'd done wrong, to promise to change. But, of course, she did not do any of those things. She was the Ice Queen, the bulldog, the tough competent lawyer who never showed her tender side. She didn't whimper. She didn't beg. She wouldn't change simply to please a man.

Jillian pressed her lips together and took the hit. "I see."

They stared at each other.

"Where are you going?" she finally asked, her chest tightening. She was having trouble catching her breath.

"I have a place to stay in Manhattan."

"Manhattan?" She tried to keep her voice controlled. Not only was he moving out, but he was also moving away. She wouldn't see him again.

"You were right all along."

She moistened her lips with her tongue. Her throat felt parched. "I was?"

"I've been hiding out. It's time to start living again. I have a job making music boxes like the one I made for Evie."

"Oh," she repeated, and then said inanely, "It is a beautiful music box."

He shifted, his gaze never leaving her face, but he said nothing.

"Um, what about the lake house?"

"The deed's never going to turn up. Obviously Sutter lost it. Besides, Blake wanted you to have the house. I was being stubborn insisting on staying here. I realize that now. The place is yours, Jillian." His eyes clouded. "I...I want you to have it."

"Tuck..." She stopped, swallowed, tasted salt. "I'm the

one who's been stubborn. This is your home; you lived here with your wife. I'm the interloper. The outsider. I should be the one to leave."

He shook his head. "You need this place, Jillian. It's given you a new start. Soon you'll take the bar exam, and I know you'll pass it. Then you'll eventually take over Sutter's law practice. Me?" He shrugged. "This house, the past, has been holding me back, keeping me from moving on with my life, and I wasn't able to see that until you showed up."

Sorrow jolted her straight to her soul. He was telling her that she'd given him the strength to leave. It served her right for daring to hope.

She'd known better. People always betrayed you or left you. Her mother had dumped her on her father's doorstep and run away. Then her father had died, leaving her to a bitter woman who resented having to raise her husband's illegitimate daughter. And, of course, there was Alex Fredericks, who'd betrayed her as well. Even her best friends had moved on with their lives, leaving her behind.

"I'm catching an early morning flight to New York."

"What's the rush?" she asked, cringing inwardly, terrified he could hear the sadness in her voice. Purposefully she shrugged, acting as if she didn't care. "I mean, it's trivia night at the Rusty Nail. We're supposed to play against Lexi and Jefferson, remember?"

"If I don't make it to New York by tomorrow, the woman's going to sublet her place to someone else. She's leaving for Europe and has to have the place rented before she takes off."

She hitched in a breath. "So this is good-bye?"

He nodded. "I just took Mutt out for a walk. He loves the snow."

"That he does."

Silence stretched between them.

"Mutt's another reason for you to keep the lake house." His eyes were all over her face, and she realized she hadn't broken his gaze either.

"So you already said good-bye to Mutt?"

"Yeah." His Adam's apple bobbed. "Brought him a juicy soup bone from the Bluebird. He's in the living room in front of the fire gnawing it up." His smile was slight.

"Thanks," she said, because she didn't know what else to say.

Finally, Tuck tore his gaze from hers and bent to pick up his suitcases, then paused. "For what it's worth?"

"Yes?" Her heart quickened. What was he going to say?

"The town pool betting on when you'd leave?"

"Yes?"

"I had today's date in the pot. Ironic, huh?"

"There goes your ten bucks." She struggled hard to keep her face neutral. She wasn't about to let him know how much she was hurting.

A horn honked outside.

"That's Ridley. He's driving me to the airport in Denver."

She nodded.

"Take care of yourself, Jillian." He looked wistful, but she refused to let it get to her.

"You too, Tuck."

"We still friends, Sally?"

"Friends," she echoed, but she knew it was a lie. They could never go back to being just friends.

Tuck stepped toward her and gave her a quick kiss on her cheek. A nice kiss. A friendly kiss. She wanted to slug him for it.

"Take care of yourself." Then without another word, he turned and walked out the door.

Jillian let him go. What else could she do? She stumbled to the living room and plunked down on the couch. The room was cold, but she was too depressed to get up and poke the embers, to add wood to the fire. Mutt, sensing her mood, came over and stuck his head in her lap. She reached out to scratch his ears. He whined his sympathy and she just broke.

The woman who never cried sat on the couch, thick tears rolling down her cheeks. She'd never had a feeling like this. Her friends had told her it was a good feeling, a wonderful feeling, but to Jillian it was pure torture.

She'd been denying it, avoiding it, pretending they were just friends, but after last night, she knew she was lying to herself. She was stone cold in love with Tuck Manning, and he wasn't able to love her back.

Two weeks after Tuck moved to Manhattan, Jillian sat on a barstool at the Bluebird, elbows on the counter, her chin propped morosely in her palms, trying her best not to think about how empty her life was now that he'd gone or how much she missed him. But it was particularly difficult when she kept picturing him totally naked, stretched out on the bed, head propped in his hand and him winking provocatively at her.

Why couldn't she get that damned man out of her head?

She clenched her teeth and pushed the cold scrambled eggs she'd ordered but didn't possess the enthusiasm to eat around on her plate. The Bluebird was decorated for Christmas, tree in the corner, lights strung around the room, pine boughs and holly and mistletoe above the door.

Hands down, Tuck was the best lover she'd ever had, bar none. She doubted there was a better lover on the planet. At least for her. It seemed he'd known without her having to tell him exactly what she needed and when she needed it. Until the unpleasant part where he'd abandoned her in the middle.

And even as they were digging out of the snow and purposefully not discussing how they were feeling, Jillian had quelled an overwhelming urge to throw herself into his arms and tell him she wanted so much more than either sex or friendship.

She wanted the kind of love he'd had with Aimee. And then he'd just packed up and moved to New York without any notice after they'd made love. Every time she thought about it, she got a painful catch in the dead center of her chest.

"You can't ever replace Aimee in his eyes," she muttered under her breath. "There's no point in trying."

So many people had abandoned her in one way or another. She'd learned that she could not depend on anyone. There was no guide, no teacher, no authority that could save her. There was only herself.

She'd spent her life holding her feelings in reserve, afraid to trust, terrified that she'd be abandoned again if she dared to give away her heart. She realized now that she'd displaced her emotions into her career. She'd used her loyalty to law as a way to avoid false starts and stops in her personal life.

But when she lost Blake and quit her job, she found something else. Salvation. That's what she had to remember. The lake house, the town, the people. She'd survive without Tuck.

Now if only she could stop thinking about him.

Snap out of it. Focus on something else. Think about studying for the bar.

But the test seemed so far away. The lonely winter loomed long.

Evie came over. "Mind if I sit down?"

"Not at all."

Evie came around from the other side of the counter and plunked down on the barstool next to her. "Eggs that bad?"

Jillian shook her head. "It's not the food. It's me."

"I'm sorry about Tuck moving to Manhattan. I miss him too. I thought you guys were working on something."

She shrugged. "Hey, it wasn't meant to be."

Evie patted her hand.

"How are you and Ridley doing?" Jillian asked, eager to get the subject off her and Tuck. "Any news on the baby front?"

To her alarm, Evie's eyes misted with tears.

"What is it? What's wrong?"

Evie clenched her jaw. "I've been putting on a brave face, but"—she swallowed—"during the storm, I went and did this vision quest thing, and I got a bad omen. Ridley says it's a good omen, but I don't believe him. I think he was just trying to placate me."

"Vision quest? What are you talking about?"

Evie explained what a vision quest was and detailed what she'd seen.

"You know, I really don't believe in that sort of thing, Evie."

"I didn't either, but when Tuck..." Evie bit down on her bottom lip.

"When Tuck what?"

"On the second anniversary of Aimee's death, Ridley stuck Tuck in the sweat lodge and he had a vision."

"Good vision or bad vision?"

"It was about you."

"Really? What did he see?"

"You'll have to ask Tuck; he didn't talk to me about it. I got all this secondhand from Ridley."

"So this vision you had," Jillian said, switching the focus back to Evie. "What was the omen?"

"I'll probably never have kids, and I want them so badly. The thing is, it's affecting our marriage. Ridley tries and he's Mr. Optimistic, but, Jillian, I'm scared we won't survive this." A tear slipped down her cheek.

"Come on, you guys really love each other. You can work this out. Can't you?"

"I don't know if love is enough. I've tried to keep the faith but..." Evie swallowed visibly as the tears streamed faster down her face. "I got my period. I was so hoping that this month—this time—after all the love we made during the blizzard...but it's just not going to happen. Faith isn't going to change reality. Babies just aren't in the cards for us."

Evie's distress stilled Jillian's heart. She wasn't a big believer in the power of love in the first place, but to think that a couple as strong as Evie and Ridley couldn't overcome their problems confirmed every negative thing she'd ever believed about love.

"I'm sorry. So there's no hope left?"

Evie wiped at her eyes, tried to smile but failed miserably. "We're going to New York to spend Christmas with my sister Desiree and her family. I have an appointment with a celebrity fertility specialist. He helps movie stars in their fifties have babies. It's gonna cost us a big chunk of our savings, but I'm desperate. If this doesn't work..." She let her words trail off again.

"I wish you the best of luck."

At that moment, the bell over the door jangled. Bill Chambers and his fiancée Lily Massey came in, bundled in snowsuits and gazing romantically into each other's eyes. Jillian felt a twinge—part jealousy, part longing, part concern for Lily, who'd torn up her prenup agreement for this man. She had no legal protection now; she was banking her future on love.

"Jillian, hi!" Lily called out, and scurried across the room toward her, Bill following in her wake. "I've been looking all over for you."

"What's up?"

"We just wanted to give you this." Lily placed a white linen card in her hand. "An official invitation to our wedding on Christmas Eve. You're still planning on coming, right?"

Why not? It wasn't like she had anywhere else to go. "Sure."

"Evie and Ridley are bailing on us." Lily gave a pretend pout.

"Family thing," Evie said.

"We understand," Bill interjected.

"But we're sooo going to miss you," Lily said with her native California inflection.

The door opened again. Lexi and Jefferson came in laughing over some shared joke. Jillian had to admit they were a good-looking couple. Over the past few weeks, Lexi had been giving her daily updates on their romance. Apparently, things were hot and heavy.

She was in the midst of a love-a-thon.

Lexi and Jefferson came over and started chatting with Lily and Bill about the wedding. Evie got up and went back to work. Jillian felt like a fifth wheel. She was about to leave when Lexi leaned over to whispered, "How you holding up?"

"Fine, fine, why wouldn't I be?"

"I know how much you're missing Tuck. I can imagine how I'd feel if Jefferson was in New York and I was stuck here."

Jillian waved a hand. "Please, I'm fine."

Lexi looked skeptical. "Are you sure? 'Cause if you want a girls night out, just you and me closing down the Rusty Nail, say the word. I'm there for you."

Jillian shook her head.

The bell over the door jangled a third time. Everyone looked over to see Sutter Godfrey cross the threshold, leaning heavily on his cane but out of his wheelchair. The entire café clapped. "Way to walk it, Sutter," Dutch called from the kitchen.

Sutter waved away the accolades. His eyes met Jillian's. "Ah," he said. "Just the lady I wanted to see."

While Sutter was dragging Jillian into the back room for a private conversation, Tuck was walking up 42nd Street. He'd been in Manhattan for two weeks and he'd yet to pick up a carving tool. He hadn't been able to work. The city noises kept him up at night. In the day, he'd stare out the window at the building across from him, seeing in his mind's eye Salvation Lake surrounded by the Rocky Mountains.

He tried to work, but his creativity fled. The wood felt cold, dead in his hands. He'd stare at the wood, willing inspiration, but nothing happened.

Stella Bagby's apartment was spacious by New York standards and was only three blocks from the hustle and bustle of Time's Square. The city was alive, dusted with snow, Christmas lights winking, people carrying brightly colored shopping bags. He used to love it here. The energy, the urgency, the audacity of the best city in the world.

But the Big Apple was no longer in his blood. His pulse didn't skip, his breathing didn't quicken, his mind didn't rev as he took it all in. His heart was still in Colorado.

He knew he looked out of place in his flannel, jeans, and work boots, but he didn't care. He walked at a Colorado pace, people zipping around him. He turned up Broadway, entered the throng of Times Square. He looked up at a theater marquis and saw to his surprise there was a revival of *Les Miserables*. Immediately he thought of Jillian.

It was their favorite musical.

His chest tightened. He glanced at his watch. The matinee started in fifteen minutes.

He imagined Jillian with him. He pictured them snuggled together in the balcony seating, whispering the lines to each other; they both knew the story so well. He wished he could share this with her.

"For old time's sake," he murmured, then walked up to the booth and bought a ticket.

While Tuck was walking into *Les Miserables*, Jillian was sitting down across from Sutter in the back room of the Bluebird.

"What did you want to see me about?" she asked.

"I found this in a desk drawer at my home office," he said, pulling a manila envelope from the inside of his jacket and sliding it across the table to Jillian.

"You have a home office?"

"Didn't I mention that?" His eyes twinkled.

"No, you didn't."

"You've been doing a good job, and I thought it was time to give you this," he said as she removed the rubber band he'd wrapped around the envelope.

A bonus? she wondered. Or maybe he'd drawn up papers to make her his partner. Her pulse accelerated.

"I've been getting community reports. Everyone likes you. Business has picked up, which I'm sure you know. Smart of me to hire you."

She didn't mention that it had been her idea. She slit open the envelope with her finger, slid out the paper inside. Her breath hung in her lungs when she saw what it was.

The deed to the lake house. Made out to Tuck.

She looked up to meet his gaze. "You found it."

"I never lost it." His eyes were sharp. The old man was not a fool.

"You had it all along. But why—"

"There's a letter inside that envelope too." He nodded. "I think you should read it now."

She found the letter and opened it with trembling fingers. Even before she saw the familiar handwriting, she knew who it was from, and hot tears caught in the back of her throat.

My dearest Jillian,

I write this letter to you after having just received news that I have an inoperable brain tumor. At most, I have six months to live. You won't be reading this until after my death, but I ask you, my dear friend, please don't grieve. I'm with my darling Aimee now. I couldn't do right by her in life, but I feel with all my heart that in death we will be reunited.

You and I never talked about faith, and until I lost my daughter, I'm not sure I had much. I made many mistakes, hurt many people. But you were the one shining star in my screwed up world. I turned you into my surrogate daughter, and I loved you like a father.

I worry about you, Jillian. You've got such an emotional wall up. It's necessary in our profession to detach, to distance ourselves from the ugly world we deal in, but you've carried it too far. Whenever you do get involved with men, it's those wretched types like Alex Fredericks. I know you're afraid to take a chance on an honest, kind man you could really love. I don't want you to make the same mistakes I made. I want you to be able to love freely, wholeheartedly, without reservation or hesitation. To that end, I must confess to a bit of subterfuge, and my old friend Sutter has agreed to play along.

Right after Aimee died, I had Hamilton Green draw up a will giving you the lake house. It was always my intention for you to have the place, but I figured that day would be a long time off. Today, the oncologist told me differently.

Even though you didn't bring your problems to me, I knew you were having a crisis of conscience over your affair with Fredericks. I also knew Tuck was grieving too hard and too long for Aimee. Maybe I shouldn't have let him stay in the lake house. Maybe if I'd pushed him, he would have started healing faster.

It doesn't matter. What does matter is that I realized you two were perfect for each other if you could only see it. Tuck is a good and honest man. You are a smart, strong woman who deserves to be loved.

Therefore, I'm deeding the house to Tuck, but

I'm having Sutter "forget" to file the deed and then "lose" it. My hope with this little beyond-the-grave matchmaking is that Tuck will fight to stay in the house because of his ties to Aimee and you'll fight to keep it because you have nowhere else to go.

Yes, I knew Newsom was going to appoint Fredericks to take my place, and I knew the egotistical bastard would accept. I also knew he'd try to force you to knuckle under and that you had too much integrity to take it. I hope you can forgive me if I've caused you any distress. That was never my intention. The lake house is your life preserver, and Tuck can be your anchor if you can learn to see your way clear to each other.

But even if it doesn't work out between you two, I do know that you have found your way to Salvation.

With all my endearing love,
Blake

During intermission, Tuck wandered out into the lobby, his mind still on Jillian. He'd barely even noticed the actors on the stage.

A group of young tween girls were chatting avidly about the musical, but Tuck didn't pay much attention to them—that is, until he heard a familiar voice urging the girls to hurry and down their refreshments before the curtain went up on the final act.

His head jerked up, and he glanced over to see Aimee's mother, Margery, ushering her charges toward their seats. Their eyes met.

"Tuck," she said, and broke into an instant smile. "I didn't know you were back in Manhattan. Why didn't you give me a call?"

Without even knowing he was going to say it, Tuck said, "I...I don't know what I'm doing here, Margery."

She looked around him. "You're alone?"

"Yes."

"Girls, go on back to your seats. I'll be with you in a minute."

Giggling, the girls took off.

"Sorry," Margery said, drawing closer to him. "Field trip."

"You're still teaching at Andover?"

"In a Manning building," she said, referring to the classrooms he'd built in Albany. "I'm so happy you're back. You've been grieving too long. It's time to share your gift with the world again."

They stood in awkward silence, theater patrons pushing past them, headed back to the auditorium. She took his elbow and pulled him out of the flow of traffic.

"I miss her, Margery."

"I know you do, Tuck. I miss her, too, but you've got to move on. Are you dating anyone?"

He thought of Jillian, shook his head.

"Why not?"

"There was someone," he said. "But I blew it. I..."

She squeezed his forearm. "Are you in love with this woman?"

Miserably, he nodded. "I tried not to fall in love with her. I felt like I was cheating on Aimee. I came to the city. I wanted to start over, but..." He swept his hand at the theater. "I came here because she loves *Les Miz* like I do. I didn't know they were having a revival."

"Aimee hated *Les Miz*," Margery said. "She hated musicals. Loved plays, though."

"I know."

Another awkward pause.

"Look, Tuck. You're only thirty. You can spend the rest of your life grieving. If you've found someone, embrace it. Aimee would understand. If the roles were reversed, you'd want her to find love again, wouldn't you?"

"Yes, yes, sure."

"Okay, then." Margery smiled softly. "I've got to get back to my girls, and you need to get back to...what's her name?"

"Jillian Samuels."

"Oh." She sounded surprised. "Blake's surrogate daughter?"

"You know about Jillian?"

Margery nodded. "I suppose there's a kind of poetic justice to it."

"You're not angry?"

"Honey," Margery said, "when you get to be my age, you realize how truly rare unconditional love is, and when you can find it, you grab it with both hands. You have my blessings, and I believe you have Aimee's as well."

Tuck went back into the theater for the last act, but he couldn't concentrate on the story. All he could do was think of Jillian and how damned much he missed her. Margery was right. He was wrong.

How had he been so blind as to throw away love? It was such a rare and precious thing. He'd been damned lucky to have a second chance at it, and he'd just walked away.

Proud, stubborn, scared.

Yeah. he was scared. That's why he'd run. Terrified that if he dared love Jillian, he'd lose her the way he lost Aimee.

So what are you going to do about it? Stay here

cowering or do something to show Jillian how much you love her?

Once the thought popped into his head, Tuck knew exactly what he had to do before he could return to her. He jumped up and ran from the theater, his heart pounding with hope.

Tuck ran down the street, dodging foot traffic, bent on finding a store that sold the highest grade mahogany in town.

Three days before Christmas, as they were waiting in the lobby of the expensive, hot-shot Fifth Avenue fertility specialist's office, Ridley opened the sack containing Evie's Christmas present. He felt compelled to give it to her here, and Ridley was not a man who ignored his instincts.

She was leafing through a baby magazine and paused to look over at him. "Are you finally going to tell me what you've got in the bag?"

"It's the reason Tuck's in New York."

"What?" She put down the magazine.

"I asked Tuck to make it for your Christmas present. Steve saw it when they came over for Thanksgiving and insisted on showing it to some art dealers in town. They went ape over it, and now Tuck's been commissioned to make a boatload of them. That's why he came back to Manhattan. The magic is back. What's in the box is bedazzling people the way his classrooms did."

"And you're just now telling me this?"

"I didn't want to ruin the surprise." Ridley took the music box wrapped in green foil from the sack and passed it to her. "Open it."

Evie eyed her husband, wondering what in the world was going on. Things had been up and down with them, mainly because her emotions had been on a roller coaster.

Ridley rolled with the punches, but sometimes he'd escape to the sweat lodge, and then she'd feel guilty for running him off with her fears.

"Babe, I just want you to know that whatever happens in there"—he nodded toward the doctor's office door—"I love you and I'm behind you one hundred percent."

"Thank you. That means the world to me."

He squeezed her hand. "Open the package."

A sweet, unexpected giddiness enveloped her, and she realized it had been a long time since she'd felt truly happy. She felt it now, in the squeeze of her husband's hand.

Evie undid the bow, lifted up the tape, slid the foil wrapping off. She opened the lid, and when she spied the cradle, her heart flip-flopped. "Oh my. This is so beautiful."

She lifted out the music box, watched the cradle rock. The carvings were intricate, delicate, sublime. "Tuck did this?"

Ridley nodded. "Your brother is an artist. He shouldn't be wasting his time making cabinets for tract homes. Steve feels the same way. It's why he brought him back to New York."

She opened the music box, and it began to play "Faith." Several people in the waiting room looked over at them.

"You gotta have faith, babe," Ridley whispered. "Faith in us. Faith in me. Faith in the baby who's coming our way."

Her nose clogged with tears. "Oh, Ridley, you're the best husband any woman could ask for."

"Mrs. Red Deer?" called the office nurse, dressed in cool, sage green scrubs, from the doorway. "We're ready for you now."

She handed the music box back to Ridley, and he stowed it in the sack. It was still playing "Faith," as the nurse led them to the examination room.

The nurse asked Ridley to wait in the hallway while Evie got undressed and the nurse put her legs in the stir-rups, covered her with a sheet, and let Ridley come into the room. He perched his big body on the thin-legged chair beside the examination table. Evie saw on his face that he was as worried as she.

"It's gonna be okay. We've got each other."

She nodded.

The door opened. The specialist came in. He intro-duced himself. Shook Ridley's hand. Then all business, he donned gloves, sat on the rolling stool, and went down at the end of the table to perform a pelvic exam on Evie while he questioned them about their fertility status.

Evie told him everything they'd tried. "We're desper-ate, Doctor," she admitted. "You're our last hope."

The specialist finished the exam, put the sheet back in place, snapped off the rubber gloves, and stood up. "I'm sorry, Mrs. Red Deer. I can't help you."

Despair unlike anything she'd ever felt swallowed Evie up whole. It was over. The dream she'd dared to dream. The vision quest was right. She had no eggs left in her bas-ket. From the sack on the floor, the music box dinged one lone note of "Faith" and then fell silent.

Where the hell did faith get you? Sorrow stomped on her soul.

Ridley got to his feet, hands clenched at his sides. "Why not? What's wrong? Why can't you help us have a baby?"

"Because." The doctor's eyes met Evie's and he smiled. "You're already pregnant."

Chapter 22

On Christmas Eve, it took every ounce of courage Jillian possessed to drive herself up to Thunder Mountain for Bill and Lily's wedding. But once she was there, she had to admit it was a beautiful location for the ceremony, and it was the perfect time of year to get married at a ski resort.

The lights were beautiful, the decorations festive. Lily was breathtaking in her white floor-length wedding dress, carrying a bouquet of white calla lilies as her father escorted her down the aisle of the intimate chapel.

Then Jillian looked up and saw him.

Tuck.

She rubbed her eyes, sure it was a mirage, but no. There was Tuck in what looked like the tux he wore on the cover of *Architectural Digest*. The Magic Man of Manhattan. He must have gotten her message that Sutter had found the lake house deed.

This is just like *When Harry Met Sally*, she thought absurdly. Except in *When Harry Met Sally*, they got together in the end. She was holding out no such hope for herself and Tuck.

Most of the town of Salvation was at the reception that followed. Evie and Ridley were there as well, Ridley strutting like the proud papa-to-be that he was. They'd celebrated Christmas early with Evie's family, then flown home to break the good news of Evie's pregnancy to Ridley's folks and the rest of Salvation.

Jillian ended up seated at a table with Sutter Godfrey and his wife. The meal was pleasant. She ate without tasting it. The tables were cleared, the band started playing, and the bride and groom had their first dance. She hadn't spotted Tuck in the crowded dining room, and she was wondering if he'd already left when her cell phone rang. She took it out of her purse.

Sutter frowned at her. "It's bad manners to take a cell phone call at the table."

"You're right," she said, and got up to walk toward the alcove.

That's when she saw him and lost her breath. "Hello," she whispered into the cell phone, her eyes on tuxedoed Tuck with his cell phone to his ear.

"Hello, Sally," he said.

Her heart fluttered. "Why, hi there, Harry."

"You're looking quite beautiful."

"Not so shabby yourself. You clean up quite nicely." She walked toward him.

His grin reeled her in.

She shut her phone.

He held out his hand. "Care to dance?"

She was going to tell him no; she meant to tell him no, but then the band started playing "Do You Believe in Magic?" and she just said, "I'd love to."

Tuck swept her onto the dance floor, his hand wrapped securely around her waist.

"I had no idea you were such a good dancer, Magic Man."

"You're not so bad yourself, Queenie."

"Did you slip the band a twenty to play this song?"

"It was a hundred."

"Big spender."

He spun her around the floor, then pulled her up close against him. "Nothing's too good for my girl."

"Your girl? Since when am I your girl?"

"Can we go somewhere and talk?"

Oh, how she wanted to hope. But she was so scared, so afraid to take that leap of faith.

"Please," he said. "I have a special Christmas present just for you."

"I don't know." She hesitated. "You did a number on me before."

He looked contrite. "Come on, Sally. Harry admits he behaved like a complete putz."

"Putz is putting it nicely," she said.

"Okay, I acted like a jerk."

"Just a jerk?"

"An ass. I was an ass."

She nodded. "True enough. What happened to your big career in Manhattan?"

"Mistake."

"How do you know this isn't the mistake?"

His eyes darkened. "Being with you was never a mistake."

"Coulda fooled me," she said lightly, but her heart was strumming. "The way you ran out of the bedroom on me that night during the blizzard."

"Forget putz, forget jerk, forget ass. I was a total chicken-shit tool."

"Mmm-hmm."

"I was scared, Jillian."

"And I wasn't?"

"You're gonna make me work for this, aren't you?"

"No one appreciates that which comes easily," she teased.

"Then you, Queenie, are supremely appreciated."

"That's all I needed to hear." She wrapped her arms around his neck, and he bent to kiss her. The minute their lips touched, she burst into flames of sexual delight. No way could she drag this out, even if she was having fun sassing him. All she wanted was to make love to him again.

"You know," he said, "they're giving sleigh rides around the resort."

"Really?"

"That sound like something you'd be interested in?"

"I might be persuaded."

Tuck escorted her out of the reception hall and led her outside, where the horse-drawn sleighs were waiting along with wool blankets and complimentary wassail. A valet also handed Tuck a box wrapped with silver paper and a bright blue foil bow.

Once they were away from the hubbub of the wedding celebration, he handed it to Jillian. "Your Christmas present."

"I...I didn't get you anything."

"You danced with me. You're on the sleigh with me. You're hearing me out. Those are the only gifts I need."

Sleigh bells on the horse jingled. The air smelled of snow and pinecones. The heat from Jillian's body warmed him from the outside in.

"Tuck..."

"Go ahead. Open it."

She unwrapped the package, took the lid off the box, and sucked in her breath.

"I made it myself," he said.

"Oh, Tuck." Tears shone in her eyes as she took the tackle box, made from mahogany wood but painted pink with yellow daisies stenciled on it. Just like the tackle box her daddy had given her.

"Undo the clasps."

She opened the metal clasps, and when she lifted the lid, it started to play "Do You Believe in Magic?" "A music box tackle box?"

"Do you like it?"

She wiped away her tears with the back of her hand.

"Jillian?" Sudden panic clutched him. She was trembling, and he was terrified she felt cornered. It was the last thing Tuck wanted to make her feel.

"It's the most wonderful present I've ever gotten," she sobbed. "Oh dammit, Tuck, you've made me bawl."

He pulled a clean tissue from his pocket and passed it to her. She dabbed at her eyes. "What's this all about? What happened? What changed?"

"After we made love and I ran out on you—because I couldn't deal with the depth of my feelings—I understood you were right that day when you accused me of being an underachiever. I had used Aimee's illness as an excuse to escape my sudden celebrity. I realized that I had to face my past and deal with it before I could come to you free and ready to love again."

"And?"

He took her hand in his, squeezed it tight. "I tried to forget you. I fought to deny we were fated. I told myself it wasn't logical. I'd already had my one great romance, and lightning doesn't strike twice, but, Jillian, it did. It has."

"What are you saying, Tuck?"

"I had a vision of you," he admitted. "In a dream. In Ridley's sweat lodge. Long before we ever met."

Jillian's eyes widened. He was confessing it to her.

"It sounds stupid now, hearing myself saying it, but it's true. It was the night of the second anniversary of Aimee's death, and I was torn up."

He told her then what happened. How he'd fallen into the lake. How Ridley had rescued him and shoved him freezing wet into the sweat lodge and made him get naked and breathe smoke and take a vision quest.

"I saw you first in the dream and then we met," he said.

Tuck was afraid she was going to tell him he was nuts. Terrified she was going to tell the driver to stop the sleigh and walk off without him. Especially when he saw her trembling. He'd made a big mistake. He shouldn't have told her any of this. It was crazy; he knew it sounded nuts, but it was the truth, and he needed her to know why he felt the way he did.

"Jillian." He reached out to touch her shoulder. "Am I freaking you out?"

She shook her head and smiled at him through the mist of tears. Her lips parted. "I saw you too."

The breath fled from his lungs. "What?"

She nodded and then told him a fantastic story about a magic wedding veil.

"I didn't think you believed in stuff like that...I thought..."

"I always wanted to believe," she whispered, "but I was so scared to believe in case it wasn't real."

"I'm real," he said, and pulled her into his arms. "And I'm here."

"Oh, Tuck."

"I never thought I'd feel the magic again. I thought one shot at love was all you got in life. I held on to Aimee too long. I know that. I also know she'd want me to be happy. To love again. To have a family."

"Are you sure?"

"I'm tired of being among the walking wounded. You made me come alive again, Queenie. You challenged me, you nurtured me, you stood up for me. Even though you never said it, you showed me exactly how much you loved me. You make me want to be the man you see in me. You saved me, Jillian. In more ways than you can ever know."

"Tell me," she whispered.

"I love you," he said, and squeezed her tight.

He was ready to risk his heart again. Jillian was worth the gamble. He loved her so much. He still loved Aimee but in the soft way of memories. And his heart was big enough to have two great loves in his life. He was a lucky, lucky man to have found Jillian, and he told her so. Kissing her and whispering his love for her over and over and over. "I love, I love you, I love you."

"I love you too," she whispered. "And I want you to know I've never said that to anyone before."

"I know how hard this is for you. I treasure your ability to say it to me now." Tuck reached out, took her hands, and laced his fingers through hers. He put his head to her forehead and looked deeply into her eyes. "You hear me on this, Queenie? I love you."

Jillian nodded. She heard him. This man loved her. He not only told her, but he'd also showed her repeatedly, and she'd just been too scared to recognize what it was or admit to herself what she was feeling in return. Too afraid there wasn't really such a thing as love this deep and wonderful. But now it was here, and she was feeling it, and she felt so stupid for not believing, not understanding. Her friends had tried to tell her, but their words of encouragement had fallen on deaf ears. She had to find out for herself.

As she looked into Tuck's eyes as deeply as he was looking into hers, she felt her consciousness shift to a whole new level of being.

For Tuck had convinced her to trust. Trust was all she needed to believe in the true miracle of love.

"My Magic Man," she murmured, and kissed him from the very depths of her faithful soul.

Epilogue

It was time to let go.

Tuck knew that as surely as he knew he loved Jillian. Loving her didn't mean he loved Aimee less. He had room in his heart for two great loves in his life, and he realized his love for Aimee had been the love of his youth, his feelings pure and simple and, honestly, in retrospect, too dependent.

The love he felt for Jillian was more mature. It was the love of his adulthood. Stronger, more complex, more autonomous. Jillian made him change and grow in ways Aimee never had. He was ready for this grown-up kind of love. Ready and unafraid.

They walked somberly down the dock together on that first day of summer, Jillian carrying the urn with Blake's ashes. They were dressed in black jeans and sweaters, black boots, and black leather jackets. They climbed into the skiff and rowed out into the middle of the lake. Tuck remembered the last time he'd been out on the lake. So much had changed since that autumn day.

The sun was warm on their faces, but the air was still chilly. From the center of the water, they could see the lake house.

Tuck's eyes met Jillian's and she nodded. Slowly, with great reverence, they said a prayer and then they said good-bye to Blake.

They sat for a long moment, not talking, just watching the water wash away the past and the sun slip down the horizon.

"It's time to go," Jillian said at last.

Tuck nodded. He dipped the oars into the water, rowing back to the lake house and giving thanks for the woman sitting across from him. Jillian had brought him back to life. He'd been emotionally dead when he'd met her, and she'd saved his soul.

The little craft glided over the gentle current, carrying them to shore. He docked the boat. Jillian climbed out and tied it up, and then she reached for his hand. He took it. Partners, the two of them.

And in each other's arms, they'd both found what they'd been searching for.

Salvation.

Dear Readers,

Writing the Wedding Veil Wishes has been such fun I hate to see the series end. If *All of Me* is your introduction to the series, I envy you getting to meet the characters for the first time. To me, one of the most endearing things about Wedding Veil Wishes is the camaraderie between these four friends. In today's hectic world we all need our women friends to help us through the ups and downs life (and romance) often throws our way.

The adventure all started in *There Goes the Bride* with Delaney Cartwright who finds that all important wish-fulfilling wedding veil in that mysterious little consignment shop in Houston, Texas. Having the courage to wish on that legendary veil for a way out of her high-society wedding led Delaney to her heart's true desire—sexy cop Nick Vinetti.

Delaney passed the veil on to wedding videographer Tish Gallagher in *Once Smitten, Twice Shy*. Some sad life circumstances have broken Tish's heart and her habit of using shopping as a solace has gotten her into deep financial trouble. But when she wishes on the veil to get out of debt and ends up with a chance to film the wedding of the President's daughter, she's stunned to learn the groom is none other than Secret Service Agent Shane Tremont, the ex-husband she never stopped loving.

In *Addicted to Love*, starry-eyed Rachael Henderson (who was born in Valentine, Texas on Valentine's Day) wishes on the veil to help her get rid of her foolish romantic notions. After all, she's been jilted at the altar—*twice*. The last time on the same day her parents inform her they're getting divorced after twenty-seven years. Disillusioned with love, she starts Romanceaholics Anonymous, only to discover the feelings she has for her childhood crush, Sheriff Brody Carlton, are anything but foolish.

And last but not least, is Jillian Samuels from *All of Me* who never believed in true love or fairytale endings. She isn't about to wish on that veil until a cruel betrayal leaves her raw and aching. Pushed to the limit, she puts on the veil, falls asleep and dreams of her beloved. The only problem is, widower Tuck Manner is still mourning the loss of his beloved wife.

It's with a fond farewell I bid Delaney, Tish, Rachael and Jillian their happily-ever-after. And I hope, as you read their stories, they will inspire you to do some wishing of your very own.

May your life be filled with love,

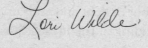

The moment Texas socialite Delaney Cartwright touches the magical wedding veil, she envisions a stranger's dark eyes and sexy lips...

Turn this page for an excerpt from the first Wedding Veil Wishes novel,

There Goes the Bride

Prologue

The summer issue of *Society Bride* declared the marriage of Houston's hottest bachelor, Dr. Evan Van Zandt, to his childhood sweetheart, oil heiress Delaney Cartwright, a classic friends-to-lovers fairy tale.

Texas Monthly, in its trendy yet folksy way, decreed their union the high-society equivalent of beef barbecue and mustard potato salad. Delaney and Evan simply belonged together.

A sentimental write-up in the *Houston Chronicle* dubbed their romance a heartwarming Lone Star love story.

Delaney's mother, Honey Montgomery Cartwright, pronounced them the perfect couple. Lavish praise indeed from a Philadelphia blue blood with impossibly high standards.

Her father grumbled, "This thing's costing us more than her liberal arts degree from Rice," as he wrote out a very large check to cover the nuptials.

And her long-deceased sister Skylar, who occasionally popped up in Delaney's dreams to offer unsolicited advice, whispered with unbridled glee that the ceremony was a glorious train wreck just waiting to happen and she insisted on front-row seating.

Skylar, being dead, could of course sit anywhere she chose. Everyone else had to cram into the River Oaks Methodist Church.

The cherrywood pews overflowed with five hundred invited guests, plus a dozen members of the press and a sprinkling of enterprising wedding crashers. The laboring air-conditioning system was no match for the double punch of a too-thick crowd and sweltering one-hundred-degree heat.

"Who gets married in Houston during August?" Delaney heard a woman murmur.

"I'm getting a heat rash in these panty hose," another woman replied.

Feeling chastised, Delaney ducked her head. She stood just outside the open door of the chapel waiting for the wedding march to commence, her arm looped through her father's.

"I heard it was originally supposed to be a Christmas ceremony, but the bride postponed it twice," the first woman said. "Do you suppose we could have a runaway situation?"

"Hmm, now that would make an interesting spread in tomorrow's society pages."

At that comment, her father tightened his grip. *No turning back now,* his clench said.

Delaney's hopes sank. Her mind spun. *A coyote would gnaw her paw off.*

The bridesmaids reached their places. Her best friend, Tish, wedding videographer extraordinaire, was filming madly. Every gaze in the place was glued to Delaney.

Everything was perfect. It was a true celebrity-style

wedding, just as her mother had planned. The purple orchids, accented with white roses, were on lavish display—in bouquets and boutonnieres, in vases and corsages. Her size-four, ten-thousand-dollar Vera Wang wedding dress fit like a fantasy. The flower girl was cute. The two-year-old ring bearer even cuter. And both children were on exemplary behavior. Delaney's antique wedding veil fetchingly framed her face, even though her scalp had been tingling weirdly ever since she put it on.

This was it.

Her big day.

The seven-piece orchestra struck the first notes of the wedding march. Dum, dum, de-dum.

Delaney took a deep breath and glanced down the long aisle festooned with white rose petals to where Evan stood at the altar. He looked stunningly handsome in his long-tailed tux, love shining in his trusting blue eyes.

Her father started forward.

But Delaney's beaded white Jimmy Choo stilettos stayed rooted to the spot. No, no, this was all wrong. It was a big mistake. She had to call it off before she embarrassed everyone. Where was her cell phone?

"Delaney Lynn Cartwright," her father growled under his breath. "Don't make me drag you."

A hard throb of distress surged through her temples. *What have you done? What have you done? What have you done?*

She forced herself to move forward. Her gaze searched for the exits. There were two on either side of the altar, and of course, the one directly behind her.

But Daddy wasn't letting go.

Closer, closer, almost there.

Evan made eye contact, smiled sweetly.

Guilt whirled like a demon tornado in the pit of her stomach. She dragged in a ragged breath.

Her husband-to-be held out his palm. Her father put her hand in Evan's.

Delaney's gaze shifted from one corner exit to the other. Too late. It was too late to call this off. What time was it anyway?

"Dearly beloved," the portly minister began, but that's as far as he got.

A clattering erupted from behind the exit door on the left.

And then there he loomed. Dressed head to toe in black. Wearing a ski mask. Standing out like crude oil in a cotton field.

Thrilled, chilled, shamefaced, and greatly relieved, Delaney held her breath.

The intruder charged the altar.

The congregation inhaled a simultaneous gasp.

The minister blinked, looked confused.

"Back away from the bride," the dark stranger growled and waved a pistol at Evan.

Excitement burst like tiny exploding bubbles inside her head. *Prop gun*, Delaney thought. *Nice touch*.

Evan stared at the masked intruder, but did not move. Apparently he had not yet realized what was transpiring.

"Move it." The interloper pointed his weapon directly at Evan's head. "Hands up."

Finally, her groom got the message. He dropped Delaney's hand, raised his arms over his head, and took a step back.

"Don't anyone try anything cute," the man commanded at the same moment he wrapped the crook of his elbow around Delaney's neck and pressed the revolver to her temple. The cold nose of it felt deadly against her skin.

Fear catapulted into her throat, diluting the excitement. Delaney dropped her bouquet. It *was* a prop gun, wasn't it?

The crowd shot to its collective feet as the stranger dragged her toward the exit from whence he'd appeared.

"Follow us and the bride gets it," he shouted dramatically just before the exit door slammed closed behind them.

"You're choking me," Delaney gasped. "You can let go now."

He ignored her and just kept dragging her by the neck toward the white delivery van parked at the back of the rectory.

A bolt of raw panic shot through her veins. What was going on here? She dug her freshly manicured fingernails into his thick arm and tried to pry herself free.

He stuck his gun in his waistband, pulled a pair of handcuffs from his back pocket, and one-handedly slapped them around her wrists.

"What is this?" she squeaked.

He did not speak. He wrenched open the back door of the van just as the congregation came spilling out of the rectory and into the street. He tossed her onto the floor, slammed the door, and ran around to the driver's side.

Delaney lay facedown, her knees and elbows stinging from carpet burn. She couldn't see a thing, but she heard anxious shouts and the sound of fists pounding the side of the vehicle.

The engine revved and the van shot forward, knocking her over onto her side.

"What's going on?" She struggled to sit. The veil fell across her face. She pushed it away with her cuffed hands and peered into the front of the van. "What's with all the rough stuff?"

He didn't answer.

She cleared her throat. Perhaps he hadn't heard her. "Nice execution," she said. "Loved the toy gun, but the handcuffs are a definite overkill."

He hit the street doing at least fifty and she tipped over again.

Her heart flipped up into her tightly constricted throat. She dragged in a ragged swallow of air. This guy was playing his role to the hilt.

When they made it to the freeway entrance ramp, he ripped off the ski mask, threw it in the seat beside him, and then turned to look back at Delaney.

Alarm rocketed through her. Saliva evaporated from her mouth. Something had gone very, very wrong.

Because the man who'd just taken her hostage was *not* the kidnapper she'd hired.

VISIT US ONLINE AT

WWW.HACHETTEBOOKGROUP.COM

FEATURES:

**OPENBOOK BROWSE AND
SEARCH EXCERPTS**

•

AUDIOBOOK EXCERPTS AND PODCASTS

•

AUTHOR ARTICLES AND INTERVIEWS

•

**BESTSELLER AND PUBLISHING
GROUP NEWS**

•

SIGN UP FOR E-NEWSLETTERS

•

**AUTHOR APPEARANCES AND TOUR
INFORMATION**

•

SOCIAL MEDIA FEEDS AND WIDGETS

•

DOWNLOAD FREE APPS

Bookmark Hachette Book Group
@ www.HachetteBookGroup.com

Find out more about Forever Romance!

Visit us at
www.hachettebookgroup.com/publishing_forever.aspx

Find us on Facebook
http://www.facebook.com/ForeverRomance

Follow us on Twitter
http://twitter.com/ForeverRomance

NEW AND UPCOMING TITLES

Each month we feature our new titles
and reader favorites.

CONTESTS AND GIVEAWAYS

We give away galleys, autographed copies,
and all kinds of exclusive items.

AUTHOR INFO

You'll find bios, articles, and links to personal websites
for all your favorite authors—and so much more.

GET SOCIAL

Connect with your favorite authors, editors, and
other Forever fans, and share what's important to you.

THE BUZZ

Sign up for our monthly romance newsletter,
and be the first to read all about it.